Grace Harlowe's High School Years

Jessie Graham Flower, A.M.

ISBN: 1514627175
ISBN-13: 9781514627174

## DEDICATION

For lovers of adventure, lovers of determination and lovers of good story telling from prior to World War I.

GRACE HARLOWE'S PLEBE YEAR AT HIGH SCHOOL
OR


The Merry Doings Of The Oakdale Freshman Girls

ACKNOWLEDGMENTS

Many thanks to Jesse Graham Flower, A.M who in real life was Josephine Chase, a prolific writer for Altemus Publishing from 1909 until around 1930. Her feel for the girls of the day went a long way to making Grace Harlowe such a widely popular character.

# CHAPTER I
## THE ACCIDENT OF FRIENDSHIPS

"Who is the new girl in the class?" asked Miriam Nesbit, flashing her black eyes from one schoolmate to another, as the girls assembled in the locker room of the Oakdale High School.

"Her name is Pierson; that is all I know about her," replied Nora O'Malley, gazing at her pretty Irish face in the looking glass with secret satisfaction. "She's very quiet and shy and looks as if she would weep aloud when her turn comes to recite, but I'm sure she's all right," she added good naturedly. For Nora had a charming, sunny nature, and always saw the best if there was any best to see.

"She is very bright," broke in Grace Harlowe decisively. "She went through her Latin lesson without a mistake, which is certainly more than I could do."

"Well, I don't like her," pouted Miriam. "I never trust those quiet little things. And, besides, she is the worst-dressed girl in——"

"Hush!" interrupted Jessica Bright, touching a finger to her lips. "Here she is."

A little, brown figure entered the room just as Miriam finished speaking. But Jessica was too late with her warning. The young girl had, without doubt, heard the cruel speech and her face flushed painfully as she pinned on a shabby old hat, slipped her arms into a thin black jacket and stepped out again without looking at the crowd of schoolmates who watched her silently.

"Miriam, I should think you'd learn to be more careful," exclaimed hot-tempered Nora, her soft heart touched by the appealing little stranger.

"Well, what difference does it make?" replied Miriam. "If Miss Pierson doesn't know already that she's the shabbiest girl in school, it's high time she found it out. I have a suspicion her mother takes in washing or something, and I mean to find it out right now. We can't invite a girl like that to our class parties and entertainments. She would disgrace us."

"Miriam," said Grace quietly, "I believe we are all privileged to invite whom we please to our homes. I intend to give a class tea next Saturday, and I mean to follow Miss Pierson right now and ask her to help me receive."

The two girls looked into each other's faces for a moment without speaking. Grace was quiet and contained, Miriam flushed and furiously angry. They had been rival leaders always at the Grammar School, but the rivalry had never come to open battle until now.

Miriam was the first to drop her eyes. She did not reply, but from that moment she was the sworn enemy of Grace Harlowe and her two friends, Nora and Jessica.

"Well, we had better hurry," said Jessica, trying to calm the troubled scene. "Nobody knows exactly where Miss Pierson lives and she will be out of sight before we can catch her."

The three girls ran lightly out of the basement of the fine old building that was the pride of Oakdale. It was large and imposing, built of smooth, gray stone, with four huge columns supporting the front portico. A hundred yards away stood the companion building, the Boys' High School, exactly like the first in every respect except that a wing had been added for a gymnasium which the girls had the privilege of using on certain days. A wide campus surrounded the two buildings, shaded by elm and oak trees. Certainly no other town in the state could boast of twin high schools as fine as these; and especially did the situation appeal to the people of Oakdale, for the ten level acres surrounding the two buildings gave ample space for the various athletic fields, and the doings of the high schools formed the very life of the place.

But we must return to our three girls who were hurrying down the shady street, followed in a more leisurely and dignified fashion by Miriam and her friends. The shabby figure of the little stranger had just turned the corner as the girls left the High School grounds.

"Come on," cried Grace breathlessly, leading the way. Having once made up her mind, she always pursued her point with a fine obstinacy regardless of opinion.

When they had come to the cross street they saw their quarry again, now making her way slowly toward the street next the river. This was the shabbiest street in Oakdale, though no one knew exactly why, since the river bank might have been the chosen site for all the handsomest buildings; but towns are as incorrigible as people, sometimes, and insist on growing one way when they should grow another, without the slightest regard for future appearances.

And so, when little Miss Pierson stopped in front of one of the smallest and meanest cottages on River Street, the girls knew she must, indeed, be very poor. The house, small and forlorn, presented a sad countenance streaked with tear stains from a leaky gutter. An uneven pavement led to the front door, which bore a painted sign: "Plain Sewing."

They paused irresolutely at the gate, and were taking counsel together when Miriam Nesbit passed with her friends. She pointed at the door and laughed.

"Really, that girl's conduct is contemptible!" exclaimed Grace, giving the wooden gate a vigorous push. "I simply won't tolerate her rudeness.

She is an unmitigated snob!" Grace knocked on the door rather sharply to emphasize her feelings. It was opened almost immediately by Miss Pierson herself, still in her hat and coat; and in her surprise and embarrassment she almost shut the door in their faces. But Jessica's gentle smile reassured her, and Grace, who was a born leader, took her hand kindly and plunged at once into the subject.

"You left school so quickly this afternoon, Miss Pierson, that I didn't have a chance to see you. I have something very particular I want to ask you to-day."

"Won't you come in?" said the other, opening the door into the parlor, which had an air of refinement about it in spite of its utter poorness.

"Anne!" called a querulous voice down the passage.

"Yes, mother, I'm coming," answered the girl, hurrying out of the room with a frightened look in her eyes. In a few moments she was back again.

"Please excuse me for leaving you," she said. "My mother is an invalid and needs my sister or me with her constantly."

"Her name is Anne, then," thought Grace. "I shall call her so at once and break the ice."

"Anne," she said aloud, "I think you know my friends, don't you— Jessica Bright and Nora O'Malley? And I am Grace Harlowe."

"Oh, yes," replied Anne, brightening at the friendly advances of the others. "I remember your names from the roll call."

"Of course," replied Grace. "But I think we should all be more to each other than roll-call acquaintances, we freshmen. I am very ambitious for our class. I want it to be the best that ever graduated from Oakdale High School, and for that reason, I think all the girls in it should try to be friends and work together to advance the cause. I'm going to start the ball rolling by giving a tea to our class next Saturday afternoon. Will you come and receive with Jessica and Nora and me?"

Anne clasped her hands delightedly for a moment. Then her eyes filled with tears and her lips trembled so that the girls were afraid she might be going to cry. Tender-hearted Jessica turned her face away for fear of showing too much sympathy.

"I'm sorry," said Anne at last, rather unsteadily, "but I am afraid I can't accept your delightful invitation. I——"

"I beg your pardon," said a voice at the door, "I didn't mean to intrude on your visitors, Anne, but I couldn't help overhearing Miss Harlowe's invitation."

A small woman, much older than Anne, but very like her in face and figure, appeared at the door.

"This is my sister," said Anne, taking the other's hand affectionately.

3

"Anne imagines she can't go, but she certainly can," went on the older Miss Pierson, calmly, not in the least embarrassed by the strange young girls. "Of course, she must go. I can arrange it easily."

"But, Mary——" protested Anne.

"Never mind, little sister," interrupted Mary, "it will be all right. Miss Harlowe, what time must she be there?"

"At four o'clock," answered Grace, rising to go, "and I am delighted that she can come. Remember, Anne, I'm counting on you to pour the lemonade. The other girls are going to help with the sandwiches and ice cream. By the way," she added, as they went down the steps, "be sure and come to the basketball meeting at the gym this afternoon."

And so it was arranged that Anne Pierson, the shabbiest and poorest girl in Oakdale High School, was to help receive at one of the prettiest and most charming houses in town. Miriam Nesbit's rudeness was to bring about a friendship between Anne Pierson and her three schoolmates that lasted a lifetime.

After the half-past two o'clock dinner, which was the universal custom in Oakdale, the chums met again at the gymnasium in the Boys' High School. Wednesdays and Saturdays were nicknamed "ladies' days" by the High School boys, for on these afternoons the girls were permitted free use of the gymnasium.

The meeting to-day was not for gymnastic exercises, however, but an important subject was to be discussed—the Freshman Basketball Team. Also the captain of the team was to be elected.

Other club meetings were in full force when the girls arrived, and the great room vibrated with the hum of voices. The three freshmen, who knew better than to interrupt sophomores and juniors at their pow-wows, made their way quietly across the hall to the appointed place of rendezvous. Of course, the entire Freshman Class did not assemble to discuss this subject. Many members were not interested in basketball, except to look on. Girls who were over studious, and not physically strong, could not at any rate play on the team, and therefore they seldom attended such meetings. Jessica Bright was one of these, nevertheless, she followed her two friends, who had always been foremost in athletics at the Central Grammar School.

The election of a captain was the first business of the meeting. That over, the captain, after due and serious consultation with a friendly cabinet, chose the players and their substitutes.

Undoubtedly Grace Harlowe had the coolest head in the class, and was the most to be relied upon at critical moments; yet Miriam Nesbit exerted a strange influence over her followers, who were almost her slaves. She was the richest of all the girls and wore the costliest clothes.

4

The parties she gave, from time to time, in her mother's large and handsome home were the talk of the place. She was also the cleverest girl in the class, and had taken undisputed first place since she was a child. She was not a close student, but seemed to absorb her lessons in half the time that it took her friends to master them. Popular she certainly was, or rather she was feared by her schoolmates. Her masterful, overpowering spirit seemed to sweep everything before it.

Grace Harlowe was quite as powerful in her way, but she had a noble, unselfish disposition and was much beloved by her friends. She stood well in her studies, but had never taken first place. Perhaps this was because she had interested herself so much in outdoor sports that she had not given enough time to study.

Both girls were handsome—Miriam tall, dark and oriental-looking, with flashing eyes and an imperious curve to her lips; Grace was also tall, with wavy, chestnut hair, fine gray eyes, regular features, a full, generous chin and cheeks glowing with health.

Miriam Nesbit had already done a good deal of lobbying when the three girls arrived on the scene. She wished to be elected captain of the team at any cost; but Grace's adherents were holding off, quietly waiting for her arrival.

"Well, here you are at last!" said Marian Barber, who had been preparing the ballots for the coming election.

Marian was the busy girl of the class, and always made herself useful.

"Is everyone here?" demanded Nora, scanning the crowd of freshmen with a view to ascertaining what her chum's chances were.

"All that intend coming," replied Miriam. "The softies stayed away, as usual."

"Suppose we wait five minutes," said Grace, looking at her watch, "and then, if no one comes, we will cast the votes."

"No, no," exclaimed Miriam impatiently. "I have an engagement and can't spare any more time. I vote that we have the election at once, without waiting another moment."

"Very well," assented Grace. "I only suggested waiting because Anne Pierson promised to come, and, of course, every girl in the class has a right to vote at the class elections."

"Anne Pierson?" cried Miriam, turning crimson with suppressed rage.

"Yes," answered Grace calmly; "but, if everybody is agreeable, suppose we go ahead."

"Agreed!" cried the others and the ballots were cast.

There was not much parliamentary practice in these class elections. Each girl wrote the name of her choice on a slip of paper and dropped it in a hat. Four of the girls then counted the votes, and the one receiving the most slips was declared elected.

The slips were dropped into the hat, amid the silence of the company. Some of the sophomores and juniors, perched on parallel bars, watched the scene with superior amusement, but no notice was taken of their half-whispered jeers.

The four girls then retired to count the votes.

"It's a tie," announced Marian Barber, returning presently; "a tie between Grace and Miriam. I wish some of the others would come and settle the matter."

"Here's some one," cried Nora. "Here's Anne Pierson. Let her cast the decisive vote."

Miriam's eyes blazed, but she held her peace. There was nothing to do but submit with an uneasy grace. But who could doubt what the outcome would be? However, she felt somewhat relieved when Grace said:

"I think we should cast the votes over again, and, according to the rules we made last year, Miriam and I should not vote, since the election rests between us."

The votes were cast again, Anne timidly dropping her slip in the hat with the others, and, as might have been expected, Grace was elected captain of the Freshman Basketball Team of the Oakdale High School.

# CHAPTER II
## THE SPONSOR OF THE FRESHMAN CLASS

"Grace," asked Mrs. Harlowe, the day of the famous freshman tea, "have you asked some of the girls to help this afternoon? Bridget can attend to the sandwiches, but someone ought to pour the lemonade and generally look after the wants of the others."

Grace was arranging a bowl of China asters on the piano in her mother's charming drawing room. The shining mahogany chairs and tables reflected the glow of the wood fire, for the day was chilly, and bright chintz curtains at the windows gave a cheerful note of color to the scene.

"Oh, yes, mother," replied Grace. "Nora and Jessica, of course, and Anne Pierson."

"And who is Anne Pierson?"

"I don't know who she is," answered Grace. "I never knew her until she entered the High School. But she is terribly poor. Her mother is an invalid and her sister takes in plain sewing. I really asked her at first because Miriam Nesbit was rude to her one day. But I'm beginning to like her so much, now, that I'm glad I did it. She's as quiet as a little mouse, but she is fast taking first place in class. I believe she will outstrip Miriam before the end of the year. Don't ask me who she is, though. I haven't the least idea, but she's all right, I can promise you that. I'm sorry for her because she is poor. They live in a little broken-down cottage on River Street."

Mrs. Harlowe looked dubious. Grace was always bringing home stray people and animals, and the mother was accustomed to her daughter's whims. The young girl was familiar to all the ragamuffins of the town slum, and when she sometimes found one gazing wistfully through the fence palings of her mother's old-fashioned garden, she promptly led him around to the kitchen, gave him a plate of food on the back steps, picked him a small bouquet and sent him off half-dazed with her gracious and impetuous kindness.

"Well, my dear, I shall be prepared for anything," exclaimed Mrs. Harlowe; "but remember that feeding people on the back steps and asking them into the parlor to meet your friends and acquaintances are two different matters altogether."

"Don't be afraid, mother," replied Grace. "You will like Anne as well as I do, once you get to know her. You must be careful not to frighten her at first. She is the most timid little soul I ever met."

Just then the front gate clicked and two girls strolled up the red-brick walk, their light organdie dresses peeping out from the folds of their long

7

capes.

"Here come Nora and Jessica," cried Grace excitedly, running to the door to meet her friends.

Mrs. Harlowe smiled. In spite of Grace's sixteen years she was still her little girl.

There was another click at the gate and Mrs. Harlowe saw through the parlor window a little, dark figure, pathetically plain in its shabby coat and hat.

"Poor little soul," thought the good woman. "How I wish I could put her into one of Grace's muslins, but, of course, I couldn't think of offering to do such a thing."

"Mother," said Grace some minutes later, when the girls had laid aside their wraps and descended into the drawing room, "this is Anne Pierson, our new friend."

Anne Pierson, small and shrinking, was dressed in a queer, old-fashioned black silk that had evidently been taken up and made short for the occasion. Mrs. Harlowe's heart was touched to the quick and she bent and kissed the young girl gently.

"How do you do, my dear?" she said kindly. "I am always glad to meet Grace's friends, and you are most welcome."

Anne was too frightened almost to speak. This was the first party she had ever attended, and the beautiful room, the girls in their light, pretty dresses, the bowls of flowers and the cheery firelight nearly stupefied her.

Mrs. Harlowe disappeared into the little conservatory off the dining room, returning in a moment with two big red roses which she pinned to Anne's dress.

"These red roses have been waiting for you all morning," she said, "and they're just in their prime now."

More guests began to arrive, and soon the room was full of young girls talking gaily together in groups or walking about, their arms around each other's waists after the manner of fifteen and sixteen.

Grace had seated Anne at the dining room table behind a large cut glass bowl which almost hid her small figure. Grace knew from experience that this would be the most popular spot in the room, and she cautioned many of her friends to be kind to the timid little stranger. She knew also that giving Anne something to keep her occupied would relieve her embarrassment. Anne conscientiously filled and refilled the glasses, and in the intervals answered the questions put to her; but never asked any herself.

Miriam Nesbit came in late with her two most intimate friends. She wore a resplendent dress of old rose crepe and a big black hat. Anne forgot her resentment when she caught sight of the vision and was lost in admiration. But she was brought sharply to her senses by a rude, sneering laugh from the ill-bred girl, who was staring insolently at the old black silk gown.

Anne flushed and hung her head.

"I am glad Mrs. Harlowe gave me the flowers," she thought. "They hide it a little, I think."

Meantime there was the bustle of a new and important arrival. Grace and her mother ushered in a charming little old lady and seated her in the place of honor, a big leather chair between the windows. She wore a gray silk dress and a lavender bonnet daintily trimmed in lace and white ostrich tips.

"Girls," said Grace, as a hush fell over the room, "there is no need for me to introduce any of you to Mrs. Gray, who is the sponsor for the freshman class."

There was a buzz of laughter and conversation again, and through the double doors Anne caught sight of the little old lady, talking gaily to her subjects, seated, like a diminutive queen, on a large throne.

"Why is she the sponsor of the class?" Anne asked of Jessica, who was hovering nearby.

"Oh, have you never heard?" returned Jessica. "Mrs. Gray's daughter died during her freshman year at High School, long ago, and ever since then, Mrs. Gray has offered a prize of twenty-five dollars for the girl who makes the highest average in her examinations at the end of the freshman year. She was made sponsor of the freshman class about ten years ago, so each year, soon after school opens, some one of the freshmen gives a tea and invites her to meet the new girls. You must come in and be introduced, too, as soon as you are through here."

"A prize of twenty-five dollars," repeated Anne. "How I wish I might win it!"

"It's even more than that," said Jessica. "For a perfect examination she offers one hundred dollars. But, needless to say, no one has ever won the hundred. It is considered impossible to pass a perfect examination in every subject."

"One hundred dollars!" exclaimed Anne. "Oh, if I only could!"

"Well, you may win the twenty-five dollars, anyway, Anne," said Jessica. "I suppose the one hundred dollar prize is beyond the reach of human beings."

"And now, young ladies," Mrs. Gray was saying, smiling at the group of girls who surrounded her, as she examined them through her lorgnette, "most of you I have known since you were little tots, and your fathers and mothers before you; but I don't know which of you excels in her studies. Is it you, Grace, my dear?"

Grace shook her head vigorously.

"No, indeed, Mrs. Gray," she replied. "I could never be accused of over study. I suppose I'm too fond of basketball."

"It won't hurt you, my dear," said the old lady, tapping the girl indulgently with her lorgnette; "the open air is much better than that of the schoolroom, and so long as you keep up an average, I daresay you won't disappoint your mother. But none of you have told me yet who leads the freshman class in her studies."

"Miriam Nesbit," said several voices in unison.

"Ah!" said Mrs. Gray, looking intently at Miriam. "So you are the gold medal girl, Miriam? Dear me, what a young lady you are growing to be! But you must not study too hard. Don't overdo it."

Mrs. Gray had gone through this same conversation every year since any of the girls could remember, and never failed to caution the head girl not to over study.

"There's no fear of that, Mrs. Gray," replied Miriam boastfully. "My lessons give me very little trouble."

"Mrs. Gray," broke in Nora O'Malley mischievously, "Miriam Nesbit has a close second in the class. The first girl who has ever been known to come up to her."

Miriam flushed, half-angry and half-pleased at the adroit compliment.

"And who may that be, my dear?" queried Mrs. Gray, searching about the room with her nearsighted blue eyes.

"It's Anne Pierson" replied Nora.

"Pierson, Pierson?" repeated the little old lady. "Why have I not met her? I do not seem to remember the name in Oakdale. But where is this wonderful young woman who is outstripping our brilliant Miriam? I feel a great curiosity to see her."

"Anne Pierson, Anne Pierson!" called several voices, while Grace began to search through the rooms and hall.

At the first mention of her name Anne had darted from her seat behind the lemonade bowl, and rushed to the nearest shelter, which was the conservatory.

Grace found her, at last, in the conservatory crouched behind a palm.

"Come here, you foolish child!" exclaimed Grace. "You are wanted at once. Why did you run and hide? Mrs. Gray—the great Mrs. Gray—wishes to meet you. Think of that!"

Anne clasped the girl's strong hand with her two small ones.

"Oh, Grace," she whispered, "won't you excuse me? I—I——"

"You what? Silly, come right along!"

Grace fairly dragged the trembling little figure into the drawing room, where a silence had fallen over the group of young girls who watched the scene.

"Tut, tut, my dear!" exclaimed Mrs. Gray gently. "You mustn't be afraid of me. I'm the most harmless old woman in the world."

Then she tried to get a glimpse of Anne's downcast, crimson face.

"I wanted particularly to meet you, child," went on Mrs. Gray, "because I hear you are a formidable rival of the best pupil in the freshman class. That is a great boast for your friends to make for you, my dear. Miriam Nesbit is a famously smart girl, I'm told. But I wanted to meet you, too, because you bear the name I love best in the world."

Here the old lady's voice became very soft, and the girls suddenly remembered that the young daughter had been called Anne. Was there not a memorial window, in the chapel of the High School, of an angel carrying a lily and underneath an inscription familiar to them all: "In Memory of Anne Gray, died in her freshman year, aged sixteen"?

The girls moved off quietly, conversing in low voices, leaving Anne alone with her new friend.

"You are a very little girl to be so clever," said Mrs. Gray, patting one of Anne's small wrists as she looked into the dark eyes. "Where do you live, dear?"

"On River Street," replied Anne undergoing the scrutiny calmly, now she found herself alone.

"River Street?" repeated Mrs. Gray, trying to recall whom she had ever known living in that strange quarter of the town. "Have you been long in Oakdale?" she went on.

"A few years, ma'am," replied Anne.

"And what is your father's business, my child?" continued the old lady remorselessly.

Anne blushed and hung her head, and for a moment there was no reply to the question. Presently she drew a sharp breath as if it hurt her to make the confession.

"My father does not live here," was what she said. "My mother is an invalid. My sister supports us with sewing. As soon as I finish in the High School, I shall teach."

Mrs. Gray put an arm around the girl's waist and drew her down beside her.

"I'm a stupid old woman, child. You must forgive me. Old people forget their manners sometimes. Will you come and see me very soon? Perhaps to-morrow after church you will take luncheon with me? I want to know you better."

She drew a card from the beaded reticule that hung at her side.

"Remember, at half-past twelve," she said, giving the girl's hand an extra squeeze as she rose to go.

After Mrs. Gray had taken her departure a free and easy atmosphere was restored and the girls began talking and laughing without the restriction of an older person's presence. Mrs. Harlowe shortly after this also left them to themselves.

"Let's do some stunts," proposed Grace. "Nora, will you give us your imitations?"

"Certainly," replied Nora, "if Miriam will promise to sing, and Jessica will do her Greek dance, and Georgie will play for us."

"All right!" came a chorus of voices.

"We've done it oft before, but we'll do it o'er again if the company so wishes," said Georgie Pine, one of the brightest and gayest girls in the class.

The others seated themselves in a semicircle, while each girl gave her little performance, and, at the conclusion, was applauded enthusiastically. Nora had a real talent for mimicry; she convulsed her audience with imitations of some of the High School teachers. When it came Miriam's turn she sat down at the piano with a queer look on her face.

"I believe she means mischief," thought Grace to herself, as she watched the girl curiously.

Miriam ran a brilliant scale up the piano, for music was another of her many accomplishments. Then she paused and turned to the others.

"I won't sing," she said, "unless Miss Pierson promises to recite us something first, Poe's 'Raven,' for instance."

Grace flushed angrily and was about to interfere when, to her surprise, Anne herself replied:

"I shall be glad to if that is the poem you like best. I always preferred 'Annabel Lee.'"

Miriam was too amazed to answer. She could never form an idea of what it cost Anne in self-control to acquiesce; but the young girl had gained a new strength that day. So many people had been kind to her, and what is more, interested in her welfare. She rose quietly and walked to the middle of the semicircle.

Grace and her chums were in an agony of fear lest poor Anne should break down, and so distress them all except the unkind Miriam. However, they need not have troubled themselves. Anne fixed her eyes on the far wall of the dining room and commenced to recite "The Raven" in a clear, musical voice that deepened as she repeated the stanzas. The girls forgot the shabby little figure in its ill-fitting black silk and saw only Anne's small, white face and glowing eyes. Not Miss Tebbs, herself, teacher of English and elocution at the High School, could have improved upon the performance.

"It was perfectly done," said Grace afterwards, telling the story to her mother. "It was almost uncanny and quite creepy toward the last."

When the performance was over the girls crowded around little Anne with eager congratulations; but, strange to say, everyone forgot that Miriam had given her promise to sing.

What the crestfallen Miriam kept wondering was: "Wherever did she learn to do it?"

# CHAPTER III
## MRS. GRAY ENGAGES A SECRETARY

Grace and her two friends, Jessica and Nora, were also invited to Mrs. Gray's luncheon the next day, after church. Grace had often taken meals in the beautiful house on Chapel Hill, but the other girls had never been privileged to do more than sit in the large, shady parlors while their mothers paid an afternoon call.

It was with some excitement, therefore, that the three girls met in front of the Catholic Church, of which Nora was a member, and strolled up the broad street together. As they passed the little Episcopal Chapel, which had given the hill its name, Anne Pierson joined them. She looked grave and excited, and there was a feverish glow in her eyes.

"Anne, my child," exclaimed Grace, who always seemed much older than the others, "how late do you study at night? I believe you are working too hard. You look tired out."

"I'm not tired," replied Anne. "I don't mind studying. Only so much has happened in the last few days! And now we're going to luncheon with Mrs. Gray. I've seen her house. It's very beautiful from the outside, more beautiful than the Nesbits', I think, because it is older and there is such a pretty garden at the side."

"Anne," said Jessica, "we're counting on you to win the prize. There is no reason why a rich girl like Miriam Nesbit should get it. She doesn't need the money, in the first place; and, in the second, she's already had enough glory to turn her head. Being beaten won't hurt her at all."

"I would rather win it," answered Anne, with passionate fervor, "than almost anything in the world. And think of the big prize of $100! If I could win that——" Words failed to express her enthusiasm and she paused and clasped her hands.

"Oh, well, we won't expect that of you," replied Grace, "Nobody could be expected to pass a perfect examination. That's an impossible achievement."

"*I* shall try, anyway," said Anne in a low voice.

Just then they were joined by a young man of about eighteen, who lifted his hat politely to them.

"May I walk with you?" he asked of Grace. "You seem to be going my way this morning."

"Certainly, David, we are going your way. We are lunching with your next door neighbor, Mrs. Gray. But you must let me introduce you to

Miss Pierson. Anne, this is Mr. Nesbit, Miriam's brother."

Anne flushed at the mention of Miriam's name and bowed distantly to the newcomer, who was a junior at the High School and quite grown-up to the young freshmen.

David Nesbit, like his sister, was tall, dark and handsome; but unlike her, he was quiet and unassuming. He, too, stood at the head of his classes, but he was not athletic, as Miriam was, and spent most of his time in the school laboratory, experimenting, or working at home on engines and machinery of his own contriving.

However, there was nothing snobbish in David's attitude. He greeted Anne as cordially as he had the others.

"We never see you now, David," continued Grace. "You are always so busy with your inventions and contrivances. What is the latest? A flying machine?"

"You guessed right the very first time," replied David. "It is just that."

"Really?" laughed the girls, incredulously, while Anne's eyes grew large with interest.

"Shall you fly around Oakdale in it?" asked Jessica.

"Oh, we are not building big ones yet," answered David. "These are little fellows. Models, you know. The big ones may come later. Six of the junior and senior fellows have been working on them all summer. We started it in the manual training course. After we had learned to hammer things out of silver, and do wood carving and a few other little useful accomplishments, I suggested a flying machine to Professor Blitz and he fell to it like a ripe peach. It was too late to do anything last spring except talk, however. But we are almost ready now, after our labors this summer."

"Ready for what?" demanded Grace. "If you are not going to fly yourselves."

"For our exhibition. Why don't you come and see it at the gym. next Friday night?"

"We can't. We aren't invited," answered Nora, tossing back her saucy little curls.

"I'll invite you," said David. "This will admit four young ladies to the High School gym.," he continued, taking out a card and writing on it, "At 7.30 Thursday evening."

"Then everybody isn't invited?" demanded Jessica.

"No, not everybody," replied David. "Just a chosen few. And you must be sure to come, too, Miss Pierson," he added, turning to Anne, who, all this time, had been silently listening to the conversation.

"I should love to," she answered, giving him a grateful glance.

"I'll leave you here," said David, turning in at a graveled driveway that led to the Nesbit house, a very large and ornate building standing far back from the street in the midst of a well-kept lawn.

"I wish Miriam would take a few lessons in manners from her brother," murmured Grace, when they were out of hearing distance.

"He is certainly one of the nicest boys in High School," said Jessica.

"If he only played football!" said Grace, with a sigh.

"And danced," added Nora.

"I don't know how to dance, nor did I ever see a game of football," said Anne.

"Meaning that Mr. David suits you, Miss Anne," said Grace teasingly.

"It was nice of him to ask me, too," was all Anne said in reply.

"How do you do, my dears?" said Mrs. Gray, a few moments later, when John, the aged butler, ushered the girls into the long, old-fashioned parlor. "You are most kind to come and cheer up a lonely old woman. I shall expect you to be very gay and tell me all the gossip of the Oakdale High School, the four of you."

"Luncheon is served, ma'am," announced John, whereat the sprightly old lady led the way to the dining room.

Over the delicious broiled chicken and other good things they discussed the affairs of the school, the new teacher in mathematics, Miss Leece, who was so unpopular; the girls' principal, Miss Thompson, beloved by all the pupils; the merits of the Freshman Basketball Team and a dozen other schoolgirl topics that seemed to delight the ears of Mrs. Gray.

"The truth is," she said, "I believe this freshman class is going to be one of the finest Oakdale High School has ever turned out. I have a feeling that I shall be very proud of my new girls, and at Christmas time I mean to do something I have never done before, if all goes well."

"Oh, do tell us what it is, Mrs. Gray," cried the girls in great excitement.

"I mean to celebrate with the largest Christmas party that's been given in Oakdale for many a long year. Grace, you shall manage it for me, and all of you shall help me decorate the tree and the house. We'll invite the freshmen boys and have a real dance with Ohlson's band for the music."

"Oh, oh!" cried the girls ecstatically, even quiet Anne joining in the chorus.

"By the way," went on Mrs. Gray, "do you know any girl who would like to come up and read to me twice a week, and write my notes for me? I'm getting to be an old woman. My eyesight is growing dim. Is there any girl who would like to earn a little pocket money? But she must have a sweet, soft voice, like Anne's here."

"Anne would be the very girl herself, Mrs. Gray," suggested Grace. "She reads and recites beautifully."

"You are not sure it would trespass on your time too much, Anne?"

observed the wily old lady. "I don't want to impose on you."

Anne's face fairly radiated with happiness. Could those girls possibly guess how much it meant to her to earn a little money! Five dollars was to her an enormous sum, and perhaps she might earn as much as that in time.

"Might I do it?" she exclaimed, beside herself with joy.

Grace turned her face away a moment. She felt almost ashamed of her own comfortable prosperity. And how like Mrs. Gray it was to do a kind thing in that way, as if Anne would be conferring a favor by accepting the position.

"Indeed, you might, my dear. And I feel myself lucky to get the brightest girl in her class, and maybe in Oakdale High School, to come and entertain me twice a week."

# CHAPTER IV

## THE BLACK MONKS OF ASIA

"Who wants to go nutting?" demanded Grace Harlowe in the basement cloakroom a few afternoons later.

"We do," came a chorus of voices.

"I don't," answered one.

"Don't you like nutting parties, Miriam?" asked Grace.

"She's too old," put in a sophomore. "This is a young people's party, I presume?"

"Well, it's not a sophomore party, at any rate," retorted Nora.

"Ma-ma, ma-ma," cried a number of other sophomores, imitating the cries of a baby.

The freshmen were nettled by the superior attitude of the older class, but they knew better than to say anything more just then.

"Never mind, girls," said Grace in a low voice, after the sophomores had strolled away, "we'll be sophomores ourselves next year. Now, all who want to join the party, meet Nora and Jessica and me at the old Omnibus House at three-thirty. And, above all, don't give the meeting place away."

"Not in a thousand years," said Marian Barber.

It was evident that Miriam Nesbit had hoped to break up the party by declining to go herself. But she was not quite strong enough in the class to divide it utterly, and she went off in a huff, with the secret wish to take revenge on somebody. As she started up Chapel Hill to her home she was joined by one of the sophomore girls, who lived across the street.

"Your plebes are getting away from you, Miriam," exclaimed the older girl in a bantering tone. "You haven't got them well in hand yet. Nutting parties should be left behind for the Grammar School pupils."

"They certainly should," replied Miriam in a disgusted tone. "It's Grace Harlowe who gets up all these foolish children's games. She's nothing but a tomboy, anyhow."

"She's the captain of the basketball team, isn't she?" asked the other dryly.

"Yes," admitted Miriam reluctantly, "but she never would have been if she hadn't brought along all her friends to vote for her."

"Whew-w-w!" whistled the sophomore. "You don't mean to say it wasn't a fair election?"

"Oh, fair enough," said Miriam, "except that I didn't bother to bring any of my special friends, and she did. I don't call that exactly fair."

"Oh, well," consoled the other, "you have a few things coming to you anyway, Miriam. You're at the head of your class, as usual, I suppose?"

Miriam nodded her head without answering. She was thinking of little Anne Pierson and what a close race they were running together. Even studying harder than she had ever had to do before, Miriam found it difficult to keep up with Anne.

"Where are they going?" asked the other girl suddenly, after they had walked along a few minutes in silence.

"Where are who going?" asked Miriam.

"Why, the nutting party, of course."

Here was Miriam's chance for revenge. The sophomores were a famously mischievous class, and this girl was one of its ringleaders. Back in Grammar School days they had played many pranks on their school fellows, and even in their freshman year they had dared to turn off all lights, one night at a dance of older schoolmates.

"If I tell, you won't give me away, will you?" asked Miriam.

"I promise," said the older girl.

"Very well, then. They meet at three-thirty at the Omnibus House on the River road."

"Good," said the sophomore. "Don't you want to come along and see the fun?"

"Don't count on me," answered Miriam, turning in at her gate, with mixed feelings of shame and triumph.

The Omnibus House, which had been chosen by Grace as the class meeting place, was an old stone building standing in the middle of an orchard. It was now in ruins, but tradition set it down as a former inn and stage coach station built before the days of railroads, and finally burned by the Indians. There was a curious hieroglyphic sign cut in a stone slab in the front wall which one of the High School professors interested in archeology had deciphered as follows: "Peace and Justice Reign Over Mount Asia Tavern."

Here the crowd of High School "plebes," as the sophomores scornfully dubbed them, met in conclave, partly to gather nuts in the woods nearby, partly to discuss class matters, but chiefly to enjoy the crisp autumn weather. The woods were still gorgeous in russets and reds, in spite of the recent heavy frosts, and there was a smell of burning leaves and dry bracken in the air. The girls skipped about like young ponies.

"If this is childish," cried Grace, "then I'd like to be a child always, for I shall play in the woods when the notion strikes me, even if I'm a grandmother."

There was a smothered snicker at this from the inside of the old stone house, but the girls were too intent on their enjoyment to notice it.

19

"Young ladies," exclaimed Nora O'Malley, trailing her cape after her to make her skirts look longer, and twisting her mouth down to give her face a severe expression, "you are not in your usual form to-day. I must ask for better preparation hereafter."

There was a peal of joyous laughter from the other girls.

"Miss Leece to a dot," cried Jessica.

"Miss Bright," went on Nora, "you will please pay attention to the lesson. If you do not, young woman, I shall have to punish you in the old-fashioned way."

"You will, will you?" cried Jessica, rushing gaily upon her friend. "Come on and try it then!"

The other girls followed, and there was a tussle to pull Nora down from the stone upon which she had clambered to protect herself.

Shrieks, struggles and wild laughter followed, while Nora fought desperately to hold her position. So absorbed were they in friendly battle that they had not noticed a troop of black-robed figures leaving the ruined Omnibus House and stealthily approaching.

Nora was the first to see the ominous circle. She stopped short, and pointed with unmistakable terror at the masked and hooded persons, who were watching them silently. There was a moment of frozen horror when the girls turned around. This was a lonely spot, too remote from any dwelling to call for help. Besides, the freshmen were outnumbered by these weird figures, who appeared not unlike monks in their somber cowls, although their faces were absolutely hidden by black masks.

The girls clustered together around the rock like a group of frightened chickens. Jessica had turned pale. She was not very robust and often overtaxed her strength to keep up with her two devoted friends.

The tallest of the masked figures then spoke in a queer, deep voice.

"Young women, are you not aware that this is a sacred spot, devoted for generations past to the Black Monks of Asia, whose home this building was before it became a roadhouse for stage coaches? Never invade this spot again with your hilarity. And now we will permit you to go, marching out single file, without looking back. But first, through your leader you must give your word never to mention this meeting to anyone. If you refuse this promise we shall punish you as only the Black Monks of Asia know how to punish persons who have offended the order. The leader will please step forward."

There was a moment's whispered conversation among the freshmen. Then Grace, urged by her friends, said:

"We promise."

"Now march out, single file, as agreed," resumed the Black Monk of Asia, his voice trembling a little with suppressed emotion of some sort.

The girls started to move out of the enclosure single file, Grace leading the procession, when a gust of wind blew the robe of the leading monk apart, disclosing a navy blue serge walking-skirt. Grace's quick eye caught sight of the skirt at once, and breaking from the line, she charged straight into the group of black monks, crying:

"Sophomores! Sophomores!"

The other girls ran after her, screaming at the tops of their voices; and there might have been almost a free fight between the two classes had not the Black Monks of Asia scattered in every direction, running at utmost speed.

"Come on back, girls," cried Grace in a disgusted tone.

She had chased a monk half-way across the orchard; then stopped to wonder what she would do if she caught the tall, black-robed individual who had indecorously caught up her skirts and was flying well ahead over the rough ground.

One by one the plebes returned to their meeting place.

"Well, that was a sell!" uttered Nora disgustedly. "How shall we ever manage to get even with those mean sophomores!"

"If we don't," exclaimed Grace, "we shall never hear the last of it in Oakdale."

"But who gave us away?" demanded Jessica. "Did anyone drop a hint to the sophomores of our secret meeting place?"

"I didn't," said one girl after another.

"Perhaps they followed us," suggested Marian Barber.

"No one followed me," asserted Grace. "I was careful to look behind and see."

"Nor me."

"Nor me," exclaimed several of her classmates.

"No," said Nora. "Somebody must have overheard and given the secret away."

"Not Mi——" but Grace stopped before she had finished the name.

The girls looked at each other.

Could Miriam Nesbit have been so false to her class?

No one replied, but each made a secret resolution to ferret out Miriam's suspected treachery if it were the last act of her life.

"Let's start home, now," said Grace. "It's too late to go nutting anyhow, and these foolish sophomores have spoiled the afternoon, for me at least. If we don't cook up something to pay them back, the name of freshman will be disgraced forever more."

However, the afternoon adventures were not at an end.

As the group of girls started toward the road, some distance away, trying not to look crestfallen, a gruff voice from the far side of the Omnibus House called:

"Hold up there!"

The girls took no notice, thinking it was more upper-class tricks.

Five rough-looking men emerged from a grove of alders which grew about the building.

The young girls were really frightened this time. No sophomore could disguise herself like this. These were undoubtedly genuine ruffians of the worst type, hungry, blear-eyed and ragged.

"What shall we do?" whispered Jessica, clinging to Grace desperately.

"Everybody run," answered her friend, trying to be calm as the five men advanced on them. But when they broke away to run toward the distant road they found their retreat cut off by the tramps, who were active enough as soon as the girls showed signs of flight. Back of them lay the dense woods into which the sophomores must have plunged and departed for town by another road. Seeing that escape was impossible, since, if some got away, others would be caught—and no girl was willing to desert her friends—the frightened plebes paused again and clustered about their leader.

"What do you want?" asked Grace of one of the men.

"First your money, then your jewelry," answered the tramp, insolently leering at her.

"But suppose we haven't any money or jewelry," replied Grace.

"So much the worse for you, then," answered the tramp in a threatening tone.

"He can have this gold bracelet," exclaimed Jessica, slipping the band from her arm.

But Grace was not listening. Her attention was absorbed by a group of people passing in a straggling line on the road. Lifting up her voice she gave the High School yell, which had been familiar to every High School boy and girl for the last twenty years:

"Hi-hi-hi; hi-hi-hi; Oakdale, Oakdale, HIGH SCHOOL!"

As she expected, the call was answered immediately, and some of the loiterers along the highway vaulted the fence at one bound.

"Help!" cried all the girls in chorus. "Help! Help!"

"It's some of the High School boys!" exclaimed Nora, in a relieved voice as the rescuers came bounding through the orchard.

The tramps looked irresolute for a moment, but when they saw that the newcomers were five boys they held their ground.

"What do you want?" said the tallest boy, with a flaming head of red hair, as he confronted one of the tramps.

"Thank heaven it's Reddy Brooks, pitcher on the sophomore baseball team!" whispered Grace, unable to conceal her joy.

"Is that any of your business, young man?" demanded the tramp, showing his teeth like an angry dog.

"It's my business to protect these young ladies," answered Reddy Brooks, "and I'll do it if I have to shed somebody's blood in the attempt."

"Ho, ho, ho!" laughed the big tramp, clapping his hands to his sides and almost dancing a jig in his amusement.

In the meantime Reddy had cast his eyes about for some kind of a weapon. There was not a stick nor stone in sight. The only thing he could find was a pile of winter apples that had evidently been collected by the owner of the orchard to be barreled next day.

Reddy made a rush for the pile, to the amazement of his fellow-students, who imagined for a moment that he was running away. They soon found out his purpose, however, when the apples came whizzing through the air with well-aimed precision.

The first one hit the biggest tramp squarely on the chin and almost stunned him. Each boy then chose his man and the five ruffians were soon running across the orchard to the wood, the boys after them, their pockets bulging with apples. Laughing and yelling like wild Indians, they pelted their victims until the men disappeared in the forest.

The girls, who had forgotten their fright in the excitement of the chase, were laughing, too, and urging on the attacks exactly as they would have done at one of the college football games. Perhaps they had had a narrow escape, but it was great fun, now, especially when Reddy Brooks threw one of his famous curved balls and hit a tramp plump on the back of the head.

"Oh," cried Nora, wiping tears of laughter from her eyes, "I never had such a good time in all my life! Wasn't it great?"

"Wasn't it though?" grinned Reddy, as the boys returned from the field of victory. "Lots more fun than throwing balls at dummies at the county fair, wasn't it, fellows?"

"You girls ought to be careful how you walk out here alone at this time of the year," said Jimmie Burke. "There are a great many tramps around now, going south in bunches to spend the winter in Palm Beach, no doubt."

"We'll never do it again," answered Grace.

"Never again!" exclaimed Nora, raising her right hand to heaven.

"I suppose Farmer Smithson will wonder what became of his apples," observed Reddy.

"Oh, well, he has so many acres of orchards, I don't suppose he'll miss this one little pile."

And the crowd started gaily off to town.

But the girls of the freshman class had not forgotten—or forgiven—the Black Monks of Asia.

All along the walk Grace was turning over and over in her mind some scheme of revenge. Nothing seemed feasible, however. The sophomores were so well up in tricks that it would be difficult to deceive them.

"Suppose," Grace proposed suddenly, aloud, "we ask David Nesbit's advice to-morrow night, when we go to the flying machine exhibition."

After that she dismissed the subject from her mind for the time being

# CHAPTER V

## ANNE HAS A SECRET

On the night of the flying machine exhibition, the four chums, for Anne had now been formally adopted by Grace and her friends, arrived somewhat early at the great arched doorway leading into the gymnasium.

They were all somewhat excited over this new experience. There had been many balloon ascensions at the State Fair, and once a dirigible airship had sailed over the town of Oakdale. But to see a real flying machine with all its grace and elegance and lightness was like stepping onto another planet where progress had advanced much faster than it had on this.

At least, so thought Anne as she followed her friends into the building. There was a sound of puffing and churning, during which David arrived in a cloud of smoke on his motor cycle.

"I mean to learn to ride one of those queer machines," exclaimed Grace from the doorway, never dreaming what an important part that very machine was one day to play in the history of Oakdale.

"All right, you're welcome to," replied David, jumping off as he stopped the motor. "Come over to the campus to-morrow afternoon, and I'll give you your first lesson."

"Is that really an invitation?" asked Grace. "For I shall accept it, if it is."

"It certainly is," answered the young man, "and I shall expect you to make a very excellent prize pupil, not like Reddy Brooks, who tumbled off and smashed his nose because he suddenly forgot how to manage the brakes."

A few other people gathered in the roomy gymnasium to see the exhibition, but the girls could see that it was a very exclusive company they had been invited to join. There were, in fact, no other girls, except Miriam Nesbit, who came late with her mother, a handsome, quiet woman to whom her son David bore a marked resemblance.

Grace and her friends spoke to Mrs. Nesbit cordially, while Miriam bowed coldly and confined all her attentions to Miss Leece, the unpopular teacher of mathematics. Miriam ignored Anne entirely.

"And now, ladies, if you will all be seated, the show will begin," announced David, leading them to the spectators' benches ranged against the wall. "Don't expect anything wonderful of mine," he added. "It's only in the first stages so far. I'm afraid she'll break down, but she's a great little machine, just the same. Isn't she, mother?"

"She is wonderful, I think, David," replied Mrs. Nesbit, who was a very shy, quiet woman, almost entirely wrapped up in her only son. Miriam had always been too much for her, and she had long since given up attempting to rule or direct her brilliant, willful daughter.

"Mrs. Nesbit," said Grace, "this is Anne Pierson, one of the brightest girls in the freshman class."

"How do you do?" said Mrs. Nesbit cordially, giving the girl her hand. "You are a newcomer, are you not? I haven't heard Miriam speak of you."

"She is a newcomer, mother, but I hear she's giving your daughter Miriam a stiff pull for first place," said David teasingly.

"I wish you'd keep quiet, David," exclaimed his sister angrily. "You always talk too much."

"Miriam!" remonstrated her mother.

"Miss Nesbit," said Miss Leece in a disagreeable, harsh voice, "will have no trouble, I think, in holding her own."

The teacher gave Anne such a glare from her pale blue eyes that the poor child shrank behind Grace in embarrassment.

"Dear, dear," murmured Mrs. Nesbit helplessly. She disliked exceedingly the scenes to which her daughter often subjected the family.

David only laughed good-naturedly.

"The exhibition is about to begin," he said, and disappeared into the room where the ships were to be put through their performances.

In a few moments six young airship builders appeared, each carrying in his arms the result of his summer's labors. There was vigorous applause from everybody except Miriam, who was too angry with her brother to enjoy the spectacle.

The aeroplanes were all copies of well-known models, except David's, which was of an entirely new and original design of his own invention. It looked something like a flying fish, the girls thought, with its slender, oblong body, gauzy fins at the sides and a funny little forked tail at the stern.

The models were too light for machinery, so rubber bands, secured criss-cross in the bows, when suddenly released with a snap gave the little ships the impetus they needed to fly the length of the gymnasium.

Only four of the six, however, were destined to fly that evening. They soared straight down the big room, as easily and gracefully as great white birds, and dropped gently when they hit the curtain at the other end, their builders running after them as eagerly as boys sailing kites. One of the models fluttered and settled down before it reached the other side, and David's machine, which had commanded most attention because it was different, started out bravely enough, its little propeller making a busy humming as it skimmed along. But it had gone hardly ten yards before it collapsed and ignominiously crashed to the floor.

"I'm glad of it," said Miriam above the din, for everyone had gathered about the young man to offer sympathy and congratulations at the same time.

"It's very, very clever, my boy," said Professor Blitz, "and you'll succeed yet, if you keep at it."

"She wouldn't go far, David," said Grace, stroking the little model, as if it had been a pet dog, "but she's the prettiest of all, just the same."

"Did it hurt it when it fell?" Anne asked him.

"I think it broke one of its little fins," laughed David. "It hurt me much more than itself, because it wouldn't be good and fly all the way."

"Anne," called Grace, "here is someone looking for you. It's a boy with a note."

Anne looked frightened as she opened a soiled looking envelope the boy handed her.

27

"Is anything the matter?" asked Jessica, seeing the expression of fear on her face.

"No—yes——," answered poor little Anne, undecidedly. "I must go home, or rather I mustn't go the way I came. Don't you think I could leave at a side entrance? I don't want to see the person who is waiting for me in front."

"Of course, child," spoke up Grace. "We'll see you home ourselves. Won't we, girls!"

"Wait until I lock up my motor cycle and I'll go along," called David. "We'll all protect Miss Anne."

"Tell him," said Anne to the boy, putting the note back in the envelope and giving it to him, "that what he asks is impossible."

"Couldn't you squeeze us into the carriage, mother?" asked David, returning presently with his hat.

"I have invited Miss Leece to drive home with us, mother," interrupted Miriam, giving her brother a blighting glance. "There is room for only one more person. Perhaps Jessica will take it."

"You are very kind," said Jessica coldly, "but I prefer to walk with the girls."

"*You'd* better walk, too, cross-patch, and learn a few manners from your friends," was David's parting advice to his sister.

"Children, children!" exclaimed Mrs. Nesbit, "don't, I beg of you, quarrel in public."

Presently the five young people had slipped out of a side door of the gymnasium and started down a back street in the direction of Anne's house. They had not gone far, however, before they became aware that they were being followed. Grace was the first to call the attention of Nora and Jessica to a long, slim figure stealing after them in the shadows.

"Here he comes," whispered Jessica. "What in the world do you suppose he wants with our poor little Anne?"

"I believe he's going to stop us," returned Grace. "He is coming nearer and nearer."

28

"Anne, I command you to wait!" called a voice from behind them.

They all stopped suddenly and Anne jumped as though she had received a shock.

A tall, theatrical-looking individual had come up to them. He wore a shabby frock coat and a black slouch hat, which he raised with an elaborate flourish when he saw the young girls.

"Pardon me, ladies," he said, "but I wish to speak with my daughter."

Anne controlled herself with an effort.

"I cannot see you now, father," she said. "It is quite late and I must get back."

"You shall not only speak to me but you shall come with me," exclaimed the man, with a sudden flare of anger. "I will not submit to disobedience again. Come at once!"

"Father, I cannot go with you," cried Anne, clinging to her friends. "I would rather be with mother and Mary. They need me more than you do and I want to go to school and study to be a teacher."

The man was now beside himself with theatrical rage.

"Miserable child!" he cried, waving his arms wildly. "I shall take you if I must by force." Breaking through the group, he seized the hand of his daughter and dragged her after him.

"Oh, save me!" cried the poor girl, struggling to release herself.

"I can't stand this! If she doesn't want to go with him, she shan't, father or no father," growled David, dashing after the pair.

"Stop, sir!" he cried, seizing Anne's other hand. "I must ask you to release this young lady at once."

"Insolent boy!" cried the other, giving each word an oratorical flourish, "are you not aware that this young lady, as you call her, is merely a child, and that she happens to be my daughter? I cannot see that you have a right to interfere in a family matter."

"But I have no proof that Miss Pierson is your daughter," retorted David. "It is enough that she doesn't want to go with you. I undertook to see her safely to her own home, this evening, and I mean to do it. After that you may settle your difficulties as you please."

"Miserable upstart!" cried the man, now so thoroughly angry that he let go Anne's hand, "I have a good mind to give you what you deserve. As for you, undutiful, wretched girl," he added, his voice rising to an emotional tremolo, "you shall be well punished for this!"

"Don't wait," whispered Anne. "If we run, we can get away, now, while he is so angry." At that they all took to their heels, David following after them, much relieved to have given Anne's father the slip without further disagreeable argument.

No one spoke until they had reached the Pierson cottage and had seen Anne safely to the front door.

"I'm so sorry!" she exclaimed at last, trying not to cry. "I wouldn't for anything have had it happen, and just when you were all beginning to like me a little. Will you forgive me?"

"Forgive you, Anne!" cried Grace. "It wasn't your fault. We are only awfully sorry for you."

"We will just forget all about it, and never speak of it to anyone," promised Jessica, taking the girl's hand kindly.

"But I want you to understand that I was right in not going," protested Anne. "Someday I will explain."

"Of course you were right," said David, "and I hope you will never be persuaded to go."

"Thank you, all, a thousand times!" came gratefully from Anne; "and good night." Then she disappeared into the cottage.

"Well, this was a night's adventure," observed Grace, as they started homeward.

"I am afraid Anne's father is a night's adventurer," muttered David. "He looks mightily like one of those strolling actors who go barnstorming through country towns."

"Poor Anne! Do you suppose he wants her to barnstorm?" asked Nora.

"I haven't a doubt of it," replied the young man. "I think you girls had better adopt that poor child and look after her."

"We have already," answered Grace. "Didn't Miriam tell you about it?"

"Miriam? No; she never tells me anything. Besides, what has she to do with it?"

The girls were silent.

"By the way," continued Grace, "speaking of barnstorming, we want to ask your advice, David. The sophomores played a mean trick on us the other day at the old Omnibus House."

"I heard something about the Black Monks of Asia," answered David, laughing.

"Can't your inventive brain devise a scheme of revenge?" went on Grace. "If we don't get even with them soon, the story will be all over town."

"Well," replied David, "I can tell you a secret I happened to have overheard when one of the sophomores was calling on Miriam. I was an eavesdropper entirely by accident, but what I heard might help some. The sophomores are going to give an initiation mask ball a week from Saturday night. Only the class and a few outsiders, among them Miriam, are to be present. Everybody is to be in fancy dress, and disguised out of all recognition. Can't you work up a scheme with that to go upon, girls?"

"We certainly can," cried Nora. "It's the chance of a lifetime."

"Just wait and see!" exclaimed Grace.

"By the way, David, you didn't happen to overhear the password, did you?" asked Jessica.

"I did," he replied. "Nothing escaped me, for I was caught in a trap. You know I don't care for that large, husky young damsel who leads the sophomores, and if I had made my presence behind the screen known, I should have had to speak to her. So I just sat still and said nothing. The password is 'Asia.'"

"They are trying to rub it in, I suppose," cried Grace. "But I think they won't be so ready to use that word after their old ball is over."

"If you want any help," offered David as he left Grace at her front door, "you know where to come for it, don't you?"

"You're a true brick, David!" said Grace. "Good night."

# CHAPTER VI

## THE SOPHOMORE BALL

There was an undercurrent of excitement in the air on the day of the sophomore ball.

The sophomores themselves were full of secrets, whispering around in groups, their faces grave with self-important expressions. This was to be their annual Initiation Ball, and many new members, after receiving initiation into the various sophomore societies, were to be invited to the gymnasium, which had been turned over to the class for the evening.

There was no end to the fun of these balls, according to feminine gossip, for no male was ever admitted and only three invitations were issued to girls of other classes. It was, in fact, to be nothing but fun and frolic, and every costume had been planned weeks ahead.

One teacher was asked to be present to keep order in case of intrusion, for the gymnasium door, on that famous night, was always besieged by youths from the Boys' High School, who roared and jeered as each cloaked and masked figure rushed under the archway and disappeared.

The freshmen, all through the day, were unusually quiet. They kept to themselves and had little to say. Miriam and her three particular friends were carefully avoided by their classmates. Miriam, herself, felt the snub at once. Had she, after all, made a mistake, and was she losing ground in the class? But her vanity was like a life buoy to her sinking hopes. She refused to see that the other girls regarded her with growing dislike.

When school was over, that afternoon, six girls strolled down the High School walk arm in arm. They were Grace and her three chums and two other girls who were popular in the freshman class.

Anne's small figure seemed almost dwarfed next to Grace, who towered half a foot her. Ever since Anne's trying scene with her father, Grace had been doubly tender and kind to her, until the young girl seemed to expand under the happy influence.

"Well, girlies, dear, we are the chosen six. I hope we shall be a credit to the class."

"Don't talk so loudly, Nora. I feel as if we were surrounded by spies to-day. Everybody has been so mysterious and queer."

"One thing is practically certain," whispered Grace: "I believe it was Miriam who told the sophomores about the Omnibus House. Why else did they invite her to their ball?"

"We can never prove it, though," said one of the others, "unless we get her up a tree some day and make her admit it."

"Remember, Anne," cautioned Grace, when they came to the cross street leading to the Pierson cottage, "eight o'clock sharp at my house! And don't bother about things. We shall have more than enough among us."

At half-past eight that night the sound of a stringed orchestra floated out on the breeze as the door of the gymnasium swung back and forth to admit disguised sophomores, who each whispered the countersign to the doorkeeper, after running the gauntlet of the waiting crowd, and slipped in.

The music was furnished by a troupe of women players especially engaged to play in this Adamless Eden. What would not the crowd of waiting boys have given for one glimpse of the ball room, where ballet girls, clowns and courtiers, Egyptian snake charmers, Mephistopholeses and Marguerites, priests and priestesses of the Orient, all whirled madly together?

Every door had been locked and bolted and every downstairs window securely closed. Ventilation was obtained through the half-open windows opening on the upper gallery, which ran around the four sides of the gymnasium. The doors to this gallery had also been locked and the only way to reach it was by steps leading up from the gymnasium.

Six masked and hooded figures swung down High · School Street together, talking and laughing in low voices. The smallest of the six appeared to stumble over her feet, and once tumbled in the road. Her friends gayly helped her up, when it was disclosed that she wore a pair of boy's shoes much too large for her.

"If we don't break our necks stumbling over these brogans," whispered the tallest girl, "we'll be lucky."

As a matter of fact, each one of the six maskers was wearing a pair of men's shoes.

"I stuffed my toes with cotton," laughed another, "but even now they are hard to manage."

Just then a motor cycle shot past them, slowed down and stopped altogether.

The rider rested it against a tree and came back.

"I recognized you by your big feet," he said in a whisper. "Grace, here's the duplicate key to the laboratory. I had some trouble getting it, but no one knows, and you'll be safe enough. I'll let myself in with the other duplicate key and lock the door. They will be sure to try it at intervals. If you get into any trouble, early in the evening, make a dash for the steps and blow your horn loud. Now, that's all, I think. I'll be hidden in the laboratory until my turn comes. Good-bye and good luck!"

In another instant he was off on his motor cycle.

Six figures, well disguised in dominoes of as many hues, presently appeared on the ball room floor, just in time for the grand march. It was a pity no one, except the lone teacher, was permitted to look at the brilliant picture. But such was the tradition of the class. After the march, ten ballet girls in tarlatan skirts, their faces concealed by little black satin masks, gave a performance. Following this, a Spanish dancer, whom the six dominoes recognized at once as the treacherous Miriam Nesbit, gave an exhibition of her skill.

"I'm going to have some fun with her," whispered the blue domino to the red one. "Just follow me and see."

The last speaker joined the dancer as the music struck up a waltz.

"That was a good day's work you did for our class, not long ago," she whispered as they danced off together.

"What do you mean?" asked the Spanish dancer.

"I mean the Black Monks of Asia. Now, do you understand?"

"But I thought it was not to be told," exclaimed the dancer, flushing under her mask.

"Only to the committee so that you might be rewarded with an invitation," whispered the domino, as she slipped away.

"*She* did confess it, and every freshman in the class shall know it to-morrow!" the emissary exclaimed privately to her friend, the red domino.

"In spite of what her brother is doing for us to-night?" returned the red domino.

"You are quite right, child. I never thought of that. Perhaps that is the very reason he is helping us get even to-night."

"I think it is," added the other, quietly.

"Girls, we must hurry up and begin," whispered another of the six dominoes. "They are all going to unmask at half-past ten."

So the unrecognized intruders slipped away, stationing themselves about the room.

Pretty soon a rumor began to spread among the dancers that there were young men present. No one knew exactly how it started, but it grew and spread with such persistency that it finally reached the ears of the chaperon.

"Some of the girls saw their feet," said her informant, "and not only their feet but their trousers, too."

The teacher rose and rapped sharply for order.

"Young ladies," she called in a loud voice, "I am sorry to disturb the dancers, but we have every reason to believe there are some men in the room. Since it is not yet time for you to unmask, it will be simple to find out who does not belong here by having you file past me. I will lift each mask myself."

The dancers accordingly arranged themselves in a long line and walked single file past the teacher. She saw only girl's faces, however, as she peeped under the masks, and the dance proceeded.

The next disturbance came when the maskers had all taken their stand at one end of the room at the request of the six dominoes, who managed to whisper to each sophomore that there was presently to be a surprise.

An expectant hush fell over the company as the six dominoes filed out of a side room and stood, for a moment, in full view of the sophomores. Then the six deliberately lifted their dominoes, disclosing trouser legs and men's shoes. Instantly the place was in pandemonium; yet before the sophomores could rush upon the intruders six long horns were blown in unison, and immediately the lights went out. In the darkness the six dominoes made for the stairs, rushed along the gallery, and were admitted to the laboratory by the duplicate key. But, just before the blue domino disappeared, she called out in a loud voice from the gallery:

"The freshmen are avenged!"

When the doors were safely closed the lights were turned on again, disclosing the sophomores blinking foolishly at each other after the sudden startling change from darkness to light.

"They are in the laboratory!" cried one. "Let's cut off their escape!"

The angry sophomores made a rush for the door.

"Hurry girls!" urged David, who had just returned to the laboratory after manipulating the lights. "They'll catch us before we know it."

But the young fugitives were too late. Just then there was the sound of many feet running up the stairs from the other door.

"How about one of the gallery doors?" asked Grace.

"They are all locked," answered David. "There only remain the skylight trap-door and the roof. Do you think you could manage it if I helped you?"

"Of course; we could manage anything," protested the freshmen girls.

It was an easy matter to climb up the ladder, and clamber through the trap-door on to the roof.

"We're just in time," whispered David. "They have found the right key to the gallery door, and they'll be coming in both ways. Crawl carefully now, girls, for heaven's sake, and don't slip!"

The seven young people began slowly to draw themselves along the gymnasium roof on their hands and knees. Fortunately, it was not a very sloping roof, and their only danger lay in their movements being heard from below. Meanwhile the gymnasium had emptied itself, and parties of enraged sophomores were engaged in searching the adjoining class rooms and passages.

"Let's surround the building on the outside," cried one of the class leaders. "They can't escape, then, by any of the fire escapes, and we are sure to catch them!"

In a few moments, David peeping over the edge of the roof, saw figures stationed at every possible exit, waiting patiently.

"Lie low," he whispered, "and crawl on your stomachs, or you're surely caught."

Soon after the seven had reached the end of the hundred feet of gymnasium, where their flight was stopped short by a blank wall where the gymnasium joined the High School building.

"Here's a pretty pass," whispered David. "I forgot about this old school wall. The only thing to do, now, is to hide behind this chimney and wait for the row to quiet down."

There they lay, as flat as possible, listening with bated breath to the sophomores below. Presently there was a sound of footsteps on the gymnasium roof and they heard Miriam's voice saying:

"They must have escaped through the trap-door in the laboratory and come along here. Wait a minute, girls, and I'll see."

"O Grace, we're caught!" groaned Jessica. "What shall we do?"

"No we aren't yet," answered Grace. "Especially if she is coming alone, and that is what I am praying for."

"I'll come with you, Miriam," called the voice of the sophomore leader.

"Why don't you take the other side?" proposed Miriam. "And I'll go around and meet you."

"Very well," came the answer.

The freshmen clutched each other and waited.

Miriam ran lightly along the roof, and came upon the seven prostrate figures so suddenly that she almost lost her balance.

"Don't speak," said Grace, in a distinct whisper, "and don't give us away. If you do, you will regret it. Remember the blue domino who waltzed with you!"

She hoped Miriam would understand what she meant and so save her from further explanation. In this Grace was right. Miriam was trapped at last. She deliberately turned and walked away without a word.

"Come on, girls," they heard her call to the others, "let's waste no more time on them." When all was quiet the seven intriguers slipped down the fire escape and disappeared in the darkness—safely escaping discovery.

# CHAPTER VII

## ALL HALLOWE'EN

"Anne," called a chorus of boys' and girls' voices, "come out and have some fun. Have you forgotten it's Hallowe'en?"

The door of the Pierson cottage opened and Anne appeared on the threshold.

"I can't," she answered; "I must study to-night."

"Oh, bother lessons!" exclaimed Grace Harlowe. "Skip them, for once, and join the crowd. We are going Hallowe'ening. Mother allowed it because David Nesbit and Reddy Brooks are along to look after us."

Anne looked longingly at the little company.

"I'll come," she sighed, "although it was my algebra I was working on. You know Miss Leece hates me, and, if I slip up, she'll be much harder than any of the other teachers."

"Hang Miss Leece!" said David promptly.

"Well, let's hang her, then," exclaimed Nora. "Let's dress her up and hang her on a limb of a tree."

"What do you mean by 'hang' her?" asked Grace, while Anne went in to put on her hat and coat.

"Don't you know?" replied Nora. "You stuff an old dress full of hay and paper, make a head out of any old thing, put a hat on it, and there you have her mighty fine."

"That's an old stunt, Nora," observed David. "Let's have something more improved and up-to-date. Suppose, for instance, we use Marian's Jack-o'-lantern for the head. I'll put some little electric bulbs in the eye holes and attach them to a battery so that we can turn her eyes off and on. And we'll ride her on a broomstick in good style."

39

"Only, nobody must know it's Miss Leece whose being effigied," urged Grace. "This must be merely for our own private satisfaction. Everybody promise not to tell."

Everybody promised; so, with Anne safely in tow, they started for Jessica's house to make the figure. Here they were not likely to be interrupted. Jessica's mother was dead and her father spent most of his evenings in his library.

Half a broomstick, with a small pumpkin attached to one end, formed the framework of Miss Leece's effigy. A cross beam gave a human touch to the shoulders and with the skeleton ready, the business of stuffing an old ulster and hanging it over the figure was simple. Tiny electric bulbs were placed in the eyes and a bonnet tied on the head with a green veil floating behind. Miss Leece, Nora insisted, always wore one growing out of her left ear. There was nothing left to do now, but to place the figure in a legless chair that had been nailed to two poles, and the procession was ready.

"She's a very fine lady," cried Grace, running ahead to get the effect of the absurd lopsided figure whose eyes glared and went out alternately. "I wish the real Miss L. could see herself now. She would know exactly what she looks like when she glares at poor little Anne in class."

"Yes, Anne," said David, "this shall be your party. We are going to give you satisfaction for your wrongs in the only way that lies in our power."

"Oh, I don't really mind her," replied Anne, "only I'm afraid she'll catch me unprepared, some day, and then I *will* get it in earnest."

"It's a perfect outrage," exclaimed Grace. "Miss Leece is so cruel to little Anne, David, that it makes my blood boil. I sometimes think she is trying to make Anne lose the freshman prize."

"The old Hessian!" cried David, who was on a sort of rampage that evening. "What shall I do to her, Anne? Give her an electric shock?" and he pressed the electric button rapidly up and down, which made the eyes glare hideously and go out several times in succession.

In a town the size of Oakdale strolling parties of boys and girls, on

Hallowe'en night, made a not unusual sight, so when our young people paraded boldly down the main street, singing and blowing horns, nothing was thought of it. What they were doing might be considered exceedingly out of place by a few straight-laced persons, but boys and girls will have their fun, even if it must sometimes be at the expense of other people.

Certainly Miss Leece was the most unpopular teacher ever employed in the High School as far back as memory could reach. She was cruel, strict and sharp-tongued. Often her violent, unrestrained temper got the better of her in the class room; then she gave an exhibition that was not good for young girls to see. Anne, especially, was the victim of her rages— poor little Anne who never missed a lesson and studied twice as hard as the other girls. Miss Leece had but one weakness, apparently, and that was Miriam Nesbit.

Twice had the faculty convened in secret session to consider Miss Leece's case, but it had been decided to keep her through the year at least, since she was engaged by contract and was moreover an excellent instructor in mathematics.

So, it was no wonder that even this early in the school year, she was the object of dislike to the High School girls. But could our girls have foreseen what the evening's fun would bring forth, they would never have been so reckless in carrying the effigy about town.

"Suppose we take her across the square," cried Reddy; "then over the bridge to the old graveyard and hang her on the limb of the apple tree just outside the wall?"

Off they started, singing at the tops of their voices:

Hang a mean teacher on a sour apple tree, Hang a mean teacher on a sour apple tree.

When they reached the center of the public square, where a big electric light shed its rays, who should spring out of the shadows, from nowhere apparently, but Miss Leece herself? Nothing escaped her sharp ears and her cold blue eyes; neither words of the song nor the figure in detail, green veil and all; nor Anne Pierson, who happened to be standing quite near the effigy at the moment.

And what was worse, and still more incriminating to the guilty merrymakers, the moment they caught sight of her they stopped singing. The eyes in the pumpkin suddenly lost their glare, and a silent procession wound its way hurriedly from the square.

"Good heavens!" cried Grace. "Why did we stop the song? If we had only gone right ahead, it wouldn't have looked half as bad."

"It was a mistake," admitted David, gravely, "especially as she seemed to have seen Anne first of all. Anne, if she walks into you to-morrow morning, you can just lay the blame on me, do you hear? I got up the whole party and I'm willing to stand for it."

"No, no," cried Anne. "That wouldn't be fair, David. I couldn't think of doing that."

"Well, you are not to get the blame, at any rate," said David, "if I have to go up and make a confession to the principal herself."

"Let's go and hang her now, anyhow," cried Reddy. "We'll take no half-way measures with old Queen Bess."

But somehow the spice of the adventure seemed to have gone out of it.

"It really would be dangerous now," said Grace. "She would be certain to hear of it and make it worse for all of us."

"Why not burn her," put in Nora, who was afraid of nothing and had often looked at the scolding teacher with such cold, laughing eyes, that even Miss Leece was disconcerted.

"Good!" cried several of the others. "We will take her down below the bridge and burn her as a witch."

No one objected to this, since the ashes of the effigy would tell no tales. Once more they started singing: "Merrily we roll along!" as they marched out of the village, crossed the bridge over the little river and finally paused on the bank below.

"Plant the pole in deep," said David, "so she won't topple, and fix her up to suit yourselves, girls, while we get the fagots."

The boys began to search about for dried sticks and twigs, while the girls were arranging the figure for her funeral pyre.

Suddenly, there was a wild war whoop. A crowd of boys dashed out of a thicket nearby, each one carrying a lighted Jack-o'-lantern on top of a pole, and surrounded the effigy of the teacher.

"Help!" cried the girls, trying to defend the absurd thing from the attack, but they were too late. One of the boys seized the pole and rushed off in the darkness.

Miss Leece, in effigy, had been kidnapped in an instant, before David and his friends had had time to realize what had happened.

"Which way did they go?" he asked breathlessly.

"Through the thicket," cried Grace.

And the whole crowd dashed after the kidnappers. It was great fun for everybody except Anne, who was too tired to keep up the chase for long, and was soon lagging behind the others. David saw her and turned back.

"You are too little for all this junketing, Anne," he said kindly. "Suppose I take you home? Shall I?"

"I wish you would, David," answered the girl. "I'm just about ready to drop, I'm so tired."

Taking her arm, he helped her over the ruts and rough places, until they finally emerged from the wood and started on the road to town.

There were many other Hallowe'en parties out that night; singing and laughing was heard in every direction.

"It's like a play," said Anne, "only everything is behind the scenes. Don't think I haven't enjoyed it, David, just because I got tired. I never played with boys and girls of my own age before. What fun it is!"

"Isn't it?" replied the young man, "I love to get out, once in a while, and have a good time like this. I find I can work all the better after it's over."

Presently the others caught up with them, breathless and laughing.

"Miss Leece is stolen," cried Grace, "before ever she was hanged or burned. I do wonder what they'll do with her."

"Oh, leave her in the woods," responded Reddy, "to scare the birds away."

"Good night, Anne," continued Grace. "David will take you home. We go this way. Don't be frightened about to-morrow. I doubt if she says anything; and if she does, we are all implicated."

The young people separated, still singing and laughing; never dreaming of the storm brewing from their evening's prank.

"Anne," pursued David, as they strolled down River Street together, "when I make my flying machine will you be afraid to take a sail with me?"

"Never," replied Anne, "but I wish it had been made in time to carry me away from Miss Leece to-morrow morning."

And Anne's words had more meaning than either of them realized at the time.

Imagine the surprise and horror of the Hallowe'en party when, next morning, they discovered the effigy of Miss Leece planted right in front of the Girls' High School!

And the teacher herself was the first to see the impious outrage.

# CHAPTER VIII

## MISS LEECE

Yes, there stood the hideous, grotesque effigy just where her abductors had left her the night before, her green veil floating in the breezes. As a figure of fun and an object of ridicule, she might not have created more than a ripple with the faculty. But it was evident that Miss Leece's function, even in effigy, was to make trouble.

And trouble was certainly brewing that memorable morning. The figure itself might never have been recognized, but a placard which had been pinned on the front of the old Ulster left no room for doubt. Across it had been inscribed in large printed letters:

"THE MOST UNPOPULAR TEACHER IN SCHOOL."

No one dared take the effigy away for fear of being implicated. Everybody had seen it, both men and women professors and the boys and girls of the two schools. But it was not until Miss Thompson, the principal of the Girls' High School, had arrived that the figure was removed.

"How could those boys have been so mean!" exclaimed Grace to her three friends just before the gong sounded. "They might have known what would happen."

There was an ominous quiet in the various class rooms all morning; but nothing was said or done to indicate just when the storm would burst. When the first class in algebra met, Anne trembled with fear, but Miss Leece, in a robin's egg-blue dress, which offset the angry hue of her complexion, was apparently too angry to trust herself to look in the direction of the young girl and the lesson progressed without incident.

However, she was only biding her time.

"Miss Pierson," she said, toward the end of the lesson, in a voice so rasping as to make the girls fairly shiver, "go to the blackboard and demonstrate this problem."

Then she read aloud in the same disagreeable voice, the following difficult problem:

"'Train A starts from Chicago going thirty miles an hour. An hour later Train B starts from Chicago going thirty-five miles an hour. How far from Chicago will they be when Train B passes Train A?'"

The girls looked up surprised. The problem was well in advance of what they had been studying and Miss Leece was really asking Anne to recite something she had not yet learned.

Anne hardly knew how to reply to the terrible woman who stood glowering at her as if she would like to crush her to bits.

"I'm sorry," said the girl. "I cannot."

"Miss Nesbit," said the teacher, "will you demonstrate this problem?"

Miriam rose with a little smile of triumph on her face and went to the blackboard, where she worked out the problem.

"Why, what on earth does the woman mean?" whispered Grace. "Are we expected to learn lessons we have never been taught and has that horrid Miriam been studying ahead?"

"I think I must be dreaming," replied Anne, looking sorrowfully at Miss Leece.

"Miss Pierson," thundered the teacher, "you are aware, I believe, that I permit no conversation in this class. Stupidity and inattention are not to be supported in any student, and I must ask you to leave the room."

Anne rose in a dazed sort of way, looking very small and shabby as she left the room.

But Miss Leece was not to come off so easily in the fight, and Anne had a splendid champion in Grace Harlowe, who could not endure injustice and was fearless where her rights or her friends' rights were concerned.

She rose quietly and faced the angry teacher, who already regretted having gone so far.

"If Miss Pierson is to be ordered from the room, Miss Leece, I shall follow her. I spoke to her first. I was naturally surprised that you gave out a problem so far in advance of our regular work. It is doubtful if any girl in the class could do it except Miriam, and she must have been prepared."

"Miss Harlowe," said Miss Leece, stamping her foot, and again giving way to rage, "I must ask you to take your seat at once and never interfere again with the way I conduct this class."

"You conduct this class with injustice and violence, Miss Leece," said Grace, turning very white, but holding herself in admirable control considering the conduct of the older woman.

"I am in no humor to be answered back this morning, Miss Harlowe, and I would advise you to be careful," continued the enraged woman. "I have had enough to try me since last night and this morning. Miss Pierson must answer to the principal for those insults, and her insubordination just now has only made matters worse."

"Miss Pierson has nothing to answer for which I have not, and I shall join her," replied Grace, and she left the room.

Miss Leece was about to continue the lesson when Jessica, pale and trembling, rose and followed her friend. Nora was next to go and in another moment there was not a girl left in the algebra class except Miriam and her four particular friends. The gong sounded as the last pupil closed the door behind her, but there was little doubt that the first class in algebra had gone on a strike.

The noon recess gong had sounded before the girls were able to meet and talk about the incident, and, during the time that intervened, Anne had received a summons in the form of a small note to meet the principal in her office at three that afternoon. She said nothing to her friends, however, and hid the envelope in her pocket.

The girls in IV. algebra gathered around their friends to hear the story.

They were indignant and expressed their readiness to join the strike out of sympathy in case there was any more trouble.

"They have no right to put such a violent woman over us," said Grace, as she nibbled at a pickle and a cracker in the locker room. "I wish they would give me the opportunity. I should be more than willing to testify to her behavior before the entire faculty and the school board combined."

Anne, herself, the center of the whole affair was very quiet. This remarkable young girl seemed to possess some secret force that she was able to draw upon when she most needed it.

"Anne, you precious child," exclaimed the impetuous Nora, "you must not get scared. Whatever happens, the whole class means to stand by you. Don't we, girls?"

"Yes," came from all sides.

"I don't think anything in particular will happen," replied Anne. "I believe Miss Leece really wants to prevent my winning the prize. That's all."

"She has certainly adopted a pet," cried Marian Barber.

"What did Miriam Nesbit mean by studying ahead like that?" exclaimed another. "It was disloyal to the whole class."

"It looks very much as if they had fixed it up between them," continued Grace. "I'm sorry about the effigy, but I won't stand that kind of favoritism. It's mean and underhanded."

After school Anne lingered in the corridor until the other girls had gone. Then she made her way slowly to the office of the principal. "Come in," came the answer to her timid knock.

Miss Thompson, the principal, was a fine woman, much beloved by the people of Oakdale where she had served as principal of the Girls' High School for many years. She had adjusted numerous difficulties in her time, but never such a knotty problem as the present one. It was incredible that Anne Pierson, who stood so well in her classes that she had already been mentioned by the faculty, should have engaged in such an escapade as Miss Leece had accused her of.

"Sit down," she said kindly to the young girl, whose small, tired face appealed to her sympathies. "What is this trouble between you and Miss Leece, Miss Pierson?" she continued, plunging into the subject.

"I do not know myself, Miss Thompson," answered Anne quietly.

"But she accuses you of rather terrible things, Miss Pierson," went on the principal, picking up a slip of paper and reading aloud, "'inattention, insubordination, impertinence and a tendency to make trouble.' Have you any answer to make to these charges?"

"No," replied Anne.

"Have you nothing to say?"

"Only that they are untrue."

"Miss Pierson," continued the principal, opening a closet door, "do you recognize this figure."

"Miss Pierson, Do You Recognize This Figure?"
89

## "Miss Pierson, Do You Recognize This Figure?"

There, hanging by its neck on a coat hook and still wearing its fantastic bonnet and green veil, was the famous effigy.

Anne looked at the absurd thing for a moment in silence. Then her eyes met Miss Thompson's, and both teacher and pupil burst out laughing.

The young girl never knew how far that laugh went to soften her present predicament. As a matter of fact, Miss Thompson had never liked the teacher in mathematics, while the small, shabby pupil appealed strongly

50

to her sympathy.

"Were you not the originator of this outrageous plot, Miss Pierson?"

Anne was silent. She could hardly say she was the originator and still she had participated.

"I will put the question in another form," said the principal. "If you were not the originator, who was?"

Still Anne made no reply.

"Miss Leece," continued the principal, "alleges that she distinctly saw you standing by the figure. She did not recognize the other faces. Do you think, Miss Pierson, that such an escapade as you engaged in last night was entirely respectful or worthy of a pupil of Oakdale High School?"

"No," replied Anne at last.

"Do you know that suspension or expulsion are the punishments for such behavior?"

Anne clasped her hands nervously. She saw the freshman prize floating away, and her eyes filled with tears, but she said nothing.

Instead of being angry, however, Miss Thompson was pleased with the girl's pluck and loyalty. But she was puzzled to know how to proceed. Her judgment and her sympathies revolted against punishing this prize pupil, and still it looked as if Miss Leece had everything on her side. A tap at the door interrupted her reflections, and Anne opened it, admitting Mrs. Gray escorted by David and Grace.

"My dear Miss Thompson," said the old lady, "I know you will consider me an interfering old woman, but when I heard that my particular child, Anne Pierson, was in trouble, I came straight to you. I want to talk the whole matter over comfortably; since it's my own freshman class that's on the rampage, I feel as if I had a right to put in a word."

"You are most welcome, Mrs. Gray," replied Miss Thompson, cordially.

She was exceedingly fond of the lonely old lady who had been a benefactor to the school in so many ways. "But what's this you say about the freshman class? I have heard nothing about it."

"Grace," said Mrs. Gray, "suppose you tell Miss Thompson what you have just finished telling me."

Then Grace related the incident in the algebra class and the long succession of insults Anne had endured from the terrible Miss Leece.

"Dear, dear," murmured Miss Thompson, "this looks like persecution and very strong favoritism on the part of Miss Leece. A thing we wish to keep out of the school as much as possible. But what about this!" and she opened the door of the closet where the pumpkin face of the effigy grinned at them grotesquely from the shadows.

"I have something to say about that, Miss Thompson," declared David. "I am the author of this 'crime' and I intend to take the blame for it. Miss Pierson had so little to do with it that we had fairly to drag her out of her own house to make her join the crowd."

"I think, Miss Thompson," put in Mrs. Gray, "that a teacher must have been exceedingly sharp and disagreeable to have inspired such nice children to this," and she pointed to the figure.

"I believe you are right," admitted the principal after a moment's thought, "and I trust, under the circumstances, that the whole affair can be settled without the interference of the School Board. Suppose you leave Miss Leece to me. And young people," she added, "if you will promise to say nothing more about the subject, I think Miss Leece may be persuaded to let the matter drop."

And so ended the Hallowe'en escapade. Miss Thompson paid a visit to Miss Leece that evening, at the teacher's rooms in Oakdale, and was closeted with her for more than an hour. No one ever knew what happened. Miss Thompson was a woman to keep her own counsel; but the affair never came up before the School Board and Miss Leece, after that, though somewhat stiff in her manner, had no more outbursts of rage for some time. Undoubtedly her display of favoritism in the algebra class had lost her the day.

Miss Thompson was a woman of fine judgment and broad and just views. She was proud of the Oakdale High Schools and the splendid classes they turned out year after year. She realized perfectly what a disturbance a woman like Miss Leece could cause and she determined to check her at every point, especially when the most prominent and finest pupils of the two schools were implicated. Therefore the offenders went scot-free and Anne was once more safe to pursue the freshman prize. Miss Leece, however, was only biding her time. While Anne had won this battle she might lose the next.

# CHAPTER IX

## THANKSGIVING DAY

"Oh, how I love Thanksgiving!" cried Grace.

"Oh, how you love turkey, you mean," exclaimed her bosom friend, Nora O'Malley.

"Yes," admitted Grace, "the turkey is a grand old bird, bless him, but football is what I really love, delightful, thrilling football. I wish I could play center on the home team. I know I could make a touchdown as well as the best of them."

The crowd of young people were seated on straw in the bottom of a large road wagon that was slowly making its way from Grace's house out to the football grounds. It was decorated with the colors of the Oakdale High School, sea-blue and white, and the girls wore blue and white rosettes and carried long horns from which dangled ribbon streamers. Numbers of Oakdale people were hurrying down the road toward the field, and the crisp autumn air vibrated with the sounds of talk and laughter. In the distance could be heard the music of the town band, which always gave a concert before the Thanksgiving game.

"And to think that little Anne has never in her life seen a football game!" exclaimed Jessica.

Anne blushed.

"Yes," she replied reluctantly, "I'll have to admit this is my very first game, but I understand the rules. Grace has explained them to me. I hope our boys will win."

"If the Dunsmore boys are in good trim, I'm afraid they'll give us a stiff pull," observed David, "but the stiffer the pull the more interesting it is to watch, so long as they don't lick us."

Just then the wagon drew up at the grounds and the boys and girls jumped out and made their way through the crowd to their seats.

Everybody in Oakdale turned out for the annual Thanksgiving football game. The professors and their wives, the teachers from the Girls' High School and all the pupils were there in full force, besides the citizens of Oakdale and their families. There was really a very large assemblage in the semicircular amphitheater which was hung with bunting and flags in honor of the great occasion, and probably not one in the whole cheerful company but had enjoyed a good Thanksgiving dinner that afternoon, so good humor beamed from every face.

"Don't you think this is a thrilling sight, Anne?" demanded Grace, for there was not a soul in Oakdale who was not vain of the High School football team, which had won for itself honors all over the state.

"Wonderful!" exclaimed Anne, clasping her hands and waiting impatiently for the performance to commence.

Just then the band struck up again, and under cover of the music David whispered to Jessica:

"Do you see that man over there to the right on the back seat, with long, dark hair and a slouch hat?"

Jessica found the individual presently, starting slightly when she saw his face.

"I do believe it's Anne's father," she whispered.

"It just is," said David, "and he's looking hard at Anne, too. I wonder if he means to make another scene."

"Poor Anne!" sighed Jessica. "She seems to have more than her fair share of troubles."

The two teams then filed out for warming-up practice; the excitement of the ensuing game drove all thought of the sinister looking Mr. Pierson out of their heads, for the time being. The first half ended in a brilliant touchdown for the High School boys, though the kick for goal failed. Immediately the place rang with the cheers of the spectators. Crowds of

55

boys rushed up and down giving the High School yell and when the noise died down somewhat the girls started the High School song:

"Here's three cheers for dear old Oakdale, God bless her, everyone!"

Anne was thrilled. Never had she enjoyed herself so much. She stood upon the seat beside Grace and waved a blue and white banner as frantically as anybody else.

"I don't think I quite understand what it's all about," she confided to David, who sat next to her, "but I am very happy all the same."

David smiled down into the radiant face. What a new dress and hat can do for one small, insignificant little person is quite wonderful sometimes. And Anne, with the money she had earned from Mrs. Gray, had replenished her wardrobe. In her neat brown suit and broad-brimmed hat she was really pretty, in a queer, quiet sort of way, David thought. He wondered if the father, hidden by rows of people, in the back, would be able to see how prosperous and well his daughter was looking. But his attention was recalled to the football field, for the next half was going against the High School, and there was apprehension among the sons and daughters of Oakdale.

"Dunsmore! Dunsmore!" cried a delegation from Dunsmore College.

But Dunsmore was not to be the victor that Thanksgiving Day. It was ordained that, just as hope had almost expired, a slender, fleet-footed young junior of the High School team should seize the ball and fly like the wind across the line. Score 10 to 1—Oakdale's score!

Immediately a terrific hubbub began. Surely the place had gone mad, Anne thought. The hundreds of spectators, including Grace and her party, had rushed from the amphitheater, clambered over the railing and dashed into the field of glory. Such yelling and roaring, such blowing of horns while the hero of the afternoon was carried about on the shoulders of his fellows, made her heart palpitate wildly. Her friends had forgotten all about her, evidently, or perhaps they thought she had followed.

"Anne," said a voice in her ear, "don't make any disturbance. I want you to come with me."

Anne turned around quickly and faced her father.

"Come at once!" he said. "I want to get out of this howling mob as soon as possible. We can talk later."

He took her hand, not urgently, and presently they found themselves on the other side of the fence surrounding the field. Anne had not meant to go, but she knew her father was quite capable of making a scene and she felt she couldn't endure it just then. Once outside, she thought she might escape. Never once, however, did he release her hand until he had her safe in one of the town hacks and they had started down the road.

When Grace and her friends finally recovered from their wild joy and excitement there was no Anne to be found.

"Perhaps she stayed in her seat," exclaimed Grace, but the place was quite empty.

David and Jessica looked about them uneasily.

"What chumps we were!" said the young man presently. "We never bothered to look after her, and now probably that old parent of hers has actually gone and kidnapped the poor child."

They searched through the crowds everywhere, but Anne was nowhere about.

At last David and Jessica confessed their suspicions to Grace.

"Oh, oh!" cried Grace, "I feel as if we were personally responsible for her! What shall we do?"

David thought a minute.

"Is there a play at the Opera House to-night?" he asked presently.

"I believe there is," replied Grace. "Why?"

"Ten to one Anne's father is acting in it," said David, "and that is the reason he happens to be in Oakdale to-day."

"That's a very brilliant idea if it happens to be true," said Jessica. "But don't you think we had better see Miss Mary Pierson before we do anything?"

"No," exclaimed Grace decisively. She was in the habit of thinking quickly and her friends usually let her have her way; but it was generally the best way. "It would be a pity to alarm her unnecessarily if we can avoid it. Anne isn't expected home until late, anyway. She is invited as are all of you to eat supper at my house. Suppose we go right to town, while David makes some inquiries at the Opera House. Then, if Anne's father is really acting in town to-night, we shall know what to do."

Accordingly, they tumbled into the road wagon, whipped up the horse and drove back to Oakdale as fast as they could go. On the way in, they saw a new bill posted on a wall, advertising a play entitled "Forsaken." It showed, in vivid colors, a young girl very ragged and tired looking, asleep on the steps of a large church.

"Let's go to the show," cried Nora, who always managed to combine amusement with duty; "that is," she added, "if Anne's father is in it. Of course, Anne will probably be somewhere about, in that case, and we could spirit her away while he is acting."

"That isn't a bad idea," answered David. "But I'd better find out a few things first. I'll come over to your house, Grace, and report," he called as he jumped out of the back of the cart.

The girls waited impatiently for his return, feeling that every moment Anne might be speeding away in some outgoing train, and they were losing valuable time. Grace had thought of consulting her mother, her best and wisest counselor at all times, but Mr. and Mrs. Harlowe had gone on a long drive to the home of Mrs. Harlowe's mother and would not return until late that night. In half an hour their patience was rewarded; the gate clicked and David ran breathlessly up the walk, joining them presently in the parlor.

"It's true," he cried excitedly. "Anne is at the Spencer Arms, probably locked up in a room. Her father is acting to-night in 'Forsaken,' and the whole company leaves town on the 11.30 train. I suppose Anne must go to the theater, for there will be no time to go back to the hotel after the play. I got the whole thing out of the clerk."

"Then we can all go to the theater," cried Nora triumphantly.

"What good will that do Anne?" demanded practical Grace.

"It may do her no good whatever," said David, "but it would be well not to lose sight of the father, even, if we must follow him to the train. And if Anne knows we are near, she will be able to get back her nerve."

"Children," cried Grace suddenly, "I have a scheme. I won't put it into action unless it's absolutely necessary, but it's bound to work."

"What is it?" demanded the others.

"I won't tell," replied Grace mysteriously, "because I may not have to use it, and I'll warn you that it's rather dangerous. But it will save Anne, and we just mustn't get caught."

# CHAPTER X

## GRACE KEEPS HER SECRET

The "best" Oakdale people did not often see the melodramas that appeared from time to time at the small opera house. Occasionally, if something really good came along, Oakdale society turned out in force and filled the boxes and the orchestra seats; but, generally speaking, the little theater was only half filled.

And such was the case on this Thanksgiving night. Most of the audience was made up of farmers out holiday-making with their families, factory girls from the silk mills and a few storekeepers and clerks.

"I am glad there are so few people here," observed Grace, looking around the scanty audience; "because, if we have to resort to my scheme, it will make it much easier and less dangerous."

"What in the world is it?" pleaded Jessica.

"Never mind," answered her friend. "I'm afraid you'll object, so I won't tell until the last minute."

Just then a wheezy orchestra struck up a march and the High School party settled down in their seats, each with a secret feeling that it was rather good fun, in spite of the peculiar reason that had taken them there.

"Here he is," said Nora, pointing to the name on the programme. "He takes the part of Amos Lord, owner of the woolen mills."

At that moment the lights went down and the music stopped short. The curtain rolled up slowly disclosing the front of a church. It was night and lights gleamed through the stained glass windows. Snow was falling and from the church came the sound of organ music playing the wedding march. The picture was really very impressive, although the music was somewhat throaty and the flakes of snow were larger than life-size.

But who was it half lying, half sitting on the church steps, shivering with cold?

The girls had not been so often to the theater that they could afford to be disdainful over almost any passable play, and from the very moment the curtain went up their interest was aroused. Certainly, there was something extremely romantic and interesting about the lonely little figure on the church steps.

"That's the heroine," whispered Jessica. "Her name is Evelyn Chase."

Then people began to go into the church. It was a wedding evidently, although the groom was a tall, lean, middle-aged individual with gray hair.

"It's Mr. Pierson himself," exclaimed Nora in a loud whisper.

The bride-to-be was young and quite pretty. She was not dressed in white, but it was plain she was the bride because she carried a bouquet and hung on the arm of Anne's incorrigible parent. As they started up the steps, what should they stumble over but the half-frozen form of the young girl!

Then, there was a great deal of acting, not badly done at all, thought David, who had had more experience in these matters than his friends. The bride refused to go on with the ceremony until the poor little thing was taken care of. The groom would brook no delay, for, oh, perfidy, he had recognized in the still figure his own child by a former wife deserted years before.

Slowly the forsaken girl regained consciousness, lifted her head from the steps, threw back her shawl, and——

"Heavens and earth, it's Anne herself!" exclaimed Grace.

It was Anne. They were so startled and amazed they nearly tumbled off their seats.

"As I live, it is Anne, and acting beautifully!" whispered David.

"Where did she learn how?" demanded Jessica. "Strange she never told it."

But they were too interested to reply, for the action of the play was excellent and the interest held until the curtain rang down on the first act.

"No wonder he wants to keep her with him," ejaculated David when the lights went up. "She is the star performer in the show."

"She is wonderful," declared Grace. "To think that little, brown, quiet thing could be so talented! I always imagined acting was the hardest thing in the world to do, but it seems as though she had always been on the stage."

"Are we still going to try to save her?" asked Nora.

"Of course," replied David. "She doesn't want to act. Didn't you hear her say so that night? She wants to go to school."

"But it seems a pity, somehow, when she is so talented."

"She's just as talented in her studies," said Grace, "and I've often heard that stage life is very hard. No, no! I intend to do my best to get Anne away this very night, if it upsets the entire town of Oakdale."

When the second act was over, and Anne had actually so moved her audience that one old farmer was audibly sobbing into a red cotton handkerchief, and the girls themselves were secretly wiping their eyes, Grace whispered to David:

"I'm going to write a note, if you'll lend me a pencil and a slip of paper, and wrap it around the stem of this chrysanthemum. When Anne appears in the next act, you go up in the box, and if she's alone an instant pitch it to her. Then she will know what she's to do."

"But what is she to do?" demanded the others.

"I won't tell," persisted Grace. "You'll object, if I do."

"All right," said David. "I'll obey you Mistress Grace, although I wish you would confide in me."

But Grace was obdurate. She would tell no one.

The last act disclosed an attic at the top of an old tenement, with dormer windows looking out on a wintry scene. Anne appeared, more ragged than ever, carrying a little basket of matches. It was evident that she was a match girl by trade, and that this was her wretched domicile. As she crept down the center of the stage, ill and wretched, for she was supposed to be about to die—David saw his opportunity. From behind the curtain of the box he tossed the chrysanthemum, which fell right at her feet.

"If she only sees it," he thought.

But apparently she didn't. Going wearily to an old cupboard, she took out a crust of bread. Then she drew the ragged curtains at the windows and lit a candle. Simultaneously the entire attic was illuminated, for stage candles have remarkable powers of diffusing light.

"Why doesn't she pick up the flower?" exclaimed Grace. "If she doesn't the scheme won't work at all."

"I believe she's going to die," whispered Nora in a broken voice.

Just then the Irish comedian appeared, puffing and blowing from the long climb he had had to the top of the house. He had come to bring help to the dying girl, but he was funny in spite of the dreary tragedy, and Nora changed her tears to laughter and began to giggle violently, burying her face in her handkerchief in her effort to control her mirth. Her laughter was always contagious, and presently her two friends were giggling in chorus.

"Do hush, Nora O'Malley!" whispered Jessica nervously. "You know that if you once get us started we'll never stop."

A countryman, sitting back of Nora, touched her on the shoulder.

"Be you laughing or crying, miss?" he asked. "It ain't a time for laughing nor yet for crying, since the young lady ain't dead yet and I don't believe she's goin' to die, either."

"She just is," exclaimed Nora, wiping the tears from her eyes. "She'll die before she gets off that bed to-night, I'll wager anything."

All this while, the chrysanthemum with the note twisted and pinned to its stem lay in the middle of the stage. In the meantime, Anne had fallen into a stupor from cold and hunger. The kind little comedian rushed about the stage, making a fire, putting on the tea kettle and stumbling over his own feet in an effort to be useful.

"Now, all the others will enter in a minute," whispered Grace disgustedly, "and she'll never get it at all."

Just then Anne turned on her pillow and opened her eyes. They looked straight at David, who was sitting in the front of the box. He pointed deliberately at the chrysanthemum.

"She sees it," said Jessica, for Anne's eyes were now fixed on the flower.

When the kind Irishman departed to spend his last cent on medicine and food for the dying girl, she rose, staggered across the stage, seized the chrysanthemum and rushed back again, just in time to be lying prone when her father entered, now a repentant and sorrowful sinner.

"It's all right," whispered Grace in a relieved tone. "I feel sure that the plan will work to perfection."

Anne *did* die a stage death, and there was not a dry eye in the house when she forgave her father, bade farewell to the entire company, who had now gathered in the attic, and her soul passed out to soft music while the lights were turned very low.

"Fire! Fire!" rang out a voice from the darkened house.

Where did the voice come from? Nora and Jessica were so startled they could only clutch each other and wonder, while Grace whispered:

"Don't move from your seats."

"Grace, was that your voice?" whispered David, who had joined the girls during the death-bed scene.

But Grace made no reply. She only put her finger to her lips as she held his arm with a detaining hand.

There was a panic in the house. The audience rushed for the doors while the actors leaped over the footlights in their mad scramble to escape. Several women's voices took up the cry of fire and the place was in wild confusion. Evidently the man who managed the lights had been too frightened to turn them on again, for the theater still remained in semi-darkness.

The four young people did not move while the audience was crowding out of the aisles.

"We might as well be suffocated as crushed," observed David. "It's a much more comfortable death, and besides I can't smell any smoke."

Grace smiled but was silent.

"I'm here at last," announced Anne's well-known voice behind them.

And there she was, still in her ragged stage dress, carrying her hat and coat on her arm.

"Why, Anne Pierson!" cried Nora, "I thought you were dead and gone."

Anne laughed.

"Not dead," she said. "But I would certainly have been gone in another half hour. We needn't hurry," she continued. "I don't believe he would ever think of looking for me inside the theater, and, for the time being, this is the safest place."

"Anne, why did you never tell us you were an actress!" demanded David.

"I was afraid to," faltered the girl. "I was afraid you would all hate me if you knew the truth. Besides, I never acted but six months in all my life. We toured in this play a year ago, and I knew the part perfectly. It would have been cruel of me not to have played to-night. The girl who usually does it was sick and there was no one to take her part. When father told me that, I knew I should have to do it this once, but if the fire panic hadn't started I couldn't have gotten away from him very easily. He would have made a terrible scene. And even then, it might have been difficult. No stranger would have helped me run away from my own father, who is determined that I shall go on the stage. He thinks I have the making of an actress. But I don't like the stage life. It is hard and ugly. I want to study, and be with girls like you." A charming smile radiated her small, intelligent face.

"Where do I come in?" asked David, looking at her.

"I think you are the best friend I have in the world, David," declared Anne. "I can never forget your kindness."

"And now, Mademoiselle Annette Piersonelli," asked David, secretly much pleased at the girl's earnestness, "can't you divest yourself of your ragged dress before we go?"

"Yes, indeed," she replied. "I am fully clothed underneath." She slipped off the stage dress and put on her hat and coat.

Meanwhile, not a soul was left in the theater except two of the ushers, who were sniffing around trying to find out where the fire scare had originated.

"There comes father," whispered Anne. "Can't we hide behind the seats?"

"Quick," cautioned David. "He's coming down the center aisle."

The five young people crouched low while the actor stalked down the aisle. But it was plain he was not looking for his daughter in the theater, for he called out to one of the ushers moving about at a distance:

"Have you seen anything of the young girl who was with the company? I lost her during the panic and I haven't been able to locate her since. I must be leaving town in a few minutes," he added, consulting his watch. "It's almost time for the train now."

"The company all left with the audience," said the usher. "I guess she went along with 'em."

"Now is our time," said Anne, when the actor had disappeared. "Suppose we go out the stage entrance and down that side street!"

Whereupon she led the way back of the boxes and into the wings, followed by her friends, who looked curiously about them at the unusual sight.

"What a queer place," said Grace, "and how smudgy the scenery looks! Are these little places dressing rooms, Anne?"

"Yes," answered Anne. "You see, it's all horrid when you are close. And the life is worse—riding almost every day on smoky trains and spending each night in a different place. The people are so different, too. I would rather go to Oakdale High School," she exclaimed, "than be the greatest actress in the world."

They were standing in one of the larger dressing rooms while Anne endeavored to wipe the powder and rouge from her face with a pocket handkerchief.

A tall figure darkened the doorway, and in the glass Anne saw the reflection of her father's face. Without a word, she ran to the open window and jumped out on the fire escape. The others followed nimbly after her. Mr. Pierson turned and rushed down the passage to the side entrance.

"Hurry, Anne!" called David. "He will meet you at the bottom if you don't."

They climbed quickly down the ladder, almost treading on each other's fingers in their haste, and in another moment they were running down an alleyway.

"Another narrow escape," cried Anne, when they were out of danger. "How shall I ever thank you, dear friends?"

"You have already discharged the debt, Anne, by letting us see you act," answered Grace.

"By the way, Grace," commanded David, "own up now. It was you, wasn't it, who started the fire panic?"

"I told you I wouldn't tell," answered Grace, "and I never shall."

"Anne, did she say anything about it in her note?" asked Nora.

"No," said Anne mysteriously, "she never mentioned the word 'fire' at all."

"I feel certain it was you who called 'fire,' Grace," said Jessica.

"I'll never, never tell," cried Grace teasingly; "so you'll never, never know."

She turned in at her own gate and to this day the mystery is still unsolved.

# CHAPTER XI

## MRS. GRAY'S ADOPTED DAUGHTERS

After Mrs. Gray's luncheon party in honor of Grace and her three friends a tiny little idea had implanted itself in her mind. As the weeks rolled on, and Christmas holidays approached, it grew and spread into a real plan which occupied her thoughts a considerable part of every day.

As a secretary Anne had turned out admirably. The only drawback was that Mrs. Gray could not see enough of her. The lonesome old lady almost lived on Anne's semi-weekly visits, but the girl was too busy to give any more of her time to reading aloud or driving with her benefactor.

Finally Mrs. Gray took a bold step. She invited the four girls to meet at another Sunday luncheon, and announced her intentions from the head of the table.

"My dear children," she said, "you are aware that I am a very old woman."

"We are not aware of anything of the sort, Mrs. Gray," interrupted Grace.

"Nevertheless I am," pursued Mrs. Gray. "A very old, lonesome person with few pleasures. I have decided, therefore, to do an exceedingly selfish thing, and give myself a real treat."

"You deserve it if anyone in the world does, Mrs. Gray," put in Jessica. "You who are always giving other people treats."

"Wait until you hear the plan, child, before you pass judgment," answered Mrs. Gray. "It's been too many years to count since I have had a really, jolly Christmas," she continued. "I have just sat here in this quiet old house, and let the holidays roll over me without even noticing them."

"Now, Mrs. Gray," exclaimed Grace, "the poor people in Oakdale would not agree with you on that point. Only last Christmas I saw your carriage stopping in front of the Flower Mission, and it was simply bursting with presents."

"Yes, yes, my dear. It is the easiest thing in the world to give presents and not so much pleasure after all. What I want is some actual fun, good Christmas cheer and plenty of young people. But I shall have to be selfish if I'm to get it all, because it will mean that I'm to rob mothers and fathers for a whole week of their children. Mr. and Mrs. Harlowe will have to learn to do without you, Grace, for seven days and nights. Your father, Jessica, must keep his own house. Nora, your brothers and sister must not expect to see you at all while you belong to me. As for my precious Anne, here, I should just like to steal her away altogether from her mother. In fact, my dears, I am going to adopt you for a whole week during the holidays and then—such larks!"

And the charming old lady looked so gay and pretty that the girls all laughed joyously.

"Do you mean that you really want us to make you a visit, Mrs. Gray?"

"I do indeed. That is the exceedingly selfish wish I have been entertaining for the last six weeks. I not only want it, but I have arranged for it already. I have made secret calls, my dears, and mothers and fathers, brothers and sisters are all most agreeable. You are to come to me a week before Christmas and must settle yourselves exactly as if you were my own children. I mean to punish any homesick girl severely by giving her an overdose of chocolate drops. Families may be visited once a day, if necessary, though I shall frown down upon too frequent absences. But, young ladies, before we get any further, tell me what you think of the plan?"

The girls were almost speechless with amazement and pleasure. To visit Mrs. Gray's beautiful home and live in a whirl of parties and fun making such as would be sure to follow was more than any of them had ever dreamed of.

"It's perfectly delightful, Mrs. Gray!" they cried almost in one breath.

"And we shall give the Christmas party together, my four daughters and I, and we'll do exactly as we choose and invite whom we please."

"Oh, oh!" exclaimed the four young girls. "Won't it be fun?"

"It will for me," said the little old lady. "And I need to have a good time. I am getting old before my time for lack of amusement. And now, my lady-birds, who else shall we invite to the house party?"

"Who else?" said Grace, somewhat crestfallen; for four intimate girl chums are invariably jealous of admitting other girls to the charmed circle.

"Do you mean what other girls, Mrs. Gray?" asked Jessica.

"No, no, child; I mean what other boys, of course. Do you think I want any more than my four nice freshmen to amuse me? But I don't think this party would be complete without four fine fellows to look after us. Who are the four nicest boys you know?"

"David," exclaimed all four voices in unison.

Mrs. Gray laughed.

"There seems to be no difference of opinion on that score," she replied; "but is David the only boy in Oakdale?"

"He's the nicest one," said Anne, who could never forget how kind David had been to her when his sister was her bitter enemy.

"Reddy Brooks is nice, too," said Nora. "He threw apples at some tramps once, and saved us from being robbed."

"Very good," said Mrs. Gray. "Reddy Brooks shall certainly be invited to the house party. I admire courage above all things."

"Then there's 'Hippopotamus' Wingate," said Jessica.

"Who?" demanded Mrs. Gray.

"His name is really 'Theophilus', but the boys have always called him 'Hippopotamus,' and now the name sticks to him and everybody forgets he has any other."

"Are you agreed on Hippopotamus, my adopted daughters?" demanded Mrs. Gray.

It was voted by acclamation, that Hippopotamus was agreeable to the company.

"And now, I have a fourth to propose," announced Mrs. Gray. "I think I should like to import my great-nephew, Tom Gray, from New York. He is a little older than these boys, perhaps. Nineteen is his age, I think, and I haven't seen him since he was a child; but he's obliged to be nice because he bears the name of one beloved by all who knew him."

"Whose name, Mrs. Gray?" asked Nora.

"That of my husband," said the old lady, softly. "The nicest Tom Gray this world has ever known." And she looked at a portrait over the sideboard of a very handsome young man dressed in the uniform of an Army officer.

"He loved his country, my dears, and fought for it nobly. He was a soldier and a gentleman," went on the old lady proudly, "and I am sorry he left no son to follow in his footsteps. He was a great hunter and traveler, too. I used to tell him if he had not loved his family so dearly, he would certainly have been a gypsy. He liked camping and tramping, and used to wander off in Upton Woods for hours at a time. He knew the names of all the trees and birds and animals that exist, I believe. But he loved his home, too, and no woods had the power to draw him away from it for long. I used to tell him he had brought a piece of the forest and put it in our front yard, for he planted all those beautiful trees you now see growing on my lawn, which my old gardener, who has been with me since I was first married, cherishes as he would his own children."

"And is young Tom Gray like him, Mrs. Gray?" interposed Grace.

"I hope so, my dear," sighed the old lady. "If he has inherited the beautiful traits of his uncle, his wholesome tastes for the outdoors and nature, he can't help being a fine fellow. But I have not seen my nephew since he was a child. He has been living here and there all these years, sometimes in America and sometimes in England. His mother and father are both dead, and he has been brought up by his mother's unmarried sisters, who are half English themselves. But he must be a nice boy, even if he has only one drop of his uncle's blood in his veins."

The girls sighed and said nothing. It was touching and beautiful to see the old lady's loyalty and devotion after all these years of loneliness; for her husband had been dead since she was a young woman. Still Mrs. Gray never brooded. She was always cheerful and happy in doing kindnesses for other people.

"If ever I marry," sentimental Jessica was thinking, "I hope it will be somebody like Mrs. Gray's husband."

"I should like to have a brother like Tom Gray," observed Grace aloud.

"Well," said Mrs. Gray, "we shall have to wait and see what the new Tom Gray is like. He may be utterly unlike *my* Tom Gray."

And the old lady sighed.

"We shall all have to get new party dresses," exclaimed Nora to change the subject. "I have been wanting one for an age and now I have a good excuse."

"Oh, yes," cried Grace enthusiastically. "Now, at last, I shall be able to get the blue silk mother promised I could have if at any time there was an occasion worthy of it."

"I'm going to ask papa to give me a lavender crepe for a Christmas present," said Jessica.

"O Mrs. Gray," continued Nora, "we are going to have such fun Oakdale can't hold us."

"I think we should have a surprise for Mrs. Gray," announced Grace. "She is doing so much for us. O girls! I have an idea."

"What!" demanded the others breathlessly, including Mrs. Gray herself, who was as full of curiosity as a young girl.

"No, no," cried Grace, "it wouldn't be a surprise if I gave it away. But it's going to require a lot of work and planning to carry it out."

"Is it big or little?" asked the dainty old lady as eager as a child to find out the secret.

"It's rather small," answered Grace.

"Fine or superfine?"

"Both," laughed Grace. "But you'll not know till Christmas night; so stifle your curiosity."

"I suppose I must wait, but it's going to be very hard," replied Mrs. Gray plaintively.

And so the party was arranged. Notes, written by Anne, were dispatched to the four boys; plans were discussed for the week's amusements, and the four girls finally started home in a state of great excitement to look over their wardrobes and furbish up their party dresses.

Only Anne had looked somewhat dubious during the conversation. How could she spend a week in a beautiful house, with parties every night and company all the time, and nothing to wear but that hideous black silk?

"Anne," called Mrs. Gray, as the young girl was about to close the front door and follow the others down the steps. "Wait a moment. I want to see you." She led Anne into the big drawing room. "Do you know that I am greatly in your debt, my child?" continued the old lady, as she drew Anne down beside her on the sofa. "I don't think I could ever possibly repay you for the good you have done me this autumn. But I am going to try, nevertheless, by making you a Christmas present before Christmas arrives. Now, when I was your age, I preferred clothes to other things. I think all young girls do; or, if they don't they are most unnatural. Therefore, child, I have decided to pay off some of my indebtedness to you by getting my dressmaker to make you some dresses, if it is agreeable to you. Why, what is this! My little girl crying?"

The tears were streaming down Anne's cheeks.

"You mustn't cry, my own child," sobbed Mrs. Gray. "For I always cry when I see other people doing it, and it's very bad for my old eyes, you know."

"You are so good to me!" said Anne. "It makes me cry because I'm so happy."

"Well, well!" exclaimed Mrs. Gray, drying her eyes and beginning to laugh. "What a couple of sillies we are, to be sure. Now go, Anne, to my dressmaker, Mrs. Harvey, who has orders to make you four dresses, two for evening and two for afternoon. Mrs. Harvey has good taste and will help you select them. But perhaps you will like the ones she and I looked at the other day. One of them I am sure you will admire. I chose it specially because it will give color to your pale cheeks."

"What is it, Mrs. Gray?" asked Anne eagerly.

"It's pink crepe de Chine, my dear."

And Anne held her breath to keep from crying again.

# CHAPTER XII

## MIRIAM PLANS A REVENGE

For weeks Miriam Nesbit had felt a sullen resentment toward her brother, David, because he persisted in being friends with at least two of the girls in Oakdale High School whom she disliked most.

When he announced, one morning at breakfast, that he had been included in Mrs. Gray's house party, his sister suddenly burst into tears of passionate rage.

"Please don't cry, Miriam, old girl," said David, who was not of a quarrelsome disposition. "I'm awfully sorry if I hurt you, but, you know, Mrs. Gray was one of my earliest sweethearts."

Which was perfectly true. When David was a little boy he used to crawl through the garden hedge and call on the charming old lady nearly every day.

David had hoped that Miriam would laugh at this, but she stormed all the more, while poor Mrs. Nesbit looked wretched.

"It isn't Mrs. Gray," sobbed Miriam. "But to think that my own brother would associate with Grace Harlowe, who is always working against me, and that common little Pierson girl whose sister takes in sewing!"

"Miriam, Miriam!" exclaimed Mrs. Nesbit, "I am shocked to hear you say such things. Because the girl is poor she is not necessarily common. Your grandfather was a poor man, too. He started his career as a machinist. You would never have had the money and position you have now if he had not become an inventor. Is it possible you would try to keep someone else from rising in life, when your own family struggled with poverty years ago?"

Miriam was silenced for a moment. She had seldom heard her mother speak so forcibly; but Mrs. Nesbit had seen, with growing misgivings, the innate snobbishness in her daughter's character, and for a long time she had been looking for an opportunity like the one that now presented itself.

David had risen during Miriam's contemptuous speech, and had turned very white; which was always a signal that his slow wrath had been kindled at last; but since he was a child he had had such admirable control of his feelings that it had often been remarked by older people. Miriam, however, knew the sign and resorted again to tears to draw attention to her own sufferings.

"You and mother have turned against me," she cried. "Mother, you have always loved David best, anyhow."

"Nonsense!" replied David. "You are a willful, selfish girl, jealous because a poor girl is getting ahead of you in your classes and because you are not included in the house party. Do you think Mrs. Gray would ask you to join those four nice girls in her house after that Miss Leece business? If you had learned to be polite and agreeable you would never have gotten into this state now." Having delivered himself of his opinion, and spent his rage, David walked out of the room and quietly closed the door after him.

"You see what you have done, Miriam," exclaimed Mrs. Nesbit. "You have made your brother angry. I have seldom seen him like that before, not since the stable man beat his dog. But don't cry, my child. It's all over now," and Mrs. Nesbit drew her daughter to her and stroked her hot forehead. "Why don't you give a house party, too?" she added after a moment's thought. "Would it give you any pleasure or help to heal your hurt feelings?"

"O mother!" exclaimed Miriam, looking up quickly. "I believe I *will* invite four girls and boys to spend Christmas week with me. Wouldn't it be fun?"

And it was in this manner that a plan for an opposition house party sprang into existence; although the son of the house had joined the other side.

All through her preparations Miriam carefully guarded the secret that she was bitterly hurt at having been left out of Mrs. Gray's party, and she meditated a revenge that was still only a half-formed idea. In the first place, she chose Julia Crosby as one of the guests of the Christmas house party; Julia Crosby the tall, mischievous sophomore who had originated the "Black Monks of Asia." Surely the two together could work out some scheme which would bring her enemies to her feet and humble little Mrs. Gray, who had dared to slight her.

Meanwhile, the holidays were approaching. The crisp, cold air resounded with the jingle of sleigh bells, for snow had fallen the first week in

December and all the sleighs in Oakdale were taken from their summer quarters.

The four chums were full of secret preparations. Grace had devised a scheme of entertainment which, in the town of Oakdale, would be unique, but it required much work and practice to perfect it. In the meantime Nora O'Malley had decided to entertain her friends at a bobbing party to start the Christmas holidays. And it was at this party that Miriam seized her first opportunity to make trouble.

"Anne, you are learned in many things, but not in outdoor fun," said Grace as the young people in mufflers and sweaters started to climb the long hill where the coasting was best.

"Do you mean to say you have never been coasting, Anne?" demanded David.

"I'm afraid I'll have to admit it," replied Anne. "To tell the truth, I never did have any fun, except reading, until I started in the High School and met all of you. You see, little city children are denied all these nice things unless they go to the parks, but it's no fun going alone."

"Well, you won't be alone now," said Hippy Wingate. "There are four to a sled, and we'll put you in the middle to keep you from getting lost in the snow."

"Look out, here comes some one!" called Grace, just as a small sled shot past them like a flash, with a laugh and a cheer from its occupants, Miriam and Reddy Brooks.

"They ought not to have done that," exclaimed David. "We couldn't see them over the knob of the hill and they might have run us down."

By this time they had reached the top of the hill, and Anne's heart bounded at the sight of the long, white track made by the sled which had just passed them and disappeared far below across a flat meadow now smooth and hard as a table top.

"Don't be frightened, Anne," said David, who sat behind her on the sled.

He pinioned her arms with his own and with a wild whoop the four young people skimmed down the hill.

There was no time to be frightened, no time even to think, as they shot through the fine bracing air like a ball from a cannon. Before they knew it, they were landed at the bottom.

"O Hippy," cried Grace, her cheeks glowing like winter berries, "I feel as if I were riding the comet. But look out for the others," for the remaining sleds followed in quick succession and the air resounded with the whoops of the boys and girls as they shot past. "Is there any sport in the world that can touch it?" she demanded of the world in general.

Three or four more such rides, and Anne felt an exhilaration she had never before known. She was climbing the hill for a final trip before the party returned to Nora's for hot chocolate and sandwiches, when she heard someone cry out just behind her. She had lingered a little to watch the sleds pass, and had failed to notice a small sled with a single occupant come over the brow of the hill well out of the beaten path and make straight for her. It was Miriam Nesbit, riding flat on her stomach and going like the wind.

"Jump to the left, Anne," cried Grace's voice, "or you'll be hurt!"

Anne looked up and saw the sled. It all happened in a flash, and how David managed to get there first she never knew; but the next instant the two were rolling over and over in the snow with Miriam on top of them and a broken sled skidding on its back down the hillside.

"It was Miss Pierson's fault," exclaimed Miriam as she pulled herself out of the snow, and the others came running to the scene of the accident. "Why didn't she get out of the way? Inexperienced people ought not to come to bobbing parties. They always get hurt."

David was binding up a cut in his wrist, which was sprinkling the snow with blood. He was too angry to trust himself to answer his sister before the others just then. They had pulled Anne out of a snowdrift and she was leaning limply against Jessica, trying to collect her senses. It seemed to her that she had been walking well out of the sled track, out of everybody's way; but it didn't make any difference since nobody was killed.

"All I can say now, Miriam," said Grace, "is that you are entirely mistaken. If you hadn't hit Anne you'd have knocked me over. I was walking just ahead of her and nobody can say I am inexperienced."

"Grace Harlowe, do you think I did it on purpose?" demanded Miriam furiously.

"I haven't insinuated anything, Miriam," replied Grace. "I simply wanted to disabuse your mind of a mistake. That was all." And she turned away from the angry girl.

All this time the other young people had said nothing. It was really an embarrassing situation, considering that David had not said a word either for or against his sister.

"I think we had better not coast any more to-night," said Nora, after a pause. "David has hurt his hand and Anne is so shaken that it would be well to give her something hot to drink. Come on, everybody."

"David, are you much hurt?" asked Grace uneasily.

"Nothing but a little cut," he said shortly, so shortly that Grace flushed. Perhaps he was angry with her for having spoken out to Miriam.

"I hope you aren't hurt much, David," said Miriam.

David made no reply.

"David," she repeated in a louder voice.

But her brother had started down the hill, his hands in his pockets. Nobody took much notice of Miriam as the young people followed after him. Reddy Brooks was secretly congratulating himself that he hadn't been riding behind her on the sled as she had wished, insisting that she wanted to do the guiding herself. It was curious, he thought, and might have resulted in a serious accident, at least to Anne if David hadn't pulled her away. If Miriam had only thought to throw herself to the right when she saw Anne in the way. Girls had no heads, anyway, that is, most girls. Grace, he decided, was almost equal to a man for coolness and good judgment. But there were few girls who could touch Grace Harlowe; and he did a series of cartwheels in the snow to emphasize his feelings, to the relief of everybody present, for the silence was becoming uncomfortable.

"Nora," said Anne when they had reached town, "if you'll excuse me I think I'll go home. I'm a little tired."

"I'll take you home, Anne," said David, who had heard her remark. "I don't feel much like partifying either after this jolt. Come along, little girl," and he tucked Anne's arm in his and marched her off without another word.

"All my party is leaving before the party," cried Nora in despair.

"No, not all," replied Hippy Wingate. "There are still a few of us left, and I promise to drink any extra chocolate you may happen to have."

"Don't give the animals sweets, Nora," exclaimed Reddy. "Especially the hippopotamus. He has a delicate stomach. You see, his keeper used to feed him chocolate drops three times a day."

Hippy grinned good-naturedly. He was a round roly-poly boy, famous for his appetite.

"Get away from here, Red Curls," he cried, hitting Reddy in the back with a snowball.

"Oh, you coward," cried Reddy, talking in a high falsetto voice, "to hit a man when his back is turned. I'll slap you for that," and he landed a snowball on Hippy's chest.

Hippy crouched behind the girls.

"I was a fool to throw at a pitcher," he cried; "he'll be sending me one of his curves in a minute."

"Hiding behind the ladies, hey?" returned Reddy, beginning to pitch snowballs at the girls.

"Let's wash his face," cried Nora to the other boys and girls coming up just then. They chased Reddy all the way to Nora's house and rolled him in the snow until he cried "enough."

Once inside Nora's cozy home, the coasters were soon doing ample justice to the good things to eat, which Nora's sister had prepared for them. Although all three of Anne's chums regretted deeply the unpleasant affair on the hill it was not mentioned again during the evening. Still, each girl felt in her heart that poor little Anne had, in Miriam Nesbit, a dangerous enemy.

## CHAPTER XIII

## CHRISTMAS HOLIDAYS

"Here's the tack-hammer, Hippy, and don't fall off the ladder, please," cautioned Grace, as she assisted Hippy Wingate to tack up an evergreen garland in Mrs. Gray's drawing room.

Not in twenty years had the old house taken on such holiday attire. Great bunches of holly and cedar filled the vases and bowls and decorated the chandeliers. Fires blazed on every hearth and the warm glow from many candles and shaded lamps brightened the fine old rooms.

"My dear young people," exclaimed Mrs. Gray, coming in just then, "how happy you make me feel! I do wish you were all really my children and could forever stay just the ages you are now."

"This house would be like the palace of everlasting youth, then, wouldn't it, Mrs. Gray?" suggested Anne.

"Until some meddlesome little Pandora came along, opened the box and let all the troubles out," interposed David, who was still feeling very bitter toward his sister Miriam, and glad to leave home for a time until his anger had cooled.

"Ah, well, we have no Pandoras here," answered Mrs. Gray, smiling on the young guests. "You are all girls and boys after my own heart, and I trust we shall have a beautiful time together. But here comes that nephew of mine, Tom Gray. I wonder if he's grown out of all recollection."

While she was speaking one of the town hacks had driven up to the steps, and there was a violent ring at the bell.

"Mr. Thomas Gray," announced the old butler at the door and Tom Gray, who had been the subject of endless speculation and conjecture, entered the room.

"If he turns out to be disagreeable or stupid or anything," the girls had been whispering, "it would be such a pity because everybody else is so nice."

Neither had the boys felt inclined to be prepossessed in Tom Gray's favor. He was a stranger, from New York, older than themselves and in college.

"I wish he wasn't going to butt in with his city manners," Reddy Brooks was thinking regretfully. "He is sure to have a swelled head and try to boss the crowd."

They had pictured him as a sort of dandy, with needle-toed patent leather shoes and a coat cut in at the waist and padded over the shoulders.

Even David had voiced a few thoughts on the subject of Tom Gray.

"I'll bet he's an English dude," he said. For Mrs. Gray's nephew had spent most of his life in England. "He'll probably carry a cane and wear a monocle."

They were not surprised, therefore, when a young man entered the room who bore out somewhat the picture they had conjured. He was tall and slender, very dapper and rather ladylike in his bearing. His alert, dark eyes were set too close together, and his face had a narrow, sinister look that made them all feel uncomfortable. He spoke with a decided English accent, in a light, flippant voice which sent a quiver of dislike up and down David's spine, and made Reddy Brooks give his right arm a vigorous twirl as if he would have liked to pitch something at the young man's head.

Mrs. Gray was the most surprised person in the room. It must be remembered that she had not seen her nephew since he was a child, and she had hoped for better things than this. However, always the most courteous and loyal of souls, she now made the best of the situation and greeted the newcomer cordially, though she did not bestow upon him the motherly kiss she had been saving.

Tom Gray bowed low over his aunt's hand.

"You are so much changed, Tom; I should hardly have known you," exclaimed the old lady, trying to conceal her disappointment and dismay. "England has weaned you away from your own country. You look as if you had just stepped out of Piccadilly."

"And so I have, aunt," replied the young man, using a very broad "a." "I have been in this country only a few months. England is the only place in the world for me, you know. I can't bear America."

Hippy Wingate gave himself an angry shake, which made all the ornaments on the mantelpiece rattle ominously.

"You must let me introduce you to my young friends, Tom," said Mrs. Gray, changing the subject quickly.

The introductions having been accomplished, she took his arm and led the way back to dinner.

"Do you think we can stand him for a week?" whispered David to Grace, as they followed down the hall.

"We'll have to," replied Grace, "or hurt Mrs. Gray's feelings. But isn't he the limit?"

"Asinine dandy!" hissed Hippy.

"I knew he'd be a Miss Nancy," exclaimed Reddy.

The girls did not express their disappointment, but as the meal progressed the conversation was strained and stupid.

"How did you leave your cousins in England, Tom?" asked Mrs. Gray, trying to keep the ball rolling and inwardly wishing she had never asked her nephew down.

"Quite well, thank you, aunt," replied Thomas Gray. "I expect to leave this beastly country and join them very soon."

"Indeed?" answered Mrs. Gray, flushing and with difficulty keeping back the tears of disappointment. To think a nephew of hers could have turned out like this!

"Do you play football?" demanded Hippy abruptly.

"Really, I don't care for the game," answered Thomas. "It's awfully rough, don't you know."

"Perhaps you prefer baseball?" suggested Grace.

"No," continued the young man, "I can't say I do. The truth is, I don't like outdoor games at all."

"What do you like, then?" demanded Nora, giving him a glance of ineffable scorn.

"I like afternoon tea," he answered, "and bridge."

Reddy almost groaned aloud, but he remembered his manners and choked his outburst of disgust.

"It is a pity," said Tom's aunt, turning her nearsighted blue eyes on him in amazement and displeasure. "Our Oakdale boys are all athletes. Even David here, the scholar and inventor, I'll venture to say, knows football and baseball as well as his friends."

"I'm not much of an inventor, Mrs. Gray," protested David. "You know my airship tumbled down before it got half way across the gym. But I shall never lose hope."

"Ah, airships?" exclaimed Thomas Gray, and deliberately taking a monocle from his pocket, he stuck it in his eye and stared at David, who choked and sputtered in his glass of water, while Hippy dropped a fork that fell on his plate with a great clatter.

Mrs. Gray raised her lorgnette and looked at her nephew.

"Thomas," she said sternly, "don't wear that thing here. It's not the custom in this town or in this country, for that matter. If you are nearsighted, buy yourself a pair of spectacles."

"Certainly, aunt, certainly; it shall be as you wish," replied Thomas, without a tinge of embarrassment. "I am so unused to America, you know."

Then Nora relieved the painful situation by laughing. She was taken with the giggles and she laughed till the tears rolled down her cheeks. The others laughed, too, even Mrs. Gray, who felt that she might give way to hysterics at any moment.

After dinner Thomas Gray detained his aunt in another room, while the girls and boys returned to the parlor. The two were closeted together for some time, and when they finally appeared, Mrs. Gray looked strangely flushed and nervous. But there was a smile on her nephew's thin lips and a dangerous flicker in his crafty eyes.

"I'll stake my last cent he's been getting money out of his poor little aunty," said David to Grace. "He's just the kind to do it."

"Poor Mrs. Gray!" exclaimed Grace. "I am so sorry for her. You can't think how she's been planning this party for months. Why did she ever ask down that wretch of a nephew? David, do try and make friends with him. Maybe there's something good in him after all, and it will help things along if Mrs. Gray feels that we want to like him."

"All right," promised David. "It goes against my grain to talk with a Miss Nancy dandy like that. It gives me a feeling in my chest like indigestion and bronchitis combined—but I'll make the effort."

So he went over and joined the Anglo-American, and began to talk with him in an easy, friendly sort of way.

"Won't you come over by the fire," he said. "I think we are going to play some games the girls have planned."

"Thanks, no," said the other, stifling a yawn. "I think I'll retire. I've had a long journey and I'm awfully knocked out. By the way, old chap," he continued, coming closer to David and whispering in his ear, which made that sensitive young man draw back with a quiver of dislike, "you couldn't favor me with a few dollars, could you? I left my check book in my portmanteau, which is still on the way and I find I haven't a cent. I'll return it to-morrow."

David regarded him with amazement. Here was a man whom he had met only an hour before, already trying to borrow money from him. Schoolboys are not likely to have money about them, but David did happen to have five dollars in his pocket.

"Certainly," was all he said, as he handed over the money.

The transaction had only taken a moment and when David drew out the five dollar bill, he was careful not to let anyone see him do it. However, Mrs. Gray, who had been out of the room, returned at the very moment the money was changing hands. In a flash she saw what her nephew had done. Without stopping to think she made straight for the two young men.

"Tom Gray," she said, speaking too low for anyone except her nephew and David to hear, "how dare you ask me for money and then borrow from one of my guests? You are a disgrace to your father, and to the name of Gray! I am ashamed of you and I command you to give that money back to David instantly."

Tom Gray was as angry as his aunt. His face went from red to white, and he looked as if he would like to break a vase or tear something to pieces.

"'Eavens, awnt, don't make a scene. I wouldn't a' awsked 'im, h'if I 'adn't needed more money. I'll pay him to-morrow."

Mrs. Gray and David were too surprised to speak. It was plain that, when Tom Gray was angry, he dropped his h's.

David looked at him curiously, then he drew the old lady's arm through his.

"Don't bother, Mrs. Gray," he said. "It was only a small loan, and I was glad to be of service. I believe Mr. Gray wants to go to bed now. He just said he was very tired. Shall I take him up?"

"If you will," replied Mrs. Gray, quieting down. "His room is next yours, David. Will you show him the way?"

"Young people," she said, going across to the boys and girls, who had gathered around the fire and were laughing and talking in low voices, "would you mind if we all went up early to-night? I feel a little out of sorts—bewildered—I don't know what. Children change so as they grow up," she added, sighing.

The poor old lady's eyes filled with tears. She slipped her arm around Anne's waist.

"You will never change, my dear boys and girls. You will all grow into fine men and women, I feel certain, and be devoted citizens of this splendid country of ours, which has always been good enough for our mothers and fathers, and ought to be quite good enough for us."

"Three cheers for America!" cried Hippy Wingate, giving his plump figure a twist like a whirling dervish.

Mrs. Gray laughed.

"Yes, indeed, my dears, America is a splendid country and every American should be proud to say so."

"And Oakdale is one of the nicest places in America," piped up Anne.

"Hurrah for Oakdale!" cried Hippy again.

"And Oakdale High School!" added Anne.

"And hurrah for the sponsor of the freshman class!" exclaimed Grace.

Whereupon they formed a circle, with Mrs. Gray in the middle, and danced about her laughing and singing:

"Hurrah for Mrs. Gray!"

The pretty, little old lady beamed happily upon her adopted family, as she called them.

"My darling children!" she cried. "Kiss me good night, every one of you, and we'll all go up to our beds."

# CHAPTER XIV

## A MIDNIGHT ALARM

The dry, cold air of the outdoors, and the warm fires inside the old house, certainly had the effect of making a very sleepy crowd of boys and girls who were not sorry, after all, to turn in early.

Grace and Anne occupied a room together so large that it could easily have been turned into two apartments and each have been the size of ordinary bedrooms.

"I'm glad our beds are close together, anyway," said Grace. "The rest of the furniture in this room seems to be miles apart."

Mrs. Gray's room was just in front; Nora and Jessica were in a smaller one back of theirs, and across the hall were the boys' rooms.

"Isn't it a wonderful old house?" replied Anne. "I never slept in such a big room in all my life. And how kind Mrs. Gray is! There is nothing she hasn't remembered."

Each girl had found on her bed a pretty dressing gown of silk and wool and beside it a pair of bedroom slippers. There was a bowl of fruit on a table, and just before they dropped off to sleep a maid brought in a tray of glasses with a pitcher of hot milk.

"Mrs. Gray says this will warm you up before you go to bed," explained the maid.

"Dear, sweet Mrs. Gray," continued Anne, as she curled up on a rug before the fire to sip the warm drink, "she has planned so many things for this party. I am so sorry she has been disappointed."

"He's not a bit like her, Anne," replied her friend, not caring to mention names. "I do wish she had never asked him."

"My only hope," said Anne, "is that we will all seem so young and childish to him that he will get bored and leave."

"Well, just strictly between us and as man to man, as David is always saying, don't you think he is horrid? He has no manners at all, and it's hard to believe he's a product of the Gray family."

"He has such shifty eyes," said Anne, "and I had a feeling that his dislike for America was all put on to shock us. I feel so warm and sleepy," she continued drowsily when the lights were put out and they had snuggled down in the soft, comfortable beds.

"I heard him drop an 'h' once," whispered Grace, in a sleepy voice.

But there was no reply. Anne was already dreaming of her four beautiful new dresses.

It might have been midnight, perhaps a little later when Grace awoke with a start. Not a sound disturbed the peace of the old house except the ticking of the clock on the mantel and the occasional crackling of dying embers in the fireplace. Yes; there was one sound and it aroused her. A loose board creaked in the floor, or was it a door which opened and closed softly? Perhaps it was nothing after all. And she closed her eyes and drew the eiderdown quilt close about her shoulders.

No; there it was again. A distinct footfall. She raised herself on her elbow and peered into the shadows. Far over at the other side of the chamber—it seemed an infinite distance just then—stood a figure. Grace looked at it calmly. She had never been a coward and she was not frightened now, only she wondered who could be invading their room at this hour. Perhaps Mrs. Gray; perhaps one of the servants. No, it was neither; of course it couldn't be because it was the figure of a man. She saw him now plainly enough hovering over the dressing table.

A small, cold hand slipped into hers. Anne was awake too. She had seen the figure and lay quite still watching it. Grace silently returned the pressure; then the two lay watching the man's stealthy motions for a moment, while Grace's mind was busy devising a plan by which the robber might be caught.

Oakdale was a quiet, prosperous place, and burglars were unusual. Occasionally the hands in the silk mills made a disturbance, and there had been a few highway robberies, but an actual house-breaker seldom troubled the law-abiding town. The two girls, as they lay watching him from under the covers, guessed that this man was a real burglar. He wore a black soft hat and carried a small electric lantern, while, with a practiced hand, he picked the lock of a small drawer in the dressing table where the girls had put their purses. Once he turned the light toward the beds. Instantly the girls' eyelids dropped and they lay as still as mice. Having satisfied himself that all was well, the prowler went on with his work, finally tiptoeing into the front room where Mrs. Gray was sleeping. Evidently he had made a circuit of the three bedrooms on that side of the house. As he slipped out Grace leaped from the bed. Now was the time for action. Putting on her dressing gown and slippers she dashed to the door leading into the hall, only to come upon the burglar again who had probably been frightened in his last venture and had retired to the hall for safety.

Fortunately he was standing with his back to her while he closed the door, and feeling that she was safe for the moment, she crouched in the shadow of the doorway. The thief evidently thought he also was safe, for he seized a large, heavy-looking valise from the floor and made straight for the steps without looking to right or left.

Now a door across the hall opened and another figure appeared. Grace trembled for a moment, fearing it might be another thief. She had always heard they traveled in pairs. But it was David, wrapped in a long gray dressing gown, looking for all the world like a monk.

He glanced up and down the hall for a moment, then tapped on the door of the next room and without waiting for an answer walked in. In an instant he was out again and had started swiftly down the stairs, Grace following him. She had intended to speak to him, but it had all taken place so quickly there was no time. David made straight for the dining room, opening the heavy door. The room was brightly lighted. In a flash, Grace saw on the table a pile of the beautiful Gray silver, brought over from England by past generations of Grays. Grace never knew what instinct prompted her to enter the dining room by the butler's pantry at the very end of the long hall. As she pushed the swinging door, she heard David say:

"You low blackguard, what do you mean by stealing your aunt's silver?"

Grace started at the mention of the word "aunt." It was, then, the wretched Tom Gray who was robbing his own relative!

"Get out!" returned the other coldly, "and attend to your own business. You are only a kid."

"Give up those things you have stolen, or I'll pound you to a jelly!" cried David, making a rush at the burglar, who dodged nimbly.

Then Grace had an inspiration, which assuredly saved David from very disagreeable consequences. Real burglars, like rattlesnakes, are not likely to be dangerous except when they are disturbed. It is then that they become dangerous characters. Grace slipped back into the pantry, swiftly opened one of the linen drawers and drew forth what turned out later to be a breakfast cloth, which was lucky because it was small and easy to manage.

When, in the next instant, she had pushed the door open, what she saw made her blood run cold. Tom Gray had whipped out a small pistol and pointed it straight at David's head.

"Get out of here, quick!" he said just as Grace opened the table cloth with a jerk and flung it over his head. A pistol shot rang out, but David had dodged in time and the bullet was buried in the mahogany wainscot back of him. The astonished burglar dropped the weapon, and began to struggle violently to release himself.

Instantly David pinioned his arms from the back. But the fellow might even then have struggled free, if Reddy Brooks and Hippy Wingate had not burst into the room, followed by Anne, who had roused them after Grace had gone. The three boys swiftly overpowered Tom Gray and tied him to a chair with cord Grace had found in the pantry.

But now, what was to be done? Undoubtedly the noise would awaken Mrs. Gray and she would have to be told that her nephew was a burglar about to make off with the family silver.

Perhaps the loss of the silver would hurt less than family disgrace.

In the midst of their council Mrs. Gray herself appeared.

"What in the world is the matter?" she demanded.

No one replied for a moment. It was a very uncomfortable situation for the young guests of the house party. If only the burglar had not been a member of the Gray family!

Then Tom Gray himself spoke.

"I must say this is a nice 'ospitable way to treat a guest and a relation. 'Ere I am taken by a lot of silly children for a burglar. I, your own nephew, awnt, who 'ad come down stairs on the h'innocent h'errand of finding some h'ice water."

Mrs. Gray looked from one to another of the silent group. Her eyes took in the silver piled on the table, the pistol on the floor and the burglar's tools and lantern.

"You are a burglar," she said, "a wretched, common thief. I knew it as soon as you entered my house last night. I could not then explain the feeling of repugnance I had, but I know now what it meant. I shall not offer hospitality to a coward, for all thieves are cowards. Boys, take what he has stolen from his pockets."

Reddy and Hippy searched the bulging pockets of the thief's coat and waistcoat, and brought forth a quantity of jewelry, watches and purses.

"Now, David," continued Mrs. Gray, firmly, "be kind enough to give me that pistol."

David obeyed her, wondering if she meant to shoot her own nephew.

Mrs. Gray pointed the pistol at the thief with as steady a hand as if she had been shooting at targets all her life.

"Untie the cords," she commanded.

They cut the cords with a carving knife.

"Now, go!" said the old lady, still pointing the pistol at his head. "Leave my house quickly. I shall not punish you, because a thief is always punished sooner or later."

Tom Gray looked immensely relieved, Grace thought, in spite of his crestfallen, hangdog air. They followed him down the hall, Mrs. Gray in the lead, until he slammed the front door after him and disappeared in the night.

Then, turning with her old, sweet manner, she continued:

"My dear children, I want to thank you for helping me rid my house of this man. I know I can depend on all of you never to mention it to anyone. It would have been a great blow to me if I had not been so angry; but now let us all go to our beds and forget this horrid episode. To-morrow we shall be as happy as ever. I am determined it shall not interfere with our good time."

# CHAPTER XV

## TOM GRAY

The company which met around the breakfast table, next morning, was entirely restored to its old gayety. There was not one member of the house party, including Mrs. Gray herself, who did not feel unbounded relief that the place was so well rid of Tom Gray.

David was glad there had been no arrest, and that the mistress of the house had with so much dignity and spirit turned out the culprit. It would have been a bad business, testifying in court against Mrs. Gray's nephew when he had been visiting in her house.

"Mrs. Gray," suggested Grace, "if you haven't made any plans this morning for us, I think we had better spend an hour or so rehearsing our surprise."

"Very well, my dear, you may spend as much time as you like at it; but if I peep over the transom, or listen through a crack in the door, you mustn't scold. I don't know that I can wait much longer to find out what it is."

"No, no! You're not to come near the third story," protested Grace. "We shall nail down the transom and stuff the keyhole with soap if you do."

"I never could stand suspense," exclaimed the old lady, shaking her head until her lace breakfast cap, with its little bows of lavender ribbon, quivered all over. "I fear I shall be tempted to break into the room before Christmas night and unearth the whole business. But tell me this much. Who is in the surprise?"

"All of us," declared Nora. "But now we'll have to get somebody to take the place of——"

She paused and blushed scarlet.

"Mr. Thomas Gray," announced the old butler at the door, with a peculiar expression on his countenance.

There was a dead silence. Mrs. Gray sat as if turned to stone, while

David half rose from his seat and Hippy seized a bread and butter knife to plunge into the heart of his enemy, if necessary.

"Aunt Rose," cried a voice outside, "aren't you glad to see me?"

A broad-shouldered, well-built young man walked into the room and kissed the old lady right in the mouth, before she could say a word. He had a sunburned, wholesome face, kindly gray eyes, light-brown hair, and wore a heavy suit of rough, blue cloth. He carried no cane; neither were his shoes pointed at the toes, and there wasn't a tinge of English in his accent except that his enunciation was unusually good.

Mrs. Gray rose from her chair and examined the young man long and carefully.

"The very image of your uncle," she cried at last, and gave him a good hug. "The very image, my dear Tom. Your old aunty has been a most egregious fool. Why didn't you come last night?"

"Didn't you get my telegram? I sent it in good time. I was delayed and had to take the night train up. I am awfully sorry if it inconvenienced you."

"You haven't inconvenienced me, my boy, except for a slight loss of sleep, and a fright and a narrow of escape from losing the family silver, which David and Grace, here, prevented."

Then Mrs. Gray sat down and burst out laughing. The others joined in and for a few minutes the breakfast table was in an uproar.

The real Tom Gray, who was the image of his uncle's portrait over the sideboard, looked from one to another of the strange faces and then began to laugh too, since it seemed to be the proper thing to do. He had one of those delightful, hearty laughs that ring out in a whole roomful of voices. When Mrs. Gray heard it she stopped short, patting her nephew on the cheek; for he was sitting beside her now in a place hastily arranged by the butler.

"Exactly your uncle's laugh. It's good to hear it again. You're a Gray, every inch of you; and, thank God, you're a fine fellow! If you had come down here with an English accent and no 'h's' and a monocle, I should have shut the door in your face. I should, indeed."

"Who, me?" demanded her nephew, forgetting his grammar in his surprise at such a state of affairs. "Not me, dear aunt. America's good enough for me. I've had lots of good times with my English cousins, but America's my home and country."

"Hurrah!" cried Hippy, dashing around the table and seizing the young man's hand. "We're glad to know you. We're proud and happy to make your acquaintance."

There was such an uproar of fun and laughter at this that Tom Gray began at last to see that something had really happened, and that his sudden and unheralded appearance had brought immense relief to the assembled company.

"Don't you think it's time somebody put me on?" he asked finally when the noise had quieted down a little.

"Tom," replied his aunt, "did you tell anyone you were coming to Oakdale for Christmas to visit me!"

"Why, yes," answered Tom after a moment's thought. "I believe I did. In fact I know I did. I was staying for a week in New York, with an English friend, Arthur Butler. I told him all about it. It was on his account that I stayed over one night. I sent the telegram by his servant, Richards."

"Ah, ha!" cried Mrs. Gray. "And pray tell us what that wretch of a servant looked like."

Tom laughed.

"Richards is quite an unusual fellow, a good servant I believe, but rather effeminate and a kind of a dandy——"

"That's the man!"

"He's the one!"

"The very fellow!"

Half a dozen voices interrupted at once.

Then Mrs. Gray explained the rather serious adventure of the night before. She ended by saying:

"I never, in my heart of hearts, really believed he was you, Tom, dear."

"The scoundrel!" exclaimed the young man. "Can't we set the police on him?"

"The police in Oakdale are slow, Tom," replied his aunt. "Slow from lack of occupation. Robbers do not flock here in great numbers."

"At least, I'll telegraph to Arthur Butler," said Tom, "and warn him. They may catch him from that end."

The telegram was accordingly sent. Likewise the police were notified, but Richards, who turned out to be a well-known English crook, made good his escape and was heard from no more.

It did not take our young people long to make the acquaintance of the real Tom Gray, nor to decide he was a fine fellow and one they could admit to their circle without regret.

"He's like a breath of fresh air," thought Grace, and indeed it was disclosed later that he intended to study forestry because he loved the country and the open air, and spent all his vacations camping out and taking long walking trips. But there was nothing of the gypsy in him. He was full of energy and ambition and infused such a wholesome vigor into whatever he did that the young people felt a new enthusiasm in his presence.

"I propose to celebrate the return of the real Tom Gray," announced Mrs. Gray, "by sending my boys and girls off on a sleighing party this afternoon. The big old sleigh holds exactly eight. Reddy, you may drive, since the roads are so familiar to you. You must all be back at six o'clock, for, remember, to-night we decorate the Christmas tree and every girl freshman in Oakdale High School must have a present on it."

Just after lunch, therefore, after a hard morning's work over Mrs. Gray's "surprise," the young people bundled into the big side-seated sleigh, and tucked the buffalo robes tightly around them. The horses snorted in the crisp, dry air; there was a jingle of merry sleigh bells as off they started down the street toward the open country.

"Jingle bells, jingle bells, Jingle all the way. Oh, what fun 'tis to ride In a one-horse open sleigh," they sang as they bowled over the well-beaten track; and Tom Gray breathed a sigh of pure delight.

"Isn't this great!" he exclaimed. "Wouldn't you rather do this than write an essay or study Latin prose composition?"

"Next to riding in an airship and skating, it's the finest thing I know of," answered David.

"Have you ever ridden in an airship?" demanded Tom.

"No, but I intend to," replied the other; for David had never for a moment relinquished his pet scheme, but worked on his experiments whenever he had a spare moment; little dreaming that one day he was to become the talk of the town.

As the sleigh passed the Nesbit house, Miriam and some of her friends were just entering her front gate. She saw the party and a shadow of black jealousy darkened her face.

"Why don't we do the same thing?" she exclaimed aloud, and in another twenty minutes she had bundled her own guests into the Nesbit sleigh, while she herself took the reins and guided the pair of spirited black horses.

"Miriam, I do wish you would let one of the boys drive," said her mother, who had come to the door to see her off.

"I prefer to do the driving, mother," replied the spoiled girl, and with a crack of the whip, the second sleighful was off after the first. It was not long before the Nesbit sleigh had met and passed the other, which was not going at a very great rate of speed. Mrs. Gray's carriage horses were much older and more staid than Miriam's pair of young blacks.

"Who is the girl in front?" asked Tom, as the sleigh flashed past.

"My sister," answered David shortly.

"She must be a pretty good driver," observed Tom.

David made no reply. He knew perfectly well that Miriam was not strong enough to hold in the black team, once the horses got the upper hand; but he hoped one of the boys would take the reins if they showed any symptoms of running away.

The early twilight was just falling when the Gray house party came to a narrow, rickety old bridge spanning the bed of a creek. Here they stopped the horses for a time, while Grace and Hippy gathered some branches of evergreen growing on the edge of a wood, just over the bridge.

Suddenly the stillness was broken by the sound of bells ringing so violently that it seemed as if all Bedlam had broken loose. Around a curve and down the road in front of them loomed Miriam's blacks, making straight for the other group. They were going like the wind, and the empty sleigh, lying on its side, was clattering behind them.

"Jump, girls!" cried Tom, while with the other boys he started to cross the bridge to intercept the horses.

If Grace had paused to reflect she might never have attempted accomplishing the daring deed that suggested itself to her. Quickly snatching off her scarlet cape, she dashed into the middle of the road, waving it before her. Perhaps the horses also thought Bedlam had been let loose. At sight of the terrifying apparition, they slackened up, snorted and reared backward.

"She is a brave girl," thought Tom Gray, as he leaped at the nearest rearing, plunging animal, while David seized the other. Far down the road came the sound of a faint halloo.

"I'll pick up the others. I suppose they are in a drift," said Reddy, as he drove off and in a few minutes returned carrying Miriam and her party. Miriam herself looked white and frightened, although she pretended to treat the affair lightly.

"A rabbit scared the horses," was all she said. "I'll let one of the boys drive us home."

"Indeed, I shan't go back in that sleigh," cried Julia Crosby.

"Perhaps you'll accept a ride in the freshman sleigh, Miss Crosby," suggested Nora; and the other girl, somewhat ashamed, was obliged to place herself at the mercy of her enemies.

"All of you girls get into Mrs. Gray's sleigh," commanded David, "and Tom and I will drive the other sleigh back." No one ever cared to disobey David when he spoke in this tone. Even his willful sister took her seat between Grace and Anne without a word and never spoke during the entire drive back, except to say good night at her own front gate.

But Grace could not refrain from one sharp little thrust.

"You seem to be unlucky with sleighs and sleds both, Miriam," she said.

## CHAPTER XVI

## THE MARIONETTE SHOW

Do you remember your first party dress? How it gave a glimpse of the throat and neck, and seemed to sweep the ground all around, although it merely reached your shoe tops?

Did you feel a thrill of pleasure when the last hook and eye was fastened and you surveyed yourself in the longest mirror in the house?

So it was with Anne in her pink crepe de Chine. Or was it really Anne, this little vision in rose color with glowing cheeks and sparkling eyes? She stood spellbound before the glass on that memorable Christmas night, and no one disturbed her for awhile. Mrs. Gray and the girls had stolen out so as not to embarrass the young girl who, for the first time, saw herself in a beautiful new silk dress exactly the color of pink rose petals, which hung in soft folds to the tips of her small pink satin slippers.

"Give her a chance, girls," whispered Mrs. Gray. "We mustn't be too enthusiastic about the difference. It might hurt her tender little feelings. But she *does* look sweet, doesn't she?"

"As pretty as a picture, Mrs. Gray," answered Grace, kissing the old lady's peach blossom cheek. "But they are coming. I hear them on the walk. We must get behind the scenes and see that everything is all ready."

The big drawing room of the Gray house was soon full of young people watching the folding doors leading into the library with expectant faces. In the hall a string orchestra was discoursing soft music and the place was filled with the hum of conversation and low laughter. Mrs. Gray, seated on the front row, in the place of honor, occasionally looked about her and smiled happily.

"Why didn't I do this long ago?" she said to herself. "But then, were there ever before such nice girls as my four adopted daughters?"

Miriam sat near, with the other members of her house party. It had been a source of much discussion whether or not to admit Julia Crosby to the freshman party. But, since she was Miriam's guest, what else was there to do?

"We shall be only heaping coals of fire on her head at any rate," hinted Jessica, "and that certainly ought to make her feel worse than if she had been left out."

After everyone was comfortably seated three loud raps were heard from behind the folding doors. Someone began to play "The Funeral March of a Marionette" on the piano, and the doors slid slowly back.

There was a murmur of surprise and wonder.

Two curtains had been stretched across the door opening above and below and two hung down at each side, leaving an oblong space in the middle in which stood a little doll theater nearly a yard and a half long and a yard high. A row of footlights across the miniature stage presently blossomed into light, and the freshman girls smiled as they recognized some of those same little bulbs that had served to illuminate the pumpkin face of Miss Leece's effigy. The music ceased and the curtains rolled back. There sat Cinderella by the kitchen fire, very stiff and straight, but weeping audibly with her little fists in her eyes. She was ten inches high and, on careful examination, it could be seen that two threads attached to her arms, and another to the back of her neck, made it possible for her to move about and use her hands in a remarkably life-like manner.

Wild applause from the audience. Well there might be, for the scene was perfect, from the old brick fireplace with an iron pot steaming on the coals to the rows of shining pans and blue dishes on a shelf at the side, all of which came from a toy shop, along with a little kitchen bench and chairs.

The cruel sisters swept in, dressed for the ball. When they spoke there were convulsive titters among the guests for the voices of the cruel step-sisters were those of Nora and Hippy. Anne read the lines of Cinderella so plaintively that Mrs. Gray shed a secret tear or two when Cinderella was left alone in the gloomy old kitchen. When the fairy godmother appeared, in a peaked red hat and a long red cape, it was Jessica who spoke the lines in a sweet, musical voice. How Cinderella rolled out the pumpkin and displayed six white mice in a trap, and how, after a brief interval of total darkness, could be seen through the open door a coach of gold in which sat Cinderella in a silken gown, need not be related here. It all took place without a single slip and the dolls went through their parts with such funny life-like motions that the boys and girls forgot they were not watching real actors.

It was the scene of the ballroom, however, which was the real triumph of the evening.

"How did those clever children ever do it?" exclaimed Mrs. Gray, aloud, when the curtain rolled back and disclosed the ballroom of the palace, with a drop curtain at the back showing a vista of marble columns and pillars. A gilt chandelier was suspended in the middle, from which stretched garlands of real smilax. There were rows of little gilt chairs against the walls filled with dolls in stiff satins and brocades. And one large throne chair with a red velvet cushion in it, on which sat the prince, who spoke with the voice of David Nesbit, and entertained his guests in royal state. After the exciting arrival of Cinderella, Nora played a minuet on the mandolin, the tinkling music of which seemed best suited to the doll drama, and the prince and Cinderella executed a dance of such intricate steps and low bows that the audience was convulsed with laughter. There were even suppressed titters from behind the scenes. This dance, which had been devised by Tom Gray and Grace, necessitated two extra threads to manipulate the feet. It was most difficult and had required long and tedious practice, but the results were quite worth all the time and trouble.

Mrs. Gray laughed till the tears rolled down her cheeks and made a personal appeal for an encore, which was given; but there was a mishap this time; Cinderella's threads became entangled and she came near to breaking her china nose. Audiences are invariably most pitiless when they are most pleased, and have no mercy on exhausted actors. At the cry of "Speech! Speech!" the Prince stepped forward and made a low bow.

"Ladies and gentlemen," he said, "we thank you for your approval and if strength and breath permitted us, and the lady had not injured her nose, we would gladly dance again for you."

Then came the last scene. The step-sisters made desperate efforts to wear the slipper; Cinderella finally retired triumphantly on the prince's arm, and the curtains closed only to open again a few moments later upon a scene which bore a strong resemblance to Oakdale High School. The fairy godmother occupied the center of the stage while the entire company of dolls were lined up on either side. Cinderella and the prince, each held the end of an open scroll, which bore a printed inscription that could be seen by the audience. It read:

"A MERRY CHRISTMAS TO THE FAIRY GODMOTHER OF THE FRESHMAN CLASS."

A scene of wild enthusiasm followed. The young people gave three cheers for Mrs. Gray and ended with the High School yell. The actors came out and were cheered each in turn.

Grace, Tom Gray and Reddy had worked the marionettes, it seemed, standing on the back of the table where the theater was placed, while the others, sitting on low stools at the sides where they could see and not be seen, read their lines which had been composed by Anne.

"It wasn't so hard as you might think," said Grace, explaining the marionettes to a group of friends. "Dressing the dolls was easy; we glued on most of their clothes, and we made the step-sisters ugly by giving them putty noses. Hippy painted the scenery and David supplied the electric lights. The threads that moved the arms and bodies were tied to little cross sticks something like a gallows, so that they could be held from above without being seen."

But the marionette show was only the beginning of the party. There was to be feasting and dancing, and, lastly, a big Christmas tree loaded with presents.

The floors were cleared. The notes of a waltz rang out, and away whirled the happy boys and girls. Anne and David, who did not dance, retired to a sofa in the library to look on.

"Are you happy, Anne, in your beautiful pink dress?" asked David, regarding her with open admiration.

"How can I help being happy?" she replied. "This is the first pretty dress that I have ever had and I never went to a party before, either."

"I never enjoyed a party before," said David, "but I'm enjoying this one. I hope, for Mrs. Gray's sake, it goes off without a hitch."

Just then Tom Gray waltzed by with Grace. They stopped when they saw their friends, and came back.

"Our efforts are certainly crowned with success," exclaimed Grace. "It's the most beautiful ball ever given in Oakdale. Everyone says so. By the way," she added, "get your partners and fall in line for the grand march to supper."

"I already have mine, all right," declared Tom Gray.

"And I think I have mine," observed David. "She's wearing a pink dress and is just about as tall as a marionette."

Anne laughed and stood on tiptoe to make herself look taller. Suddenly she caught the eye of Miriam Nesbit, who was lingering in the doorway, watching the scene with an expression that the circumstances and holiday surroundings hardly seemed to justify.

"I wonder if the party will go off without a hitch," thought Anne, as they joined the grand march into the dining room.

When the beautiful, illuminated tree had been disburdened of all its presents and the guests were well advanced on their supper, Mrs. Gray approached Anne, carrying an oblong box, neatly done up in white tissue paper tied with red ribbons. Pinned to the ribbon with a piece of holly was a Christmas card on which was printed in fancy lettering "A Christmas Thought."

"Why, what is this, Mrs. Gray?" demanded Anne, rather excited, while many of the boys and girls gathered around her and some stood on chairs in order to see what the mysterious box contained.

"I know no more than you, dear," replied the old lady. "A man left it at the door a moment ago, and one of the servants gave it to me. Why don't you open it and see?"

Anne hesitated. Something told her not to open the box, but how could she help it with dozens of her friends waiting eagerly to see what was in it?

"Hurry up, Anne, aren't you curious to see what it is?" someone called.

"It looks like flowers," said another.

"Or candy," observed a third.

And still Anne's fingers lingered on the bow of red ribbon. Was there anyone in the world who could be sending her a box that night? Certainly not her mother nor her sister, nor any of her friends who had exchanged presents in the morning. Mrs. Gray evidently had not sent it and there was no one else in her small list of friends who would have taken the trouble.

"Anne, you funny child, don't you see we are all waiting impatiently?" said Grace at last.

Anne slipped off the ribbons and opened the package. In the box was some object, carefully done up in more tissue paper.

"It looks like a mummy," exclaimed Hippy.

Untying the wrappers, Anne held up to the curious view of the others a large doll.

At first she hardly comprehended what it was and held it out at arms' length looking at it wonderingly. It was dressed as a man in a black suit with a long Prince Albert coat, very crudely made on close inspection, but still cut and fitted to give the right effect. The face had been cleverly changed with paint and putty, and pinned on the head was a black felt hat, constructed out of the crown of an old one evidently, in which had been sewn some lank black hair.

A card was tied around the doll's neck, and some one looking over

Anne's shoulder read aloud the following inscription written upon it:

"Why have imitation actors when you can get real ones?"

Anne gave a gasp.

Who could have played this cruel trick upon her? She knew her four friends had never spoken of the happenings of Thanksgiving night, but such secrets would leak out in spite of everything, and there may have been others in the audience who had recognized her. Moreover, her father himself would not have hesitated to tell who she was, so that it was not difficult to understand how the story had spread.

But who would have the heart to hold her father up to ridicule in this way, and to cause her such secret pain and unhappiness? While her thoughts were busy, David had seized the doll and wrapped it up again. He was very angry, but it was wiser to keep silent.

"What was it, dear?" demanded Mrs. Gray, who had not been able to hear the message written on the card.

"Just a silly trick on Anne, Mrs. Gray," replied David, for Anne was too near to tears to trust the sound of her own voice.

"Something about actors, wasn't it?" asked Julia Crosby, who was hovering near, and before she could be stopped, she had snatched the doll from Anne's lap. The covers fluttered to the floor and the others pressed eagerly around to get a glimpse of it.

David leaped to his feet so vigorously that he upset a chair.

"Give that back!" he commanded. "It is not yours."

"Give That Back! It Is Not Yours."

177

## "Give That Back! It Is Not Yours."

"I will not," answered Julia Crosby. "Neither is it yours."

"I say you will," cried David, furiously, losing his temper completely. "Get it if you can!" challenged the girl, darting through the crowd with David at her heels. Suddenly there was a crash, a startled cry and the great fir tree with all its ornaments and lighted candles fell to the floor.

# CHAPTER XVII

## AFTER THE BALL

Yes, here was the hitch that Anne had secretly dreaded and which the other girls had anxiously hoped to avoid.

She had not dreamed what it would be, but she had felt it coming all evening, ever since she had seen Miriam hovering near the library door. And, in a way, Miriam was connected with the disaster. Had not Miriam's guest and chum exceeded all bounds of politeness by prying into other people's affairs? No doubt, as she fled from David, her dress had caught in one of the branches of the tree and so pulled it over.

All this darted through Anne's head as she stood leaning against the wall while the room was fast filling with smoke and the pungent odor of burning pine.

Suddenly, someone at her elbow deliberately called "Fire! Fire!" These were the same ominous words she had heard Thanksgiving night, only they seemed now more alarming, more threatening. Who could be so foolish, so ill-advised as to scream those agitating words in a roomful of girls and boys already keyed up to a high pitch of excitement? Anne turned quickly and confronted Miriam.

"Don't do that!" exclaimed Anne. "You will only make matters worse."

Miriam looked at her scornfully, although it was evident she had not noticed her before.

"Be quiet, spy," she hissed, "and don't make trouble."

"I suspect you of making a great deal," returned Anne, calmly.

She was not afraid of this passionate, spoiled girl, and only the fact that Miriam was the sister of David, her devoted friend, kept Anne from saying more.

In another moment, the entire Christmas tree was in a bright blaze. Anne had climbed up to a chair, and thence to the table that the crowd had pushed against her as it ran. Anne was about to leap to the floor when Grace and Tom Gray dashed in with an armful apiece of wet blankets.

With the help of the others they spread the blankets over the burning tree and the blaze was extinguished almost as soon as it was born.

"No harm has been done," said Tom. "The canvas covering saved the floor and fortunately all the furniture has been taken out anyhow. It's all right, Aunt Rose. Nobody hurt; nothing damaged. I never heard of a more accommodating fire in my life."

"Open the windows now and let out the smoke," ordered Mrs. Gray, "and, if you have all finished eating, I think you had better come into the drawing room while the servants clear out this debris. Tom, please tell the musicians to play a waltz. I do not want my guests to carry away any unpleasant impressions of this house."

The music struck up and the dance began again.

"Well," said Grace, "no one need feel badly about the fire, because a Christmas tree generally has to be burned, anyway, and nothing of value but the ornaments was destroyed. So everything is all right."

"It was all my fault," exclaimed David, in a contrite voice. "Mrs. Gray, you will have to forgive me before I can enjoy a clear conscience again. If it hadn't been for that lumbering sophomore, Julia Crosby, I should never have lost my temper the way I did."

"My dear David," cried Mrs. Gray, patting him affectionately on the arm, "you couldn't do anything I would disapprove of. If you wanted to rescue Anne's doll I am sure you had some excellent reason for it."

Mrs. Gray had not heard the history of Anne's father, for Grace and her friends had kept the secret well, and Anne, herself, had never cared to tell the story. She was a quiet, reserved girl who talked little of her own affairs.

"He *did* have a good reason, Mrs. Gray," put in Grace, "and it was enough to make him lose his temper. Julia Crosby is everlastingly playing practical jokes and getting people into trouble. However, I don't suppose she upset the tree on purpose," she added, thoughtfully.

"Well, well," exclaimed Mrs. Gray, "let us forget all about it and wind up the party with a Virginia reel. Tom and Grace must lead it off, and Anne, you and David watch the others so that when it comes your turn you will be able to dance it yourselves."

So it was that Mrs. Gray's freshman Christmas ball ended as gaily as it had started, with a romping, joyous Virginia reel. There was not a soul, except the little old lady herself, who did not join the two long lines stretching from one end of the rooms to the other and when it came Anne's turn, she was not afraid to bow and curtsey as the others had done, for she had quickly mastered the various figures of the dance. Moreover, was she not wearing a beautiful dress of pink crepe de Chine? After all a pretty dress does make a great difference. Anne felt she could never have danced so well in the old black silk.

When the reel was over the boys and girls joined hands and formed an immense circle about their charming hostess, whirling madly around her as they cried:

"Three cheers for Mrs. Gray!"

The old lady was very happy. She waved her small, wrinkled hands at them and called out over the din:

"Three cheers for my dear freshmen boys and girls!"

At length, when the hands of the clock pointed to two, and the last of the dancers had departed, Mrs. Gray sank into a chair exhausted.

"I am tired," she said, "but I never in my life had such a good time!"

Was there ever a girl in the world who did not want to exchange confidences with her best friends after a party?

Grace and Anne, therefore, were not surprised when two figures in dressing gowns and slippers stole into their room, crouching on the rug before the fire.

"We've all sorts of things to say," exclaimed Nora, "else we wouldn't think of keeping you up so late. In the first place, wasn't it perfectly delightful?"

"Grand!" sighed the others.

"Everything except that one accident, and the thing that caused it," answered Grace.

"By the way, Anne, where is the doll?" asked Jessica.

Anne produced it from its box.

"Here it is," she said sadly. "But it was a cruel joke. Can you imagine who could have done it?"

"I have several suspicions," answered Grace, "but I make no accusations without grounds."

The four girls examined the doll carefully.

"My poor father!" exclaimed Anne, her eyes filling with tears.

"I'll tell you what, girls," cried Nora suddenly, "there's more to this than just Anne's secret. How did anyone know we were going to have a marionette show? Didn't we keep it dark?"

"Yes," they answered.

"Perhaps it got out through the servants," suggested Jessica.

"It certainly is rather an underhanded business," cried Grace, "for whoever did this not only must have bribed one of Mrs. Gray's servants, but also must have some way or other raked up Anne's secret. It was evidently someone who had a grudge against you, poor dear," she added, patting Anne on the cheek.

"Girls!" exclaimed Jessica, who all this time had been looking the doll over carefully, "where have you seen this material before?" She pointed at the fancy red waistcoat the doll was wearing.

"It has a familiar look," answered Nora.

"It looks to me very much like a red velveteen suit I saw somewhere once upon a time," observed Grace.

"You did see it, Grace. But it was—how long ago? Two or more years, wasn't it?"

"I know," cried Nora. "Miriam Nesbit's!"

"Sh-h-h!" warned Grace. "Remember David. He's just across the hall."

"And he must never know," added Anne, "not if she sent me a dozen dolls."

"But I haven't finished," continued Jessica. "I feel exactly like a detective on the scent. This doll is wearing something else that is familiar to us all. Anne, you have seen it, I am sure."

They scanned the doll eagerly. The shabby black suit was made of some indescribable material that might have come from anywhere. The red velveteen waistcoat they had already identified. Then came a little white cotton dickey, with a high standing collar and then——

"The tie!" cried Nora. "The green tie! Is that it, Jessica?"

"You are right," answered Jessica. "Have you never seen that green silk before?"

Grace was in a brown study.

Anne could not recall it and Nora was groping in the dark.

"I'll tell you this much," said Jessica, who loved a mystery; "It just matches a certain veil——"

"Miss Leece!" exclaimed Grace. "It's a piece of the trimming on an old dress she sometimes wears."

"Exactly," said Jessica. "Who, having once seen it could ever forget it?"

And so Miss Leece and Miriam had combined forces against poor little Anne!

## CHAPTER XVIII

## A WINTER PICNIC

"Aunt Rose," exclaimed Tom Gray, several mornings after the Christmas dance, "I have a scheme; but, before I ask your permission to carry it out, I want you to grant it."

"Why do you ask it at all, then, Tom, dear?" answered his aunt.

"Because we want your seal and sanction upon the undertaking," replied Tom, giving the old lady an affectionate squeeze. "Is it granted, little Lady Gray?" he asked.

"I am merely groping about in the dark, my boy, but I trust to your good sense not to ask me anything too outrageous. Tell me what it is quickly, so that I may know exactly how deeply I am implicated."

"Well," said Tom, "here's the scheme in a nutshell. I want to give a picnic."

Mrs. Gray groaned.

"A picnic, boy? Whoever heard of a picnic in mid-winter. What mad notion is this?"

"But you have given your consent, aunty, and no honorable woman can go back on her word."

"So I have, child, but explain to me quickly what a winter picnic is so that I may know the worst at once."

"A winter picnic is a glorious tramp in the woods, with a big camp-fire at noon, for food, warmth and rest, and then a tramp back again."

"And can I trust to you to take good care of my four girls? Anne and Jessica are not giants for strength. You must not walk them too far, or let them get chilled; and, if you find they are growing tired, you must bring them straight back."

"On my word of honor, as a gentleman and a Gray, I promise," said Tom, solemnly.

"And you will all be in before dark?" continued Mrs. Gray.

"We promise," continued the young people.

"Wear your stoutest shoes and warmest clothing," she went on.

"We promise," they cried.

"And we want a lot of lunch, aunt," said Tom coaxingly, "and some nice raw bacon for cooking and eating purposes."

"You shall have everything you want," said Mrs. Gray, "but who will carry the lunch?"

"We will distribute it on the backs of our four pack mules," replied Grace. "But Hippy must carry the coffee-pot. He's not to be trusted with food."

"Now, wouldn't it be a remarkable sight to see a pack mule eating off his own back!" observed Hippy. "There are several animals that can turn their heads all the way around, I believe, but not the human animal."

"We had better start as soon as possible," broke in Tom. "Hurry up, girls, and get ready, while the servants fix the lunch."

In half an hour eight young people, well muffled and mittened, started off toward the open country. It was a clear, cold day and the snow-covered fields and meadows sparkled in the sunshine.

"If I were a gypsy by birth, as well as by inclination," declared Tom, as they trudged gayly along, "I should take to the road in the early spring, and never see a roof again until cold weather."

"But being a member of a respectable family and about to enter college, you have to sleep in a bed under cover?" added David.

"It's partly that," said Tom, "and partly the cold weather that is responsible for my good behavior two thirds of the year. If I lived in a warm climate all the year around, every respectable notion I had would melt away in a week and I'd take to the open forever."

"I have never been in the woods in the winter time," said Anne. "Are they very beautiful?"

"One of the finest sights in the world," cried Tom enthusiastically, his wholesome face glowing from his exercise.

Just then they climbed an old stone wall and entered a forest known as "Upton Wood," which covered an area of ten miles or more in length and several miles across.

"It is beautiful," said Anne as she gazed up and down the wooded aisles carpeted in white. "It is like a great cathedral. I could almost kneel and pray at one of these snow covered stumps. They are like altars."

"The fault I find with the woods in winter," observed Grace, "is that there is nothing to do in them, no birds and beasts to make things lively, no flowers to pick, no brooks to wade in. Just an everlasting stillness."

"I admit there's not much social life," replied Tom. "The inhabitants either go to sleep or fly south, most of them. But don't forget the rabbits and squirrels and——"

"And an occasional bear," interrupted Reddy. "They have been seen in these parts."

"Worse than bears," said Hippy. "Wolves!"

"Goodness!" ejaculated Tom. "You are doing pretty well. I didn't know this country was so wild. But that's going some."

"Oh, well, as to that," said David, "nobody has ever really seen anything worse than wildcats, and we have to take old Jean's word for it about the wolves. He claimed to have seen wolves in these woods three years ago. As a matter of fact they chased him out, and he was obliged to turn civilized for three months."

"Who is old Jean?" asked Tom, much interested.

"He is a French-Canadian hunter who has lived somewhere in this forest for years. He comes into town occasionally, looking like Daniel Boone, dressed in skins with a squirrel cap, and carrying a bunch of rabbits that he sells to the butchers."

"He's a great sight," said Grace. "I saw him on his snowshoes one day. He was coming down Upton Hill, where we coasted, you know, Anne, and he sped along the fields faster than David's motor cycle."

They had been walking for some time over the hard-packed snow and were now well into the forest, which hemmed them in on every side and seemed to stretch out in all directions into infinite space.

"Reddy, are you perfectly sure we won't get lost in this place?" demanded Jessica at last.

They had been walking along silently intent on their own thoughts. Perhaps it was the grandeur of the great snow-laden trees that oppressed them; perhaps the vast loneliness of the place, where nothing was stirring, not even a rabbit.

"We're all right," returned Reddy. "My compass tells me. We go due north till we want to start home and then we can either turn around and go back due south or turn west and go home by the road."

"I have neither compass nor watch," said Hippy, "but nature's timepiece tells me that it's lunch time. This cold air gives me an appetite."

"Gives you one?" cried David. "You old anaconda, you were born with an appetite. You started eating boiled dumplings when you were two years old."

"Who told you so?" demanded Hippy.

"Never mind," said David. "It's an old story in Oakdale."

"Let's feed the poor soul," interposed Grace. "It would be wanton cruelty to keep him waiting any longer."

"He'll have to make the fire, then," said Reddy. "Make him pay for his dumplings if he wants 'em so early."

"All right, Carrots," cried Hippy. "I'll gather fagots and make a fire, just to keep you from talking so much."

"I'll help you, Hippy," said Nora. "I'm not ashamed to admit that I am very hungry too. It's the people who are never able to eat at the table, and then go off and feed up in the pantry, who always manage to shirk their work."

The others all laughed.

"Let's make a fair division of labor," put in Grace, "so as to prevent future talk."

While some of them gathered sticks and dried branches, the others began clearing away the snow in an open space, where the fire could be built.

Anne and Jessica unpacked the luncheon and poured some coffee from a glass jar into a tin pot to be heated, while Tom peeled several long switches and impaled pieces of bacon on the ends to be cooked over the fire, which was soon blazing comfortably.

"How do you like this, girls?" he asked presently, when the broiling bacon began to give out an appetizing smell and the hot coffee added its fragrance to the air. "How's this for a winter picnic?"

"I like it better than a summer picnic," interposed Hippy. "The food is better and there are no gnats."

"Gnats are very fond of fat people," said Reddy. "They drink down their blood like—circus lemonade."

"Get busy and give me some coffee, Red-head," said Hippy, who sat on a stump and ate energetically, while the others were broiling their slices of bacon.

"Here, Hippy," said Nora, pouring out a steaming cupful, "if it wasn't interesting to watch you store it away, perhaps I wouldn't wait on you hand and foot like this."

"This is the best way in the world to cook bacon," said Tom, holding his wand over the fire with several pieces of bacon stuck on the forked ends.

"A very good method, if your stick doesn't burn up," replied Anne. "There! Mine fell into the fire. I knew it would."

Meantime, Jessica and Grace were frying the rest of the slices in a pan.

"That's good enough, but this is better and quicker," said Grace. "There's no reason for dispensing with all the comforts of a home just because you choose to be a woodsman, Tom."

They never forget how they enjoyed that luncheon, devouring everything to the ultimate crumb and the final drop of hot coffee.

Although it was bitterly cold, they did not feel the chill. The brisk walk, the warm fire and their hearty meal had quickened their blood, and even Anne, the smallest and most delicate of them all, felt something of Tom's enthusiasm for the deep woods.

At last it was time to start again.

The boys were trampling down the fire while the girls began stowing the cups and coffee-pot into a basket. The woods seemed suddenly to have grown very quiet.

"How still it is," whispered Anne. "I feel as if everything in the world had stopped. There is not a breath stirring."

"Perhaps it has," answered Grace. "But we mustn't stop, even if everything else has, now that the fire is out, or we'll freeze to death."

She was just about to call the others briskly, for the air was beginning to nip her cheeks, when something in the faces of the four boys made her pause.

They were standing together near the remains of the fire, and seemed to be listening intently.

Not a sound, not even the crackling of a branch disturbed the stillness for a moment and then, from what appeared to be a great distance, came a long, howling wail, so forlorn, so weird, it might have been the cry of a spirit.

"What is it?" whispered the other girls, creeping about Grace.

"I think we'd better be hurrying along, now, girls," said David in a natural voice. "It's getting late."

"You can't deceive us, David," replied Grace calmly. "We know it's wolves."

## CHAPTER XIX

## WOLVES!

Wolves! The name was terrifying enough. But their cry, that long-drawn-out, hungry call, gave the picnickers a chill of apprehension.

"We must take the nearest way out of the wood, Reddy," exclaimed Tom. "They are still several miles off, and, if we hurry, we may reach the open before they do."

All started on a run, David helping Anne to keep up with the others while Reddy looked after Jessica. Nora and Grace were well enough trained in outdoor exercise to run without any assistance from the boys. Indeed, Grace Harlowe could out-run most boys of her own age.

"Go straight to your left," called Reddy, consulting his compass as he hurried Jessica over the snow.

Again they heard the angry howl of the wolves, and the last time it seemed much nearer.

"It's a terrible business, this running after a heavy meal," muttered Hippy, gasping for breath as he stumbled along in the track of his friends. "I'll make a nice meal for 'em if they catch me," he added, "and it looks as if I'd be the first to go."

"Reddy, are you sure you're right?" called Tom. "The woods don't seem to be thinning out as they are likely to do toward the edge."

"Keep going," called Reddy, confident of the direction. "You see, we had gone pretty far in, but I believe the open country is about a mile this way."

A mile? Good heavens! Jessica and Anne were already stumbling from exhaustion, while Hippy was quite winded. Another five minutes of this and at least three of the party would be food for wolves, unless something could be done. So thought David, who, breathless and light headed, was now almost carrying Anne.

"Hurrah!" cried Grace, who had been running ahead of the others. "Here's Jean's hut!"

There, sure enough, right in front of them, was a little house built of logs and mud.

Had it been put in that particular spot years ago just to save their eight lives now? Anne wondered vaguely as she blindly stumbled on.

As Grace lifted the wooden latch of the door, she looked over her shoulder. Not three hundred yards away loped five gaunt, gray animals. Their tongues hung limply from the sides of their mouths and their eyes glowered with a fierce hunger.

"Hurry!" she cried, in an agony of fear. "Oh, hurry!"

Tom and David were carrying Anne now, while Jessica was half staggering, assisted by Nora and Reddy. Hippy, the perspiration pouring from his face, brought up the rear, and they had scarcely pulled him in and barred the door before the wolves had reached the hut and were leaping against the walls howling and snarling.

Nobody spoke for some time. Those who were not too tired were busy thinking.

What was to be done? Eight young people, on a bitter cold winter afternoon, shut up in a hut in the middle of a forest while five half-starved wolves besieged the door.

Presently Tom Gray began to look about him.

There was a fireplace in the hut, which, by great good luck, contained the remains of a large backlog. More fuel was stacked in the corner, chiefly brushwood and sticks. He made a fire at once and the others gathered around the blaze, for they felt the penetrating chill now, after their rapid and exhausting flight through the forest.

"Here's a rifle," exclaimed Grace, who was also exploring, while Tom kindled the fire.

"Good!" cried Tom. "Let's see it. It may be our salvation."

He seized the gun and examined the barrel, but, alas, there was only one shot left in it. They searched the hut for more cartridges, but not one could they find.

In the meantime the wolves, which might have been taken for large collie dogs at a little distance, were trotting around the house, leaping against the door and windows and occasionally giving a blood-curdling howl.

"Suppose you feed me to them?" groaned Hippy. "You could get almost to Oakdale before they finished me."

The suggestion seemed to break the apprehensive silence that had settled down upon them, and they burst out laughing, one and all; even Anne, who was lying on a bearskin in front of the fire.

"I suppose the beasts were driven down from the hills by hunger, and when they smelled the fat bacon frying, the woods couldn't hold them," observed David. "I have always heard that a hungry wolf could smell something to eat on another planet."

"Well, what are we going to do?" demanded Nora. "If we leave this charming abode of Jean's, we shall be eaten alive, and if we stay in it we shall starve."

"You won't starve for a while yet, child. You have only just eaten. You remind me of the story of the people who were locked up in a vault in a cemetery. They divided the candle into notches and decided to eat a notch apiece every day. They had just finished the last notch, and were expecting to die at any moment of starvation, when somebody unlocked the door, and how long do you suppose they had been shut up!"

"Several days, I suppose," answered Nora, "since they appeared to have eaten several notches."

"Not at all," replied David. "Only three hours."

"I'd rather be in a vault, with the dead, than out here," observed Hippy.

"Are we such poor company as all that, Fatty!" laughed Reddy.

"I've made a great find," announced Tom Gray in the midst of their chatter. He was standing on a bench examining something on a shelf suspended from the ceiling.

"What?" demanded the others in great excitement.

"A pair of snowshoes," he answered.

There was a disappointed silence.

"Well, don't all speak at once," said Tom at last. "Don't you agree with me that it's a great find?"

"We are sorry we can't enthuse," answered David, "but we fail to see how snow shoes can help us out of our present predicament."

"Nobody here knows how to use them," continued Reddy, "and even if he did, he couldn't out-run a pack of wolves."

"I know how to use them," exclaimed Tom. "I learned it in Canada a few winters ago, but I will admit I couldn't beat the wolves in a race. However, the shoes may come in handy yet."

Just then one of the wolves threw his body against the door and the small cabin shook with the force of the blow.

"By Jove!" exclaimed David, "I thought they had us then. Another blow like that and the old latch might give way."

They looked about them for something to place against the door, but there was not a stick of furniture in the room. Even the bed, in one corner, was made of pine boughs and skins.

"I wonder how there happens to be only five wolves," said Anne. "I thought they went about in large packs."

"They are probably mama and papa and the whole family," replied Hippy. "The smallest, friskiest ones, I think, are young ladies, by the way they switched along behind the others and hung back kind of shy-like."

"Now, Hippy Wingate, don't tell us such a romance as that," warned Grace, "when you were so winded you could hardly look in front of you, much less behind you."

At that moment there was another crash against the door while two gray paws and the tip of a pointed muzzle could be seen on one of the window sills.

"It's almost three o'clock," said Tom Gray, looking at his watch. "I think we'll have to do something, or we shall be penned here all night. Now, what shall it be? Suppose we have a friendly council and consider."

"All right," said David; "the meeting is open for suggestions. What do you advise, Anne?"

Anne smiled thoughtfully.

"I have no advice to offer," she said, "unless you shoot one of the wolves and let the others eat him up. Perhaps that would take the edge off their appetites."

"No, that would only serve as an appetizer," answered David. "After they had eaten one member of the family they would be still hungrier for another."

"And yet that isn't a half bad idea," said Tom, "and for two reasons. Did you notice a path which began at the hut and which was evidently Jean's trail? I saw it from the corner of my eye as I ran."

No, the others had not noticed anything of the sort. But who would stop to think of trails with a pack of hungry wolves at his heels?

Tom's training in the woods had taught him to take in such details, and consequently he had noticed it particularly. Moreover, the trail led straight to the left, presumably toward the west.

"Now, this is what I propose to do," he continued, taking down the snowshoes and looking over their straps and fastenings carefully. "Reddy, who, I hear, is a good shot, must climb up at one of the windows and shoot the first wolf he sees. Eating the dead wolf would probably occupy the attention of his brothers for some ten minutes or so—perhaps longer. While they are busy I shall make off on the snowshoes. With that much of a start, and with plenty of tasty human beings close at hand, I doubt if they even follow me. If they do, why I'll just shin up a tree. But I believe I can beat them. I'm pretty good on snowshoes."

"Tom Gray, you shan't do it!" cried Grace. "It may mean sure death. How do you know the wolves won't seize you the moment you open the door? Besides, you don't know the way. Suppose you should get lost?"

"No, no," insisted Tom. "None of these things will happen. I know positively that a hungry wolf will stop chasing a human being and eat up a dead wolf, or a shoe, or a rug, or anything that happens to be thrown to him. I never was surer of anything in my life than that I can get away from here before the beasts know it."

There was a storm of protestation from the others, but Tom Gray finally overruled every objection and they reluctantly consented to let him go.

It was arranged that Reddy should stand on a bench by one of the small windows and attract the attention of the wolves by throwing out a rabbit skin that was nailed to one of the walls. While the beasts were tearing this to pieces he was to shoot one of them. Furthermore, the instant the live wolves had finished devouring the dead one, Reddy was to pitch out another skin, of which there were many about the hut, of foxes, rabbits and other small animals, which the trapper had collected.

This, they agreed, would probably keep the wolves occupied for awhile, until Tom had got a good start down the trail.

Tom slipped his feet in the snowshoes and stood by the door waiting. While the wolves howled and fought over the rabbit skin, bang went the rifle.

"I got him!" cried Reddy.

In an instant Tom Gray had flung open the door and was off down the trail.

As he had expected, the live wolves were hungrily eating the dead one and had not apparently even noticed his departure.

The boys and girls in the hut sat breathlessly waiting, while Reddy watched the famished animals gorge themselves with the blood and fresh meat of their comrade.

Reddy had rolled up a fox skin into a small bundle, and was prepared to pitch it out to them the moment they had finished.

Just as they had lapped the last drop of blood, he cast out the skin. They sniffed at it a moment, gave a long, disapproving howl, that sent the cold chills down the spines of the prisoners, and then made off down the trail after Tom Gray.

Reddy gave a loud exclamation and jumped down from the bench.

"*They have followed Tom!*" he cried, in a high state of excitement.

There was a long pause.

"We'll have to go, then," said David finally. "Girls, you are safe as long as you stay inside the hut, and some of us at least will be able to bring help before long."

With that, all three of the boys, for Hippy was no coward, in spite of his size and appetite, rushed out of the hut and disappeared in the wood.

The afternoon shadows were beginning to lengthen when Grace fastened the latch and returned to the fire where her three friends sat silent, afraid to speak for fear of giving way to tears.

## CHAPTER XX

## THE GRAY BROTHERS

The four girls never knew how long they waited that afternoon in the hunter's cabin. It might have been only minutes, but the minutes seemed to drag themselves into hours. The uncertain fate of the boys, the tragedy that surely awaited perhaps all of them made the situation almost unbearable.

Grace piled the fireplace high with the remaining wood, but the blaze could not keep away the chill that crept over them as the sun sank behind the trees. They shivered and drew nearer together for comfort.

Should they ever see their four brave friends again?

And David?

Anne could endure it no longer. She rose and began to move about the hut. There lay her coat and hat. Almost without knowing what she did she put them on, pulled on her mittens and tied a broad, knitted muffler around her ears.

"Girls," she said suddenly. She had gone about her preparations so quietly the other three had not even turned to see what she was doing. "I'm going. I don't want any of you to go with me, but I would rather die than stay here all night without knowing what has happened to David and the others."

"Wait a moment," cried Grace, "and I'll go, too. It would be unbearable not to know—and if we meet the wolves, why, then, as Tom said, we can climb a tree. Poor Tom!" she added sadly. "I wonder where he is now."

Nora and Jessica rose hastily.

"Do you think I'd stay?" cried Nora. "Not in a thousand years!"

"Anything is better than this," exclaimed Jessica, as she drew on her wraps and prepared to follow her friends into the woods.

Grace opened the door, peering out into the gathering darkness.

"There is not a living thing in sight," she said. "We'd better hurry, girls; it will soon be dark." Then the four young girls started down the trail and were soon out of sight.

When Tom Gray left old Jean's hut, with nothing between him and the ravenous wolves, except the angle of a wall, he took a long, gliding step, his body swinging gracefully with the motion, and was off like the wind, under a broad avenue of trees. But he had not gone far before one of the straps loosened and his foot slipped. He fell headlong, but was up instantly.

It took a few moments to tighten the strap, and it must have been then that the wolves caught the scent, and after hurriedly finishing the meal in hand, galloped off for another without taking the slightest notice of the fox skin that Reddy had tossed to them. Tom made a fresh start, feeling more confident on his feet than he had at first, and he was well under way when he heard the howl of the wolves behind him. Gathering all his energies together he managed to keep ahead of them until the woods became less dense, and he saw through the interlacing branches the open meadows and fields.

"They are too hungry to leave off now," he said to himself as he hurriedly searched the valley below for the nearest farmhouse. In front of him was a very high, steep hill, that same hill, in fact, where Nora's coasting party had taken place. Glancing behind him, he caught a glimpse of the gray brothers trotting through the forest.

"I'll take the hill," he thought. "It's quickest and there must be some kind of a refuge below." With long, swift glides he reached the knob which had hidden Miriam's sled from view as she bore down on Anne the night of the coasting party.

The wolves were right behind him now, and unless something turned up he hardly dared think what would happen.

But Tom Gray had always possessed an indomitable belief that things would turn out all right. It seemed absurd to him that he was to be food for wolves when he had still a long and delightful life before him. Certainly he would not give up without a struggle.

Perhaps it was this fine confidence that his destiny was not yet completed that gave him the strength which now promised to save him. As he fled down the hill he saw below an old oak tree whose first branches had been lopped off. Exerting every atom of strength in him, just as he reached the bottom Tom gave a leap. He caught the lowest limb with one hand, pulled himself up and calmly took his seat in the crotch of the tree.

He was just in time. The wolves were at his heels, snarling and snapping like angry dogs. The boy regarded them from his safe perch and burst out laughing.

Tom Gray Escapes from the Wolves.

211

## Tom Gray Escapes from the Wolves.

"So I fooled you, did I, you gray rascals?" he said aloud. "You think you'll keep me here all night, do you, old hounds? Well, we'll see who wins out in the long run."

Meanwhile, the wolves ran about howling disconsolately while Tom sat in the branches of the tree, rubbing his hands and arms to keep warm. He had removed the snowshoes and was just contemplating climbing to the top of the tree to keep his blood circulating, when three figures appeared on the brow of the hill.

"As I live, it's the boys," he said to himself. "Go back!" he yelled, waving a red silk muffler. "Climb a tree quickly!"

They had seen and heard him, and making for the nearest tree, each shinned up as fast as he could.

"Here's a howdy-do," said Tom to himself. "Four boys treed by wolves and night coming on."

Yet he swung his legs and whistled thoughtfully, while the others shouted to him, but he could not hear what they said, for the wind was blowing away from him. In the meantime the wolves did not all desert him and he could only wait patiently, with the others, for something to turn up.

What did turn up was a good deal of a shock to all of them.

Grace, Jessica, Nora and Anne suddenly emerged from the forest, standing out in bold relief on the brow of the hill.

The three boys at the top of the hill all jumped to the ground at once.

"Run for the trees," cried David, for the wolves had caught the new scent and had started toward them on a dead run.

"Crack, crack," went a rifle. Instantly the first wolf staggered and fell backward.

How was it that the boys had not noticed before that the girls were not alone?

Another shot and a second wolf ran almost into their midst, gave a leap and fell dead. One more dropped; and the sole surviving wolf beat a frenzied retreat.

"We found old Jean!" cried Grace. "Wasn't it the most fortunate thing in the world? And now nobody is killed and we are all safe and I'm so happy!" She gave the old hunter's arm a squeeze.

Old Jean, enveloped in skins from top to toe, smiled good-naturedly.

"It was the Bon Dieu, mademoiselle, who have preserve you. Do not t'ank ole Jean. It was the Bon Dieu who put it in ole Jean's haid to set rabbit trap to-night."

He would accept neither money nor thanks for shooting the wolves.

"I will skin them. It is sufficient."

It was not long before eight very tired and very happy young people were seated around Mrs. Gray's dinner table. Grace was a little choky and homesick for her mother, now that all the danger was over, but the week of the house party was almost up, so she concealed her impatience to be home again.

The softly shaded candles shed a warm glow over their faces, and the logs crackled on the brass andirons. They looked into each others' eyes and smiled sleepily.

Had it all been a dream, their winter picnic, or was old Jean at that very moment really nailing wolf skins to his wall?

## CHAPTER XXI

## THE LOST LETTER

Spring was well advanced, full of soft airs and the sweet scents of orchards in full bloom.

Through the open windows of the schoolroom Grace could hear the pleasant sounds of the out of doors. The tinkle of a cow bell in a distant meadow and the songs of the birds brought to her the nearness of the glorious summer time.

She chewed the end of her pencil impatiently, endeavoring to withdraw her attention from the things she liked so much better than Latin grammar and algebra. Examinations were coming, those bugbears of the young freshman, and then vacation. A vision of picnics crossed her mind, of long days spent out of doors, with luncheon under the trees and tramps through the woods. Yet, before all these joys, must come the inevitable final test, the race for the freshman prize. Although, after all, only two would really enter the race, Miriam and Anne. Nobody else would think of competing with these two brilliant students.

How tired Anne looked! She had done nothing but study of late. No party had been alluring enough to beguile her from her books. She had even discontinued her work with Mrs. Gray, and early and late toiled at her studies.

"She will tire herself out," Grace thought, and made a resolution to take Anne with her on a visit to her grandmother's in the country just as soon as the High School doors were closed for the summer.

Miriam was not studying so hard. But then she never did anything hard. She simply seemed to absorb, without taking the trouble to plod. She had been very defiant of late, Grace thought, and more insolent than ever before. She and Miss Leece were "thicker" than was good for Miriam, considering that teacher's peculiar disposition to flatter and spoil her. However, that was none of Grace's business, and certainly Miss Leece had been careful since the sound rating Miss Thompson had given her.

Just then the gong broke in upon Grace's reflections. With a sigh of relief she closed her book and strolled with her friends down to their usual meeting place in the locker room.

There was but one topic of conversation now, the freshman prize.

"Anne," predicted Nora, "you just can't help winning it! I don't believe it's in you to make a mistake. Miss Leece always gives you the hardest problems, too, but she can't stump little Anne."

Anne smiled wearily. It was well examinations were to begin in two days. In her secret soul she felt she could not hold out much longer. Moreover, Anne was worried about family affairs. She had received a letter, that morning, which had troubled her so much that she had been on the point, a dozen times, of bursting into tears. However, if she won the prize—not the small one, but the *big* one—the difficulty would be surmounted.

Another worry had crept into her mind. She had lost the letter. A little, wayward breeze had seized it suddenly from her limp fingers and blown it away. She knew the letter was lurking somewhere in a corner of the schoolroom, and she had hoped to find it when the class was dismissed. But the missing paper was nowhere in sight when she had searched for it during recess. Perhaps it had blown out the window, in which case it would be brushed up by the janitress and never thought of again. Not for worlds would Anne have had anyone read that letter.

It was during the afternoon session, in the middle of one of the schoolroom recitations, that she caught sight of her letter again. But after the class was dismissed and she had made haste to the corner of the room, where she thought she had seen it under a desk, it was not there. Disappointed and uneasy Anne put on her hat and started home.

All afternoon she worried about it. Perhaps it was because she was so tired that she was especially sensitive about the letter being found by someone else. If that someone else should read the contents, she felt it would mean nothing less than disgrace.

"You look exhausted, child," said Anne's sister Mary, who was weary herself, having worked hard all day on a pile of spring sewing Mrs. Gray had ordered. "Why don't you take a walk and not try to do any studying this afternoon?"

"I think I will, sister," replied Anne; and, pinning on her hat, she left her small cottage and started toward High School Street.

Turning mechanically into the broad avenue shaded by elm trees, she strolled along, half-dreaming and half-waking. She was so weary she felt she might lie down and sleep for twenty years, and like Rip Van Winkle awaken old and gray. It was foolish of her to be so uneasy about that letter.

Was it a premonition that compelled her to return to the schoolroom and search again for it? Perhaps the old janitress might have found it. The young girl quickened her pace. She must hurry if she wanted to catch the old woman before the latter closed up for the night.

Anne had not thought of looking behind. Her mind, so trained to concentration, was now bent only upon one object. But would it have swerved her from her present purpose, even if she had noticed Miss Leece following her?

The High School was still open, although Anne could not find the janitress. Perhaps the old woman was asleep somewhere. On several occasions she had been found sleeping soundly when she should have been brushing out schoolrooms and mopping floors. Anne was determined, however, to give one good, thorough search for her letter and she accordingly mounted to the floor where the freshmen class room was situated and entered the large, empty recitation room.

She looked long and carefully under the desks and benches, even going through the scrap baskets, but there was no sign of the letter. Then she went into some of the other class rooms, but her search was unrewarded.

"What's the use?" she asked herself at last. "It's sure to have been destroyed. I think I'll just have to give it up, and try to rest a little before to-morrow, or I'll never be fit to try for that prize."

As she started down the broad staircase she heard the rasping voice of Miss Leece mingling with the principal's cool, well-modulated tones. Anne paused a moment, watching the two figures below. Miss Leece looked up and caught her eye, but Miss Thompson was engaged in unlocking the door, and did not see the little figure lingering on the steps.

Just as the door opened, another door slammed violently, and the next moment Anne heard footsteps running along a small passage that crossed the corridor. Leaning far over the rail she caught a glimpse of a figure. It was—no, Anne could not be certain of the identity. But it looked like— well, never mind whom. Anne meant to keep the secret, for it was evident that the person had been bent on mischief, else why slam a door and run at the approach of Miss Thompson! And now Anne heard the door open again and Miss Thompson's voice calling: "Who is there?" But there was no answer. Deep down in Anne's heart there crept a vague suspicion.

## CHAPTER XXII

## DANGER AHEAD

MY DEAR GRACE:

Will you come and see me at my office after school to-day? I have something very important to discuss.

Sincerely yours,

EMMA THOMPSON.

Grace read the letter over twice. What in the world could Miss Thompson want to discuss with her? Perhaps she had not been doing well enough in her classes. But Grace rejected the idea. She always kept up to the average, and it was only those who fell below who ever received warnings from the principal.

Perhaps it was—well, never mind, she would wait and see. As soon as school was over she hurried to the principal's office and tapped on the door.

"Well, Grace, my dear," said Miss Thompson, as the young girl entered, "did my note frighten you?"

"No, indeed," replied Grace; "I had a clear conscience and I don't expect to fail in exams to-morrow, although I am not so studious as Anne Pierson or Miriam."

"Of course you don't expect to fail, my dear," said the principal, kindly, for, of all the girls in the school, Grace was her favorite. "I didn't bring you here to scold you. But I have something very serious to talk about. While I have threshed out the matter with myself, I believe I might do better by talking things over with one of my safest and sanest freshman."

"Why, what has happened, Miss Thompson?" asked Grace curiously.

"First, let me ask you a few questions," answered the principal. "Tell me something about the competition for the freshman prize. Which girl do you think has the best chance of winning it?"

"I know whom I want to win," replied Grace innocently. "Anne, of course, and I believe she will, too. While Miriam is more showy in her recitations, Anne is much more thorough, and she studies a great deal harder. The fact is, I am afraid she is making herself ill with studying. But she is determined to win not the little prize, but the big one, which is more than even Anne can do, I believe. Whoever heard of having every examination paper perfect?"

"It has not been done so far," admitted Miss Thompson, "but why is Anne so bent on winning the prize? Is it all for glory, do you think?"

"Anne is very poor, you know, Miss Thompson," said Grace simply.

"So she is," replied the principal, "and the child needs the money." Miss Thompson paused a moment, looking thoughtfully out over the smooth green lawn. "Grace," she resumed, finally, "I have something very serious to tell you. Two days ago I made a discovery that may change the fate of the freshman prize this year considerably. You know I keep the examination questions here in my desk. That is, the originals. A copy is now at the printers. So, you see, I have only one set of originals. I had occasion to come back to my office quite late the day of the discovery, and, as I let myself in at that door," she pointed to the door leading into the corridor, "what I thought was a gust of wind slammed the door leading into the next room which I usually keep shut and bolted on this side. My desk was open and the freshman examination papers undoubtedly had been tampered with. I could tell because they are usually the last in the pile and they were all on top and quite disarranged. Whoever had been here, had heard my key in the lock, and without waiting to close the desk had fled by the other door. I feel deeply grieved over this matter. I should never think of suspecting any of my fine girls of such trickery; and, yet, who else could it have been except one of the freshmen?"

"Oh, Miss Thompson, this is dreadful," exclaimed Grace, distressed and shocked over the story. "I don't believe there's a girl in the class who would have done it. There must be some mistake."

"That is why I sent for you, Grace," said the principal. "I want your advice. Now Anne——"

"*Anne?*" interrupted Grace horrified. "You don't suppose, for a minute, Anne would be dishonest? Never! I won't stay and listen any longer," and she rushed to the door.

Miss Thompson followed, placing a detaining hand on her arm.

"You are right, Grace, to be loyal to your friend," said the principal, always just and kind under the most trying circumstances; "but Anne, I must tell you, is under suspicion."

"Why?" demanded Grace, almost sobbing in her anger and unhappiness.

"The afternoon of the discovery Anne was here long after school hours. She was seen by two people wandering about the building."

"Who were the people?" demanded Grace incredulously.

"The janitress, who saw her from the window of another room, and—Miss Leece."

"I thought so," exclaimed Grace, with a note of triumph in her voice. "It is Miss Leece, is it, who is trumping up all this business? I tell you, I don't believe a word of it, Miss Thompson. Anne would no more do such a thing than I would, and I am going to fight to save her if it takes my last breath. Do you know how hard she has worked to win this prize? Simply all the time. I believe, if she knew what you suspected, it would kill her. I believe it's some tale Miss Leece has made up. And besides, why shouldn't she have come back to the building? Perhaps she forgot a book or something. I'd just like to know what Miss Leece was doing here at that time of day."

"She came here to meet me on business," answered Miss Thompson. "That is why she knows something of the unfortunate affair. She was with me when I found my desk had been broken open and the papers disturbed. She also heard the other door slam and it was then she told me of having seen Anne wandering about the building for which, as you say, there might have been a dozen reasons; I believe, as firmly as you do, that the child is incapable of cheating, and I intend to leave no stone unturned to get at the truth. But there is still another fact against Anne that is very black." The speaker took from a drawer a slip of folded paper. "This was found in the building," she continued, "and since it was an open letter, without address and under the circumstances, so important, it was read and the contents reported to me. I have since read it myself and I now ask you to read it."

DEAR ANNE:

I must have one hundred dollars at once, or go somewhere for a long time. I foolishly signed a friend's name to a slip of paper. I didn't know he would be so hard, but he threatens to prosecute unless I pay up before the end of next week. I know you have rich friends. I have been hearing of your successes. Perhaps the old lady, Mrs. G., will oblige you. I trust to your good sense to see that the hundred must be forthcoming, or it will mean disgrace for us all.

Your father,

J. P.

Grace limply held the letter in one hand.

"Oh, poor, poor Anne!" she groaned, wiping away the tears that had welled up into her eyes and were running down her cheeks.

"I feel just as you do, my child," went on Miss Thompson. "I am deeply, bitterly sorry for this unfortunate child. But you will agree with me that she has had a very strong motive for winning the prize." Grace nodded mutely.

"By the way," she asked presently, when she had calmed herself, "who was it that found the letter?"

"Miss Leece again," replied Miss Thompson, hesitatingly.

"There, you see," exclaimed Grace excitedly, "that woman is determined to ruin Anne before the close of school. I tell you, I won't believe Anne is guilty. It has taken just this much to make me certain that she is entirely innocent. Is there no clue whatever to the person who copied the papers?"

"Yes," answered Miss Thompson, "there is. This had been shoved back in the desk under the papers. It does not belong to me, and it could not have gotten into my desk by any other means. I suppose, in her hurry to copy the freshmen sheets, whoever she was, laid it down and forgot it."

Miss Thompson produced a crumpled pocket handkerchief. Grace took it and held it to the light. There were no marks or initials upon it whatever; it was simply a cambric handkerchief with a narrow hemstitched border, a handkerchief such as anyone might use. It was neither large nor small, neither of thin nor thick material.

"There's nothing on it," said Grace. "I suppose the stores sell hundreds of these."

"That's very true," answered the principal, "but I hoped you would be familiar enough with your friends' handkerchiefs to recognize this one."

"No," replied Grace, "I haven't the least idea whose it is. Wait a moment," she added quickly, smelling the handkerchief; "there is a perfume on it of some sort. Did you notice that?"

"I did," replied Miss Thompson. "It was one of the first things I did notice. I am very sensitive to perfumes; perhaps because I dislike them on clothing. But I waited for you to find it out for yourself. In fact, my dear, this will be the only means of trapping the person. Now, what perfume is it, and who in the class uses it? I am not familiar with perfumes, but I thought perhaps you were. And now, I will tell you that this is the reason I sent for you. The reason I showed you this letter, which has only been seen by one other person besides myself—Miss Leece, of course. I do not wish to tell anyone else about this matter. I do not care to put the subject before the School Board for discussion. I do not believe, any more than you, that Anne is guilty and I have taken you into my confidence because I believe you are the one person in the world who can help me in this predicament. Miss Leece, of course, intends to do everything in her power to bring the child 'to justice.' But, until I give her permission, she will hardly dare to speak of it. So far, we three are the only people who know what has happened. In the meantime, I shall turn over this handkerchief to you. Keep it carefully and be very guarded about what you do and say. You are a young girl," she continued, taking Grace's hand and gazing full into her honest eyes, "but I have a great respect for your judgment and discretion, and that is the reason I am asking for your help in this very delicate matter. You may rest assured that I shall do nothing whatever; at least, not until after examinations. I have an idea that we may get a clue through them. We must save Anne, whose life would be utterly ruined by such a false accusation as this. And I feel convinced that it is false."

"Well, I can tell you one thing, Miss Thompson," returned Grace as she opened the door, "and that is Anne Pierson never used any perfume in her life. She hasn't any to use."

Miss Thompson nodded and smiled.

"I was sure of that," she called.

Grace had little time to lose. The examinations, which took place the next day and the day after, would undoubtedly bring matters to a crisis.

She took the handkerchief from her pocket and sniffed at it. Neither was she familiar with perfumes, and this odor was new to her. Suddenly an idea occurred to her and she made straight for the nearest drugstore.

"Mr. Gleason," she demanded of the clerk in charge, "could you tell me what perfume this is?"

The druggist sniffed thoughtfully at the handkerchief for some seconds.

"It's sandalwood," he said at last. "We received some in stock a week ago."

# CHAPTER XXIII

## IN THE THICK OF THE FIGHT

How examinations loom up on the fatal day, like monstrous obstacles that must be overcome! How the hours slip past, with nothing to break the stillness save the scratching of pens on foolscap paper, while each student draws upon the supply of knowledge stored up during the winter months!

A fly buzzes on the window pane; a teacher rises, tiptoes slowly about the room and sits down again. She can do nothing, now, but keep watch on the pairs of drooping shoulders and the tired, flushed faces.

Anne was so absorbed in her work that she was oblivious to everything about her. Her pen moved with precision over her paper and her copy was neat and clear.

It was the second day of the examinations and she felt that her fate would soon be decided; but she was too tired now to worry. She worked on quietly and steadily. She had almost finished, and, as she answered one question after another, she was more and more buoyed up by the conviction that she would win the prize.

Miriam had finished her work. Her impatient nature would not permit her to do anything slowly. As she gave a last flourishing stroke with her pen, she leaned back, looking about her. She smiled contemptuously as her eyes rested on Anne.

"What a shabby, slow little creature she is!" Miriam murmured. "It would be a disgrace for a girl like me to be beaten by her. I'll never endure it in the world."

It was not long before the girls had all finished and turned in their papers to the teacher in charge.

"Oh, glorious happy day!" cried Nora, as she sped joyously down the corridor. "Examinations are over, and now for a good time!"

A dozen or more of the freshman class had been invited to Miriam's to a tea to celebrate the close of school. Anne, of course, was not invited; but Grace and her friends had received invitations and promptly accepted them.

Grace had taken Nora and Jessica into her confidence to some extent. She needed their help, but she had not mentioned the letter from Anne's father. The three girls met early by appointment, at the Harlowe house, to discuss matters before going to Miriam Nesbit's.

"Here's a list of the people in Oakdale," said Nora, "who have bought sandalwood perfume. I have been to four drug stores and all the dry goods stores."

Grace took the list and read:

"'Mrs. I. Rosenfield, Miss Alice Gwendolyn Jones, Mr. Percival Butz, etc.' Good heavens!" she cried, "there's not a single person on this list who has anything to do with Oakdale High School. Mr. Percival Butz," she laughed. "The idea of a man buying perfume. Really, girls," she added in despair, "we've been wasting our time. I can't see that any of us has made the least headway. I have called on almost every freshman in the class and inquired what her favorite perfume is, and I know some of them thought I was silly. Anyway, not one of them claimed to use sandalwood."

"The stupidest girls would be the ones who would be most likely to want to copy the papers," observed Jessica, "but those girls are much too nice to believe such horrid things about. I went to see Ellen Wiggins and Sallie Moore yesterday afternoon. Neither of them use perfume. Sallie Moore told me she had an orris root sachet that had almost lost its scent. Which reminds me," she continued, "why couldn't this handkerchief have been scented by some other means than just perfume. Perhaps it was put into a mouchoir case with sandalwood powder."

"Why, of course," exclaimed Grace. "Jessica, I never thought of asking who had been buying sachet powders. You have a great head."

"Must I go back and ask all those storekeepers for more lists?" demanded Nora.

"No, child," replied Grace. "Just give us time to think first."

"It's time to go to Miriam's anyhow," observed Jessica. "Perhaps some sort of inspiration will come on the way," and the three girls set out for the tea party.

As they paused to admire the beautiful flower beds on the Nesbit lawn Jessica said:

"Have you inquired Miriam's favorite perfume?"

"Oh, yes," answered Grace. "She said she liked them all and had no favorites."

"Why are all these strange young women breaking into my premises?" demanded a voice behind them.

"David Nesbit," cried Grace, "where have you been all this time? You never seem to find the time to come near your old friends anymore."

"I have been busy, girls," replied David. "Never busier in my life. But I believe I've struck it at last. It will not be long, now, before I turn into a bird."

"Oh, *do* show it to us!" cried Grace. "Where is the model?"

"In my workroom," he replied. "If you are very good, and will promise to say nothing to the others, I'll give you a peep this afternoon. When I signal to you from the music room, by sounding three bass notes on the piano, start upstairs and I'll meet you on the landing. You may ask why this mystery? But I know girls, and if all those chattering freshmen are allowed to come into my room they are sure to knock over some of the models, or break something, and I couldn't stand it."

The three girls entered the large and imposing drawing room where Miriam, in a beautiful pink mulle, trimmed with filmy lace insertions, received them with unusual cordiality; and presently they all repaired to the dining room where ice cream and strawberries were served with little cakes with pink icing. It was, as a matter of fact, a pink tea, and Miriam's cheeks were as pink as her decorations. She looked particularly excited and happy. Each of the three chums had just swallowed her last and largest strawberry, saved as a final relish, when three low notes sounded softly on the piano in the adjoining room.

In the hum of conversation nobody had noticed David's signal except Grace and her friends, who strolled into the music room where he was waiting.

"Come along," he said, leading the way up the back stairs, "and please consider this as a special mark of attention from the great inventor who has never yet made anything go. Where's Anne?"

"I suppose she is resting," answered Grace. "She had just about reached the end of her strength to-day."

"But she'll win the prize, I hope," continued David.

"We are all sure of it," answered Grace, in emphatic tones.

David opened the door into his own private quarters, which consisted of a large workroom with a laboratory attached, where he had once worked on chemical experiments until he had become interested in flying machines.

"Here they are," he exclaimed, walking over to a large table in the workroom. "I have three models, you see, and each one works a little better than the other. This last one, I believe, will do the business." He pointed to a graceful little aeroplane made of bamboo sticks and rice paper.

"Isn't it sweet?" exclaimed the girls in unison.

"And it has a name, too," continued David unabashed. "I've called her 'Anne,' because, while she's such a small, unpretentious-looking little craft, she can soar to such heights. There is not room here to show you how good she is, but we'll have another gymnasium seance some day soon, Anne must come and see her namesake."

"There!" cried Grace in a tone of annoyance. "I have jagged a big place in my dress, David Nesbit, on a nail in your table. Why do you have such things about to destroy people's clothes?"

"But nobody who wears dresses ever comes in here," protested David, "except mother and the maid, and they know better than to come near this table. Can't I do something? Glue it together or mend it with a piece of sticking plaster?"

"No, indeed," answered the girl. "Just get me a needle and thread, please. I don't want to go downstairs with such a hideous rent in my dress."

"Why, of course," assented David. "Why didn't I think of it sooner? Mother will fix you up," and he opened the door into the hall and called "mother!"

Mrs. Nesbit came hurrying in. She never waited to be called twice by her son, who was the apple of her eye.

"My dear Grace," she exclaimed when she saw the tear, "this is too bad. Come right into my room and I'll mend it for you."

So it happened that Grace was presently seated in an armchair in Mrs. Nesbit's bedroom, while the good-natured woman whipped together the jagged edges of the rent.

"What a beautiful box you have, Mrs. Nesbit," said Grace, pointing to a large carved box on the dressing table.

"Do you like it?" replied the other. "I'm fond of it, probably because I was so happy when I bought it years ago while traveling abroad with my husband. It smells as sweet as it did when it was new," she added, placing the box in Grace's lap.

Nora and Jessica, who had been hovering about the room, now came over to see the sweet-scented box. How strangely familiar was that pungent perfume which floated up to them. Where had they smelled it before?

"It is made of carved sandalwood," continued Mrs. Nesbit, opening the lid, "and I have always kept my handkerchiefs in it, you see——"

"Mother!" called David's voice from the hall, and Mrs. Nesbit left the room for a moment.

"Sandalwood!" gasped Grace.

Yes, it was the same perfume that now faintly scented the famous handkerchief.

There was a pile of handkerchiefs in the box. Grace lifted the top one and sniffed at it. She examined the border carefully and the texture.

"It looks like stealing," she whispered, "but I must have this handkerchief. I'll return it afterwards," and she slipped the handkerchief into her belt.

Nora and Jessica had exchanged significant glances, while Nora's lips had formed the words, "exactly like the other one."

In the meantime Miss Thompson had been closeted with Anne Pierson for half an hour in the principal's office. By special request she had arranged to have Anne's examination papers looked over immediately and sent to her. The papers were therefore the first to receive attention from each teacher, and were then turned over to Miss Thompson, who hurried with them into her office and locked the door behind her.

"It would be a pity if they were too perfect," she said to herself. "That would tell very much against Anne, I fear."

But, as her eyes ran over them, she shook her head dubiously. They were marvels of neatness and not one cross or written comment marred their perfection. At the foot of each sheet the word "perfect" had been written. Some of the teachers had even added notes stating that no errors of any sort had been found, while one professor had paid Anne the very high compliment of stating that the perfection of her examination papers had not been a surprise. Never in that teacher's experience had he taught a more brilliant pupil. Miss Thompson looked with interest at the algebra papers. If this had not come up, she thought, Miss Leece would certainly have managed to find a flaw somewhere, even if she had had to invent one. But under the circumstances, it was more to that wily woman's purpose to give Anne her due. For Miss Leece knew that a perfect examination paper would tell more against the young girl than for her.

It was after this that Miss Thompson had her talk with Anne, a very kindly, interested talk, in which the young girl's prospects, her work and health had all come under consideration. And then in the gentlest possible way Miss Thompson had produced the letter.

"Is this yours, Anne?" she asked.

Anne started violently.

"O Miss Thompson," she cried, making a great effort to keep back her tears, "where did you find it? I spent one entire afternoon here looking for it. It was the very day you and Miss Leece were here."

"Oh, you saw us then," replied the principal. "And where were you?"

"I was outside on the steps," replied Anne. "Didn't Miss Leece mention it? She looked up and saw me just as you unlocked the door. Then the other door slammed and someone hurried down the passage. I saw her, too, but——"

"But what, Anne?" asked the principal slowly.

"But I am not sure who it was."

"Have you an idea?"

"I could only guess from the outline of her figure," replied Anne. "And it wouldn't be fair to tell her name unless I had seen her plainly. It might have been someone else."

Anne had a suspicion that something had happened, and that Miss Thompson had brought her here to find out what she knew. But she never dreamed that she herself was under suspicion.

One thing had struck Miss Thompson very forcibly. Miss Leece had known all along that Anne was on the staircase at the very moment the other person was slamming the door in their faces. And yet Miss Leece was determined to condemn Anne to the faculty that very night. She had said so in as many words, in defiance of the principal's arguments against such a course.

"Well, good night, my child," she said at last, giving Anne a motherly kiss. "You have done a good winter's work and I am proud of you."

Anne hurried away, clutching the letter in her hand. She wondered if Miss Thompson had read it, and somehow she didn't mind so much after all. The principal seemed to her the very embodiment of all that was good and kind.

Miss Thompson was destined to have several callers that afternoon. In a few moments Grace hurried in, breathless and excited.

"Look at that, Miss Thompson," cried the girl, thrusting a handkerchief into her hand. "Look at it and smell it."

"Well," replied the principal, "I've seen it before and smelled it before, too. Only you've had it washed and ironed, haven't you!"

Grace took a crumpled handkerchief from her pocket.

"Here's the real one," she cried triumphantly.

The two handkerchiefs were certainly identical in shape and material and both were perfumed with sandalwood.

"Where did you get this one?" demanded the principal.

"From Mrs. Nesbit's sandalwood handkerchief box," whispered Grace slowly.

"You think it was then——?"

"Yes," replied Grace. "I'm certain of it. It's as plain as daylight. She borrowed her mother's handkerchief."

"Dear, dear!" exclaimed the principal. "How very foolish! How very unnecessary! And all because she couldn't endure to be beaten! Do you know," she continued presently, "that Miss Leece intends to denounce Anne before the faculty to-night? My authority can't stop her, and I don't believe the similarity of these two handkerchiefs will either."

"Miss Thompson," exclaimed Grace, "I tell you I know perfectly well that woman is going to try to ruin Anne for the sake of Miriam. I have known it for months. Why, at Mrs. Gray's Christmas party she did a thing that is too outrageous to believe," and here Grace opened a bundle she had brought with her and produced the marionette of James Pierson.

Miss Thompson was shocked at the recital of the story. She, too, recognized the green silk tie, although she had no recollection of Miriam's red velveteen suit, a piece of which formed the waistcoat. But there was something about that green silk which stuck in the memory. Probably because it was so ugly, having a semi-invisible yellow line running through it.

"Yes," she said, "I remember it very well. It was the trimming on a blouse Miss Leece wore last autumn. I do not believe anyone could forget such a hideous piece of material."

Miss Thompson paused a moment and considered.

"My dear," she continued presently, "I believe this is all I shall need to confront Miss Leece with. Your bringing it to me at this moment shows most excellent judgment. It may prevent a painful scandal in the school, as well as saving Anne from disgrace. As for the two handkerchiefs, the evidence is too slight to make any open accusations; but at any rate you may leave both with me. I may need them in my interview with Miss Leece. I may as well tell you I am anticipating a pretty stiff battle with her. I don't believe I should have won with only the handkerchiefs."

"Oh, I hope we can save Anne, Miss Thompson," cried Grace.

"I earnestly hope so, too," replied the principal. "It would be too heart breaking to have the child go down under this false accusation; and aside from that, such scandals are bad for the school and I would rather deal with them privately than have them made public. But run along now, dear. You have done nobly and deserve a prize yourself."

A knock was heard, and as Grace departed through one door Miss Leece opened the other.

"If Miss Thompson only wins this battle!" the young girl exclaimed to herself. "I want to believe she will, but I know that terrible Miss Leece will make a tremendous fight."

She joined her friends, who were waiting for her outside.

"Girls," she cried, "pray for Anne to-night!"

Nora, good little Catholic that she was, went straight to her church and burned two candles before the altar of the Holy Virgin, while she offered up a humble petition for Anne's deliverance; while Grace and Jessica, in their own bedrooms, that night prayed reverently and earnestly that Anne might be saved from her enemies. Thus were Anne's three devoted friends working and praying for her while she slept the sleep of exhaustion.

# CHAPTER XXIV

## THE FRESHMAN PRIZE

Graduation night in Oakdale High School was one of the great social events of the year. The floor and galleries of Assembly Hall were invariably packed with an enthusiastic audience; for the two schools united at the ceremony of graduation and the senior class formed a mixed company on the stage.

Most of the pupils attended commencement and the freshman class of the Girls' High School was always there in full to witness the triumph of one of its members, who was called forth from the audience to receive the usual freshman prize of twenty-five dollars.

The identity of the winner was always kept a secret until the great night, when she was summoned from the audience to the stage and presented with the money before the entire assembly.

The readers can imagine, therefore, the uncertainty and trepidation that fluttered in the hearts of our four girls as they sat together in the center of the great hall. Anne had passed through a dozen stages of emotions, both hopeful and otherwise, and had finally steeled herself to give up all thought of winning either of the prizes.

Miriam, confident and handsome, sat near them. She wore a beautiful white dress trimmed with lace, and her thick, black plaits were twisted around her head like a coronet.

"She's all dressed up to step up on the stage and get her twenty-five," whispered Nora to Jessica.

"Perhaps she already knows she's going to get it," answered Jessica doubtfully. "Perhaps Miss Leece has told her."

"If Miss Leece knew it, she would certainly have told her," answered Grace, leaning over so that Anne could not hear her; "but I feel sure Miss Thompson has managed it somehow, although I kept hoping all day she would send me a note or something. It may be she hated to tell me the bad news."

Hippy Wingate and Reddy Brooks came down the aisle in immaculate attire. David followed behind, pale and silent.

Did David suspect anything about his sister? Grace wondered. Certainly he had directly or indirectly been the means of balking every one of Miriam's schemes for injuring Anne. Perhaps Miriam had told him she was to win the prize, and he was thinking of Anne's disappointment. All three boys paused when they saw their friends of the Christmas house party. Hippy leaned over to say:

"Hello, girls! Can you guess what has brought us here to-night, all dressed up in our best?"

"Not unless it was to show off your clothes," replied Nora.

"To see Miss Anne Pierson win the freshman prize. Simply that, and nothing more."

"But I don't expect to win it, Hippy," protested Anne.

"If you don't, you aren't the girl we took you for, then," replied Hippy. "I heard from a young person in your class that you hadn't made a mistake in six months."

"But just as many people think Miriam will win," said Anne. "Look at all the people congratulating her already."

Surely enough Miriam's friends had rallied around her at the final test, and numbers of girls and boys and grown people, too, were already prophesying victory.

Just then the audience composed itself, for the exercises were about to begin. Soft music was heard and the graduates filed out and took their seats.

Immediately they were seated, Mrs. Gray, in a beautiful lavender silk gown and a white lace bonnet trimmed with violets, swept down the aisle, bowing and smiling right and left.

"Girls!" cried Grace delightedly, looking over her shoulder, "guess who is with our precious little Mrs. Gray?"

"Tom Gray!" cried the others in unison, just as Tom Gray himself appeared opposite them and waved his hat, regardless of the many eyes fastened upon him, for Mrs. Gray was an important personage not only at these annual assemblages, but in Oakdale itself, of which she had always been a most generous and loyal citizen.

Mrs. Gray nodded cordially when she saw the girls, but shook her head over Anne's pale, drawn little face.

As the ceremonies proceeded after the opening prayer, Anne felt herself drifting further and further away. She was a little boat on a troubled, restless sea, with the noise of the waves in her head, and only occasionally did she hear some one's voice reading a graduating essay or making a speech—she couldn't tell which. She remembered there was a piano solo, very loud and crashing, it seemed to her, and there was a tremendous humming sound. The sea was growing very rough, she thought. A storm was brewing somewhere. Then the wind died down again, there was a complete and utter silence and she seemed to be entirely alone.

"I have great pleasure in announcing," she dimly heard a voice say, "that the annual freshman prize, so generously donated always by Mrs. Gray, is awarded this year to one of the most brilliant and remarkable pupils who has ever studied in Oakdale High School. My language, in this instance, may appear to be rather extravagant, but the pupil, who has been under the eye of the faculty for many months because of her most excellent standing, has achieved a unique success in the history of the school. I may say that she has turned in a set of examination papers absolutely perfect in every detail, and it is with real delight I announce that she has won not only the usual smaller prize of twenty-five dollars, but the premium always offered at the same time, but never before won by any pupil of this school, of one hundred dollars, for a flawless examination. I would, therefore, ask Miss Anne Pierson to come to the platform, that I may have the honor of delivering both prizes to her."

Such a shout as arose after this remarkable speech had never before been heard at a high school graduation. The freshman class was fairly mad with joy, while Hippy and Reddy yelled themselves hoarse.

"Anne!" cried Grace. "Wake up, Anne! Are you asleep, child? Go up to the platform. Miss Thompson is waiting for you."

Tears of joy and relief were rolling down Grace's cheeks as she urged Anne to rise from her seat.

Anne stood up, half dazed, still wondering what it was all about, and made her way through a sea of faces to the platform.

"Hurrah!" roared the pupils of the High School in one voice.

"Hi-hi-hi! Hi-hi-hi! Oakdale, Oakdale, HIGH SCHOOL!"

This was an honor usually accorded only to football and baseball heroes.

When Anne reached the platform she appeared so small and plain, in her simple white muslin frock, that people looked at her wonderingly. It was not everyone in Oakdale who was familiar with the little, dark-haired girl.

"My dear," said Miss Thompson, very handsome and imposing in a gray silk dress, "I am happy to be the one to hand you these two prizes. You have worked hard and richly deserve them both. I am sure everyone in this house to-night is glad that your winter's unceasing labors are crowned with success, and I now recommend you to take a good rest, for such prizes are only earned by earnest and hard application, and hard work carries with it, sometimes, its own penalty." (She placed special emphasis on these last words.) "You have indeed earned the right to a happy vacation."

Two bouquets were handed over the footlights at this point, one a beautiful bunch of pink roses and the other of lilies of the valley.

Mrs. Gray had sent the roses Grace felt sure. It was her custom always to send such a bouquet to the one who carried off the prize. But who had sent the lilies of the valley?

"Very likely David," Grace said to herself, watching the boy's face as Anne took the flowers from the usher.

Had he known then that his sister had lost the prize, or was his faith in Anne so great?

But something had happened.

Suddenly the waves, which for the last half hour had been roaring and tossing about Anne, seemed to submerge her completely. She felt a horrid sensation of sickness for a moment; and then down, down she sank to the bottom of nothing, carrying her flowers and prizes with her.

"She's fainted!" cried someone. "The poor, little, tired girl has fainted!"

A tall young graduate picked up the small, limp figure and carried her off the stage as easily as if she had been a child. The closing exercises were then resumed, the benediction pronounced and the audience filed out somewhat silently.

Grace and her friends hurried around behind the scenes, where they found Mrs. Gray in the act of placing a smelling-salts bottle to Anne's nostrils, while Tom Gray and David Nesbit were cooling her temples with lumps of ice. "She is conscious at last!" exclaimed the old lady, as Anne opened her eyes. "It was entirely too much excitement for this delicate, worn-out child. Tom, order the carriage. I mean to take her straight to my own house and nurse her myself. I am the only person in this town who has time to give her all the care and attention she needs. I feel like such a lazy, good-for-nothing old woman when I see all these bright young people winning prizes and doing so many clever things."

"How you do go on, Mrs. Gray," said David. "You know very well you are the brightest, youngest and prettiest girl in Oakdale."

Anne sat up at this moment, and looked into the faces of her best friends leaning over her anxiously.

"I thought the boat capsized just as I was about to win the race," she said faintly.

"The little boat did capsize, dear," answered Mrs. Gray gently, "but not until after you had won the race. And now, if you are well enough to let this strong nephew of mine carry you, we are going to take you right home. Are all my Christmas children here?" she continued, looking about her. Hippy and Reddy had joined the group just then. "Yes, here you are. Tom and I can't take you all up in the carriage, but I want you to follow us, if your parents and guardians have no objections. I have arranged a little supper to celebrate Anne's victory. I am sorry she can't come to her own party, but she may hear all about it afterwards and the rest of you shall make merry for her."

Not long after, six young people strolled up Chapel Hill in the moonlight, talking gayly of the happy days they had spent together with Mrs. Gray; for Richards, the burglar, seemed now a sort of joke to them, and even the terrible recollection of the wolves was softened by time, and they could only laugh at poor Hippy's plight when his breath gave out and his legs refused their office.

"Oh, well," exclaimed Hippy, pretending to be much offended, "it is a very good idea to remember only the funny things and forget the dangerous ones, when all's said and done. But if I'd have had a stroke of apoplexy just as that young lady wolf began to lick my heels, you wouldn't have been so merry over the recollection."

"Well," retorted Nora, "we would have been just about going into half mourning, by now, and that's always a cheerful thought."

"Grace," whispered Jessica, taking advantage of the talk of the others not to be overheard, "did you notice Miriam when Miss Thompson began her speech?"

"No," answered Grace, "I was too intent upon Anne to look at Miriam. Why?"

"Well," continued Jessica, "you remember that Miss Thompson mentioned no names until almost the very end of the speech!"

"Yes," answered the other; "I remember it particularly, because I kept wishing she would hurry and get to the point."

"Exactly," went on Jessica, "and Miriam thought she had won the prize."

"How do you know, Jessica! How could you tell?"

"Oh, in a hundred different ways. I could tell by the smile on her face that she took every compliment to herself. Lots of people were watching her, too, and I couldn't help feeling a little sorry for her, because she is one of those people who just can't stand losing. When Miss Thompson reached the place where she was about to ask Anne to step up and get the prize, Miriam half rose in her seat. Mrs. Nesbit pulled her back in the nick of time. I honestly believe she would have reached the stage before Anne did, if her mother hadn't stopped her. Hippy told me they left before the benediction. I suppose Miriam was not equal to the mortification."

"I thought perhaps Miss Thompson would have mentioned her name as coming second in the contest," said Grace. "She usually does, you know. But there were good reasons, and plenty, why she shouldn't this time, I suppose. And to think, Jessica, that Miriam need never have done that dreadful thing. She would probably have passed second in the class anyway, and copying the papers didn't help her one little bit."

Mrs. Gray reported Anne to be much better. She had taken some nourishing broth and gone to bed, and she was at that moment sleeping soundly.

So there was no cause for anything but good cheer at the supper party.

And here let us leave them around Mrs. Gray's hospitable table. For, is it not better to say farewell rejoicing so that no shadows may darken the memory we shall carry with us during the long months of separation?

Before Oakdale High School welcomes her children back again, David will sail abroad with his mother and sister; Grace and Anne will set off for the country to visit Grace's grandmother; the others and their families will scatter to various summer resorts, while Mrs. Gray will seek a cool spot in the mountains.

However, in the next volume, which will be entitled, "GRACE HARLOWE'S SOPHOMORE YEAR AT HIGH SCHOOL; Or, the Record of the Girl Chums in Work and Athletics," we shall again meet the four girls and their friends. This book, the record of the girl chums in athletics, tells of the exciting rivalries of the sophomore and junior basketball teams, culminating in a final hard-fought battle. Again Grace Harlowe distinguishes herself by her bravery and good judgment, and again Miriam Nesbit will do her best to thwart her at every point. And we may learn what Anne Pierson did with the prize money.

THE END.

Grace Harlowe's Sophomore

Year at High School

OR

**The Record of the Girl Chums**

**in Work and Athletics**

**By**

**JESSIE GRAHAM FLOWER, A.M.**

Author of Grace Harlowe's Plebe Year at High School, Grace Harlowe's Junior Year at High School, Grace Harlowe's Senior Year at High School, etc.

Illustrated

PHILADELPHIA

HENRY ALTEMUS COMPANY

1911

# CHAPTER I

# A DECLARATION OF WAR

"Anne, you will never learn to do a side vault that way. Let me show you," exclaimed Grace Harlowe.

The gymnasium was full of High School girls, and a very busy and interesting picture they made, running, leaping, vaulting, passing the medicine ball and practicing on the rings.

In one corner a class was in progress, the physical culture instructor calling out her orders like an officer on parade.

The four girl chums had grown somewhat taller than when last seen. A rich summer-vacation tan had browned their faces and Nora O'Malley's tip-tilted Irish nose was dotted with freckles. All four were dressed in gymnasium suits of dark blue and across the front of each blouse in letters of sky-blue were the initials "O.H.S.S." which stood for "Oakdale High School Sophomore." They were rather proud of these initials, perhaps because the lettering was still too recent to have lost its novelty.

"Never mind," replied Anne Pierson; "I don't believe I shall ever learn it, but, thank goodness, vaulting isn't entirely necessary to human happiness."

"Thank goodness it isn't," observed Jessica, who never really enjoyed gymnasium work.

"It is to mine," protested Grace, glowing with exercise and enthusiasm. "If I couldn't do every one of these stunts I should certainly lie awake at night grieving over it."

She gave a joyous laugh as she vaulted over the wooden horse as easily and gracefully as an acrobat.

"I'd much rather dance," replied Anne. "Ever since Mrs. Gray's Christmas party I've wanted to learn."

157

"Why Anne," replied Grace, "I had forgotten that you don't dance. I'll give you a lesson at once. But you must first learn to waltz, then all other dancing will be easy."

"Just watch me while I show you the step," Grace continued.

"Now, you try it while I count for you."

"One, two, three. One, two, three. That's right. Just keep on practicing, until you are sure of yourself; then if Jessica will play for us, I'll waltz with you."

"With pleasure," said Jessica, "Anne must learn to waltz. Her education in dancing mustn't be neglected another minute."

Anne patiently practiced the step while Jessica played a very slow waltz on the piano and Grace counted for Anne. Then the two girls danced together, and under Grace's guidance Anne found waltzing wasn't half as hard as she had imagined it would be.

By this time the gymnasium was almost empty. The class in physical culture had been dismissed, and the girls belonging to it had withdrawn to the locker rooms to dress and go home. The four girl chums were practically alone.

"I do wish the rest of the basketball team would put in an appearance," said Grace, as she and Anne stopped to rest. "We need every minute we can get for practice. The opening game is so very near, and it's really difficult to get the gymnasium now, for the juniors seem to consider it their especial possession. One would think they had leased it for the season."

"They are awfully mean, I think," said Nora O'Malley. "They weren't at all nice to us last year when we were freshmen and they were sophomores. Even the dignity of being juniors doesn't seem to improve them any. They are just as hateful as ever."

"Most of the juniors are really nice girls, but it is due to Julia Crosby that they behave so badly," said Jessica Bright thoughtfully, "She leads them, into all kinds of mischief. She is a born trouble-maker."

"She is one of the rudest girls I have ever known," remarked Nora with emphasis. "How Miriam Nesbit can tolerate her is more than I can see."

"Well," said Grace, "it is hardly a case of toleration. Miriam seems really fond of her."

"Hush!" said Anne, who had been silently listening to the conversation. "Here comes the rest of the team, and Miriam is with them."

Readers of the preceding volume of this series, "GRACE HARLOWE'S PLEBE
YEAR AT HIGH SCHOOL," need no introduction to Grace Harlowe and her girl chums. In that volume was narrated the race for the freshman prize, so generously offered each year by Mrs. Gray, sponsor of the freshman class, and the efforts of Miriam Nesbit aided by the disagreeable teacher of algebra, Miss Leece, to ruin the career of Anne Pierson, the brightest
pupil of Oakdale High School. Through the loyalty and cleverness of Grace and her friends, the plot was brought to light and Anne was vindicated.

Many and varied were the experiences which fell to the lot of the High School girls. The encounter with an impostor, masquerading as Mrs. Gray's nephew, Tom Gray, the escape from wolves in Upton Woods, and Mrs. Gray's
Christmas ball proved exciting additions to the routine of school work.

The contest between Grace and Miriam Nesbit for the basketball captaincy, resulting in Grace's subsequent election, was also one of the interesting features of the freshman year.

The beginning of the sophomore year found Miriam Nesbit in a most unpleasant frame of mind toward Grace and her friends. The loss of the basketball captaincy had been a severe blow to Miriam's pride, and she could not forgive Grace her popularity.

As she walked across the gymnasium followed by the other members of the team, her face wore a sullen expression which deepened as her eyes rested upon Grace, and she nodded very stiffly to the young captain. Grace, fully aware of the coldness of Miriam's salutation, returned it as courteously as though Miriam had been one of her particular friends. Long before this

Grace had made up her mind to treat Miriam as though nothing disagreeable had ever happened. There was no use in holding a grudge.

"If Miriam once realizes that we are willing to overlook some things which happened last year," Grace had confided to Anne, "perhaps her better self will come to the surface. I am sure she has a better self, only she has never given it a chance to develop."

Anne did not feel quite so positive as to the existence of Miriam's better self, but agreed with Grace because she adored her.

The entire team having assembled, Grace lost no time in assigning the players to their various positions.

"Miriam will you play one of the forwards?" she asked.

"Who is going to play center?" queried Miriam ignoring Grace's question.

"Why the girls have asked me to play," replied Grace.

"If I cannot play center," announced Miriam shrugging her shoulders, "I shall play nothing."

A sudden silence fell upon the group of girls, who, amazed at Miriam's rudeness, awaited Grace's answer.

Stifling her desire to retort sharply, Grace said "Why Miriam, I didn't know you felt that way about it. Certainly you may play center if you wish to. I am sure I don't wish to seem selfish."

This was too much for Nora O'Malley, who deeply resented Miriam's attitude toward Grace.

"We want our captain for center," she said. "Don't we, girls?"

"Yes," chorused the girls.

It was a humiliating moment for proud Miriam. Grace realized this and felt equally embarrassed at their outspoken preference.

Then Miriam said with a contemptuous laugh, "Really, Miss Harlowe, I congratulate you upon your loyal support. It is a good thing to have friends at court. However, it is immaterial to me what position I play, for I am not particularly enthusiastic over basketball. The juniors are sure to win at any rate."

A flush mounted to Grace's cheeks at Miriam's insulting words. Controlling her anger, she said quietly: "Very well, I will play center." Then she rapidly named the other players.

This last formality having been disposed of, the team lined up for practice. Soon the game was at its height. Miriam in the excitement of the play, forgot her recently avowed indifference toward basketball and went to work with all the skill and activity she possessed.

The basketball team, during its infancy in the freshman class had given splendid promise of future fame. Grace felt proud of her players as she stopped for a moment to watch their agile movements and spirited work. Surely, the juniors would have to look out for their laurels this year. Her blood quickened at thought, of the coming contests which were to take place during the course of the winter between the two class teams. There were to be three games that season, and the sophomores had made up their minds to win all of them. What if the junior team were a famous one, and had won victory after victory the year before over all other class teams?
The sophomores resolved to be famous, too.

In fact, all of Grace's hopes were centered on the coming season. Napoleon himself could not have been more eager for victory.

"We must just make up our minds to work, girls," she exhorted her friends. "I would rather beat those juniors than take a trip to Europe."

Nor was she alone in her desire. The other girls were just as eager to overthrow the victorious juniors. It was evident, so strong was the feeling in the class, that something more than a sense of sport had stirred them to this degree of rivalry.

The former freshman class had many scores against the present juniors. As sophomores, the winter before, they had never missed an opportunity to annoy and irritate the freshmen in a hundred disagreeable ways. "The Black Monks of Asia" still rankled in their memories. Moreover, was not

Julia Crosby, the junior captain? She was the same mischievous sophomore who had created so much havoc at the Christmas ball. She was always
playing unkind practical jokes on other people. It is true, she was an intimate and close friend of Miriam Nesbit, but they all were aware that Miriam was a law unto herself, and none of them had ever attempted to explain certain doings of hers in connection with Julia Crosby and her friends during the freshman year.

Grace's mind was busy with these thoughts when the door of the gymnasium opened noisily. There was a whoop followed by cries and calls and in rushed the junior players, most of them dressed in gymnasium suits.

Julia Crosby, at their head, had come with so much force, that she now slid halfway across the room, landing right in the midst of the sophomores.

"I beg your pardon," said Grace, who had been almost knocked down by the encounter, "I suppose you did not notice us. But you see, now, that we are in the midst of practicing. The gym. is ours for the afternoon."

Julia Crosby looked at her insolently and laughed.

How irritating that laugh had always been to the rival class of younger girls. It had a dozen different shades of meaning in it--a nasty, condescending contemptuous laugh, Grace thought, and such qualities had no right to be put in a laugh at all, since laughing is meant to show pleasure and nothing else. But Julia Crosby always laughed at the wrong time; especially when there was nothing at which to laugh.

"Who said the gym. was yours for the afternoon?" she asked.

"Miss Thompson said so," answered Grace. "I asked her, this morning, and she gave us permission, as she did to you last Monday, when the boys were all out at the football grounds."

"Have you a written permission?" asked Julia Crosby, laughing again, so disagreeably that hot-headed Nora was obliged to turn away to keep from saying something unworthy of herself.

"No," answered Grace, endeavoring to be calm under these trying circumstances, but her voice trembling nevertheless with anger. "No, I have no written permission and you had none last Monday. You know as well as I do that the boys principal is willing to lend us the gym. as often as we like during football season, when it is not much in use; and that Miss Thompson tries to divide the time as evenly as possible among the girls."

"I don't know anything about that, Miss Harlowe," said Julia Crosby. "But I do know that you and your team will have to give up the gymnasium at once, because our team is in a hurry to begin practicing."

Then a great chattering arose. Every sophomore there except Miriam Nesbit raised a protesting voice. Grace held up her hand for silence, then summoning all her dignity she turned to Julia Crosby.

"Miss Crosby," she said, "you have evidently made a mistake. We have had permission to use the gymnasium this afternoon, which I feel sure you have not had. It was neither polite nor kind to break in upon us as you did, and the least you can do is to go away quietly without interrupting us further."

"Really, Miss Harlowe," said Julia Crosby, and again her tantalizing laugh rang out, "you are entirely too hasty in your supposition. As it happens, I have the best right in the world to bring my team to the gym. this afternoon. So, little folks," looking from one sophomore to another in a way that was fairly maddening, "run away and play somewhere else."

"Miss Crosby," cried Grace, now thoroughly angry, "I insist on knowing from whom you received permission. It was not granted by Miss Thompson."

"Oh, I did not stop at Miss Thompson's. I went to a higher authority. Mr. Cole, the boys' principal, gave me a written permission. Here it is. Do you care to read it?" and Julia thrust the offending paper before Grace's eyes.

This was the last straw. Grace dashed the paper to the floor, and turned with flashing eyes to her tormentor.

"Miss Crosby," she said, "if Professor Cole had known that Miss Thompson had given me permission to use the gymnasium, he would never have given you this paper. You obtained it by a trick, which is your usual method of gaining your ends. But I want you to understand that the sophomore class will not tamely submit to such impositions. We evened our score with you as freshmen, and we shall do it again this year as sophomores.

Furthermore, we mean to win every basketball game of the series, for we should consider being beaten by the juniors the deepest possible disgrace.

I regret that we have agreed to play against an unworthy foe."

With her head held high, Grace walked from the gymnasium, followed by the other members of her team, who were too indignant to notice that Miriam had remained behind.

## CHAPTER II

## THE WAY OF THE TRANSGRESSOR

Once outside the gymnasium, Grace's dignity forsook her, and she felt a wild desire to kick and scream like a small child. The contemptible conduct of the junior team filled her with just rage. With a great effort at self-control she turned to the other girls, who were holding an indignation meeting in the corridor.

"Girls," she said, "I know just how you feel about this, and if we had been boys there would have been a hand-to-hand conflict in the gymnasium to-day."

"I wish we hadn't given in," said Nora, almost sobbing with anger.

"There was really nothing else to do," said Anne. "It is better to retire with dignity than to indulge in a free-for-all fight."

"Yes," responded Grace, "it is. But when that insufferable Julia Crosby poked Professor Cole's permit under my nose, I felt like taking her by the shoulders and shaking her. What those juniors need is a good, sound thrashing. That being utterly out of the question, the only thing to do is to whitewash them at basketball."

"Three cheers for the valiant sophomores!" cried Nora, "On to victory! Down with juniors!"

The cheers were given with a will, and by common consent the crowd of girls moved on down the corridor that led to the locker room.

The sophomore locker room was the particular rendezvous of that class in general. Here matters of state were discussed, class gossip retailed, and class friendships cemented. It was in reality a sort of clubroom, and dear to the heart of every girl in the class. To the girls in their present state of mind it seemed the only place to go. They seated themselves on the benches and Grace took the floor.

"Attention, fellow citizens and basketball artists," she called. "Do you solemnly promise to exert yourselves to the utmost to repay the juniors for this afternoon's work?"

"We do," was the answer.

"And will you pledge your sacred honor to whip the juniors, no matter what happens!"

"We will," responded the girls.

"Anne!" called Grace. "You and Jessica are not players, but you can pledge your loyalty to the team anyhow. I want you to be in this, too. Hold up your right hands."

"We will be loyal," said both girls, holding up their right hands, laughing meanwhile at Grace's serious expression.

"Now," said Grace, "I feel better. As long as we can't get the actual practice this afternoon let's lay out a course of action at any rate, and arrange our secret signals."

"Done," cried the girls, and soon they were deep in the mysteries of secret plays and signs.

Grace explained the game to Anne, who did not incline towards athletics, and had had little previous opportunity to enjoy them.

Anne, eager to learn for Grace's sake, became interested on her own account, and soon mastered the main points of the game.

"Here is a list of the secret signals, Anne," said Grace. "Study it carefully and learn it by heart, then you will understand every move our team makes during the coming games. I expect you to become an enthusiastic fan."

Anne thanked her, and put the paper in her purse, little dreaming how much unhappiness that same paper was to cause her.

The business of the afternoon having been disposed of, the girls donned street clothing and left the building, schoolgirl fashion, in groups of twos and threes.

On the way out they encountered several of the victorious juniors, who managed to make their presence felt.

"Oh," said Nora O'Malley, "those girls ought to be suppressed."

"Never mind," put in Anne. "You know 'the way of the transgressor is hard.' Perhaps those juniors will get what they deserve yet."

"Not much danger of it. They're too tricky," said Jessica contemptuously.

Anne's prophecy was to be fulfilled, however, in a most unexpected manner.

There had been one unnoticed spectator of the recent quarrel between the two classes. This was the teacher of physical culture, Miss Kane, who had returned to the gymnasium for a moment, arriving just in time to witness the whole scene. She, too, had had trouble at various times with the junior class, particularly Julia Crosby, who invariably tried her patience severely. She had been heard to pronounce them the most unruly class she had ever attempted to instruct. Therefore her sympathies were with the retreating sophomores, and with set lips and righteous indignation in her eye, she resolved to lay the matter before Miss Thompson, at the earliest opportunity.

Miss Thompson listened the next day with considerable surprise to Miss Kane's account of the affair. No one knew the mischievous tendencies of the juniors better than did the principal. Ordinary mischief she could forgive, but this was overstepping all bounds. She had given the sophomore class permission to use the gymnasium for the afternoon, and no other class had the least right to take the matter over her head. She knew that Professor Cole was entirely innocent of the deception practised upon him, so she resolved to say nothing to him, but deal with the junior team as she deemed best. One thing was certain, they should receive their just deserts.

Miss Thompson's face, usually calm and serene, wore an expression of great sternness as she faced the assembled classes in the study-hall the following morning. The girls looked apprehensively at each other, wondering what was about to happen. When their beloved principal looked like that, there was trouble brewing for some one. Miss Thompson, though a strict disciplinarian, was seldom angry. She was both patient and reasonable in her dealings with the pupils under her supervision, and had their utmost confidence and respect. To incur her displeasure one must commit a serious offense. Each girl searched her mind for possible delinquencies There was absolute silence in the great room. Then the principal spoke:

"I must ask the undivided attention of every girl in this room, as what I am about to say relates in a measure to all of you.

"There are four classes, representing four divisions of high school work, assembled here this morning. Each one must be passed through before the desired goal—graduation—is reached.

"The standard of each class from freshmen to seniors, should be honor. I have been very proud of my girls because I believed that they would be able to live up to that standard. However it seems that some of them have yet to learn the meaning of the word."

Miss Thompson paused. Nora cast a significant look toward Jessica, who sat directly opposite her, while Julia Crosby fidgeted nervously in her seat, and felt suddenly ill at ease.

"Good-natured rivalry between classes," continued Miss Thompson, "has always been encouraged, but ill-natured trickery is to be deplored. A matter has come to my ears which makes it necessary for me to put down with an iron hand anything resembling such an evil.

"You are all aware that I have been very willing to grant the use of the gymnasium to the various teams for basketball practice, and have tried to divide up the time as evenly as possible. Two days ago I gave the members of the sophomore team permission to use the gymnasium for practice. No other team had any right whatever to disturb them, yet I understand that another team did commit that breach of class etiquette, drove the rightful possessors from the room and occupied it for the remainder of the afternoon. The report brought to me says that the young women of the sophomore team conducted themselves with dignity during a most trying situation."

Miss Thompson turned suddenly toward the junior section.

"The members of the junior basketball team will please rise," she said sternly.

There was a subdued murmur throughout the section, then one after another, with the exception of Julia Crosby, the girls rose.

"Miss Crosby," said the principal in a tone that brooked no delay, "rise at once! I expect instant obedience from every pupil in this school."

Julia sulkily rose to her feet.

"Miss Crosby," continued Miss Thompson, "are you not the captain of the junior team?"

"Yes," answered Julia defiantly.

"Did you go to Professor Cole for permission to use the gymnasium last Thursday?"

"Yes."

"Why did you not come to me?"

Julia hung her head and made no reply.

"I will tell you the reason, Miss Crosby," said the principal. "You already knew that permission had been granted the sophomore team, did you not?"

"Yes," said Julia very faintly.

"Very well. You are guilty of two serious misdemeanors. You purposely misrepresented matters to Professor Cole and deliberately put aside my authority; not to mention the unwomanly way in which you behaved toward the sophomore team. Every girl who aided and abetted you in this is equally guilty. Therefore you will all learn and recite to me an extra page in history every day for two weeks. The use of the gymnasium will be prohibited you for the same length of time, and if such a thing ever again occurs, the culprits will be suspended without delay. You may be seated."

The dazed juniors sank limply into their seats. The tables had been turned upon them with a vengeance. A page of history a day was bad enough, but the loss of the gymnasium privilege was worse. The opening game was only two weeks off, and they needed practice.

Julia Crosby put her head down on her desk and wept tears of rage and mortification. The rest of the girls looked ready to cry, too.

The first bell for classes sounded and the girls picked up their books. At the second bell they filed out through the corridor to their various recitation rooms. As Grace, who had stopped to look for a lost pencil, hurried toward the geometry classroom, she passed Julia Crosby, who was moping along, wiping her eyes with her handkerchief. Julia cast an angry glance at Grace, and hissed, "tale-bearer."

Grace, inwardly smarting at the unjust accusation walked on without answering.

"What did I tell you about the way of the transgressor?" said Anne to Grace, as they walked home from school that day.

"It certainly is hard enough this time," said Grace. "But," she added, as she thought of Julia Crosby's recent accusation, "the way of the righteous isn't always easy."

# CHAPTER III

## A GENEROUS APPEAL

The juniors themselves hardly felt the weight of their punishment more than did Grace Harlowe. Her heart was set on winning every basketball game of the series. But she wished to win fairly and honestly. Now, that the juniors had been forbidden the use of the gymnasium, the sophomores might practice there to their heart's content. But was that fair? To be sure the juniors had deserved their punishment, but what kind of basketball could they play after having had no practice for two weeks? Besides, Julia Crosby blamed her for telling what had occurred in the gymnasium. She had gone to Julia, earnestly avowing innocence, but Julia had only laughed at her and refused to listen.

All this passed rapidly through Grace's mind as she walked toward the High School several mornings later. Something must be done, but what she hardly knew. The game could be postponed, but Grace felt that the other girls would not care to postpone it. They were heartily glad that the junior team had come to grief, and showed no sympathy for them.

"There's just one thing to be done," sighed Grace to herself. "And that's to go to Miss Thompson and ask her to restore the juniors their privilege. I hate to do it, she was so angry with them. But I'll do what I can, anyway. Here goes."

Miss Thompson was in her office when Grace entered rather timidly, seating herself on the oak settee until the principal should find time to talk to talk with her.

"Well, Grace, what can I do for you?" said Miss Thompson, looking up smilingly at the young girl. "You look as though you carried the cares of the world upon your shoulders this morning."

"Not quite all of them, but I have a few especial ones that are bothering me," replied Grace. Then after a moment's hesitation she said, "Miss Thompson, won't you, please, restore the juniors their gymnasium privilege?"

Miss Thompson regarded Grace searchingly. "What a peculiar request to make, Grace. Don't you consider the juniors' punishment a just one?"

"Yes," said Grace earnestly, "I do. But this is the whole trouble. The first basketball game between the juniors and the sophomores is scheduled to take place in less than two weeks. If the juniors do not practice they will play badly, and we shall beat them. We hope to win, at any rate, but we want to feel that they have had the same chances that we have had. If they do fail, they will say that it was because they had no opportunity for practice. That will take all the sweetness out of the victory for us."

"I think I see," said Miss Thompson, smiling a little. "It is a case of the innocent suffering with the guilty, isn't it? Personally, I hardly feel like restoring these bad children to favor, as they sadly needed a lesson; but since you take the matter so seriously to heart; I suppose I must say 'yes.'"

"Thank you so much, dear Miss Thompson," said Grace with shining eyes, "and now I want to ask one more favor. Julia Crosby believes that I reported her to you that day. Of course you know that I did not. Will you please tell her so? Her accusation has made me very unhappy."

Miss Thompson looked a trifle stern. "Yes, Grace," she said, "I will attend to that, too."

Grace turned to go, but Miss Thompson said. "Wait a moment, Grace, I will send for Miss Crosby."

Julia Crosby heard the summons with dismay. She wondered what Miss Thompson could have to say to her. The principal's reprimand had been so severe that even mischievous Julia felt obliged to go softly. Another performance like the last might cut short her High School career. So she let the sophomores severely alone. She was, therefore, surprised on entering the office to meet Grace Harlowe face to face.

"Miss Crosby," said Miss Thompson coldly, "Miss Harlowe has just asked me to restore the junior team their gymnasium privilege. Had any other girl asked this favor I should have refused her. But Miss Harlowe, in spite of the shabby way in which she has been treated, is generous enough to overlook the past, and begs that you be given another chance. It is only for her sake that I grant it.

"Also, Miss Crosby, I received no information from Miss Harlowe or any of her team regarding your recent rude conduct in the gymnasium. The report came from an entirely different source. You may go; but first you may apologize to Miss Harlowe, and thank her for what she has done."

With a very poor grace, Julia mumbled a few words of apology and thanks and hurried from the room. The principal looked after her and shook her head, then turning to Grace, she asked, "Well, Grace, are you satisfied?"

Grace thanked her again, and with a light heart sped towards the study hall. Once more she could look forward to the coming game with pleasant anticipations.

Julia Crosby had already informed the junior players of the rise in their fallen fortunes. When school was over they gathered about their leader to hear the story. Now, Julia, if possible felt more bitter toward Grace than formerly. It galled her to be compelled to accept anything from Grace's hands, and she did not intend to let any more of the truth be known than she could help. This was too good an opportunity to gain popularity to let slip through her fingers So she put on a mysterious expression and said:

"Now, see here, girls, I got you into all that trouble, and I made up my mind to get you out again. Just go ahead and practice for all your worth, and don't worry about how it all happened."

"Well," said Alice Waite, "it was awfully brave of you to go to Miss Thompson, even if you are too modest to tell of it. Wasn't it, girls?"

"Yes," chorused the team. "Three cheers for our brave captain."

Julia, fairly dazzled at her own popularity, smiled a smile of intense satisfaction. She had produced exactly the impression that she wished.

"What on earth are those juniors making such a fuss about?" inquired Nora O'Malley, as the four chums strolled across the campus toward the gate. The junior team, headed by Julia, was coming down the walk talking at the top of their voices.

"Nothing of any importance, you may be sure," said Jessica Bright. "'Shallow brooks babble loudest,' you know."

"They seem to be 'babbling' over Julia Crosby just now," said Anne, who had been curiously watching the jubilant juniors.

"No doubt she has just unfolded some new scheme," said Nora sarcastically, "that will be practiced on the sophomores at the first opportunity."

"Doesn't it seem strange," said Grace, who had hitherto offered no comments, "that we must always be at sixes and sevens with the juniors?

Such a spirit never existed between classes before. I wonder how it will all end?"

"Don't worry your dear head over those girls, Grace," said Anne, patting Grace's hand. "They aren't worth it."

"Oh, look girls!" exclaimed Nora suddenly. "There is David Nesbit, and he is coming this way. I haven't seen him for an age."

"Good afternoon, girls," said David, lifting his cap. "It is indeed a pleasure to see you."

"Why, David," said Grace, "you are quite a stranger. Where have you been keeping yourself?"

Anne also looked her pleasure at seeing her old friend.

"I have been very, very busy with some important business of my own," said David in a mock-pompous tone. Then he announced: "I am going to give a party and I am going to invite all of you. Will you come?"

"We will!" cried Nora. "Dressed in our costliest raiment, at that."

"Never mind about the fine clothes," said David, laughing. "This is to be a plain, every-day affair."

"Who else is invited, David?" asked Jessica.

"Only one other girl beside yourselves has had the honor of receiving an invitation."

"Miriam?" queried Grace, unable to conceal a shade of disappointment in her tone.

"No, no; not Miriam," answered Miriam's brother.

Grace looked relieved. If Miriam joined the party, something unpleasant was sure to happen. Miriam treasured a spite against Anne for winning the freshman prize, and never treated her with civility when they chanced to meet. Grace knew, too, that Miriam's attitude toward her was equally hostile. She wondered if David knew all these things about his sister.

Whatever he did know of Miriam and her deep-laid plans and schemes, he divulged to no one. None of the girls had ever heard him say a word against his sister; although they felt that he deeply disapproved of her jealousy and false pride.

"You haven't guessed her name yet," smiled David. "She is one of my best friends, girls. She has been my sweetheart ever since I was a young man of five. She's one of the prettiest girls in Oakdale, she's sixty years young, and her name is——"

"Dear Mrs. Gray, of course!" exclaimed Grace delightedly.

"And has she accepted your invitation?" asked Anne.

"She has," replied David, "and will come in her coach and four, or rather her carriage and two. You ordinary mortals will be obliged to walk, I fear."

"But why does she use her 'coach and four,' When she lives in the palace just next door?" rhymed Nora.

"Very good, my child," commented David. "However, what I was about to say was this: My party is not to be in a house. It is an open-air party. We are to meet at the Omnibus House, to-morrow afternoon at four o'clock. Two very distinguished gentlemen have also been invited—Mr. Reddy Brooks and Mr. Hippy Wingate."

A shout of laughter went up from the girls

"Distinguished, indeed," cried Nora. "It will be a delightful party I am sure."

"Shall we bring food for Hippy!"

"No," laughed David. "Let him eat the apples he finds on the ground. If we feed him on every festive occasion he will soon be too fat to walk, and we shall have to roll him about on casters."

"What a terrible fate," said Anne smiling.

"Well, girls? do you promise to attend?"

"Yes? indeed!" cried the four girls.

"Be sure not to surprise us with a disappointment."

"The main thing is not to disappoint you with the surprise," were his parting words.

"If all boys were as nice as David the world would be a better place!" exclaimed Grace. "I suppose you can guess what the object of this party is."

"Never mind, don't mention it," said Jessica in a low tone. "Here come some other girls, and if they knew what we know, there would be a multitude instead of a select, private party at the Omnibus House to-morrow."

# CHAPTER IV

## AN UNFORTUNATE AVIATOR

It was an unusual entertainment that David had provided for his little circle of intimate friends in the old orchard surrounding the Omnibus House. There was a look of intense excitement in his eyes, as he stood awaiting his guests, the following afternoon. Mrs. Gray had already arrived, and, leaving her carriage to wait for her near the entrance, now stood by David and helped him receive.

"It's good to see all my children together again," she exclaimed, giving Anne a gentle hug; for ever since her Christmas house party she had acquired a sort of proprietary feeling toward these young people. "I only wish Tom Gray were to be with us to-day. I should like him to have a share in the surprise; for you may be sure there is to be a surprise. David would never have asked us to this lonely place for nothing."

"David is a good old reliable, Mrs. Gray," cried Hippy. "Certainly if I had imagined for a moment that he would disappoint us, I never should have dragged my slight frame all this distance."

"Good, loyal old Hippy," replied David. "The surprise is ready, but even if it had not been, there is no exercise so beneficial to stout people as walking."

"Well, bring it on, bring it on," exclaimed Reddy. "We are waiting patiently."

"Curb your impatience, Sorrel Top," said David. "Just follow me, and see what I have to show you."

They helped little Mrs. Gray, who was nimble in spite of her years, through a broken gap in the wall of the Omnibus House. The old ruin was more picturesque than, ever in its cloak of five-leafed ivy which the autumn had touched with red and gold. A lean-to had been built against the back wall of the building, fitted with a stout door on the inside and a pair of doors on the outside.

"I rented this plot of land from the farmer who owns the orchard," explained David, taking a key from his pocket and opening the door in the stone wall. "This was about the best place I could think of for experiments, partly because it's such a lonesome place, and partly

177

because there is a clear open space of several hundred yards back here without a tree or bush on it."

It was dark inside until he had opened the double doors in the opposite wall, when the slanting light showed them an aëroplane; not a little gymnasium model this time, but a full-fledged flying machine, a trim and graceful object, even at close view.

"David," cried Anne joyously, "you don't mean to say you've gone and done it at last?"

"I have," answered David gravely; "and I've made two trips with pretty good success each time."

Then everyone talked at once. David was the hero of the hour.

"David, my dear boy," cried Mrs. Gray. "To think that I should live to see you an aviator!"

"I'm a long way from being one, yet, Mrs. Gray," answered David. "My bird doesn't always care to fly. There are times when she'd rather stay in her nest with her wings folded. Of course, I haven't nearly perfected her yet, so I don't want it mentioned in town until I get things in shape. But I couldn't wait until then to show it to you, my dear friends, because you were all interested in it last year."

"Well, well, come on and fly," cried Hippy. "My heart is palpitating so with excitement that I am afraid it will beat once too often if something doesn't happen."

"I was waiting for my helper," answered David, "but he appears to be late. You boys will do as well."

"Who is your helper, David?" asked Anne.

"You could never guess," he replied smiling, "so I'll have to tell you. It's old Jean, the hunter."

"Why, the dear old thing!" cried Grace. "To think of him leaving his uncivilized state to do anything so utterly civilized and modern as to help with a flying machine."

"And he does it well, too," went on David. "He is not only thoroughly interested but he keeps guard out here in case any one should try to break in. There are his cot and things in the corner. He sleeps in the open unless it rains. Then he sleeps inside."

As the old hunter did not put in an appearance David decided to wait no longer.

"Why can't we all help?" asked Grace. "What must we do? Please tell us."

"All right," answered David, "just give it a shove into the open space, and you'll see how she gradually rises for a flight."

After making a careful examination of all the parts of the aëroplane, and starting the engine, David took his seat in the machine.

Then the two boys, assisted by Grace and Nora, pushed it swiftly out into the broad open space back of the ruin.

Suddenly the machine began to rise. Slowly, at first, then seeming to gather strength and confidence like a young bird that has learned to fly at last, it soared over the apple trees. David, white, but very calm, quietly worked the levers that operated the little engine. When he had risen about a hundred feet, he began to dip and soar around the orchard in circles. He appeared to have forgotten his friends, watching anxiously below. He did not notice that little Mrs. Gray's knees had suddenly refused to support her, nor that she had sat flat on the ground in a state of utter bewilderment at the sight of his sudden flight. David looked far across at the beautiful rolling meadows, and fields dotted with farmhouses and cottages. How he loved the fertile valley, with its little river winding in and out between green banks! It was all so beautiful, but it was time to descend. He must not give his pet too much liberty, or he might rue his indiscretion. He headed his machine for the open space back of the Omnibus House, and began the descent. Then, something snapped, and he fell. He remembered as he fell the look of horror on the up-raised faces of his friends, and then everything became a blank.

It all happened in a flash, much too quickly to do anything but stand and wait until the aëroplane had crashed to the ground, but it seemed much longer, and Anne remembered later that she had felt a curious impulse to run away and hide. If David were to meet his death through this new toy, she could not endure to stay and see it happen.

But David was far from dead. He was only stunned and dizzy from the swift descent. He had not been high enough from the ground when the accident occurred to sustain serious injuries. They lifted him from the machine and laid him upon the grass, while Reddy ran to the brook and brought back his cap filled with water.

Mrs. Gray produced her smelling salts which she always carried with her. "Not for my own use, my dears," she always said, "but for the benefit of other people."

Reddy loosened David's collar and dashed the water into his face; while Hippy chafed the unconscious boy's wrists.

Presently David opened his eyes, looking vaguely about. He had a confused idea that something had happened to him, but just what it was he could not think. He looked up into the anxious faces of his friends who stood around him. Then he remembered.

"I'm not hurt," he said in a rather weak voice. Then he sat up and smiled feebly at the company. "I just had the wind knocked out of me. I am sure no bones are broken. How about my pet bird? Has she smashed her little ribs?"

"No, old fellow," exclaimed Hippy in a reassuring tone, for Hippy had never been able to endure the sight of suffering or disappointment. "Her wings are a good deal battered, that's all. But are you all right, old man?" he added, feeling David's arms and legs, and even putting an ear over his heart.

"It's still beating, you foolish, old fat-head," said David, patting his friend affectionately on the back.

In the meantime Anne had helped Mrs. Gray to her feet.

"I declare, I feel as though I had dropped from the clouds myself," said the old lady, wiping her eyes. "I am so stunned and bewildered. David, my dear boy, if you had been seriously hurt I should never have forgiven myself for allowing you to fly off like that. What would your poor mother say if she knew what had happened?"

"It won't be necessary to break the news to her, Mrs. Gray," said David. "I shall be as good as new inside of a few minutes. It's my poor little bird here who has received the injuries. Look at her poor battered wings! I think I know just what caused my sudden descent though, and I'll take care it doesn't happen again."

David then began a minute examination of his damaged pet, and soon located the trouble. His friends listened, deeply interested, as he explained the principles of aviation, and showed them how he had carried out his own ideas in constructing his aëroplane. Grace, who had a taste for mechanics, asked all sorts of questions, until Hippy asked her if she intended building an aëroplane of her own.

"I may," replied Grace, laughing. "You know that girls have as much chance at the big things of the world to-day, as boys."

"Well, if you do, let me know," responded Hippy, "and I'll write an epic poem about you that will make the world sit up and take notice."

"Then I am assured of fame beforehand," laughed Grace.

"Look!" said Nora suddenly. "Who are those people coming across the orchard? Doesn't that look like Julia Crosby and some of her crowd?"

"Yes," exclaimed Grace, "it is, and Miriam is with them."

"Then help me get my aëroplane into the shed quickly," exclaimed David. "You know that the Crosby girl is not a favorite with me." Then he added half to himself, "I don't see why Miriam insists on going around with her so much."

The boys lost no time in getting the aëroplane into the house, David slammed the doors, and triumphantly turned the key in the lock just as Miriam and her party came up.

With a quick glance Miriam's eyes took in the situation. She bowed courteously to Mrs. Gray, whom she dared not slight; included Grace, Nora and Jessica in a cool little nod, and stared straight past Anne. Then turning to her brother she said, "David, show Miss Crosby and her friends your aëroplane, they wish to see it."

A look of grim determination settled about David's mouth. Looking his sister squarely in the face, he said, "I am sorry to seem disobliging but I cannot show your friends my aëroplane and I am surprised to find that they know I have one."

Miriam reddened at this, but said insolently, "If you can invite other people to see it, you can show it to us."

There was an uncomfortable silence. Mrs. Gray looked surprised and annoyed. The peaceful old lady, disliked scenes of any kind. Grace and her chums, knowing that Miriam was only making herself ridiculous, felt embarrassed for her. Then Julia Crosby laughed in her tantalizing irritating way.

That settled the matter as far as David was concerned.

"You are right," he said, "I could show my flying machine to you and your friends if I cared to do so. However, I don't care to. Knowing that I wished my experiment to be kept a secret, you came here with the one idea of being disagreeable, and you have succeeded. I am sorry to be so rude to my own sister, but occasionally the brutal truth is a good thing for you to hear, Miriam."

Miriam was speechless with anger, but before she could frame a reply, Mrs. Gray said soothingly "Children, children don't quarrel. David, it is getting late. We had better go. I suppose it is of no use to ask any of you athletic young folks to ride back to town." With a little bow to Miriam and her discomfited party, Mrs. Gray turned toward where her carriage awaited her, followed by David and his friends.

After bidding her good-bye, the young people took the road to town. For David's sake all mention of the recent unpleasantness was tacitly avoided, though it was uppermost in each one's mind.

"I have one thing to be thankful for," said Grace to Anne, as she turned in at her own gate, "and that is that Miriam Nesbit isn't my sister."

As for Miriam, her feelings can be better imagined than described. She sulked and pouted the whole way home, vowing to get even with David for daring to cross her. Julia Crosby grew rather tired of Miriam's tirade, and left her with the parting advice that she had better forget it.

When Miriam reached home she immediately asked if David had come in. Receiving an affirmative reply, she went from room to room looking for him, and finally found him in the library. He was busy with a book on aviation. She snatched the book from him, threw it across the room and expressed her opinion of himself and his friends in very plain terms. Without a word David picked up his book and walked out of the library, leaving her in full possession of the field.

# CHAPTER V

## ON THE EVE OF BATTLE

But little time remained before the first basketball game of the series between the sophomores and juniors. Both teams had been untiring in their practice. There had been no further altercations between them as to the use of the gymnasium, for the juniors, fearing the wrath of Miss Thompson, were more circumspect in their behavior, and let the sophomore team strictly alone.

"They are liable to break out at any time, you can trust them just as far as you can see them and no farther, and that's the truth," cried Nora O'Malley. The sophomore players were standing in the corridor outside the gymnasium awaiting the pleasure of the juniors, whose practice time was up.

"They are supposed to be out of here at four o'clock," continued Nora, "and it's fifteen minutes past four now. They are loitering on purpose They don't dare to do mean things openly since Miss Thompson lectured them so, but they make up for it by being aggravating."

"Never mind, Nora," said Grace, smiling at Nora's outburst. "We'll whip them off the face of the earth next Saturday."

"Well, I hope so," said Nora, "I am sure we are better players."

"What outrageous conceit," said Jessica, and the four girls laughed merrily.

"By the way, Grace," said Anne, "I want to ask you something about that list you gave me. I don't quite understand what one of those signals means."

"Trot it out," said Grace. "I'll have time to tell you about it before the practice actually begins."

Anne took out her purse and began searching for the list. It was not to be found.

"Why, how strange," she said. "I was looking at it this morning on the way to school. I wonder if I have lost it. That would be dreadful."

She turned her purse upside down, shaking it energetically, but no list fell out.

"Oh, never mind," said Grace, seeing Anne's distress. "It's of no consequence. No one will ever find it anyway. Suppose it were found, who would know what it meant?"

"Yes, but one would know," persisted Anne, "because I wrote 'Sophomore basketball signals' on the outside of it. Oh, dear, I don't see how I could have been so careless."

"Poor little Anne," said Jessica, "she is always worried over something or other."

"Now see here, Anne," said Grace, "just because you lost a letter last term and had trouble over it, don't begin to mourn over those old signals. No one will ever see them, and perhaps you haven't lost them. Maybe you'll find them at home."

"Perhaps I shall," said Anne brightening.

"Now smile Anne," said Nora, "and forget your troubles. There is no use in crossing bridges before you come to them."

This homely old saying seemed to console Anne, and soon she was eagerly watching the work of the team, her brief anxiety forgotten.

That night she searched her room, and the next day gave her desk in school a thorough overhauling, but the list of signals remained missing.

The sophomore players with their substitute team met that afternoon in the gymnasium. It was their last opportunity for practice. Saturday they would rise to victory or go down in ignominious defeat. The latter seemed to them impossible. They had practiced faithfully, and Grace had been so earnest in her efforts to perfect their playing that they were completely under her control and moved like clockwork. There was no weak spot in the team. Every point had been diligently worked over and mastered. They had played several games with the freshmen and had won every time, so Grace was fairly confident of their success.

"Oh, girls," she cried, wringing her hands in her earnestness, "don't make any mistakes. Keep your heads, all of you. I am convinced we are better players than the juniors, even if they did get the pennant last year. For one thing I don't think they work together as well as we do, and that's really the main thing. Miriam, you missed practice yesterday. You are going to stay to-day, aren't you?"

Miriam nodded without replying. She was busy with her own thoughts. She wished she could hit upon some way to humiliate Grace Harlowe. But what could she do? That was the question. The members of the team adored their gray-eyed, independent young captain, therefore she would have to be very careful.

She had been steadily losing ground with her class on account of her constant association with the juniors, and the slightest misstep on her part would jeopardize her place on the team. She had a genuine love for the game, and since she couldn't play on the junior team, she concluded it would be just as well not to lose her place with the sophomores. In her heart she cared nothing for her class. She had tried to be their leader, and Grace had supplanted her, but now Grace should pay for it.

All this passed through Miriam's mind as she covertly watched Grace, who was reassuring Anne for the fiftieth time, not to worry over the lost signals.

"Don't tell anyone about it," she whispered to Anne. "You may find them yet."

Anne shook her head sorrowfully. She felt in some way that those signals were bound to make trouble for her.

"By the way, girls," said Grace, addressing the team, "has any one any objection to Anne and Jessica staying to see the practice game? They have seen all our work and are now anxious to see the practice game. They know all the points, but they want to see how the new signal code works."

"Of course not," answered the girls. "We won't turn Oakdale's star pupil out of the gym. Anne shall be our mascot. As for Jessica, she is a matter of course."

"I object," said Miriam. "I object seriously."

"Object?" repeated Grace, turning in amazement to Miriam. "Why?"

"You know that it is against all basketball rules to allow anyone in the gymnasium during practice except the regular team and the subs. If we follow our rules then we shall be certain that nothing we do reaches the ears of the juniors. We have always made an exception of Jessica, but I don't think we should allow anyone else here."

"And do you think that Anne Pierson would carry information?" exclaimed Grace sharply. "Really, Miriam, you are provoking enough to try the patience of a saint. Just as if Anne, who is the soul of honor, would do such a thing."

An indignant murmur arose from the girls. They were all prepared to like little Anne, although they did not know her very well.

"How can you say such things, Miriam?" cried Nora.

"I didn't say she would," said Miriam rather alarmed at the storm she had raised. "But I do think it is better to be careful. However, have it your own way. But if we lose the game——"

She paused. Her judgment told her she had said enough. If anything did happen, the blame would fall on Grace's shoulders.

Anne, deeply hurt, tried to leave the gymnasium but the girls caught her, and brought her back again. She shed a few tears, but soon forgot her grief in the interest of the game.

"Girls," said Grace, as she and Nora and Jessica walked down the street that night after leaving Anne at her corner, "we must look out for Anne. It is evident from the way Miriam acted to-day that she will never lose an opportunity to hurt Anne's feelings. I thought perhaps time would soften her wrath, but it looks as though she still nursed her old grudge."

How true Grace's words were to prove she could not at that time foresee.

"Well," said Nora, "Anne is one of the nicest girls in Oakdale, and if Miriam knows when she's well off she'll mind her own business."

The day before the game, as Grace was leaving school, she heard David's familiar whistle and turned to see the young man hurrying toward her, a look of subdued excitement upon his face.

"I've been looking all over for you, Grace," he said, as he lifted his cap to her. "I have something to tell you. This afternoon after school, Reddy, Hippy and I went out to the old Omnibus House. I wanted to show the fellows some things about my machine. While we were out there who should appear but Julia Crosby and some more of her crowd. They were having a regular pow-wow and were in high glee over something. We kept still because we knew if they saw us they'd descend upon us in a body. They stayed a long time and Julia Crosby made a speech. I couldn't hear what she said, but it seemed to be about the proper thing, for her satellites applauded about every two minutes. Then they got their heads together and all talked at once. While they were so busy we skipped out without being noticed. I thought I'd better tell you, for I have an idea they are putting up some scheme to queer you in the game to-morrow; so look out for them."

"Thank you, David," answered Grace. "You are always looking after our interests. I wonder what those juniors are planning. They are obliged to play a fair game, for they know perfectly well what will happen if they don't. Miss Thompson will be there to-morrow, and they know she has her eye on them."

"Put not your trust in juniors," cautioned David. "They may elude even her watchful eye."

"You are coming to see us play to-morrow, aren't you, David?" asked Grace.

"I'll be there before the doors are open, with Reddy and Hippy at my heels," responded David. "Good-bye, Grace. Look out for squalls to-morrow."

# CHAPTER VI

## THE DEEPEST POSSIBLE DISGRACE

A feeling of depression swept over Grace Harlowe as she looked out the window the next morning. The rain was falling heavily and the skies were sullen and gray.

"What a miserable day for the game," was her first thought. "I do hope the rain won't keep people away. This weather is enough to discourage any one."

All morning she watched anxiously for the clouds to lift, going from window to door until her mother told her to stop fretting about the weather and save her strength for the coming game.

The game was set for two o'clock, but at one, Grace put on her raincoat and set out for the High School. She knew she was early, but she felt that she couldn't stay in the house a minute longer.

One by one the sophomore team and its substitutes assembled, but the rain had dampened their spirits and the enthusiasm of the past few days had left them.

Grace looked worried, as she noticed how listless her players seemed. She wished it had been one of those cold, crisp days that set the blood tingling and make the heart beat high with hope.

Still Grace felt confident that her team would rise to the occasion when the game was called. They were two well-trained, too certain of their powers to ever think of failing.

The bad weather had evidently not depressed the spirits of their opponents. The juniors stood about laughing and talking. Julia Crosby moved from one girl to the other whispering slyly.

"Wretch!" thought Grace. "How disagreeable she is. She was born too late. She should have lived in the middle ages, when plotting was the fashion. She is anything but a credit to her class and dear old Oakdale High School."

Grace's rather vehement reflections were cut short by the approach of Miss Thompson, who stopped to say a word of cheer to the girls before taking her seat in the gallery.

"Well, Grace," she said, "this is a rather bad day outside, but still there will be a few loyal souls to cheer you on to victory. May the best man win. You must put forth every energy if you expect to conquer the juniors, however. They have held the championship a long time."

"They will not hold it after to-day if we can help it," answered Grace. "We feel fairly sure that we can whip them."

"That is the right spirit," said Miss Thompson. "Confidence is first cousin to success, you know."

"Was there ever a teacher quite like Miss Thompson?" asked Nora as the principal left them to take her seat in the gallery.

"She is a dear," said Marian Barber, "and she's on our side, too."

"There's the referee now!" exclaimed Grace. "Now, girls, make up your minds to play as you never played before. Remember it's for the honor of the sophomores."

By this time the gallery was half filled with an audience largely composed of High School boys and girls. A few outsiders were present. Mrs. Harlowe had come to see her daughter's team win the game, she said; for she knew that Grace's heart was set on victory.

The referee, time-keeper and scorer chosen from the senior class took their places. The whistle blew and the teams lined up. There was a round of loud applause from the fans of both teams. The players presented a fine appearance. The earnest, "do or die" expression on every face made the spectators feel that the coming game would be well worth seeing.

The rival captains faced each other, ready to jump for the ball the instant it left the referee's hands. There was a moment of expectant silence; then the referee put the ball in play, the whistle blew and the game began. Both captains sprang for the ball, but alas for the sophomores, Julia Crosby caught it and threw it to the junior right forward. It looked for a minute as though the juniors would score without effort, but Nora O'Malley, who was left guard, succeeded so effectually in annoying her opponent that when the bewildered goal-thrower did succeed in throwing the ball, it fell wide of the basket. It had barely touched the floor before there was a rush for it, and the fun waxed fast and furious.

During the first five minutes neither side scored; then the tide turned in favor of the juniors and they netted the ball.

Grace Harlowe set her teeth, resolving to play harder than ever. The juniors should not score again if she could help it. Nora had the ball and was dribbling it for dear life. Grace signaled her team, who responded instantly; but, to their consternation, the juniors seemed to understand the signal as fully as did their own team, and quickly blocking their play, scored again.

There was a howl of delight from the junior fans in the gallery. The sudden triumph of the enemy seemed to daze the sophomores. They looked at their captain in amazement, then sprang once more to their work. But the trend the game was taking had affected them, and in their desperate efforts to score they made mistakes. Miriam Nesbit ran with the ball and a foul was called, which resulted in the juniors scoring a point.

Nora O'Malley, in her excitement, caught the forward she was guarding by the arm, and again a foul was called; this time, however, the juniors made nothing from it. But the precious time was flying and only four minutes of the first half remained. Again Grace signaled for another secret play, and again the juniors rose to the occasion and thwarted her.

It was maddening.

The score stood 7 to 0 in favor of the juniors. Miriam Nesbit had the ball now, and was trying to throw it. She stood near the junior basket. Eluding her guard, who was dancing about in front of her, she made a wild throw. Whether by accident or design it was hard to tell, but the ball landed squarely in the junior basket. A whoop went up from the gallery. The whistle blew and the first half was over. The score stood 9 to 0 in favor of the enemy. The last two points had been presented to the juniors.

Up in the gallery discussion ran rife. The admirers of the juniors were loud in their praise of the superior ability of the team. The junior class, who were sitting in a body at one end of the gallery, grew especially noisy, and were laughing derisively at the downfall of the sophomores.

Miss Thompson was puzzled.

"I cannot imagine what ails my sophomores," she said to the teacher next to her. "I understood that they were such fine players. Yet they don't seem to be able to hold their own. It looks as though their defeat were inevitable, unless they do some remarkable playing during the next half."

Mrs. Harlowe, too, was disappointed. She wondered why Grace had boasted so much of her team.

"After all, they are little more than children," she thought. "Those juniors seem older to me."

As for Grace and her team—they were sitting in a room just off the gymnasium gloomily discussing the situation. Tears of mortification stood in Nora's eyes, while Grace was putting forth every effort to appear calm. She knew that if she showed the least sign of faltering all would be lost. Her players must feel that she still had faith in their ability to win.

"We are not beaten yet, girls," she said, "and I believe we shall make up in the last half what we lost in the first. Work fast, but keep your wits about you. Don't give the referee any chance to call a foul, we can't spare a minute from now on. When I give the signal for a certain play, be on the alert, and please, please don't any of you present those juniors with any more points. I'm not blaming you, Miriam, for I know that last throw of yours was an accident, but I could have cried when that ball went into the basket."

Miriam's face flushed; then realizing that all eyes were turned toward her, she said sarcastically:

"Really, Miss Harlowe, it's so kind of you to look at it in that light. However, anyone with common sense would have known without being told that I never intended that ball for the juniors."

"I am not so sure of that," muttered Nora, who, seeing the hurt look that crept into Grace's eyes at Miriam's words, immediately rose in behalf of her captain.

Miriam whirled on Nora.

"What did you say?" asked Miriam angrily.

Before Nora could answer the whistle blew. Intermission was over and the second half was on. The teams changed baskets and stood in readiness for work. Once more Grace and Julia Crosby faced each other. There was a malicious gleam in Julia's eye and a look of determination in Grace's. With a spring, Grace caught the ball as it descended and threw it to Nora, who, eluding her guard, tossed it to Miriam. With unerring aim Miriam sent the ball into the basket and the sophomores scored for the first time.

Their friends in the gallery applauded vigorously and began to take heart, but their joy was short-lived, for as the play proceeded the sophomores steadily lost what little ground they had gained. Try as they might, they could make no headway. Grace called for play after play, only to find that in some inexplicable way the enemy seemed to know just what she meant, and acted accordingly.

The game neared its close and the sophomores fought with the desperation of the doomed. They knew that they could not win save by a miracle, but they resolved to die hard. The ball was in Miriam's hands and she made a feint at throwing it to Nora, but whirled and threw it to Grace, who, divining her intention, ran forward to receive it. There was a rush on the part of the juniors. Julia Crosby, crossing in front of Grace, managed slyly to thrust one foot forward. Grace tripped and fell to the floor, twisting one leg under her. The ball rolled on, and was caught by the enemy, who threw it to goal just as the whistle sounded for the last time. The juniors had won. The score stood 17 to 2 in their favor. The scorer attempted to announce it, but her voice was lost in the noisy yells of the junior class in the gallery.

The fact that Grace Harlowe still sat on the gymnasium floor passed for a moment unnoticed. In the final grand rush for the ball, the other players failed to see that their valiant captain still occupied the spot where she fell. Tumbles were not infrequent, and Grace was well able to take care of herself.

Anne Pierson alone saw Julia Crosby's foot slide out, and, scenting treachery, hastily left her seat in the gallery. She ran as fast as she could to where Grace sat, reaching her a few seconds after the whistle blew.

"Good little Anne," called Grace. "You have come to my rescue even though the others have deserted me. Perhaps you can help me up. I tried it, but my ankle hurts every time I try to stand."

Her face was very white, and Anne saw that she was in great pain.

By this time Grace's team, realizing she was not with them, began looking about, and rushed over to her in a body. David, Reddy and Hippy appeared on the scene, as did Mrs. Harlowe, accompanied by Miss Thompson. Excitement reigned. The boys lifted Grace to her feet; but she cried with pain and would have fallen had they not held her.

"She has sprained her ankle!" exclaimed Miss Thompson. "How did it happen, Grace? I did not see you fall."

"I don't know, Miss Thompson," said Grace faintly. "It all happened so quickly I didn't have time to think about it."

"It certainly is a shame," cried Anne. "And I know——"

Just then Grace gave Anne a warning glance and shook her head slightly. Anne closed her lips and was silent.

"What were you saying, Anne?" asked Miss Thompson.

But Anne had received her orders.

"I am so sorry that Grace has been hurt," she said lamely.

A carriage was ordered and Grace was taken home, Anne and Mrs. Harlowe accompanying her. Mrs. Harlowe sent for their physician, who bandaged the swollen ankle, and told Grace that the sprain was not serious. She refused, however, to go to bed, but lay on the wide lounge in the sitting room.

"Just keep quiet for a few days, and you'll be all right," said Dr. Gale. "You girls are as bad as boys about getting hard knocks. It looks as though basketball were about as barbarous as football."

"It is a dear old game, and I love it in spite of hard knocks," said Grace emphatically.

"I like your spirit, Grace," laughed Dr. Gale. "Now, remember to treat that ankle well if you want to appear again in the basketball arena."

"Grace," said Anne, after the doctor had gone. "You know how it happened, don't you?"

"Yes," answered Grace, after a little hesitation. "I do."

"What are you going to do about it?" asked Anne.

"I don't know," said Grace. "I am not sure it was intentional."

"Grace," said Anne with decision, "it was intentional. I watched her every minute of the game, for I didn't trust her, and I saw her do it. I was so angry that when Miss Thompson asked how it happened I felt that I must tell, then and there. It was you who prevented me. I think such a trick should be exposed."

"What a vengeful little Anne," said Grace. "You are usually the last one to tell anything."

She took Anne's hand in hers.

"It's just this way, Anne," she continued. "If I were to tell what Julia Crosby did, Miss Thompson might forbid basketball. That would be dreadful. Besides, the juniors would hardly believe me, and would say it was a case of sour grapes, on account of the sophomores losing the game. So you see I should gain nothing and perhaps lose a great deal. I believe that people that do mean things are usually repaid in their own coin. Julia didn't really intend to hurt me. Her idea was to prevent me from getting the ball. Of course it was dishonorable and she knew it. It is strictly forbidden in basketball, and if her own team knew positively that she was guilty, it would go hard with her. There is honor even among thieves, you know."

There was a brief silence. Grace lay back among the cushions, looking very white and tired. Her ankle pained her severely, but the defeat of her beloved team was a deeper hurt to her proud spirit.

Anne sat apparently wrapped in thought. She nervously clasped and unclasped her small hands.

"Grace," she said, "don't you think it was queer the way the juniors seemed to understand our signals. They knew every one of them. I believe that they found that list and it is all my fault. I had no business to lose it. I felt when I couldn't find it that it would fall into the wrong hands and cause trouble. I don't care for myself but if the girls find it out they will blame you for giving it to me. You know what Miriam said the other day. Now she will have a chance to be disagreeable to you about it."

Anne was almost in tears.

"Anne, dear," said Grace soothingly, "don't worry about it. I am not afraid to tell the girls about that list, and I shall certainly do so. They will understand that it was an accident, and overlook it. Besides, we are not sure that the juniors found it. I will admit that everything points that way. You know David warned us that they had some mischief on hand. If they did find it, the only honorable thing to do was to return it. They are far more at fault than we are, and the girls will agree with me, I know."

But Anne was not so confident.

"Miriam will try to make trouble about it, I know she will. And I am to blame for the whole thing," she said.

Grace was about to reply when Mrs. Harlowe appeared in the door with a tray of tempting food.

Anne rose and began donning her wraps.

"Won't you stay, Anne, and have supper with my invalid girl?" said Mrs. Harlowe.

"Please do, Anne," coaxed Grace. "I hate eating alone, and having you here takes my mind off my pain."

Anne stayed, and the two girls had a merry time over their meal. Grace, knowing Anne's distress over the lost signals, refused to talk of the subject. Jessica and Nora, David, Hippy and Reddy dropped in, one after the other, to inquire for Grace.

"There is nothing like accidents to bring one's friends together," declared Grace, as the young people gathered around her.

"I told you to look out for squalls, Grace," said David. "But you didn't weather the gale very well."

"Those juniors must have been eavesdropping when you made your signal code. They understood every play you made. By George, I wonder if that were the meaning of that pow-wow the other day. Someone must have put Julia Crosby wise, and that's why she called a meeting at the Omnibus House. It's an out-of-the-way place, and she thought there was no danger of being disturbed.

"Who could have been mean enough to betray us?" cried Nora. "I am sure none of the team did, unless——" Nora stopped short.

She had been on the point of using Miriam's name, but remembered just in time that Miriam's brother was present.

"If we knew the girl who did it, we'd certainly cut her acquaintance," said Reddy Brooks.

"Never again should she bask in the light of our society," said Hippy dramatically.

"None of our friends would do such a thing," said David soberly. Then, turning to Anne, "What's your opinion on the subject, Queen Anne?"

But Anne could find no answer. She simply shook her head.

Grace, knowing Anne's feelings over the affair, came to the rescue.

"Anne's opinion and mine are the same. We feel sure that they knew our signals, but we believe they accidentally hit upon the knowledge. There is no use in crying over spilt milk. We shall have to change all our signals and take care that it doesn't happen again. And now let's talk of something more agreeable, for basketball is a sore subject with me in more than one sense." The talk drifted into other channels much to Anne's relief.

"I have an idea!" exclaimed Hippy.

"Impossible," said Reddy. "No one would ever accuse you of such a thing."

"Be silent, fellow," commanded Hippy. "I will not brook such idle babbling." He strutted up and down the room, his chest inflated and one hand over his heart, presenting such a ridiculous figure that he raised a general laugh.

"Speak on, fat one. I promise not to make any more remarks," said Reddy.

"I propose," said Hippy, pausing in his march, "that we give an impromptu vaudeville show for the benefit of Miss Grace Harlowe, once an active member of this happy band, but now laid on the shelf—couch, I mean—for repairs."

"Done," was the unanimous reply.

"Now," continued Hippy, "get cozy, and the show will begin. Miss Nora O'Malley will open the show by singing 'Peggy Brady,' as only an Irish colleen of her pretensions can."

Nora rose, looked toward Jessica, who went at once to the piano to accompany her, and sang the song demanded with a fascinating brogue that always brought forth the applause of her friends. She responded to an encore. Then Anne's turn came, and she recited "Lasca." Hippy next favored the company with a comic song, which caused them to shout with laughter. Jessica did her Greek dance for which she was famous. The performance ended with an up-to-date version of "Antony and Cleopatra," enacted by David, Reddy and Hippy, with dialogue and stage business of which Shakespeare never dreamed.

It was a product of Hippy's fertile brain, and the boys had been rehearsing it with great glee, in view of appearing in it, on some fitting occasion, before the girls.

David, gracefully draped in the piano cover, represented Egypt's queen, and languished upon Marc Antony's shoulder in the most approved manner. Reddy, as the Roman conqueror left nothing to be desired. The star actor of the piece, however, was Hippy, who played the deadly asp. He writhed and wriggled in a manner that would have filled a respectable serpent with envy, and in the closing scene bit the unfortunate Cleopatra so venomously that she howled for mercy, and instead of dying gracefully, arose and engaged in battle with his snakeship.

Grace forgot her sprained ankle and laughed until the tears rolled down her cheeks. "You funny, funny boys," she gasped, "how did you ever think of anything so ridiculous!"

"Hippy perpetrated the outrage," said David "and we agreed to help him produce it. We have been practicing it for two weeks, only we don't generally end up with a scuffle. I hope you will pardon us, Grace, but the desire to shake that husky Egyptian reptile was irresistible."

"There is nothing to pardon," replied Grace, "and we have only thanks to offer for the fun you have given us."

"It was indeed a notable performance," agreed Nora.

"Girls and boys," said Anne, "it is almost ten o'clock and Grace ought to be in bed. I move that we adjourn." "Second the motion," said David. "We have been very selfish in keeping poor Grace up when she is ill."

"Poor Grace is glad you came, and isn't a bit tired," replied Grace, looking fondly at her friends. "You must all come to see me as often as you can while I am laid up. I shall be pretty lonely for a few days."

The young folks departed, singing "Good Night, Ladies" as they trooped down the walk.

"What a pleasure it is to have such dear, good friends," thought Grace as she lay back on her couch after they had gone. "They are well worth all the loyalty I can give them."

She went to sleep that night unconscious of how soon her loyalty to one of them would be put to the test.

## CHAPTER VII

## GATHERING CLOUDS

"A sprained ankle is not so serious," declared Grace from her nest among the sofa cushions. It was the Monday after the game. Her various sympathetic classmates were seated about the Harlowe's comfortable living room. A wood fire crackled cheerfully in the big, open fireplace, while a large plate of chocolate fudge circulated from one lap to another.

"Jessica, will you pour the chocolate?" continued Grace to her friend, who rose at once to comply with her request. "Anne, will you help serve, please?"

Anne accordingly drew about the room a little table on wheels, containing on its several shelves plates containing sandwiches, cookies and cakes.

"Trust to the Harlowe's to have lots of good things to eat," exclaimed Marian Barber. "It must be fun to be laid up, Grace, if you can give a party every afternoon."

"I must entertain my friends when they are kind enough to come and see me," answered Grace. "But some people think sandwiches poor provender unless they are the fancy kind, with olives and nuts in them. Miriam, for instance would never serve such plain fare to her company as cream cheese sandwiches."

"Here comes Miriam up the walk now," cried Jessica. "She looks as though she had something on her mind."

Presently the door opened and Miriam was ushered in. Grace wondered a little at her call, considering the unfriendly spirit Miriam had recently exhibited toward her. She greeted Miriam cordially. The laws of hospitality were sacred in the Harlowe family, and not for worlds would Grace have shown anything but the kindest feeling toward a guest under her own roof.

Miriam accepted the chair and the cup of chocolate tendered her, ignoring the plate of cakes offered by Anne. She looked about her like a marksman taking aim before he fires. There was a danger signal in either eye.

"She is out for slaughter," thought Nora.

"Well, Miriam, what's the news?" said Marian Barber good-naturedly. "You have a mysterious, newsy look in your eye. Is it good, bad or indifferent?"

"How did you guess that I had news?" inquired Miriam. Then without waiting for an answer she went on. "I certainly have, and very unpleasant news, at that."

"Out with it," said Nora, "and don't keep us in suspense."

"Well," said Miriam, "I suppose you all noticed how the juniors outwitted us at every point last Saturday? We put up a hard fight, too. The reason of it was that they knew every one of our signals."

"How dreadful!" "How did they get their information?" "Who told you so?" were the exclamations that rose from the assembled girls.

Grace had raised herself to a sitting position and was steadily regarding Miriam, who, well aware of that keen, searching gaze, deliberately continued:

"What makes the matter so much worse is the fact that we were betrayed by a member of our own class."

"Oh, Miriam, you don't mean that?" said Jessica.

"I am sorry to say that it is true," replied Miriam, "and I am going to put the matter before the class."

"Tell us who it is, Miriam," cried the girls. "We'll fix her!"

"Miriam," said Grace in a tone of quiet command that made every girl look toward her, "you are to mention no names while in my house."

Miriam's face flamed. Before she could reply, however, Grace went on. "Girls you must realize the position in which Miriam's remarks place me.

She is sure that she knows who betrayed our signals, and is willing to name the person. Suppose she names some girl present. Think of the feelings of that girl, my guest, yet not safe from accusation while here. I should prove a poor sort of hostess if I allowed the honor of any of my friends to suffer while in my house.

"The place to discuss these things is in school. There every girl stands on an equal footing and can refute any charges made against her. I wish to say that I have a communication to make which may put a different face on the whole matter. I know something of the story of those signals. When I go back to school I shall call a meeting of the basketball team and its subs. and tell them what I know about it; but not until then. Furthermore it is not strictly a class matter, as it pertains to the basketball players alone. Therefore anyone outside the team has no right to interfere. Please don't think me disagreeable. It is because I am trying to avoid unpleasant consequences that I am firm about having no names mentioned here."

"You Need Mention No Names While in My House."

There was an absolute silence in the room. The girls had a deep regard for Grace on account of her frank, open nature and love of fair play; but Miriam had her own particular friends who had respect for her on account of her being a Nesbit. She had a faculty of obtaining her own way, too, that seemed, to them, little short of marvellous, and she spent more money than any other girl in Oakdale High School. It was therefore difficult to choose between the two factions.

Nora broke the embarrassing pause.

"Grace is right as usual," she said, "and none of you girls should feel offended. What's the use of wasting the whole afternoon quarrelling over an old basketball game? Do talk about something pleasant. The sophomore ball for instance. Do you girls realize that we ought to be making some plans for it? It's the annual class dance, and should be welcomed, with enthusiasm. We've all been so crazy over basketball that we've neglected to think about our class responsibilities. We ought to try to make it a greater success than any other dance ever given by a sophomore class. We must call a meeting very soon, not to fight over basketball, but to make arrangements for our dance."

Nora's reminder of the coming ball was a stroke of diplomacy on her part.

What school girl does not grow enthusiastic over a class dance? A buzz of conversation immediately arose as to gowns, decorations, refreshments and the thousand and one things all important to a festivity of that kind.

Miriam seeing that it was useless to try to raise any further disturbance, cut her call short, taking with her several girls who were her staunch upholders.

Those who remained did not seem sorry at her departure, and Grace drew a breath of relief as the door closed upon the wilful girl. She had at least saved Anne from a cruel attack, but how much longer she could do so was a question. Miriam would undoubtedly bring up the subject at the first class meeting, and Grace was not so sure, now, that the girls would be willing to overlook the loss of the signals when she told them of it.

"I shall be loyal to Anne, no matter what it costs me," she decided. "She has done nothing wrong, and Miriam will find that she cannot trample upon either of us with impunity. As for Jessica and Nora, I know they will agree with me."

Under cover of conversation, Grace whispered to Jessica that she wished her to remain after the others had gone, and to ask Nora and Anne to do the same.

When the last of the callers had said good-bye, and the four chums had the room to themselves, Grace told Nora and Jessica about Anne's mishap, and how utterly innocent of blame she was.

"Do you mean to tell me that Miriam meant Anne when she said she could name the girl?" demanded Nora.

"She did, indeed," replied Anne, "and if it had not been for Grace she would have made things very unpleasant for me."

"Humph," ejaculated the fiery Nora, "then all I have to say is that I don't see how a nice boy like David ever happened to have a horrid hateful, scheming sister like Miriam. Stand up for Anne? Well I rather think so! Let Miriam dare to say anything like that to me."

"Or me," said Jessica.

"I knew you girls would feel the same as I do," said Grace. "Anne has some true friends, thank goodness. You see Miriam is basing all her suppositions on the fact that Anne was allowed to come to practice. She doesn't know anything about the loss of the signals. You remember she objected to Anne seeing the practice game. Now she will try to show that she was right in doing so."

"Let her try it," said Jessica, "She'll be sorry."

"I am not so sure of that," said Anne quietly. "You know that Miriam has plenty of influence with certain girls, while I am only a stranger about whom no one cares except yourselves and the boys and Mrs. Gray.

"You are the brightest girl in school just the same," said Nora, "and that counts for a whole lot. Miss Thompson likes you, too, and our crowd is not to be despised."

"You are the dearest people in the world," responded Anne gratefully. "Please don't think that I am unappreciative. You have done far too much for me, and I don't want you to get into trouble on my account. As long as you girls care for me, I don't mind what the others think."

"Don't say that Anne," said Jessica. "You don't know how mean some of those girls can be. Don't you remember the junior that was cut by her class last year? Of course, she did something for which she deserved to be cut, but the girls made her life miserable. The story went through every class, and she got the cold shoulder all around. She's not here this year. Her father sent her away to school, she was so unhappy. You remember her, don't you?" turning to Grace and Nora.

Both girls nodded. The story of the unfortunate junior loomed up before them. Every girl in High School knew it.

"We can only hope that history will not repeat itself," said Grace thoughtfully. "Of course, I don't mean that there is any similarity between the two cases. That girl last year was untruthful and extremely dishonorable. It is perfectly ridiculous to think of placing the blame for those signals upon Anne. If the girls are silly enough to listen to Miriam's insinuations, then they must choose between Miriam and me. Anne is my dear friend, and I shall stick to her until the end."

## CHAPTER VIII

## THE PRICE OF FRIENDSHIP

It was a week before Dr. Gale pronounced Grace fit to return to school. When she did make her appearance, she was hailed with delight by her schoolmates and made much of. Miss Thompson greeted her warmly. She was very fond of Grace, and had expressed great concern over the young girl's accident. It was unusual for a girl to receive so serious an injury during a game, as all rough play was strictly forbidden.

The principal had kept the members of both teams after school and questioned them closely. No one had seen Grace fall, nor realized that she was hurt until she had been discovered sitting on the gymnasium floor. Miss Thompson had a vague suspicion of foul play on the part of the juniors, but was unable to find out anything.

"Athletics for girls have always been encouraged in this school," she had said. "Rough play is disgraceful. If I found that any member of any High School basketball organization, either directly or indirectly, caused the injury of an opponent, I should forbid basketball for the rest of the season at least, and perhaps absolutely. Tripping, striking and kicking are barred out of the boys' games and will certainly not be tolerated in those of the girls."

As Grace was returning to the study hall from geometry recitation that morning, she encountered Julia Crosby. Julia glanced at her with an expression half fearful, half cunning, as though she wondered if Grace knew the truth about her fall.

Grace returned the look with one of such quiet contempt and scorn that Julia dropped her eyes and hurried along the corridor.

"How could she have been so contemptible?" thought Grace.

"I wonder if she'll tell," thought Julia. "She evidently knows I was responsible for her tumble. My, what a look she gave me. I wonder if that snippy little Anne Pierson knows about it, too. Very likely she does, for Grace Harlowe tells her all her business. If they do say anything I'll take good care no one believes it."

She was so absorbed in her own ruminations that she crashed into the dignified president of the senior class with considerable force, much to the glee of Nora, who happened to be near enough to catch the icy expression on the senior's face as Julia mumbled an apology.

At recess Grace notified the members of the basketball team and their substitutes that she had called a meeting to take place that afternoon at three o'clock in the sophomore locker room. "Only the basketball people are requested to be present," she concluded, "so don't bring any of the rest of the class."

At three o'clock precisely the last member had arrived. Every girl took particular pains to be there, for most of them had been at the Harlowe's on the day that Grace had silenced Miriam.

The meeting promised to be one of interest, for had not Grace Harlowe said that she would tell them something about the betrayed signals?

"Girls," Grace began, "you all know that although it is against the rules to allow any outsider to witness our practice, we have always made an exception in favor of Jessica. You all have perfect confidence in Jessica, I am sure. Since practice began this fall we have allowed Anne to come to it, too. You remember I asked permission for her to see the practice game, because I knew her to be absolutely trustworthy."

Here Nora nodded emphatically, Miriam tossed her head and smiled mockingly, while the rest of the girls looked a trifle mystified.

"Anne," continued Grace, "did not understand many of our plays, so I wrote out a list of signals for her, to study and learn by heart, telling her to destroy them as soon as she was sure she knew them. Unfortunately, she lost them, and at once told me about it. She felt very unhappy over it; but I told her not to worry, because I never supposed their loss would make any difference.

"When the game was well under way and the juniors began to block our plays, it flashed across me that in some way they had found that list. Anne, who has a mania for labeling everything, had written 'Sophomore basketball signals' across the paper; so, of course, any one who found it would know exactly what the list meant.

"We were warned that the juniors held a meeting at the Omnibus House a day or so before the game, and that they meant mischief. I never thought, however, they would be quite so dishonorable.

"I would have told you this before the game, but was afraid it would confuse and worry you. I am sure that you will agree with me, and absolve Anne from all blame."

"I don't agree with you at all," flashed Miriam, "and I am glad to have a chance to speak my mind. I told you before the game that I objected to Miss Pierson watching our practice, that it was against the rules, but no attention was paid to what I said. If you had taken my advice the result would have been far different. I have no doubt Grace believes that Miss Pierson lost the list, but I am not so easily deceived. I believe she deliberately handed it over to the juniors, and every loyal member of the team should cut her acquaintance."

"Miriam Nesbit," cried Nora. "You haven't the least right to accuse Anne Pierson of any such thing. She is too honorable to think of it, and she has no love for the junior class either. She isn't even friendly with them. If anyone is to be accused of treachery, I should say that there are members of the team far more friendly with the juniors than poor little Anne."

This was a direct slap at Miriam, who winced a little at Nora's words.

"Well," said Marian Barber quickly, "it stands to reason that no member of the team would be foolish enough to help the enemy. I don't know anything about Miss Pierson, but I do know that I overheard Julia Crosby telling some girl in her class that the sophomores could thank one of their own class for their defeat."

"When did you hear her say that?" queried Miriam sharply.

"Yesterday morning. I was walking behind her, and she was so busy talking she didn't notice me."

"You girls can draw your own conclusions," said Miriam triumphantly. "That simply proves what I have said."

"That simply proves nothing at all," exclaimed Grace Harlowe, who had been too angry to trust herself to speak. "You are making a very serious charge against Anne without one bit of ground on which to base your suspicions. You have always disliked her because she won the freshman prize, and you know nothing whatever against her."

"No," said Miriam scornfully, "nor anything to her credit either. Who is she, anyway? The daughter of a strolling third-rate actor, who goes barnstorming about the country, and she has been on the stage, too. She has a very good opinion of herself since Mrs. Gray and certain Oakdale girls took her up, but I wouldn't trust her as far as I could see her. Why should girls of good Oakdale families be forced to associate with such people? I suppose she wanted to be on good terms with the juniors, too, and took that method of gaining her point."

"That is pure nonsense," exclaimed Nora. "Don't you think so, girls?"

But the other girls made no reply. They were thinking hard. Suspicion seemed to point in Anne's direction. What a pity Grace had been so rash about taking Anne up if her father were a common actor. Miriam was right about not caring to associate with Anne. After all, they knew very little about her. Grace Harlowe was always picking queer people and trying to help them.

"I think we ought to be very careful about taking outsiders into our confidence," firmly said Eva Allen, one of the team. "I didn't know Miss Pierson had ever been an actress." There was a note of horror in her voice as she pronounced the last word. "I have always heard that they were very unreliable people," said another miss of sixteen.

Grace was in despair. She felt that she had lost. By dragging up Anne's unfortunate family history, Miriam had produced a bad impression that she was powerless to efface.

"Girls," she said, "you ought to be ashamed of yourselves. You know perfectly well that Anne is innocent. If you wish to be my friend you must be Anne's also. Please say that you believe her."

"Count on me," said Nora.

But the other sophomores had nothing to say.

Grace looked about her appealingly, only to meet cold looks and averted faces. Miriam was smiling openly.

"The meeting is adjourned," said Grace shortly, and without another word she went to her locker and began taking out her wraps. Nora followed her, but the majority of the girls walked over to the other end of the room and began to talk in low tones with Miriam.

Grace realized that her team had deserted her for Miriam. It was almost unbelievable. She set her lips and winked hard to keep back the tears which rose to her eyes. Then, followed by her one faithful friend, she walked out of the locker room, leaving her fickle classmates with their chosen lea

## CHAPTER IX

## AN UNSUCCESSFUL INTERVIEW

There were two subjects of interest under discussion in the sophomore class. One was the coming ball, the other the story of the lost signals, which had gone the round of the class. The general opinion seemed to be that Anne had betrayed the team, and with the unthinking cruelty of youth, the girls had resolved to teach her a lesson. Miriam's accusation had been repeated from one girl to another, with unconscious additions, until Anne loomed up in the light of a traitor, and was treated accordingly.

Grace had told Anne the next day the details of the meeting, and in some measure prepared her for what would undoubtedly follow. Anne had laughed a little at the account of Miriam's remarks regarding her father, and the girls' evident disapproval of the theatrical profession.

"How silly they are," she said to Grace, who felt secretly relieved to know that Anne was not mortally hurt over Miriam's attack. "They don't know anything about professional people. Of course, there are plenty of worthless actors, but some of them are really very fine men and women. Miriam may abuse my family all she chooses, but I do feel unhappy to think that those girls believe me dishonorable and under-handed."

"They wouldn't if they had any sense," responded Grace hotly, "I never believed that those girls could be so snobbish. I always thought them above such petty meanness. Don't pay any attention to them, Anne. They aren't worth it. I am going to interview Julia Crosby and make her acknowledge that she wasn't referring to you the other day. There is something queer about it all. I believe that there is some kind of secret understanding between Miriam and Julia; that this is a deliberate plot on their part to injure you and humiliate me, and I shall find out the truth before I am through."

"But what has Julia Crosby against me?" queried Anne, "I hardly know her."

"She hasn't forgotten the way David defended you at Mrs. Gray's Christmas ball last year," answered Grace, "Besides, you're a sophomore. Isn't that a good enough reason?"

"I suppose it is," said Anne wearily.

Grace kept her word and hailed Julia Crosby on the following afternoon as she was leaving the High School. It seemed a favorable opportunity for Julia was alone.

"Miss Crosby," said Grace coldly. "I should like to speak to you about a very important matter."

"There's nothing to hinder you, Miss Harlowe," replied Julia brusquely. "I'm here. Are you sure that it really is important?"

She stopped and eyed Grace insolently.

"I am very sure that it is important, Miss Crosby," said Grace. "Not long ago a certain sophomore overheard you telling a member of your class that we sophomores could thank a girl in our class for our basketball defeat. A certain girl had already been unjustly accused of betraying our signals. When your remark was repeated to the team, they immediately decided that you meant her. Since then her classmates have taken the matter up and are determined to cut her acquaintance."

"Well what has all this childish prattle to do with me?" demanded Julia rudely.

"It has this to do with you, that you can set the matter right by saying it was not Anne. You know perfectly well she had nothing to do with it. I don't know how you got those signals, but I do know that Anne never gave them to you."

"Did I say that she did?" asked Julia.

"No," said Grace, "neither did you say that she didn't."

"Very true," replied Julia in a disagreeable tone, "and I don't intend to say so either. She may or she may not have given them to me. I'll never tell. She's a snippy, conceited, little prig, and a little punishment for her sins will do her good."

"You are a cruel, heartless girl," cried Grace angrily. "Knowing Anne to be innocent, you refuse to clear her name of the suspicion resting upon it. Let me tell you one thing. I know who tripped me the day of the game, and so does Anne. If you don't clear Anne instantly, I shall go straight to Miss Thompson with it."

Grace's threat went home. Julia stood in actual dread of the principal. It looked as though the tables had been turned at last. If Grace went to Miss Thompson what a commotion there would be!

In a moment, however, Julia recovered herself. What was it Miss Thompson had said about rough play? Ah, Julia remembered now, and with the recollection of the principal's words came the means of worsting Grace Harlowe in her efforts to vindicate Anne.

"You may go to Miss Thompson if you think it wise," she said with a malicious smile, "but I wouldn't advise it—that is, unless you have gotten over caring for basketball."

"What do you mean?" asked Grace. Then like a flash she understood. If she should tell Miss Thompson the truth, the principal would believe her. Julia would receive her just deserts but, oh, bitter thought, there would be no more basketball that season.

Grace felt that she had no right to sacrifice the pleasure of so many others, even for Anne's sake. It would only increase the feeling against both Anne and herself, and after all, Julia might still hold out in her insinuations against Anne.

"How can you be so contemptible?" she said to her smiling enemy. "You never win anything honestly. I see it is useless for me to appeal to you for something which you cannot give, and that is fair play!" With a slight bow, Grace walked quickly away, leaving Julia a little astonished at her sudden departure and not at all pleased at Grace's frankly expressed opinion.

Grace lost no time in relating to Anne her fruitless interview with the junior captain.

"I am so humiliated to think I failed. I expected that threatening to tell Miss Thompson would bring her to her senses, but she is too cunning for me," sighed Grace.

The two girls were walking home from school.

"Shall you tell Nora and Jessica?" asked Anne.

"No," said Grace. "Let us keep the sprained ankle part of the story a secret. They are loyal to you, at any rate, and Nora would be so angry. I am afraid I couldn't keep her from going straight to Miss Thompson and making a general mess of things. I am so sorry, Anne, dear, but I guess we shall have to weather the gale together. It will die out after a while, just as all those things do. Hush! Don't say anything now. Here come Nora and Jessica."

"What do you think!" cried Nora. "Edna Wright is giving a party next Saturday, and she isn't going to invite either you or Anne."

"How shocking!" said Grace. "We shall both die of grief at having been slighted."

She spoke lightly, and no one but Anne guessed how much the news hurt her.

"We are not going," declared Nora, "and we told her so."

"What did she say?" asked Grace.

"We didn't give her time to answer," said Nora, "but rushed off to find you. The whole thing is perfectly ridiculous! The idea of a lot of silly little school girls thinking they own the earth. It's all Miriam's fault. She has tried to be leader of her class ever since it was organized but mark what I say, she'll never accomplish it. Pride will get a fall, one of these days, and I hope I'll be around when it happens."

"Never mind, Nora," said Grace soothingly. "Anne and I don't care. We'll give a party at the same time, to our own crowd. I'll tell you what we'll do. We will have a surprise party for Mrs. Gray. I'll write to Tom Gray and ask him to come down for next Saturday. That will be a double surprise to dear Mrs. Gray."

"Fine!" cried Jessica. "We'll have Hippy and Reddy and David. Then our circle will be complete. The other crowd will be furious. Those boys are all popular, and I know that Edna intends to invite them."

"Let's tell them at once, then," said Nora, "before the other girls get a chance."

The boys were promptly invited. Grace sent a note to Tom Gray, who found it possible to get away for the week end.

Reddy, Hippy and David received invitations to the other party, but politely declined. Miriam endeavored to point out to her brother the folly of his conduct, but David simply stared at her and said nothing. He knew to what lengths her jealousy had carried her during the freshman year, and although Nora had entirely omitted his sister's name from the conversation when telling him of the recent trouble that had arisen, still David felt that Miriam was at the bottom of it.

Failing to elicit any response from her brother, she flew into a rage and did not speak to him for a week, while David went serenely on his way, and let her get over it as best she might.

The surprise party proved a success. Mrs. Gray's delight at seeing her "Christmas children" and having her beloved nephew with her was worth seeing. The young people did all the "stunts" they knew for her entertainment, and the boys repeated their Shakespearian performance for the old lady, who laughed until she could laugh no more.

It was their turn to be surprised, however, when the old butler suddenly appeared and announced that supper was served. Mrs. Gray had held a word of conversation with him directly after their arrival, which resulted in an array of good things calculated to tempt the appetite of any healthy boy or girl.

After supper they had an old-fashioned "sing," with Jessica at the piano, ending with "Home, Sweet Home" and the inevitable "Good Night, Ladies."

"I'm sure we had a better time than the other crowd," said Nora as they all walked down the street.

"Of course," said Grace, but a little feeling of sadness swept over her as she realized for the first time in her short life she had been slighted by any of her school friends.

# CHAPTER X

# THE SOPHOMORE BALL

It was the night of the sophomore ball. For a week past the class had been making preparations. The gymnasium had been transformed into a veritable bower of beauty. Every palm in Oakdale that could be begged, borrowed or rented was used for the occasion. Drawing rooms had been robbed of their prettiest sofa cushions and hangings, to make attractive cozy corners in the big room.

The walls were decorated with evergreens and class banners, while the class colors, red and gold, were everywhere in evidence. The sophomores had been recklessly extravagant in the matter of cut flowers, and bowls of red roses and carnations ornamented the various tables, loaned by fond mothers for the gratification of sophomore vanity.

The girls had worked hard to outdo previous sophomore affairs, and when all was finished the various teachers who were invited to view the general effect were unanimous in their admiration.

Once a year each of the four High School classes gave some sort of entertainment. Readers of "GRACE HARLOWE'S PLEBE YEAR" will remember the masquerade ball given by the sophomores, now juniors, and the active part taken by Grace and her chums in that festivity.

The present sophomores had decided to make their ball a larger affair than usual, and had sent out invitations to favored members of the other classes. An equal number of boys had been invited from the boys' High School, and the party promised to be one of the social events of Oakdale.

Mrs. Gray and a number of other prominent women of Oakdale, were to act as patronesses. Mrs. Harlowe, usually a favorite chaperon with Grace's crowd, had been ignored for the first time, and Grace was cut to the quick over it. As for Grace herself, she had not been appointed to a single committee. Prominent heretofore in every school enterprise, it was galling to the high-spirited girl to be deliberately left out of the preparations. Nora had been asked to help receive and Jessica had been appointed to the refreshment committee, but on finding that Grace was being snubbed, both had coldly declined to serve in either capacity.

The four chums held more than one anxious discussion as to the advisability of even attending the ball.

"I think we ought to go, just to show those girls that we are impervious to their petty insults," declared Grace. "We have as much right there as anyone else, and I am sure the boys we know will dance with us whether the rest of the girls like it or not. Besides, Mrs. Gray will be there, and she will expect to see us. She doesn't know anything about this trouble, and I don't want her to know. It would only grieve her. She is so fond of Anne. By all means we must go to the ball. Wear your prettiest gowns and act as though nothing had happened."

That night, the four young girls, in their party finery, sat waiting in the Harlowe's drawing room for their escorts—David, Hippy and Reddy. Anne wore the pink crepe de chine which had done duty at Mrs. Gray's house party the previous winter. Grace wore an exquisite gown of pale blue silk made in a simple, girlish fashion that set her off to perfection. Nora was gowned in lavender and wore a corsage bouquet of violets that had mysteriously arrived that afternoon, and that everyone present suspected Hippy of sending. Jessica's gown was of white organdie, trimmed with tiny butterfly medallions and valenciennes lace.

In spite of the possibility that she and Anne might be the subject of unpleasant comment, Grace made up her mind to enjoy herself. She was fond of dancing, and knew that she would have plenty of invitations to do so. David would look after Anne, who was not yet proficient enough in dancing to venture to try it in public.

"If only Miriam and Julia Crosby behave themselves!" she thought, "for, of course, Julia will be there. Miriam will see that she gets an invitation."

Grace thrilled with pride as she entered the gymnasium. How beautifully it had been decorated and how well everything looked. She was so sorry that the girls had seen fit to leave her out of it all. Then she remembered her resolution to forget all differences and just have a good time.

Miriam, gowned in apricot messaline trimmed with silver, was in the receiving line with half a dozen other sophomores. Grace and her party would be obliged to exchange civilities with the enemy. She wondered what Miriam would do. David solved this problem for her by taking charge of the situation. Walking straight up to Miriam, he said a few words to her in a low tone. She flushed slightly, looked a trifle defiant then greeted the girls coldly, but with civility. The other sophomores followed her example, but Grace breathed a sigh of relief as they walked over to where Mrs. Gray, in a wonderful black satin gown, sat among the patronesses.

"My dear children, I am so glad to see all of you!" exclaimed the sprightly old lady. "How fine all my girls look. You are like a bouquet of flowers. Grace is a bluebell, Anne is a dear little clove pink, Nora is a whole bunch of violets and Jessica looks like a white narcissus."

"Where do we come in?" asked David, smiling at Mrs. Gray's pretty comparison.

"Allow me to answer that question," said Hippy. "You are like the tall and graceful burdock. Reddy resembles the common, but much-admired sheep sorrel, while I am like that tender little flower, the forget-me-not. Having once seen me, is it possible to forget me!" He struck an attitude and looked languishingly at Nora.

"I'll forget you forever if you look at me like that," threatened Nora.

"Never again," said Hippy hastily. "Bear witness, all of you, that my expression has changed."

Just then the first notes of the waltz "Amoreuse" rang out, and the gymnasium floor was soon filled with High School boys and girls dressed in their best party attire. The dances followed each other in rapid succession until supper was announced. This was served at small tables by the town caterer.

Mrs. Gray and her adopted children occupied two tables near together and had a merry time. Many curious glances were cast in their direction by the other members of the sophomore class.

Some of the girls wondered whether it was a good thing to cut Anne Pierson's acquaintance. She was certainly a friend of Mrs. Gray, and Mrs. Gray was one of the most influential women in Oakdale. Frances Fuller, a worldly-minded sophomore, dared to intimate as much to Miriam Nesbit, who replied loftily:

"If Mrs. Gray knew as much about Miss Pierson as we do, she would probably not care for her any longer."

"It's a pity someone doesn't tell her," said Julia Crosby, ever ready for mischief.

"Oh, someone will have the courage yet," answered Miriam, "and when she does, that will end everything as far as Miss Pierson is concerned. Mrs. Gray can't endure anything dishonorable."

Just then a young man claimed Miriam for the two-step about to begin, and Julia wandered off, leaving Frances to digest what had been said. The more the latter thought about it, the more she felt that Mrs. Gray ought to be warned against Anne. She decided that she had the courage; that it was her duty to do so.

Without hesitating, she blundered over to where Mrs. Gray sat for the moment.

"Mrs. Gray," Frances began, "I want to tell you something which I think you ought to know."

"And what is that, my dear?" asked the old lady courteously, trying vainly to remember the girl's face.

"Why, about Miss Pierson's true character," replied the girl.

"Miss Pierson's true character?" repeated Mrs. Gray. "I don't understand what you mean."

"That she is dishonorable and treacherous. She betrayed the sophomore basketball signals to the juniors, and then denied it, when her class had positive proof against her. Besides, her father is a disreputable actor, and she was an actress before she came here. We thought if you knew the truth you wouldn't uphold any such person." Frances paused. She thought she had made an impression upon her listener.

Mrs. Gray sat silent. She was too deeply incensed to trust herself to speak. Frances looked complacent. She evidently hoped to be commended for her plain speaking. Then Mrs. Gray found her voice.

"Young woman," she said, "you ought to be ashamed of yourself. What can you hope to gain by saying unkind things about a nice, gentle, little girl who is in every respect worthy of all the love and regard that can be given her? I do not know what you can be thinking of to speak so slightingly of one of your classmates, and I am sorry to be obliged to remind you that it is the height of ill breeding to abuse a person to his or her friends."

With these words, Mrs. Gray turned her back squarely upon the dazed girl, who slowly arose, and without looking at Mrs. Gray, walked dejectedly across the room. But Miriam Nesbit lost one supporter from that minute on.

"Hateful things," said the mortified Frances, looking towards Julia and Miriam. "I believe they are more to blame than Miss Pierson ever thought of being."

When Grace paused at Mrs. Gray's side after the two-step, she saw plainly that the old lady was much agitated.

"Grace," she said quickly, "what is all this nonsense about Anne?"

"O Mrs. Gray," cried Grace. "Who could have been so unkind as to tell you? We didn't want you to know. It is all so foolish."

"But I want to know," said the old lady positively. "Anne is so very dear to me, and I can't allow these hare-brained girls to make damaging statements about her. Tell me at once, Grace."

Grace reluctantly gave a brief account of her recent disagreement with her class and the unpleasantness to which Anne had been subjected.

"What does ail Miriam Nesbit? She used to be such a nice child!" exclaimed Mrs. Gray. "Really, Grace, I feel that I ought to go straight to Miss Thompson with this."

Grace's heart sank. That was just what she did not want Mrs. Gray to do.

"Dear Mrs. Gray," she said, patting the old lady's hand, "it is better for us to fight it out by ourselves. If Miss Thompson knew all that had happened, she would forbid basketball for the rest of the season. She is awfully opposed to anything of that kind, and would champion Anne's cause to the end, but Anne would rather let matters stand the way they are, than lose us our basketball privilege. You see, the juniors have won the first game, and if basketball were stopped now we would have no chance to make up our lost ground. I firmly believe that all will come right in the end, and I think the girls will get tired of their grudge and gradually drop it. Of course it hurts to be snubbed, but I guess we can stand it. We have some friends who are loyal, at any rate."

"I suppose you are right, my dear," responded the old lady. "It is better for old folks to keep their fingers out of young folk's pies. But what did that pert miss mean about Anne's father being an actor? I had an idea he was dead."

So Grace told Mrs. Gray the story of Anne's father, beginning from where he had intercepted Anne on her way from the aëroplane exhibition during her freshman year, up to the time of the arrival of his letter begging for money.

"Anne used her freshman prize money last year to help him out of trouble. He forged a friend's name for one hundred dollars, and would have had to go to prison had she not made good the money he took, I always wanted you to know about it, Mrs. Gray, but Anne felt so badly over it, she begged me never to tell anyone."

"Your story explains a great many things I never before understood," said Mrs. Gray. "That doll that was sent to the Christmas party last year, for instance. But how did Miriam find out about it?"

"We don't know," said Grace. "Her doings are dark and mysterious. Find out she did; and she has told the story with considerable effect among the girls."

"It is too bad," mused Mrs. Gray. "I should like to right matters were it possible, but as long as you don't wish it, my dear, I suppose I must let you fight it out by yourselves. But one thing I am sure of, Anne shall never want for a friend as long as I live. Now run along and have a good time. I've kept you here when you might have been dancing."

"I have loved being with you," said Grace. "I shall not tell Anne about what was said," she added in a lower tone.

"That is right, Grace," responded Mrs. Gray. "No need of hurting the child's feelings."

During the balance of the evening nothing occurred to discomfit either Grace or Anne. To be sure there was a marked coolness exhibited by most of their classmates, but David took charge of Anne and saw to it that nothing disturbed her. Grace, who was a general favorite with the High School boys of Oakdale, could have filled her programme three times over. She was the embodiment of life and danced with such apparent unconcern that the mind of more than one sophomore was divided as to whether to cleave to Miriam or renew their former allegiance to Grace.

It was well after one o'clock when the "Home, Sweet Home" waltz sounded. The floor was well filled with dancers, for the majority of the guests had remained until the end of the ball. As the last strains of the music died away the sophomores sent their class yell echoing through the gymnasium. It was answered by the various yells of the other classes, given with true High School fervor. Each class trying to outdo the other in the making of noise.

Sleepy chaperons began gathering up their charges. The sophomore ball was a thing of the past.

"These late hours and indigestible suppers are bound to break down my delicate constitution yet," Hippy confided to Nora.

"In that case I shall make it a point to see that you don't receive any more invitations to our parties," Nora answered cruelly. "Then you can stay at home and build up that precious health of yours."

"Don't mention it," replied Hippy hastily. "I would rather become an emaciated wreck than deprive myself of your society."

"It was simply glorious," said Anne to Grace as they stood waiting for their carriage, "and was there ever such a nice boy as David!"

Grace pressed Anne's hand by way of answer. She knew that David had understood the situation and had taken care to steer Anne clear of shoals, and Grace determined that no matter what Miriam might say or do in future, for David's sake it should be overlooked.

# CHAPTER XI

## A LION AT LAST

It was a week before the last borrowed decoration reposed in its original place, and fully that long before the echoes of the sophomore ball died out. It was pronounced the most successful class function given in Oakdale for a number of years, and the sophomores felt justly proud of themselves. Miriam Nesbit took particular pains to point out that the success of the affair was in no way due to Grace Harlowe, and many of the girls who had hitherto believed that Grace was a necessary factor in High School fun, decided that they had perhaps overrated her ability.

Grace was fully cognizant of their change of heart, and spent more than one unhappy hour over it, but outwardly she carried herself as though unaware of the many little ill-natured stabs directed toward her. Anne, who was completely ignored, took it philosophically, her only regret being the fact that Grace had been dragged into difficulties on her account.

Thanksgiving had come and gone. The High School boys had played their usual game of football with a neighboring school and whipped them to a standstill, David had played on the team and covered himself with glory by making a sensational touchdown. The girl chums had worn his colors and shrieked themselves hoarse with joy over the prowess of their friend.

Miriam, secretly proud of her brother, resolved to make a like record for herself during the next basketball game, which was to take place during the following week. She believed that it was the last touch needed to make her the avowed leader of her class. She even dreamed that the basketball captaincy might one day be hers. To be sure Grace had Nora on her side, and Nora was one of the regular players, but the other two players were Miriam's faithful allies. That made three against two, and the second team had practically declared in her favor. Grace would have to do differently if she expected to keep the captaincy.

Meanwhile Grace was finding the captaincy of a team divided against itself anything but satisfactory. The girls, with the exception of Nora, obeyed her orders indifferently and as though under protest. It was almost impossible to get every member to come to practice. Some one of them invariably stayed away. On one occasion she spoke rather sharply to the team about it, but her earnest words were received with sullen resentment.

"What is the use of working ourselves to death simply to have our game handed over to the enemy?" one girl had muttered.

Grace colored at this thrust, but closed her lips tightly and made no reply. But the attitude of her team worked upon her mind, and she lost confidence in herself. She realized that a new and injurious influence was at work, and she was powerless to stem the tide of dissension that had arisen.

The practice game was played on the afternoon before the contest, and not even Jessica was there to witness it, although she had formerly been taken as a matter of course. When invited to attend practice she had scornfully refused it.

"No, thank you," she said. "If anything should go wrong to-morrow I'd be accused of treachery. No one's reputation is safe in this class." At which remark several sophomores had the grace to blush.

The day dawned bright and clear. Grace arrived at the gymnasium long before the others. She was worried and anxious over the behavior of her team. She was half afraid that some one of them would absent herself, in which case one of the substitutes would have to be called, and Grace doubted whether they could be relied upon.

Two months before, she had been certain that there were no players like those of the sophomore organization. Now she had no confidence in them or herself. She had a faint hope that when the game opened, her players would forget their grievances and work for the honor of the sophomores. She would do her best at all events, and Nora could be depended upon, too. All this passed rapidly through Grace's mind as she waited for the team to appear.

The spectators were arriving in numbers. The gallery was almost full, and it still lacked fifteen minutes of the time before the game would be called. The proverbial little bird had been extremely busy, and all sorts of rumors regarding the two teams were afloat. The juniors were, as usual, seated in a body and making a great deal of unnecessary noise. The members of the sophomore class were scattered here and there. Anne and Jessica sat with three or four of the girls who had refused to pay any attention to the talk about Anne. A dozen or more of Miriam's flock sat together watching for the appearance of their favorite. Occasionally they glanced over toward Anne, whispered to each other, and then giggled in a way that made Anne wince and Jessica feel like ordering them out of the gallery.

Grace and Nora stood talking together at one end of the gymnasium. Grace kept an anxious eye on the clock. It was five minutes of two and Miriam had not arrived. "Would she dare to stay away?" Grace wondered. At two minutes of two there was a burst of applause from the section of the gallery where Miriam's admirers were seated. Grace glanced quickly around to see what had caused it, and beheld Miriam serenely approaching, a satisfied smile on her face. She had waited until the last minute in the hope of making a sensation, and had not been disappointed. Then the game began.

Julia Crosby and Grace Harlowe once more faced each other on the field of action. This time Grace won the toss and sent the ball whizzing to the goal thrower, who tried for goal and caged the ball without effort. This aroused the sophomores, and Grace could have danced for joy as she saw that they were really going to work in earnest. The juniors were on the alert, too. If they won to-day that meant the season's championship. If they won the third game, that meant a complete whitewash for the sophomores.

So the juniors hotly contested every inch of the ground, and the sophomores found that they had their hands full. The first half of the game closed with the score 8 to 6 in favor of the juniors.

During the intermission of twenty minutes between halves, the sophomores retired to the little room off the gymnasium to rest. The outlook was indeed gloomy. It was doubtful whether they could make up their loss during the last half. Marian Barber, Eva Allen and Miriam whispered together in one corner. Grace sat with her chin in her hand, deep in thought, while Nora stood staring out the window trying to keep back the tears. Two or three of the substitutes strolled in and joined Miriam's group. The whispering grew to be a subdued murmur. The girls were evidently talking about Grace, hence their lowered voices. Their long-suffering captain looked at them once or twice, made a move as if to join them, then sat down again. Nora's blood was up at the girls' rudeness. She marched over to the group and was about to deliver her opinion of them in scathing terms, when the whistle sounded. There was a general scramble for places. Then the ball was put in play and the second half began.

The sophomores managed to tie the score during the early part of the last half, and from that on held their own. They fought strenuously to keep the juniors from scoring. When the juniors did score, the plucky sophomores managed to do the same soon after. There were two more minutes of the game, and the score stood 10 to 10. It looked as though it might end in a tie. One of the juniors had the ball. With unerring aim she threw it to goal. It never reached there, for Miriam Nesbit made a dash, sprang straight into the air and caught the ball before it reached its destination. Quick as a flash she threw it to Nora, who threw it to Marian Barber. The latter being near the basket threw it to goal without any trouble.

Before the juniors could get anywhere near the ball the whistle blew and the game closed. Score 12 to 10. The sophomores had won.

The noise in the gallery was deafening. Miriam's sensational playing had taken every one by storm. A crowd of sophomores rushed down to the gymnasium and began dancing around her singing their class song. Her cheeks were scarlet and her eyes blazed with triumph. She was a lion at last, and now the rest would follow. She felt sure that she would be asked to take the place of Grace as captain. She had shown them what she could do. Grace had done nothing but cause trouble. The team would be better off without her.

Anne and Jessica were waiting in the corridor for Grace and Nora. The two players rapidly changed their clothes and soon the chums were walking down the quiet street.

"Well," said Jessica, "Miriam has done it at last."

"She has, indeed," responded Grace, "and no one begrudges her her glory. She made a star play and saved the day for us. She is loyal to the team even if she doesn't like their captain."

"I don't know about that," said Nora, "I think she might have exerted herself during the first game if she wanted so much to show her loyalty. She was anything but a star player, then. I have no faith in her, whatever. She cares for no one but herself, and that star play was for her own benefit, not because of any allegiance to her team. She's up to something, you may depend upon that."

"Oh, Nora, don't be too hard on her. She deserves great credit for her work. Don't you think so, girls?" Grace turned appealingly to Anne and Jessica.

"It was a remarkable play," said Anne.

Jessica made no answer. She would not praise Grace's enemy, even to please Grace.

"You may say what you please," said Nora obstinately, "I shall stick to my own convictions. The way those girls stood in the corner and whispered during intermission was simply disgraceful. Mark my words, something will come of it."

"Oh, here comes David on his motorcycle," called Anne delightedly.

David slowed up when he saw the girls, alighted and greeted them warmly. He at once congratulated them on their victory.

"I congratulate you on having a star player for a sister," said Grace. "It must run in the family." She referred to his late football triumphs.

David flushed with pleasure, more at the compliment paid to his sister than the one meant for him.

"Sis can come up to the mark when she wants to," he said earnestly. "I hope she repeats the performance." Then he abruptly changed the subject. That one little speech revealed to his friends the fact that he understood the situation and longed with all his heart for a change of tactics on the part of his sister.

## CHAPTER XII

## THE WAYS OF SCHOOLGIRLS

The clang of the gong announced the end of school for the day, but some of the sophomores lingered in their locker-room.

They had a very disagreeable communication to make that afternoon, to one of their class, and now that the time had come were inclined to shrink from the ordeal.

"I think Miriam should break the news herself," observed Marian Barber, "as long as she is to succeed Grace."

"Miriam isn't here," said Eva Allen, "she went home early. She told me she could not bear to see anyone unhappy. She is so sensitive you know?" Eva Allen was devoted to Miriam's cause.

"Oh, I don't know about that," said practical Marian. "She'll make a good captain, however, because she has showed more loyalty to the team than Grace has."

Marian firmly believed what she said. She had never been an ardent admirer of Miriam, and had at first stubbornly refused to repudiate Grace. But Miriam had little by little instilled into her the idea of Grace's incompetency, until Marian, who thought only of the good of the team, became convinced that a change of captains was advisable. Miriam's brilliant playing in the recent game was the final touch needed, and now Marian was prepared to do what she considered was her absolute duty.

"Suppose we write Grace a letter," suggested one of the substitutes, "as long as no one seems anxious to tell her."

"Hush," exclaimed Eva Allen, holding up her finger. "Here come Nora and Jessica. I know they are going to make a lot of fuss when they hear the news. Suppose we go back to the classroom and write the letter. We can all sign our names to it, and then we'll be equally to blame."

The conspirators accordingly trooped into the corridor, just as Nora and Jessica were about to enter the locker-room.

"What in the world is the matter now?" called Jessica. "You girls looks as guilty as though you'd stolen a gold mine."

"Wait and see," said Eva with a rather embarrassed laugh, as she hurried after the others up the stairs.

"Do you know, Jessica, I believe they're up to some hateful mischief. What did I tell you the other day? Those girls have given Grace the cold shoulder more than ever, since the game. They have been following Miriam about like a lot of sheep. Grace notices it, too, and it makes her unhappy, only she's too proud to say so."

"Never mind," said Jessica soothingly. "They'll be sorry some day. Miriam's influence won't last. Grace did perfectly right in standing by Anne, and you and I must always stand by Grace. Grace is a fine captain, and——"

"What are you saying about me?" demanded Grace herself, walking into the locker-room with Anne.

Jessica blushed and was silent, but Nora said glibly, "Oh, Jessica just now said that you made a fine captain." Then she went on hurriedly, "I think our chances for winning the championship are better than ever, don't you?"

"The juniors have been practicing like mad since their defeat," mused Grace. "They will make a hard fight next time. Miss Thompson told me yesterday that she never saw better work in basketball than ours last Saturday. I am so proud of my team, even though they haven't been very nice to me lately. My whole desire is for them to win the final game. I suppose a captain has about the same feeling toward her players that a mother has toward her daughters. She is willing to make any sacrifice in order to make fine girls of them."

"And you are a fine captain," cried Anne. "I felt so proud of you the other day. You handled your team so well. Knowing how hateful they have been, it was wonderful to see you give your orders as though nothing had happened. No other girl could have done it."

"That is a nice compliment, Anne, dear," said Grace pleased with the words of praise from her friend, for the bitterness of her recent unpopularity had made her heart heavy.

At that moment the sophomores whom Jessica and Nora had encountered filed into the room.

Each girl wore a self-conscious expression. Eva Allen carried an envelope in her hand. She was confused and nervous.

Once inside the door the girls paused and began a whispered conversation. Then Eva Allen tried to push the envelope into another girl's hand; but the girl put her hands behind her back and obstinately refused to take it. There was another whispered conference with many side glances in Grace's direction.

Nora stood scowling savagely at the group. She noticed that it consisted of the basketball team and its substitutes. They were all there except Miriam.

"If you have any secrets, girls," remarked Grace in a hurt tone, "please postpone the telling of them for a few minutes. I am going, directly."

She opened her locker and drew out her coat and hat, trying to hide the tears that filled her eyes.

Then Marian Barber impatiently took the envelope from Eva and stepped forward. She had made up her mind to get the whole thing over as rapidly as she could.

"Er—Grace," she said, clearing her throat, "er—the team has——"

"Well, what is it?" exclaimed Nora, irritated beyond her power of endurance. "Why don't you speak out, instead of stuttering in that fashion? I always did detest stuttering."

"Marian has a note for you, Grace," interposed one of the substitutes growing bolder.

Marian placed the note in Grace's hand and turned slowly away. Up to that minute she had believed that what they were about to do was for the best; but all at once the feeling swept over her that she had done a contemptible thing. She turned as though about to take the envelope from Grace, but the latter had already opened it, and unfolding the paper began reading the contents aloud.

"Dear Grace," she read, "after a meeting to-day of the members of the regular and substitute sophomore basketball teams, it was decided that your resignation as captain of the same be requested.

"We are sorry to do this, but we believe it is for the good of the team. We feel that you cannot be loyal to its interests as long as you persist in being a friend of one of its enemies."

The names of the players, with the exception of Nora's and Miriam's, were signed to this communication.

After she had finished reading Grace stood perfectly still, looking searchingly into the faces of her classmates. She was trying to gain her self-control before speaking to them.

She could hardly realize that her own team had dealt this cruel blow. For the first time in her life she had received a real shock. She took a long deep breath and clenched her hands. She did not wish to break down before she had spoken what was in her mind.

Nora was muttering angrily to herself. Jessica looked ready to cry, while Anne, pale and resolute, came over and stood by Grace. She felt that she had been the primary cause of the whole trouble. She had borne the girls' unjust treatment of herself in silence, but, now, they had visited their displeasure upon Grace, and that was not to be borne.

"How dared you do such a despicable thing?" she cried. "You are cruel, unfeeling, and oh, so unjust. You accused me of something I would scorn to do, and not satisfied with that, visited your petty spite upon a girl who is the soul of truth and honor. You may say what you choose about me, but you shall not hurt Grace, and if you don't immediately retract what you have written I will take measures which may prove most unpleasant to all of you."

Just what Anne intended to do she did not know, but her outburst had its effect on the conspirators, and they squirmed uneasily under the lash of her words. Perhaps, they had misjudged this slender, dark-eyed girl after all.

Before Anne could say more, Grace spoke quietly.

"Sit down, all of you," she said at last, with a sweetness and dignity that was remarkable in so young a girl. "I have something to say to you. It is curious," she went on, "that I was just talking about our basketball team when you came into the room. I had said to Nora, Jessica and Anne that I wanted more than anything else in the world to beat the junior team. Miss Thompson had been praising the team to me, and I said to the girls that I thought I loved it just as a mother loves her daughters. There is no sacrifice I wouldn't make to keep up the team's good work, and that is the reason why I am going to make a sacrifice, now, and decline to resign. If I had been a poor captain, you would have had a right to ask for my resignation But I haven't. I have been a good, hard-working, conscientious captain, and I have made a success of the team. None of you can deny it. If you took a new captain at this stage it might ruin everything, and I tell you I have thought too much about it; I have set my heart on it so firmly that it would just break if we lost the deciding game."

Her voice broke a little. Nora was sobbing openly. It was hard work for Grace to control her own tears.

"Of course," she went on, clearing her throat and raising her voice to steady it, "it will be a sacrifice for me to keep on being your captain when you don't want me. It's no fun, I can assure you. Perhaps none of you has ever felt the hurt that comes of being turned out by people who were once fond of you. I hope you never will. I am still fond of all of you, and some day, perhaps, you will see that you have made a mistake. At any rate, I decline to resign my place. It was given to me for the year, and I won't give it up."

Grace turned her back and walked to the window. She had come at last to the end of her strength. She leaned against the window jamb and wept bitterly.

But the address of Mark Anthony over the dead body of Cæsar was not more effective than this simple schoolgirl's speech. Every girl there melted into tears of remorse and sympathy.

"Oh, Grace," cried Marian Barber, "won't you forgive us? We never dreamed it would hurt you so. Now that I look back upon it, I can't see how we could have asked you to do it. We did believe that Miss Pierson betrayed us; but after all, that had nothing to do with your being captain of the team. I think you have been a great deal more loyal than we have. I want to say right here, girls, that I apologize to Grace and scratch my name off the list."

She took a pencil, dashing it through her signature, which was the first one on the letter.

One by one each of the other girls put a pencil stroke through her name.

Then they pinned on their hats, slipped into their coats and left the room as quickly as possible. They were all desperately ashamed; each in her secret heart wished she had never entered into the conspiracy.

They had given the captaincy to Grace, and after all, they had no right to take away what they had freely given, and for no better reason than that Grace was loyal to a friend whom they distrusted.

It was a cruel thing that they had done. They admitted it to each other now, and wished they had never listened to Miriam Nesbit.

Speaking of Miriam, who was to tell her that she had not supplanted Grace after all, as captain of the team.

"You are all cowards," exclaimed Marian Barber still buoyed up by her recent emotions, "I am not afraid of Miriam, or anyone else, and I'll undertake to tell her."

But at the last moment she determined to break the news by letter.

In the meantime, Miss Thompson had quietly entered the locker-room, where Grace and her three chums were still standing.

"Grace," said the principal, "I was passing by and I could not help overhearing what has been said, and while I don't care to enter into the little private quarrels of my girls, I want to tell you that you made a noble defense of your position. I am very proud of you, my child." Miss Thompson put her arms around the weeping girl and kissed her. "I wish every girl in my school would make such a stand for her principles. You were right not to have resigned. Always do what your judgment tells you is right, no matter what the result is, and don't give up the captaincy!"

# CHAPTER XIII

## A SKATING PARTY

The holidays had come and gone, and the pupils of Oakdale High School had resigned themselves to a period of hard study. The dreaded mid-year examinations stared them in the face, and for the time being basketball ardor had cooled and a surprising devotion to study had ensued.

Since the day that Grace had refused to give up her captaincy there had been considerable change in the girls' attitude toward her. She had not regained her old-time popularity, but it was evident that her schoolmates respected her for her brave decision and treated her with courtesy. They still retained a feeling of suspicion toward Anne, however, although they did not openly manifest it.

Miriam Nesbit had been inwardly furious over the outcome of her plan to gain the captaincy, but she was wise enough to assume an air of indifference over her defeat. Grace's speech had made considerable impression on the minds of even Miriam's most devoted supporters and she knew that the slightest slip on her part would turn the tide of opinion against her.

Grace was in a more cheerful frame of mind than formerly. She felt that all would come right some day. "Truth crushed to earth shall rise again," she told herself, and the familiar saying proved very comforting to her.

Winter had settled down on Oakdale as only a northern winter can do. There had been snow on the ground since Thanksgiving, and sleigh rides and skating parties were in order.

Grace awoke one Saturday morning in high good humor.

"To-day's the day," she said to herself. "Hurrah for skating!"

She hurried through her breakfast and was donning her fur cap and sweater, when Anne, Jessica and Nora, accompanied by David, Hippy, Reddy and, to her surprise and delight, Tom Gray, turned in at her gate.
"'Oh, be joyful, oh, be gay, For there's skating on the bay,'" sang Hippy.
"Meaning pond, I suppose," laughed Grace, as she opened her front door.
"Meaning pond?" answered Hippy, "only pond doesn't rhyme with gay."

"You might say, "'Oh, be joyful, oh, be fond, For there's skating on the pond,'" suggested David.

"Fond of what?" demanded Hippy.

"Of the person you've asked to skate with you," replied David, looking toward Anne, who stood with a small pair of new skates tucked under her arm.

"I shall be initiated into all the mysteries of the world soon," she observed, smiling happily. "Last year it was coasting and football and now it's dancing and skating. When I once get these things on, David, I'll be like a bird trying its wings, I'll flop about just as helplessly."

"I'm awfully glad to see you, Tom," said Grace, "I did not expect to see you until Easter."

"Oh, I couldn't keep away," laughed Tom. "This is the jolliest place I know."

"Good reason," said Reddy, "we are the real people."

"Stop praising yourself and listen to me," said Hippy. "Our pond has frozen over in the most obliging manner. It's as smooth as glass. Let's go there to skate. There's a crowd of boys and girls on it already."

The pond on the Wingate estate was really a small lake, a mile or more in circumference. While it froze over every winter, the ice was apt to be rough, and there were often dangerous places in it, air-holes and thin spots where several serious accidents had occurred.

Therefore, Wingate's Pond was not used as much as the river for skating; but this winter the ice was as smooth and solid as if it had been frozen artificially, so the High School boys and girls could not resist the temptation to skim over its surface.

"Isn't it a fine sight?" asked Grace, as they came in view of the skaters who were circling and gliding over the pond, some by twos and threes, others in long rows, laughing and shouting.

A big fire burned on the bank, rows of new-comers sat near it, fitting on their skates.

"Away with dull care!" cried Hippy, as he circled gracefully over the ice; for, with all his weight, Hippy was considered one of the best skaters in Oakdale.

"Away with everything but fun," finished Grace who could think of nothing save the joy of skating. "Come along, Anne. Don't be afraid. David and I will keep you up until you learn to use those tiny little feet of yours."

Anne's small feet went almost higher than her head while Grace was speaking, and she sat flat down on the ice.

"No harm done," she laughed, "only I didn't know it could possibly be so slippery."

They pulled her up, David and Grace, and put her between them with Tom Gray on the other side of Grace as additional support, and off they flew, while Anne, keeping her feet together and holding on tightly, sailed along like a small ice boat.

"This will give you confidence," explained David, "and later on you can learn how to use your feet."

But Anne hardly heard him, so thrilled was she by the glorious sensation. As they flew by, followed by Hippy and Nora, with Reddy and Jessica, she caught glimpses of many people looking strangely unfamiliar on skates. Miriam passed, gliding gracefully over the ice with a troop of sophomores at her heels. There were many High School boys "cracking the whip" in long rows of eight or more, while there were some older people comfortably seated in sleigh chairs which were pushed from behind, generally by some poor boys in Oakdale, who stood on the bank waiting to be hired.

"Now, we'll have a lesson," exclaimed David when they had reached the starting point again, while the others lost themselves in the crowd. Anne was a good pupil, but she was soon tired and sat down on a bench near the bank.

"Do go and have a good skate yourself, David," she insisted. "I'll rest for awhile and look on."

But it was far too cold to sit still.

"I'll give myself a lesson," she said. "This is a quiet spot. All the others seem to have skated up to the other end."

As she was carefully taking the strokes David had taught her, with an occasional struggle to keep her balance, she heard a great shouting behind her. The next instant, someone had seized her by the hand.

"Keep your feet together!" was shouted in her ear, and she found herself going like the wind at the end of a long line of girls. They were juniors, she saw at once, and it was Julia Crosby at the whip end who had seized her by the hand.

Anne closed her eyes. They were going at a tremendous rate of speed, it seemed to her, like a comet shooting through the air. Then, suddenly, the head of the comet stood still and the tail swung around it, and Anne, who represented the very tip of the tail and who hardly reached to Julia Crosby's shoulder, felt herself carried along with such velocity that the breath left her body, her knees gave way and she fell down in a limp little bundle. Julia Crosby instantly let go her hand and the impetus of the rush shot her like a catapult far over the ice into the midst of a crowd of skaters.

But the juniors never stopped to see what damage had been done. They quickly joined hands again, and were off on another expedition almost before Anne had been picked up by David and Hippy.

"It's that Julia Crosby again," cried David. "I wish she would move to Europe. I'd gladly buy her a ticket. The town of Oakdale isn't big enough to hold her and other people. She's always trying to knock somebody off the side of the earth."

Anne went home, tired and bruised. She had had enough of skating for one morning David returned to join the others; for this was not the last of the day's adventures and Julia Crosby, before sunset, was to repent of her cruelty to Anne.

In the meantime Grace and Tom had skated up to the far end of the pond.

"Well, Grace," said Tom, "how has the world been using you? I suppose you have been adding to your laurels as a basketball captain."

"Far from it," said Grace a trifle sadly. "Miriam Nesbit is star player at present."

They skated on for some time in silence. Tom felt there was something wrong, so he tactfully changed the subject.

"Who is the girl doing the fancy strokes?" he asked, pointing to Julia Crosby, who, some distance ahead of them, was giving an exhibition of her powers as a maker of figure eights and cross-cuts.

"That's the junior captain," answered Grace. "I hope she won't fall, because she's heavy enough to go right through the ice if she should have a hard tumble."

"Suppose we stop watching her," suggested Tom. "I don't want to see her take a header, and people who show off on skates always do so, sooner or later."

They changed their course toward the middle of the pond, while Julia, who was turning and circling nearer the shore, watched them from one corner of her eye.

Suddenly Grace stopped.

"Julia! Julia!" she cried. "Miss Crosby!"

"What's the matter?" demanded Tom.

"Don't you see the danger flag over there? She will skate into a hole if she keeps on. The ice houses are near here, and I suppose it is where they have been cutting ice."

"Hello-o!" cried Tom, straining his lungs to reach the skater, who looked back, gave her usual tantalizing laugh and skated on.

"You are getting onto thin ice," screamed Grace in despair, beckoning wildly. "Stop! Stop!"

Julia Crosby was skating backwards now, facing the others.

"Catch me if you can," she called, and the wind carried her words to them as they flew after her.

Then Grace, who had been anxiously watching the skater and not the ice, stumbled on a piece of frozen wood and fell headlong. She lay still for an instant, half stunned by the blow, but even in that distressful moment she could hear the other girl's derisive laughter.

Tom called again:

"You'll be drowned, if you don't look where you are going."

"Why don't you learn to skate?" was Julia's answer.

"O Tom," exclaimed Grace. "Leave me. I'll soon get my breath. Do go and stop that girl. The pond's awfully deep there."

"Miss Crosby," Tom Gray called, "won't you wait a minute? I have something to tell you."

"Catch me first!" she cried.

She turned and began skating for dear life, bending from the waist and going like the wind.

"I think I'll try and catch her from the front," he said to himself. "I don't propose to tumble in, too, and leave poor Grace to fish, us both out."

With arms swinging freely, he made for the center of the pond. As he whizzed past the girl, he turned with a wide sweep and came toward her, pointing at the same time to the white flag. But it was too late. In her effort to outstrip him, Julia slid heavily into the danger zone.

There was a crash and a splash, then down she went into the icy water, followed by Tom, who had seized her arm in a fruitless effort to save her.

For an instant Tom was paralyzed with the coldness of the water. Still, keeping a firm grip on the arm of the girl who had been responsible for his ice bath, he managed to clutch the ledge of ice made by their fall with his free hand.

"Take hold of the ice and try to help yourself a little," commanded Tom.

Julia made a half-hearted attempt, and managed to grasp the ledge, but her hold was so feeble that Tom dared not withdraw his support He was powerless to act, and they would both drown unless help came quickly.

# CHAPTER XIV

# A BRAVE RESCUE

Grace was still where she had fallen, cooling a large, red lump on her forehead by applying her handkerchief first to the ice and then to the swollen place, when she suddenly felt herself to be entirely alone in the world.

"Everybody has gone home to dinner!" she exclaimed, as she glanced over her shoulder at the other end of the pond, now denuded of skaters.

Then she shifted her position, looking for Tom and Julia. She had never dreamed, when she saw her friend go whizzing across the ice, that he had not caught the reckless girl in time to warn her of her danger.

In a flash she saw the empty expanse of ice before her. She leaped to her feet, balancing herself with difficulty, for her head was still dizzy from the blow.

"Tom! Tom Gray!" she called. "Where are you?"

"Run for help!" came the answer. In another moment she saw them clinging to a broken ledge of ice, Tom supporting Julia Crosby.

As for the junior captain, she was weeping bitterly, and making no attempt to help herself.

Grace anxiously scanned the expanse of the ice. It was nearly a mile to the other end of the pond, and the last group of skaters had disappeared over the brow of the hill.

"You must think quickly," she said to herself.

Her eyes took in the other shore. Not a soul was there, not a dwelling of any sort; nothing but the great ice house that stood like a lonely sentinel on the bank. Yet something seemed to tell her that help lay in that direction.

Once before, in a moment of danger, Grace had obeyed this same impulse and had never regretted it. Once again she was following the instinct that might have seemed to another person anything but wise.

Skating as she had never skated before, Grace Harlowe reached the shore in a moment. Here, dropping to the bank, she quickly removed her skates, then ran toward the ice house, feeling strangely unaccustomed to walking on the ground after her long morning on skates.

"What if I am off on a wild-goose chase?" she said to herself. "Suppose there is no one there?" She paused for an instant and then ran on faster than before.

"I shall find help over there, I know I shall," she thought as she hurried over the frozen ground and made straight for the ice house. There was no time to be lost. Tom and Julia were liable to be sucked under and drowned while she was looking for help.

Grace pushed resolutely on. In the meantime hardly four minutes had really elapsed since the skaters had tumbled into the water.

On the other side of the ice house she came abruptly upon a man engaged in loading a child's wagon with chips of wood.

"Help!" cried Grace. "Help! Some people have broken through the ice. Have you a rope?"

The man made no answer whatever. He did not even look up until Grace shook him by the shoulder.

"There is no time to lose," she cried. "They may drown at any moment. Come! Come quickly, and help me save them."

The man looked at her with a strange, far-away expression in his eyes.

"Don't you hear me?" cried Grace in an agony of impatience. "Are you deaf?"

He shook his head stupidly, touching his ears and mouth.

"Deaf and dumb!" she exclaimed in despair.

Holding up two fingers, Grace pointed toward the water. Then she made a swimming motion. Perhaps he had understood. She could not tell, but her quick eye had caught sight of a long, thin plank on the shore.

Pulling off one of her mittens, she showed him a little pearl and turquoise ring her mother had given her for a birthday present, indicating that she would give it to him if he would help her. Then she seized one end of the plank and made a sign for him to take the other; but the stubborn creature began to unload the chips from the wagon.

Grace ran blindly ahead, dragging the plank alone.

"He's feeble-minded," she quivered. "I suppose I shall have to work this thing by myself."

When she had reached the bank, Grace heard him trotting behind her with his little wagon. In another moment there was a tug at the board. She turned and shook her fist angrily at him; but, without regarding her in the least, he lifted the plank and rested it on the wagon. Then motioning her to hold up the back end, he started on a run down the bank.

"The poor soul thinks he's a horse, I suppose," she said to herself, "but what difference does it make, if we can only get the plank to Tom and Julia?"

Grace soon saw, however, that the idea was not entirely idiotic. Later she was to offer up a prayer of thanks for that same child's wagon. The deaf and dumb man was wearing heavy Arctic rubbers, which kept him from slipping; while Grace, whose soles were as smooth as glass, kept her balance admirably by means of the other end of the plank.

Tom and Julia Crosby had now been nearly ten minutes in the water. Twice the ice had broken under Tom's grasp, while Julia, who seemed unable to help herself, had thrown all her weight on the poor boy, while she called wildly for help and heaped Grace with reproaches for running away.

"If it were not for the fact that it would be the act of a coward," exclaimed Tom at last, his teeth chattering with cold, "I would let go of your arm and give up the job of supporting you in this ice water for talking about Grace like that. Of course she has gone for help. Haven't you found out long ago that she is the right sort?"

"Well, why did she go in the wrong direction?" sobbed Julia. "Everybody is over on the other bank. There is nothing but an ice house over here."

"You may trust to her to have had some good, sensible reason," retorted Tom loyally.

"I don't think I can keep up much longer," exclaimed Julia, beginning to cry again.

"Keep on crying," replied Tom exasperated. "It will warm you—and remember that I am doing the keeping up. I don't see that you are making any special effort in that direction."

Once Tom had endeavored to lift Julia out of the hole, and he believed, and always insisted, in telling the story afterwards, that if she had been willing to help herself it could have been accomplished. But Julia Crosby, triumphant leader of her class, and Julia Crosby cold and wet as a result of her own recklessness, were two different beings altogether.

"Grace Harlowe has left us to drown," she sobbed. "I am so wretched. She is a selfish girl."

"No such thing," replied Tom vigorously. "Here she comes now, bringing help as I expected I should think you'd be ashamed of yourself." He gave a sigh of relief when he saw Grace and the strange man approaching at a quick trot, the wagon and plank between them. His confidence in Grace had not been misplaced. He felt that they would soon be released from their perilous predicament.

Grace and the Strange Man Quickly Approached.

"All right," called Grace cheerfully as she approached. "Keep up a little while longer. We'll have you both out in a jiffy."

Both rescuers slid the plank on the ice until one end projected over the hole.

Then the man and Grace both lay flat down on the other end and Grace called "ready."

Julia Crosby seized the board and pulled herself out of the water, safe, now, from the breaking of thin ice at the edge.

"Now, Tom," cried Grace.

But Julia's considerable weight had already weakened the wood. When Tom attempted to draw himself up, crack! went the board, and a jagged piece broke off. This would not have been so serious if the ice had not given way. Then, into the water, with many strange, guttural cries, slipped the deaf and dumb man. Grace herself was wet through by the rush of water over the ice, and just saved herself by slipping backward.

There was still a small portion of the plank left, and, with Julia Crosby's help, Grace thought they might manage to pull the two men out.

But Julia looked hardly able to help herself. She sat shivering on the bank trying to remove her skates.

"Julia," called Grace desperately. "You must help me now or these two men will drown. Help me hold down this plank."

Aroused by Grace's appeal, Julia meekly obeyed, and, still shivering violently, knelt beside Grace on the plank. But it was too short; when Tom Gray seized one end of it he nearly upset both the girls into the water.

"Oh, what shall we do?" cried Grace in despair when suddenly there came the thought of the little wagon.

Quickly untwisting a long muffler of red silk from about her neck, Grace tied it securely in the middle, around the cross piece of the tongue of the stout little vehicle. Then she pushed it gently until it stood on the edge of the hole. Giving one end of the muffler to Julia, Grace took the other herself.

"Catch hold of the tail piece, Tom," she cried.

Fortunately the ice was very rough where the girls were standing, or they would certainly have slipped and fallen. They pulled and tugged until gradually the ice in front of them, with Tom's additional weight on it, instead of breaking began to sink. But Tom Gray was out of the hole now; helped by the wagon he slipped easily along the half-submerged ice, then finally rolled over with a cry of relief upon the firm surface.

In the same way they pulled out the deaf and dumb man, who had certainly been brave and patient during the ordeal, although he had uttered the most fearful sounds.

As soon as his feet touched the solid ice, he seized his wagon and made for the bank. Grace, remembering she had promised him her ring, hurried after him, but she was chilled to the bone and could not run. By the time she reached the bank he had rounded the corner of the ice house and was out of sight.

"He evidently doesn't care to be thanked," said Tom Gray as Grace returned to where he and Julia stood waiting.

"We had better get home as soon as possible or we'll all be laid up with colds."

The three half-frozen young people made their way home as best they could. Their clothes had frozen stiff, making it impossible for them to hurry. Julia Crosby said not a word during the walk, but when she left them at the corner where she turned into her own street, she said huskily: "Thank you both for what you did for me to-day, I owe my life to you."

"That was a whole lot for her to say," said Grace.

"She ought to be grateful," growled Tom. "She was the cause of all this mess," pointing to his wet clothes.

"I believe she will be," said Grace softly, "After all, 'It's an ill wind that blows no one good.'"

Grace's mother was justly horrified when Grace, in her bedraggled condition, walked into the living room. She insisted on putting her to bed, wrapping her in blankets and giving her hot drinks. Grace fell into a sound sleep from which she did not awaken until evening. Then she rose, dressed and appeared at the supper table apparently none the worse for her wetting.

Meanwhile Tom Gray had gone to his aunt's, given himself a brisk rubbing down and changed his wet clothing for another suit he fortunately happened to have with him. Thanks to his strong constitution and vigorous health, he felt no bad effects.

He then went down to the kitchen, asked the cook for a cup of hot coffee, and, after hastily swallowing it, rushed off to find David, Hippy and Reddy and tell them the news. He was filled with admiration for Grace.

"She is the finest, most resolute girl I ever knew!" he exclaimed as he finished his story.

"Hurrah for Grace Harlowe!" shouted Reddy.

"Let's go down to-night and see if she's all right?" suggested David.

Before seven o'clock the four boys were on their way to the Harlowe's. They crept quietly up to the living-room window. Grace sat by the fire reading. Very softly they began a popular song that was a favorite of hers. Grace's quick ears caught the sound of the music. She was out of the house like a flash, and five minutes later the four boys were seated around the fire going over the day's adventure.

"The deaf and dumb man who helped you out is quite a character," said Hippy. "I know him well. He used to work for my father. He isn't half so foolish as he looks, either. As for that wagon you used as a life preserver, I am proud to say that it was once mine."

"It must have been made especially strong," observed Reddy.

"It was. Hickory and iron were the materials used, I believe. I played with it when but a toddling che-ild," continued Hippy, "and also smashed three before my father had this one made to order. "Twas ever thus from childhood's earliest hour,'" he added mournfully. "I always had to have things made to order."

There was a shout of laughter at Hippy's last remark. From infancy Hippy had been the prize fat boy of Oakdale.

"It's only seven o'clock," said David. I move that we hunt up the girls and have a party. That is, if Grace is willing."

"That will be fine," cried Grace.

Hippy and Reddy were dispatched to find Nora and Jessica. While David took upon himself the pleasant task of going for Anne. Tom remained with Grace. He had a boyish admiration for this straightforward, gray-eyed girl and made no secret of his preference for her.

Inside of an hour the sound of girls' voices outside proclaimed the fact that the boys' mission had not been in vain. The girls had been informed by their escorts of the afternoon's happenings, but Grace and Tom were obliged to tell the story all over again.

"I hope Julia Crosby's ice bath will have a subduing effect upon her," said Nora. "I am glad, of course, that she didn't lose her life, but I'm not sorry she got a good ducking. She deserved something for the way she dragged Anne into that game of crack the whip."

"Let's talk about something pleasant," proposed Reddy.

"Me, for instance," said Hippy, with a Cheshire cat grin. "I am a thing of beauty, and, consequently, a joy forever."

"Smother him with a sofa pillow!" commanded Tom. "He is too conceited to live."

Reddy seized the unfortunate Hippy by the back of the neck, while David covered the fat youth with pillows until only his feet were visible and the smothering process was carried on with great glee until Nora mercifully came to his rescue.

## CHAPTER XV

## A BELATED REPENTANCE

The following Monday as Grace Harlowe was about to leave the schoolroom, Julia Crosby's younger sister, one of the freshman class, handed her a note. It was from Julia, and read as follows:

"DEAR GRACE:

"Will you come and see me this afternoon when school is over? I have a severe cold, and am unable to be out of bed. I have something I must say to you that cannot wait until I get back to school.

"Your sincere friend,

"JULIA"

"Oh, dear!" thought Grace. "I don't want to go up there. Her mother will fall upon my neck and weep, and tell me I saved Julia's life. I know her of old. She's one of the weeping kind. I suppose it's my duty to go, however."

Grace's prognostication was fulfilled to the letter. Mrs. Crosby clasped her in a tumultuous embrace the moment she entered the hall. Grace finally escaped from her, and was shown up to Julia's room.

She looked about her with some curiosity. It was a light airy room, daintily furnished. Julia was lying on the pretty brass bed in one corner of the room. She wore a dressing gown of pale blue eiderdown, and Grace thought she had never seen her old enemy look better.

"How do you do, Julia?" she said, walking over to the bed and holding out her hand to the invalid.

"Not very well," responded Julia hoarsely. "I have a bad cold and am too weak to be up."

"I'm sorry," said Grace, "the wetting didn't hurt me in the least. But, of course, I wasn't in the water like you were. It didn't hurt Tom, either."

"I'm glad you are both all right," said Julia.

She looked solemnly at Grace, and then said hesitatingly, "Grace, I didn't deserve to be rescued the other day. I've been awfully mean to you." She buried her face in the bed clothing and sobbed convulsively.

"Julia, Julia, please don't cry," said Grace, her quick sympathy aroused by the distress of another. "Did you think we would leave you to drown? You would have done the same for me. Don't you know that people never think of petty differences when real trouble arises?"

She laid her hand upon the head of the weeping girl. After a little the sobs ceased and Julia sat up and wiped her eyes.

"Bring that chair over and sit down beside me, Grace. I want to tell you everything," she said. "Last year I was perfectly horrid to you and that little Pierson girl, for no earthly reason either, I thought it was smart to annoy you and torment you. After we had the quarrel that day in the gymnasium, I was really angry with you, and determined to pay you back.

"You know, of course, that I purposely tripped you the day of the basketball game. I was awfully shocked when I found you had sprained your ankle, but I was too cowardly to confess that I did it. Miss Thompson would have suspended me from school. I didn't know whether you knew that I had done it until I met you that day in the corridor, and the way you looked at me made me feel miserable. Then we got hold of your signals."

She paused.

Grace leaned forward in her chair in an agony of suspense.

"Julia," she said, "I don't care what you did to me; but won't you please say that Anne didn't give you those signals?"

"Miss Pierson did not give them to me," was the quick reply.

"I'm so glad to hear you say it," Grace answered. "I knew she was innocent, but the girls have distrusted her all year. She lost the list accidentally, you know, but they wouldn't believe that she did."

"Yes, I heard that she did," said Julia. "The list was given to me, but I am not at liberty to tell who gave it. It was not your Anne, although I was too mean to say so, even when I knew that she had been accused. I'll write you a statement to that effect if you want me to do so. That will clear her."

"Oh, Julia, will you truly? I want it more than anything else in the whole world. A statement from you will carry more weight with the girls than anything I could possibly tell them. It will convince the doubters, you know. There are sure to be some who will insist on being skeptical."

Acting under Julia's direction, Grace brought a little writing case from a nearby table, Julia opened it, selected a sheet of paper and wrote in a firm, clear hand:

"To the members of the sophomore class, and to all those whom it may concern:

"The accusation made against Anne Pierson last fall regarding the betrayal of the basketball signals to the junior team is false. Our knowledge of these signals came from an entirely different source.

"JULIA CROSBY,
Capt. Junior Team."

"And now," concluded Julia, "I have done something toward straightening out the mischief I made. Will you forgive me, Grace, and try to think of me as your friend?"

"With all my heart," replied Grace, kissing her warmly. "And I am so happy to-day. Just think, the junior and sophomore classes will be at peace at last."

The two girls looked into each other's eyes, and both began to laugh.

"After two years' war the hatchet will be buried," said Julia a little tremulously.

"Oh, Julia!" exclaimed Grace, hopping about, "I've a perfectly splendid idea!"

"What is it?" asked Julia breathlessly.

"Let's have a grand blow out and bury the hatchet with pomp and ceremony. We'll have speeches from both classes, and a perfectly gorgeous feed afterwards. You break the news to your class and I'll endeavor to get my naughty children under control once more. I believe some of them love me a little yet," she smiled.

"Of course, they do," said Julia stoutly. "I must say I don't see why they were so hateful to you, even if Anne Pierson were under suspicion. I know I am to blame for helping the grudge along," she added remorsefully, "but I am, not the only one."

"I know," said Grace quickly. "There are lots of things I'd like to say, but for certain reasons of my own I shall not say them. You understand, I think."

Julia nodded. She did, indeed, understand, and the full beauty of Grace Harlowe's nobility of spirit was revealed to her.

"You are the finest, squarest girl I ever knew, Grace," she said admiringly.

"Nonsense," laughed Grace, flushing a little at the tribute paid her by the once arrogant junior captain. "You don't know me at all. I have just as many faults as other girls, with a few extra ones thrown in. I have no claim to a pedestal. I hope we shall be friends for the rest of our schooldays and forever after. You will be a senior next year, and I shall be a junior. It's time we put by childish quarrels, and assumed the high and mighty attitude of the upper classes. It is our duty to become a living example to erring freshmen."

Both girls laughed merrily; then Grace rose to go. She kissed Julia good-bye and walked out of the house as though on air. Her cup of happiness was full to the brim. She carefully tucked the precious paper away in her bag and sped down the street on winged feet.

The incredible had come to pass. Her old-time enemy had become her friend. She wondered if it could have ever come about by any other means. She doubted it. She had always heard that "Desperate cases require desperate remedies." The happenings of the past week seemed conclusive proof of the truth of the saying. Furthermore, she believed in the sincerity of Julia Crosby's repentance. It was more than skin deep. She felt that henceforward Julia would be different. Best of all, she had the reward of her own conscience. In being true to Anne she had been true to herself.

## CHAPTER XVI

## AN OUNCE OF LOYALTY

When the girls of the sophomore class entered their locker-room the next day they found a notice posted to the effect that a class meeting would be held after school in the locker-room at which all members were earnestly requested to be present.

There was considerable speculation as to the object of the meeting, and no one knew who had posted the notice. Grace kept her own counsel. She wished to take the class by surprise, and thus make Anne's restoration to favor complete.

At recess Nora and Jessica brought up the subject, but found that Grace apparently wished to avoid talking about it.

"You'll attend, won't you, Grace?" asked Anne.

"Of course," said Grace hastily. "Will you excuse me, girls? I have a theorem to study."

She felt that if she stayed a minute longer she would tell her friends the good news and spoil her surprise.

"What makes Grace act so queerly to-day?" said Jessica. "I believe she knows something and won't tell us."

"I'll make her tell it," said Nora, and ran after Grace. But just then the gong sounded and recess was over.

As soon as school was dismissed for the day, the entire sophomore class crowded into the locker-room. They were curious to know what was in the wind. Every member was present, and Grace felt a secret satisfaction when Miriam Nesbit, looking rather bored, sauntered in.

There was a confused murmur of voices. The girls chattered gayly to each other, as they waited for someone to call the meeting to order. When Grace left the corner where she had been standing with her three friends, and stood facing her classmates, the talking instantly ceased.

"Girls," she said, "I suppose you wonder who called this meeting, and why it was called? I wrote the notice you all read this morning. I have something to tell you which I hope you will be glad to hear."

"At the beginning of the school year, some things happened that caused unpleasant suspicions to rest upon a member of our class. You all know who I mean. It has caused her and her friends a great deal of unhappiness, and I am glad to be able at last to bring you the proof that she has been misjudged."

Grace paused and looked about her. She noted that Miriam had turned very pale.

"Just as I suspected," thought Grace, "she really did have a hand in that signal affair."

Then she continued.

"A few days ago I had occasion to call upon the junior captain, Miss Crosby. While there, she assured me that the juniors did receive our signals, but that Miss Pierson had absolutely nothing to do with the matter. I was not sure that you would care to take my word, alone, for this"—Grace couldn't resist this one tiny thrust—"so she very kindly gave me the assurance in writing, signed by herself."

Grace then unfolded the paper and in a clear voice read Julia's statement.

There was not a sound in the room. Grace stood waiting. She had done her part, the rest lay with her classmates.

Nora and Jessica had their arms around Anne, who had begun to cry quietly. The relief was so great that it had unnerved her. Then Marian Barber sprang to Grace's side and seized her by the hand.

"Listen, girls," she cried, "I want to acknowledge for the second time that I am heartily ashamed of myself. We have all been nasty and suspicious toward Anne. We never gave her a chance to defend herself, we just went ahead and behaved like a lot of silly children. I am sorry for anything I have ever said about her, and I want to tell you right here that I consider Grace Harlowe the ideal type of High School girl. I only wish I were half as noble and courageous. I suppose you all wonder why Grace went to see Julia Crosby. Well I'll tell you. I found out about it from Julia's sister this morning."

"Oh Marian, please don't," begged Grace, rosy with confusion.

But the girls cried in chorus, "Tell us, Marian! Don't mind Grace!"

When Marian had finished many of the girls were in tears. They crowded around Anne and Grace vying with each other in trying to show their good will. Then Eva Allen proposed three cheers for Grace and Anne.

They were given with a will. The noise of the ovation bringing one of the teachers to the door with the severe injunction, "Young ladies please contain yourselves. There is too much noise here."

The girls dispersed by twos and threes, until Marian Barber and the chums were the only ones left.

"I have a motto," said Marian, "that I shall bring here to-morrow and hang in the locker-room. If I had paid more attention to it, it would have been better for me."

"What is it, Marian?" asked Jessica.

"Wait and see," replied Marian. "Oh, it's a good one, and appropriate, too."

After saying good-bye to Marian the four chums walked on together.

"Are you happy, Anne, dear?" said Grace, slipping her hand into Anne's.

Anne looked up at Grace with a smile so full of love and gratitude that Grace felt well repaid for all she had endured for friendship's sake.

"Everything has turned out just like the last chapter in a book," sighed Nora with satisfaction "The sinner—that's Julia Crosby—has repented, and the truly good people—Anne and Grace—have triumphed and will live happy forever after."

The girls laughed at Nora's remark.

"Now I can go on planning for our big game without being afraid that the girls will stay away from practice and do things to annoy and make it hard for me," said Grace happily. "I know that we shall win. I feel so full of enthusiasm I don't know what to do. Oh, girls, I forgot to tell you that Julia Crosby and I have a perfectly splendid plan. But I promised not to say anything to anyone about it until she comes back to school."

"How funny it sounds to hear you talk about having plans with Julia Crosby," said Jessica laughing. "You will make Miriam Nesbit jealous if you take Julia away from her."

"By the way, girls!" exclaimed Nora, "what became of Miriam? I saw her enter the locker-room, but she wasn't there when Marian Barber began her speech. I know she did not remain, because I looked for her and couldn't find her."

"I saw her go," said Grace quietly, "That is the only part of this story that doesn't end well. She doesn't like Anne or me any better than before and never will, I'm afraid. She influenced the girls against us, after the first game, and you remember what she said at the basketball meeting, don't you, Nora?"

"Yes," responded Nora, "I do, and if she hadn't been David's sister I would have told her a few plain truths, then and there."

"I said at the beginning of the year that I believed Miriam had a better self," said Grace thoughtfully. "I still believe it, and I am not going to give her up yet."

"I don't envy you the task of finding it," said Jessica.

"I wonder what Marian Barber's motto is?" mused Anne. "She said it would be a good one."

"I have no doubt of that. Marian Barber doesn't usually do things by halves when once she starts," said Jessica. "I am surprised that she ever allowed herself to be drawn into Miriam's net. She seems awfully sorry for it now."

"Oh, girls," cried Nora suddenly. "I have a half a dollar."

"Really?" said Jessica. "I didn't suppose there was that much money in Oakdale."

"My sister gave it to me this morning," Nora went on, ignoring Jessica's remark. "I am supposed to buy a new collar with it, but if you are thirsty——"

"I am simply perishing with thirst," murmured Grace.

Five minutes later the four girls were seated in the nearest drug store busily engaged with hot chocolate, while they congratulated Nora on having spent her money in a good cause.

The sophomores smiled to themselves next morning at Marian's motto. It hung in a prominent place in the locker-room and read: "An ounce of loyalty is worth a pound of cleverness."

# CHAPTER XVII

## BURYING THE HATCHET

It was some days before Julia Crosby was able to return to school, but when she did put in an appearance, she lost no time in taking her class in hand and bringing about a much-needed reform. The part played by Grace Harlowe in Julia's rescue had been related by her to various classmates who had visited her during her illness, and Grace found that the older girls were inclined to lionize her more than she cared to be. She received praise enough to have completely turned her head had she not been too sensible to allow it to do so.

After holding a conference with Julia, the two girls sent out notices to their respective classes that a grand reunion of the two classes would take place on the next Saturday afternoon at one o'clock, at the old Omnibus House, providing the weather permitted. A tax of twenty-five cents apiece was levied on the members of both classes. "Please pay your money promptly to the treasurer of your class," ended the notices, "if you wish to have plenty to eat. Important rites and ceremonies will be observed. You will be sorry if you stay away, as an interesting program is promised. Please keep this notice a secret."

"The field back of the Omnibus House is an ideal place for the burial," Julia told Grace. "It was there that the 'Black Monks of Asia' held their revel and were unmasked by the freshmen. Besides, it's quiet and we shan't be disturbed."

Grace agreed with her, and the two girls outlined the proceedings with many a chuckle.

The junior and sophomore classes had been requested to go directly to the Omnibus House.

"It would be great to have both classes march out there, but we should have the whole of Oakdale marching with us before we arrived at the sacred spot," observed Grace, with a giggle.

"If we don't have a lot of freshmen to suppress it will be surprising. I do hope the girls haven't told anyone," Julia answered. "By the way, we have a hatchet at home that will be just the thing to bury. It is more like a battle-ax than anything else, and looks formidable enough to represent the feeling that the juniors and sophomores are about to bury. Now, Grace, you must prepare a speech, for we ought to have representative remarks from both classes. Then Anne Pierson must recite 'The Bridge of Sighs,' after I have made it over to suit the occasion. We'll have to have some pallbearers. Three girls from each class will do."

Julia planned rapidly and well. Grace listened attentively. The junior captain had remarkable energy. It was easy to see why Julia had always headed her class. Julia in turn, was equally impressed with Grace's ability. A mutual admiration society bade fair to spring up between the two, so recently at swords' points.

On Saturday the weather left nothing to be desired. It seemed like a day in late spring, although it was in reality early March. At one o'clock precisely the two classes, with the exception of one member, assembled. Julia Crosby acting as master of ceremonies, formed the classes in two lines, and marched them to the middle of the field. Here, to their complete mystification, they saw a large hole about four feet in depth had been dug.

"Who on earth dug that hole, and what is it for?" inquired a curious sophomore.

"Hush!" said Julia Crosby reverently. "That is a grave. Be patient. Curb your rising curiosity. Soon you shall know all."

"Assistant Master Harlowe, will you arrange the esteemed spectators, so that the ceremony may proceed?"

Grace stepped forward and solemnly requested the girls to form a double line on each side of the opening. The shorter girls were placed in the front rows.

"The sophomores will now sing their class song," directed the master of ceremonies.

When the sophomores had finished, the juniors applauded vigorously.

The juniors' song was next in order and the sophomores graciously returned the applause.

"I will now request the worthy junior members Olive Craig, Anne Green and Elsie Todd, to advance. Honorable Assistant Master Harlowe, will you name your trusted followers?"

Grace named Nora, Jessica and Marian Barber who came to her side with alacrity.

"During the brief space of time that we are obliged to absent ourselves, will every guest keep her roving eyes bent reverently on the ground and think about nothing. It is well to fittingly prepare for what is to come."

With this Julia marched her adherents down the field and around the corner of the Omnibus House. She was followed by Grace and her band. There was a chorus of giggles from the chosen helpers that was sternly checked by Julia.

Before their eyes stood a large, open paste-board box lined with the colors of both classes, in which reposed the Crosby hatchet, likened to a battle-ax by Julia. Its handle was decorated with sophomore and junior ribbons, and around the head was a wreath of immortelles. A disreputable looking sheaf of wheat lay across the end of the box.

There was a smothered laugh from Nora, whose quick brain had grasped the full significance of the thing.

"This is not an occasion for levity," reprimanded Grace sternly. "Laughing will not be tolerated."

Three twisted ribbon handles of sophomore colors and three of junior ornamented either side of the box. Each girl grasped a handle.

"We will proceed with the ceremony," directed Julia. "Lift up the box."

This was easier said than done. The handles were so close together that the girls hardly had room to step. The journey was finally accomplished without any further mishap than the sliding off of the wheat sheaf. This was hastily replaced by Jessica before its fall had been marked by the eagle eye of the master of ceremonies, who marched ahead with her assistant.

When the box had been carefully deposited at one side of the "grave," Julia Crosby took her place beside it, and assuming a Daniel Webster attitude began her address.

"Honored juniors and sophomores. We have met together to-day for a great and noble purpose. We are about to take a step which will forever after be recorded among the doughty deeds of Oakdale High School. It will go down in High School history as the glorious inspiration of a master mind. We are going to unfurl the banner of peace and bury the hatchet.

"Since the early days of our class history, war, cruel war, has raged between the august bodies represented here to-day. On this very field many moons ago the gallant sophomores advanced upon the, then, very fresh freshmen, but retreated in wild confusion. It is therefore fitting that this should be the place chosen for the burial of all grudges, jealousies and unworthy emotions that formerly rent our breasts."

Here Julia paused to take breath.

The girls cheered wildly.

Julia bowed right and left, her hand over her heart. When the noise had subsided, she continued. She bewailed junior misdeeds and professed meek repentance. She dwelt upon the beauty of peace and she begged her hearers henceforth to live with each other amicably.

It was a capital address, delivered in a mock-serious manner that provoked mirth, and did more toward establishing general good feeling than any other method she might have tried. In closing she said:

"The hatchet is the symbol of war. The wheat-sheaf represents our elderly grudge; but the immortelles are the everlasting flowers of good will that spring from the planting of these two. We will now listen to a few remarks from the pride of the sophomore class, Assistant Master of Ceremonies Grace Harlowe."

Grace attempted to speak, but received an ovation that made her flush and laughingly put her hands over her ears. When she was finally allowed to proceed, she delivered an oration as flowery as that of the master of ceremonies.

When the cries of approbation evoked by Grace's oration had died away, it was announced that the "renowned elocutionist," Miss Anne Pierson, would recite a poem appropriate to the occasion. Anne accordingly recited "The Bridge of Sighs," done over by Julia Crosby, and beginning:

"Take it up gingerly;
Handle with care;
'Tis a relic of sophomore
And junior warfare."

The intense feeling with which Anne rendered this touching effusion, caused the master of ceremonies to sob audibly and lean so heavily upon her assistant for support that that dignified person almost pitched head first into the opening, and was saved from an ignominious tumble by one of her attendants. This was too much for the others, who, forgetting the solemnity of their office, shrieked with mirth, in which the spectators were not slow to join.

"I think we had better wind up the ceremony," said Julia with great dignity. "These people will soon be beyond our control."

The attendants managed to straighten their faces long enough to assist in the concluding rites that were somewhat hastily performed, and the master of ceremonies and her assistants held an impromptu reception on the spot. "Now," said Julia Crosby, "we have done a good day's work for both classes. I only hope that no prying freshmen hear of this. They will be sure to come here and dig up what we have gone to such pains to bury. They have no respect for their superiors. However, you have all behaved yourselves with true High School spirit, and I wish to announce that you will find a spread awaiting you around the corner of the Omnibus House."

There was a general hurrah at this statement, and the guests rushed off to the spot designated.

Grace had held an earnest conference with old Jean, and the result showed itself in the row of tables rudely constructed to fit the emergency. He it was who had dug the "grave." He now sat on the steps waiting to build a fire, over which Grace had planned to make coffee for the hungry girls whose appetites had been whetted by the fresh air.

The money contributed by the classes had been used to good advantage by Grace and Julia, and piles of tempting eatables gladdened the eyes of the guests.

For the next half hour feasting was in order. Juniors and sophomores shared cups; as the supply of these were limited. At the end of that time the last crumb of food had disappeared and the girls stood in groups or walked about the field, discussing the various features of school life.

Some one proposed playing old-fashioned games, and soon "puss in the corner," "pom-pom-pull-away," and "prisoner's goal" were in full swing. "This brings back one's Grammar School days, doesn't it?" said Nora to Grace. They were deep in a game of prisoner's goal, and stood for a moment waiting for the enemy to move toward them.

"I haven't had such a good, wholesale romp for ages," answered Grace, and was off like the wind to intercept Eva Allen as she endeavored to make a wide detour of their goal.

The hours slipped by on wings. The start home was made about five o'clock. The juniors and sophomores trooped back to Oakdale arm in arm, singing school songs and making the welkin ring with their joyous laughter. The people of Oakdale smiled at the procession of happy girls and wondered what particular celebration was in order.

When the center of town was reached the party broke up with a great deal of laughing and chattering, the girls going their separate ways in the best of spirits.

"I've had a perfectly fine time," declared Grace, as she said good-bye to her chums, "and how glad I am that we are all friends again."

She quite forgot when she made that statement that Miriam Nesbit had not honored the reunion with her presence.

# CHAPTER XVIII

## AT THE ELEVENTH HOUR

One more excitement was to quicken the pulses of the sophomores before they settled down to that long last period of study between Easter holidays and vacation.

The great, decisive basketball game with the juniors was now to take place.

Grace, in conclave with her team, had gone over her instructions for the hundredth time. They had discussed the strong points of the juniors and what were their own weak ones.

Miriam Nesbit was sullen at these meetings; but in the practice game she had played with her usual agility and skill, so the girls felt that she was far too valuable a member of the team for them to mind her humors.

"Everybody is coming to-morrow to see us play," exclaimed Nora in the locker-room, at the recess on Friday. "I don't believe the President's visit would create more excitement, really," she added with a touch of pride.

"Did you know," interposed Anne, "that the upper class girls are calling Grace and Julia Crosby 'David and Jonathan'?"

This was also an amusing piece of news at which the other girls laughed joyously. In fact, there was no such feeling of depression before this game as had affected the class when the first game was played. The sophomores were cheerful and confident, awaiting the great battle with courage in their hearts.

"Be here early, girls," cautioned Grace, as they parted after school that day. "Perhaps we may get in a little practice before the people begin to come."

Grace hurried through her own dinner as fast as she could, on the eventful Saturday.

"I shall be glad when this final game is over, child," exclaimed Mrs. Harlowe anxiously, "I really think you have had more athletics this winter than has been good for you, what with your walking, and skating, dancing, and now basketball."

"You'll come, won't you, mother?" cried Grace, seizing her hat and rushing off without listening to Mrs. Harlowe's comments. "We are sure to win," she called as she waved her a good-bye kiss.

There was no one in the school building when Grace got back; that is, no one except the old janitress, who was sweeping down the corridor, as usual. The other girls had not been so expeditious and Grace found the locker-room deserted.

With trembling eagerness she was slipping on her gymnasium suit and rubber-soled shoes, when she suddenly remembered that she had left her tie in the geometry classroom. She had bought a new one the day before, placed it in the back of her geometry and walked out of the classroom, leaving book, tie and all behind.

"I'll run up and get it right away, before the others come," she said to herself.

Running nimbly up the broad stairway, she entered the deserted classroom and hurried down the aisle to the end of the room where she usually sat during recitation.

"Here it is," she murmured, taking it out of the book and tying it on. Then, sitting down at the desk, she rested her chin in her hands. The quiet of the place was soothing to her excited nerves, and since it was so early she would rest there for a moment and think.

Grace might have dreamed away five minutes when she heard the distant sound of voices below.

"Dear me," she exclaimed, laughing, "they'll scold me for not being on time. I must hurry." So she hastened up the aisle to the door, which was shut, although she had not remembered closing it after her.

She turned the knob, still smiling to herself, but the door stuck fast. It was locked!

Grace was so stunned that for a moment she hardly comprehended what had happened. She sat down and tried to collect her thoughts. Locked up in an upper classroom on the afternoon of the great game!

She tried the one other door in the room. It also was locked. As for the great windows, they were too large for her to push up without a pole.

"I'll try calling," she said. "They may hear me."

But her calls were fruitless, and beating and knocking on the door panels seemed nothing but muffled sounds in the stillness.

"Oh! Oh!" she cried, rushing wildly from doors to windows and back again. "What shall I do! What shall I do?"

In the meantime, it was growing late. The sophomores had assembled and were confidently waiting for their captain.

"She's late for the first time," observed one of the girls, "but we'll forgive her under the circumstances."

"Maybe she's in the gymnasium," suggested Anne, hurrying off to look for her friend. In spite of herself she felt some misgivings and she meant to lose no time in finding her beloved Grace.

The gallery was already half full of people. Anne moved about looking for David, or someone who could help her. Just then Mrs. Harlowe appeared at the door.

"Where is Grace, Mrs. Harlowe?" Anne demanded eagerly.

"I don't know, dear," answered Mrs. Harlowe "She ate her dinner and went off in such a hurry that I hardly had time to speak to her. She told me she wanted to get back to meet the girls."

Anne ran back to the locker-room.

"Grace left home hours ago," she cried. "I just felt that something had happened."

Jessica opened Grace's locker.

"Grace must be in the building," she exclaimed "Here are her clothes."

The girls began to rush about wildly, looking for their captain in the various rooms on the basement floor.

In a few moments a junior came to the door.

"The game will be called in ten minutes," she said. "Are you ready?"

"Yes," answered Nora calmly. "Be careful," she whispered. "Don't let them know yet."

Anne ran again to the gymnasium.

"I'll get David this time," she said to herself. "Something will have to be done if Grace is to be found in time."

David was sitting at one side of the gallery with Reddy and Hippy.

He looked very grave when Anne whispered the news to him. The place was packed with impatient spectators. The junior team was already standing on the floor talking in low voices as they waited impatiently for their opponents to appear at the opposite end.

"She must be somewhere in the building," David ejaculated. "That is if she has on her gymnasium suit. Have you looked upstairs yet?"

"No," replied Anne, "but we have been all through the downstairs' rooms."

As they ran up the steps they heard the shrill whistle that summoned the players to their positions.

"Come on," cried Nora. "Miriam, you will have to take Grace's place, and Eva Allen will substitute for you."

It still lacked a few moments of the toss up; the whistle having been blown sooner to hurry the dilatory sophomores, who seemed determined to linger, unaccountably, in the little side room.

But in that brief time a remarkable change had taken place in the demeanor of Miriam Nesbit. Two brilliant spots burned on her cheeks, and her black eyes flashed and glowed with happiness. The other girls were too downcast and wretched to notice the transformation. They walked slowly into the gymnasium and stood, ill at ease and downcast, at their end of the hall.

A wave of gossip had spread quickly over the audience, that sat waiting with breathless interest for the appearance of the tardy sophomore.

What had happened? Had there been an accident?

No; it was all a mistake. There they were. And tremendous applause burst forth, which died down almost as soon as it had begun. Where was Grace Harlowe, the daring captain of the sophomore team, who had boasted that her team would win the game if it took their last breath to do it?

There was a great craning of necks as the spectators looked in vain for the missing Grace.

Hippy dropped his chin upon his breast disconsolately.

"I feel limp as a rag," he groaned. "Where, oh, where, is our gallant captain? I'll never believe Grace deserted her post."

In the meantime poor Grace, locked in the upper classroom, had concentrated all her thoughts and mental energies on a means of making her escape in time. She sat down quietly, and, folding her hands, began to consider the situation. In looking back long afterwards upon this tragic hour, it seemed to her that it was the blackest moment of her life. The walls were thick. The doors heavy and massive. The ceilings high. There was no possibility of her cries being heard below. It is true she might break a window, but what good would that do? She couldn't jump down three stories into a stone court below. She went to the window and looked out.

"If I hung by this window sill," Grace said aloud, "I believe my feet would just reach the cornice of the second-story window."

Seizing a heavy ruler from one of the desks, she ran to the window and deliberately smashed out all the plate glass in the lower sash. Then, hoisting herself onto the sill, she looked down from what seemed to be rather a dizzy height. But nerve and determination will accomplish anything, and Grace turned her eyes upward.

"I shall do it," she kept saying to herself over and over.

Clinging to the window sill, she gradually let herself down until her feet touched the top of the cornice underneath. Then, steadying herself she looked down. The cornice ledge was quite broad; broad enough to kneel on, in fact. She was glad of this, for she had intended to kneel on it, whatever its width.

With infinite caution, she gradually slipped along the ledge until she was kneeling. Resting her elbows on the stone shelf, she lowered herself to the next window sill. There she stood for a moment, looking in at the empty classroom.

The door into the corridor stood open, and as she clung to the narrow ledge, her face pressed against the window, she wondered how she was going to get in.

"Unless I butt my head against this plate glass," she exclaimed, "I really don't think I can make it. I can't kick in the glass, for fear of losing my balance."

Suddenly she heard her name called.

"Grace! Grace! Where are you?"

First it was David's voice, and then Anne's, and then the two together, echoing through the empty corridors and classrooms.

"I'm here," she answered. "Help! Help!"

Fortunately, they were passing the door at that instant and heard her muffled cries.

"Here," she cried again, and they saw her at last, clinging desperately to the window ledge.

"I don't dare open the window," exclaimed David, thinking aloud. "The slightest jar might make her lose her balance. Grace," he cried, "I'll have to break out the upper sash. Lower your head as much as possible and close your eyes."

Another instant, and Grace was crouching in a shower of broken glass, which fell harmlessly on her back and the top of her head. David knocked off the jagged pieces at the lower end, and Grace climbed nimbly over the sash.

"There's no time for explanations now," she cried. "I was mysteriously locked in. Has the game been called?"

David looked hurriedly at his watch.

"You have just a minute and a half," he exclaimed, and the three ran madly down the steps and into the gymnasium just as the whistle blew and the girls took their places.

When Grace, covered with dust, a long, red scratch across one cheek, rushed into the gymnasium, wild applause shook the walls of the building, for the honor of the sophomore class was saved.

# CHAPTER XIX

## THE GREAT GAME

It was a pitched battle from the very beginning.

The junior team was in splendid trim, and they played with great finish and judgment; but the sight of Grace, one side of whose face was tinged with blood that had risen to the surface from the deep scratch, seemed to spur the sophomores to the most spectacular and brilliant plays.

Only one girl lagged, and was not in her usual trim. It was Miriam Nesbit, whose actions were dispirited and showed no enthusiasm. Her shooting was so inaccurate that a wave of criticism spread over the audience, and the members of her own class watched her with deep anxiety. When the first half ended, however the sophomores were two points to the good.

"Grand little players!" cried Hippy, expressing his joy by kicking both feet against the wooden walls as hard as he could, while he clapped his hands and roared with all his might.

"The gamest little team I ever saw," answered Reddy.

But David, who had resumed his seat beside them, made no reply. He rose presently and went to find his sister, who was sitting somewhat apart from the other girls in gloomy silence.

"What's the matter with you, sister?" he asked gently. "You are not playing as well as usual. I expected you, especially, to do some fine work to-day. On the contrary, you have never played worse."

Miriam looked at her brother coldly.

"Why should I help them when they have dishonored me?" she demanded fiercely.

"How have they dishonored you, Miriam?" asked David.

"By making me the last in everything; putting me at the foot," she said, stifling a sob of anger.

David looked at his sister sorrowfully. He saw there was no reasoning with her in her present state of mind; yet knowing her revengeful spirit, he dreaded the consequences.

"Miriam," he said at last, speaking slowly, "perhaps, some day, you will learn by experience that the people who give a square deal are the only ones who really stay at the head. They always win out; and those who are not on the level——" He stopped. A sudden suspicion had come into his mind.

"You don't mean to say that it was you who——"

But he didn't finish. Instead, he turned on his heel and walked away. In one glance he had read Miriam's secret. Now he understood that look of wild appeal, baffled rage, mortification and disappointment, all jumbled together in her turbulent soul.

"Did she really want it so badly as all that?" he thought, "or was it only her insatiable desire never to be beaten?"

In the meantime, Grace, surrounded by a circle of her school-fellows, was telling them the history of her imprisonment. Miss Thompson and Mrs. Harlowe had made their way across the floor to the crowd of sophomores; Mrs. Harlowe to find out whether her daughter's cheek had been seriously cut, which it had not, and the principal to ask a few questions.

"Did it look like a trick, Grace?" she asked when she had heard the story.

"I hardly know, Miss Thompson. I feel certain that I left the door open when I went in. The janitress may have locked it without seeing me."

"Perhaps," answered Miss Thompson thoughtfully, "but the rule of locking the larger classrooms after school hours has never been followed that I know of. There is really no reason for it, and it might cause some delay in the morning, in case Mrs. Gunby were not around to unlock the doors."

"You will have to send a bill to father for all the broken glass," laughed Grace. "I shouldn't have been here at this moment if I hadn't done some smashing."

Miss Thompson smiled.

"You were perfectly right to do it, my dear. It was an exhibition of good judgment and great courage. As for the bill, certainly the victim of an employee's stupidity should not be held accountable for costs. But we won't disturb you now with any more questions. You deserve to win the game and I hope with all my heart you will."

266

There was still a little time left and Grace determined to improve those shining moments by having a talk with Miriam.

Miriam never looked up when Grace approached her. Her dark brows were knit in an ugly frown and her eyes were on the floor.

"Miriam, aren't you glad I got out of prison in time?" asked Grace cordially.

"I suppose so," answered Miriam, looking anywhere but at Grace.

"Is there anything the matter with you to-day?" continued Grace.

"No," answered Miriam shortly.

"Your playing is not up to mark. The girls are very uneasy. Won't you try to do a little better next half?"

There was a childlike appeal in Grace's voice that grated so on Miriam's nerves, at that moment that she deliberately turned and walked away, leaving Grace standing alone.

"Wait a minute, Miriam," called Nora, who, with some of the other sophomores, had been watching the scene. "You aren't ill to-day, are you?"

"No," replied Miriam angrily.

"Because, if you are really ill, you know," continued Nora, "your sub. could take your place. Anna Ray can play a great deal better game than you played the first half."

Miriam turned on Nora furiously, and was about to make one of her most violent replies, when the whistle blew and the girls flew to their places.

Julia Crosby and Grace smiled at each other in the most friendly fashion as they stood face to face for the last time that season. There was nothing but good-natured rivalry between them now.

The referee balanced the ball for an instant, her whistle to her lips. Then the ball shot up, her whistle sounded and the great decisive last half had begun.

Grace managed to bat the ball as it descended in the direction of one of her eager forwards who tried for the basket and just missed it. The juniors made a desperate attempt to get the ball into their territory, but the sophomores were too quick for them, and Nora made a brilliant throw to goal that caused the sophomore fans to cheer with wild enthusiasm.

It was a game long to be remembered. Both teams fought with a determination and spirit that caused their fans in the gallery to shout themselves hoarse. The juniors made some plays little short of marvelous, and five minutes before the last half was over the score stood 8 to 6 in favor of the sophomores.

"This game will end in a tie if they're not careful," exclaimed Hippy. "No, Nora has the ball! She'll score if anyone can! Put her home, Nora!" he yelled excitedly.

Nora was about to make one of the lightning goal throws for which she was noted, when like a flash Miriam Nesbit seized the ball from her, and attempted to make the play herself. But her aim was inaccurate. The ball flew wide of the basket and was seized by a junior guard. The tie seemed inevitable.

A groan went up from the gallery. Then a distinct hiss was heard, and a second later the entire sophomore class hissed Miriam Nesbit.

Miss Thompson rose, thinking to call the house to order, but sat down again, shaking her head.

"They know what they are about," she said, for Grace herself did not know the game any better than the principal. "It was inexcusable of Miriam, inexcusable and intentional. In attempting to gratify her own vanity she has prevented her side from scoring at a time when all personal desire should be put aside. She really deserves it."

But the score was not tied after all, for the junior guard fumbled the ball, dropped it and before she could regain possession of it, it was speeding toward Marian Barber, thrown with unerring accuracy by Grace. Up went Marian's hands. She grasped it, then hurled it with all her might, straight into the basket. Five seconds later the whistle blew, with the score 10 to 6.

The sophomores had won.

The enthusiastic fans of both classes rushed out of the gallery and down the stairs to the gymnasium. Two tall sophomores seized Grace and making a chair of their hands, carried her around the gymnasium, followed by the rest of the class, sounding their class yell at the tops of their voices.

The story of Grace's imprisonment and escape out of the third story window went from mouth to mouth, and her friends eagerly crowded the floor in an effort to speak to her. There were High School yells and class yells until Miss Thompson was obliged to cover her ears to deaden the noise.

Miss Thompson made her way through the crowd to where Grace was standing in the midst of her admiring schoolmates. The principal took the young captain in her arms, embracing her tenderly.

Surely no one had ever seen Miss Thompson display so much unrestrained and candid emotion before. There were tears in her eyes, her voice trembled when she spoke.

"It was a great victory, Grace, I congratulate you and your class. You have fought a fine, courageous battle against great odds. Many another girl who had climbed out of a third-story window, without even a rope to hold by, would have little strength left to play basketball much less to win the championship. I am very proud of you to-day, my dear," and she kissed Grace right on the deep, red scratch that marred her cheek.

"She is a girl after my own heart," Miss Thompson was thinking, as she hurried to her office. "Grace has faults, of course, but on the other hand, she is as honest as the day, modest about her ability, unselfish and with boundless courage. Certainly she is a splendid influence in a school, and I wish I had more pupils like her."

It was with difficulty that Grace extricated herself from her admiring friends and, accompanied by her chums, made for the locker room to don street attire.

Now that it was all over the reaction had set in, and she began to feel a little tired, although she was almost too happy for words. She walked along, dimly alive to what the girls were saying.

Nora was still upset over Miriam Nesbit's lawless attempt to score, and sputtered angrily all the way down the corridor. "I should think Miriam Nesbit would be ashamed to show her face in school, again, after this afternoon's performance," Nora declared.

"Did you see what David did?" queried Jessica.

"Yes, I did," said Anne.

"What was it?" asked Grace, coming out of her day dream.

"The minute the girls began to hiss Miriam, he got up and walked out of the gymnasium," Jessica replied. "I believe he was so deeply ashamed of what she did that he couldn't bear to stay."

"Well, he found Grace, and rescued her in time for the game," said Anne. "That must be some consolation to him. I don't see how you got locked in, Grace. Are you sure you didn't close the door after you. It has a spring lock, you know."

"I thought I left it open," mused Grace, "but I might have unconsciously pulled it to."

"It is very strange," replied Anne, in whose mind a vague suspicion had taken root. Then she made a mental resolve to do a little private investigating on her own account.

When Grace reached home that night she found two boxes awaiting her.

"Oh, what can they be?" she cried in great excitement, for it was not every day that she found two imposing packages on the hall table, at the same time, addressed to her.

"Open them and see, little daughter," replied Grace's father, pinching her unscratched cheek.

The one was a large box of candy from her classmates, the contents of which they helped to devour the next day.

The other box held a bunch of violets and lilies of the valley. In this were two cards, "Mrs. Robert Nesbit" and "Mr. David Nesbit."

"Poor old David!" thought Grace, as she buried her nose in the violets. "He is trying to atone for Miriam's sins."

## CHAPTER XX

## A PIECE OF NEWS

After the excitement of the famous game came a great calm. The various teachers privately congratulated themselves on the marked improvement in lessons, and were secretly relieved with the thought that basketball was laid on the shelf for the rest of the school year.

Miriam Nesbit left Oakdale for a visit the Monday after the game, and did not return for two weeks. The general opinion seemed to be that she was ashamed of herself; but the expression on her face when she did return was not indicative of either shame or humility. She was more aggressive than before, and looked as though she considered the whole school far beneath her. She refused to even nod to Grace, Nora, Anne or Jessica, while Julia Crosby remarked with a cheerful grin that she guessed Miriam had forgotten that they had ever been introduced.

During the Easter holidays, Tom Gray came down and his aunt gave a dinner to her "adopted children" in honor of her nephew. Nora gave a fancy dress party to about twenty of her friends, while Grace invited the seven young people to a straw ride and a moonlight picnic in Upton Wood.

The days sped swiftly by, and spring came with her wealth of bud and bloom. During the long, balmy days Grace inwardly chafed at schoolbooks and lessons. She wanted to be out of doors. As she sat trying to write a theme for her advanced English class, one sunny afternoon during the latter part of April, she glanced frequently out the window toward the golf links that lay just beyond the High School campus. How she wished it were Saturday instead of only Wednesday. That very day she had arranged to play a game of golf with one of the senior class girls, who had made a record the previous year on the links. Grace felt rather flattered at the notice of the older girl, who was considered particularly exclusive, and rarely if ever paid any attention to the lower class girls. She had accidentally learned that Grace was an enthusiastic golfer, and therefore lost no time in asking her to play.

"I was awfully surprised when she asked me to play," confided Grace to her chums on the way home from school that afternoon.

"Oh, that's nothing," said Jessica. "She ought to feel honored to think you consented. You are really an Oakdale celebrity, you know."

"Please remember when you are basking in the light of her senior countenance that you once had friends among the sophomores," said Nora in a mournful tone.

"I consider both those remarks verging on idiotic," laughed Grace. "Don't you, Anne?"

"Certainly," replied Anne. "But let me add a word of caution. Don't allow this mark of senior caprice to turn your head. Remember you are——"

"You're worse than the others," cried Grace, "Let's change the subject."

Saturday proved a beautiful day, and with a light heart Grace started for the links with her golf bag strapped across her shoulder. The senior whose name was Ethel Post, sat waiting for her on one of the rustic benches set under a tree at one side of the starting place. She greeted Grace cordially and the two girls set to work without delay to demonstrate their prowess as golfers. The caddies, two small boys of Oakdale, who could be hired at the links by anyone desiring their services, carried the girls' clubs and hunted lost balls with alacrity.

Miss Post found that Grace was a foeman worthy of her steel. The young girl's arm was steady, and she delivered her strokes with decision. Grace came out two holes ahead.

Miss Post was delighted. "I hope you will golf with me often, Miss Harlowe," she said cordially. "It is so seldom one finds a really good player."

"I am fond of all games and outdoor sports," replied Grace, "but I like basketball best of all. Did you attend any of our games during the winter, Miss Post?"

"No," answered the senior. "I am not much interested in basketball. I really paid no attention to it this year, and haven't attended a game since I was a freshman. Speaking of basketball," continued Miss Post, "I picked up a paper last fall with a whole lot of basketball plays written on it. It was labeled 'Sophomore basketball signals,' and I turned it over to one of the girls in your class. She happened to be on the team, too, and seemed very glad to get it. I presume it was hers, although she didn't say so."

At the mention of the word signals, Grace pricked up her ears. As Miss Post innocently told of finding the list, Grace could hardly control herself. She wanted to get up and dance a jig on the green. She was about to learn the truth at last.

Trying to keep the excitement she felt out of her voice, Grace asked in a low tone, "Whom did you return it to, Miss Post?"

"Why, Miss Nesbit," was the answer. "I was inside the campus when I found it, and just then she passed me on the walk. I knew she was a sophomore, and thought it best to get rid of it, as I would probably have forgotten all about it, and it never would have been returned."

"Quite true," Grace replied, but she thought to herself that a great deal of unhappiness might have been avoided if Miss Post had only forgotten.

The talk drifted into other channels. Miss Post told Grace that she expected to sail for Europe as soon as school was over. In the fall she would return and enter Wellesley. She had crossed the ocean once before, and had done the continent. This time she intended to spend all of her time in Germany. Grace decided her new acquaintance to be a remarkably bright girl. At any other time she would have listened to her with absorbed interest, but try as she might, Grace could not focus her attention on what was being said. One thought was uppermost in her mind, that Miriam was the real culprit.

What was to be done about it? She would gain nothing by exposing Miriam to her classmates. There had been too much unpleasantness already. If there was only some way that Miriam could be brought to see the folly of her present course. Grace decided to tell Anne the news that night and ask her advice.

## CHAPTER XXI

## ANNE AND GRACE COMPARE NOTES

During the walk home from the links, Grace kept continually thinking, "I knew it was Miriam. She gave them to Julia." She replied rather absent-mindedly to Miss Post's comments, and left the older girl with the impression that Miss Harlowe was not as interesting as she had at first seemed.

Grace escaped from the supper table at the earliest opportunity, and seizing her hat, made for Anne's house as fast as her feet would take her. Anne opened the door for her.

"Oh, Anne, Anne! You never can guess what I know!" cried Grace, before she was fairly inside the house.

"Of course, I can't," replied Anne, "any more than you can guess what I know."

"Why, do you know something special, too?" demanded Grace.

"I do, indeed. But tell me your news first, and then I'll tell you mine," said Anne, pushing Grace into a chair.

"Mine's about Miriam," said Grace soberly.

"So is mine," was the reply, "and it's nothing creditable, either."

"Well," began Grace, "you know I went over to the golf links to-day with Ethel Post of the senior class."

Anne nodded.

"We were sitting on a bench resting after the game, and the subject of basketball came up. Before I knew it, she was telling me all about finding the list of signals you lost last fall. She gave them to one of our class, you can guess who."

"Miriam," said Anne.

"Yes, it was Miriam. I always suspected that she had more to do with it than anyone else. She gave Julia the signals, because she wanted to see me humiliated, and fastened suspicion on you to shield herself. She knew that I had boasted, openly, that my team would win. When Julia gave me the statement that cleared you in the eyes of the girls, she told me that she was under promise not to tell how she obtained the signals. But I'm sure she knew that I suspected Miriam. What do you think we ought to do about it?"

Grace looked anxiously at Anne.

"I don't know, yet," Anne replied. "Now listen to my news. I have felt ever since the game that your getting locked up was not accidental. I don't know why I felt so, but I did, nevertheless. So I set to work to find out if anyone else had been around there that day. I went to the janitress and asked her if she had noticed any one in the corridors before half past one. That was about the time that people began to come, you know. She said she hadn't. She was down in the basement and didn't go near the upstairs classrooms until after two o'clock. But when she did go up there she found this."

Anne held up a curious scarab pin that Grace immediately recognized. It was one that Miriam Nesbit often wore, and was extremely fond of.

"It's Miriam's," gasped Grace. "I wonder why——" She stopped. The reason Miriam had not made her loss known was plain. She was afraid to tell where and when she had lost her pin.

"I see," said Grace slowly. "It looks pretty bad, doesn't it? But why didn't the janitress take it straight to Miss Thompson? That's what she usually does with articles she finds."

"She missed seeing Miss Thompson that Saturday," said Anne. "When I hunted her up early Monday morning, in order to question her, she asked me if I had lost a pin. She said she had just returned one to Miss Thompson, and told me where she found it. I asked her to describe the pin, and at once recognized it. Every girl in school knows that scarab of Miriam's. There is nothing like it in Oakdale.

"For a minute I didn't know what to do. Don't you remember when Miriam first had it? She showed it to Miss Thompson, and Miss Thompson spoke of how curious it was. I knew that Miss Thompson would not be apt to forget it. I hurried up to her office and found her with the pin in her hand. She had sent for Miriam, but the messenger came back with the report that Miriam wasn't in school. She laid the pin down and said, 'What is it, Anne?' So I just asked her if she would let me have the pin. Of course, she looked surprised, and asked me if I knew to whom it belonged. I told her I did. Then she looked at me very hard, and asked me to tell her exactly why I wanted it. But, of course, I couldn't tell her, so I didn't say anything. Then she said: 'Anne, I know without being told why you want this pin. I am going to give it to you, and let you settle a delicate matter in your own way. I am sure it will be the right one.'"

"Anne Pierson, you bad child!" exclaimed Grace. "To think that you've kept this to yourself ever since the game. Why didn't you tell me?"

"I wanted to think what to do about it, before telling even you," Anne replied. "Yesterday I had a long talk with David. He knows everything that Miriam has done since the beginning of the freshman year. He feels dreadfully about it all. I think you and I ought to go to her and tell her that we are willing to forget the past and be her friends."

"It would do no good," said Grace dubiously. "She would simply laugh at us. I used to have dreams about making Miriam see the evil of her ways, but I have come to the conclusion that they were dreams, and nothing more."

"Let's try, anyway," said Anne. "David says she seems sad and unhappy, and is more gentle than she has been for a long time."

"All right, we'll beard the lion in her den, the Nesbit on her soil, if you say so. But I expect to be routed with great slaughter," said Grace with a shudder. "When do we go forth on our mission of reform?"

"We'll call on her to-morrow after school," Anne replied, "and don't forget that you once made the remark that you thought Miriam had a better self. You told me the day you read Julia Crosby's statement to the girls that you wouldn't give her up."

"I suppose that I shall have to confess that I did say so," laughed Grace. "But that was before she locked me up. She is so proud and stubborn that she will probably take the olive branch we hold out and trample upon it. After all, it really isn't our place to hold out olive branches anyway. She is the one who ought to eat humble pie. I feel ashamed to think I have to tell her what I know about her."

"So do I," responded Anne. "It's horrid to have to go to people and tell them about their misdeeds. I wouldn't propose going now if it weren't for David. He seems to think that she would be willing to behave if someone showed her how."

"All right," said Grace, "we'll go, but if we encounter a human tornado don't say I didn't warn you."

"That's one reason I want to go to her house," replied Anne. "If we approach her at school she is liable to turn on us and make a scene, or else walk off with her nose in the air. If we can catch her at home perhaps she will be more amenable to reason. But, if, to-morrow, she refuses to melt and be forgiven, then I wash my hands of her forever.

## CHAPTER XXII

## A RESCUE AND A REFORM

It was with considerable trepidation that Anne and Grace approached the Nesbit gate the following afternoon.

"I feel my knees beginning to wobble," Grace observed, as they rang the bell. "This business of being a reformer has its drawbacks. How had we better begin?"

"I don't know, the inspiration to say the right thing will probably come, when we see her," said Anne.

"If she behaves in her usual manner, I shall have a strong inspiration, to give her a good shaking," said Grace bluntly.

To their relief, the maid who answered the bell informed them that Miriam had gone out for a walk.

"Do you know which way she went?" Grace asked.

"I think, miss, that she went toward Upton Wood. She often walks there," replied the maid.

The girls thanked her and started down the walk.

"Miriam ought never to walk, alone, in Upton Wood, especially this time of year," remarked Grace. "There are any amount of tramps lurking around. If David knew it he would be awfully provoked."

"Let's walk over that way, and perhaps we'll meet her," suggested Anne. "Now that we've started, I hate to turn back. If we don't see her to-day, we'll keep on putting it off and end up by not seeing her at all."

"That's true," Grace agreed.

The two girls strolled along in the direction of Upton Wood, thoroughly enjoying their walk. Occasionally, they stopped to gather a few wild flowers, or listen to the joyous trill of a bird. They were at the edge of the wood, when Grace suddenly put up her hand.

"Hush!" she said. "I hear voices."

Just then the cry Help! Help! rang out.

"That's Miriam's voice," cried Grace.

Glancing quickly about for a weapon, Grace picked up a good-sized stick she found on the ground, and ran in the direction of the sound, Anne at her heels.

Miriam was struggling desperately to free herself from the grasp of a rough, unkempt fellow who had her by the arm and was trying to abstract the little gold watch that she wore fastened to her shirtwaist with a châtelaine pin.

The tramp stood with his back to the approaching girls. Before he was aware of their presence, Grace brought her stick down on his head with all the force she had in her strong, young arms.

With a howl of pain he released Miriam, whirling on his assailant. Grace hit him again, the force of her second blow knocking him over.

Before the man could regain his feet the three girls were off through the wood. They ran without looking back until fairly out in the open field.

"I don't see him," panted Grace, halting to get her breath. "I guess he's gone."

Anne was pale and trembling. The run out of the woods had been almost too much for her. As for Miriam, she was sobbing quite hysterically.

"Don't cry, Miriam," soothed Grace, putting her arm around the frightened girl. "He can't hurt you now. I am so glad that we happened along. You ought never to go into Upton Wood alone, you know."

Miriam gradually gained control of herself. Wiping her eyes, she asked, "How did you ever happen to be out here just at the time I needed help?"

"To tell the truth, we were hunting for you," Grace replied. "Your maid said that you had gone toward Upton Wood. We walked on, expecting every minute to meet you. Then we heard you scream and that's all."

"It's not all," said Miriam quickly. "I know I have been a wretch. I have made things unpleasant for you two girls ever since we started in at High School. I made fun of Anne, and tried to make her lose the freshman prize. I sent her that doll a year ago last Christmas, knowing that it would hurt her feelings. But the things I did last year aren't half as bad as all I've done this year, I gave——"

"That's just what we came to see you about, Miriam," interrupted Grace. "We know that you gave the signals to Julia, and we know that you locked me in the classroom the day of the big game."

Miriam flushed with shame and her lip quivered.

Seeing her distress, Grace went on quickly:

"The janitress found your scarab pin just outside the door on the day of the game. Anne has it here for you."

Anne fumbled in her purse and drew out the pin.

"But how did you get it?" asked Miriam faintly, as she took the pin with evident reluctance.

"Miss Thompson gave it to me," Anne answered.

Miriam looked frightened. "Then she knows——"

"Nothing," said Grace softly. "As soon as Anne heard that Miss Thompson had your pin and knew where it had been found, she went right to the office and asked Miss Thompson to give it to her. Miss Thompson thought from the first that I had been the victim of a trick. Anne knew that the finding of your pin would make her suspect you. She had already sent for you when Anne reached the office. Luckily you weren't in school. Anne asked permission to return the pin to you. She wouldn't give any reason for asking. Finally Miss Thompson handed it to her, and told Anne she was sure she would do what was right."

"You owe a great deal to Anne, Miriam," Grace continued, "for if she had not gone to Miss Thompson I am afraid you would have been suspended from school. Miss Thompson would have had very little mercy upon you, for she knew about those examination papers last June."

Miriam looked so utterly miserable and ashamed at Grace's words, that Anne hastened to say:

"I would have given you your pin at once, Miriam, but you were away from school. Then David told me how unhappy you seemed. I hadn't said a word to anyone about the pin until I told Grace. We decided to come and see you, and say that we were willing to 'let bygones be bygones' if you were. We thought it was right to let you know that we knew everything. There is only one other person who knows. That person is your brother."

"He knew I locked you up the day of the game," faltered Miriam, "The way he looked at me has haunted me ever since. He thinks me the most dishonorable girl in the world." She began to cry again.

Anne and Grace walked along silently beside the weeping girl. They thought it better to let her have her cry out. She really deserved to spend a brief season in the Valley of Humiliation.

They had now left the fields and were turning into one of the smaller streets of Oakdale.

"Miriam," said Grace, "try and brace up. We'll soon be on Main Street and you don't want people to see you cry, do you? Here," extracting a little book of rice powder paper from her bag, "rub this over your face and the marks of your tears won't show."

Miriam took the paper gratefully, and did as Grace bade her. Then she straightened up and gave a long sigh, "I feel like that man in Pilgrim's Progress, after he dropped his burden from his back," she said. "The mean things I did never bothered me until just lately. After I saw that my own brother had nothing but contempt for me, I began to realize what a wretch I was, and the remorse has been just awful."

It was David, after all, who had been instrumental in holding up the mirror so that his stubborn sister could see herself as others saw her. Although she had quarreled frequently with him, she had secretly respected his high standard of honor and fine principles. The fear that he despised her utterly had brought her face to face with herself at last.

"Anne has always wanted to be friends with you, Miriam," Grace said earnestly as they neared the Nesbit home. "You and I used to play together when we were little girls in the grammar school. It's only since we started High School that this quarreling has begun. Let's put it all aside and swear to be friends, tried and true, from now on? You can be a great power for good if you choose. We all ought to try to set up a high standard, for the sake of those who come after. Then Oakdale will have good reason to be proud of her High School girls."

They had reached the gate.

Miriam turned and stretched out a hand to each girl. There was a new light in her eyes. "My dear, dear friends," she said softly.

A shrill whistle broke in upon this little love feast and the three girls looked up. David was hurrying down the walk, his face aglow.

"I whistled to attract your attention. I was afraid you girls would go before I could reach you. Mother wants you girls to come in for dinner. She saw you from the window. Don't say you can't, for I'm going to call on the Piersons and Harlowes right now and inform them that their daughters are dining out to-night. So hurry along now, for mother's waiting for you."

A minute later he had mounted his motorcycle and was off down the street, going like the wind.

The girls entered the house and were warmly greeted by Mrs. Nesbit. She and David had viewed the little scene from the window. She had deeply deplored Miriam's attitude toward Grace and her chums. It was with delight that she and David had watched the three girls stop at the gate and clasp hands. She therefore hurried her son out to the girls to offer them her hospitality.

Anne had never before entered the Nesbit home. She thought it very beautiful and luxurious. Miriam put forth every effort to be agreeable, and the time passed so rapidly that they were surprised when dinner was announced.

After dinner, Miriam, who was really a brilliant performer for a girl of her age, played for them. Anne, who was a music-hungry little soul, listened like one entranced. David, seeing her absorption, beckoned to Grace, who stole softly out of the room without being observed.

Once out in the hall the two young people did a sort of wild dance to express their feelings.

"You are the best girl a fellow ever knew," said David in a whisper. "How did you do it?"

"I'll tell you some other time," whispered Grace, who had cautioned the girls to say nothing of the adventure for fear of frightening Miriam's mother. "Let's go back before they notice we're gone."

"Anne is too wrapped up in music to pay any attention to us. Come on up to my workshop. I want to show you something I'm working at in connection with my aëroplane. We can talk there, without being disturbed. I want to know what worked this transformation. It is really too good to be true. I've always wanted Miriam to be friends with Anne, but I had just about lost all hope."

Grace followed David up the stairs and through the hall to his workshop, which was situated at the back of the house.

"Now," said the young man, as he pushed forward a stool for his guest, "fire away."

Grace began with their call at the house, their walk in search of Miriam, and their adventure with the tramp, modestly making light of her own bravery. When she had finished, David held out his hand, his face glowing with appreciation "Grace," he said, "you've more spirit and courage than any girl I ever knew. You ought to have been a boy. You would have done great things."

Grace felt that this was the highest compliment David could pay her. She had always cherished a secret regret that she had been born a girl.

"Thank you, David," she said, blushing, then hastily changed the subject. "Tell me about your aëroplane. Is it still at the old Omnibus House?"

"Yes," David answered. "I had it here all winter, but I moved it out there again about a month ago."

"I should like to see it again," said Grace. "I didn't have time to look at it carefully the day you invited us out there."

"I'll take you over any time you want to go," said David. "Oh, better still, here's a duplicate key to the place. You can take the girls and go over there whenever you please, without waiting for me. You are the only person that I'd trust with this key, Grace," he added gravely. "I had it made in case old Jean or I should lose those we carry. I wouldn't even let the fellows have one, for fear they might go over there, get careless and do some damage."

"It's awfully good of you, David," Grace replied as she took the key. "I'll be careful not to lose it. I'll put it on my watch chain. It's such a small key it is not likely it will be noticed."

Grace took from her neck the long, silver chain from which her watch was suspended. She opened the clasp, slid the key on the chain and tucked both watch and key snugly into her belt.

"There," she said, patting it, "that can't get lost. My chain is very strong. I prefer a chain to a pin or fob, because either one is so easy to lose."

"That's sensible," commented David. "Girls wouldn't be eternally losing their watches if they weren't so vain about wearing those silly little châtelaine pins."

"Why, David Nesbit!" exclaimed Grace, glancing up at the mission clock on the wall. "It's almost nine o'clock! I had no idea it was so late. Let's go down at once."

They returned to the parlor to find Anne and Miriam deep in some foreign photographs that Miriam had collected during her trip to Europe the previous summer.

"How I should love to see Europe," sighed Anne. "I'm going there someday, though, if I live," she added with a sudden resolution.

"Mother and father have promised me a trip across as a graduation gift. Maybe you'll be able to go, too, by that time, Anne," said Grace hopefully.

"Perhaps I shall, but I'm afraid it's doubtful," said Anne, smiling a little.

"We've had a fine time, Miriam," said Grace, "but we really must go. Mother will worry if I stay any later."

"Please come again soon," said Miriam, kissing both girls affectionately. "I have a plan to talk over with you, but I can't say anything about it now. I must consult mother first. You'll like it, I'm sure."

"Of course we shall," responded Grace. "Good night, Miriam, and pleasant dreams."

"They are the nicest girls in Oakdale, and I shall try hard to be like them," thought Miriam, as she closed the door. "David is right. It certainly pays to be square."

# CHAPTER XXIII

## GRACE MEETS A DISTINGUISHED CHARACTER

June had come, bringing with it the trials and tribulations of final examinations. The days grew long and sunny. Roses nodded from every bush, but the pupils of Oakdale's two High Schools were far too busy to think about the beauty of the weather. Golf, tennis, baseball and other outdoor sports were sternly put aside, and the usual season of "cramming" set in. Young faces wore an almost tragic expression, and back lessons were reviewed with desperate zeal.

Grace Harlowe had crammed as assiduously as the rest, for a day or two. She was particularly shaky on her geometry. She went over her theorems until she came to triangles, then she threw the book down in disgust. "What's the use of cramming?" she said to herself. "If I keep on I won't even be able to remember that 'the hypotenuse of a right-angled triangle is equal to the sum of the squares of the other two sides.' I'm in a muddle over these triangles now. I'll find the girls and get them to go to the woods with me. I really ought to collect a few more botany specimens."

Grace's specimens were a source of keen delight to her girlish heart. She didn't care so much about pressing and mounting them. It was the joy she experienced in being in the woods that, to her, made botany the most fascinating of studies. She poked into secluded spots unearthing rare specimens. Her collection was already overflowing; still she could never resist adding just a few more.

She was doomed to disappointment as far as Nora and Jessica were concerned. Both girls mournfully shook their heads when invited to specimen-hunting, declaring regretfully they were obliged to study. Anne was at Mrs. Gray's attending to the old lady's correspondence. This had been her regular task since the beginning of the freshman year, and she never failed to perform it.

"Oh, dear, I wish examinations and school were over," Grace sighed impatiently. "I can't go to the woods alone, and I can't get any one to go with me. I suppose I'll have to give it up and go home. No, I won't, either. I'll go as far as the old Omnibus House. There are lots of wild plants in the orchard surrounding it, and I may get some new specimens."

With her basket on her arm, Grace turned her steps in the direction of the old house. She had not been there since the day of their reunion. She smiled to herself as she recalled the absurdities of that occasion.

After traversing the orchard several times and finding nothing startling in the way of specimens, Grace concluded that she might as well have stayed at home.

She walked slowly over to the steps and sat down, placing the basket beside her. "How lonely it seems here to-day," she thought. "I wonder where old Jean is? I haven't seen him for an age." Then she fell to musing over the school year so nearly ended. Everything that had happened passed through her mind like a panorama. It had been a stormy year, full of quarrels and bickering, but it was about to end gloriously. Anne and Miriam had become the best of friends, while she and Julia Crosby were daily finding out each other's good qualities There was nothing left to be desired.

Grace started from her dream and looked at her watch. It was after six o'clock. She had better be getting back.

She rose and reached for her basket.

Suddenly a figure loomed up before her. Grace started in surprise, to find herself facing a tall, thin man with wild, dark eyes. He stood with folded arms, regarding her fixedly.

Grace Found Herself Facing a Tall, Thin Man.

"Why, where——" but she got no further, for the curious new-comer interrupted her.

"Ah, Josephine," he said, "so I have found you at last."

"My name isn't Josephine at all. It's Grace Harlowe, and you have made a mistake," said Grace, endeavoring to pass him. But he barred her way, saying sadly:

"What, do you, too, pretend? Do you think I do not know you? I, your royal husband, Napoleon Bonaparte."

"Good gracious," gasped Grace. "He's crazy as can be. However shall I get away from him?"

The man heard the word "crazy" and exclaimed angrily: "How dare you call me crazy! You, of all people, should know I am sane. I have just returned from Isle of St. Helena to claim my empire. For years I have been an exile, but now I am free, free." He waved his arms wildly.

"Yes, of course I know you, now," said Grace, thinking to mollify him. "How strange that I didn't recognize you before."

Then she remembered reading in the paper of the preceding night of the escape of a dangerous lunatic from the state asylum, that was situated a few miles from Oakdale. This must be the man. Grace decided that he answered the description the paper had given. She realized that she would have to be careful not to anger him. It would require strategy to get clear of him.

"It's time you remembered me," returned Napoleon Bonaparte, petulantly. "They told me that you had died years ago, but I knew better. Now that I have found you, we'd better start for France at once. Have you your court robes with you? And what have you done with your crown? You are dressed like a peasant." He was disdainfully eyeing her brown, linen gown.

In spite of her danger, Grace could scarcely repress a laugh. It all seemed so ludicrous. Then a sudden thought seized her.

"You see, I have nothing fit to travel in," she said. "Suppose you wait here for me while I go back to town and get my things? then I can appear properly at court."

"No you don't," said Napoleon promptly, a cunning expression stealing into his face. "If you go you'll never come back. I need your influence at the royal court, and I can't afford to lose you. I am about to conquer the world. I should have done it long ago, if those villains hadn't exiled me, and locked me up."

He walked back and forth, muttering to himself still keeping his eye on Grace for fear that she might escape.

"Oh, what shall I do?" thought the terrified girl. "Goodness knows what he'll think of next. He may keep me here until dark, and I shall die if I have to stay here until then, I must get away."

Grace knew that it would be sheer folly to try to run. Her captor would overtake her before she had gone six yards, not to mention the fit of rage her attempted flight would be likely to throw him into.

She anxiously scanned the neighboring fields in the hope of seeing old Jean, the hunter. He was usually not far away. But look as she might, she could discover no sign of him. There was only one thing in her favor. It would be light for some time yet. Being June, the darkness would not descend for two hours. She must escape, but how was she to do it!

She racked her brain for some means of deliverance, but received no inspiration. Again she drew out her watch. Then her eye rested for a second on the little key that hung on her watch chain. It was the key to the lean-to in which David kept his aëroplane. Like a flash the way was revealed to her. But would she be able to carry out the daring design that had sprung into her mind? She would try, at any rate. With an unconcern that she was far from feeling, Grace walked carelessly toward the door of the lean-to.

The demented man was beside her in a twinkling He clutched Grace by the arm with a force that made her catch her breath.

"What are you trying to do!" he exclaimed, glaring at her savagely. "Didn't I tell you that you couldn't go away!"

He held her at arm's length with one hand, and threateningly shook his finger at her.

"Remember, once and for all, that I am your emperor and must be obeyed. Disregard my commands and you shall pay the penalty with your life. What is the life of one like you to me, when I hold the fate of nations in my hands? Perhaps it would be better to put an end to you now. Women are ever given over to intriguing and deception. You might betray me to my enemies. Yet, I believed you loyal in the past. I——"

"Indeed I have always been loyal, my emperor," interrupted Grace eagerly. "How can you doubt me?"

Her situation was becoming more precarious with every minute. She must persuade this terrible individual that she was necessary to his plans, if she wished to get away with her life.

"I have your welfare constantly at heart," she continued. "Have you ever thought of flying to our beloved France? In the shed behind me is a strange ship that flies through the air. Its sails are like the wings of a bird, and it flies with the speed of the wind. It waits to carry us across the sea. It is called an aëroplane."

"I have heard of such things," said Napoleon. "When I was in exile, a fool who came to visit me showed me a picture of one. He told me it could fly like a bird, but he lied. I believe you are lying, too," he added, looking at her suspiciously.

"Let me prove to you that I am not," Grace answered, trying to appear calm, though ready to collapse under the terrible strain of the part she was being forced to play. "Do you see this key? It unlocks the door that leads to the flying ship. Would you not like to look at it?" she said coaxingly.

"Very well, but be quick about it I have already wasted too much time with you. I must be off before my enemies find me."

"You must release my arm, or I cannot unlock the door," Grace said.

"Oh, yes, you can," rejoined Napoleon, not relaxing his grip for an instant. "Do you think I am going to run any risk of losing you?"

As she turned the key he swung her to one side, and, opening the door, peered cautiously in. For a moment he stood like a statue staring in wonder at David's aëroplane, then with a loud cry that froze the blood in Grace's veins, he threw up his arms and rushed madly into the shed, shouting, "We shall fly, fly, fly!"

With a sob of terror Grace slammed the door and turned the key. She was not an instant too soon. Napoleon Bonaparte reached it with a bound and threw himself against it, uttering blood-curdling shrieks. The frightful sounds came to Grace's ears as she tore across the field in the direction of

Oakdale. Terror lent wings to her feet. Every second was precious. She did not know how long the door would stand against the frantic assaults of the maniac.

She had reached the road, when, to her joy and relief, she beheld half a dozen men approaching. Stumbling blindly toward them, she panted out: "The crazy man—I—locked—him—in—the Omnibus House. Here—is—the key." She gave a long, shuddering sigh, and for the first time in her life sturdy Grace Harlowe fainted.

The men picked her up tenderly.

"Here, Hampton," said one of them, "take this child over to the nearest house. She is all in. By George, I wonder whether she has locked that lunatic up? Something has certainly upset her. We'd better get over there right away and see what we can find out."

The man addressed as Hampton picked Grace up as though she had been a baby and carried her to a house a little further up the road.

Meanwhile the men hurried on, arriving at the Omnibus House just as Napoleon succeeded in breaking down the door. Before he could elude them, he was seized by five pairs of stalwart arms. He fought like a tiger, making it difficult to bind him. This was finally accomplished though they were obliged to carry him, for he had to be tied up like a papoose to keep him from doing damage. He raved continually over the duplicity of Josephine, threatening dire vengeance when he should find her.

When Grace came to herself she looked about her in wonder. She was lying on a comfortable couch in a big, cheerful sitting room. A kindly faced woman was bathing her temples, while a young girl chafed her hands.

"Where am I?" said Grace feebly. "Did Napoleon get out?"

"Lie still and rest, my dear," said Mrs. Forrest, "Don't try to exert yourself."

Grace sat up and looked about her. "Oh, I know what happened. I fainted. How silly of me. I never did that in my life before. I had a terrible scare, but I'm all right now."

The man who had carried her to the house came forward.

"My name is Hampton, miss. I am a guard over at the asylum. Those other men you saw are employed there, too. We were looking for one of our people who escaped night before last. He nearly killed his keeper. He's the worst patient we have out there. Thinks he's Napoleon. Judging from your fright, I guess you must have met him. Did you really lock him in that old house?"

"Indeed I did," answered Grace, who was rapidly recovering from the effects of her fright. "He took me for the Empress Josephine." She related all that had happened, ending with the way she locked his emperorship in.

"Well, all I've got to say is that you're the pluckiest girl I ever came across," said the man admiringly, when Grace had finished.

But she shook her head.

"I never was so frightened in my life before. I shall never forget his screams."

It was after eight o'clock when Grace Harlowe arrived at her own door. The man Hampton had insisted on calling a carriage, so Grace rode home in state. As she neared the house she saw that the lawn and porch were full of people.

"What on earth is the matter!" she asked herself. As she alighted from the carriage her mother rushed forward and took her in her arms.

"My darling child," she sobbed. "What a narrow escape you have had. You must never, never wander off alone again."

"Why, mother, how did you know anything about it?"

"When you didn't come home to supper I felt worried, for you had not told me that you were invited anywhere. Then Nora came down to see you, and seemed surprised not to find you at home. She said you had gone on a specimen hunt after school. I became frightened and sent your father out at once to look for you. He met the keepers with that dreadful man," said Mrs. Harlowe, shuddering, "and they described you, telling him where you were and how they had met you. Your father went straight out to the Forrests. I suppose you just missed him."

Grace hugged her mother tenderly. "Don't worry, mother. I'm all right. What are all these people standing around for?"

"They came to see you, of course. The news is all over town. Everyone is devoured with curiosity to hear your story."

"It looks as though I had become a celebrity at last," laughed Grace.

She was obliged to tell the story of her adventure over and over again that night to her eager listeners. Her chums hung about her adoringly. Hippy, Reddy and David were fairly beside themselves.

"Oh, you lunatic snatcher," cried Hippy, throwing up his hat to express his feelings.

"You never dreamed that the little key you gave me would prove my salvation," said Grace to David, as her friends bade her good night. "It surely must have been fate."

# CHAPTER XXIV

## COMMENCEMENT

Examinations had ceased to be bug-bears and kill joys to the young idea of Oakdale. The last paper had been looked over, and the anxious hearts of the majority of the High School pupils had been set at rest. In most cases there was general rejoicing over the results of the final test. Marks were compared and plans for the next year's course of study discussed.

The juniors were about to come into their own. When the present seniors had been handed their diplomas, and Miss Thompson and Mr. Cole had wished them god-speed, the present juniors would start on the home stretch that ended in commencement, and a vague awakening to the real duties of life.

The senior class stood for the time being in the limelight of public attention. It was the observed of all observers. Teas were given in honor of its various members, and bevies of young girls in dainty summer apparel brightened the streets of Oakdale, during the long sunny afternoons.

It was truly an eventful week. Grace Harlowe gave a tea in honor of Ethel Post, which was a marked social success. The two girls had become thoroughly well acquainted over their golf and had received great benefit from each other's society. Miss Post's calm philosophical view of life had a quieting effect on impulsive Grace, while Grace's energy and whole-hearted way of diving into things proved a stimulus to the older girl.

It was Tuesday afternoon and class day. High School girls in gala attire were seen hurrying up the broad walk leading to the main door of the school building.

It was the day of all days, to those about to graduate. Of course, receiving one's diploma was the most important feature, but class day lay nearest the heart.

The exercises were to be held in the gymnasium.

The junior and senior classes had brought in half the woods to beautify the big room, and Oakdale gardens had been ruthlessly forced to give up their wealth of bud and bloom in honor of the occasion.

It was customary for the seniors to invite the junior class, who always sat in a body at one side of the gymnasium; while the seniors sat on the opposite side. The rest of the space was given up to the families of the seniors and their friends. Lucky, indeed, were those who could obtain an invitation to this most characteristic of class functions.

The four girl chums had been among the fortunate recipients of invitations. A very pretty picture they made as they followed the usher, one of the junior class, to their seats.

Grace wore a gown of pale blue organdie that was a marvel of sheer daintiness. Jessica, a fetching little affair of white silk muslin sprinkled with tiny pink rosebuds; while Anne and Nora were resplendent in white lingerie gowns. Anne's frock was particularly beautiful and the girls had exclaimed with delight over it when they first caught sight of her.

It was a present from Mrs. Gray, Anne told them. She had fully expected to wear her little white muslin, but the latter had grown rather shabby and she felt ashamed of it. Then a boy appeared with a big box addressed to her. Wrapped in fold after fold of tissue paper lay the exquisite new gown. Pinned to one sleeve was a note from Mrs. Gray, asking her to accept the gift in memory of the other Anne—Mrs. Gray's young daughter—who had passed away years ago. There were tears in Anne's eyes as she told them about it, the girls agreeing with her that there was no one in the world quite so utterly dear as Mrs. Gray.

"I'm glad we're early," whispered Nora. "We can watch the classes come in. See, that place is for the juniors. It is roped off with their colors and the other side belongs to the seniors."

"How fine the gym. looks," remarked Anne. "They certainly must have worked hard to fix it up so beautifully."

"Julia Crosby is largely responsible for it," answered Grace. "She has the most original ideas about decorations and things. You know the juniors always decorate for the seniors. It's a sacred duty."

"Did you know that Julia was elected president of her class?" asked Jessica.

"Oh, yes," said Grace, "she told me about it the other day. Oh, girls, here they come! Doesn't Ethel Post look sweet? There's Julia at the head of her class."

"It is certainly great to be a graduate," sighed Nora.

"Speaking of graduation," said Grace, "did you know that David has put off his graduation for another year! He wished to finish school with Hippy and Reddy. They have planned to enter the same college. So our little crowd will be together for one more year."

"How nice of him," cried the girls.

"Yes, isn't it! I'll be awfully sorry when my turn comes," responded Grace. "I'm sure I shall never care for college as I do for this dear old school."

"You can't tell until you've tried it," said Nora wisely.

The two classes had now seated themselves, and an expectant hush fell upon those assembled. The first number on the program was a song by the senior glee club. This was followed by the salutatory address, given by a tall dignified senior. The class poem came next, and was received with enthusiasm. The other numbers followed in rapid succession, each being applauded to the echo. The class grinds were hailed with keen relish. Each girl solemnly rose to take her medicine in the form of mild ridicule over some past harmless folly.

The class prophecy provoked ripples of merriment from the audience.

Grace chuckled with glee at the idea of exclusive Ethel Post becoming the proprietor of a moving-picture show at Coney Island. The futures prophesied for the other members of the class were equally remarkable for their impossibility.

At last nothing remained but the senior charge and the junior reply. The president of the senior class rose, and facing the juniors poured forth her final words of advice and counsel. She likened them to a baby in swaddling clothes, and cautioned them to be careful about standing on their feet too early. It was the usual patronizing speech so necessary to class day.

Julia Crosby smiled a little as the senior exhorted her hearers to never forget the dignity of their station. She was thinking of the day she crashed into that young woman, in the corridor. The senior president had manifested the dignity of her station then.

Julia straightened her face and stepped forward to make her reply. She thanked the president for her solicitude and tender counsel. She humbly acknowledged that the juniors were helpless infants, entirely innocent of the wicked world. They realized that they needed proper nourishment and exercise. There was one consolation however, they were daily growing larger and wiser, and their lungs were strong. If all went well they hoped to be healthy, well-grown seniors, capable of giving sage advice to those who would follow them.

Grace's face was full of eager appreciation as she listened to Julia's clever speech. How greatly she had changed, and what a power she would be in her class during the senior year. Grace felt that her sophomore year, though dark in the beginning, was about to end in a blaze of glory.

Julia sat down amid demonstrations of approval. Then the first notes of "Auld Lang Syne" sounded on the piano, and the entire audience, led by the senior glee club, rose to their feet to join in that sweetest of old songs whose plaintive melody causes heart strings to tighten and eyes to fill.

The four chums silently joined hands as they sang, and mentally resolved that with them "auld acquaintance" should never "be forgot."

There was a second's pause after the song was done. Then clear on the air rose the senior class yell. That broke the spell. Those who had felt lumps rising in their throats at the music, laughed. A buzz of conversation began, and soon the graduates were surrounded by their families and friends.

The gymnasium gradually cleared. The seniors hurried off to their banquet on the lawn and one more class day glided off to find its place with those of the past.

"Wasn't it perfectly lovely?" sighed Jessica, as they made their way out.

"I think commencement week has even more thrills in it than Christmas," Nora replied. "Wait till we have our class day. You shall write the class poem, Anne, and Jessica the song."

"I speak for the class prophecy," said Grace.

"That leaves nothing for me but the grinds. But that job would be greatly to my taste," said Nora.

"What about the rest of the class?" inquired Anne, smiling at this monopoly of class honors. "Are we to carry off all the glory!"

"Without a doubt," Jessica answered. "After us there are no more."

"Be sure to come to my house for supper Thursday evening," said Grace. "We are to go to commencement together, you know. The boys are coming, too."

The chums parted with many expressions of satisfaction over the pleasant afternoon's entertainment.

Thursday evening found them impatiently awaiting the boys.

"I suppose they all stopped to fuss and prink," said Nora, as she peered through the vines that screened the porch. "Men are, truly, vainer than girls. There they come around the corner, now. I really believe Hippy is growing fatter. He looks awfully nice to-night, though," she hastily added.

Hippy had a friend in Nora.

"Did you know that Tom Gray is in town?" asked David, as he took his place beside Anne and Grace. The latter carried an immense bouquet of red roses to give to Ethel Post.

"Oh, how nice!" exclaimed Grace. "I suppose he'll be there to-night with dear Mrs. Gray."

"Yes, they are going," said David. "I don't believe Mrs. Gray has missed a commencement for the last twenty years."

"I wonder who'll get the freshman prize this year?" mused Grace. "I hope it goes to some girl who really needs it. I know one thing; there will be no claimant for the hundred dollar prize this year. Anne broke the record."

"Indeed she did," said David, looking fondly at Anne. "To be in company with Oakdale's star prize winner is a great honor."

"Oh, don't," said Anne who hated compliments.

"Very well, if you spurn the truth," replied David. "By the way, I have an invitation to deliver. Miriam wants all of you to come up to our house the minute the exercises are over to-night. Never mind if it is late. Commencement comes but once a year."

"De-lighted," chorused the chums.

"Hush," said Hippy. "Make no uproar. We are about to enter the sacred precincts of Assembly Hall. I feel that on account of my years of experience I must make myself responsible for the behavior of you children. Smother that giggle, Nora O'Malley," he commanded, looking at Nora with an expression of severity that set oddly on his fat, good-natured face.

This made the whole party laugh, and Hippy declared, disgustedly, that he considered them quite ignorant of the first principles of good behavior.

They were seated in the hall at last, and for the next two hours listened with serious attention to the essays and addresses of the graduates.

Grace had sent Ethel Post her roses as soon as she entered the hall, and had the pleasure of seeing them in her friend's hands.

The diplomas were presented, and the freshman prize given out. It was won by a shy-looking little girl with big, pleading, brown eyes. Grace watched her closely as she walked up to receive it and resolved to find out more about her.

"She looks as though she needed friends," was her mental comment.

Anne, too, felt drawn toward the slender little girl. She recalled her freshman commencement and her total collapse after the race had been won.

"I hope that little girl has friends as good and true as mine," she whispered to Grace.

"Don't you think she looks lonely?" Grace asked.

"She surely does," returned Anne. "Let's find out all about her."

"Done," Grace replied.

As soon as the exercises were over the young people hurried over to where Tom Gray and his aunt stood talking with friends.

"Well, well," sighed the old lady joyously, "here are all my own children. I am so glad to see you. I understand that I am too late with my invitation for an after gathering. Miriam has forestalled me," she added, placing her arm around Miriam, whose face glowed with pleasure at the caress.

"She has invited me, too, so I am not to complain. As many as there are room can ride in my carriage. The rest will have go in Tom's."

"Tom's?" was the cry, "When did he acquire a carriage?"

"Come and see it," was Tom's reply.

They all trooped out, Hippy leading the van.

"I wish to be the first to look upon the miracle," he cried.

"It's a peach," he shouted, as the others came up, and he was right.

"O Tom, isn't it great?" Grace exclaimed.

Directly in front of Mrs. Gray's carriage stood a handsome Packard car.

"Aunt Rose gave it to me, to-day," he explained, his face glowing. "It has been waiting a week for me. Come on, everybody, and we'll get up steam and fly to Nesbit's."

Of course everyone wanted to ride in the new car. David and Anne decided, however, to go with Mrs. Gray, and with a honk! honk! the automobile was off.

The Nesbit home was ablaze with light. Mrs. Nesbit stood in the wide hall waiting to receive Miriam's guests.

"The first thing to do is to find food," declared David, leading the way to the dining room.

The whole party exclaimed with admiration at the tastefully decorated table. A huge favor pie in the shape of a deep red rose ornamented the center, the ribbons reaching to each one's place. There were pretty, hand-painted place cards, too, tied with red and gold, the sophomore colors.

Mrs. Gray occupied the place of honor at the head of the table. She was fairly overflowing with happiness and good cheer, as she beamed on first one and then another of her children.

The young people did ample justice to the delicious repast served them. The favor pie created much amusement, as the favors were chosen to suit the particular personality of each guest. After every one had finished eating, a season of toasts followed.

"Here's to dear Mrs. Gray," said David, raising his glass of fruit punch, "May she live to be one hundred years old, and grow younger every day. Drink her down."

Mrs. Gray proposed a toast to Mrs. Nesbit, which was drunk with enthusiasm. Presently everyone had been toasted, then Miriam rose and begged permission to speak.

It was unanimously granted.

"I suppose you all think I invited you here to-night for the express purpose of having a good time," she said. "So I did. But now that you are here, I want to talk to you about a plan that I hope you will like. It rests with you whether or not it materializes. You know that we have a cottage at Lake George, although we do not always spend our summers there. But I want to go there this year, and you can make it possible for me to do so."

"We'll carry your luggage and put you on the train, if that will help you out any," volunteered Hippy.

Miriam laughed. "That isn't enough," she said. "I want every one of you to go, too, Now don't say a word until I'm through. Mother has given her consent to a house party, and will chaperon us. Don't one of you refuse,for I shall pay no attention to you. You simply must come. We are to start next Tuesday, and stay as long as we like. So you'll have to make your preparations in a hurry. We'll meet at the station next Tuesday morning at 9.30. That's all."

Then what a babble arose. Grace and Nora were in high glee over the proposed trip. They were sure of going. Anne was rather dubious at first, but Grace overruled her objections, and made fun of Jessica for saying she had promised to visit her aunt.

"Go and visit your aunt afterwards, Jessica. Remember, she is a secondary matter when compared to us," she said laughingly.

"I shall take my car," said Tom. "That will help things along."

"Mother has promised me one," remarked David, "so we'll have plenty of means of conveyance.

"How sorry I am that you can't go, too, Aunt Rose," exclaimed Tom regretfully.

"Nonsense," replied his aunt, "you don't want an old woman at your heels all the time. Besides, I must visit my brother in California this summer. I haven't seen him for several years."

"Let's drink to the success of the house party," cried Reddy, "and pledge ourselves to be on time next Tuesday morning. Drink her down."

When next we meet our Oakdale boys and girls, they will have returned to their books after a long happy summer. In "GRACE HARLOWE'S JUNIOR YEAR AT HIGH SCHOOL"; Or, "FAST FRIENDS IN THE SORORITIES," the girl chums will appear as members of a High School sorority. Here the reader will make the acquaintance of Eleanor Savell, a clever but exceedingly willful girl, whose advent in Oakdale High School brings about a series of happenings that make the story one of absorbing interest. The doings of a rival sorority, organized by Eleanor, the contest for dramatic honors between Eleanor and Anne Pierson and the mischievous plot against the latter originated by the former and frustrated by Grace Harlowe, are among the features that will hold the attention and cement the reader's friendship for the girl chums.

## THE END

Jessie Graham Flower, A.M.

Grace Harlowe's Junior Year
at High School

OR

Fast Friends in the Sororities

By
JESSIE GRAHAM FLOWER, A.M.

Author of Grace Harlowe's Plebe Year at High School, Grace Harlowe's
Sophomore Year at High School, Grace Harlowe's Senior
Year at High School, etc.

Illustrated

PHILADELPHIA
HENRY ALTEMUS COMPANY

COPYRIGHT, 1911, BY HOWARD E. ALTEMUS

# CHAPTER I

## A NEW ARRIVAL

"Next to home, there is really nothing quite so satisfying as our dear old High School!" exclaimed Grace Harlowe, as she entered the locker-room and beamed on her three friends who stood nearby.

"It does seem good to be back, even though we have had such a perfectly glorious summer," said Jessica Bright. "We are a notch higher, too. We're actually juniors. This locker-room is now our property, although I don't like it as well as the one we had last year."

"We'll get accustomed to it, and it will seem like home inside of two weeks," said Anne Pierson philosophically. "Everything is bound to change in this world, you know. 'We must put ourselves in harmony with the things among which our lot is cast.'"

"Well, Marcus Aurelius, we'll try to accept your teaching," laughed Grace, who immediately recognized the quotation as coming from a tiny "Marcus Aurelius Year Book" that Anne kept in her desk and frequently perused.

"I wonder what school will bring us this year?" mused Nora O'Malley, as she retied her bow for the fifth time before the mirror and critically surveyed the final effect. "We had a stormy enough time last year, goodness knows. Really, girls, it is hard to believe that Miriam Nesbit and Julia Crosby were at one time the banes of our existence. They come next to you three girls with me, now."

"I think that we all feel the same about them," replied Grace. "Miriam is a perfect dear now, and is just as enthusiastic over class matters as we are."

"It looks as though everything were going to be plain sailing this year," said Jessica. "There isn't a disturbing element in the class that I know of. Still, one can never tell."

"Oh, here come Eva Allen and Marian Barber," called Grace

delightedly, and rushed over to the newcomers with outstretched hands.

By this time girls began to arrive rapidly, and soon the locker-room hummed with the sound of fresh, young voices. Coats of tan were compared and newly acquired freckles deplored, as the girls stood about in groups, talking of the delights of the summer vacation just ended.

To the readers of "GRACE HARLOWE'S PLEBE YEAR AT HIGH SCHOOL," and "GRACE HARLOWE'S SOPHOMORE YEAR AT HIGH SCHOOL," the girl chums have become familiar figures. It will be remembered how Grace Harlowe and her friends, Nora O'Malley and Jessica Bright, during their freshman year, became the firm friends of Anne Pierson, the brilliant young girl who won the freshman prize offered each year to the freshmen by Mrs. Gray. The reader will recall the repeated efforts of Miriam Nesbit, aided by Miss Leece, the algebra teacher, to disgrace Anne in the eyes of the faculty, and the way each attempt was frustrated by Grace Harlowe and her friends. Mrs. Gray's house party, the winter picnic in Upton Wood, and Anne Pierson's struggles to escape her unworthy father all contributed toward making the story stand out in the reader's mind.

In "GRACE HARLOWE'S SOPHOMORE YEAR," the girl chums were found leading their class in athletics. Here, Miriam Nesbit, still unsubdued, endeavored once more to humiliate Anne Pierson, and to oust Grace from her position as captain of the basketball team, being aided in her plan by Julia Crosby, captain of the junior team, against whom the sophomores had engaged to play a series of three games. Grace's brave rescue of Julia Crosby during a skating party and the latter's subsequent repentance restored good feeling between the two classes, and the book ended with the final conversion of Miriam after her long and stubbornly nursed enmity.

David Nesbit's trial flight in his aëroplane, Grace's encounter with the escaped lunatic, who imagined himself to be Napoleon Bonaparte, were among the features which made the book absorbing from start to finish.

The clang of the first bell broke in upon the chattering groups, and obedient to its summons, the girls moved slowly out of the locker-room and down the corridor, talking in subdued tones as they strolled toward the study hall.

Miss Thompson stood at her desk, serene and smiling, as the girls filed in.

"How well Miss Thompson looks," whispered Grace to Anne as they neared their seats. "Let's go up and see her when this session is over. It's sure to be short this morning."

It was customary on the opening of school for the members of the various classes to take their seats of the previous year. Then the sections were rearranged, the seniors taking the seats left by the graduates, and the other classes moving up accordingly. The first day of school amounted to really nothing further than being    assigned to one's seat and getting used to the idea of school again. Miss Thompson usually addressed the girls on the duty of High School students, and the girls went forth full of new resolutions that last for at least a week.

Grace looked curiously about her. She wondered if there were to be many new girls that year. The present freshmen, direct from the Grammar Schools, sat on the front seats looking a trifle awed at the idea of being academic pupils, and feeling very strange and uncomfortable under the scrutiny of so many pairs of eyes.

Her glance wandered toward the new sophomore class, as though in search of someone, her eyes brightening as she caught sight of the brown-eyed girl who had won the freshman prize the previous June. The latter looked as helpless and friendless as when Grace first saw her step up on the platform to receive her money. "I shall certainly find out more about that child," she decided. "What is her name? I heard it at commencement, but I have forgotten it."

Taking a leaf from a little note-book that she always carried, Grace wrote: "Do you see the freshman-prize girl over among the sophomores? What is her name? I can't remember." Then, folding the paper, she tossed it to Anne, who nodded; then wrote, "Mabel Allison," and handed it to the girl sitting opposite her, who obligingly passed it over to Grace.

With a nod of thanks to Anne, Grace glanced at the paper and then at the owner of the name, who sat with her hands meekly folded on her desk, listening to Miss Thompson as though her life depended upon hearing every word that the principal uttered.

"I want all my girls to try particularly this year to reach a higher standard than ever before," Miss Thompson concluded, "not only in your studies, but in your attitude toward one another. Be straightforward and honorable in all your dealings, girls; so that when the day comes for you to receive your diplomas and bid Oakdale High School farewell, you can do so with the proud consciousness that you have been to your schoolmates just what you would have wished them to be to you. I know of no better preparation for a happy life than constant observation of the golden rule.

"And now I hope I shall have no occasion to deliver another lecture during the school year," said the principal, smiling. "There can be no formation of classes to-day, as the bulletins of the various subjects have just been posted, and will undoubtedly undergo some changes. It would be advisable, however, to arrange as speedily as possible about the subjects you intend to take, as we wish to begin recitations by Friday at the latest, and I dare say the changes made in the schedule will be slight."

Then the work of assigning each class to its particular section of the study hall began. The seniors moved with evident pride into the places reserved for the first class, while the freshmen looked visibly relieved at having any place at all to call their own. Immediately after this the classes were dismissed, and a general rush was made to the end of the great room, where the bulletins were posted.

Grace, Nora, Anne and Jessica wished to recite in the same classes as far as could be arranged, and a lively confab ensued as to what would be best to take. They all decided on solid geometry and English reading, as they could be together for these classes, but the rest was not so easy, for Nora, who loathed history, was obliged to take ancient history to complete her history group, the other girls having wisely completed theirs the previous year. Jessica wanted to take physical geography, Anne rhetoric, and Grace boldly announced a hankering for zoölogy.

"How horrible," shuddered Jessica. "How can you bear to think of cutting up live cats and dogs and angleworms and things".

"Oh, you silly," laughed Grace. "You're thinking of vivisection. I wouldn't cut up anything alive for all the world. The girls did dissect crabs and lobsters, and even rabbits, last year, but they were dead long before they ever reached the zoölogy class."

"Oh," said Jessica, somewhat reassured, "I'm glad to hear that, at any rate."

"That makes three subjects," said Nora. "Now we want one more. Are any of you going to be over ambitious and take five?"

"Not I," responded Grace and Jessica in chorus.

"I shall," said Anne quietly. "I'm going to learn just as much as I can while I have the chance."

"Well," said Jessica, "you're different. Five studies aren't any harder for you than four for us."

"Thank the lady prettily for her high opinion of your ability, Anne," said Grace, laughing. "She really seems to be sincere."

"She's too sincere for comfort," murmured Anne, who hated compliments.

"We haven't settled on that fourth subject yet," interposed Nora.

"Why don't you all take French, it is such a beautiful language," said a soft voice behind them. "I'm sure you'd like it."

The four girls turned simultaneously at the sound of the strange, soft voice, to face a girl whose beauty was almost startling. She was a trifle taller than Grace and beautifully straight and slender. Her hair was jet black and lay on her forehead in little silky rings, while she had the bluest eyes the girls had ever seen. Her features were small and regular, and her skin as creamy as the petal of a magnolia. She stood regarding the astonished girls with a fascinating little smile that was irresistible.

"Please excuse me for breaking in upon you, but I saw you from afar, and you looked awfully good to me." Her clear enunciation made the slang phrase sound like the purest English. "I have just been with your principal in her office. She told me to come here and look over the list of subjects. Do you think me unpardonably rude?" She looked appealingly at the four chums.

"Why, of course not," said Grace promptly, recovering in a measure from her first surprise. "I suppose you are going to enter our school, are you not? Let me introduce you to my friends." She named her three chums in turn, who bowed cordially to the attractive stranger.

"My name is Grace Harlowe. Will you tell me yours?"

"My name is Eleanor Savell," replied the new-comer, "and I have just come to Oakdale with my aunt. We have leased a quaint old house in the suburbs called 'Heartsease.' My aunt fell quite in love with it, so perhaps we shall stay awhile. We travel most of the time, and I get very tired of it," she concluded with a little pout.

"'Heartsease'?" cried the girls in chorus. "Do you live at 'Heartsease'?"

"Yes," said the stranger curiously. "Is there anything peculiar about it?"

"Oh, no," Grace hastened to reply. "The reason we are interested is because we know the owner of the property, Mrs. Gray, very well."

"Oh, do you know her?" replied Eleanor lightly. "Isn't she a dainty, little, old creature? She looks like a Dresden shepherdess grown old. For an elderly woman, she really is interesting."

"We call her our fairy godmother," said Anne, "and love her so dearly that we never think of her as being old." There had been something about the careless words that jarred upon Anne.

"Oh, I am sure she is all that is delightful," responded Miss Savell, quickly divining that Anne was not pleased at her remark. "I hope to know her better."

"You are lucky to get 'Heartsease,'" said Grace. "Mrs. Gray has refused over and over again to rent it. It belonged to her favorite brother, who willed it to her when he died. She has always kept it in repair. Even the furniture has not been changed. I have been there with her, and I love every bit of it. I am glad to know that it has a tenant at last."

"Mrs. Gray knew my aunt years ago. They have kept up a correspondence for ever so long. It was due to her that we came here," said Eleanor.

"Is your aunt Miss Margaret Nevin?" asked Anne quietly.

"Why, how did you know her name?" cried Eleanor, apparently mystified. "'This is getting curiouser and curiouser.'"

The four girls laughed merrily.

"Anne is Mrs. Gray's private secretary," explained Jessica. "She tends to all her correspondence. I suppose you have written more than one letter to Miss Savell's aunt, haven't you, Anne!"

"Yes, indeed," replied Anne. "Her name is very familiar to me."

"What class are you girls in?" said Eleanor, abruptly changing the subject. "Or aren't you all in the same class?"

"We are all juniors," laughed Nora, "and proud of it. Our green and callow days are over, and we have entered into the realm of the upper classes."

"Then I shall enter the junior class, too, for I choose to hob-nob with you girls. Don't say you don't want me, for I have made up my mind; and it is like the laws of the Medes and Persians, unchangeable."

"We shall be glad to welcome a new classmate, of course," responded Grace. "I hope you will soon be one of us. Did Miss Thompson say that you would have to take examinations?"

"She did, she did," answered Eleanor ruefully. "Still I'm not much afraid. I've studied with a tutor, so I'm pretty well up in mathematics and English. I can speak French, German, Italian and Spanish almost as well as English. You know I've lived most of my life abroad. I'll manage to pass somehow."

"I should think you would," exclaimed Anne admiringly. "I hope you pass, I'm sure. Perhaps you'll be too far advanced for our class."

"Never fear, my dear," said Eleanor. "My heart is with the juniors, and leave it to me not to land in any other class. But, really, I've bothered you long enough. I must go back to your principal and announce myself ready to meet my fate. I hope to know you better when examinations have ceased to be a burden and the weary are at rest. That is, if I survive."

With a gay little nod, and a dazzling smile that revealed almost perfect teeth, she walked quickly down the long room and out the door, leaving the girl chums staring after her.

"What an extraordinary girl!" said Jessica. "She acts as though she'd known us all her life, and we never set eyes on her until she marched in and calmly interrupted us ten minutes ago."

"It doesn't seem to make much difference whether or not we like her. She has decided she likes us, and that settles it," said Grace, smiling. "What do you think of her, Anne? You are a pretty good judge of character."

"I don't know yet," replied Anne slowly. "She seems charming. She must be awfully clever, too, to know so many languages, but——"

"But what?" queried Nora.

"Oh, I don't know just what I want to say, only let's proceed slowly with her, then we'll never have anything to regret."

"Come on, girls," said Jessica impatiently. "Let's hurry. You know we promised to meet the boys as soon as school was over."

The girl chums walked out of the study hall, each with her mind so full of the new girl, who had so suddenly appeared in their midst, that the proposed call upon Miss Thompson was entirely forgotten.

# CHAPTER II

## CONFIDENCES

"I am the bearer of an invitation," announced Anne Pierson as the four girls collected in one corner of the locker-room during the brief recess allowed each morning.

"Mrs. Gray wishes to see us all at four o'clock this afternoon. We are to dine with her and spend the evening, and the boys are invited for the evening, too. So we will have just time enough after school to go home and dress."

"You had better meet at my house, then," said Grace, "for it's on the way to Mrs. Gray's. Good-bye. Be sure and be there at a quarter of four at the latest."

Promptly at the appointed time the girls hurried up the Harlowe walk. They were met at the door by Grace, who had been standing at the window for the last ten minutes with hat and gloves on, impatiently waiting their arrival.

As they neared Mrs. Gray's beautiful home, Anne said in a low tone to Grace, who was walking with her, "I suppose Mrs. Gray has a double motive in asking us up here to-day. I believe she wants to talk to us about Eleanor Savell. Miss Nevin called on Mrs. Gray yesterday and they were in the parlor together for a long time. After Miss Nevin had gone, Mrs. Gray told me that Miss Nevin was anxious that Eleanor should associate with girls of her own age. That is the reason she brought her to Oakdale."

"Hurry up, you two," called Nora, who had reached the steps. "How you do lag to-day."

"You will hear more of this later," whispered Anne.

Mrs. Gray stood in the wide hall with hands outstretched in welcome. She kissed each girl affectionately, but her eyes lingered upon Anne, who was plainly her favorite. The old lady had become so accustomed to the sympathetic presence of the quiet, young girl that it seemed, at times, as though her own daughter had come back to her once more.

"Come right into the library and make yourself comfy," cried Mrs. Gray cheerily. "I spend most of my time there. The view from the windows is so beautiful, and as one grows old, one resorts more and more to book friendships."

"What shall we do with you, Mrs. Gray, if you keep on insisting that you are old?" said Grace. "You're not a day older at heart than any of the rest of us. Here, sit down in this nice, easy chair, while we take turns telling you just how young you are."

"It is due to my adopted children that I am not a cross, crotchety, complaining old woman," said Mrs. Gray, allowing Grace to seat her in the big leather-covered arm chair.

"Now, what does your Majesty crave of her loyal subjects?" inquired Grace, bowing low before the little, old lady.

"Very well, if I am queen, then I must be obeyed. Draw up your chairs and sit in a circle. I want to tell you a little story. That is partly my reason for inviting you here this afternoon, although you know you are welcome whenever you choose to come."

"Is it a fairy story, dear Mrs. Gray, and does it begin with 'Once upon a time'?" queried Jessica.

"It is a story of real life, my child, but I'll begin it like a fairy tale if you wish it."

"Oh, please begin at once," said Grace, who, at eighteen, was as fond of a story as she had been at six.

"Well, 'once upon a time,' there were two sisters. They were really only half sisters, and the one was almost twenty years older than the other. The mother of the elder sister had died when she was about fifteen years of age, and two years later the father had married a beautiful young Irish girl of very good family, who loved him dearly in spite of the difference in their ages.

312

"After they had been married a little over two years, a little girl came to them, and the older sister loved the tiny baby as dearly as she loved her beautiful, young step-mother."

"Why, that sounds very much like Grimm's fairy tales!" exclaimed Nora. "Only the book people are all kings and queens, but this is even better because the heroine is actually Irish."

There was a general laugh over Nora's remark in which Mrs. Gray joined.

"It's a case of Ireland forever, isn't it Nora?" said Grace teasingly.

"'Fine and dandy are the Irish,'" said Nora with a grin, quoting from a popular song she had heard in a recent musical comedy. "But stop teasing me, and let Mrs. Gray go on with her story."

"When the baby sister, whose name was Edith, was about three years old, the beautiful young mother died and left the husband inconsolable. A year later he was killed in a railroad accident, and the elder sister, named Margaret, was left with only little Edith to comfort her. The father had been a rich man, so they had no anxiety about money, and lived on year after year in their beautiful old home, with everything heart could wish.

"As Edith grew older, she developed a decided talent for music, and when she was fifteen Margaret decided to take her abroad and allow her to enter one of the great conservatories of Europe. They went to Leipsic, and Edith, who had high hopes of one day becoming a concert pianiste, continued her studies under the best instructors that money could procure. Things ran along smoothly until Edith met a young Italian named Guido Savelli, who was studying the violin at the same conservatory. His brilliant playing had already created a sensation wherever he appeared, and he gave promise of being a virtuoso.

"He fell violently in love with Edith, who had her mother's beautiful blue eyes and the combination of white skin and black hair that go to make an Irish beauty. She returned his love, and after a brief engagement they were married, much against the wishes of Margaret, who thought them both too young and impressionable to know their own minds."

"And did they live happy ever after?" asked Grace eagerly.

"That is the sad part of my story," said Mrs. Gray, sighing. "They were anything but happy. They both had too much of the artistic temperament to live peaceably. Besides, Guido Savelli was thoroughly selfish at heart. Next to himself, his music was the only thing in the world that he really cared for. When they had been married for about a year and a half he played before the king, and soon became the man of the hour. He neglected his beautiful young wife, who, in spite of their frequent quarrels, loved him with a pure and disinterested affection.

"Finally he went on a concert tour through the principal European cities, and she never saw him again. She wrote him repeatedly, but he never answered her letters, and she was too proud to follow him. She had one child, a baby girl, named Eleanor, who was the sole comfort of the heartbroken mother."

At this juncture Anne and Grace exchanged significant glances.

"When Eleanor was about a year old, the mother wrote Guido Savelli once more, begging him to come to her, if only for the sake of his child, but either he never received the letter or else paid no attention to it, for she received no reply. She relapsed into a dull, apathetic state, from which the repeated efforts of her sister failed to arouse her. The following winter she contracted pneumonia and died, leaving her sister the sole guardian of Eleanor."

"How long ago did all this happen, dear Mrs. Gray?" queried Nora eagerly, "and is little Eleanor living?"

"It was sixteen years ago, my dear," replied Mrs. Gray, "and the reason that I have told you this long tale is because the baby girl is almost a woman now, and——"

"The girl is Eleanor Savell and we met her the other day," broke in Grace excitedly, forgetting for an instant that she had interrupted Mrs. Gray. "She is going to live at 'Heartsease' and—— oh, Mrs. Gray, please pardon me for interrupting you, I was so excited that I didn't realize my own rudeness."

"Granted, my dear," smiled the old lady. "But how did you happen to meet Eleanor? They arrived only a few days ago."

Grace rapidly narrated their meeting and conversation with Eleanor, while Mrs. Gray listened without comment. When Grace repeated Eleanor's remark about having made up her mind, the old lady looked a little troubled. Then her face cleared and she said softly:

"My dear Christmas children, I am very anxious that for her own sake you should become well acquainted with Eleanor. Her aunt was here yesterday, and we had a long talk regarding her. Eleanor is an uncommon girl in many respects. She has remarkable beauty and talent, but she is frightfully self-willed. Her aunt has spoiled her, and realizes too late the damage she has done by having allowed her to grow up on the continent. They have lived in France, Germany, Italy and Spain, with an occasional visit to America, and Eleanor has always done just as she pleased. For years her aunt has obeyed her slightest whim, but as she grows older she grows more like her father, and her aunt wants her to have some steadying influence that will put a curb on her unconventional tendencies.

"When she wrote me of Eleanor, I wrote her about my girls, and offered her 'Heartsease.' She was delighted with the whole thing and lost no time in getting here. So now you understand why I have told you all this. I want you to promise me that you will do what you can for this motherless girl."

"But we felt sure we should like her when we saw her the other day," said Nora. "She seemed so sweet and winning."

"So she is. She has her father's winning personality, and a good deal of his selfishness, too," replied Mrs. Gray. "You won't find her at all disagreeable. But she is reckless, self-willed, defiant of public opinion and exceedingly impulsive. I look to you girls to keep her out of mischief."

"Well, we'll try, but I never did pride myself on being a first-class reformer," said Grace, laughing.

"Where is her father now?" asked Anne. "Is it possible that he is the great Savelli who toured America two years ago?"

"He is the man," said Mrs. Gray. "He is a wonderful musician. I heard him in New York City. I shall never forget the way he played one of Liszt's 'Hungarian Rhapsodies.' I must caution you, girls, never to mention Eleanor's father to her. She has been kept in absolute ignorance of him. When she is twenty-one her aunt will tell her about him. If she knew he was the great Savelli, she would rush off and join him to-morrow, she is so impulsive. She has the music madness of both father and mother. Her aunt tells me she is a remarkable performer on both violin and piano."

"But why shouldn't she go to her father if he is a great musician?" said Jessica. "And why is she called Savell, if her name is Savelli?"

"Because, my dear, her father has never evinced the slightest desire to look up his own child. Even if he had, he is too irresponsible and too temperamental to assume the care of a girl like Eleanor," Mrs. Gray answered. "No, Eleanor is better off with her aunt. As to her name, her aunt hates everything Italian, so she dropped the 'I' and made the name Savell."

"My," said Nora with a sigh. "She is almost as remarkable as a fairy princess, after all."

"Oh, I don't know," replied Grace quickly. "Her life, of course, has been eventful, but I believe if we are to do her any good we shall just have to act as though she were an everyday girl like the rest of us. If we begin to bow down to her, we shall be obliged to keep it up. Besides, I have an idea that I am as fond of having my own way as she is."

"Dinner is served," announced John, the butler.

The four girls arose and followed Mrs. Gray to the dining room. During the dinner Eleanor was not again mentioned, although she occupied more or less of the four girls' thoughts.

Later on, David, Hippy and Reddy appeared and a merry frolic ensued. It was after ten o'clock before the little party of young folks prepared to take their departure.

"Remember, I rely upon you," whispered Mrs. Gray to Grace as she kissed her good night. Grace nodded sympathetically, but went home with an uneasy feeling that playing the guardian angel to Eleanor would be anything but a light task.

## CHAPTER III

## AN AUTUMN WALKING EXPEDITION

"It is simply too lovely to go home to-day," exclaimed Grace Harlowe to her three chums as they strolled down High School Street one sunny afternoon in early October. "I move that we drop our books at my house and go for a walk."

"I'm willing to drop my books anywhere and never see them again," grumbled Nora O'Malley, who was not fond of study.

"I ought to go straight home," demurred Anne Pierson, "but I'll put pleasure before duty and stay with the crowd."

"What about you, Jessica?" asked Grace.

"You couldn't drive me home," replied Jessica promptly.

"Very well," laughed Grace, "as we are all of the same mind, let's shed these books and be off."

After a brief stop at Grace's home, the four girls started out, keenly alive to the beauty of the day. The leaves on the trees were beginning to lose their green and put on their dresses of red and gold. Though the sun shone brightly, the air was cool and bracing, and filled one with that vigor and joy of living which makes autumn the most delightful season of the year.

Once outside the gate, the chums unconsciously headed in the same direction.

"I believe we all have the same place in mind," laughed Grace. "I was thinking about a walk to the old Omnibus House."

"'Great minds run in the same channel,'" quoted Jessica.

"I haven't been out there since the spread last year," said Anne.

"I have," said Grace, with a slight shudder. "I am not likely to forget it, either."

"Well we are not apt to meet any more Napoleon Bonapartes out there," said Nora, referring to Grace's encounter with an escaped lunatic, fully narrated in "GRACE HARLOWE'S SOPHOMORE YEAR AT HIGH SCHOOL."

318

They were nearing their destination when Anne suddenly exclaimed: "Look, girls. Someone is over at the old house. I just saw a man go around the corner!"

The girls looked quickly in the direction of the house. Just then a figure appeared, stared at the approaching girls and began waving his hat wildly, at the same time doing a sort of war dance.

"It's another lunatic," screamed Jessica. "Run, girls, run!"

"Run nothing," exclaimed Nora. "Don't you know Reddy Brooks when you see him? Just wait until I get near enough to tell him that you mistook him for a lunatic. Hurrah! David and Hippy are with him."

"Well, well, well!" exclaimed Hippy as the girls approached. "Here is Mrs. Harlowe's little girl and some of her juvenile friends. I'm very glad to see so many Oakdale children out to-day."

"How dare you take possession of the very spot we had our eye on?" asked Grace, as she shook hands with David.

"I came over to try my bird before I have it sent home for the winter," replied David. "I was just locking up."

"And the exhibition is all over," cried Grace in a disappointed tone. "I'm so sorry. You see, I still have a hankering for aëroplanes."

"There wasn't any exhibition, after all," said David. "It wouldn't fly worth a cent to-day. I shall have to give it a complete overhauling when I get it back to my workshop. What are you girls doing out this way?"

"Oh, we just came out to walk, because it was too nice to stay indoors," said Anne. "And now we are particularly glad we came."

"Not half as glad as I am," replied David, looking at her with a smile.

"Speaking of walking," remarked Hippy, "I have decided to go in for a little on my own account. Object, to become a light weight. Is there anyone who will encourage me in this laudable resolution, and beguile me while I go 'galumphing' over the ground?"

"Oh, I know something that would be perfectly fine!" exclaimed Nora, hopping about in excitement.

"Watch her," cried Hippy. "She is about to have a conniption. She always has them when an idea hits her. I've known her for years and——"

"Make him stop," appealed Nora to David and Reddy, "or I won't tell any of you a single thing."

"I'll desist, merely to please the Irish lady, not because I'm afraid of you two long, slim persons," said Hippy, cleverly dodging both David and Reddy.

"Suppose we go on a walking expedition," said Nora. "We can start early some Saturday morning, with enough lunch to last us all day, and walk to the other side of Upton Wood and back. My sister would be glad to go with us, so that will settle the matter of having an older person along. We can have the whole day in the woods, and the walk will do us all good. We won't have many more chances, either, for winter will be upon us before we know it. It's a shame to waste such perfect days as these."

"What a perfectly lovely stunt!" exclaimed Grace. "We'll write to Tom Gray, and see if he can't come, too. The walking expedition wouldn't be complete without him."

"I'll write to him to-night," said David. "I certainly should like to see the good old chap."

"Will there be plenty to eat?" asked Hippy. "I always feel hungry after such strenuous exercise as walking. I am not very strong, you know."

"Hear him," jeered Reddy. "One minute he vows to walk until he reaches the skeleton stage, and the next he threatens to kick over all his vows by overeating."

"I didn't say anything about overeating," retorted Hippy. "I merely stated that there are times when I feel the pangs of hunger."

"Stop squabbling," said Jessica, "and let's lay some plans."

"Where shall we lay them?" innocently asked Hippy.

"Nowhere, if you're not good," said Nora eyeing him severely.

Then an animated discussion began, and the following Saturday was agreed upon, the weather permitting, as the best time to go.

Saturday turned out fair, and by nine o'clock the entire party were monopolizing the Harlowe's veranda.

"Well, are we all ready?" said Tom Gray, as he glanced at his watch. "Everybody scramble. One, two, three, walk."

Eight highly excited boys and girls accompanied by Miss Edith O'Malley, hustled down the steps, waving good-bye to Mrs. Harlowe as she stood on the veranda and watched them out of sight.

The lunch had been divided into four packages and each boy strapped a package to his shoulder. Grace wore a little knapsack fitted to her back with two cross straps. "There's nothing in it but some walnut fudge that I made last night, but I couldn't resist wearing it. It belonged to my grandfather," she confided to the girls when they had exclaimed over it.

"My, but it's great to be here," said Tom Gray to Grace as they entered Upton Wood. "I'm so glad I could come."

"So are we," she replied. "A lark in the woods wouldn't be half the fun with our forester missing."

"Back to nature for me, every time," he exclaimed, taking a deep breath and looking about him, his face aglow with forest worship.

"I love the woods, too," said Grace, "almost enough to wish I were a gypsy."

On down the shady wood road they traveled, sometimes stopping to watch a squirrel or a chipmunk or to knock down a few burrs from the chestnut trees they occasionally found along the way. Once they stopped and played hide and seek for half an hour. By one o'clock they were ravenously hungry. Hippy clamored incessantly for food.

"Let us feed him at once, and have peace," exclaimed Nora. "I'm hungry, too. It seems an age since breakfast."

A halt was made and the contents of two of the lunch packages were arranged on a little tablecloth at the foot of a great oak. The hungry young folks gathered around it and in a short time nothing remained of the lunch excepting the packages reserved for supper.

"I move we all take a half hour's rest and then go on," said David. "We still have a mile to go before we are through the wood. We'll feel more like walking after we've rested a little."

"Let us all sit in a row with our backs against this fallen tree and tell a story," said Grace. "Hippy, you are on the end, so you can begin it, then after you have gone a little way, Nora must take up the narrative, and so on down the line until the story is finished."

"Fine," said Hippy. "Here goes:"

"Once upon a time, in the heart of a deep forest, there lived a most beautiful prince. He had all that heart could wish; still he was not happy, for, alas, he was too fat."

At this statement there was a shout of laughter from his listeners, at which Hippy, pretending anger, glared ferociously and vowed that he would not continue. Nora thereupon took up the narrative and convulsed her hearers with the remedies tried by the fat prince to reduce his weight. Then the story was passed on to Anne. With each narrator it grew funnier, until the party screamed with laughter over the misfortunes of the ill-starred prince.

Hippy ended the tale by marrying the hero to a princess who was a golf fiend and who forced the poor prince to be her caddy.

"From the day of his marriage he chased golf balls," concluded Hippy, "and the habit became so firmly fixed with him that he even rose and chased them in his sleep. He lost flesh at an alarming rate, and three months after his wedding day they laid him to rest in the quiet churchyard, with the touching epitaph over him, 'Things are not what they seem.'"

Hippy buried his face in his handkerchief and sobbed audibly until David and Reddy pounced upon him and he was obliged to forego his lamentations and defend himself.

"It's time to move," said Tom Gray, consulting his watch. "I don't believe we'd better go on through the wood. We'll have to about face if we expect to get home before dark."

So the start back was made, but their progress was slow. A dozen things beguiled them from the path. Tom's trained eye spied a wasp's nest hanging from a limb. It was as large as a Japanese lantern and a beautiful silver-gray color. Anne stopped to pick some ground berries she found nestling under the leaves. Then they all started in wild pursuit of a rabbit, and in consequence had difficulty in finding the road again. Finally they all grew so hungry they sat down and disposed of the remaining food.

"How dark it is growing," exclaimed Jessica, as they again took the road. "It must be very late."

"It's after four o'clock," replied David, "and there's a storm coming, too. I think we had better hurry. I don't fancy being caught in the woods in bad weather. Hustle, everybody."

As they hurried along the path a blast of wind blew full in their faces. The whole forest seemed suddenly astir. There were strange sounds from every direction. The branches creaked and the dry leaves fell rattling to the ground by hundreds. Another gust of wind filled their eyes and nostrils with fine dust.

"Don't be frightened," called Tom. "Follow me."

He led the way with Reddy, but the storm was upon them before they had gone ten steps. The wind almost blew them off their feet and black darkness settled down over the woods. They could just see the outlines of the trees as they staggered on, a blinding rain drenching them to the skin.

Tom divided the party into two sections, four in one and five in the other. They were to hold each other's hands tightly and keep together. Frequent flashes of lightning revealed the woods in a tremendous state of agitation and it seemed better to be moving than to stand still and watch the terrifying spectacle.

On they stumbled, but suddenly came to grief, for the four in front fell headlong over a tree that had been blown across the path, and the other five hearing their cries of warning too late, followed after.

By the time they had picked themselves up the storm had grown so furious that they could only press miserably together and wait for it to pass.

Suddenly Tom amazed them all by putting his hands to his mouth and blowing a strange kind of hollow whistle that sounded like the note of a trumpet.

He repeated the whistle again and again. "You may not believe it," he said between calls, "but the hunter who taught me this, told me never to use it unless I was in dire need. Then help of some sort would surely come. It is called the Elf's Horn."

"Did you ever try it before," asked Reddy curiously.

"No," he answered, "I never did. I suppose it's only superstition, but I love hunter's lore. Perhaps it may work. Who knows?"

"Hello-o-o!" cried a voice seemingly close by. "Hello-o-o!"

"Where are you?" called Tom.

"This way," answered the voice, and a light flashed a little distance off, revealing to them a man waving a lantern with one hand and beckoning with the other. One and all dashed toward the light, feeling that shelter was at hand.

"It must be a hunter," panted Tom, "and he has heard the Elf's Horn."

It was a hunter, and none other than old Jean. Their blind wandering had taken them straight to the hunter's cabin.

"It is Mademoiselle Grace and her friends," cried the old man with delight. "When the sky grow so dark, I take my lantern and go out to my trap I have set this morning. Then I hear a strange whistle, many times, and I think someone get lost and I cry 'hello,' and you answer and I find mademoiselle and her friends."

"That was the Elf's Horn, Jean," replied Tom, "and you heard because you are a hunter."

"I know not what monsieur mean by Elf Horn, but I hear whistle, anyhow, and come," remarked the old man, smiling.

The others laughed.

"It's a shame to spoil it," replied David, "but I am afraid your Elf's Horn and Jean's helloing were just a coincidence."

"Coincidence or not," replied Tom good-naturedly, "my faith in the fairy horn is now unshakable. I shall use it again if I ever need to."

Before a blazing fire kindled by Jean in the big fireplace, the whole party dried themselves. The old hunter listened to the story of their mad scramble through the woods with many expressions of sympathy.

It was eight o'clock when the storm had abated sufficiently to allow them to sally forth, and in a short time they were in Oakdale.

Fifteen minutes later they were telling Mr. and Mrs. Harlowe just how it all happened.

## CHAPTER IV

## GRACE MAKES A DISCOVERY

The Monday after the walking expedition, Grace Harlowe set out for school full of an idea that had been revolving in her busy brain for weeks. The time had come for herself and for her three chums to bind themselves together as a sorority. As charter members, they would initiate four other girls, as soon as proper rites could be thought of. It should be a Greek letter society. Grace thought "Phi Sigma Tau" would sound well. Aside from the social part, their chief object would be to keep a watchful eye open for girls in school who needed assistance of any sort.

Mrs. Gray's anxiety over Eleanor Savell had set the bee in Grace's bonnet buzzing, and now her plans were practically perfected. All that remained to be done was to tell her three friends, and consult them as to what other four girls would be eligible to membership.

Her proposition was hailed with acclamation by Anne, Nora and Jessica. Miriam Nesbit, Marian Barber, Eva Allen and Eleanor Savell were chosen as candidates and promptly notified to report at Jessica's home the next Thursday evening for initiation. They at once accepted the invitation and solemnly promised to be there.

"'Where are you going, my pretty maid?'" said David Nesbit, stopping directly in front of Grace Harlowe as she hurried toward the Bright home the following Thursday evening.

Grace laughed merrily, dropped a little curtsy and recited, "I'm going to an initiation, sir, she said."

"'And may I go with you, my pretty maid?'" replied David, bowing low.

"No boys allowed there, sir, she said."

"That settles it," sighed David. "I suppose a sorority is about to come to the surface. Am I right, and will you take me along?"

"Yes, we are going to initiate members into our new sorority, but you can't come, so you might as well be resigned to fate," retorted Grace. "We didn't receive invitations to your fraternity initiations."

"Be kind to Anne, won't you. Tell her she has my sympathy," said David solemnly.

"Anne is a charter member, if you please," laughed Grace. "She is spared the ordeals of initiation. But Miriam will not escape so easily. She is one of the candidates."

"Ah, ha!" exclaimed David. "That's what she was so mysterious over. I tried to find out where she was going, but she wouldn't tell me. By the way, where does the affair take place?" he added, trying to look innocent.

"Don't you wish you knew?" teased Grace. "However, you shan't find out from me. I know too well what would happen if you boys traced us to our lair. But I must go or I shall be late. Good night, David. Please be good and don't follow me. Promise me you won't."

"I never make rash promises," answered David, smiling. "Be merciful to the candidates." Lifting his cap, the young man hurried off and turned the corner without looking back.

"I wonder what I had better do," Grace mused. "I know perfectly well that David Nesbit won't go away. He will wait until he thinks I am far enough up the street and then he'll follow me. As soon as he finds out where I am going he'll rush back and hunt up Hippy Wingate and Reddy Brooks. Goodness knows what the three of them will plan."

She decided to turn down a side street, go back one block and into the public library. She could easily leave the library by the side entrance and cut across Putnam Square. That would mislead David, although no doubt he would find them before the evening was over.

Grace lost no time in putting her plan into action. As she hurried into the library she looked back, but saw no sign of David. When she reached Putnam Square she almost ran along the broad asphalt walk. It was fifteen minutes past seven by the city hall clock, and she did not wish to be late. The girls had agreed to be there by half past seven. She was almost across the square when her ear caught the sound of a low sob. Grace glanced quickly about. The square was practically deserted, but under one of the great trees, curled up on a bench, was a girl. Without an instant's hesitation Grace made for the bench. She touched the girl on the shoulder and said, "You seem to be in distress. Can I do anything to help you?"

Then Grace gave a little surprised exclamation. The face turned toward her was that of Mabel Allison, the freshman prize girl. The glare from the neighboring light revealed her tear-swollen eyes and quivering lips. She gave Grace one long, agonized look, then dropped her head on her arm and sobbed harder than ever.

"Why, Miss Allison, don't cry so," soothed Grace. "Tell me what your trouble is. Perhaps I can be of some service to you. I've wanted to know you ever since you won the freshman prize last June, and so has Anne Pierson. She won the prize the year before, you know."

The girl nodded, but she could not sufficiently control herself to speak.

Grace stood silently waiting until the other should find her voice. A moment more and Mabel Allison began to speak in a plaintive little voice that went straight to Grace's heart:

"You are Grace Harlowe. I believe every girl in Oakdale High School knows you. I have heard so much about you, but I never dreamed that you'd ever speak to me."

"Nonsense," replied Grace, laughing. "I'm just a girl like yourself. There isn't anything remarkable about me. I'm very glad to know you, Miss Allison, but I am sorry to find you so unhappy. Can't you tell me about it?" she coaxed, sitting down on the bench and slipping one arm around the shabby little figure.

Mabel's lip quivered again. Then she turned impulsively toward Grace and said: "Yes; I will tell you, although no one can help me. I suppose you don't know where I live or anything about me, do you?"

"No," replied Grace, shaking her head, "but I'd be glad to have you tell me."

"Well," continued Mabel, "I'm an orphan, and I live with Miss Brant. She——"

"Not that horrible, miserly Miss Brant who lives in that ugly yellow house on Elm Street?" interrupted Grace in a horrified tone.

"Yes, she is the one I mean," continued Mabel. "She took me from an orphan asylum two years ago. I hated her the first time I ever saw her, but the matron said I was old enough to work, that I'd have a good home with her and that I should be paid for my work. She promised to send me to school, and I was wild to get a good education, so I went with her. But she is perfectly awful, and I wish I were dead."

Her voice ended almost in a wail.

"I don't blame you," said Grace sympathetically. "She has the reputation of being one of the most hateful women in Oakdale. I am surprised that she even allows you to go to school."

"That's just the trouble," the girl replied, her voice husky. "She's going to take me out of school. I shall be sixteen next month, and exempt from the school law. So she is going to make me stop school and go to work in the silk mill. I worked there all through vacation last summer, and she took every cent of my wages. She took my freshman prize money, too."

"What a burning shame!" exclaimed Grace indignantly. "Haven't you any relatives at all, Miss Allison, or anyone else with whom you could stay?"

Mabel shook her head.

"I don't know anything about myself," she said. "I was picked up on the street in New York City when I was three years old, and as no one claimed me, I was put in an orphanage. There was one woman at the orphanage who was always good to me. She remembered the day they brought me, and she said that I was beautifully dressed. She always believed that I had been stolen. She said that I could tell my name, 'Mabel Isabel Allison,' and that I would be three years old in November, but that I couldn't tell where I lived. Whenever they asked me I cried and said I didn't know. She wanted to save my clothes for me, thinking that by them I might someday find my parents, but the matron took them away from her, all but three little gold baby pins marked 'M.I.A.' She hid them away from the matron. When she heard I was to go with Miss Brant, she kissed me, and gave them to me. She was the only person that ever cared for me."

The tears stood in Grace's eyes.

"You poor, little thing!" she cried. "I care for you, and I'm going to see if I can do something for you. You shan't stop school if I can help it. I can't stay with you any longer, just now, because I am going to Miss Bright's and I am late. It is eight o'clock, you see."

The girl gave a little cry of fright.

"Oh, I didn't think it was so late. I know Miss Brant will be very angry. She will probably beat me. I am still carrying the marks from the last whipping she gave me. She sent me out on an errand, but I felt as though I must be alone, if only for a few minutes. That's why I stopped in the square."

"Beat you!" exclaimed Grace. "How dare she touch you? Why, I never had a whipping in my life! I won't keep you another minute, but wait for me outside the campus when school is out to-morrow. I wish to talk further with you."

"I'll come," promised Mabel, her face lighting up. Then she suddenly threw both arms around Grace's neck and said, "I do love you, and I feel that someone cares about me at last." Then, like a flash, she darted across the square and was soon lost to Grace's view.

"Well, of all things!" Grace remarked softly to herself. "I think it's high time we organized a sorority for the purpose of aiding girls in distress."

"You're a prompt person. Did you really decide to come?" were the cries that greeted her from the porch as she opened the Bright's gate.

"Save your caustic comments," said Grace as she handed Jessica her hat. "I have a tale to tell."

"Out with it!" was the cry, and the girls surrounded Grace, who began with her meeting with David, and ended with the story of Mabel Allison.

"You haven't heard anything of those boys yet, have you?" she asked when she had finished.

"Not yet," said Nora, "but never fear, the night is yet young."

"Where is Eleanor Savell?" asked Grace, noticing for the first time that Eleanor was not present. "You promised to go for her, didn't you, Anne?"

"I did go," replied Anne, "but she wouldn't come. She said she'd come sometime when she felt like it. She was playing on the violin when the maid let me in, and how she can play! She wanted me to stay there with her and didn't seem to understand why I couldn't break my engagement with you girls. She said that she always kept her engagements unless the spirit moved her to do something else."

"Is Eleanor Savell the girl who comes into the study hall every morning after opening exercises have begun?" asked Marian Barber.

"Yes," Grace answered. "I forgot for a moment that you and Eva and Miriam hadn't met her. She is really very charming, although her ideas about punctuality and school rules are somewhat hazy as yet. She lives at 'Heartsease,' Mrs. Gray's property. I am disappointed because she will not be here to-night. She seemed delighted when I asked her to join our society."

"As long as we know she isn't coming, don't you think we should begin the initiation?" asked Nora. "It is after eight o'clock and we can't stay out too late, you know."

"Very well," said Grace. "Blindfold the candidates."

The three girls meekly submitted to the blindfolding, and the chums were about to lead them to the initiation chamber, when the ringing of the door bell caused them to start.

"It's David and the boys," said Jessica. "Shall I tell them that they can't come in?"

"Of course," responded Nora. "You and Grace go to the door, while Anne and I stay here with our victims. Be careful they don't play you a trick."

The two girls cautiously approached the door, opening it very slowly, and saw—not the three boys—but Eleanor. She smiled serenely and said: "Good evening. I decided, after all, that I would come."

"Come right in," said Jessica cordially. "I am so glad you changed your mind and came. The initiation is about to begin. Have you ever belonged to a secret society?"

"Never," replied Eleanor. "But now that I'm here, I am willing to try it."

"Come this way."

"Girls," said Grace, addressing the three blindfolded girls, "this is Eleanor Savell. You can't see her yet, but you may all shake hands with her. She is to be your companion in misery."

Eleanor laughed, shook hands with the others and graciously allowed Nora to tie a handkerchief over her eyes.

"All ready! March!" called Grace, and the eight girls solemnly proceeded to the initiation chamber.

## CHAPTER V

## THE PHI SIGMA TAU

At the door a halt was called.

"Prepare to jump," commanded Grace in a deep voice. "One, two, three! Jump down! Be careful!"

The four candidates gave four uncertain jumps and experienced the disagreeable sensation usually felt in attempting to jump downward when on level ground. This was one of the oldest and mildest forms of initiation, but Nora had insisted upon it, and giggled violently as the four girls prepared for a long leap. Even Grace, who was conducting the ceremony with the utmost seriousness, laughed a little at the picture they made.

"They'll do anything you tell them," whispered Nora. Which was perfectly true. To show fear or reluctance in obeying the demands made upon one, was to prove one's self unworthy of membership in the Phi Sigma Tau.

"Let the music begin," said Grace.

There was a faint snicker as Anne, Nora and Jessica raised three combs, wrapped in tissue paper, to their lips and began the "Merry Widow" waltz, with weird effect.

"You must waltz around the room fifteen times without stopping," continued Grace, "and then sit down in the four opposite corners of the room, on the cushions provided for you."

The girl chums retreated to the doorway of the room, that had previously been cleared of almost all the furniture, to watch the movements of their victims as they endeavored to circle the room the required number of times. They lost their count, bumped each other at every turn, and at last staggered dizzily toward what they thought were the corners of the room. Miriam Nesbit made straight for the door in which the chums stood, and Grace was obliged to take her by the shoulders and gently steer her in the opposite direction. Eleanor, after groping along one side of the room for a corner, was the first to find one, and sank with a sigh of relief upon the pile of cushions. The other girls had not been so successful. They all endeavored to sit in the same corner at once, and Grace was obliged to go to the rescue, and lead two of them to opposite sides of the initiation chamber.

"In order to become successful members of this society, it is necessary for you to sing. You may all sing the first verse and the chorus of any song you know, only be sure that you don't choose the same song, and don't stop until you have finished," directed Grace. "Begin after I have counted three. I will wait for a minute while you choose your song. The orchestra will accompany you."

There was considerable subdued laughter from the orchestra, who had been instructed to play "The Star Spangled Banner," oblivious of whatever the candidates might sing.

"One, two, three!" counted Grace, and the concert began.

Eva Allen chose "John Brown's Body." Miriam Nesbit, "Old Kentucky Home." Marian Barber, "Schooldays," while Eleanor contributed "The Marseillaise" in French. The orchestra dutifully burst forth with "The Star Spangled Banner," and the effect was indescribable.

The orchestra broke down before they reached their chorus, and the accompaniment ended in a shriek of suppressed mirth, but the candidates went stolidly on without a smile and finished almost together.

"Very well done," commended Grace. "I see you will be valuable additions to the society."

The girls were then put through a series of ridiculous tests that the four chums had devised. They were made to dip their hands in water charged with electricity, caress a mechanical rubber snake that wriggled realistically, drink a cup of boneset tea apiece, and were directed finally to bare their arms for the branding of the letters of the society.

The branding was done with a piece of ice, pressed hard against their bare arms, and the shock made the victims gasp for a second and wonder if they really were being burned.

"You will now hold up your right hands and repeat after me," said Grace, "I do solemnly swear that I will faithfully execute my duties as a member of the Phi Sigma Tau, and will, to the best of my ability, preserve, protect and defend its laws."

This done, the girls received the grip of the society, the handkerchiefs were removed from their eyes and they were pronounced full-fledged members.

"That oath has a rather familiar sound," remarked Miriam Nesbit, trying to recollect where she had heard it before.

"I know," she said at last. "It's the oath of office taken by the President of the United States at inauguration, only you changed it to suit this sorority."

"You've guessed it exactly," replied Grace. "I chose it because it sounded so much more expressive than to say, 'May my bones be crushed and my heart cut out if ever I am unfaithful to my vows.'"

There was a general laugh at this, the girls agreeing that Grace's choice was infinitely less blood-thirsty.

"Now that you have so bravely endured the trials of initiation, you shall receive your reward," declared Jessica. "Follow me."

She led the way to the dining room, where a bountiful lunch awaited them, to which, after the manner of hungry school girls, they did full justice.

"By the way," said Grace, after they had returned to the sitting room and were comfortably settled, "you never said one word about my freshman prize girl. I thought you would be awfully interested in her. For the benefit of the new members, I will say that this society was organized with a definite object, that of helping others. We are to look after girls who have no one to make things pleasant or happy for them. Why, do you know that there are quite a number of girls attending High School who come from other places, and who have to spend the holidays at their boarding houses without any fun at all? Look at this poor, little Allison girl. She works for her board in the winter, and in the mill in the summer, and now that miserable Miss Brant is going to take her out of school, and she is getting along so well, too."

"Isn't it a pity," said Anne, "that people like her can't understand that if a girl were allowed to finish her education, she could earn so much more in the long run than she could by working year after year in a mill?"

"We might go to Miss Brant and explain that to her," said Nora. "Perhaps she would listen to us."

"I don't believe so," replied Grace. "Besides, she might be very angry and take her spite out on poor Mabel. If we could only get Mabel away from her. But if she has legally adopted her we couldn't do anything. Besides, where would she go if we did get her away?"

"I'll tell you what I'll do," said Jessica thoughtfully. "I'll ask papa about it. Lawyers always know everything about such things. Maybe he could find out if Miss Brant has any real claim upon her."

"That's a good idea," said Miriam Nesbit. "If we can get her away from that hateful old wretch, the sorority could adopt her. She could stay with each one of us for a month. That would be eight months, and at the end of that time she would have finished her sophomore year. Then she could get something pleasant to do through the summer vacation. That would give her some money for clothes for next year. Perhaps by that time we could find some nice people for her to stay with, or if we liked her well enough, we could go on having her with us. I'll ask my mother to-morrow, and you girls might do the same."

"Miriam Nesbit, what a perfectly lovely plan!" exclaimed Grace Harlowe with rapture. "I feel sure mother would let me have her."

"She can come here any time," said Jessica. "Papa allows me to do as I like."

"'First catch your bird,'" said Nora wisely. "Don't plan too much, until you find out whether you can snatch her from the dragon's claws."

"I feel sure we shall win," replied Grace confidently. "What do you girls think of it?" she asked, turning to Eva, Marian and Eleanor, who had so far expressed no opinion.

"Count us in," said Eva and Marian in a breath.

"And you, Eleanor?" asked Grace.

"She can live at our house forever, if she doesn't disturb me," replied Eleanor lazily. "My aunt won't care, either. When we lived in Spain she used to help every beggar we came across, and Spain is a land of beggars. She never can resist an appeal for charity."

There was a sudden silence. Then Grace said gently, although she felt irritated at Eleanor's careless speech: "I don't think Mabel Allison could really be called a beggar; and if we adopt her, we ought never to let her think that we consider her a dependent. Of course we know very little about her yet, but I think she will prove worthy. I am to see her to-morrow, and perhaps it would be better to talk a little more with her before we tell Jessica's father about it."

Eleanor looked at Grace with an amused smile.

"How serious you girls are," she said. "Is it school that makes you so? If it is, I don't think I shall stay long. I like to drift along and do only what my inclination prompts me to do. I hate responsibility of any sort."

"Perhaps you will feel differently about school after a while," said Anne quietly. "This is my third year in Oakdale High School, and I never had any good times until I came here. As for responsibility, it is a good thing to learn to be responsible for one's self, if for no one else."

"Well, perhaps you are right, but I am sure that if you had never lived long enough in one country to become acclimated, you wouldn't feel very responsible, either," said Eleanor in such rueful tones that the girls laughed, although they secretly disapproved of Eleanor's inconsequential attitude.

"Did you think the examinations hard?" asked Jessica of Eleanor.

"Oh, no," replied Eleanor lightly. "I had an English governess who was with us for five years. She drilled me thoroughly in English and mathematics. I loathed them both, but studied them merely to show her that I could master them. Miss Thompson said my work was good, and that if I were ambitious she would put me in the senior class, but I held out for the juniors and finally got my own way. If you are going to take such a serious view of this gay world, however, perhaps I'll wish I had joined the seniors, after all. No, I don't mean that. I'm awfully glad to know you, and feel honored at being a member of your sorority. Only I don't expect to ever be a very useful one. My aunt has spoiled me, and I frankly admit it. So, you see, there is no hope for me." She spread out both hands in a deprecating manner and shrugged her shoulders exactly as a French woman might have done.

"I am sure we like you, just as you are," said Eva Allen warmly. She had been rather impressed with Eleanor.

"Do you see the time?" said Nora, suddenly pointing to the old-fashioned clock in the corner. "Half past ten! I must go this minute. Sister will be worried."

335

She immediately made for her hat and coat, the others following suit, with the exception of Eleanor, who was to wait until the coachman came for her.

Once the girls were outside the gate, Marian Barber broke out with: "What a queer girl that Eleanor Savell is. She is beautiful and fascinating, but I don't know whether I like her or not."

"You must like her," said Grace. "You know the members of this society must stand by each other."

"But why did you ask her to join, Grace?" persisted Marian. "She is different from the rest of us. I don't believe we shall get along with her very well."

"I'll tell you girls a secret," replied Grace. "Anne and Nora already know it. Mrs. Gray wants us to be nice to Eleanor for a number of reasons, and, of course, we wish to please her. Anne, Jessica, Nora and I were talking about it the other day, and while we were laying plans for this sorority, we decided to ask Eleanor to join. We thought we could learn to know her better, and she would eventually become a good comrade."

"It sounds ridiculous to talk about helping a clever girl like Eleanor, but from her conversation to-night you can see that she needs some wholesome advice occasionally," said Nora bluntly. "Mrs. Gray seems to think we can be of some use in that direction, so we are trying to carry out her theory."

"I think I understand the situation," said Miriam Nesbit, "and will do all I can to be nice to her, if she doesn't attempt to patronize me. I couldn't stand that. I know I used to do it. I suppose that's why it seems so unendurable to me now."

"David Nesbit didn't disturb us, after all," remarked Eva Allen. "It's a wonder those boys didn't put tick-tacks on the windows or do something like that."

The girls had come to the turn of the street, and were about to pass the only really lonely spot during their walk. It was an old colonial residence, the surrounding grounds extending for a block. It had been untenanted for some time, as the owners were in Europe, although both house and grounds were looked after by a care-taker. On the other side of the street was a field where the small fry of Oakdale usually held their ball games.

"I always hate passing this old house," said Marian Barber. "It is so terribly still back there among those pines. I don't——"

She stopped short, an expression of terror overspreading her good-natured face, as she mutely pointed toward the old house. Three ghostly figures swathed in white stole out from the shadow of the pines and glided down the wide, graveled drive toward the gate. Their appearance was terrifying. Their faces were white as their robes, and blue flames played about their eyes. They carried out in every particular the description of the regulation churchyard ghost.

For an instant the six girls stood still, regarding those strange apparitions with fascinated terror. Then Eva Allen and Marian Barber shrieked in unison and fled down the street as fast as their legs would carry them. Grace, Nora, Anne and Miriam stood their ground and awaited the oncoming specters, who halted when they saw that the girls did not intend to run.

"High School boys, on a lark," whispered Grace to her friends. "Let's charge them in a body."

With a bound she reached the drive, closely followed by the other girls. The ghostly three evidently considering discretion the better part of valor, left the drive and took to their heels across the lawn. But Grace, who was well in the lead, caught the last fleeing ghost by its robe and held on for dear life. There was a sound of rending cloth as the apparition [Pg 65]bounded forward, then it caught its specter toe on a tuft of long grass and fell forward with a decidedly human thud.

The girls surrounded it in an instant. Before it had time to rise, Grace snatched off a white mask smeared around the eye-holes with phosphorus, which explained the flame like effect, and disclosed the sheepish face of James Gardiner, one of the sophomore class.

"Oh, let a fellow up, will you?" he said, with a sickly grin.

"You bad boy!" exclaimed Grace. "What do you mean by dressing up like this? Don't you know you might frighten some timid person terribly?"

"Initiation," said the youth, with a grin, rising on his elbow and looking as though he would like to make a sudden break for liberty. "Part of the sacred obligations of the 'Knights and Squires' frat. Three fellows of us were initiated to-night. This was the last stunt."

"Well, I suppose under those circumstances we shall have to forgive you. Did you appear to anyone else?" asked Grace.

"Only to that old crank Miss Brant. She was scared out of her wits," replied James, laughing. "Two of your crowd got out in a hurry, too, didn't they?"

"I suppose I shall have to confess that they did," replied Grace. "If I were you, James, I'd take off that costume and hurry away. Miss Brant is liable to inform the police, and they might not look at initiation stunts as we do."

"That's right," said James, looking a trifle alarmed. "Wonder where the fellows went. I'd better put them on. We never thought of that. If you girls will excuse me, I'll hunt them up."

"Certainly," said the girls. "Good night, James."

"Good night," replied the youth. "You girls are all right. Can't scare you." With a nod to them he started across the grass on the run, his ghostly garments trailing behind him.

"I'm glad that wasn't David," said Anne as James disappeared. "I was afraid when first I saw them that they might be our boys. I didn't feel frightened at all, after what Grace had said about meeting David."

"Eva and Marian didn't show any great amount of courage," said Nora, laughing. "I wonder if they ran all the way home."

"There they are ahead of us," said Anne.

True enough, the two girls stood on the corner waiting for the others to come up.

"Why don't you hurry on home?" called Nora. "'The goblins will git you, ef you don't watch out.'"

"Don't tease," said Marian Barber, looking rather foolish. "We are awfully sorry we ran away, but when I saw those awful white figures coming toward us, I just had to run and so did Eva. Who on earth were they, and where did they go?"

In a few words Grace told her what had happened.

"That horrid James Gardiner. I'll never speak to him again," cried Eva Allen. "I hope he didn't recognize us. He'll tell everyone in school about it."

"I don't think he did," replied Grace. "Oh, look, girls! Here comes Officer Donavan! I was right when I said that Miss Brant would notify the police."

"I hope she got a good scare," remarked Nora wickedly. "As for the ghosts, they are very likely at home by this time."

# CHAPTER VI

## A VISIT TO ELEANOR

The next day, when Grace, in company with her chums, left the school building, they beheld the shabby little figure of Mabel Allison waiting for them just outside the campus. She looked shy and embarrassed when she saw the four girls bearing down upon her, and seemed half inclined to run away. Grace greeted her cordially and introduced her to her chums, whose simple and unaffected manners soon put her at her ease.

"I am so glad you waited," said Grace cordially. "I have told my three friends about you, as I knew they would be as much interested in you as I am. We have made a plan and if we can carry it out, you will be able to go to school until you graduate."

"You are very good to take so much trouble for me," said Mabel, the tears springing to her eyes; "but I'm afraid it won't do any good."

"Don't be down-hearted," said Nora sympathetically. "You don't know Grace Harlowe. She always does whatever she sets out to do."

"She's a regular fairy godmother," said Anne softly. "I know from experience."

"Such flattery is overwhelming," murmured Grace. "I regret that I'm too busy to bow my thanks. But to get down to the business of the hour—tell me, Mabel, dear—did this Miss Brant legally adopt you when she took you from the orphanage, or are you bound to her in any way?"

"I don't know," said the girl, her eyes growing big with wonder. "I never thought about it. I don't believe, however, that she has any legal claim upon me."

"Is there any way in which you can find out?" asked Anne.

"Why, yes," replied Mabel. "I could write the woman at the orphanage who was good to me. She is still there, and several times she has written to me, but Miss Brant read her letters first and then tore them up. Her name is Mary Stevens, and she would surely know!"

"Then write to her at once," said Grace, "and tell her to send her letter in an outside envelope addressed to me. Your whole future depends upon her answer."

Grace thereupon related to her their conversation of the previous night.

"As soon as you find out about Miss Brant's claim, we shall take the matter to Jessica's father, who is a lawyer. He will help us," Grace concluded. "Then when you are free,we shall have something else to tell you. Just be patient for a few days, and don't be afraid. Everything will come right."

"How can I ever thank you all?" said Mabel, taking one of Grace's hands between hers and looking at her with a world of gratitude in her eyes. "I will write to-night. I must go now or I shall be home late. Forgive me for hurrying away, but I daren't stay," she added piteously. "You know that I should like to. Good-bye, and thank you again."

"Good-bye," called Grace. "I'll let you know as soon as I hear from Mary Stevens."

"What a sweet little girl she is," said Jessica. "I should like to keep her with me all the time."

"She is a nice child," said Grace, "and she deserves something better than her present fate."

"To change the subject," said Nora, "has any one seen Eleanor to-day? She was not in English or geometry, although she may have come in late."

"I don't believe she was in school at all," said Anne. "Maybe the initiation was too much for her."

"Oh, I don't know. She didn't seem to mind it," remarked Jessica. "She will hear from Miss Thompson if she makes a practice of staying out of school. Attendance is one of the chief requisites in Miss Thompson's eyes."

"I suppose we ought to call on Eleanor before long," mused Grace. "She has invited us, and it's our duty to call on her first. Anne has already been there. Suppose we go over now; that is, unless you girls have something else to do."

It was decided at once that they could go, and soon the four chums were walking briskly down the street in the direction of "Heartsease." It was an Indian summer day and the girls congratulated themselves on having taken advantage of it. As school had closed at half past two, it was not yet four o'clock. They would have plenty of time for their call without hurrying themselves. So they strolled along, laughing and chatting in the care-free manner that belongs alone to the school girl.

As they neared the house one and all exclaimed at the beauty of the grounds. The lawn looked like a great stretch of green velvet, while the trees were gorgeous in their autumn glory of crimson and gold, with here and there a patch of russet by way of contrast. Over at one side were clumps of pink and white anemones; while all around the house and in the garden beds that dotted the lawn many-colored chrysanthemums stood up in brave array.

"What a delightful place 'Heartsease' is," cried Grace as she paused just inside the gate to feast her eyes upon its beauty. "Sometimes I think that autumn is the finest season of the year, and then again I like spring better."

"What difference does the season make, so long as we have a good time?" said Nora blithely. "I haven't any preference. They're all good."

"Eleanor will be surprised to see us," remarked Grace, as she rang the bell.

"Let's hope she will appreciate the honor of having four such distinguished persons descend upon her at one time," said Anne.

"Is Miss Savell in?" asked Grace to the trim maid who answered her ring.

"Yes, miss," replied the maid. "Come in. Who shall I say is here?"

"Say to Miss Savell that Grace Harlowe and her friends would like to see her."

The maid soon reappeared and led the girls down the wide, old-fashioned hall, and, somewhat to their surprise, ushered them into the dining room, where they beheld Eleanor, arrayed in a dainty white house gown, dining alone.

She arose as they entered and came forward with both hands outstretched. "How are the Phi Sigma Taus to-day?" she asked. "It was awfully nice of you to come and see me."

"We thought you might be ill," said Nora. "We missed you at school to-day."

"Oh, no," replied Eleanor serenely. "I am perfectly well. I really didn't feel like going to school to-day, so I stayed in bed until eleven o'clock. I am just having lunch now. Won't you join me? I am keeping house by myself this afternoon. My aunt is dining with Mrs. Gray."

"Thank you," said Grace, speaking for the girls. "We all have supper at half past six and must save our appetites for that."

"We usually dine about eight o'clock," said Eleanor. "We acquired the habit of dining late from living on the continent. But, come, now. I have finished my lunch. I want you to see where I live, almost entirely, when in the house."

The girls followed her up the broad staircase and down the hall. Every inch of the ground was familiar to Grace. She had been there so often with Mrs. Gray. "Oh, you have the suite at the back," she exclaimed. "I love those two rooms."

"You will find them somewhat changed," remarked Eleanor as she opened the door and ushered the girls into the most quietly luxurious apartment they had ever seen. Even Miriam Nesbit's room could not compare with it.

"What a beautiful room!" exclaimed Grace, looking about her with delight. "I don't wonder you like to spend your time in it. I see you have your own piano."

"Yes," replied Eleanor. "My aunt sent to New York for it. The one downstairs in the drawing room is all right, but I like to have this one handy, so that I can play whenever the spirit moves me. This is my bedroom," she continued, pushing aside the silken curtains that separated the two rooms. The girls exclaimed over the Circassian walnut furniture and could not decide as to which room was the prettier.

"Eleanor," said Grace solemnly, "you ought to be a very happy girl. You have everything a heart can wish. Think of poor little Mabel Allison."

"Oh, don't let's think about disagreeable things," said Eleanor lightly. "Sit down and be comfy and I'll play for you. What shall I play?"

"Do you know the 'Peer Gynt' suite?" asked Grace. "I love 'Anitra's Dance.'"

Without answering, Eleanor immediately began the "Peer Gynt" music and played the entire suite with remarkable expression.

"How well you play!" exclaimed Jessica with eager admiration in her voice, as Eleanor turned around on the stool after she had finished. "I should love to hear you play on the violin. Anne heard you the other night, and told us about it."

"I love the violin better than the piano, but it sounds better with a piano accompaniment. Don't you girls play?"

"Jessica does," chorused her friends.

"Oh, I never could play, after hearing Eleanor," said Jessica blushing.

"Come on," said Eleanor, taking her by the arm and dragging her over to the piano. "You can accompany me. What do you play?"

"Do you know Raff's 'Cavatina'?" asked Jessica a trifle shyly.

"By heart," answered Eleanor. "I love it. Wait and I'll get the music for you."

After a moment's search she produced the music, picked up her violin, and, after tightening a string, announced herself ready.

The girls listened, spellbound. It seemed as though Eleanor's very soul had entered into the violin. They could not believe that this was the capricious Eleanor of half an hour before.

"Whatever she may do in future," thought Grace, as she listened to the last plaintive notes of the "Cavatina," "I'll forgive her for her music's sake. One has to make allowances for people like her. It is the claim of the artistic temperament."

"Please play once more," begged Nora. "Then we must go. It's almost six o'clock."

Eleanor chose Nevin's "Venetian Love Song," and Jessica again accompanied her.

"You play with considerable expression," said Eleanor, as Jessica rose from the piano stool.

"How could I help it?" replied Jessica, smiling. "You inspired me."

Eleanor accompanied the four girls down the walk to the gate and repeatedly invited them to come again.

"It's your turn to come and see us now," said Grace. "Do you think you will go to school to-morrow, Eleanor? Miss Thompson dislikes having the girls stay out."

"I can't help what Miss Thompson dislikes," returned Eleanor, laughing. "What I dislike is of more importance to me. I dare say I shall go to-morrow, providing I get up in time."

"What an irresponsible girl Eleanor is," remarked Anne, as they walked along. "I am afraid we can't do much for her. She doesn't seem much interested in school and I don't think she is particularly impressed with our sorority."

"Anne," said Jessica, "you have seen Miss Nevin, her aunt. Tell us how she looks."

"She is tall," replied Anne, "and has beautiful dark eyes. Her hair is very white, but her face looks young, only she has the saddest expression I ever saw on any one's face."

"I should think she would look sad after seventeen years of Eleanor's whims," remarked Nora bluntly. "It would wear me out to be with her continually, she is so changeable."

"Mrs. Gray told me," remarked Anne, "that Miss Nevin's life had been one long sacrifice to the pleasure of others. First her father, then her step-sister and now Eleanor. She was engaged to be married to a young English officer, and he died of fever while stationed in India. So, there is reason for her sad expression."

"I once read, somewhere," said Jessica sentimentally, "that "Tis better to have loved and lost than never to have loved at all.'"

"Humph!" said Nora. "If I am ever foolish enough to fall in love, I certainly don't want to lose the object of my devotion."

"You can't very well," said Grace slyly, "for from all present indications I should say that he is too fat to get lost."

And Nora was obliged to explain elaborately to the laughing girls, all the way home, that the object of her future devotion would not be a fat man.

# CHAPTER VII

## THE CLAIM OF THE "ARTISTIC TEMPERAMENT"

When Eleanor returned to school the following morning, she found that what Miss Thompson "disliked" was, after all, of considerable importance. Directly after opening exercises the principal sent for her and asked the reason for her absence of the day before. On finding that Eleanor had no plausible excuse, but had absented herself merely because she felt like it, Miss Thompson thereupon delivered a sharp little lecture on unnecessary absence, informing Eleanor that it was the rule of the school to present a written excuse for absence, and that a verbal excuse would not be accepted.

"I will overlook it this time, Miss Savell," Miss Thompson said, "because you are not as yet thoroughly acquainted with the rules of this school, but do not let it occur again. And I must also insist upon punctuality in future. You have been late a number of times."

With these words the principal turned to her desk and resumed the writing she had been engaged in when Eleanor entered.

For a second, Eleanor stood regarding Miss Thompson with angry eyes. No one had ever before dared to speak sharply to her. She was about to tell the principal that she was not used to being addressed in that tone, but the words would not come. Something in the elder woman's quiet, resolute face as she sat writing checked the willful girl, and though she felt deeply incensed at the reprimand, she managed to control herself and walked out of the office with her head held high, vowing to herself that Miss Thompson should pay for what Eleanor termed "her insolence."

All morning she sulked through her classes, and before closing time had managed to incur the displeasure of every teacher to whom she recited.

"What ails her to-day?" whispered Nora to Jessica.

It was geometry hour, and Miss Ames, the geometry teacher, had just reproved Eleanor for inattention.

Nora shook her head. She dared not answer, as Miss Ames was very strict, and she knew that to be caught whispering meant two originals to work out, and Nora hated originals.

When the bell rang at the close of the hour, Eleanor walked haughtily by Miss Ames, giving her a contemptuous look as she passed that made the teacher tighten her lips and look severe. Grace, who was directly behind her, saw both the look and the expression on the teacher's face. She felt worried for Eleanor's sake, because she saw trouble ahead for her unless she changed her tactics. If Eleanor could only understand that she must respect the authority of her various teachers during recitation hours and cheerfully comply with their requests, then all might be well. Since Miss Leece had left the High School at the close of Grace's freshman year, she could not conscientiously say that she disliked any of her teachers. They had been both kind and just, and if Eleanor defied them openly, then she would have to take the consequences. To be sure, Eleanor might refuse to go to school, but Grace had an idea that, lenient as Miss Nevin was with her niece, she would not allow Eleanor to go that far. Grace decided that she would have a talk with Eleanor after school. It would do no harm and it might possibly do some good.

She hurried down to the locker-room that afternoon in order to catch Eleanor as she left school. She had just reached there when Eleanor walked in, looking extremely sulky. She jerked her hat and coat from her locker, hastily donned them, and, without looking at Grace, left the room.

"She looks awfully cross," thought Grace. "Well, here goes," and she hurried after Eleanor, overtaking her at the entrance to the school grounds.

"What's the matter, Eleanor?" she asked. "Didn't you care to wait for me?"

Eleanor looked at her with lowering brows. "I hate school," she said vehemently. "I hate the teachers, and I hate Miss Thompson most of all. Every one of those teachers are common, low-bred and impertinent. As for your Miss Thompson, she is a self-satisfied prig."

"You must not say such things of Miss Thompson, Eleanor," said Grace firmly. "She doesn't deserve them. She is one of the finest women I have ever known, and she takes a warm interest in every girl in school. What has she done that you should speak of her as you do?"

"She called me into her office this morning and made a whole lot of fuss because I didn't have a written excuse for yesterday's absence," said Eleanor angrily. "When I told her that I stayed at home because I felt inclined to do so, she almost had a spasm, and gave me another lecture then and there, ending up by saying that it must not occur again. I should like to know how she knew I was absent yesterday."

"Miss Thompson always knows when a girl is absent," replied Grace. "The special teachers report to her every day. It is the rule of this school for a girl to present her excuse at the office as soon as she returns; then her name is taken off the absent list. If she is absent the second day, then a messenger is sent to her home to find out the cause. I suppose that when Miss Thompson looked over the list, she remembered seeing you at opening exercises, so of course sent for you."

"She is a crabbed old maid," said Eleanor contemptuously, "and I despise her. I'll find some way to get even with her, and all the rest of those teachers, too."

"You will never get along in school, Eleanor," answered Grace gently, "if you take that stand. The only way to be happy is to——"

"Please don't preach to me," said Eleanor haughtily. "It is of no use. I am not a child and I understand my own business thoroughly. When I saw you girls the first day of school, I thought that you were full of life and spirit, but really you are all goody-goodies, who allow those teachers to lead you around by the nose. I had intended to ask Aunt Margaret to take me out of this ridiculous school, for some of the people in it make me tired, but I have changed my mind. I shall stay for pure spite and show that stiff-necked principal of yours that I am a law unto myself, and won't stand her interference."

"Stop a moment, Eleanor. I am going no farther with you," said Grace, flushing, "but I should just like to say before I leave you that you are taking the wrong view of things, and you'll find it out sooner or later. I am sorry that you have such a poor opinion of myself and my friends, for we cherish nothing but the friendliest feelings toward you."

With this, Grace walked away, feeling more hurt over Eleanor's rudeness than she cared to show.

As she turned out of High School Street she heard a familiar call, and, glancing up the street, saw her three chums waiting for her on the corner.

"We saw you just as you tackled Eleanor," said Nora, "so we kept away, for we thought after to-day's performances she wouldn't be in a very good humor."

"What was the matter with her to-day?" asked Jessica curiously. "She behaved like a bad child in English this morning, followed it up in geometry; and Anne says that in rhetoric class Miss Chester lost all patience with her and gave her a severe lecturing."

"I might as well tell you at once that Eleanor's opinion of us is far from flattering," said Grace, half laughing, although there was a hurt look on her face. "She says we are all goody-goodies and that we make her tired. She also requested me to mind my own business."

"She said that to you? Just wait until the next time I see her," blustered Nora, "I'll tell her what I think of her."

"On the contrary, we must treat her better, if anything, than before," said Anne quietly. "Don't you remember we promised Mrs. Gray that we would try to help her?"

"Yes, I remember all that; but I can't bear to have any one say horrid things to Grace," grumbled Nora.

"What a queer girl she is," said Jessica. "Yesterday she treated us as though we were her dearest friends, while to-day she scorns us utterly. It's a case of 'blow hot, blow cold.'"

"That is because she has the artistic temperament," replied Anne, smiling.

"You may say what you like about the artistic temperament," said Nora, "but in my opinion it's nothing more nor less than just plain temper."

## CHAPTER VIII

## ELEANOR THROWS DOWN THE GAUNTLET

"The Phi Sigma Tau is to have a special meeting to-night at Jessica's," called Grace Harlowe to Nora O'Malley as the latter entered the locker-room at the close of school one day about two weeks after the initiation at Jessica's.

"Does Jessica know it?" inquired Nora.

"Not yet," replied Grace, "but she will as soon as she comes in. I rushed down here the minute the last bell rang, because I wanted to be here when the girls come in. You are the first, however."

"Why are we to hold a meeting?" asked Nora, her curiosity aroused.

"Wait and see," replied Grace, smiling. "Of what use is it to hold a meeting, if I tell you all the business beforehand?"

"All right," said Nora, "you keep your secrets and I'll keep mine."

"What have you heard that's new?" asked Grace.

"Wait and see," replied Nora, with a grin of delight. "I am saving my news for the meeting."

By this time the remaining members of the Phi Sigma Tau, with the exception of Eleanor Savell, had come into the locker-room, and had been promptly hailed by Grace. Marian Barber, Miriam Nesbit and Eva Allen after agreeing to be at Jessica's, at eight o'clock, had gone their separate ways.

"Everyone excepting Eleanor has been told," said Grace. "I really don't know how to approach her. She has been so distant of late."

"Don't wait to ask her," said Nora decidedly. "She won't attend the meeting."

"How do you know?" asked Jessica.

350

"I'll tell you to-night," answered Nora mysteriously, "but I know positively that she won't come, because she is going to have company at 'Heartsease.' Now I've told you more than I intended to, and I shall not say another word until to-night."

"Come on then," said Grace, "we won't wait any longer. Jessica, will you ask your father if he will be at liberty for a few minutes this evening?"

"Certainly," replied Jessica.

"Oh, I know now whom it's all about," cried Nora gleefully. "Mary Stevens."

"You have guessed it," said Grace, "but, like yourself, I decline to talk until to-night."

Before eight o'clock the seven girls had taken possession of the Bright's big, comfortable sitting room and were impatiently waiting for Grace to tell her news.

"Before I tell you what is on my mind," said Grace, "we ought to have a president, vice president and secretary for this worthy organization. I move therefore that we choose Miriam Nesbit for president of this sorority. Those in favor say 'aye.' We'll dispense with seconding the motion."

There was an instant's pause, then a chorus of "ayes" burst forth.

"Contrary, 'no.'"

The only "no" was from Miriam.

"We appreciate the fact that you are too polite to vote for yourself, Miriam," said Grace, "but your 'no' doesn't amount to a row of pins. You're elected, so come over here and occupy the chair of state. Long live the president of the Phi Sigma Tau."

Miriam, flushed with pleasure, then took the seat that Grace had vacated. She had not expected this honor and was deeply touched by it. Her summer with her girl chums at Lake George had made her an entirely different girl from the Miriam of old. Admiration for Grace and her friends had taken the place of the old animosity. Although the chums had not taken her into their inner circle, still they made much of her, and she came nearer to being one of them than any other girl in the junior class.

"I am sure I thank you all," began Miriam, "and now we must have a vice president and a secretary."

Grace and Anne were elected with enthusiasm to the respective offices, then Miriam requested Grace to tell the other members what was on her mind.

After addressing the chair, Grace began: "I know you will all be glad to hear that Mabel has received a letter from Mary Stevens. It was addressed to me on the outside envelope and Mabel has given me permission to open and read it to you. She is willing for us to do whatever we think best. I won't attempt to read all the letter, only that part that interests us.

"Here it is: 'I am so sorry about the way in which you are treated, but glad to know that you have found friends at last. Miss Brant has no claim on you whatever. She took you from the orphanage with the understanding that if you did not suit her she was to be allowed to send you back. The matron asked her why she did not adopt you, or at least appoint herself your guardian, and she said that under no circumstances would she do so; that she wanted a good maid of all work, not a daughter. I enclose a statement from the matron to this effect. I would have advised you before this to leave her, but you are too young to drift about the world alone. I hope that when I next hear from you, you will be in happier surroundings. I have always believed that your parents were people of means and that you were lost or stolen when a baby. Perhaps if they are still living you will find them some day.'"

"That is about all we need," said Grace, as she folded the letter and put it back in the envelope. "The next thing to do is to see Mr. Bright."

"I'll go for him at once," said Jessica, and darted off to the library, where her father sat reading. He rose, and, tucking his daughter's arm in his, walked out to the sitting room, where the Phi Sigma Tau eagerly awaited him.

"Well, well!" he exclaimed, smiling at the circle of girls. "What's all this? Am I invited to be present at a suffragette's meeting or is Jessica simply anxious to show me what nice friends she has?"

"No compliments allowed," laughed Grace. "We wish to ask your advice about something."

"I am at your service," said Jessica's father, making her an elaborate bow. "Command me as you will."

"'Tis well, most reverend sir. I thank you," said Grace, with a curtsy. "Now sit you down, I pray, for presently I have a tale to tell."

Having conducted Mr. Bright with great ceremony to the arm chair in the corner, Grace established him with many low bows, much to the amusement of the girls, with whom Jessica's father was a great favorite. Then Grace began with her meeting with Mabel Allison and ended with the letter from Mary Stevens, enclosing the matron's statement.

"Now, those are all the facts of the case, Mr. Bright," she concluded. "Will it be possible for us to get Mabel away from Miss Brant, or can Miss Brant hold her against her will?"

"Miss Stevens' letter and the matron's statement are sufficient," answered Mr. Bright. "This woman cannot hold your little friend. Miss Brant will in all probability be very angry, and attempt to brave the matter out. Suppose you and Jessica and I go down there together, Grace, and see what we can do?"

"O Mr. Bright!" cried Grace, clasping her hands delightedly, "will you, truly? Then let's go to-morrow and bring Mabel back with us."

"Very well; you and Jessica meet me at my office at four o'clock to-morrow afternoon," said Mr. Bright. "But what do you girls intend to do with her, once you get her? You can't adopt her, you know."

"She is to take turns living with us, papa," said Jessica, slipping her

353

hand into her father's. "May she come here first? I'd love to have her."

Mr. Bright drew Jessica to his side. "My dear child, you know that you may do as you please about it. I feel sure that she must be the right sort of girl, or you and your friends wouldn't have become interested in her. Try her, and if you like her, then she is welcome to stay as long as she chooses. I think it would do you good to have a girl of your own age in the house."

"Three cheers for Mr. Bright," cried Nora.

The cheers were given with a will, then the girls joined hands and danced around Jessica's father, sounding their class yell until he broke through the circle and made a rush for the library, his fingers to his ears.

"Now that we have that question settled," said Miriam Nesbit, after the girls were once more seated, "I think we ought to have a sorority pin."

"I think," began Eva Allen, "that my brother would design a pin for us. He is very clever at that sort of thing."

"Let's have a monogram," exclaimed Grace. "Old English letters of gold on a dull-green enamel background. We can get them up for about two dollars and a half apiece. Is that too expensive?"

The girls, who, with the exception of Anne, had small allowances of their own, expressed themselves satisfied; while Anne determined that for once she was justified in yielding to wild extravagance.

"That's settled," said Miriam. "The next thing to do is——"

But a loud ring of the door bell interrupted her speech and caused the whole party to start.

"Someone to see papa," said Jessica. "Go on with what you were saying, Miriam."

But before Miriam had a chance to continue, the maid entered the room, a letter in her hand.

"Here's a letter, Miss Jessica," she said. "But it's such a quare name on the outside, I be wondering if it's fur yerself and no other?"

Jessica looked at the envelope. It was addressed to the "Phi Sigma Tau, care of Miss Jessica Bright."

"Why, who in the world can this be from? I thought no one outside knew the name of our society as yet," said Jessica as she opened the end of the envelope. Then she turned the page, glanced at the signature, and gave a little cry of surprise.

"Just listen to this, girls!" she exclaimed, and read:

"'TO THE PHI SIGMA TAU:

"'After initiating me into your ridiculous society, you have seen fit to call a meeting of the members without directly notifying me, therefore I wish to withdraw from your sorority, as I feel that I have been deeply insulted. I have this satisfaction, however, that I would not have met with you to-night, at any rate. I am entertaining some girls in your class this evening, whom I find far more congenial than any previous acquaintances I have made in Oakdale. We are about to organize a sorority of our own. Our object will be to enjoy ourselves, not to continually preach to other people. I am deeply disappointed in all of you, and assure you that I am not in the least desirous of continuing your acquaintance.

"'Yours sincerely,
"'ELEANOR SAVELL.'"

"Well, of all things!" exclaimed Nora O'Malley. "She says she is deeply insulted because we didn't invite her, but that she didn't intend to come, at any rate. There's a shining example of consistency for you!"

"Who on earth told her about the meeting?" said Jessica. "We didn't wait to ask her to-day."

"I shall have to confess that I am the guilty one," said Eva Allen. "You didn't say anything to Miriam, Marian and me about Eleanor, and when I left the locker-room I went back upstairs after a book I had forgotten. I met Eleanor on the stairs and told her about the meeting, and that you were waiting in the locker-room for her. You must have left before she got there, and, of course, she thought you did it purposely."

"Oh, dear, what a mess," sighed Grace. "I didn't mean to slight her. But Nora said she knew, positively, that Eleanor was entertaining some guests to-night, so I didn't wait. By the way, Nora, what was that news of yours that you were so mysterious about this afternoon?"

"Just this," replied Nora. "That Edna Wright told me, that I needn't think we were the only people that could have a sorority. I asked her what she meant, and she said that she and Rose Lynton and Daisy Culver had been invited out to Eleanor's to-night for the purpose of forming a very select club of their own. I am sorry I didn't tell you while in the locker-room, but you would insist on having secrets, so I thought I'd have one, too."

"Well, it can't be helped now," said Grace. "It is a pity that Eleanor has taken up with Edna Wright. She is the only girl in the class that I really dislike. She is frivolous and empty-headed, and Eleanor is self-willed and lawless. Put them together, and they will make a bad combination. As to the other two girls, they are sworn friends of Edna's."

"I think," said Nora, "that our reform movement is about to end in a glaring fizzle."

"How can we reform a person who won't have anything to do with us?" asked Jessica scornfully.

"Let us hold her place in this sorority open for her, and let us make it our business to be ready to help her if she needs us," said Anne thoughtfully. "Like all spoiled children, she is sure to get into mischief, and just as sure to come to grief. Mark my words, some day she'll be glad to come back to the Phi Sigma Tau."

# CHAPTER IX

## THE RESCUE PARTY

It was with mingled feelings of excitement and trepidation that Grace Harlowe and Jessica Bright hurried toward the office of the latter's father the following afternoon. Now that they were fairly started on their mission of rescue, they were not quite so confident as to the result. To be sure they had unlimited faith in Jessica's father, but it was so much easier to talk about taking Mabel away from Miss Brant than to do it.

"I'm terribly afraid of facing her," confided Jessica to Grace. "She is the terror of Oakdale, you know."

"She can't hurt us," said Grace. "Your father will do all the talking. All we need to do is to take charge of Mabel, after Miss Brant gives her up."

"Well, young ladies," said Mr. Bright, as the two girls entered his office, "I see you are prompt in keeping your appointment. Let us go at once, for I must be back here at five o'clock."

"What are you going to say to that terrible woman, papa?" shuddered Jessica as they neared the Brant home. "I'm afraid she'll scratch your eyes out."

"Am I really in such serious danger?" asked Mr. Bright in mock alarm. "I am glad I brought you girls along to protect me."

"You haven't any idea what a crank she is, Mr. Bright," laughed Grace. "She fairly snarled at us the other day, when we were coming from school, because she said we were taking up the whole sidewalk. Poor little Mabel, no wonder she has a scared look in her eyes all the time."

"Well, here we are," responded Mr. Bright, as he rang the bell. "Now for the tug of war."

As he spoke the door was opened by Mabel, who positively shook in her shoes when she saw her visitors. "Don't be frightened," whispered

Grace, taking her hand. "We have come for you."

"May I speak with Miss Brant?" asked Mr. Bright courteously, as they stepped into the narrow hall.

Before Mabel had time to answer, a tall, raw-boned woman, with a hard, forbidding face, shoved her aside and confronted them. It was Miss Brant herself.

"Well, what do you want?" she said rudely.

"Good afternoon," said Mr. Bright courteously. "Am I speaking to Miss Brant?"

"I guess likely you are," responded the woman, "and you better state your business now, for I've no time to fool away on strangers."

"You have a young girl with you by the name of Mabel Allison, have you not?" asked Mr. Bright.

"Yes, I have. What's the matter with her? Has she been gettin' into mischief? If she has, I'll tan her hide," said Miss Brant, with a threatening gesture.

"On the contrary," replied Mr. Bright, "I hear very good reports of her. Has she lived with you long?"

"That's none of your business," snapped Miss Brant. "If you've come here to quiz me and pry around about her, you can get right out, for I'm not answering any fool questions."

"I will not trouble you with further questions," replied Mr. Bright, "but will proceed at once to business. I have come to take Miss Mabel away with me. She has found friends who are willing to help her until she finishes her education, and she wishes to go to them."

"Oh, she does, does she?" sneered the woman mockingly. "Well, you just take her, if you dare."

"Have you legally adopted her?" asked Mr. Bright quietly.

"That's none of your business, either. You get out of my house or I'll throw you out and these two snips of girls with you," almost screamed Miss Brant.

"That will do," said Mr. Bright sternly. "We will go, but we shall take Miss Mabel with us. I am a lawyer, Miss Brant, and I have positive proof that this child is not bound to you in any way. You took her from the orphanage on trial, exactly as you might hire a servant. You did not even take the trouble to have yourself appointed her guardian. You agreed to pay her for her work, but blows and harsh words are the only payment she has ever received at your hands. She wishes to leave you because she can no longer endure life with you. You haven't the slightest claim upon her, and she is perfectly free to do as she chooses. She is not of age yet, but as you are not her guardian, you had no right to take money that she has earned from her, and she can call you to account for it if she chooses. However, you have imposed upon her for the last time, for she shall not spend another hour under your roof."

"You touch her if you dare. She shan't leave this house," said the woman in a furious tone.

"Mabel," said Mr. Bright to the young girl, who was cowering at one end of the hall, "get your things and come at once. We will wait for you. As for you," turning to Miss Brant, "if you try to stop her, you will soon find yourself in a most unpleasant position. I am certain that if you think back for an instant you will realize that you have forfeited all right to object."

For a moment Miss Brant stood speechless with anger, then in her wrath she poured forth such a flood of abuse that the rescue party stared in amazement. Never had they seen such an exhibition of temper. When Mabel appeared, her shabby hat in her hand, Miss Brant reached forward and tore the hat from her.

"Don't you dare leave my house with any of my property, you baggage," she hissed. "I paid for that hat and for the clothes you're wearing, and you'll send every stitch you've on back to me, or I'll have you arrested for stealing."

"Come on, Mabel," said Grace, putting her arm around the shrinking little figure. "Don't pay any attention to her. She isn't worth bothering over. You can send her back her ridiculous things. You are going to be happy now, and forget all about this cruel, terrible woman."

"You brazen imp, you," screamed the woman, and rushed at Grace, who stood perfectly still, looking the angry woman in the face with such open scorn in her gray eyes that Miss Brant drew back and stood scowling at her, her hands working convulsively.

"Come, girls," said Mr. Bright. "We have no more time to waste. If you have anything to say to me, Miss Brant, you can always find me at my office on East Main Street. The clothing now worn by Miss Mabel will be returned to you in due season. Good afternoon."

Mr. Bright, bowing politely, motioned to the three young girls to precede him, and the party went quietly down the walk, leaving Miss Brant in the open door, shaking her fist and uttering dire threats.

As for Mabel, she collapsed utterly, crying as though her heart would break. Grace and Jessica exerted every effort to quiet her sobs, and after a little she looked up, and, smiling through her tears, said brokenly: "I can't believe that it's all true—that I shall never have to go back there again. I'm afraid that it's all a dream and that I'll wake up and find her standing over me. Can she get me again?" she said, turning piteously to Mr. Bright.

"My dear little girl," he said, taking her hand, "she can't touch you. I'll adopt you myself before I'll let you go back to her. Now run along with Jessica and forget all about what has passed. Good-bye, Grace. You see, your rescue party proved a success. Good-bye, daughter. Take good care of Mabel. I'll have to hurry now, or miss my appointment."

Mr. Bright beamed on the three girls, raised his hat and hurried down the street, leaving them to proceed slowly toward Jessica's home. Passersby glanced curiously at the hatless, shabby young girl, as she walked between Grace and Jessica, clinging to their hands as though expecting every minute to be snatched from them.

"Well, girls," said Grace, "here is my street. I must leave you now. Be good children, and——"

She was interrupted by an exultant shriek, and a second later five girls appeared as by magic and gleefully surrounded the rescue party. The Phi Sigma Tau was out in full force.

"Hurrah!" shrieked Nora, waving her school bag. "'We have met the enemy and they are ours.' Tell us about it quickly. Why didn't you let me go along? I was dying to cross swords with that old stone face."

Then everyone talked at once, surrounding Mabel and asking her questions until Grace said, laughing: "Stop it, girls; let her get used to you gradually. Don't come down on her like an avalanche."

Mabel, however, was equal to the occasion. She answered their questions without embarrassment, and seemed quietly pleased at their demonstrations.

"You are the child of the sorority now, Mabel," said Miriam Nesbit, "and we are your adopted mothers. You will have your hands full trying to please all of us."

"Stop teasing her," said Anne, "or she'll run away before she is fairly adopted."

"It is very uncertain as to whether she will ever go further than my house," said Jessica calmly. "I need Mabel more than do the rest of you, but perhaps if you're good I'll loan her to you occasionally. Come on, Mabel, let's go home before they spoil you completely."

"Considering the fact that the Bright family did two thirds of the rescuing, I suppose we shall have to respect your claim," said Nora, "but remember, Jessica, that generosity is a beautiful virtue to cultivate."

# CHAPTER X

## JULIA PERFORMS A SACRED DUTY

"What have we ever done that we should be so neglected?" said David Nesbit, swinging himself from his motorcycle and landing squarely in front of Grace Harlowe and Anne Pierson while they were out walking one afternoon.

"Why, David Nesbit, how can you make such statements?" replied Grace, looking at the young man in mock disapproval. "You know perfectly well that you've been shut up in your old laboratory all fall. We have scarcely seen you since the walking party. You have even given football the go by, and I'm so sorry, for you were a star player last year."

"I see you have discovered the secrets of my past life," replied David, laughing. "That's what comes of having a sister who belongs to a sorority. However, you folks are equally guilty, you've all gone mad over your sorority, and left Hippy and Reddy and me to wander about Oakdale like lost souls. I hear you've adopted a girl, too. Reddy is horribly jealous of her. He says Jessica won't look at him anymore."

"Reddy is laboring under a false impression," said Anne. "He is head over heels in football practice and has forgotten he ever knew Jessica. As for Hippy, Nora says that he is studying night and day, and that he is actually wearing himself away by burning midnight oil."

"Yes, Hippy is studying some this year," replied David. "You see this is our senior year, and we are going to enter the same college next year, if all goes well. You know Hippy never bothered himself much about study, just managed to scrape through. But now he'll have to hustle if he gets through with High School this year, and he's wide awake to that fact."

"Under those circumstances, Hippy is forgiven, but not you and Reddy!" said Grace severely. "You'll have to have better excuses than football and experiments."

"I'll tell you what we'll do to square ourselves," said David, smiling. "We'll take you girls to the football game next Thursday. It's Thanksgiving Day, you know, and Oakdale is going to play Georgetown College. Reddy's on the team, but Hippy and I will do the honors."

362

"Fine," replied Grace. "But are you willing to burden yourselves with some extra girls? You see it's this way. One of the things that our sorority has pledged itself to do this year is to look up the stray girls in High School, and see that they are not lonely and homesick during holiday seasons. I used to know nearly all the girls in school, but ever so many new ones have crept in, and some of them have come here from quite a distance, on account of the excellence of our High School. After we adopted Mabel Allison, we began looking about us for other fish to fry, and found out about these girls. So every girl in the sorority has invited one or more of these lonely ones for Thanksgiving Day. They are to come in the morning and stay until the lights go out, which will be late, for mother has consented to let me have a party and all those new girls are to be the guests of honor.

"Mrs. Gray is in it, too. She insists on having Anne with her on Thanksgiving, although Anne had invited two girls to her house," continued Grace. "Mrs. Gray had planned a party for us, but when we told her what we were about to do, she gave up her party and agreed to go to mine instead, on condition that Anne's family, plus Anne's two guests, should have dinner with her."

"Bless her dear heart," said David, "she is always thinking of the pleasure of others. Now about the football game. Bring your girls along and I'll do my best to give them a good time, although I'm generally anything but a success with new girls. However, Hippy makes up for what I lack. He can entertain a regiment of them, and not even exert himself. Now I must leave you, for I have a very important engagement at home."

"In the laboratory, I suppose," said Anne teasingly.

"Just so," replied David. "Good-bye, girls. Let me know how many tickets you want for the game." He raised his cap, mounted his machine and was off down the street.

"It will seem good to have a frolic with the boys again, won't it?" said Grace to Anne as they strolled along.

"We do seem to be getting awfully serious and settled of late," replied Anne. "Why, this sorority business has taken up all our spare time lately. We've had so many special meetings."

"I know it," replied Grace, "but after Thanksgiving we'll only meet once in two weeks, for I must get my basketball team in shape, and you see all the members belong to the society."

"You ought to do extra good work this year," observed Anne, "for the team is absolutely harmonious. Last season seems like a dream to me now."

"It was real enough then," replied Grace grimly. "I have forgiven, long ago, but I have not forgotten the way some of those girls performed last year. It was remarkable that things ever straightened themselves. The clouds looked black for a while, didn't they?"

Anne pressed Grace's hand by way of answer. The sophomore year had been crowded with many trials, some of them positive school tragedies, in which Anne and Grace had been the principal actors.

"What are you two mooning over?" asked a gay voice, and the two girls turned with a start to find Julia Crosby grinning cheerfully at them.

"O Julia, how glad I am to see you at close range!" exclaimed Grace. "Admiring you from a distance isn't a bit satisfactory."

"Business, children, business," said Julia briskly. "That's the only thing that keeps me from your side. The duties of the class president are many and irksome. At the present moment I've a duty on hand that I don't in the least relish, and I want your august assistance. Will you promise to help before I tell you?"

"Why, of course," answered Grace and Anne in the same breath. "What is it you want us to do?"

"Well, it seems that some of your juniors are still in need of discipline. You remember the hatchet that we buried last year with such pomp and ceremony?"

"Yes, yes," was the answer.

"This morning I overheard certain girls planning to go out to the Omnibus House after school to-morrow and dig up the poor hatchet and flaunt it in the seniors' faces the day of the opening basketball game, simply to rattle us. Just as though it wouldn't upset your team as much as ours. It's an idiotic trick, at any rate, and anything but funny. Now I propose to take four of our class, and you must select four of yours. We'll hustle out there the minute school is over to-morrow, and be ready to receive the marauders when they arrive. Select your girls, but don't tell them what you want or they may tell someone about it beforehand."

"Well, of all impudence!" exclaimed Anne. "Who are the girls, Julia? Are you sure they're juniors?"

"The two I heard talking are juniors. I don't know who else is in it. They'll be very much astonished to find us 'waiting at the church'—Omnibus House, I mean," said Julia, "and I imagine they'll feel rather silly, too."

"Tell us who they are, Julia," said Grace. "We don't want to go into this blindfolded."

"Wait and see," replied Julia tantalizingly. "Then you'll feel more indignant and can help my cause along all the better. I give you my word that the girls I overheard talking are not particular friends of yours. You aren't going to back out, are you, and leave me without proper support?"

"Of course not," laughed Grace. "Don't worry. We'll support you, only you must agree to do all the talking."

"I shall endeavor to overcome their insane freshness with a few well-chosen words," Julia promised. "Be sure and be on hand early."

Grace chose Anne, Nora, Jessica and Marian Barber, the latter three being considerably mystified at her request, but nevertheless agreeing to be on hand when school closed. They were met at the gate by Julia and four other seniors, and the whole party set out for the Omnibus House without delay.

Grace walked with Julia, and the two girls found plenty to say to each other during the walk. Julia was studying hard, she told Grace. She wanted to enter Smith next year.

"I don't know where I shall go after I finish High School," said Grace. "Ethel Post wants me to go to Wellesley. She'll be a junior when I'm a freshman. You know, she was graduated from High School last June and she could help me a lot in getting used to college. But I don't know whether I should like Wellesley. I shall not try to decide where I want to go for a while yet."

"Wherever we are we'll write and always be friends," said Julia, and Grace warmly acquiesced.

As they neared the old Omnibus House they could see no one about.

"We're early!" exclaimed Julia. "The enemy has not arrived. Thank goodness, it's not cold to-day or we might have a chilly vigil. Now listen, all ye faithful, while I set forth the object of this walk." She thereupon related what Grace and Anne already knew.

"What a shame!" cried Marian Barber. "It isn't the hatchet we care for, it's the principle of the thing. Give them what they deserve, Julia."

"Never fear," replied Julia. "I'll effectually attend to their case. Now we'd better dodge around the corner and keep out of sight until they get here. Then we'll swoop down upon them unawares."

The avengers hurriedly concealed themselves at the side of the old house where they could not be seen by an approaching party.

They had not waited long before they heard voices.

"They're coming," whispered Julia. "There are eight of them. Form in line and when they get nicely started, we'll circle about them and hem them in. I'll give you the signal."

The girls waited in silence. "They have trowels," Julia informed them from time to time. "They have a spade. They've begun to dig, and they are having their own troubles, for the ground is hard. All ready! March!"

Softly the procession approached the spot where the marauders were energetically digging. Grace gave a little gasp, and reaching back caught Anne's hand.

The girl using the spade was Eleanor.

"Now I'm in for it," groaned Grace. "She's down on me now, and she'll be sure to think I organized the whole thing." For an instant Grace regretted making the promise to Julia, before learning the situation; then, holding her head a trifle more erect, she decided to make the best of her unfortunate predicament.

"It isn't Julia's fault," she thought. "She probably knows nothing about our acquaintance with Eleanor; besides, Eleanor has no business to play such tricks. Edna Wright must have told her all about last year."

Her reflections were cut short, for one of the girls glanced up from her digging with a sudden exclamation which drew all eyes toward Julia and her party.

"Well, little folks," said Julia in mock surprise, "what sort of a party is this? Are you making mud pies or are you pretending you are at the seashore?"

At Julia's first words Eleanor dropped the small spade she held and straightened up, the picture of defiance. Her glance traveled from girl to girl, and she curled her lip contemptuously as her eye rested on Grace and Anne. The other diggers looked sheepishly at Julia, who stood eyeing them in a way that made them feel "too foolish for anything," as one of them afterwards expressed it.

"Why don't you answer me, little girls?" asked Julia. "Has the kitty stolen your tongue?"

This was too much for Eleanor.

"How dare you speak to us in that manner and treat us as though we were children?" she burst forth. "What business is it of yours why we are here? Do you own this property?"

"Mercy, no," replied Julia composedly. "Do you?"

"No," replied Eleanor a trifle less rudely, "but we have as much right here as you have."

"Granted," replied Julia calmly. "However, there is this difference. You are here to make mischief and we are here to prevent it, and, furthermore, are going to do so."

"What do you mean?" retorted Eleanor, her eyes flashing.

"Just this," replied Julia. "Last year the girls belonging to the present senior and junior classes met on this very spot and amicably disposed of a two-year-old class grudge. Emblematic of this they buried a hatchet, once occupying a humble though honorable position in the Crosby family, but cheerfully sacrificed for the good of the cause.

"Yesterday," continued Julia, "I overheard two juniors plotting to get possession of this same hatchet for the purpose of flaunting it in the faces of the seniors at the opening basketball game. Therefore I decided to take a hand in things, and here I am, backed by girls from both classes, who are of the self-same mind."

"Really, Miss Crosby," said Edna Wright, "you are very amusing."

"My friends all think so," returned Julia sweetly, "but never mind now about my amusing qualities, Edna. Let's talk about the present situation."

She looked at Edna with the old-time aggravating smile that was always warranted to further incense her opponent. It had its desired effect, for Edna fairly bristled with indignation and was about to make a furious reply when she was pushed aside by Eleanor, who said loftily, "Allow me to talk to this person, Edna."

"No," said Julia resolutely, every vestige of a smile leaving her face at Eleanor's words. "It would be useless for you to attempt to be spokesman in this matter, because you are a new girl in High School and know nothing of past class matters except from hearsay. But you have with you seven girls who do know all about the enmity that was buried here last spring, and who ought to have enough good sense to know that this afternoon's performance is liable to bring it to life again.

"If you girls carry this hatchet to school and exhibit it to the seniors on the day of the game you are apt to start bad feeling all over again," she said, turning to the others. "There are sure to be some girls in the senior class who would resent it. Neither class has played tricks on the other since peace was declared, and we don't want to begin now.

"That's the reason I asked Grace to appoint a committee of juniors and come out here with me. I feel sure that under the circumstances the absent members of both classes would agree with us if they were present. Digging up a rusty old hatchet is nothing, but digging up a rusty old grudge is quite another matter. We didn't come here to quarrel, but I appeal to you, as members of the junior class, to think before you do something that is bound to cause us all annoyance and perhaps unhappiness."

There was complete silence after Julia finished speaking. What she had said evidently impressed them. Eleanor alone looked belligerent.

"Perhaps we'd better let the old hatchet alone," Daisy Culver said sullenly. "The fun is all spoiled now, and everyone will know about it before school begins to-morrow."

"Daisy, how can you say so?" exclaimed Grace, who, fearing a scene with Eleanor, had hitherto remained silent. "You know perfectly well that none of us will say anything about it. Why, we came out here simply to try to prevent your doing something that might stir up trouble again between the senior and junior classes. There isn't a girl here who would be so contemptible as to tell anyone outside about what has happened to-day."

This was Eleanor's opportunity. Turning furiously on Grace, her eyes flashing, she exclaimed: "Yes, there is one girl who would tell anything, and that girl is you! You pretend to be honorable and high-principled, but you are nothing but a hypocrite and a sneak. I would not trust you as far as I could see you. I have no doubt Miss Crosby obtained her information about this affair to-day from you, and that everyone in school will hear it from the same source. You seem determined to meddle with matters that do not concern you, and I warn you that if you do not change your tactics you may regret it.

"You seem to think yourself the idol of your class, but there are some of the girls who are too clever to be deceived. They do not belong among the number who trail tamely after you, either. And now I wish to say that I despise you and all your friends, and wish never to speak to any of you again. Come on, girls," she said, turning to the members of her party, who had listened in silent amazement to her attack upon Grace. "Let us go. Let them keep their trumpery hatchet."

With these words she turned and stalked across the field to the road, where her runabout stood. After an instant's hesitation, she was followed by Edna, Daisy Culver and those who had come with her. Henceforth there would again be two distinct factions in the junior class.

"Good gracious," exclaimed Julia Crosby. "Talk about your human whirlwinds! What on earth did you ever do to her, Grace?"

But Grace could not answer. She was winking hard to keep back the tears. Twice she attempted to speak and failed. "Never mind her, dear," said Julia, slipping her arm about Grace, while the other girls gathered round with many expressions of displeasure at Eleanor's cruel speech.

"I can't help feeling badly," said Grace, with a sob. "She said such dreadful things."

"No one who knows you would believe them," replied Julia. "By the way, who is she? I know her name is Savell and that she's a recent arrival in Oakdale, but considering the plain and uncomplimentary manner in which she addressed you, you must have seriously offended her ladyship."

"I'll tell you about her as we walk along," replied Grace, wiping her eyes and smiling a little.

"Yes, we had better be moving," said Julia. "The battle is over. No one has been killed and only one wounded. Nevertheless, the enemy has retired in confusion."

# CHAPTER XI

## WORRIES AND PLANS

Although the girls belonging to Julia's party were silent concerning what happened at the Omnibus House, the story leaked out, creating considerable discussion among the members of the two upper classes. Julia Crosby had a shrewd suspicion that Edna Wright had been the original purveyor of the news, and in this she was right. Edna had, under pledge of secrecy, told it to a sophomore, who immediately told it to her dearest friend, and so the tale traveled until it reached Eleanor, with numerous additions, far from pleasing to her. She was thoroughly angry, and at once laid the matter at Grace's door, while her animosity toward Grace grew daily.

But Grace was not the only person that Eleanor disliked. From the day that Miss Thompson had taken her to task for absence, she had entertained a supreme contempt for the principal of which Miss Thompson was wholly unaware until, encountering Eleanor one morning in the corridor, the latter had stared at her with an expression of such open scorn and dislike that Miss Thompson felt her color rise. A direct slap in the face could scarcely have conveyed greater insult than did that one insolent glance. The principal was at a loss as to its import. She wisely decided to ignore it, but stored it up in her memory for future reference.

The sorority that Eleanor had mentioned in her letter to the Phi Sigma Tau, was now in full flower. The seven girls who had accompanied her to the Omnibus House were the chosen members. They wore pins in the shape of skulls and cross bones, and went about making mysterious signs to each other whenever they met. The very name of the society was shrouded in mystery, though Nora O'Malley was heard to declare that she had no doubt it was a branch of the "Black Hand."

Eleanor was the acknowledged leader, but Edna Wright became a close second, and between them they managed to disseminate a spirit of mischief throughout the school that the teachers found hard to combat.

Grace Harlowe watched the trend that affairs were taking with considerable anxiety. Like herself, there were plenty of girls in school to whom mischief did not appeal, but Eleanor's beauty, wealth and fascinating personality were found to dazzle some of the girls, who would follow her about like sheep, and it was over these girls that Grace felt worried. If Eleanor were to organize and carry out any malicious piece of mischief and they were implicated, they would all have to suffer for what she would be directly responsible. Grace's heart was with her class. She wished it to be a class among classes, and felt an almost motherly anxiety for its success.

"What does ail some of our class?" she exclaimed to Anne and Nora one day as they left the school building. "They seem possessed with imps. The Phi Sigma Tau girls and a few of the grinds are really the only ones who behave lately."

"It's largely due to Eleanor, I think," replied Anne. "She seems to have become quite a power among some of the girls in the class. She is helping to destroy that spirit of earnestness that you have tried so hard to cultivate. I think it's a shame, too. The upper class girls ought to set the example for the two lower classes."

"That's just what worries me," said Grace earnestly. "Hardly a recitation passes in my class without some kind of disturbance, and it is always traced to one of the girls in that crowd. The juniors will get the reputation among the teachers this year that the junior class had last, and it seems such a pity. I overheard Miss Chester tell Miss Kane the other day that her junior classes were the most trying of the day, because she had to work harder to maintain discipline than to teach her subject."

"That's a nice reputation to carry around, isn't it!" remarked Nora indignantly. "But all we can do is to try harder than ever to make things go smoothly. I don't believe their society will last long, at any rate. Those girls are sure to quarrel among themselves, and that will end the whole thing. Or they may go too far and have Miss Thompson to reckon with, and that would probably cool their ardor."

"O girls!" exclaimed Grace. "Speaking of Miss Thompson, reminds me that I have something to tell you. What do you suppose the latest is?"

"If you know anything new, it is your duty to tell us at once, without making us beg for it," said Nora reprovingly.

"All right; I accept the reproof," said Grace. "Now for my news. There is talk of giving a Shakespearian play, with Miss Tebbs to engineer it, and the cast to be chosen from the three lower classes. The seniors, of course, will give their own play later."

"How did you find out?" asked Anne.

"Miss Thompson herself told me about it," replied Grace. "She called on mother yesterday afternoon, and, for a wonder, I was at home. She said that it was not positively decided yet, but if the girls did well with the mid-year tests, then directly after there would be a try out for parts, and rehearsals would begin without delay."

"How splendid!" exclaimed Anne, clasping her hands. "How I would love to take part in it!"

"You will, without doubt, if there is a try out," replied Grace. "There is no one in school who can recite as you do; besides, you have been on the stage."

"I shall try awfully hard for a part, even if it is only two lines," said Anne earnestly. "I wonder what play is to be chosen, and if it is to be given for the school only?"

"The play hasn't been decided upon yet," replied Grace, "but the object of it is to get some money for new books for the school library. The plan is to charge fifty cents apiece for the tickets and to give each girl a certain number of them to sell. However, I'm not going to bother much about the play now, for the senior team has just sent me a challenge to play them Saturday, December 12th. So I'll have to get the team together and go to work."

"We're awfully late this year about starting. Don't you think so?" asked Nora.

"Yes," admitted Grace. "I am just as enthusiastic over basketball as ever, only I haven't had the time to devote to it that I did last year."

"Never mind, you'll make up for lost time after Thanksgiving," said Anne soothingly. "As for me, I'm going to dream about the play."

"Anne, I believe you have more love for the stage than you will admit," said Grace, laughing. "You are all taken up with the idea of this play."

"If one could live in the same atmosphere as that of home, then there could be no profession more delightful than that of the actor," replied Anne thoughtfully. "It is wonderful to feel that one is able to forget one's self and become someone else. But it is more wonderful to make one's audience feel it, too. To have them forget that one is anything except the living, breathing person whose character one is trying to portray. I suppose it's the sense of power that one has over people's emotions that makes acting so fascinating. It is the other side that I hate," she added, with a slight shudder.

"I suppose theatrical people do undergo many hardships," said Grace, who, now that the subject had been opened, wanted to hear more of Anne's views of the stage.

"Unless any girl has remarkable talent, I should advise her to keep off the stage," said Anne decidedly. "Of course when a girl comes of a theatrical family for generations, like Maud Adams or Ethel Barrymore, then that is different. She is practically born, bred and brought up in the theatre. She is as carefully guarded as though she lived in a little village, simply because she knows from babyhood all the unpleasant features of the profession and how to avoid them. There is some chance of her becoming great, too. Of course real stars do appear once in a while, who are too talented to be kept down. However, the really great ones are few and far between. When I compare my life before I came here with the good times I have had since I met you girls, I hate the very idea of the stage.

"Only," she concluded with a shame-faced air, "there are times when the desire to act is irresistible, and it did make my heart beat a little bit faster when I heard about the play."

"You dear little mouse," said Grace, putting her arm around Anne. "I was only jesting when I spoke about your love for the stage. I think I understand how you feel, and I hope you get the best part in the play. I know you'll make good."

"She certainly will," said Nora. "But, to give the play a rest and come down to everyday affairs, where shall we meet to go to the football game?"

"Let me see," said Grace. "The game is to be called at three o'clock. I suppose we shall all be through dinner by half past two. You had better bring your girls to my house. Each of you is to have two and Jessica has one besides Mabel. I am to have three; I found another yesterday. David promised to get me the tickets. I wonder how he and Hippy will enjoy chaperoning thirteen girls?"

"I won't have the slightest chance to talk to Hippy," grumbled Nora, "and he has neglected us shamefully of late, too."

"Never mind, you can have him all to yourself at my party," consoled Grace. "By the way, girls, do you think it would be of any use to invite Eleanor?"

"Eleanor?" exclaimed Nora. "After what she has said to you! You might as well throw your invitation into the fire, for it's safe to say that she will do so when she receives it."

Nevertheless, Grace wrote a cordial little note to Eleanor that evening, and two days later she received Eleanor's reply through the mail. On opening the envelope the pieces of her own note fell out, with a half sheet of paper containing the words, "Declined with thanks."

## CHAPTER XII

## A RECKLESS CHAUFFEUR

Thanksgiving Day dawned bright and clear, with just enough frost in the air to make one's blood tingle. It had been a mild fall, with a late Indian summer, and only one or two snow flurries that had lasted but a few hours. This was unusual for Oakdale, as winter generally came with a rush before the middle of November, and treated the inhabitants of that northern city to a taste of zero weather long before the Christmas holidays.

It was with a light heart that Grace Harlowe ate her breakfast and flitted about the house, putting a final touch here and there before receiving her guests. Before eleven o'clock everything was finished, and as she arranged the last flower in its vase she felt a little thrill of pride as she looked about the pretty drawing room. Before going upstairs to dress, she ran into the reception hall for the fourth time to feast her eyes upon a huge bunch of tall chrysanthemums in the beautiful Japanese vase that stood in the alcove under the stairs. They had come about an hour before with a note from Tom Gray saying that he had arrived in Oakdale that morning, had seen the boys and would be around to help David and Reddy at the "girl convention," as he termed it.

Grace was overjoyed at the idea of seeing Tom Gray again. They had been firm friends since her freshman year, and had entertained a wholesome, boy-and-girl preference for each other untinged by any trace of foolish sentimentality.

As she dressed for dinner, Grace felt perfectly happy except for one thing. She still smarted a little at Eleanor's rude reply to her invitation. She was one of those tender-hearted girls who disliked being on bad terms with any one, and she really liked Eleanor still, in spite of the fact that Eleanor did not in the least return the sentiment.

Grace sighed a little over the rebuff, and then completely forgot her trouble as she donned the new gown that had just come from the dressmaker. It was of Italian cloth in a beautiful shade of dark red, made in one piece, with a yoke of red and gold net, and trimmed with tiny enameled buttons. It fitted her straight, slender figure perfectly and she decided that for once she had been wise in foregoing her favorite blue and choosing red.

The party that evening was to be a strictly informal affair. Grace had suspected that the girls whom the members of the Phi Sigma Tau were to entertain were not likely to possess evening gowns. In order to avoid any possibility of hurt feelings, she had quietly requested those invited to wear the afternoon gowns in which they would appear at the game.

Before one o'clock her guests had arrived. They were three shy, quiet girls who had worshiped Grace from a distance, and who had been surprised almost to tears by her invitation. Two of them were from Portville, a small town about seventy miles from Oakdale, and had begun High School with Grace, who had been too busy with her own affairs up to the present to find out much about them.

The other girl, Marie Bateman, had entered the class that year. She had come from a little village forty miles south of Oakdale, was the oldest of a large family, her mother being a widow of very small means. As her mother was unable to send her away to school, she had done clerical work for the only lawyer in the home town for the previous two years, studying between whiles. She had entered the High School in the junior class, determining to graduate and then to work her way through Normal School. By dint of questioning, Grace had discovered that she lived in a shabby little room in the suburbs, never went anywhere and did anything honest in the way of earning money that she could find to do.

The realization of what some of these girls were willing to endure for the sake of getting an education made Grace feel guilty at being so comfortably situated. She determined that the holidays that year should not find them without friends and cheer.

After a rousing Thanksgiving dinner, in which the inevitable turkey, with all its toothsome accompaniments, played a prominent part, the girls retired to Grace's room for a final adjustment of hair and a last survey in the mirror before going to the game. High School matters formed the principal theme of conversation, and Grace was not surprised to learn that Eleanor had been carrying things with a high hand in third-year French class, in which Ellen Holt, one of the Portville girls, recited.

"She speaks French as well as Professor La Roche," said Miss Holt, "but she nearly drives him crazy sometimes. She will pretend she doesn't understand him and will make him explain the construction of a sentence over and over again, or she will argue with him about a point until he loses his temper completely. She makes perfectly ridiculous caricatures of him, and leaves them on his desk when class is over, and she asks him to translate impertinent slang phrases, which he does, sometimes, before he realizes how they are going to sound. Then the whole class laughs at him. She certainly makes things lively in that class."

The sound of the bell cut short the chat and the four girls hurried downstairs to greet Jessica, Mabel and the girls who were the Bright's guests. Nora and Anne, with their charges, came next, and last of all David, Tom and Hippy paraded up the walk, in single file, blowing lustily on tin horns and waving blue and white banners. A brief season of introduction followed, then Grace distributed blue and white rosettes with long streamers that she had made for the occasion, to each member of the party. Well supplied with Oakdale colors, they set out for the football grounds, where an immense crowd of people had gathered to see the big game of the season.

"I shall never forget the first football game I saw in Oakdale," said Anne to David as they made their way to the grandstand. "It ended very sensationally for me."

"I should say it did," replied David, smiling. "Confidentially, Anne, do you ever hear from your father?"

"Not very often," replied Anne. "He is not liable to trouble me again, however, because he knows that I will not go back to the stage, no matter what he says. He was with the western company of 'True Hearts' last year, but I don't know where he is now, and I don't care. Don't think I'm unfeeling; but it is impossible for me to care for him, even though he is my father."

"I understand," said David sympathetically. "Now let's forget him and have a good time."

"Hurrah! Here comes the band!" shouted Hippy.

The "Oakdale Military Band" took their places in the improvised bandstand and began a short concert before the game with the "Stars and Stripes," while the spectators unconsciously kept time with their feet to the inspiring strains.

When the two teams appeared on the field there were shouts of enthusiasm from the friends of the players, and the band burst forth with the High School song, in which the students joined.

After the usual preliminaries, the game began, and for the next hour everything else was forgotten save the battle that waged between the two teams.

Miriam Nesbit, Eva Allen and Marian Barber, with their guests, joined Grace's party, and soon the place they occupied became the very center of enthusiasm. Reddy, who was playing left end on the home team, received an ovation every time he made a move, and when towards the end of the game he made a touchdown, his friends nearly split their loyal throats in expressing their approval.

It was over at last, and Oakdale had won a complete victory over the Georgetown foe, who took their defeat with becoming grace. As soon as Reddy could free himself from the grasp of his school fellows, who would have borne him from the field in triumph if he had not stoutly resisted, he hurried to his friends, who showered him with congratulations.

"O you Titian-haired star!" cried Hippy, clasping his hands in mock admiration. "You are the rarest jewel in the casket. Words fail to express my feelings.

"'O joy, O bliss, O rapture! Let happiness now hap!

I am a sea of gurgling glee, with ecstasy on tap.'"

Hippy recited this effusion in a killing falsetto voice, and endeavored to embrace Reddy fervently, but was dragged back by Tom and David, to Reddy's visible relief.

"He's the idol of the hour. Don't put your irreverent hands on him," was David's injunction.

"But I adore idols," persisted Hippy. "Let me at him."

"Quit it, fat one!" growled Reddy, with a grin. "I'll settle with you later."

With gay laughter and jest, the young folks made their way from the grounds and started down the road toward home.

The whole party, walking four abreast, had just turned the curve where the road ended and Main Street began, when there was a hoarse honk! honk! and a runabout decorated in blue and white, containing Eleanor and Edna Wright, bore down upon them at lightning speed. The girls, uttering little cries of alarm, scattered to both sides of the road, with the exception of Mabel Allison, who, in her hurry to get out of the way, stumbled and fell directly in the path of the oncoming machine.

## CHAPTER XIII

## A THANKSGIVING FROLIC

But sudden as had been Mabel's fall, Grace Harlowe was equal to the emergency. With a bound she reached the middle of the road, seized Mabel and dragged her back just as the runabout passed over the place where she had fallen. It almost grazed her outstretched hand, then shot on down the road without slackening its speed for an instant.

There was a cry of horror from the young folks that ended in a sigh of relief. David and Tom Gray quickly raised Mabel to her feet and turned to Grace, whose face was ghastly, while she trembled like a leaf. The reaction had set in the moment she realized that Mabel was safe. Jessica and Nora had both begun to cry, while the faces of the others fully expressed their feelings.

"Grace," said Tom in a husky voice, "that was the quickest move I ever saw any one make."

Grace drew a long breath, the color returned to her pale face and in a measure she recovered herself.

"Someone had to do something," she said weakly. "I was the nearest to her, that's all. Are you hurt, Mabel, dear?" she asked, turning to the young girl, who stood by Jessica, looking white and dazed.

"It came so suddenly," she faltered, "I couldn't get up. It was awful!" She shuddered, then burst into tears, burying her face in Jessica's shoulder.

"There, there," soothed Jessica, wiping her own eyes. "It's all right now. Stand up straight and let me brush your coat. You are all mud."

"Here come the would-be murderesses now," cried Hippy. "They actually managed to stop and turn around, and now they are coming this way. One of them is my pet abomination—Miss Wright. She used to call me 'fatty' when I was little, and I've never forgiven her. But who is the reckless young person playing chauffeur? She ought to be put in jail for exceeding the speed limit."

"Hush!" said Grace. "Here she is."

The runabout had stopped and Eleanor alighted. Ignoring the four chums, she walked up to Miriam Nesbit.

"Will you please tell me if anyone is hurt?" she asked pettishly. "I saw someone fall, but couldn't stop the machine. I supposed the highway was for vehicles, not pedestrians four abreast."

"Miss Savell, you have just missed running over Miss Allison," said Miriam coldly. "Had it not been for Miss Harlowe, there would have been a serious accident. I should advise you to drive more carefully in future, or you may not escape so easily another time."

Eleanor flushed at these words and said haughtily, "I did not ask for advice, I asked for information."

"Very true," replied Miriam calmly, "but you see I have given you both."

"You are the most ill-bred lot of girls I have ever seen," returned Eleanor crossly, "and I think you are making a great deal of unnecessary fuss over a small matter. Why didn't your prize orphan get out of the way with the rest of you? Besides, you have no right to block a public highway, as you did. I am very sorry I came back at all."

Turning on her heel, she walked back to the runabout, climbed in and drove down the road like the wind, apparently indifferent as to what comment her heartless behavior might create.

"Who on earth is that girl?" inquired Reddy Brooks. "She has about as much sympathy as a stone."

"That is Eleanor Savell," replied Anne Pierson, "and she can be nice if she wishes, but she doesn't like us very well. That's why she was so hateful."

"So that's the famous Eleanor?" said Tom Gray in a low tone to Grace. "Aunt Rose was telling me about her this morning at breakfast. I supposed she was a great friend of yours."

"She was, but she isn't," returned Grace. "That's rather indefinite. However, I'll tell you about it as we go back."

"She certainly can't complain as far as looks are concerned," said Hippy. "She must have yards of blue ribbon that she won at baby shows when but a mere infant."

"Attention, boys and girls," cried Grace. "Let us forget what has happened and have just as good a time to-night as we can. We mustn't spoil the party."

"I move that we give Grace Harlowe a special round of applause for being a heroine," cried Hippy. "Hurrah!"

His example was quickly followed and the noise of the cheering brought people to their doors to see what the excitement was about.

"Do stop," protested Grace. "People will begin asking all sorts of questions."

"Don't interfere with our simple pleasures," expostulated Hippy. "Let us howl in peace. High School yell next, please."

By the time the party had reached the center of the town where their ways parted, the shadow cast by the near accident had almost disappeared.

By eight o'clock that evening the last guest had arrived, and the Harlowe's hospitable home was the scene of radiant good cheer. Mrs. Gray, enthroned in a big chair in one corner of the drawing room, was in her element, and the young folks vied with each other in doing her homage. The sprightly old lady was never so happy as when surrounded by young folks. She had a word or smile for each one, and the new girls who had at first felt rather timid about meeting her, were soon entirely at ease in her presence.

The greater part of the furniture had been removed from the big living room and the floor had been crashed; while a string orchestra that made a specialty of playing for parties had been hired for the pleasure of those who cared to dance.

As dancing was the chief amusement at nearly all of the young people's parties in Oakdale, the floor was filled from the beginning of the first waltz until supper was announced. This was served at two long tables in the dining room, Mrs. Gray occupying the seat of honor at the head of one, and Miss Thompson, who was a favorite at High School parties, the other. There were miniature ears of corn, turkeys, pumpkins and various other favors appropriate to Thanksgiving at each one's place. In the center of one table stood two dolls dressed in the style of costume worn by the Pilgrim fathers and mothers. They held a scroll between them on which was printed the Thanksgiving Proclamation. In the center of the other table were two dolls, one dressed in football uniform, a miniature football under its arm, while the other, dressed as a High School girl, held up a blue banner with O. H. S. on it in big, white letters.

This had been Grace's idea. She had dressed the dolls with the idea of contrasting the first Thanksgiving with that of to-day. There was a great craning of necks from those at the one table to see the central figures on the other, but soon every one settled down to the discussion of the dainties provided for them.

The supper ended with a toast to their young hostess, which was drunk standing, and then the guests repaired to the drawing room, where impromptu stunts were in order. Everyone was obliged to do something, if only to make a remark appropriate to the occasion. Nora sang, Anne recited, Grace and Miriam did a Spanish dance that they had practiced during vacation with remarkable spirit and effect. Jessica was then detailed to play, and under cover of her music, Tom, Reddy, David and Hippy left the room, Tom returning presently to announce solemnly that an original one-act drama, entitled "The Suffragette," written by Mr. Wingate and presented by a notable cast, would be the next offering.

After a moment's wait, Hippy, Reddy and David appeared, and were greeted with shouts of laughter. Reddy minced along in a bonnet and skirt belonging to Mrs. Harlowe, while Hippy wore a long-sleeved gingham pinafore of Grace's, which lacked considerable of meeting in the back, and was kept on by means of a sash. After deliberately setting their stage in full view of the audience at one end of the room, the play began, with David as the meek, hen-pecked husband, Hippy as the neglected child, who wept and howled continuously, while Reddy played the unnatural wife and mother, who neglected her family and held woman's suffrage meetings in the street.

The dialogue was clever, and the action of the sketch so ridiculous that the audience laughed from the first line until the climax, especially when the suffragette was hustled off to jail by Tom Gray, in the rôle of a policeman, for disturbing the peace, while her husband and child executed a wild dance of joy as she was hauled off the scene, protesting vigorously.

The applause was tremendous and the cast were obliged to bow their thanks several times before it subsided. Songs, speeches and recitations followed rapidly until everyone had contributed something in the way of a stunt. Then the guests formed two long lines from the living room straight through the big archway into the drawing room, and soon a Virginia reel was in full swing, led off by Mr. Harlowe and Mrs. Gray, who took her steps as daintily as when she had danced at her first party so many years before.

After the reel, the young folks romped through "Paul Jones," and then the party broke up, all declaring that never before had they had quite such a good time.

As Grace sleepily prepared for bed, she felt a little thrill of pride at the success of her party, and her only regret was the fact that of all those invited, Eleanor was the only one who had refused to be present.

## CHAPTER XIV

## ELEANOR FINDS A WAY

Now that Thanksgiving was past, basketball became the topic of the hour. The juniors had accepted the challenge of the senior class, and had agreed to play them on Saturday, December 12, at two o'clock, in the gymnasium. Only two weeks remained in which to practice. Their sorority enthusiasm had so completely run away with them that they had even neglected basketball until now. Therefore Grace Harlowe lost no time in getting Miss Thompson's permission to use the gymnasium, and promptly notified her team and the subs. to meet there, in gymnasium suits, prepared to play, that afternoon.

The instant the last bell sounded on lessons, ten girls made for their lockers, and fifteen minutes later the first team and the subs. were moving toward the gymnasium deep in the discussion of the coming game and their chances for success over their opponents.

A brief meeting was held, and the girls were assigned to their positions. Grace had fully intended that Miriam should play center, but when she proposed it, Miriam flatly refused to do so, and asked for her old position of right forward.

"You are our captain," she declared to Grace, "and the best center I ever saw on a girls' team. It would be folly to change now. Don't you agree with me, girls?"

Nora was detailed as left forward, while Marian Barber and Eva Allen played right and left guards. The substitutes were also assigned their positions and practice began.

Before they had been on the floor twenty minutes the girls were thoroughly alive to the joy of the game and worked with the old-time dash and spirit that had won them the championship the previous year. Now that they were in harmony with each other, they played with remarkable unity, and after an hour's practice Grace decided that they were in a fair way to "whip the seniors off the face of the earth."

"I never saw you girls work better!" she exclaimed. "It will be a sorry day for the seniors when we line up on the twelfth."

"There'll be a great gnashing of senior teeth after the game," remarked Nora confidently.

"Do you know, girls," said Grace, as they left the gymnasium that afternoon, "I am sorry that Eleanor won't be peaceable. I wanted her to like every bit of our school life and thought she'd surely be interested in basketball. I suppose she will stay away from the game merely because we are on the team. It is really a shame for her to be so unreasonable."

"Grace Harlowe, are you ever going to stop mourning over Eleanor?" cried Miriam impatiently. "She doesn't deserve your regret and is too selfish to appreciate it. I know what I am talking about because I used to be just as ridiculous as she is, and knowing what you suffered through me, I can't bear to see you unhappy again over someone who is too trivial to be taken seriously."

"You're a dear, Miriam!" exclaimed Nora impulsively.

It was the first time that the once haughty Miriam had ever referred publicly to past shortcomings, although from the time she and Grace had settled their difficulties at the close of the sophomore year, she had been a changed girl.

"Where are Anne and Jessica to-day?" asked Eva Allen.

"Anne and Jessica have refused point blank to honor us with their presence during practice," announced Nora. "I asked Jessica to-day, and she said that they didn't want to know how we intended to play, for then they could wax enthusiastic and make a great deal more noise. It is their ambition to become loud and loyal fans."

"What a worthy ambition," said Marian Barber, with a giggle. "They are such noisy creatures already." There was more laughing at this, as Anne and Jessica were by far the quietest members of the sorority.

"Remember, we practice to-morrow after school," called Grace as she separated from her team at her street.

As she walked slowly down the quiet street, deep in thought, her ear caught the sound of an approaching automobile, and she looked up just in time to see Eleanor drive by in her machine. Grace nodded to her, but her salutation met with a chilly stare.

"How childish she is," thought Grace. "I suppose she thinks that hurts me. Of course it isn't exactly pleasant, but I'm going to keep on speaking to her, just the same. I am not angry, even if she is; although I have far greater cause to be."

But before the close of the week Grace was destined to cross swords with Eleanor in earnest, and the toleration she had felt was swallowed up in righteous indignation.

During the winter, theatrical companies sometimes visited Oakdale for a week at a time, presenting, at popular prices, old worn-out plays and cheap melodramas. These companies gave daily matinées as well as evening performances, and the more frivolous element of High School girls had in time past occasionally "skipped school" to spend the afternoon in the theatre. By the girls, this form of truancy was considered a "lark," but Miss Thompson did not look at the matter in the same light, and disciplined the culprit so severely whenever she found this to be the cause of an afternoon's absence that the girls were slow to offend in this respect.

All this Eleanor had heard, among other things, from Edna Wright, but had paid little attention to it when Edna had told her. Directly after cutting Grace Harlowe, she had turned her runabout into Main Street, where a billboard had caught her eye, displaying in glaring red and blue lettering the fact that the "Peerless Dramatic Company" would open a week's engagement in Oakdale with daily matinées.

Eleanor's eyes sparkled. She halted her machine, scanning curiously the list of plays on the billboard. "The Nihilist's Daughter" was scheduled for Thursday afternoon, and Eleanor decided to go. She wasn't afraid of Miss Thompson. Then, possessed with a sudden idea, she laughed gleefully. At last she had found a way to effectually annoy the principal.

# CHAPTER XV

# A WOULD-BE "LARK"

Eleanor Savell and the seven girls who formed their sorority were the first to enter the study hall on Tuesday morning. As soon as a girl from any of the three lower classes appeared she was approached by some of the former and a great deal of whispering and subdued laughter went on. A few girls were seen to shake their heads dubiously, and a number of those termed "grinds" were not interviewed. The majority, however, appeared to be highly delighted over what they heard, one group standing near one of the windows, of which Eleanor was the center, laughed so loudly that they were sent to their seats.

Among the number to whom nothing was said were the members of the Phi Sigma Tau, and as the morning advanced they became fully aware that something unusual was in the wind. Several times they caught sight of a folded paper being stealthily passed from one desk to another, but as to its contents they had no idea, as it was not handed to any one of them.

At recess there was more grouping and whispering, and Grace was puzzled and not a little hurt over the way in which she and her friends were ignored. Such a thing had not happened since the basketball trouble the previous year.

"Eleanor started that paper, whatever it is," said Nora O'Malley to the Phi Sigma Tau, who stood in a group around her desk. "She was here when I came in this morning, and I was early, too. It is some masterpiece of mischief on her part, or she wouldn't take the trouble to get here on time."

"Here comes Mabel," said Jessica. "Maybe she has seen the paper. Mabel, dear, did you see that paper that has been going the rounds this morning?"

Mabel nodded.

"What was written on it, Mabel?" asked Grace curiously.

Mabel looked distressed for a moment then she said, "I wish I might tell you all about it, but I gave my word of honor before I read it that I wouldn't mention the contents to anyone."

"Then, of course, we won't ask you," said Anne Pierson quickly. "But tell us this much—is it about any of us?"

"No," replied Mabel. "It isn't. It is something I was asked to sign."

"And did you sign it?" asked Jessica.

"I certainly did not," responded Mabel. "It was——" she stopped, then flushed. She had been on the point of telling. "I am sorry I ever saw it," she continued. "I can't bear to have secrets and not tell you."

"That's all right, Mabel," said Marian Barber, patting her on the shoulder. "We don't want you to tell. If it doesn't concern us we don't care, do we, girls?"

"No, indeed," was the reply.

Just then the bell sounded and the girls returned to their seats with the riddle still unsolved. Nothing more was seen of the mysterious paper, and Grace came to the conclusion that it had been nothing important, after all.

On Wednesday, aside from a little more whispering and significant glances exchanged among the pupils, not a ripple disturbed the calm of the study hall. It was therefore a distinct and not altogether pleasant surprise when Miss Thompson walked into the room, dismissed the senior class and requested the three lower classes to remain in their seats.

After the seniors had quietly left the study hall, Miss Thompson stood gravely regarding the rows of girls before her. Her eyes wandered toward where Eleanor sat, looking bored and indifferent, and then she looked toward Grace, whose steady gray eyes were fixed on the principal's face with respectful attention.

"I don't believe Grace is guilty, at any rate," thought Miss Thompson; then she addressed the assembled girls.

"Something has come to my ears, girls," said the principal, "that I find hard to credit, but before you leave here this afternoon I must know who is innocent and who is guilty."

Miss Thompson paused and a number of girls stirred uneasily in their seats, while a few glanced quickly toward Eleanor, who was looking straight ahead, the picture of innocence.

"You all know," continued the principal, "that it is strictly forbidden for any pupil to absent herself from school for the purpose of attending a circus, matinée or any public performance of this nature. I have so severely disciplined pupils for this offence that for a long time no one has disobeyed me. I was, therefore, astonished to learn that a number of girls, regardless of rules, have taken matters into their own hands and have decided to absent themselves from school to-morrow in order to attend the matinée to be given in the theatre. Such a decision is worse than disobedience—it is lawlessness. Unless a severe example is made of the offenders, the standard of the school will be lowered. Therefore, I intend to sift this matter to the bottom and find out what mischievous influence prompted this act of insubordination.

"Report says that this movement originated in the junior class, and that a paper has been circulated and signed by certain pupils, who pledged themselves to play truant and attend the matinée to-morrow."

The eyes of Grace and her chums turned questioningly toward Mabel Allison, who nodded slightly in the affirmative.

So that was what all the whispering and mystery had meant. Grace inwardly congratulated herself on having kept clear of the whole thing. None of her friends were implicated, either. Even Mabel had refused to sign.

"I have dismissed the senior class, because I have been assured of their entire ignorance of the plot. What I insist upon knowing now, is who are the real culprits, beginning with the girl who originated the paper to the last one who signed it. I am going to put every girl on her honor, and I expect absolutely truthful answers. The girls who signed the paper I have mentioned will rise."

There was a moment of suspense, then Eleanor Savell proudly rose from her seat. Her example was followed, until two thirds of the girls present were standing. The principal stood silently regarding them with an expression of severity that was decidedly discomfiting.

"That will do," she said curtly, after they had stood for what seemed to them an age, but was really only a couple of minutes.

"You may be seated. The girl who composed and wrote that agreement will now rise and explain herself."

Without hesitating, Eleanor rose and regarded the principal with an insolent smile. "I wrote it, Miss Thompson," she said clearly. "I wrote it because I wished to. I am sorry you found out about it, because it has spoiled all our fun."

There was a gasp of horror at Eleanor's assertion. No one had ever before spoken so disrespectfully to their revered principal.

"Miss Savell," said the principal quietly, although her flashing eyes and set lips showed that she was very angry, "if you have that paper in your possession, bring it to me at once, and never answer me again as you did just now. You are both disrespectful and impertinent."

But Miss Thompson's anger toward Eleanor was nothing compared with the tempest that the principal had aroused in Eleanor. The latter flushed, then turned perfectly white with rage. Still standing, she reached down, picked up a book from her desk and took from it a paper. "This," she said, in a low tense voice, "is the paper you wish to see. I do not choose to let you see it, therefore I shall destroy it."

Then she deliberately tore the offending paper into shreds and scattered them broadcast.

"I hope you understand that I am not afraid of you or any other teacher in this school," she continued. "I have never been punished in my life, therefore I am not liable to give you the first opportunity. I despise you, because you are a ridiculous prig, and I am glad of an opportunity to tell you so. As for the persons who told you about our plan, words cannot express my contempt for them, and right here I accuse Grace Harlowe

392

and her sorority of getting the information from Mabel Allison yesterday and carrying it to you. They are all tale-bearers and sneaks."

With these words, Eleanor angrily flung the book she held on the desk and walked down the aisle toward the door, but Miss Thompson barred her way.

"Stop, Miss Savell," she commanded. "You shall not leave this room until you have apologized to the girls whom you have unjustly accused and to me. I will not tolerate such behavior."

Eleanor glared at the principal, whose face was rigid in its purpose, then sank into the nearest vacant seat, saying defiantly: "You may keep me here all night if you like, but, I meant what I said, and I shall retract nothing."

Nevertheless she did not again attempt to leave the room. She had met with a will stronger than her own and she realized it.

Ignoring Eleanor's final remark, Miss Thompson once more turned her attention to the matter in hand.

"Those girls who are not in any way implicated in this matter are dismissed," she said.

About one third of the girls arose and prepared to leave the study hall, the Phi Sigma Tau being among the number. Grace motioned the girls to hurry. She wished to leave the room with her friends before Miss Thompson noticed them. She knew the principal would insist on an apology from Eleanor, and neither she nor her friends wished it. For the first time since Eleanor had chosen to cut their acquaintance Grace was thoroughly angry with her. She could not forgive Eleanor for having accused her and her friends of carrying tales before almost the entire school; therefore a forced apology would not appease her wounded pride. She drew a breath of relief when the eight girls were safely outside the study hall door.

"Hurry up," she said. "We'll talk when we get outside school. Don't stop for a minute. If Miss Thompson notices that we are gone, she'll send after us."

The girls silently donned their wraps and fled from the building like fugitives from justice. Once on the street a lively confab ensued, all talking at once.

"Let's take turns talking," cried Grace, laughing. "We shall understand each other a little better."

"Now, what do you think of Miss Eleanor?" cried Nora. "She has certainly shown her true colors this time."

"I never heard of anything more unjust than the way she accused us, when we knew nothing about her old plan," said Marian Barber.

"It was abominable," said Eva Allen.

The other girls expressed their disapproval in equally frank terms.

"I suppose it did look as though I told you girls," said Mabel Allison, who had joined them at the gate. "You know I was with you at recess, right after the paper had been passed to me. I don't think Miss Savell intended me to see it. It was passed to me by mistake."

"Very likely," agreed Grace. "I wonder who did tell Miss Thompson. I saw several girls with the paper, but hadn't the remotest idea what it was all about. You know Miss Thompson is awfully down on 'skipping school.' She threatened last year to suspend Edna Wright for it."

"There will be weeping and wailing in the 'Skull and Crossbones' crowd,'" exclaimed Nora. "They are all in this mix-up, and if they aren't suspended, they'll be lucky."

"Are you going to stand up for Eleanor now, in the face of what she said about all of us before those girls, Grace?" asked Marian Barber hotly.

"No," said Grace shortly. "She deserves to be punished. The things she said to Miss Thompson were disgraceful, and I shall never forgive her for the way she spoke of us."

"I wouldn't say that, Grace," remarked Anne. "You can never tell what may happen to change your views."

"It will have to be something remarkable in this instance," replied Grace grimly, as she bade the girls good-bye. "Remember, girls, basketball practice again to-morrow, and the rest of the week. Miss Thompson has promised me the gymnasium. Please make it a point to be on hand."

"Good-bye, Grace," chorused her friends, and went on down the street discussing the probable fate of the would-be truants.

To return to those youthful transgressors. They were spending a most uncomfortable half hour with Miss Thompson. She was merciless in her denunciation of their conduct, and the terror of suspension arose in more than one mind, as they listened to her scathing remarks. It had all seemed a huge joke when they planned it, but there was nothing funny about it now. When, with the exception of Eleanor, the principal dismissed them, they filed decorously out, very uneasy in mind. Miss Thompson had taken their names, but had not stated their punishment and it was certain that they would be made to feel the full weight of her displeasure.

When the last girl had disappeared the principal turned to Eleanor. "I will listen to your apology, Miss Savell," she said coldly. Eleanor looked scornfully at the principal, and was silent.

"Do you intend to obey me, Miss Savell?" asked Miss Thompson.

Still there was no answer.

"Very well," continued Miss Thompson. "Your silence indicates that you are still insubordinate. You may, therefore, choose between two things. You may apologize to me now, and to-morrow to the girls you have accused of treachery, or you may leave this school, not to return to it unless permitted to do so by the Board of Education."

Without a word Eleanor rose and walked haughtily out of the room.

## CHAPTER XVI

## THE JUNIORS FOREVER

When the four classes assembled Thursday morning, every girl, with the exception of Eleanor, was in her seat. Her absence created considerable comment, and it was a matter of speculation as to whether she had purposely absented herself or really had been suspended.

After conducting opening exercises, Miss Thompson pronounced sentence on the culprits. They were to forfeit their recess, library and all other privileges until the end of the term. They must turn in two themes every week of not less than six hundred words on certain subjects to be assigned to them. If, during this time, any one of them should be reported for a misdemeanor, they were to be suspended without delay.

Their penalty was far from light, but they had not been suspended, and so they resolved to endure it as best they might.

Grace Harlowe felt a load lifted from her mind when Miss Thompson publicly announced that she had not received any information from either Mabel Allison or the Phi Sigma Tau.

"Thank goodness, none of us were concerned in that affair," she told the members of her basketball team at recess. "There are two girls on the sophomore and three on the freshman team whose basketball ardor will have to cool until after the mid-year exams."

"You might know that some of those silly freshmen would get into trouble," said Nora scornfully.

"'Twas many and many a year ago,

In an age beyond recall,

That Nora, the freshman, lowly sat

At one end of the study hall."

recited Anne Pierson in dramatic tones.

There was a burst of laughter from the girls at this effusion, in which Nora herself joined.

"What a delicate way of reminding me that I once was a freshman!" she exclaimed.

"Anne has a new accomplishment," said Grace. "She can spout poetry without trying."

"Small credit is due me," said Anne, smiling. "Anyone can twist 'Annabel Lee' to suit the occasion."

"By the way, Anne," said Grace, "as you are a poet, you must compose a basketball song to-day, and I'll see that the juniors all have copies. It's time we had one. Let me see what would be a good tune?"

"'Rally Round the Flag,'" suggested Miriam Nesbit. "That has a dandy swing to it."

Grace hummed a few bars.

"The very thing," she exclaimed. "Now, Anne, get busy at once. You'd better sing the tune to yourself all the time you're writing it, then you'll be sure to put more dash and spirit into it."

"I wish the day of the game were here," said Jessica plaintively. "I have been practicing a most encouraging howl. Hippy, David and Reddy have a new one, too. Reddy says it's 'marvelously extraordinary and appallingly great.'"

"I can imagine it to be all that and more if Hippy had anything to do with its origin," said Nora.

"Wasn't it nice of Miss Thompson to exonerate us publicly?" asked Anne.

"She is always just," replied Grace. "I can't understand how Eleanor could be so rude and disagreeable to her. She has disliked Miss Thompson from the first."

"I wonder whether she apologized to Miss Thompson last night,"

397

mused Grace.

"I feel sure that she didn't, and I am just as sure that she won't get back until she does."

"We shall manage to exist if she doesn't," said Jessica dryly. She felt a personal grudge against Eleanor for her accusation against Mabel, who had grown very dear to her and whom she mothered like a hen with one chicken.

"She'll probably appear at the game in all her glory," said Miriam Nesbit. "She can go to that, even though she is on bad terms with the school."

The recess bell cut short the conversation and the girls returned to their desks with far better ideas of the coming game than of the afternoon's lessons.

Saturday, December 12, dawned cold and clear, and the girls on both teams were in high spirits as they hustled into their respective locker-rooms and rapidly donned their gymnasium suits. The spectators had not yet begun to arrive, as it was still early, so the girls indulged in a little warming-up practice, did a few stunts and skipped about, overflowing with animal spirits.

Julia Crosby and Grace took turns sprinting around the gymnasium three times in succession, while Miriam Nesbit timed them, Grace finishing just two seconds ahead of Julia.

By a quarter of two the gallery was fairly well filled and by five minutes of two it was crowded. The juniors, with the exception of Eleanor Savell's faction, arrived in a body, gave the High School yell the moment they spied their team, and then burst forth with the basketball song, led by Ruth Deane, a tall junior, who stood up and beat time with both hands. Anne had composed the song the week before. The juniors had all received copies of the words and had learned them by heart. They now sang with the utmost glee, and came out particularly strong on the chorus, which ran:

"The juniors forever, hurrah, fans, hurrah!

Our team is a winner, our captain's a star.

And we'll drive the senior foe, from the basket every time.

Shouting the war cry of the juniors."

There was a great clapping of hands from the admirers of the juniors at this effort, but the seniors promptly responded from the other end of the gallery to the tune of Dixie, with:

"The seniors are the real thing.

Hurrah! Hurrah!

Our gallant team now takes its stand,

And all the baskets soon will land.

We shout, we sing, the praises of the seniors."

Hardly had the last notes died away, when the referee blew the whistle and the teams hustled to their positions. Grace and Julia Crosby faced each other, beamed amiably and shook hands, then stood vigilant, eyes on the ball that the referee balanced in her hands. Up it went, the whistle sounded and the two captains sprang straight for it. Grace captured it, however, and sent it flying toward Miriam, who was so carefully guarded that she dared not attempt to make the basket, and after a feint managed to throw it to Nora, who tried for the basket at long range and missed.

There was a general scramble for the ball, and for five minutes neither team scored; then Marian Barber dropped a neat field goal, and soon after Grace scored on a foul. The junior fans howled joyfully at the good work of their team. The seniors did not intend to allow them to score again in a hurry. They played such a close guarding game that, try as they might, the juniors made no headway. Then Julia Crosby scored on a field goal, making the score 3 to 2. This spurred the junior team on to greater effort, and Miriam made a brilliant throw to basket that brought forth an ovation from the gallery. This ended the first half, with the score 5 to 2 in favor of the juniors.

"They'll have to work to catch up with us now," said Nora O'Malley triumphantly to the members of the team, who sat resting in the little side room off the gymnasium.

"We have the lead, but we can't afford to boast yet," replied Grace. "The seniors played a fine game last half, and they'll strain every nerve to pile up their score next half."

"We shall win," said Miriam Nesbit confidently. "I feel it in my bones."

"Let's hope that your bones are true prophets," laughed Marian Barber.

"O girls!" exclaimed Eva Allen from the open door, in which she had been standing looking up at the gallery. "Eleanor is here. She and her satellites are sitting away up on the back seat of the gallery."

"Where?" asked Nora, going to the door. "Oh, yes, I see her. She looks as haughty as ever. It's a wonder she'd condescend to come and watch her mortal enemies play."

"I suppose she hopes we'll lose," said Marian Barber. "That would fill her with joy."

"Then we'll see that she goes away in a gloomy frame of mind," said Nora, "for we're going to win, and don't you forget to remember it."

Just then the whistle blew, and there was a scramble for places. This time Julia Crosby won the toss-up, and followed it up with a field goal. Then the seniors scored twice on fouls, tying the score. The juniors set their teeth and waded in with all their might and main, setting a whirlwind pace that caused their fans to shout with wild enthusiasm and fairly dazed their opponents. Grace alone netted four foul goals, and the sensational playing of Nora and Miriam was a matter of wonder to the spectators, who conceded it to be the fastest, most brilliant half ever played by an Oakdale team. The game ended with the score 15 to 6 in favor of the juniors, whose loyal supporters swooped down upon them the moment the whistle blew and pranced about, whooping like savages.

"That was the greatest game I ever saw played under this roof," cried David, wringing Grace's hand, while Hippy hopped about, uttering little yelps of joy. Reddy circled about the victors almost too delighted for words. He was filled with profound admiration for them.

"The boys' crack team couldn't have played a better game," he said solemnly, and the girls knew that he could pay them no higher compliment, for this team was considered invincible by the High School boys.

"Perhaps we'll challenge you some day, Reddy," said Grace mischievously.

"I believe you'd win at that," he said so earnestly that everyone laughed.

"It was a great triumph," said Jessica proudly, as she stood with Mabel and Anne in the locker-room while the girls resumed street clothing. "And my new howl was a success, too."

"Glad to know that," said Grace. "There were so many different kinds of noises I couldn't distinguish it."

"There was one noise that started that was promptly hushed," said Anne. "You heard it, too, didn't you Jessica?"

"Oh, yes, girls, I intended telling you before this," replied Jessica. "Just before the last half started, Miss Thompson and Miss Kane came in and walked to the other end of the gallery. Well, Eleanor and her crowd saw them, and what do you suppose they did?"

"Hard to tell," said Nora.

"They hissed Miss Thompson. Very softly, you may be sure," continued Jessica, "but it was hissing, just the same. For a wonder, she didn't hear it, but every girl in the junior class did. They were sitting down front on the same side as Eleanor's crowd. You know what a temper Ruth Deane has and how ferocious she can look? Well, the minute she heard it she went back there like a flash, looking for all the world like a thunder cloud. She talked for a moment to Edna and Eleanor. They tossed their heads, but they didn't hiss anymore."

"What did Ruth say to them?" asked Grace curiously. "It must have been something remarkable, or they wouldn't have subsided so suddenly."

"It was," giggled Jessica. "She told them that if they didn't stop it instantly, the juniors would pick them up bodily, carry them downstairs to the classroom and lock them in until the game was over."

"How absurd!" exclaimed Grace. "They would never have dared to go that far."

"I don't know about that," said Nora O'Malley. "Ruth Deane is a terror when she gets fairly started. Besides, she would have had both High Schools on her side. Even the boys like Miss Thompson."

"It was an effectual threat at any rate," said Jessica. "They left before the game was over. Perhaps they were afraid of being waylaid."

"I suppose they couldn't bear to see us win," said Grace. "But, O girls, I am so proud of our invincible team. It was a great game and a well-earned victory."

"We ought to celebrate," said Miriam. "Come on. Here we are at Stillman's."

Without waiting for a second invitation, the Phi Sigma Tau trooped joyfully into the drug store.

## CHAPTER XVII

## THE LAST STRAW

The days glided by rapidly. The Christmas holidays came, bringing with them the usual round of gayeties. Thanks to the Phi Sigma Tau, the lonely element of High School girls did not lack for good cheer. As at Thanksgiving, each member of the sorority entertained two or more girls on Christmas and New Year's, and were amply repaid for their good deed by the warm appreciation of their guests.

Tom Gray came down for the holidays, bringing with him his roommate, Arnold Evans, a fair-haired, blue-eyed young man of twenty, who proved himself thoroughly likable in every respect. He lost no time in cultivating Miriam's acquaintance, and the two soon became firm friends.

Tom gave a dinner to his roommate, inviting "the seven originals," as he expressed it, and Miriam, who felt that at last she really belonged in the charmed circle. David was even more pleased than his sister over the turn affairs had taken. To have Miriam a member of his own particular "crowd" had always been David's dearest wish, and the advent of Arnold Evans had done away with Miriam being the odd one. So the circle was enlarged to ten young people, who managed to crowd the two weeks' vacation with all sorts of healthful pleasures.

There were coasting and sleighing parties, and on one occasion a walk to old Jean's hut in Upton Wood, where they were hospitably entertained by the old hunter, who had smilingly pointed to the wolf skins on the wall, asking them if they remembered the winter day two years before when those same skins held wolves who were far too lively for comfort. Then the story of their escape had to be gone over again for Arnold's benefit.

They had stayed until the moon came up, and, accompanied by the old hunter, had walked back to Oakdale in the moonlight.

After the holidays came the brief period of hard study before the dreaded mid-year examinations. Basketball enthusiasm declined rapidly and a remarkable devotion to study ensued that lasted until examinations began. By the last week in January, the ordeal was past.

Eleanor Savell had not yet returned to school. Whether or not she would be allowed to return was a question that occasioned a great deal of discussion among three lower classes of girls. Edna Wright and the other members of the sorority organized by Eleanor were loud in their expressions of disapproval as to Miss Thompson's "severity" toward Eleanor. They talked so freely about it, that it reached the principal's ears. She lost no time in sending for them, and after a session in the office, they emerged looking subdued and crestfallen; and after that it was noted that when in conversation with their schoolmates, they made no further allusion to Miss Thompson's methods of discipline.

There was a faint murmur of surprise around the study hall one morning, however, when Miss Thompson walked in to conduct the opening exercises, accompanied by Eleanor, who, without looking at the school, seated herself at the desk nearest to where the principal stood.

When the morning exercises were concluded, Miss Thompson nodded slightly to Eleanor, who turned rather pale, then rose, and, facing the school, said in a clear voice:

"I wish to apologize to Miss Thompson for impertinence and insubordination. I also wish to publicly apologize to the members of the Phi Sigma Tau for having accused them of treachery concerning a certain matter that recently came up in this school."

"Your apology is accepted, Miss Savell. You may take your own seat," said the principal.

Without looking to the right or left, Eleanor walked proudly up the aisle to her seat, followed by the gaze of those girls who could not refrain from watching her. The Phi Sigma Tau, to a member, sat with eyes straight to the front. They had no desire to increase Eleanor's discomfiture, for they realized what this public apology must have cost her, although they were all equally puzzled as to what had prompted her to humble herself.

Eleanor's apology was not due, however, to a change of heart. She still despised Miss Thompson as thoroughly as on the day that she had manifested her open scorn and dislike for the principal.

As for Grace and her friends, Eleanor was particularly bitter against them, and laid at their door a charge of which they were entirely innocent.

Eleanor had told her aunt nothing of her recent trouble in school, but had feigned illness as an excuse for remaining at home. After attending the basketball game her aunt had told her rather sharply that if she were able to attend basketball games, she was certainly able to continue her studies. Eleanor had agreed to return to school the following Monday, and had started from home at the usual time with no intention whatever of honoring the High School with her presence. She passed the morning in the various stores, lunched in town and went to a matinée in the afternoon. In this manner she idled the days away until the holiday vacation came, congratulating herself upon her success in pulling wool over the eyes of her long-suffering aunt.

But a day of reckoning was at hand, for just before the close of vacation Miss Thompson chanced to call at Mrs. Gray's home while Mrs. Gray was entertaining Miss Nevin, and the truth came out.

When Miss Nevin confronted her niece with the deception Eleanor had practiced upon her, a stormy scene had followed, and Eleanor had accused Grace Harlowe of telling tales to Mrs. Gray, and Mrs. Gray of carrying them to her aunt. This had angered Miss Nevin to the extent that she had immediately ordered Eleanor to her room without telling her from whom she had received her information.

For three days Eleanor had remained in her room, refusing to speak to her aunt, who, at the end of that time, decreed that if she did not at once apologize roundly and return to school her violin and piano would both be taken from her until she should again become reasonable.

In the face of this new punishment, which was the severest penalty that could be imposed upon her, Eleanor remained obdurate. Her violin and piano were removed from her room and the piano in the drawing room was closed. Still she stubbornly held out, and it was not until the day before the beginning of the new term that she went to her aunt and coldly agreed to comply with her wishes, providing she might have her violin and piano once more.

Aside from this conversation they had exchanged no words, and Eleanor therefore entered school that morning still believing the Phi Sigma Tau to be at the bottom of her misfortune.

In spite of her recent assertion that she could not forgive Eleanor, Grace's resentment vanished at sight of her enemy's humiliation. A public apology was the last thing that either she or her friends desired. Her promise to Mrs. Gray loomed up before her. If Eleanor really did believe the Phi Sigma Tau innocent, then perhaps this would be the opportunity for reconciliation. After a little thought, she tore a sheet of paper from her notebook and wrote:

"DEAR ELEANOR:

"The members of the Phi Sigma Tau are very sorry about your having to make an apology. We did not wish it. We think you showed a great deal of the right kind of courage in making the public apology you did both to Miss Thompson and to us. Won't you come back to the Phi Sigma Tau?

"YOUR SINCERE FRIENDS."

At recess Grace showed the note to her friends. She had signed her name to the note and requested the others to do the same. Here she met with some opposition. Nora, Marian Barber and Eva Allen were strongly opposed to sending it. But Jessica, Anne and Miriam agreed with Grace that it would be in fulfillment of the original promise to Mrs. Gray to help Eleanor whenever they could do so. So the Phi Sigma Tau signed their names and the note was passed to Eleanor directly after recess.

She opened it, read it through, and an expression of such intense scorn passed over her face that Nora, who sat near her and who was covertly watching her, knew at once that Grace's flag of truce had been trampled in the dust.

Picking up her pen, Eleanor wrote rapidly for a brief space, underlined what she had written, signed her name with a flourish, and, folding and addressing her note, sent it to Grace.

Rather surprised at receiving an answer so quickly, Grace unfolded the note. Then she colored, looked grave and, putting the note in the back of the text-book she was holding, went on studying.

By the time school was over for the day, the girls of the Phi Sigma Tau knew that Eleanor had once more repudiated their overtures of friendship and were curious to see what she had written.

"Don't keep us in suspense. Let us see what she wrote," exclaimed Nora O'Malley as the seven girls crossed the campus together.

"Here it is," said Grace, handing Nora the note.

Nora eagerly unfolded the paper and the girls crowded around, reading over her shoulder, Grace walking a little apart from them. Then Nora read aloud:

"To the Phi Sigma Tau:

"Your kind appreciation of my conduct in the matter of apology is really remarkable, coupled with the fact that your inability to refrain from discussing my personal affairs with Mrs. Gray forced this recent humiliation upon me. To ask me to return to your society is only adding insult to injury. I am not particularly surprised at this, however. It merely proves you to be greater hypocrites than you at first seemed.

"Eleanor Savell."

"Well, of all things!" exclaimed Marian Barber. "Grace Harlowe, if you ever attempt to conciliate her again, I'll disown you."

"What does she mean by saying that we discussed her affairs with Mrs. Gray?" cried Jessica impatiently. "We have always tried to put her best side out to dear Mrs. Gray, and you all know it."

"The best thing to do," said Anne, smiling a little, "is to tell Mrs. Gray all about it. We might as well live up to the reputation Eleanor has thrust upon us. It isn't pleasant to admit that we have failed with Eleanor, but it isn't our fault, at any rate. I am going there this afternoon. I'll tell her."

"May I go with you, Anne?" asked Grace.

"You know I'd love to have you," Anne replied.

"As long as I was the first to agree to look out for Eleanor, I have decided I had better be with you at the finish," said Grace, as the two girls walked slowly up the drive.

"The finish?" asked Anne. "Why do you say that, Grace?"

"You've heard about the last straw that broke the camel's back, haven't you?" asked Grace. "Well, Eleanor's note is the last straw. I know I said that once before, and I broke my word. I don't intend to break it again, however. I am going to ask Mrs. Gray to release me from my promise."

## CHAPTER XVIII

## THE PLAY'S THE THING

Excitement ran high in the three lower classes one morning in early February when Miss Thompson requested that those interested in the production of a Shakespearian play go to the library directly after school, there to discuss the situation.

When the gong sounded dismissal, about sixty girls with dramatic aspirations made for the library. The Phi Sigma Tau entered in a body. They had decided at recess to carry away as many laurels as possible, providing they could get into the cast.

Miss Tebbs, teacher of elocution; Miss Kane, teacher of gymnastics, and Miss Thompson stood at one side of the library talking earnestly as they noted each newcomer.

"Oh, look!" whispered Jessica, clutching Nora's arm. "There's Eleanor and her crowd."

"Then look out for squalls," replied Nora. "She'll try to be the whole cast, and will get a magnificent case of sulks if she can't have her own way."

"Sh-h-h," warned Eva Allen. "She'll hear you. Besides, Miss Thompson is going to speak."

The principal held up her hand for silence and the groups of girls engaged in subdued conversation ceased talking and turned their attention toward her.

"You are all aware that each year the senior class gives a play, which they choose, manage and produce with no assistance save that given by Miss Tebbs," said the principal. "So far the three lower classes have never given a play. Some time ago Miss Tebbs suggested that as we need money for special books in the library which our yearly appropriation does not cover, we might present a Shakespearian play with good effect, choosing the cast from the freshman, sophomore and junior classes.

"The first thing to be thought of is the play itself. After due consideration, we decided that 'As You Like It' is better suited to our needs than any of the other Shakespearian dramas. In it are twenty-one speaking characters, besides numerous lords, pages and attendants. We shall probably use about fifty girls, thus making it an elaborate production. By the attendance this afternoon I should imagine that you are heartily in favor of our project and that we shall have no trouble in making up the cast. As Miss Tebbs has charge of the situation, I yield the floor to her. She will explain to you about the giving out of the parts."

There was an enthusiastic clapping of hands as Miss Thompson smiled and nodded to the girls, then left the room. Miss Tebbs then stated that on Friday afternoon after school there would be a "try out" for parts in the gymnasium, in order to find out what girls were most capable of doing good work in the cast. Just what the test would be had not been decided. It would be well, however, to study the chosen play and become familiar with it; also each girl must bring a copy of the play with her. If the girls wished to ask any questions, she would answer them as far as possible. Miss Kane would help with the posing and coaching when the thing was fairly started.

The girls crowded around Miss Tebbs and Miss Kane, asking all sorts of questions.

"One at a time, girls," laughed Miss Tebbs. "I have not asked you to enact a mob scene."

Under cover of the confusion, Grace and her three friends slipped out of the library.

"'The play's the thing,'" quoted Nora, "and me for it."

"That is for the judges to decide," said Jessica sagely. "Perhaps they won't even look at you."

"Do you think anyone could see my Irish countenance and fail to be impressed?" demanded Nora.

"Really and truly, Nora, the more you travel with Hippy, the more you talk like him," remarked Grace.

"I consider that a compliment," replied Nora, laughing. "Hippy says awfully funny things."

"Look at our little Anne," said Jessica. "She is actually dreaming. Tell us about it, dear."

"I was thinking of the play," said Anne dreamily. "I do so want a part, if only a little one."

"You'll be chosen for Rosalind, see if you aren't," predicted Grace.

"Oh, no," said Anne. "Someone else will be sure to get that. Besides, I'm too short."

"But, Anne, you've had stage experience," said Jessica. "You ought to get it."

"Not in a Shakespearian play," replied Anne, shaking her head. "I might not do well at all with that kind of part."

"Never fear, you'll be the star before you know it," said Nora.

By Friday, there was nothing on the school horizon save the cherished play. Before school, at recess, and even in classes it was the topic of the hour. To the eager girls the day seemed particularly long, and a heartfelt sigh went up when the dismissal gong rang.

As the four chums hurried toward the gymnasium, Anne suddenly caught Grace by the arm with a faint gasp of surprise. Glancing quickly down at her friend to ascertain the cause of Anne's sudden agitation, Grace saw her friend's eyes following the figure of a tall, distinguished-looking man who was just disappearing down the corridor leading to the gymnasium.

"What's the matter, Anne?" asked Grace. "Do you know that man?"

"No," replied Anne, "but I know who he is."

"He must be a remarkable person, considering the way you gasped and clutched me," laughed Grace.

"That man is Everett Southard, the great Shakespearian actor," said Anne almost reverently. "I saw him in 'Hamlet' and his acting is wonderful."

"No wonder you were surprised," said Grace.

"It fairly takes my breath. I've seen ever so many pictures of him and read magazine articles about him. What do you suppose he is doing in Oakdale, and at the High School—of all places?"

"Time will tell," said Nora. Then she suddenly clasped her hands. "O girls, I know! He's here for the try-out!"

"Why of course he is," exclaimed Grace. "Now I remember Miss Tebbs showed me a magazine picture of him one day last year, and told me that she had known him since childhood. Besides, he is playing a three-night engagement in Albany. I read it in the paper last night. It's as plain as can be. Miss Tebbs has asked him to run up here and pick out the cast."

"Good gracious," said Jessica. "I shall retire in confusion if he looks at me. I won't dare aspire to a part now, and I had designs on the part of Phebe."

"Don't be a goose," said Nora. "He's only a man. He can't hurt you. I think having him here will be a lark. Won't some of those girls put on airs, though. There he is talking with Miss Tebbs now."

The girls entered the gymnasium to find there nearly all of those who had attended the first meeting in the library increased by about a score of girls who had decided at the last minute to try for parts. Eleanor stood at one end of the great room, with Edna Wright and Daisy Culver. Grace thought she had never seen Eleanor looking more beautiful. She was wearing a fur coat and hat far too costly for a school girl, and carried a huge muff. Her coat was thrown open, disclosing a perfectly tailored gown of brown, with trimmings of dull gold braid. She was talking animatedly and her two friends were apparently hanging on every word she uttered.

"No wonder Eleanor has an opinion of herself," said Nora. "Look at Daisy and Edna. They act as though Eleanor were the Sultan of Turkey or the Shah of Persia, or some other high and mighty dignitary. They almost grovel before her."

"Never mind, Nora," said Grace. "As long as you retain your Irish independence what do you care about what other girls do?"

"I don't care. Only they do act so silly," said Nora, with a sniff of contempt.

"Sh-h-h!" said Jessica softly. "Miss Tebbs is going to call the meeting to order."

A hush fell over the assembled girls as Miss Tebbs stepped forward to address them.

"I am very glad to see so many girls here," she said. "It shows that you are all interested in the coming play. Although you cannot all have parts, I hope that you will feel satisfied with the selection made this afternoon. In order that each member of the cast may be chosen on her merit alone, my old friend, Mr. Southard, kindly consented to come from Albany for the sole purpose of giving us the benefit of his great Shakespearian experience. Allow me to introduce Mr. Everett Southard."

412

He was greeted with a round of applause, and after bowing his thanks, the eminent actor plunged at once into the business at hand.

He spoke favorably of the idea of an all-girl cast, saying that each year many girls' colleges presented Shakespearian plays with marked success. The main thing to be considered was the intelligent delivery of the great dramatist's lines. The thing to do would be to find out what girls could most ably portray the various characters, it would be necessary to try each girl separately with a few lines from the play. In order to facilitate matters, he suggested that those girls who really desired speaking parts step to one side of the room, while those who wished merely to make the stage pictures, step to the other.

Out of the eighty girls, about thirty-five only stepped over to the side from which the principal characters were to be chosen. Many of the girls had no serious intentions whatever regarding the play, and the awe inspired by Mr. Southard's presence made them too timid to venture to open their mouths before him. Jessica, whose courage had fled, would have been among the latter if Nora had not seized her firmly by the arm as she prepared to flee and marched her over with the rest of the Phi Sigma Tau. Eleanor and Edna Wright were among the junior contestants, while there was a good showing of sophomores and freshmen.

Mr. Southard took in the aspirants with keen, comprehensive glance. His eyes rested a shade longer on Eleanor. She made a striking picture as she stood looking with apparent indifference at the girls about her. Then his quick eye traveled to Grace's fine face and graceful figure, and then on to Anne, whose small face was alive with the excitement of the moment.

A breathless silence had fallen over the room. Every eye was fixed on the actor, who stood with a small leather-covered edition of "As You Like It" in his hand. Miss Tebbs stood by with a pencil and pad. The great try-out was about to begin.

## CHAPTER XIX

## THE TRY OUT

"Will the young lady on the extreme right please come forward?" said Mr. Southard pleasantly, indicating Marian Barber, who rather timidly obeyed, taking the book he held out to her. At his request, she began to read from Orlando's entrance, in the first scene of the fourth act. She faltered a little on the first two lines, but shortly regained her courage and read on in her best manner. When she had read about a dozen lines he motioned for her to cease reading, said something to Miss Tebbs, who made an entry on her pad, and beckoned to the girl next to Marian to come forward.

Straight down the line he went, sometimes stopping a girl at her third or fourth line, rarely allowing them to read farther than the eleventh or twelfth.

Nora was the second Phi Sigma Tau to undergo the ordeal. As she briskly delivered the opening lines, the actor stopped her. Taking the book from her, he turned to the part where Touchstone, quaintly humorous, holds forth upon "the lie seven times removed."

"Read this," he said briefly, holding out the book to Nora.

Nora began and read glibly on, unconsciously emphasizing as she did so. Down one page she read and half way through the next before Mr. Southard seemed satisfied.

Then he again held conversation with Miss Tebbs, who nodded and looked smilingly toward Nora, who stood scowling faintly, rather ill-pleased at attracting so much attention.

"It looks as though Nora had made an impression, doesn't it!" whispered Jessica to Grace, who was about to reply when Mr. Southard motioned to her. Grace, who knew the scene by heart, went fearlessly forward, and read the lines with splendid emphasis. Marian and Eva Allen followed her, and acquitted themselves with credit. Then Eleanor's turn came. Handing her coat, which she had taken off and carried upon her arm, to Edna Wright, she walked proudly over, then, without a trace of self-consciousness, began the reading of the designated lines. Her voice sounded unusually clear and sweet, yet lacked something of the power of expression displayed by Grace in her rendering of the same scene. When she had finished she handed the book back with an air of studied indifference she was far from feeling. She had decided in her own mind that Rosalind was the part best suited to her, and felt that the honor now lay between herself and Grace. No other girls, with the exception of Nora, had been allowed to read as much of any scene as they two had been requested to read.

But Eleanor had reckoned without her host, for there was one girl who had not as yet come to the front. The girl was Anne Pierson, who in some mysterious manner had been all but overlooked, until Miss Tebbs spied her standing between Grace and Nora.

"Can you spare us a moment more, Mr. Southard?" said Miss Tebbs to the actor, who was preparing to leave. "You have almost missed hearing one of my best girls. Come here, Anne, and prove the truth of my words."

Grace drew a long breath of relief. She had eagerly awaited Anne's turn and was about to call Miss Tebbs's attention to Anne, just as that teacher had observed her.

As most of the girls present had heard Anne recite, there was a great craning of necks and a faint murmur of expectancy as she took her place. They expected her to live up to her reputation and she had scarcely delivered the opening line before they realized that she would not disappoint them.

Her musical voice vibrated with expression and the mock-serious bantering tones in which she delivered Rosalind's witty speeches caused Mr. Southard to smile and nod approvingly as she gave full value to the immortal lines. Her change of voice from Rosalind to Orlando was wholly delightful, and so charmingly did she depict both characters that when she ended with Orlando's exit she received a little ovation from the listening girls, in which Mr. Southard and Miss Tebbs joined.

"She's won! She's won! I'm so glad," Grace said softly to Nora and Jessica. "I wanted her to play Rosalind, and I knew she could do it. Look, girls! Mr. Southard is shaking hands with her."

True enough, Anne was shyly shaking hands with the great actor, who was congratulating her warmly upon her recent effort.

"I have never before heard an amateur read those lines as well as you have to-day, Miss Pierson," he said. "I am sure Rosalind will be safe with you, for few professional women could have done better. If I am anywhere near here when your play is enacted, I shall make it a point to come and see it."

Shaking hands warmly with Miss Tebbs and bowing to the admiring girls, Mr. Southard hurriedly departed, leaving his audience devoured with curiosity as to the chosen ones.

Anne stood perfectly still, looking rather dazed. The unexpected had happened. She was to have not only a part, but the best part, at that. The girls gathered eagerly about her, congratulating her on her success, but she was too overcome to thank them, and smiled at them through a mist of tears.

"Look at Eleanor," whispered Nora to Grace. "She's so angry she can't see straight. She must have wanted to play Rosalind herself. I told you she'd sulk if she couldn't be the leading lady."

Grace glanced over toward Eleanor, who stood biting her lip, her hands clenched and her face set in angry lines.

"She looks like the 'Vendetta' or the 'Camorra' or some other Italian vengeance agency, doesn't she?" said Nora with a giggle.

Grace laughed in spite of herself at Nora's remark, but regretted it the next moment, for Eleanor saw the glances directed toward her and heard Nora's giggle. She turned white and half started toward Grace, then stopped, and, turning her back upon the Phi Sigma Tau, began talking to Edna Wright.

Just then Miss Tebbs, who had been busy with her list, announced that she would now name the cast, and all conversation ceased as by magic.

Miriam Nesbit was entrusted with the "Duke, "while Marian Barber was to play "Frederick," his brother. Jessica was in raptures over "Phebe," while Nora had captured "Touchstone," Eva Allen, "Audrey," and, to her great delight, Grace was told that she was to play "Orlando," with Eleanor as "Celia." The other parts were assigned among the sophomores and freshmen who had made the best showing, Mabel Allison getting the part of Jacques.

"You will report for rehearsal next Tuesday afternoon after school, when typewritten copies of your parts will be handed you," said Miss Tebbs, as she was about to leave the room.

The moment Miss Tebbs ceased talking the girls began, as they gathered in little groups around the lucky ones and gave vent to their feelings with many exclamations of approval and congratulation. Several girls approached Eleanor, but she fairly ran from them and hurried out of the gymnasium after Miss Tebbs with Edna Wright and Daisy Culver at her heels.

"There goes Eleanor after Miss Tebbs," observed Marian Barber. "What do you suppose she's up to now?"

"Oh, never mind her," said Nora impatiently. "You'll see enough of her during rehearsal. It will be so pleasant to rehearse with her, considering that she isn't on speaking terms with any of us."

Had the girl chums known then what Eleanor "was up to," it would have been a matter of surprise and indignation to all of them. After imperiously commanding her satellites to wait for her in the corridor, Eleanor overtook Miss Tebbs just outside Miss Thompson's office.

"I want to speak to you, Miss Tebbs," said Eleanor as the teacher paused, her hand on the doorknob.

"Well, what can I do for you, Miss Savell?"

"I want to speak to you about the play. I wish to play Rosalind," said Eleanor with calm assurance.

"But, my dear child, Anne Pierson is to play Rosalind," replied Miss Tebbs. "Mr. Southard particularly commended her work. Did you not hear what he said?"

"Oh, yes; I heard him complimenting her," replied Eleanor complacently, "but I feel sure that I can do more with it than she can. I did not do my best work to-day. Besides, Miss Pierson is too short. I am certain of making a better appearance."

"What you say about appearance is quite true, Miss Savell," replied Miss Tebbs frankly. "Beyond a doubt you would make a beautiful Rosalind; but I am convinced that no other girl can enact the part with the spirit and dash that Miss Pierson can. Your part of Celia is very well suited to you, and you can win plenty of applause playing it. You must understand, however, that once having given out a part, I should not attempt to take it from the girl I had given it to simply because some other girl desired it. That would be both unfair and unjust. The only thing I could promise you would be to allow you to understudy Rosalind in case anything happened to Miss Pierson. Would you care to understudy the part?"

Eleanor was silent for a moment. Miss Tebbs, looking a trifle impatient, stood awaiting her reply.

"I should like to do that," Eleanor said slowly, a curious light in her eyes. "Thank you very much, Miss Tebbs."

"You are welcome," replied the teacher. "Be sure and be prompt at rehearsal next Tuesday."

As Miss Tebbs entered the office, Eleanor turned and walked slowly down the corridor.

"So Miss Tebbs thinks I ought to be satisfied with 'Celia,'" she muttered. "Very well, I'll rehearse Celia, but I'll understudy Rosalind, and it will be very strange if something doesn't happen to Miss Pierson."

# CHAPTER XX

## THE ANONYMOUS LETTER

After the parts had been given out, rehearsals for the play went merrily on. There were many hitches at first, but finally things settled down to smooth running order, and as the time for its presentation approached Miss Tebbs had good reason to feel jubilant. Each girl seemed bent on distinguishing herself, and that teacher was heard laughingly to declare that she had an "all star cast."

In spite of rehearsals, Grace Harlowe's team found time for a few basketball games, and whipped the senior team twice in succession, much to the disgust of Captain Julia Crosby, who threatened to go into deep mourning over what she called "her dead and gone team." She even composed a mournful ditty, which she sang in their ears in a wailing minor key whenever she passed any of them, and practically tormented them, until they actually did win one hard-fought victory over the juniors, "just to keep Julia from perpetrating her eternal chant," as one of them remarked.

Eleanor had outwardly settled down to the routine of school work in a way that surprised even her aunt. But inwardly she was seething with rebellion toward Miss Thompson and hatred of the Phi Sigma Tau. She had fully determined that Anne Pierson should never play Rosalind, and had hit upon a plan by which she hoped to accomplish her ends. The Phi Sigma Tau were completely carried away with Anne's impersonation of Shakespeare's heroine, and any blow struck at Anne would be equally felt by the others. Anne had been absent from one rehearsal and thus Eleanor had had an opportunity to show her ability. She had done very well and Miss Tebbs had praised her work, though in her secret heart Eleanor knew that Anne's work was finer than her own. But the means of gratifying her own personal vanity blinded her to everything except the fact that she wanted to play Rosalind regardless of Anne's superior ability.

To settle Miss Thompson was not so easy a matter, and though Eleanor racked her brain for some telling method of vengeance, no inspiration came until one afternoon in early March. Professor La Roche, irritated to the point of frenzy, ordered her from his class, with instructions to report herself to Miss Thompson. As she entered the open door of the principal's office she noticed that the room was empty of occupants. She stopped, hesitated, then went softly in, a half-formed idea in her mind that did not at first assume definite shape.

"If Miss Thompson comes in, I suppose I shall have to report myself," thought Eleanor. "While I'm here, I'll just look about and see if I can't find some way to even up that public apology she made me make."

Gliding over to the open desk, she ran her eye hastily over the various papers spread out upon it. At first she found nothing of importance, but suddenly she began to laugh softly, her face lighted with malicious glee.

"Here's the wonderful paper that Miss Tabby Cat Thompson is going to read before the 'Arts and Crafts Club' to-morrow," she murmured. "I heard her telling Miss Chester about it yesterday. She said it took her six weeks to prepare it on account of the time she spent in looking up her facts. It will take me less than six minutes to dispose of it."

Seizing the essay with both hands, she tore it across, and then tore it again and again, until it was literally reduced to shreds. These she gathered into a heap and left in the middle of the desk. Glancing about to see that no one was near, she was about to step into the corridor when she heard the sound of approaching footsteps. Quick as a flash she flung open the door of the little lavatory just outside the office and concealed herself just as a girl turned from the main corridor into the short passage leading to the principal's office. Eleanor, holding the door slightly ajar, peered stealthily out at the new-comer, who was none other than Grace Harlowe.

Having no recitation that hour, Grace had run up to the office to obtain Miss Thompson's permission to use the gymnasium that afternoon for basketball practice. A hasty glance inside the office revealed to Grace that the principal was not there. She hesitated a moment, walked toward the desk, then turned and went out again.

The moment she turned the corner, Eleanor darted out of the lavatory and fled down the corridor, just as the bell rang for the end of the period. In a moment the main corridor was filled with girls from the various classrooms, and, joining them, Eleanor entered the study hall without reporting her dismissal from French class.

She was somewhat nervous and trembled a little at the thought of her near discovery, but felt not the slightest qualm of conscience at her ruthless destruction of another's property. On the contrary, she experienced a wicked satisfaction, and smiled to herself as she pictured Miss Thompson's consternation when the latter should discover her loss. Best of all, the principal would never find out who did it, for Eleanor vowed never to admit her guilt.

She decided to go at once to Professor La Roche and apologize, so that he would not report her to Miss Thompson. Without a doubt an effort would be made to find the culprit, and if it were proven that she did not return to the study hall as soon as dismissed from French, she might be asked to account for it, and thus call down suspicion upon herself.

On her way to rhetoric recitation, she stopped at Professor La Roche's door, greatly astonishing him by a prettily worded apology, which he readily accepted and beamed upon her with forgiving good-nature. Feeling that she had bridged that difficulty, Eleanor entered the classroom to find Miss Thompson talking in low, guarded tones to Miss Chester, who looked both, shocked and surprised. She caught the words "entirely destroyed," "serious offence" and "investigate at once," Then the principal left the room and Miss Chester turned to the class and began the recitation.

To Eleanor's surprise, nothing was said of the matter that day. School was dismissed as usual, and the girls went out without dreaming that on the morrow they would all be placed under suspicion until the person guilty of the outrage was found .

The following morning, after opening exercises, Miss Thompson stated briefly the destruction of her paper.

"I was out of my office barely ten minutes," she said, "yet when I returned someone had ruthlessly torn the essay to bits and left the pieces piled in the middle of my desk. As I had spent considerable time and research in getting the subject matter together, the destruction of the paper is particularly annoying. Whoever was contemptible enough to engage in such mischief must have known this. It looks like a deliberate attempt to insult me. It is hard to believe one of my girls guilty, yet it is not probable that anyone outside could be responsible. A girl who would willfully do such a thing is a menace to the school and should be removed from it. I am not going to any extreme measures to find the miscreant. Were I to question each girl in turn I fear the offender might perjure herself rather than admit her guilt. But I am confident that sooner or later I shall know the truth of the matter."

As Miss Thompson concluded, she looked over the roomful of girls who sat watching her with serious faces. Which one of them was guilty? Time alone would tell.

At recess that morning the subject of the play was for once forgotten in the excitement occasioned by the principal's recent disclosure. Groups of girls indignantly denied even the thought of such mischief.

"I don't believe Miss Thompson would ever suspect us of any such thing," remarked Jessica to her friends.

"Of course not, goose," replied Grace. "She knows us too well for that."

But it was with a peculiar apprehension of something unpleasant that Grace answered a summons to the principal's office just before school closed for the day.

"Grace," she said, as the young girl entered the office, "were you in my office yesterday afternoon between half past one and a quarter of two?"

"Why, yes, Miss Thompson. I came to ask permission to use the gymnasium, but you were out, so I came back and asked you just before school closed."

"Yes, I remember that you did," replied the principal. "However, I want you to read this."

Grace took the paper, looking rather perplexed, and read:

"Ask Miss Harlowe what she was doing in your office between half past one and a quarter of two yesterday."

"A PASSERBY."

"Why—why——" stammered Grace, her eyes growing large with wonder. "I don't understand. I came here at that time, for I looked at the clock as I came in, but I was only here for a second."

Then the truth dawned upon her. "Why, Miss Thompson," she cried, "you surely don't think I tore up your essay?"

"No, Grace, I don't," replied the principal. "But I believe that the one who wrote this note is the one who did do it, and evidently wishes to fasten the guilt upon you. It looks to me as though we had a common enemy. Do you recognize either the paper or the writing?"

"No," replied Grace slowly, shaking her head. "Vertical writing all looks alike. The paper is peculiar. It is note paper, but different from any I ever saw before. It looks like——"

She stopped suddenly, a shocked look creeping into her eyes.

"What is it, Grace?" said Miss Thompson, who had been closely watching her.

"I—just—had a queer idea," faltered Grace.

"If you suspect any one, Grace, it is your duty to tell me," said the principal. "I cannot pass lightly over such a piece of wanton destruction. To clear up this mystery, should be a matter of vital interest to you, too, as this letter is really an insinuation against you."

Grace was silent.

"I am waiting for you, Grace," said the principal. "Will you do as I wish?"

The tears rushed to Grace's eyes. "Forgive me, Miss Thompson," she said tremulously, "but I can tell you nothing."

"You are doing wrong, Grace, in withholding your knowledge," said the older woman rather sternly, "and I am greatly displeased at your stubbornness. Ordinarily I would not ask you to betray any of your schoolmates, but in this instance I am justified, and you are making a serious mistake in sacrificing your duty upon the altar of school-girl honor."

"I am sorry, Miss Thompson," said Grace, striving to steady her voice. "I value your good opinion above everything, but I can tell you nothing you wish to know. Please, please don't ask me."

"Very well," responded the principal in a tone of cold dismissal, turning to her desk.

With a half-stifled sob, Grace hurried from the room. For the first time, since entering High School, she had incurred the displeasure of her beloved principal, and all for the sake of a girl who was unworthy of the sacrifice. For Grace had recognized the paper. It was precisely the same style of paper on which Eleanor Savell had declined her Thanksgiving invitation.

## CHAPTER XXI

## BREAKERS AHEAD

The dress rehearsal for "As You Like It" was over. It had been well nigh perfect. The costumes had for the most part been on hand, as the senior class of five years previous had given the same play and bequeathed their paraphernalia to those who should come after. Rosalind's costumes had to be altered to fit Anne, however, on account of her lack of stature. Also the lines in the text where Rosalind refers to her height underwent some changes. The final details having been attended to, Miss Tebbs and Miss Kane found time to congratulate each other on the smoothness of the production, which bade fair to surpass anything of the kind ever before given. There was not a weak spot in the cast. Anne's work had seemed to grow finer with every rehearsal.

She had won the repeated applause of the group of teachers who had been invited to witness this trial performance. Grace, Nora, Eleanor and Miriam had ably supported her and there had been tears of proud joy in Miss Tebbs's eyes as she had watched the clever and spirited acting of these girls.

"Be sure and put your costumes exactly where they belong," called Miss Tebbs as the girls filed off the stage into the dressing room after the final curtain. "Then you will have no trouble to-morrow night. We want to avoid all eleventh-hour scrambling and exciting costume hunts."

Laughing merrily, the girls began choosing places to hang their costumes in the big room off the stage where they were to dress. Anne, careful little soul that she was, piled her paraphernalia neatly in one corner, and taking a slip of paper from her bag wrote "Rosalind" upon it, pinning it to her first-act costume.

"The eternal labeler," said Nora, with her ever-ready giggle, as she watched Anne. "Are you afraid it will run away, little Miss Fussbudget!"

"No; of course not," said Anne, smiling. "I just marked it because—
—"

"You have the marking habit," finished Jessica. "Come on, girls. Don't tease Anne. Let her put tags on herself if she wants to. Then a certain young man who is waiting outside for her will be sure to recognize her. Has anyone seen that Allison child? It's time she put in an appearance."

"Just listen to Grandmother Bright," teased Anne. "She is hunting her lost chick, as usual."

With merry laugh and jest the girls prepared for the street. Grace and her friends were among the first to leave, and hurried to the street, where the boys awaited them.

"Hurrah for the only original ranters and barnstormers on exhibition in this country," cried Hippy, waving his hat in the air.

"Cease, Hippopotamus," said Nora. "You are mistaken. We are stars, but we shall refuse to twinkle in your sky unless you suddenly become more respectful."

"He doesn't know the definition of the word," said David.

"How cruelly you misjudge me," said Hippy. "I meant no disrespect. It was a sudden attack of enthusiasm. I get them spasmodically."

"So we have observed," said Nora dryly. "Let's not stand here discussing you all night. Come on up to my house, and we'll make fudge and have things to eat."

"I have my car here," said David. "Pile into it and we'll be up there in a jiffy."

"It's awfully late," demurred Grace. "After ten o'clock."

"Never mind that," said Nora. "Your mother knows you can take care of yourself. You can 'phone to her from my house."

In another minute the young people had seated themselves in the big car and were off.

"Did you see Eleanor's runabout standing there?" Nora asked Grace.

"Yes," replied Grace. "I was rather surprised, too. She hasn't used it much of late."

"How beautiful she looked to-night, didn't she?" interposed Jessica.

"Are you talking of the would-be murderess, who froze us all out Thanksgiving Day?" asked Hippy. "What is her latest crime?"

Grace felt like saying "Destroying other people's property and getting innocent folks disliked," but refrained. She had told no one of her interview with Miss Thompson. Grace knew that the principal was still displeased with her. She was no longer on the old terms of intimacy with Miss Thompson. A barrier seemed to have sprung up between them, that only one thing could remove, but Grace was resolved not to expose Eleanor—not that she felt that Eleanor did not richly deserve it, but she knew that it would mean instant expulsion from school. She believed that Eleanor had acted on the impulse of the moment, and was without doubt bitterly sorry for it, and she felt that as long as Eleanor had at last begun to be interested in school, the thing to do was to keep her there, particularly as Mrs. Gray had recently told her of Miss Nevin's pleasure at the change that the school had apparently wrought in Eleanor.

Could Grace have known what Eleanor was engaged in at the moment she would have felt like exposing her without mercy.

During the first rehearsals Grace, secretly fearing an outbreak on Eleanor's part, had been on the alert, but as rehearsals progressed and Eleanor kept strictly to herself, Grace relaxed her vigilance.

Directly after the chums had hurried out of the hall to meet the boys, Miss Tebbs had decided that opening the dressing room on the other side of the stage would relieve the congestion and insure a better chance for all to dress. Calling to the girls who still remained to move their belongings to that side, Miss Tebbs hurried across the stage to find the janitor and see that the door was at once unlocked. By the time the door was opened and the lights turned on the remaining girls flocked in, their arms piled high with costumes.

Foremost among them was Eleanor. Hastily depositing her own

costumes in one corner of the dressing room, she darted across the stage and into the room from which she had just moved her effects.

It was empty. She glanced quickly about. Like a flash she gathered up a pile of costumes marked "Rosalind," covered them with her long fur coat and ran through the hall and down the steps to where her runabout was stationed. Crowding them hastily into the bottom of the machine, she slipped on her coat, made ready her runabout and drove down the street like the wind, not lessening her speed until she reached the drive at "Heartsease."

The young people passed a merry hour at Nora's, indulging in one of their old-time frolics, that only lacked Tom Gray's presence to make the original octette complete.

"We'll be in the front row to-morrow night," said Hippy, as the young folks trooped out to the car. "I have engaged a beautiful bunch of green onions from the truck florist, Reddy has put all his money into carrots of a nice lively color, the exact shade of his hair, while I have advised Davy here to invest in turnips. They are nice and round and hard, and will hit the stage with a resounding whack, providing he can throw straight enough to hit anything. He can carry them in a paper bag and——"

But before he could say more he was seized by David and Reddy and rushed unceremoniously into the street, while the girls signified their approbation by cries of "good enough for him" and "make him promise to behave to-morrow night."

"I will. I swear it," panted Hippy. "Only don't rush me over the ground so fast. I might lose my breath and never, never catch it again."

"Oh, let him go," said Nora, who had accompanied them down the walk. "I'll have a private interview with him to-morrow and that will insure his good behavior."

"Thank you, angel Nora," replied Hippy gratefully. "You will be spared any obnoxious vegetables, even though the others may suffer."

"For that you walk," said David, who had dropped Hippy and was engaged in helping the girls into the machine.

"Never," replied Hippy, making a dive for the automobile. "I shall sit at the feet of the fair Jessica. Reddy will be so pleased."

"Everyone ready?" sang out David, as he took his place at the wheel after cranking up the machine.

"All ready, let her go," was the chorus, and the machine whizzed down the street.

## CHAPTER XXII

## AS YOU LIKE IT

The big dressing rooms on each side of the stage at Assembly Hall were ablaze with light. There was a hum of girlish voices and gay laughter, and all the pleasant excitement attending an amateur production prevailed. The dressing had been going on for the last hour, and now a goodly company of courtiers and dames stood about waiting while Miss Tebbs and Miss Kane rapidly "made up their faces" with rouge and powder. This being done to prevent them from looking too pale when in the white glare of the footlights.

Miriam Nesbit as the "Duke" looked particularly fine, and the girls gathered around her with many exclamations of admiration. Nora's roguish face looked out from her fool's cap in saucy fashion as she flitted about jingling her bells. Grace made a handsome Orlando, while Jessica looked an ideal shepherdess.

"Where's Anne?" said Grace as Nora paused in front of her. "I haven't see her to-night. I suppose she's over in the other dressing room. Miss Tebbs said that some of the costumes were moved over there after we left last night. What time is it? I didn't wear my watch to-night because I didn't want to risk losing it."

"It's almost half past seven," said Jessica. "I asked Miss Tebbs for the time just a few minutes ago."

"Let's go and find Anne at once, then," said Nora. "It's getting late, and she surely is dressed by this time. Then we'll look through the hole in the curtain at the house. People are beginning to arrive."

"Wait a minute," said Jessica. "There's Mabel. Doesn't she look great as Jacques? Come here, dear," called Jessica.

Mabel Allison joined the three girls, who hurried across the stage to the other dressing room in search of Anne Pierson.

"Why, I don't see her here," cried Grace, making a quick survey of the room. "She must be somewhere about, for——"

"There she goes now," exclaimed Nora, who stood in the door, looking out on the stage, "and she has her hat and coat on. How strange. I wonder if she knows how late it is?"

Sure enough, Anne was hurrying toward the opposite dressing room.

The three girls made a rush for her.

"Why, Anne," said Grace. "What is the matter? We thought you had dressed over here and were looking for you."

"Girls," replied Anne, "I've been on a wild-goose chase. I can't stop to tell you about it now, but you shall hear as soon as I have a chance. Will you help me with my costume and make-up? I'm awfully late, and haven't a minute to spare."

"Why of course we will," said Grace. "Give me your hat and coat, dear. Where did you put your costumes? It won't take you long to dress, for most of the girls are dressed and over on the other side, so you have the place to yourself."

"Over in that corner," replied Anne, taking off her collar and unfastening her white shirt waist. "Don't you remember, I labeled them and you laughed at me for doing so?"

"Of course we do," said Nora, making a dive for the corner where Anne had piled her costumes the previous night. "They're not here," she announced after a brief but thorough search. "Miss Tebbs must have had them moved to the other room. She opened it last night after we left. Grace, you help Anne, and Jessica and Mabel and I will run across and look for them." With these words, Nora was off, the other two girls at her heels.

"Tell me what kept you, Anne," said Grace, as the latter began arranging her hair for the first act.

"Grace," said Anne rather tremulously, "I won't wait until the others come back to tell you why I came so late. Just after I had finished my

431

supper and was putting on my wraps a boy came to the door with this note." Anne went over to where her coat hung and took out an envelope. Drawing a note from it, she silently handed it to Grace, who read:

"MY DEAR ANNE:

"Will you come up to my house before going to the hall? I wish to give you something to wear in the play.

"Yours affectionately,
"ROSE R. GRAY."

"Why, how unlike Mrs. Gray to send for you at the eleventh hour," said Grace in a puzzled tone. "No wonder you were late. What did she give you?"

"Nothing," replied Anne. "It was a trick. She never wrote the note, although the writing looks like hers, and so does the paper. She was very indignant over it and sent me back in the carriage, telling the coachman to return for her, for of course she will be here to-night. I would have arrived much later if I had been obliged to walk. I ran almost all the way up there. You know Chapel Hill is quite a distance from my house."

"I should say so," replied Grace. "Who could have been so mean? Anne, why do you suppose——" Grace stopped suddenly and stared at Anne. "Anne do you think that Eleanor could have written it?" she said slowly, as though reluctant to give voice to her suspicion.

"I am afraid so," replied Anne. "She is the only one who could profit by my being late. Yet if she did write the note, she should have realized that going to Mrs. Gray's would scarcely keep me away long enough to miss my first entrance. You know I don't come on until the second scene."

"There is something more behind this," said Grace, "and I'm going to find out, too." She darted to the door and opened it upon Nora and Jessica, who were on the threshold.

"We can't find them," they cried in alarm, "but we told Miss Tebbs and she'll be here in a minute."

"We didn't say a word to anyone else," said Nora, "because they must be somewhere about, and there is no use in stirring up a lot of unnecessary excitement."

"Wise little Nora," said Grace, patting her on the shoulder. "Here comes Miss Tebbs now." She stepped courteously aside to allow the teacher to enter the dressing room, then, following her, closed the door.

"What is this I hear about losing your costumes, Anne?" asked Miss Tebbs rather impatiently. "I cautioned the girls last night about taking care of their things."

Anne flushed at the teacher's curt tones.

"I put them all in that corner, plainly marked, before I left here last night," she answered. "When I came here to-night they were gone."

"That is strange," said the elder woman. "Have you made a thorough search for them in the other room?"

"We've gone over every inch of the ground," exclaimed Jessica, "and we can't find a trace of them. We didn't ask any of the girls about them, because if we couldn't find them we feel sure the others couldn't. So we just kept quiet."

"I don't know what is to be done, I'm sure," said Miss Tebbs in an anxious tone. "It is eight o'clock now and the curtain is supposed to run up at 8.15. I can hold it until 8.30, but no longer. The house is already well filled. You might get through the first act in a borrowed gown, Anne, but what can you do in the second? You know how that costume had to be altered to fit you. If it can be found before the second act, all will be well, but suppose you go on in the first act, and it can't be found, what then? You will spoil the whole production by appearing in an incorrect or misfit costume, besides bitterly disappointing the two girls who will have to give up their costumes to you. It is doubly provoking, because Mr. Southard is here to-night, and is particularly anxious to see your work."

"Miss Tebbs," exclaimed Grace, "Eleanor Savell has a complete 'Rosalind' outfit. She had it made purposely. One of the girls told me so.

You know she understudies Anne. Couldn't Anne use that?"

"Impossible, Grace," said Miss Tebbs. "Eleanor is taller than Anne. Anne's lack of height is her one drawback. If she had not shown such exceptional talent, 'Rosalind' would have certainly fallen to Miss Savell or yourself. I am very sorry, but it looks as though Miss Savell will have to play Rosalind after all, and she must be notified at once."

The three chums turned to Anne, who was biting her lip and trying hard to keep back her tears. Nora and Jessica looked their silent sympathy, but Grace stood apparently wrapped in thought.

Miss Tebbs moved toward the door, but as she placed her hand on the knob Grace sprang eagerly forward.

"Miss Tebbs," she cried, "don't ask Miss Savell. I believe I can find those costumes yet. Wait here and in five minutes I'll tell you whether I have succeeded. Please don't ask me what I am going to do. Just trust me and wait. You will let me try, won't you?" she pleaded.

"Certainly, my child," said Miss Tebbs, "but remember time is precious. I'll give you five minutes, but if——"

"I'll be back in that time," cried Grace, and was gone, leaving Miss Tebbs and the three chums mystified but faintly hopeful.

Across the stage she flew and into the other dressing room. The object of her search was not there. Out she rushed and collided with a girl who was about to enter.

"Pardon me," said Grace, glancing up, then seized the girl by the arm. "Eleanor Savell," she exclaimed sternly. "You know where Anne's costumes are. Don't attempt to deny it."

Eleanor looked contemptuously at Grace and tried to shake herself free, but Grace's grasp tightened.

"Answer me," she said. "Where are they?"

"Let me go," said Eleanor angrily. "You are hurting my arm. What do I care about Miss Pierson's costumes?"

"You will care," replied Grace. "For if you don't instantly tell me where they are, I shall call the whole cast and expose you."

"If you do, you will merely make yourself ridiculous," hissed Eleanor, her eyes blazing. "What grounds have you for such an accusation?"

"I can't prove that you are responsible for their disappearance, but I do know that you shall not play 'Rosalind,' if the costumes are never found."

"How can you prevent me!" asked Eleanor in insolent tones. "You are not running this production."

"I have no time to waste in arguing the matter," returned Grace with admirable self-control. "What I want is the truth about the costumes and you must answer me."

"'Must,'" repeated Eleanor, raising her eyebrows. "That is putting it rather strongly. No one ever says 'must' to me."

"I say it to you now, Eleanor, and I mean it," said Grace. "I am fully convinced that you have hidden Anne's costumes and I am equally certain that you are going to produce them at once."

"Then you are laboring under a delusion," replied Eleanor, with a disagreeable laugh, "and I should advise you to devote that tireless energy of yours, to minding your own business."

"This is my business," replied Grace evenly, "and if you wish to avoid any unpleasantness you will make it yours."

"Your threats do not alarm me," sneered Eleanor. "I am not easily frightened."

"Very well," replied Grace, looking steadily at her enemy. "I see that I shall be obliged to call Miss Thompson back here and tell her who destroyed her essay. Knowing that, do you suppose you can make her believe that you did not hide Anne's costumes?"

Eleanor's insolent expression turned to one of fear. "No," she gasped, "don't call Miss Thompson. You know she hates me, and will disgrace me in the eyes of the girls."

"And you richly deserve it, Eleanor," replied Grace, "but if you produce Anne's costumes at once, I'll agree to say nothing. Hurry, for every second is precious."

"I can't get them," wailed Eleanor. "What shall I do?"

"Where are they?" asked Grace, with compressed lips.

"At—'Heartsease,'" said Eleanor, and burst into tears.

"Oh, what a mess," groaned Grace. "It will take an hour to go there and back. Oh, I must act quickly. Let me think. Mrs. Gray's coachman would drive me out, but those horses are so slow. Eleanor," she exclaimed, turning to the weeping girl, "is your runabout outside?"

"Yes," sobbed Eleanor.

"Then that settles it," cried Grace. "I will go after the things. Tell me where to find them. Have you a latch key? I can't bother to ring after I get there."

"I'll go and get my key," said Eleanor, wiping her eyes. "They're in the wardrobe in my bedroom."

"All right, wait for me at the door and don't say a word. Here come some of the girls."

Though the time had seemed hours to Grace, her interview with Eleanor had lasted barely five minutes. She hurried back to where Miss Tebbs and the three chums awaited her, followed by the curious eyes of a number of the cast, who wondered vaguely why Grace Harlowe was rushing around at such a rate.

"Borrow a gown for Anne, Miss Tebbs, for the first act," she cried. "I'll have the missing costumes here in time for the second. Only I can't play Orlando. Miriam will have to play it; she's my understudy, you know. Ethel Dumont can play Miriam's part. They've rehearsed both parts, and will be all right. Please don't refuse me, Miss Tebbs, but let me

436

go. It's for Anne's sake. Nora, please bring me my street clothes."

As she spoke, Grace began rapidly divesting herself of her costume.

"Very well, Grace, have your own way," replied the teacher reluctantly. "I'll go at once and get a gown for Anne. But don't dare to fail me."

"Thank you, Miss Tebbs. I'll not fail." Slipping into her long coat and seizing her fur hat, Grace made for the street, stopping for an instant to take the key from Eleanor, who stood waiting at the door.

"Can you manage the machine?" faltered Eleanor.

"Yes," said Grace curtly. "Go in at once. If you are seen, the girls are apt to ask questions that you may find hard to answer truthfully."

"Thank goodness, David and Tom taught me something about automobiles last summer," thought Grace as she prepared to start, "or I should have been powerless to help Anne to-night. I am going to exceed the speed limit, that's certain." A moment later she was well into the street and on her way to "Heartsease." It was a memorable ride to Grace. It seemed as though the runabout fairly flew over the ground.

"I've only been ten minutes on the way," she breathed as she neared her destination. Leaving the runabout outside the grounds, she ran up the drive, and, inserting her key in the door, opened it softly and entered the wide, old-fashioned hall. Up the steps she hurried, meeting no one, for Miss Nevin was at Assembly Hall and the servants' quarters were at the back of the house. Knowing the house as she did, Grace went straight to Eleanor's room and to the wardrobe. Sure enough, Anne's missing costumes were lying in a neat heap on the floor. Assuring herself that everything was there, Grace piled them up in her arms and sped softly down the stairs, opened the door, and in a twinkling was down the drive and into the runabout.

She drove back even faster than she had come. As she passed the city hall clock she drew a breath of relief. It was ten minutes of nine. The first act was hardly half over. Leaping from the machine with the lost costumes she ran triumphantly into the dressing room.

437

"Here she is," shrieked Nora in delight. "I knew she'd make good."

"Are they all there, Grace," anxiously inquired Miss Tebbs. "You dear, good child. Where did you find them?"

"That is a mystery which even Sherlock Holmes can never solve," replied Grace, laughing. "Where's Anne?"

"She's on just now with Celia," replied Miss Tebbs, "and is playing up to her usual form, but she is very nervous and almost broke down after you left. She feels that you made too great a sacrifice for her in giving up your part."

"Nonsense," said Grace. "Why should I have sacrificed the star to my own personal vanity? Miriam Nesbit can play Orlando as well as I, and makes a more striking appearance at that."

"I don't agree with you, Grace, for you were an ideal 'Orlando,'" replied Miss Tebbs. "However it's too late for regret, and the best I can do now is to make you assistant stage manager. Some of those girls need looking after. Miss Savell had a bad case of stage fright and almost had to be dragged on. She forgot her lines and had to be prompted. She's all right now, but I am devoutly thankful she didn't play 'Rosalind,' for she certainly would not have done justice to it."

Grace smiled grimly as she listened to Miss Tebbs. She could not feel sorry at Eleanor's recent agitation. Now that the excitement was over, Grace felt her anger rising. Eleanor's thirst for glory and revenge had been the means of losing Grace the part that she had so eagerly looked forward to playing, not to mention the narrow escape Anne had run. Still, on the whole, Grace felt glad that so far no one knew the truth.

"I think I'll go into the wings. It's almost time for the curtain," she said to Miss Tebbs. But before she could reach there, the curtain had rung down and the audience were calling for Celia and Rosalind, who took the call hand in hand. Then Rosalind took two calls and bowed herself into the wings and straight into Grace's arms.

"O Grace, how could you do it?" said Anne, with a half sob. "You gave up your part for me. It's too much. I shan't——"

"You shall," replied Grace, hugging her. "Run along and put on male attire. I found your stuff and some time I'll tell you where, but not now."

The play progressed with remarkable smoothness, and the various actors received unstinted applause from the audience, but from first to last Anne was the star. Her portrayal of Rosalind left little to be desired. Time after time Mr. Southard led the applause, and was ably seconded by Hippy, Reddy, David and Tom, who fairly wriggled with enthusiasm.

Next to Anne, Nora, perhaps, came second. Her delivery of Touchstone's lines was delightful and she kept the audience in a gale of mirth whenever she appeared.

It was over at last. The closing line of the Epilogue had been spoken by Rosalind, and she had taken five curtain calls and retired with her arms full of flowers. The principal actors in the play had been well remembered by friends, and the dressing rooms looked like a florist's shop.

"I'm so sorry. I'd like to begin all over again," said Nora, as she rubbed her face with cold cream to take off her make-up.

"There's an end to all things," said Jessica practically, "and really I'm glad to get back into everyday clothes."

"Hurry up, slowpokes," said Grace Harlowe, popping her head in the door. "Tom Gray is here. He and David are waiting outside with their cars. We are all going up to Nesbit's for a jollification given in honor of Rosalind, who is at present dressed in everyday clothes and shaking hands with the great Southard. He and Miss Tebbs are going, too, and so is Mrs. Gray."

"Come in, Grace, and tell us where you found Anne's costumes," said Nora, giving her cheeks a final rub. "We're devoured with curiosity."

"'Thereby hangs a tale,'" replied Grace, "but I refuse to be interviewed to-night. I'll see you outside. If you're not there in three minutes, I'll put Hippy on your trail."

Closing the door, Grace walked slowly toward the entrance. The majority of the girls had gone. Anne still stood talking with Mr. Southard and Miss Tebbs.

"Grace, come here and speak to Mr. Southard," called Miss Tebbs. "Has Nora gone? Mr. Southard wishes to congratulate her and you, too." "She'll be out in a couple of minutes," said Grace, as she advanced to greet the great actor. "But I am not in line for congratulations, as I was not in the play."

"I am very sorry that you could not play Orlando to-night. I remember your work at the try-out," said Mr. Southard in his deep, musical voice. "Miss Tebbs has told me of the sacrifice you made. You deserve double congratulations for the part you played behind the scenes."

"It was nothing," murmured Grace, her color rising. "If you are ready, suppose we go. Mrs. Gray wishes you and Mr. Southard to go in her carriage, Miss Tebbs. The rest of us will go in the two automobiles." As they moved toward the door, Grace left them. Going back to the dressing room, she rapped sharply on the door. "Last call! Look out for Hippy!" she cried, then hurried to catch up with the others. But before she reached them she was confronted by Eleanor.

"I've been waiting to see you ever since the play was over," said Eleanor sullenly. Grace looked at her in silence. "Well?" she said coldly. "What are you going to do about to-night—and everything?" asked Eleanor. "Are you going to tell Miss Thompson?"

"So far I have told nothing, Eleanor," said Grace sternly. "You deserve no clemency at my hands, however, for you have repeatedly accused myself and my friends of carrying tales. Something we are above doing. You have refused our friendship and have been the means of estranging Miss Thompson and myself.

"When first you came to High School, I promised Mrs. Gray that I would help you to like High School life. For that reason I have overlooked lots of things, but to-night caps the climax, and I tell you frankly that I thoroughly despise your conduct, and if ever again you do anything to injure myself or my friends, I shall not hesitate to bring you to book for it." Eleanor stood clenching her hands in impotent rage. Grace's plain speaking had roused a tempest in her.

"I hate you, Grace Harlowe, fifty times more than ever before," she said, her voice shaking with anger. "I intended to leave this miserable school at the end of the year, but now I shall stay and show you that you cannot trample upon me with impunity."

Without answering, Grace walked away, leaving Eleanor to stare moodily after her.

## CHAPTER XXIII

## THE JUNIOR PICNIC

With the first days of spring, the longing to throw down her books and fairly live in the open returned to Grace Harlowe with renewed force.

"I do wish school were over," she said with a sigh to her three chums, as they strolled home one afternoon in May. "I don't mind studying in the winter, but when the spring comes, then it's another matter. I long to golf and play tennis, and picnic in the woods and——"

"That reminds me," said Nora, interrupting her, "that last fall the juniors talked about giving a picnic instead of a ball. We didn't give the ball, so it's up to us to go picnicking."

"That's a fine suggestion, Nora," said Jessica. "I move we post a notice in the locker-room and have a meeting to-morrow after school.

"I can't be there," said Anne regretfully. "To-morrow is one of my days at Mrs. Gray's, but whatever you do will suit me."

"Awfully sorry, Anne," said Grace. "We might call it for the day after to-morrow."

"No, no," protested Anne. "Please don't postpone it on my account."

The notice was duly posted in a conspicuous place in the locker-room the next day, and the entire class, with the exception of Anne, met in one of the smaller rooms off the gymnasium at the close of the afternoon session.

"Esteemed juniors and fellow-citizens," said Grace, after calling the meeting to order. "It is true that no one has particularly requested me to take charge of this meeting, but as I posted the notice, I feel that I am responsible for your presence here to-day. We have before us two matters that need attention. One is the annual entertainment that the junior class always gives, the other the election of class officers. Last year we gave a ball, but this year so far we have done nothing. I move that we proceed at once to elect our president, vice president, secretary and treasurer, and then decide what form of entertainment would be advisable."

"Second the motion," said Nora.

"All those in favor say 'aye,' contrary, 'no.'"

"Carried," said Grace, as no dissenting voices arose. "Nominations for president are now in order."

"I nominate Grace Harlowe for president," exclaimed Miriam Nesbit, springing from her seat.

"Second the motion," said Eva Allen.

It was carried with enthusiasm before Grace had time to protest.

"I nominate Miriam Nesbit for president," said Grace.

This was also seconded and carried. Then Edna Wright rose and nominated Eleanor Savell. This closed the nominations for president, and the matter when put to vote resulted in Grace's election by a majority of ten votes over Miriam, Eleanor having received only five. It was plain to be seen that in spite of the rival faction, Grace held first place in the hearts of most of her class. Miriam Nesbit was elected vice president, Marian Barber treasurer, and, rather to Grace's surprise, Eleanor was chosen as secretary, Edna Wright again nominating her after doing some vigorous whispering among the two back rows of girls. The only other girl proposed being one who was not particularly popular in the class.

"I always suspected Edna Wright's lack of sense," whispered Nora to Jessica. "The idea of nominating Eleanor for secretary when she knows how Eleanor hates the Phi Sigma Tau, and doesn't speak to any of us. I certainly didn't vote for her."

"Nor I," responded Jessica. "Funny Grace would never tell us about that costume business. I know Eleanor was mixed up in it."

"Of course," nodded Nora, and turned her attention to the meeting just in time to hear Grace put the motion for the picnic and say "aye" with the others.

The date for the affair was set for the following Saturday, the weather permitting, and it was generally agreed that Forest Park, a natural park about twelve miles from Oakdale, would be an ideal place to picnic. A refreshment committee was appointed, also a transportation committee. The girls were requested to pay fifty cents apiece to the treasurer.

"If we find that this is not enough, we will levy another tax," Grace announced.

"I'm not positive about the first collection," muttered Nora. "I'm perpetually broke."

"So am I," said Jessica. "My allowance lasts about two days, and then I am penniless for the rest of the month."

The details having been disposed of, the members decided to meet in front of the High School the following Saturday morning at nine o'clock. The transportation committee was to have two big picnic wagons in readiness and the juniors went home with pleasant anticipations of a day in the woods.

"Won't it be fun?" exclaimed Grace joyously, as she walked down the street, the center of the Phi Sigma Tau.

"Great," said Miriam Nesbit. "I suppose we could all squeeze into David's automobile."

"I believe we'd better not," replied Grace. "It might create bad feeling among the girls. We don't want them to feel that we think ourselves too exclusive to ride with them."

"I'll wager anything Eleanor and Edna won't go with the crowd," said Eva Allen.

"I don't know about that," remarked Nora O'Malley. "Eleanor has just been elected secretary, therefore it behooves her to keep on the right side of those who elected her."

"She owes her office to Edna Wright," said Marian Barber, "and also to the fact that her opponent, Miss Wells, is not popular. For my part, I think Miss Wells would have been a better secretary. We could at least have gotten along peaceably with her. I can't see why Eleanor accepted, knowing she would have to act with us in class matters."

"I have noticed that ever since the play she has been trying to gain a footing in the class," said Miriam Nesbit thoughtfully. "She has gone out of her way to be nice to girls that she used to snub unmercifully. We are the only ones she keeps away from. I believe she will try to influence the rest of the class against us."

"She'll have to hurry up if she does it this term," said Nora.

"Perhaps she won't come back to school next year, she is so changeable," said Jessica hopefully.

"Yes, she will," said Grace, taking part in the discussion for the first time since it had touched on Eleanor.

"How do you know?" was the question.

"She told me so the night of the play," was Grace's answer. "Girls, I have never told you about what happened that night. Anne knows, but, you see, it particularly concerned her. I was too angry at the time to trust myself to tell anyone else. As members of the same sorority, I know that you can be trusted not to repeat what I shall tell you."

In a few words Grace told the story of Eleanor's treachery, omitting, however, the part concerning Miss Thompson. She had decided to reveal that to no one.

"Well, of all things," said Nora O'Malley. "I knew she was to blame. So she threatened revenge, did she?"

"Yes," replied Grace. "That is why I have told you this. Be careful what you do. Never give her a chance to take advantage of you in any way, for she is determined to make mischief. Now let us forget her, and talk about the picnic."

With the talk of the picnic, Grace's warning soon passed from the

445

girls' minds. They had no knowledge of the trials that their senior year was to bring them or how fully the truth of Grace's words was to be proved.

The day of the picnic dawned fair and cloudless. By nine o'clock a merry party of laughing, chattering girls had gathered in front of the High School, where the two immense wagons generally used by Oakdale picnickers, each drawn by four horses, awaited them. For a wonder everyone was on time, and the start was made with a great fluttering of handkerchiefs, accompanied by enthusiastic cheers and High School yells. As they rattled down the street people paused and looked smilingly after them. Oakdale was very proud of her High School boys and girls, and enjoyed seeing them happy.

The Phi Sigma Tau were seated in one end of the second wagon, with the exception of Grace, who had perched herself on the driver's seat, and was holding an animated conversation with the driver, old Jerry Flynn, whom everyone knew and liked. Grace always cultivated old Jerry's acquaintance whenever she had the chance. To-day he was allowing her to drive, while, with folded hands, he directed her management of the lines. Grace was in her element and gave a sigh of regret as they sighted the park. "I could go on driving four horses forever, Mr. Flynn," she exclaimed. "Do let me drive going back?"

"Sure yez can, miss," said the good-natured Irishman, "and it's meself'll hellup yez, and show yez how to do it."

The committee on entertainment had provided a series of races and contests for the morning. After lunch there would be a tennis match, and then the girls could amuse themselves as they chose; the start home to be made about six o'clock.

Grace and Nora decided to enter the hundred-yard dash. "The prize is a box of stationery bought at the ten-cent store, so I am anxious to win it," Nora informed them. "In fact, all the prizes came from that useful and overworked place. I was on the purchasing committee."

"I shall enter the one-legged race. I always could stand on one foot like a crane," announced Jessica, "and hopping is my specialty."

There was an egg and spoon race, a walking match, an apple-eating contest, with the apples suspended by strings from the low branch of a tree, to be eaten without aid from the hands, and various other stunts of a similar nature.

The morning passed like magic. Each new set of contestants seemed funnier than the preceding one. Nora won the coveted box of stationery. Jessica ably demonstrated her ability to out hop her competitors, while Eva Allen covered herself with glory in the apple contest.

Grace, after losing the hundred-yard dash, laughingly refused to enter the other contests. "I mean to win at tennis this afternoon," she said, "so I'm not going to waste my precious energy on such little stunts."

After the midday luncheon had been disposed of, the entire class repaired to the tennis court at the east end of the park. A match had been arranged in which Grace and Miriam Nesbit were to play against Ruth Deane and Edna Wright, who was an indefatigable tennis player, and therefore figured frequently in tennis matches held in Oakdale. At the last minute, however, Edna pleaded a severe headache and recommended Eleanor in her place.

"But I never have played with her," protested Ruth Deane, "and how do I know whether she can play?"

"Try her," begged Edna. "I have played with her and she is a wonder."

It was with considerable surprise and some misgiving that Grace discovered that Eleanor was to play. "I seem fated to oppose her," Grace thought. "I wonder at her consenting to play against us. I'll keep my eye on her, at any rate, for I don't trust her."

Grace's fears were, in this instance, groundless, for Eleanor played a perfectly fair game from start to finish, and proved herself a powerful antagonist. Her serves were as straight and accurate as a boy's, and she played with great spirit and agility. Indeed, the sides were so evenly matched that junior excitement rose high and numerous boxes of Huyler's were wagered against the result. The game stood forty-all. Two vantages scored in succession were needed by one side to win. Grace forgot everything but the fact that she desired the victory. With her, going into a game meant winning it. Five minutes later the match was over. She and Miriam had won against worthy opponents.

"That was an evenly matched game," exclaimed Nora, as Grace and Miriam strolled to where their friends were seated upon the grass. "You played like professionals."

"Eleanor is a better player than Edna Wright," said Grace. "Her serves are wonderful. We had all we could do to hold our own."

"There's a trout brook over there," said Nora, "and I had forethought enough to borrow a fishing rod and line from Hippy. It is jointed, so it didn't get in any one's way. I left it with the lunch baskets. Therefore, as I'm not afraid of angle worms, I'm going to dig some bait and fish. Want to come?"

"Not I," laughed Anne. "Miriam and I are going up under the trees and read Browning."

"The idea of going to a picnic and reading!" exclaimed Jessica. "Come on, girls, let's go with Nora." She hastily rose, brushed off her gown and followed in Nora's wake, accompanied by Eva and Marian.

"Come with us, dear," said Anne to Grace, who stood looking dreamily toward a patch of woods to the left.

"No indeed," replied Grace. "I'm going to explore a little in those woods yonder."

"Don't go far," called Anne anxiously, as Grace turned to go.

"I won't," she answered. "See you later."

As she reached the cool shadows of the little strip of woods she drew a long breath. How delightful it was to hear the rustle of the leaves over her head, and tread upon Nature's green carpet of soft, thick moss. Forgetful of her promise, Grace wandered farther and farther on, gathering the wild flowers as she went. She found plenty of trilliums and violets, and pounced with a cry of delight upon some wild pink honeysuckle just opening. After stripping the bush, she turned into a bypath that led straight up a little hill which rose before her. Scrambling up the hill, Grace reached the top and looked about her. Nestling at the foot of the elevation on the side opposite to the one she had climbed stood a small one-story cottage.

"How funny," thought Grace. "I didn't know there was a house anywhere near here. I'm going down there for a drink of water. I'm awfully thirsty."

Suiting the action to the words, Grace hurried toward the cottage. As she neared it she noticed that the door was wide open. "Someone is at home, that's certain," she said to herself. "I hope they won't be cross at my asking for a drink. Why," she exclaimed, "there's no one living here at all. I think I'll venture in, perhaps there's a well at the back of the house."

Entering, she found that the cottage consisted of but two rooms. The front one was absolutely bare, but the back one contained an old stove, a broken-down sink and a rickety chair. At one side was a good-sized closet. Opening it, Grace found nothing save a dilapidated old coat. Just then she caught the sound of rough voices just outside the cottage.

"I tell ye, Bill, we've got to do the job to-night and hike for the West on that train that goes through Oakdale at 3.15 in the morning," said a voice that was almost a growl.

"I'm wid yer, Jim," answered another voice in correspondingly savage tones. "Even to layin' a few out stiff if dey gets in de way."

Grace listened. She heard heavy footsteps, and, peeping into the room, she saw a burly figure outlined in the front door in the act of entering. She glanced toward the back door. It was closed and fastened with a bolt. If she could slip out that way, she could make a run for the picnic grounds, but she dared not try to pass the two men who had just appeared. The few words of their conversation proved them to be lawless. Noiselessly she slipped into the closet and drew the door almost shut. She would hide until they had gone. They were not likely to linger long in the cottage.

Minute after minute went by, but the intruders showed no signs of leaving.

"What shall I do?" Grace breathed, wringing her hands. "They're real, downright burglars of the worst sort, and they're planning a robbery. It's getting late, too, and the girls will soon be going back. Oh, I must get out of here, but I won't try to go until I find out whose house they're going to rob."

The men talked on, but, listen as she might, Grace could get no clue.

"There ain't a soul on the joint except the judge and one old servant," growled Bill. "The rest o' the bunch'll be at the weddin' of one o' the girls. I laid low and heard 'em talkin' about it to-day. The judge's got money in the house, too. He always keeps it around, and that old Putnam place is pretty well back from the road."

Grace waited to hear no more. She had obtained the information she sought. They were going to rob and perhaps murder good old Judge Putnam.

Slipping quietly out of the closet, she approached the back door and cautiously took hold of the bolt. To her joy it moved easily. Exercising the greatest care in sliding it back, she lifted the latch. It made no sound, and, holding her breath, she softly swung open the door and ran on tiptoe around the corner of the house. Throwing away her bouquet as she ran, she made for a clump of underbrush at one side of the cottage. Here she paused, and hearing no disturbance from inside, she continued her flight. But she had lost her sense of direction, and after fifteen minutes' wandering was about to despair of finding her way, when she espied the honeysuckle bush that she had stripped earlier in the afternoon. This put her on the right track, but she was farther away from the picnic grounds than she had supposed, and when tired and breathless she at last reached them, it was only to find them deserted. The party had gone back to town without her.

Grace stood staring about her in blank dismay. It was nearing seven o'clock, and she was twelve miles from Oakdale. Why hadn't the girls waited? Grace felt ready to cry, then the vision of the poor old judge, alone and at the mercy of the two ruffians, flashed before her.

"I'll walk to Oakdale," she said, with a determined nod of her head. "And I'll not stop for an instant until I notify the police."

Grace never forgot that lonely walk. The darkness of a moonless night settled down upon her before she had gone three miles, but she would not allow herself to think of fear. She stumbled frequently as she neared her journey's end, and her tired body cried out for rest, but she pushed resolutely on, almost sobbing with relief as she entered the suburbs of the town. It was nearly eleven by the city hall clock when she hurried up the steps of the police station.

"Well, well!" said Chief Burroughs, as Grace rushed unceremoniously into his office. "Here's the lost girl now. I just received word that you were missing. Your father and one of my men left here not five minutes ago. They went to the livery to hire a rig."

"Oh, try and stop them, Mr. Burroughs," cried Grace excitedly. "'Phone the livery and tell them that I'm here. Then listen to me, for I've walked all the way from Forest Park and there's no time to lose."

"Walked from Forest Park?" exclaimed the chief, as he turned to the 'phone. "Why that's a good twelve miles and———"

"I know," interrupted Grace, then was silent, for the chief had begun talking to the livery.

"It's all right," he said, hanging up. "They'll be here directly. Caught them just in the nick of time, however. Now what's on your mind, Grace?"

"They're going to rob old Judge Putnam," Grace burst forth incoherently. "He's all alone. Oh, do send someone out there quickly, or it may be too late. Isn't there a telephone in the judge's house? He ought to be warned."

"Who's going to rob the judge? What are you talking about, my child?" asked the chief. "No, the judge has no 'phone. He thinks them a nuisance."

Grace rapidly told of her adventure in the woods, and her escape from the cottage. Before she had finished Chief Burroughs had begun to act. Summoning three special policemen, he narrated briefly what he had just heard, and five minutes later Grace had the satisfaction of knowing that, fully armed, they were well on their way to the Putnam estate.

"I can't understand why the girls didn't miss me," she said to the chief, as she sat awaiting her father's appearance.

"Miss Bright and Miss O'Malley, who were in the second wagon, thought you were in the first with Miss Pierson and Miss Nesbit, and vice versa," replied the chief. "The second wagon broke down when about half way home. It took over half an hour to get it fixed, so when it did arrive the girls in the head wagon had all gone home. Your mother grew uneasy when ten o'clock came, so she telephoned your friends, and on comparing notes you were found to be among the missing."

"What a mix-up," laughed Grace. "No wonder I wasn't missed. I'm sorry mother was uneasy, but she'll forgive me when she hears my tale. Oh, I hope nothing has happened to the poor old judge."

"Well, we'll soon know," replied the chief. "Now, you just take it easy and rest until your father comes. You need it after a twelve-mile walk. Of all the brave little girls——"

The ringing of the telephone cut the chief short.

Grace gave a long sigh and leaned back in the big chair. She was so tired. Her eyelids drooped——

"Well, I declare!" said the chief, as he turned from the telephone, for Grace was fast asleep.

# CHAPTER XXIV

## CONCLUSION

The special policemen sent out to the Putnam estate were not doomed to disappointment. After an hour's waiting, their patience was rewarded, and the two housebreakers appeared upon the scene. Before they could do any damage they were apprehended and a bag containing a complete outfit of burglar's tools was taken away from them. They fought desperately, but without avail, and were marched to jail to await their hearing.

Judge Putnam was greatly agitated over the affair. He had a large sum of money in the house, not to mention old family silver and other valuables.

"I realize I've had a narrow escape," he exclaimed to the chief the next day. "I might have been murdered in cold blood. I'll have a burglar alarm put in at once and a telephone, too. I had no business to let all the servants except old James go for the night. Who did you say brought the news? Tom Harlowe's little girl? She always was a wide awake youngster. I wonder what I can do for her to show her that I appreciate her bravery?"

"I don't believe she'd accept anything, Judge," replied the chief. "She's not that sort."

"We shall see. We shall see," said the judge, rubbing his hands. "I have a plan I think she'll listen to."

In the meantime, on reaching home Grace had been cried over by her mother and put to bed as though she were a baby. The story had been told by her chums throughout the school the next day, and Grace found herself the "observed of all observers."

"Any of you would have done the same," she said when surrounded by a bevy of admiring schoolmates.

"That's what you always say," exclaimed Nora. "But let me tell you I should have been in hysterics if I had been left alone in the dark twelve miles from nowhere."

Judge Putnam did not at once make his plan known to Grace. He called, thanking her and complimenting her on her bravery and presence of mind.

453

"I shall have something to ask you when school closes, my dear child," he said as he rose to go. "Something that concerns you and your friends, and you mustn't say 'no' to an old man."

"What on earth does he mean?" said Grace to her chums, as she repeated the judge's words. "I shall be eaten up with curiosity until school closes."

"Wish to goodness it was over now," growled Nora O'Malley. "I don't believe the last of June will ever come."

The morning after commencement, eight highly excited girls gathered on the Harlowe's veranda. Grace had received a note from Judge Putnam requesting that the Phi Sigma Tau call upon him at ten o'clock that morning.

"Do hurry," said Jessica, as they neared the judge's beautiful home. "The sooner we get there the sooner we'll know."

"Good morning, young ladies," said the judge, bowing with old-time gallantry as James ushered the eight girls into the library. "You look like a garden of roses. There's nothing like youth; nothing like it. Sit down and make yourselves comfortable while I tell you why I asked you to come and see an old man."

"You are just like Mrs. Gray, Judge," said Grace, "always imagining yourself old, when you know you're just a great big boy."

"Very pretty, my dear," chuckled the judge. "But if I am as young as you say, then I must do something to keep young. Now, the way I propose doing it is this: I have a camp up in the Adirondacks that needs attention, so I wrote my youngest sister about it and she agrees with me. She is going up there this week with a couple of servants to open the bungalow and put it in readiness for eight girls who call themselves the Phi Sigma Tau, providing their fathers and mothers can spare them for a few weeks. Do you think they will care to go?"

"Oh-h-h-h! How lovely!" breathed the eight girls in concert.

"Care to go? Well I should say so. It will be the greatest lark ever," cried Grace.

"If you know any young men who can make themselves useful, we might invite them. I don't like the idea of being the only boy, you know."

"David and Tom," said Grace and Anne.

"Hippy can go, I'm sure," said Nora.

"Not to mention Reddy and Arnold Evans," murmured Jessica, with a glance at Miriam.

"It looks as though I shall not lack masculine company," remarked the judge, with twinkling eyes. "Tell your parents that my sister will write them."

"I move that we give three cheers and the High School yell for Judge Putnam, and then go straight home and get proper permission," cried Grace.

The cheers were given with a will, and after shaking hands with the judge, the girls said good-bye.

"How did Judge Putnam know about the Phi Sigma Tau; even to its name?" asked Marian Barber curiously.

"Lots of people know of it," remarked Eva Allen.

"Girls," said Grace earnestly, "don't you think our society has been a success so far?"

"Yes, indeed," was the united answer.

"Our sorority has made us fast friends, loyal to each other, through good and evil report," she continued. "Let us resolve now, that during our senior year we will stand firmly together, and make the Phi Sigma Tau represent all that is best and most worthy in High School life."

When next we meet Grace Harlowe and her girl chums, they will have entered upon their senior year at High School. In "GRACE HARLOWE'S SENIOR YEAR AT HIGH SCHOOL; Or, The Parting of the Ways," we shall learn how the Phi Sigma Tau kept their sorority pledge. Eleanor Savell will again seek revenge, and Grace Harlowe will once more prove herself equal to the occasion. Those who have followed the "High School Girls" through three years of school life cannot fail to be interested in what befell these lovable everyday girls during their senior year.

**THE END**

Grace Harlowe's Senior Year at High School

OR

The Parting of the Ways

BY JESSIE GRAHAM FLOWER, A. M.

Author of Grace Harlowe's Plebe Year at High School, Grace Harlowe's
Sophomore Year at High School, Grace Harlowe's Junior Year at High
School, etc.

# CHAPTER I

# A PUZZLING RESEMBLANCE

"Oakdale won't seem like the same place. What shall we do without you?" exclaimed Grace Harlowe mournfully.

It was a sunny afternoon in early October, and Grace Harlowe with her three chums, Anne Pierson, Nora O'Malley and Jessica Bright, stood grouped around three young men on the station platform at Oakdale. For Hippy Wingate, Reddy Brooks and David Nesbit were leaving that afternoon to begin a four years' course in an eastern college, and a number of relatives and friends had gathered to wish them godspeed.

Those who have read "GRACE HARLOWE'S PLEBE YEAR AT HIGH SCHOOL" need no introduction to these three young men or to the girl chums. The doings of these merry girls made the record of their freshman year memorable indeed. The winning of the freshman prize by Anne Pierson, despite the determined opposition and plotting of Miriam Nesbit, also aspiring to that honor, Mrs. Gray's Christmas party, the winter picnic that ended in an adventure with wolves, and many other stirring events furnished plenty of excitement for the readers of that volume.

In "GRACE HARLOWE'S SOPHOMORE YEAR AT HIGH SCHOOL" the interest of the story was centered around the series of basketball games played by the sophomore and junior classes for the High School championship. In this volume was narrated the efforts of Miriam Nesbit, aided by Julia Crosby, the disagreeable junior captain, to discredit Anne, and force Grace to resign the captaincy of her team. The rescue of Julia by Grace from drowning during a skating party served to bring about a reconciliation between the two girls and clear Anne's name of the suspicion resting upon it. The two classes, formerly at sword's points, became friendly, and buried the hatchet, although Miriam Nesbit, still bitterly jealous of Grace's popularity, planned a revenge upon Grace that nearly resulted in making her miss playing on her team during the deciding game. Grace's encounter with an escaped lunatic, David Nesbit's trial flight in his aëroplane, were incidents that also held the undivided attention of the reader.

In "GRACE HARLOWE'S JUNIOR YEAR AT HIGH SCHOOL" the four chums appeared as members of the famous sorority, the "Phi Sigma Tau," organized by Grace for the purpose of helping needy High School girls.

In that volume Eleanor Savelli, the self-willed, temperamental daughter of an Italian violin virtuoso, furnished much of the interest of the book. The efforts of Grace and her chums to create in this girl a healthy, wholesome enjoyment for High School life, and her repudiation of their friendship, and subsequent attempts to revenge herself for fancied slights and insults, served to make the story absorbing.

The walking expedition through Upton Wood, the rescue of Mabel Allison, an orphan, by the Phi Sigma Tau, from the tender mercies of a cruel and ignorant woman with whom she lived, proved interesting reading.

The class play in which Eleanor plotted to oust Anne Pierson, the star, from the production and obtain the leading part for herself, the discovery of the plot at the eleventh hour by Grace, enabling her to balk Eleanor's scheme, were among the incidents that aroused anew the admiration of the reader for capable, wide-awake Grace Harlowe.

The seven young people on the platform looked unusually solemn, and a brief silence followed Grace's wistful question. Saying good-bye threatened to be a harder task than any of them had imagined it to be. Even Hippy, usually ready of speech, wore a look of concern decidedly out of place on his fat, good-humored face.

"Do say something funny, Hippy!" exclaimed Nora in desperation. "This silence is awful. In another minute we'll all be weeping. Can't you offer something cheerful?"

Hippy fixed a reflective eye upon Nora for an instant, then recited in a husky voice:

"Remember well, and bear in mind, That fat young men are hard to find."

There was a shout of laughter went up at this and things began to take a brighter turn.

"Now will you be good, Nora?" teased David.

"Humph!" sniffed Nora. "I knew his sadness was only skin deep."

"After all," said Anne Pierson, "why should we look at the gloomy side. You are all coming home for Thanksgiving and the time will slip by before we realize it. It's our duty to send you boys away in good spirits, instead of making you feel blue and melancholy."

"Anne always thinks about her duty," laughed Jessica, "but she's right, nevertheless. Let's all be as cheerful as possible."

"I hear the train coming," cried Grace, always on the alert. "Do write to us, won't you, boys! Please don't forget to send us some pictures of the college."

"Yes, don't let that new Eastman of yours go to waste, Reddy," said Nora.

"I will make Hippy pose the minute we strike the college campus," laughed Reddy, "and you shall have the first results, providing they are not too terrifying."

"I want pictures of the college, not the inmates," retorted Nora.

"Inmates!" cried Hippy. "One would think she was speaking of a lunatic asylum or a jail. I forgive you, Nora, but it was a cruel thrust. Here comes the train. Get busy, you fellows, and make your fond farewells to your families, who will no doubt be tickled pink to get rid of you for a while."

With that he made a rush to where his father and brother stood. David turned to his mother and sister Miriam, kissing them affectionately, while Reddy grasped his father's hand with silent affection in his eyes.

The last good-byes were reserved for the four chums, who felt lumps rise in their throats in spite of their recently avowed declaration to be cheerful.

Nora shoved a white box tied up with blue ribbon into Hippy's hand just as he was about to board the train.

"It's walnut fudge," she said. "But it isn't all for you. Be generous, and let David and Reddy have some, too."

"Good-bye. Good-bye. Don't forget us," chorused the chums as the train pulled out, while the young men waved farewell from the open windows.

"I hope I won't be called upon to say good-bye to any more of my friends for a blue moon!" exclaimed Grace. "I hate good-byes. When it comes my turn to go to college I believe I shall slip away quietly without saying a word to a soul except mother."

"You know you couldn't leave your little playmates in such a heartless manner," said Jessica. "We'd visit you in nightmares the whole of your freshman year if you even attempted such a thing."

"Oh, well, if you are going to use threats I expect I shall have to forego my vanishing act," said Grace, with a smile.

The four girls had walked the length of the platform and were about to turn in at the entrance leading to the street when Grace suddenly clutched Anne, pointing, and crying out, "Oh, look! look!"

Three pairs of eyes were turned instantly in the direction of her finger, just in time to see a dark blue touring car crash against a tree at the foot of the hilly street leading down to the station.

Its two occupants, the chauffeur and a woman who sat in the tonneau, were thrown out with considerable force and lay motionless at one side of the street.

In a twinkling the four girls had reached the woman's side. Grace knelt beside her, then sat down on the pavement, raising the stranger's head until it rested in her lap. The woman lay white and still, although on placing a hand to her heart Grace found that it was beating faintly. Calling for water, she dashed it in the woman's face, without any noticeable results.

By this time a crowd had collected and several men were busy with the chauffeur, who was conscious, but moaned as though in pain.

"Do go for a doctor, please," Grace cried to her chums. "I am afraid this woman is badly hurt."

"Here's Dr. Gale now," exclaimed Anne as the old doctor came hurrying across the street.

"Hello, what's the matter here?" he called. "It's a good thing I happened to be driving by."

"Oh, Dr. Gale, do look at this poor woman. She must have struck her head, for she lies as though she were dead."

Kneeling beside the stranger, the doctor busied himself with her, and after a little time the woman opened her eyes and gazed vaguely about, then again relapsed into unconsciousness.

"Whom does she resemble?" thought Grace. "Her face has a familiar look, though I am sure I have never before seen her."

"Stand back and give her air," ordered the doctor, and the circling crowd fell back a little.

"Grace, look out for her while I order the ambulance and see to this man."

The doctor bustled over to the injured chauffeur, and began his examination.

"Broken arm," he said briefly. "Send them both to the hospital."

The ambulance proved large enough to hold both victims of the accident and the attendant took them in charge, and signaled the driver, who headed for the city hospital, leaving the crowd to examine the big car.

"It's pretty badly damaged," said one man. "It must have hit that tree with a terrific crash. Skidded, I suppose."

"Come on, girls," said Anne. "There is no use in staying here any longer. We've had excitement enough for one day."

"I should say so," shuddered Jessica. "I hope that woman doesn't die. We must go to the hospital to-morrow and inquire for her."

"Of course," responded Anne. "What a sweet face she had, and her eyes were such a beautiful brown, but they haunted me. There is something so familiar about them."

"Why, that's just what I thought, too!" cried Grace. "Who is it she resembles?"

"Give it up," said Nora. "Although I noticed it, too."

Jessica alone made no remark. Her face wore a puzzled frown, as though she were searching her memory for something.

"Oh, well, what's the use of worrying over a resemblance," said Nora. "I wonder what days visitors are allowed at the hospital."

"By the way, Jessica," said Anne, "where is Mabel! She usually waits for you."

"Mabel is—" began Jessica. Then she stopped, her eyes filling with wonder, almost alarm. "Girls," she cried, her voice rising to an excited scream. "I know who that woman resembles! She looks like Mabel Allison."

## CHAPTER II

## WHAT THE DAY BROUGHT FORTH

For a second the three girls fairly gasped at Jessica's discovery. Grace was the first to speak.

"You have hit the nail on the head, Jessica. That's why her face seemed so familiar. The resemblance is striking."

The four girls glanced from one to another, the same thought in mind. Perhaps the mystery of Mabel Allison's parentage was to be solved at last.

Those who have read "GRACE HARLOWE'S JUNIOR YEAR AT HIGH SCHOOL" will recall how the Phi Sigma Tau became interested in Mabel Allison, a young girl taken from an orphanage by Miss Brant, a woman devoid of either gentleness or sympathy, who treated her young charge with great cruelty.

It will be remembered that through the efforts of Grace and Jessica, aided by Jessica's father, Miss Brant was forced to give Mabel up, and she became a member of the Bright household, and the especial protegee of the Phi Sigma Tau.

Grace and her friends had always believed Mabel to be a child of good family. She had been picked up in the streets of New York when a baby, and taken to the police station, where she had been held for some time, but on remaining unclaimed, had been sent to an orphanage outside New York City, where she had spent her life until she had been brought to Oakdale by Miss Brant.

Although Mabel had been in the Bright household but a few months, Jessica, who was motherless, had become deeply attached to her, while Jessica's father was equally fond of the young girl.

She had spent her vacation with the Phi Sigma Tau, who were the guests of Judge Putnam, a prominent Oakdale citizen, and his sister at their camp in the Adirondacks. The judge had conceived a great affection for her, and on hearing her story had offered to adopt her.

This proved a cross to Jessica, who was torn between her desire to keep Mabel with her, and the feeling that the opportunity was too great for

Mabel to refuse. Mabel had left the decision to Jessica, and the judge was still awaiting his answer.

"I might have known something would happen to take her away," almost wailed Jessica. "First, the judge, and now—"

"Don't be a goose, Jessica," said Nora stoutly, "and don't jump at the conclusion that this strange woman is a relative of Mabel's. There are lots of chance resemblances."

"Of course there are," consoled Grace. "When we go to the hospital to-morrow we'll find no doubt that our stranger is named 'Smith' or 'Brown' or anything except 'Allison.'"

"Don't worry, dear," said Anne, slipping her hand into Jessica's. "No one will take your one chicken from you."

"I don't know about that," responded Jessica gloomily. "I feel in my bones that something terrible is going to happen. I suppose you girls think me foolish about Mabel, but I've no mother or sister, and you know yourselves what a dear Mabel is."

"Forget it," advised Nora wisely. "We've had enough to harrow our young feelings to-day. Let's go and drown our sorrows in sundaes. I'll treat until my money gives out, and then the rest of you can take up the good work."

"Who will go to the hospital with me to-morrow!" asked Grace when they were seated around a table at Stillman's.

"Let me see. To-morrow is Sunday," said Jessica. "I'm afraid I can't go. Papa is going to take Mabel and me for a drive."

"I'll go with, you," volunteered Nora.

"And I," said Anne.

"Good girls," commended Grace. "Meet me here at three o'clock. I am fairly sure that visitors are allowed on Sunday, but if I am mistaken we can at least go to the office and inquire for our stranger."

The three girls met in front of Stillman's at exactly three o'clock the following afternoon, and set out for the hospital.

"Visitors are allowed on Sunday from three until five," remarked Grace as they strolled down Main Street. "I telephoned last night to the hospital. Our stranger is not seriously hurt. She is badly shaken up, and awfully nervous. If she feels more calm to-day we may be allowed to see her."

"What is her name?" asked Anne.

Grace looked blank, then exclaimed: "Why, girls, how stupid of me! I forgot to ask. I was so interested in hearing about her condition that I never thought of that."

"Well, our curiosity will soon be satisfied in that respect," said Nora, "for here we are at the hospital."

"We should like to see the woman who was thrown from the automobile yesterday afternoon," said Grace to the matron. "Is she able to receive visitors?"

"Oh, yes," replied the matron. "She is sitting in a wheeled chair on the second-story veranda. Miss Elton," she called to a nurse who had just entered, "take these young women up to the veranda, they wish to see the patient who has 47."

"What is her—" began Grace. But at that moment a nurse hurried in with a communication for the matron. Grace waited a moment, bent on repeating her question, but the nurse said rather impatiently, "This way, please," and the opportunity was lost.

The three girls began to feel a trifle diffident as they approached the stranger who was seated in a wheeled chair in a corner of the veranda.

"Visitors to see you, madam," said the nurse curtly, halting before the patient. "Be careful not to over-exert yourself," and was gone.

The woman in the chair turned quickly at the nurse's words, her eyes resting upon the three girls.

Grace felt a queer little shiver creep up and down her spine. The resemblance between the stranger and Mabel Allison was even more remarkable to-day.

"How do you do, my dears," said the woman with a sweet smile, extending her hand in turn to the three girls. "Under the circumstances I am sure you will pardon me for not rising."

Her voice was clear and well modulated.

"Please don't think of it," cried Grace. "We saw the accident yesterday. We were afraid you were seriously injured, and we couldn't resist coming to see you. I am Grace Harlowe, and these are my friends Nora O'Malley and Anne Pierson."

"I am very pleased to know you," responded the stranger. "It is so sweet to know that you thought of me."

"Miss Harlowe was the first to reach you, after your accident," said Anne, knowing that Grace herself would avoid mentioning it. "She held your head in her lap until the doctor came."

"Then I am deeply indebted to you," returned the patient, again taking Grace's hand in hers, "and I hope to know you better. I dearly love young girls."

She motioned them to a broad settee near her chair.

"There!" she exclaimed. "Now I can look at all of you at the same time. I am far more able to appreciate you to-day than I was at this time yesterday. It was all so dreadful," she shuddered slightly, then continued.

"I have never before been in an accident. I had been spending a week with some friends of mine who have a place a few miles from here called 'Hawk's Nest.' Perhaps you know of it?"

The three girls exchanged glances. "Hawk's Nest" was one of the finest estates in that part of the state, and the Gibsons who owned it had unlimited wealth.

"I was summoned to New York on business and had barely time to make my train. Mrs. Gibson's chauffeur had been running the car at a high rate of speed, and just as we reached the little incline above the station, the machine skidded, and we crashed into that tree. I felt a frightful jar that seemed to loosen every bone in my body, and remembered nothing further until I came back to earth again, here in the hospital."

"You opened your eyes, once, before the ambulance came," said Grace.

"Did I!" smiled the stranger. "I do not remember it. But, really, I am very rude! I have not told you my name."

"It's coming," thought Grace, unconsciously bracing herself. Nora and Anne had also straightened up, their eyes fastened on the speaker.

"My name is Allison," said the woman, wholly unaware of the bombshell she had exploded. "I am a widow and quite alone in the world. My husband died a number of years ago."

"I knew it, I knew it," muttered Grace.

"What did you say, my dear?" asked Mrs. Allison.

But Grace was silent. The woman was too nervous as yet to hear the news. Perhaps after all the name was a mere coincidence.

Anne, understanding Grace's silence, hurriedly took up the conversation.

"Are you familiar with this part of the country?" she asked.

"I have not been here for a number of years," replied Mrs. Allison, "although my friends, the Gibsons, have sent me repeated invitations. Mrs. Gibson and I went through Vassar together."

"We expect to go to college next year," said Grace. "We are seniors in Oakdale High School."

"The years a young girl spends in college are usually the happiest of her whole life," said Mrs. Allison, with a sigh. "Everything is rose colored. She forms high ideals that help to sweeten life for her long after her college career is over. The friendships she forms are usually worthwhile, too. Mrs. Gibson and I have kept track of one another even since graduation. We have shared our joys and sorrows, and in my darkest hours her loyal friendship and ready sympathy have been a heaven-sent blessing to me."

"We three girls are sworn friends," said Grace, "and we have another chum, too. She was very sorry that she could not come to-day. She will be glad to know that you are so much better. Her name is Jessica Bright. She was with us at the station yesterday."

"I should like to meet her," said Mrs. Allison, "and I thank her for her interest in me. I really feel as though I had known you three girls for a long time. I wish you would tell me more of yourselves and your school life."

"There isn't much to tell," laughed Grace. "The life of a school-girl is not crowded with many stirring events."

"You have no idea of how much has happened to Grace, Mrs. Allison, since we began High School," interposed Nora. "She never will talk about the splendid things she has done for other people. She is the president of her class, the captain of the senior basketball team, too, and the most popular girl in Oakdale High School."

"I refuse to plead guilty to the last statement!" exclaimed Grace. "Believe me, Mrs. Allison, there are a dozen girls in High School who are far more popular than I."

"There is only one Grace Harlowe," said Anne, with conviction.

"It is a case of two against one, Miss Grace," laughed Mrs. Allison. "I insist upon hearing about some of your good works."

"It's really time for us to go, girls," said Grace, laughing a little. She rose and held out her hand to the older woman.

"You are very cruel," smiled Mrs. Allison. "You arouse my curiosity and then refuse to satisfy it. But you cannot escape so easily. You must come to see me again before I leave here. I shall not try to return to the Gibsons before Wednesday. I expect Mr. Gibson here to-morrow and he will attend to my New York business for me. If I had accepted his offer in the first place, I might have spared myself this accident. However, I am glad, now. It has brought me charming friends. For I feel that we shall become friends," she added, stretching out both hands. "When will you come again?"

"On Tuesday afternoon after school," replied Grace promptly. "And we will bring Miss Bright, too, unless she and Mabel have some other engagement."

There was purpose in Grace's last remark. She wished to see if the name "Mabel" made any impression upon her listener, and therefore kept her eyes fixed upon Mrs. Allison.

As Grace carelessly mentioned the name she saw an expression of pain flit across Mrs. Allison's fine face.

"I shall be glad to see Miss Bright," she said quietly. "Is the 'Mabel' you speak of her sister?"

"No," replied Grace hastily, "she is a girl friend. May we bring her with us?"

"Do so by all means," rejoined Mrs. Allison. "She bears the name I love best in all the world." An expression of deep sadness crept into her face as she uttered these words, and she looked past her callers with unseeing eyes. "Good-bye, Mrs. Allison," said Grace, and the older woman roused herself with a start.

"Good-bye, my dears," she responded. "Be sure to come to me on Tuesday."

"We'll be here," chorused the three girls. "Take good care of yourself."

Not a word was spoken until they reached the street.

"Well!" exclaimed Grace. "What do you think of the whole thing?"

"I think there are several people due to get a shock," said Nora emphatically.

"I am sorry for Jessica," said Anne. "It will be very hard for her to give Mabel up."

"Then you think—" said Grace, looking at Anne.

"I am reasonably sure," replied Anne quietly, "from what I have heard and seen to-day that Mabel is no longer motherless."

## CHAPTER III

## WHAT HAPPENED IN ROOM FORTY-SEVEN

As the last period of study drew to an end on Tuesday afternoon, the hearts of the four girl chums beat a trifle faster than usual. What if after all their conjectures were to prove erroneous, and Mabel Allison was not the long-lost daughter of the woman in the hospital? All they had to go by was the remarkable resemblance between the two, and the slight emotion displayed by Mrs. Allison at the mention of Mabel's name.

When Grace had repeated the details of their call at the hospital to Jessica, the latter had turned very white, but had said bravely, "I expected it. We will go with you on Tuesday. Shall I prepare Mabel for it?"

"No," Grace had replied. "We may find ourselves mistaken, and think what a cruel disappointment it would be to Mabel. I don't mean by that Jessica, that Mabel is anxious to leave you, but you know perfectly well that the desire of Mabel's life is that she may someday find her parents."

In almost utter silence the four chums, accompanied by Mabel Allison, crossed the campus and turned into High School Street at the close of the afternoon session on Tuesday. Each girl seemed busy with her own thoughts.

"What has come over you girls?" inquired Mabel curiously. "When four of the liveliest girls in school become mum as the proverbial oyster, surely something is going to happen."

"'Coming events cast their shadows before'" said Anne half dreamily.

"Well, I wish they'd stop casting shadows over my little playmates then," laughed Mabel.

At this remark Grace made an effort to appear unconcerned.

"Are you going to play on the junior basketball team this year, Mabel?" she asked, by way of changing the subject.

"I don't know," replied Mabel. "I feel as though I ought to study every minute I am in High School, in order to be more thoroughly capable of earning my own living. I don't expect to be forever dependent upon my friends."

"Dependent, indeed," sniffed Jessica. "You know perfectly well, you bad child, that papa and I have been the gainers since you came to us, and now—" she stopped just in time.

"'And now,' what?" asked Mabel.

"Here we are at the hospital," broke in Nora without giving Jessica time to answer.

The little party waited what seemed to them an interminable length of time; although it was in reality not more than five minutes before the attendant returned with the news that they might see the patient in 47.

Grace had purposely voiced their request in so low a tone that Mabel had not heard her mention the patient's name, and she accompanied the four girls without the faintest idea of what their call might mean to her.

"Now for it," breathed Grace, as they paused at the door of 47.

"Come in," said a sweet voice, in answer to the attendant's knock, and the five girls were ushered into Mrs. Allison's presence.

"How are my young friends, to-day!" she cried gayly, rising from the easy chair in which she was sitting and coming forward with out-stretched hands.

"Very well, indeed," replied Grace, Anne and Nora in a breath as they shook hands.

"Mrs. Allison," said Grace hurriedly, "these are my friends, Miss Jessica Bright and Miss Mabel Allison."

The woman who was in the act of acknowledging the introduction to Jessica started violently when Grace pronounced Mabel's name, dropped Jessica's hand and began to tremble as she caught sight of Mabel, who stood behind Jessica, an expression of amazement in her brown eyes, that the patient's name should be the same as her own.

"Who—who—" gasped the woman, pointing at Mabel, then overcome sank into her chair, covering her face with her hands.

Grace sprang to her side in an instant, kneeling beside her chair.

"Mrs. Allison," she cried impulsively. "Forgive me. I should not have startled you so. I did not really know, although I felt sure that—"

But Mrs. Allison had uncovered her face and was looking eagerly at Mabel, who stood the picture of mystification.

"Who is that young girl who bears the name of my baby, and where did she come from?" asked the patient hoarsely.

"Speak to her," whispered Jessica, pushing Mabel forward.

"I am Mabel Isabel Allison——" began Mabel, but before she could proceed further the woman had risen, and clasping the girl in her arms, began smoothing her hair and kissing her, laughing and crying hysterically. "You are my baby girl that I lost long ago, my own little Mabel. I know it. I know it."

"Mrs. Allison," said Grace firmly, placing her arm around the sobbing woman, who seemed to have entirely lost control of her emotions, "try and be calm. There is so much to tell. Will you listen to me? And you must sit down, you were not strong enough for this. We should have waited."

Mrs. Allison partially released Mabel from her embrace, though she still held her hand, and allowed Grace to gently push her back toward her chair.

"I don't quite understand you, my dear," she said brokenly. "But I am sure that I have found my own dear little child."

"And I am sure of it, too," replied Grace. "In fact, we have suspected it since the day we first saw you at the station. We noticed the marked resemblance between you and Mabel, and when you told us your name was Allison we all felt that you might be Mabel's mother. Do you feel strong enough to hear our story and to tell us yours?"

"Tell me quickly," exclaimed Mrs. Allison eagerly, recovering in a measure from her violent agitation. "I must know the truth. It seems incredible that I should find my lost baby girl alive and in good hands. I am surely dreaming. It cannot be true. Yet she has the same sweet, serious expression in her brown eyes that she had in babyhood. Even her middle name, Isabel, that her father insisted upon giving her because it is mine!"

Anne, dreading another outbreak, gently interposed. "Try and be calm, Mrs. Allison, while we tell you about Mabel."

Then Anne began with the winning of the freshman prize by Mabel at the close of her freshman year, and the interest she had aroused in the girl chums, and followed with the story of her adoption by the Phi Sigma Tau.

Mrs. Allison listened in rapt attention until Anne had finished. "God is good," she murmured. "A higher power surely willed that Mabel should find true and worthy friends."

Then she began questioning Mabel about her life in the orphanage. Did Mabel have any recollection of the day she was brought there? Had Mary Stevens, the attendant, ever described the clothing that she had worn when found?

"I have the baby pins I wore with me. Jessica asked me to wear them to-day," replied Mabel, who looked like a person just awakened from a deep sleep. She had not yet reached a full comprehension of what it all meant.

"Let me see them," cried Mrs. Allison.

Mabel mechanically detached one of the little gold pins from her collar and handed it to Mrs. Allison, who examined it closely for a moment, then dropping it with a little cry, again clasped Mabel in her arms.

"They are the pins I had specially made and engraved for you," she said. "There is no longer any doubt. You are my lost child."

At these words a light of complete understanding seemed to dawn upon Mabel, and with a cry of rapture she wound her arms about her mother's neck.

It was a joyful, though rather a trying moment for the four chums, who were seized with a hysterical desire to laugh and cry in the same breath. Grace made a slight motion toward the door, which her friends were not slow to comprehend. It was her intention to slip quietly away and leave the mother and daughter alone with their new-found happiness.

Before she could put her plan into execution, however, Mrs. Allison divined her intention and turning quickly toward her, said, "Don't go, Grace. I feel as though you girls belonged to me, too. Besides, you have not heard my part of this story yet."

"Perhaps you are hardly strong enough to tell us after so much excitement," deprecated Grace.

"My dear, I feel as though I had just begun to live," answered Mrs. Allison. "The past has been one long dreary blank. If you only knew the years of agony I have passed through. When you hear my story you will understand why this reunion is little short of miraculous.

"My home is in Denver. Mabel was born there," continued Mrs. Allison. "Fourteen years ago this summer my husband and I decided to spend the summer in Europe, taking with us our baby daughter, Mabel, and her nurse.

"On the morning that we were to sail, circumstances arose that made it necessary for my husband and myself to be in New York until almost sailing time. He therefore sent the nurse, a French woman, who was thoroughly familiar with the city, on ahead to the vessel, with Mabel in her care. We had barely time to catch the boat and were met by the nurse, who said that she had left Mabel asleep in one of the state rooms engaged for us. It was not until we had put out to sea that we discovered that Mabel was missing, and a thorough search of the ship was at once made. The nurse persisted in her statement that Mabel went aboard with her. Every nook and cranny of the ship was overhauled, but my child could not be found, and the supposition was that she had in some way fallen overboard.

"I was distracted with grief, and nearly lost my reason, and when we reached the other side I passed into a long illness. It was many weeks before I returned to consciousness of my affairs, and the terrible realization that my baby was gone forever. I felt as though I could not face the future without her. I had scarcely recovered from the first shock attending my great loss, when my husband contracted typhoid fever and died after an illness of five weeks.

"We were in Florence, Italy, at the time and I prayed that I might die, too. It was during those dark hours that Mrs. Gibson proved her friendship for me. She sailed for Italy the instant she received the cablegram announcing my husband's death, and brought me back to America with her. I spent a year with her in her New York home, before returning to Denver. Since then I have never been east until this summer.

"Four months ago I received a letter from the nurse who had charge of Mabel on the day of her disappearance. It was a great surprise to me, as she had left us directly after we landed with the intention of returning to France. But the news the letter contained was a far greater surprise, for she stated that Mabel had never gone aboard the vessel.

"The nurse had had some personal business to attend to before going aboard, and in order to save time had taken Mabel with her. In some inexplicable manner Mabel had strayed from her side. She had made frantic search for the child and finally, not daring to go to us with the truth, had conceived the idea of making us believe that she had taken Mabel aboard the ship. She had bribed the purser, a Frenchman whom she knew, to corroborate her story, and had succeeded in her treacherous design.

"She wrote that she had longed over and over again to confess the truth, but had not dared to do so. She had heart trouble, she said, and her days were numbered. Therefore she felt that she must confess the truth before it became too late.

"You can imagine," said Mrs. Allison, "the effect this letter had upon me. For fourteen years I had mourned my child as dead. It seemed infinitely worse to hear that she had not died then, but was perhaps alive, and in what circumstances?

"The day I received the letter I took the train for the east, wiring the Gibsons to meet me, and aided by them engaged the best detective service upon the case. There was little or nothing to furnish us with a clue, for the nurse's lying statement had misled us; we were out at sea before we knew positively that Mabel had disappeared, and my long illness in Europe, followed by my husband's death kept me from instituting a thorough search of New York City.

"I was bound for New York in answer to a summons from the men engaged on the case, when this accident occurred. Mr. Gibson had offered to make the journey for me, but I felt that I alone must hear the first news—and to think that through that blessed accident I stumbled upon my little girl." She ceased speaking and with streaming eyes again clasped Mabel in a fond embrace.

The chums found their own eyes wet, during this recital, but of the four, Jessica appeared to be the most deeply moved. Mabel had meant more to her than to the others, and she found herself facing the severest trial that had so far entered her young life. She drew a deep breath, then went bravely over to Mrs. Allison, saying with quivering lips:

"It is very, very hard to give Mabel up. She is the child of our sorority, but she belongs most of all to me. She is the dearest girl imaginable, and neither hardship nor poverty have marred her. She is sweet, unselfish and wholesome, and always will be. I am glad, glad, glad that her dream has at last been realized, and I should be the most selfish girl in the world if I didn't rejoice at her good fortune."

She smiled through her tears at Mabel, who rushed over to her and exclaimed:

"Jessica, dearest, you know perfectly well how much I do and always shall love you, and Grace and Anne and Nora, too."

The four girls lingered a few moments, then said good-bye to Mrs. Allison and Mabel, who was to remain for the present with her mother. She kissed her friends tenderly, promising to see them the next day.

"I'll be in school to-morrow unless mother needs me here," she said with such a world of fond pride in her voice that the girls who had so willingly befriended her felt that their loss was a matter of small consequence when compared with the glorious fact that Mabel had come into her own.

## CHAPTER IV

## GRACE TURNS IN THE FIRE ALARM

"I wonder what sort of excitement we shall have next?" remarked Grace Harlowe to her three friends one afternoon as they gathered in the senior locker-room, before leaving school.

Three weeks had elapsed since Mabel Allison and her mother had met in Room 47 of the hospital, and many events had transpired in that short space of time.

The girl chums had been entertained at "Hawk's Nest" by Mrs. Gibson, and were in consequence the most important persons in the Girls' High School. They had found Mrs. Gibson charming, and had been invited to repeat their visit at an early date. Mabel's story had circulated throughout Oakdale, and she and her friends were the topic of the hour.

The one cloud on their horizon had been the fact of the inevitable separation. They had begged and entreated Mrs. Allison to take up her residence in Oakdale for the balance of Mabel's junior year, but on account of home matters she had been unable to comply with their wishes. So Mabel had departed for Denver with her mother, while the chums had kissed her and cried over her and had extracted a laughing promise from Mrs. Allison to bring her to Oakdale during commencement week to witness the graduation of the Phi Sigma Tau.

"It seems as though we have done nothing but say good-bye to people ever since school began," said Anne Pierson with a little sigh.

"I know it," exclaimed Nora. "First our boys, then Mabel, and—"

"And now all we can do is to wonder who will fade away and disappear next," finished Grace. "Promise me that none of you will run away from Oakdale, or elope, or do anything that can be classed under the head of vanishing."

"Oh, I think we're all rooted to the spot for this year," said Jessica, "but what about next? Nora and I will be in a conservatory, Grace will be in college and Anne—where will you be, Anne?"

"Goodness knows," replied Anne. "I'd like to try for a scholarship, but how on earth would I support myself even if I were fortunate enough to win?"

"Don't worry about that," said Grace quickly. "That is for that all-wise body, the Phi Sigma Tau, to consider. We will be your ways and means committee, Anna."

"Oh, I couldn't think of weighing you girls down with my cares," replied Anne soberly. "I must work out my own salvation."

By this time they had turned out of High School Street and were moving in the direction of Grace's home, where the majority of their chats took place, when Nora suddenly exclaimed in a low tone:

"Look, girls, there is Eleanor Savelli!"

"Where? where?" demanded three eager voices, as their owners followed Nora's glance.

"Across the street," replied Nora. "Don't let her know that we are looking at her."

Sure enough, on the opposite side of the street, Eleanor Savelli was to be seen strolling along in company with Edna Wright and Daisy Culver, two seniors who had been her faithful followers since her advent in Oakdale.

"Excitement number one," remarked Nora. "The fair Eleanor comes and our peace of mind departs. I had cherished vain hopes that she wouldn't favor us with the light of her countenance this year, even though she did inform Grace of her laudable desire to stay with the seniors for pure spite."

"Never mind, Nora," said Jessica, "I don't believe she'll worry herself about us, even though she did make dire threats."

"Remember what I told you last year, girls," said Grace in a tone of admonition. "Be careful what you do and say whenever she is near. She despises the Phi Sigma Tau and would revenge herself upon us at the slightest opportunity. She comes of a race who swear vendettas."

"She better not swear any when I am around," retorted Nora with spirit, "or she will find that the Irish are equal to the occasion."

"Don't excite yourself needlessly, Nora," laughed Anne. "That splendid Hibernian energy of yours is worthy of a better cause."

"How provoking!" suddenly exclaimed Grace. "I've left my library book in the gym. and it's a week overdue now. I shall simply have to go back and get it. It's only three o'clock," she added, consulting her watch. "Who will go with me?"

"Of what use is it for all of us to go," complained Nora. "We'll wait right here for you and you can hurry faster by going alone."

"All right, lazy, unsocial creatures," said Grace good-humoredly. "I'm off. Be sure you wait."

She hurried in the direction of the High School and in an incredibly short time was running down the corridor of the wing that led to the gymnasium. Remembering that she had laid her book on the window sill, Grace lost no time in securing it, and taking it under her arm waited toward the door. Suddenly the faint smell of smoke was borne to her nostrils.

She sniffed the air, then murmured, "I wonder what's burning. The smell seems to come from over there. Perhaps I'd better look around. It won't take a second."

She slowly retraced her steps, looking carefully about her. There was no smoke to be seen. She turned to go, then impelled by some mysterious influence, her eye traveled to the door of the small room at the left of the gymnasium.

With a cry of consternation she sped across the floor, flung open the door and staggered back, choked by a perfect volume of smoke that issued from within. The interior of the room was in flames.

To think was to act. Unless help arrived speedily their beloved gymnasium would soon be a thing of the past. Grace tore through the corridor like a wild girl, and darted out the door and across the campus. There was a fire alarm on the street below the High School, and toward this she directed her steps.

Pausing an instant before the box, she looked about her for something with which to break the glass. Spying a small boy strolling toward her, a baseball bat in his hand, she pounced upon him, seized the bat before he knew what had happened and smashed the glass with one blow. Giving the ring inside a vigorous pull, Grace shoved the bat into the hands of the astonished youngster and made for the nearest telephone.

Hurrying into Stillman's, she discovered to her disgust that the telephone was in use, but a moment later she was at the door and again out on the street. Her quick ear had caught the clang of the bell on the fire engines, and the thing to do now was to go back to her chums with the news—and then off to the fire.

"The gymnasium is on fire!" she cried, as she neared the spot where they awaited her. "Hurry, all of you! Perhaps we may be of some help."

Her three friends needed no second invitation and throwing all dignity to the winds, raced down the street in the direction of the burning building. When they reached the High School smoke was issuing from the windows of the gymnasium, and from the roof and chimneys, and situated as it was like a connecting link between the two buildings, it was an easy matter for the flames to spread in either direction.

Even in the short time it had taken Grace to turn in the alarm, the fire had made tremendous headway, and great tongues of flame shot up toward the sky. The roof had caught and was burning rapidly, although the firemen played a constant stream upon it.

As the fire grew hotter, the other companies were called out, and soon the entire Oakdale Fire Department was at work.

Ropes had been stretched around the burning part of the building to keep venturesome citizens outside the fire belt. Grace stood as close as she dared, Nora, Anne and Jessica at her side.

"Oh, do, do save our gymnasium!" she shrieked, as several firemen hurried past her.

"Can't do it, miss," replied one of them. "It's a goner. If we save the school we'll do well, let alone the gymnasium."

Long and strenuously the firemen fought the hungry flames. The wind was in the wrong direction, and helped to fan the blaze. One of the gymnasium walls fell in with a terrific crash, almost carrying with it two firemen who had been playing a stream from the rung of a ladder that leaned against it. There was a cry of horror from the assembled crowd that changed to a sigh of relief when it was discovered that the two men had saved themselves by leaping.

"Oh, if only I were a man," breathed Grace, as she watched the firemen's efforts to gain control of the situation. "I wouldn't stay here a moment. I'd be in the thick of the fight."

"Hold her girls, or she'll dash straight over the ropes," said Nora.

"I'd like to," retorted Grace. "It's dreadful to stand here unable to help and see our dear old gym. go, and perhaps our school, too."

"Well, you turned in the alarm, and that's a whole lot," declared Jessica stoutly. "If you hadn't seen the blaze when you did things might be a good deal worse. As it is, I believe they are getting the fire under control."

"It does look that way," exclaimed Anne. "See, the flames are dying out over on that side. Oh, if it would only rain and help things along."

"I believe it will rain before night. The clouds look heavy and threatening," declared Nora, squinting at the sky.

"The weather prophet has come to town," smiled Anne.

For the next hour the girls stood eagerly watching the gallant work of the firemen. A dense crowd, composed largely of High School boys and girls, packed the campus, while people blocked the streets outside the gates. Intense excitement prevailed, and when it became evident that the main building was safe a mighty cheer went up from the crowd.

"Bless their hearts!" exclaimed Grace. "They are just as fond as we are of Oakdale High School. But, oh, girls, where are we going to play basketball!"

The girls looked at each other in dismay.

"What is life without basketball?" said Nora sadly.

"True enough," said Anne, "but even though the gym. is gone we still have our school. It would be simply terrible to have had it go in our senior year."

"No doubt the gym. will be rebuilt at once," remarked Jessica.

"I am not so sure of that," replied Grace. "My father belongs to the common council, and I heard him tell mother the other day that the High School had been refused an appropriation that they had asked for."

"Oh, well, then, we High School pupils will raise the money ourselves," said Nora lightly.

"That idea is worth looking into," said Grace eagerly. "We might help a great deal."

"Grace has the 'Busy Little Helper' stunt on the brain," jeered Jessica.

"Anything to keep matters moving," laughed Grace. "I'm an advocate of the strenuous life. But seriously, girls, how splendid it would be to feel that we had been instrumental in rebuilding the gymnasium."

"Fine," agreed Nora. "We used to sing a song in kindergarten when I was very young and foolish that started out, 'We are little builders,' although at that time I never expected to really become one."

"Nora," said Grace severely, "you have all Hippy's bad traits and some of your own thrown in."

It was nearing six o'clock before the four friends left the scene of the fire and started for home. Nora's prediction of rain proved true, for just as they made their way across the campus the rain began to come down in torrents, wetting them to the skin, but in no respect dampening their joy over the fact that this shower had come just in time to save their High School from further ravage by the flames.

## CHAPTER V

## NORA BECOMES A PRIZE "SUGGESTER"

"The thing to do is to decide just what we want, and then go ahead with it."

Grace Harlowe energetically addressed her remarks to the members of the Phi Sigma Tau, who had taken possession of the Harlowe's comfortable living room.

It was Saturday afternoon, and a special meeting had been called with the object of discussing the best way to get money for the rebuilding of the gymnasium, that the fire had completely destroyed, although the splendid efforts of the firemen had prevented the flames from extending to the main buildings, and the rain had completed their good work.

Grace had allowed no grass to grow under her feet, but had gone to the root of the matter the day following the fire, and found that the school could expect no assistance from the city or the state that year. She had thereupon racked her usually fertile brain for money-making schemes, but so far had settled on nothing, so she had called in her friends, and the Phi Sigma Tau had been in council for the past half hour without having advanced a single prolific idea.

"Think hard, girls," begged Grace. "We simply must do something that will make Oakdale sit up and take notice, and incidentally spend their money."

"We might give a play or a concert," suggested Eva Allen.

"Not original enough to draw the crowd," vetoed Nora O'Malley. "Besides, the sophomore class has already begun to make plans for a play. While the other three classes are making plans we ought to go ahead and astonish the natives. The early stunt catches the cash, you know," concluded Nora slangily.

"Well, what would you suggest as a cash-catching stunt?" asked Anne. "You are generally a prize suggester."

"We might have a bazaar," said Nora after a moment's thought, "with ever so many different booths. We could have a gypsy camp, and tell fortunes, and we could have some Spanish dancers, and, oh, lots of things. We could have it in Assembly Hall and have tents with all these shows going on."

"Oh, splendid!" cried Grace. "And we could get the High School mandolin club for an orchestra. If we hurried we could have it week after next, on Thanksgiving night."

"And we could have a Mystery Auction," interposed Marian Barber eagerly.

"What on earth is a 'Mystery Auction'?" inquired Nora and Jessica in a breath.

"Why we write notes to everyone in Oakdale, asking for some kind of contribution, anything from a jar of pickles to hand-painted china. Then all these things are tied up in packages and auctioned off to the highest bidder. There is a whole lot of money in it, for people often try to outbid each other, and the fun of the thing is that no one knows what he or she is bidding on."

"Marian Barber," exclaimed Grace, "that's a positive inspiration! You clever, clever girl!"

"Oh, don't think for a minute that I originated the idea," said Marian hastily. "A cousin of mine wrote me about it last winter. They had a 'Mystery Auction' at a bazaar that was held in the town she lives."

"Well it's a brilliant idea at any rate, and I can see us fairly coining money. Now we must all work with a will and put the affair through in fine style," responded Grace warmly.

"Oh, girls, the boys will be at home in time for it!" exclaimed Jessica in rapture.

"Sure enough," said Nora, "and won't I make Hippy work. He'll lose pounds before his vacation is over. Grace, you must write and ask Tom Gray to come."

Now that the question of the bazaar was settled, the Phi Sigma Tau went to work with a will. The services of the majority of the seniors were enlisted and notes were written to everyone in Oakdale who was likely to feel even a faint interest in the movement. Eva Allen's brother, who was an artist, made a number of attractive posters and these were tacked up in public places where they at once attracted attention.

The Oakdale National Guard loaned tents, and public-spirited merchants willingly loaned draperies, flags, banners, and in fact, almost anything they were asked for.

As for donations, they fairly poured in, and the girls watched the growing collection with mingled rapture and despair.

"We'll have to sit up every night this week in order to get all these things wrapped," sighed Grace, on the Monday afternoon before Thanksgiving, as she stood resting after a spirited rehearsal of the dance that she and Miriam Nesbit were to do, and which was to be one of the features of the gypsy camp.

"And the decorating is only about half done, too," she continued. "Thank goodness school closed to-day. We'll just have to live here until Thursday, and work, work, work."

"'Clear the way for progress on the fly,'" sang out a voice behind them, and the group of startled girls turned to face a stout young man who charged into their midst with a hop, skip and a jump.

"Hippy!" shrieked Nora in delight. "And David and Reddy, and yes— Tom, too!"

"'Oh, frabjous day, calloooh, callay,'" cried Hippy shaking hands all around. "It seems ages since I saw you girls. How well you all look, only you're not looking at me. These other good-for-nothing fellows are getting all the attention. Hello, Miriam," he called to Miriam Nesbit, who ran eagerly across the floor to meet the newcomers. "There's a prize package for you, too. It's outside the door shaking the snow off its coat."

Miriam flushed and laughed a little, then hurried over to greet Arnold Evans, who had just entered the hall.

"Oh, boys, you don't know how good it seems to have you all here again," said Grace, after the first greetings had been exchanged, as she beamed on the young men. "You're just in time to go to work, too. We've oodles of things to wrap for the 'Mystery Auction,' and Hippy you must be auctioneer. You can do it to perfection."

"Tell us all about this affair. I received rather indefinite accounts of it in the exceedingly brief letters that I have been favored with of late," said Tom Gray, fixing a reproachful eye upon Grace.

"Please forgive me, Tom," begged Grace, "but really I've been so busy of late that I just had to cut my letters short. Come on around the hall with me, and I'll tell you about all the stunts we've planned. Come on, everybody," she called, turning to the young people grouped about, "and remember, that I expect some original suggestions from you boys."

Around the hall they went, stopping before each tent, while the girls explained its purpose.

"What's this to be?" asked Tom, as he stopped at one corner of the hall that was closely curtained. "May I enter?"

"Mercy, no," gasped Grace, catching him by the arm as he was about to move aside one of the heavy curtains. "That's Eleanor Savelli's own particular corner. None of us know what is behind those curtains. You see, Eleanor hasn't spoken to any of us since last year. When we first talked about having this bazaar we decided to make it a senior class affair. We didn't care to go to Eleanor and ask her to help, because she hasn't been nice to any of the Phi Sigma Tau, but we asked Miss Tebbs and Miss Kane, two of the teachers who are helping with this, to ask Eleanor to do something. You know she plays so well, both on the violin and piano, then, too, the greater part of her life has been spent abroad, so she surely must have lots of good ideas.

"When first Miss Tebbs asked her she refused to have anything to do with it. Then she suddenly changed her mind and has been working like a beaver ever since. Miss Tebbs says her booth is beautiful."

"If I'm not mistaken here she comes now," said Tom suddenly. "I never saw her but once before, yet hers is a face not easily forgotten."

"Yes, it is she," replied Grace. "Let us walk on."

Eleanor Savelli, gowned in a tailored suit of blue and looking particularly beautiful, walked haughtily by and disappeared behind the heavy green curtain.

"She is certainly a stunning girl!" was Tom's low-voiced exclamation, "but, oh, what a look she gave you, Grace!"

"Did she?" replied Grace, with an amused smile. "That doesn't worry me. She has repeated that performance so often that I have grown used to it."

"Look out for her just the same," advised Tom.

"Where do we jollificate, to-night?" asked Hippy, as Grace and Tom joined them again.

"Right here," said Nora with decision. "No fudge, no hot chocolate, no cakes, nothing except work until this bazaar is over, then we'll have a spread that will give you indigestion for a week. Do you solemnly promise to be good and not tease for things to eat, but be a ready and willing little toiler?"

"I do," said Hippy, holding up his right hand. "Do you assure me that the spread you just mentioned is no myth?"

"I do," said Nora, "also that the indigestion, shall be equally realistic."

"Lead me to it," said Hippy. "I swear in this hour that—"

But Hippy never finished his speech, for Eleanor Savelli suddenly darted into the group with flashing eyes and set lips.

"How dared you meddle with my booth during my absence!" she cried, looking from one to the other of the astonished young people. "And what have you done with my things!"

There was a brief silence. Then Nora O'Malley spoke very coolly.

"Really, Miss Savelli, we haven't the remotest idea of what you are speaking."

"You know perfectly well of what I am speaking," retorted Eleanor. "I might have expected as much, however."

"I repeat," said Nora firmly, "that we do not know what you mean, and I am not used to having my word questioned. You will have to explain yourself if you expect to get a definite reply."

"Very well," replied Eleanor, with a toss of her head. "Last night I spent a great deal of time in arranging the booth over which I have been asked to preside. On coming here to-day I find that everything has been rearranged, completely spoiling the effect I had obtained. You and your friends are the only ones who have been here this afternoon. It looks like a clear case of spite on your part."

During Eleanor's angry outburst the boys looked decidedly uncomfortable, then by common consent moved away a little. This was a matter that the girls alone could settle.

Then Miriam Nesbit stepped forward with all the dignity that she could summon to her aid.

"Miss Savelli," she said quietly, "it is absolutely childish and ridiculous for you to make the assertions you have. No one of us has the slightest curiosity as to either you or your arrangements. This is not the first time that you have publicly accused us of meddling. Now I want you to understand once and for all that this must cease. You should not jump at conclusions and then vent your rage upon innocent bystanders.

"This much I will say as a matter of information, that we were not the only ones here this afternoon, as several of your particular friends spent some time in your booth, and I should advise that you call them to account and let us alone. Come on, girls," she said, turning to Grace and her friends, "we mustn't waste any more time."

With this Miriam turned her back squarely upon Eleanor, and without giving her time to reply, walked to the other end of the hall.

The girls were not slow in joining her, and in a moment Eleanor was left alone in the middle of the hall, with the unpleasant realization that for once she had overshot.

## CHAPTER VI

## THE THANKSGIVING BAZAAR

The bazaar was at its height. No one would have guessed that staid old Assembly Hall could lend itself to such levity.

At one end a band of gypsies had pitched their tents in true Romany fashion. There were dark-eyed gypsy maids in gaudy clothing, who gayly jingled their tambourines and wheedled good-natured sightseers into their main tent with extravagant stories of the wonderful Romany dancing girls whose unequaled dancing might be seen for the small sum of ten cents. While aged gypsies crouched here and there croaking mysteriously of their power to reveal the future, and promising health, wealth and happiness to those who crossed their out-stretched palms with silver.

In front of one of the tents several gypsy boys sat grouped in picturesque attitudes, industriously twanging guitars and mandolins. The whole encampment was lighted by flaring torches on the ends of long poles, and was the final touch needed to give the true gypsy effect.

The rest of the space in the hall had been given up to booths. There was, of course, a Japanese booth, while across from it several Mexican seniors and senoritas were doing an enterprising novelty and post-card business under the red, white and green flag of Mexico.

There was a cunning little English tea shop, where one could refresh one's self with tea, cakes and jam, not to mention the booth devoted to good old Ireland, presided over by Nora O'Malley who, dressed as an Irish colleen, sang the "Wearing of the Green" and "The Harp That Once Thro' Tara's Hall," with true Irish fervor, while she disposed of boxes of home-made candy tied with green ribbon that people bought for the pleasure of hearing her sing.

Next to the gypsy encampment, however, the feature of the evening was the booth entrusted to Eleanor Savelli. It was a veritable corner in Italy, and it may be said to Eleanor's credit that she had worked untiringly to carry out her idea. She had furnished the peasant costumes for herself and three of her friends, and knew exactly how they were to be worn, and had spared no expense in the matter of fruit and flowers which were to be sold at a good profit. There were little bags of home-made confetti that were sure to be popular and various other attractive features truly Italian that Eleanor had spent much time and trouble in procuring and arranging.

There had been a heated altercation, however, between Eleanor and Edna Wright on the day after Eleanor had astonished Grace and her friends by her fiery outburst, Edna having admitted that she had been responsible for the changes that had aroused Eleanor's ire.

A quarrel had ensued, in which Edna, having been worsted, had retired from the field in tears, refusing to have anything further to do with Eleanor or her booth. At this juncture Miss Tebbs had appeared on the scene, and peace was restored, although Edna was still taciturn and sulky, and displayed little interest in what went on around her.

From the moment the doors were opened the citizens of Oakdale looked inside, feeling particularly good-natured after their Thanksgiving dinners, and prepared to spend their money.

"It's perfectly wonderful what these children have managed to do on nothing whatever," Miss Thompson was saying, as she and Mrs. Nesbit, in the guise of sightseers, were strolling down the middle of the hall.

"It looks to me like a scene from an opera," replied Mrs. Nesbit.

"Yes, we are all very prosperous and clean comic opera gypsies, Mrs. Nesbit," said Hippy Wingate, who had come up just in time to hear Mrs. Nesbit's remark.

"Why, Hippy Wingate, I never should have recognized you. You look like the big smuggler in 'Carmen.' I have forgotten his name."

"I am a smuggler, Mrs. Nesbit," put in Hippy mysteriously. "But don't give me away. It's not lace goods I've brought over the border, nor bales of silk and such things. Isn't that what gypsies are supposed usually to smuggle?"

"I believe it is," answered Mrs. Nesbit. "At least they always appear in plays and pictures seated at the foot of a high, rocky cliff in some lonely spot, with bales and casks and strange looking bundles about. No one would be heartless enough to ask what was inside the bundles, but I have always had a strong suspicion that it was excelsior."

"What have you been smuggling, Hippy?" asked Miss Thompson. "I wonder you managed to get it past that line of watchful gipsy girls."

"I won't give it away," replied Hippy. "It's a surprise. You'll see, and I wager it will be the talk of the place before the evening is over."

"Is it animal, vegetable or mineral, Hippy?" demanded Mrs. Nesbit.

"Animal," replied Hippy. "Very much animal."

"Now, what in the world," the two women exclaimed, their curiosity piqued.

"Hippy, I wish you would come on and get to work," called Grace over her shoulder, as she hurried past, and Hippy darted after her, remembering that he had not done a thing that evening to assist the girls.

"How fine Grace Harlowe does look, Mrs. Nesbit," remarked Miss Thompson, "and how I shall miss her when she leaves the High School! The time goes too quickly to suit me, when all these nice girls leave us for college."

Miss Thompson still cherished a deep regard for Grace, although, since the circumstance of Grace's refusal to betray Eleanor, narrated in "GRACE HARLOWE'S JUNIOR YEAR AT HIGH SCHOOL," the two had never returned to quite the same footing as formerly.

Grace was, indeed, the picture of a beautiful gipsy girl who in romance turns out not to be a gipsy at all, but a princess stolen in her youth. She wore a skirt of red trimmed in black and yellow, a full white blouse and a little black velvet bolero. Around her waist she had tied a gayly colored sash, while on her head was a gipsy headdress bordered with gold fringe.

"Hippy," commanded Grace, "will you please take this gong and announce that the auction is about to begin!"

"Certainly, certainly," answered Hippy. "Anything to oblige the ladies."

He mounted a chair and beat on the Japanese gong.

"This way, ladies and gentlemen. Come right this way! The 'Mystery Auction' will now commence. It is a sale of surprises. You never know what you are going to draw, but it's sure to be something nice. Everybody step this way, please. These interesting and mysterious packages are to be sold each to the highest bidder. But no man knoweth what he draweth. It is the way of life, ladies, but that's where the fun comes in, and it's sportsmanlike to take your chances, gentlemen."

By this time Hippy had drawn a crowd of curious people about the booth devoted to that purpose, in which were piled dozens of packages of various shapes and sizes, all done up in white tissue paper and tied with red ribbons.

Hippy picked up the first bundle.

"Is there anyone here who will make a bid on this interesting package?" he cried. "It may contain treasure. Who knows? It may contain fruits from the tropics, or the spices of Araby, or—"

"I'll bid ten cents," called a voice.

"Ten cents!" exclaimed Hippy in mock horror. "I ask you, dear friend, can our gymnasium be builded upon ten cents? Is there no one here who is thinking of our late, lamented gymnasium? Have we already forgotten that dear, departed hall of youthful pleasures, cut down in the flower of its youth so tragically?"

Hippy's voice rang out like an old-time orator's, and someone bid twenty-five cents. But the bidding ended there, and Farmer Benson got the package, which on being opened, was found to contain a beautiful little lacquer box. This was a lucky beginning. If the packages all held such treasures they were well worth bidding on. Then the fun grew fast and furious. Everybody began bidding, and a pound of sugar actually went for five dollars, to old Mr. McDonald, who had obstinately refused to give up to his opponent, Mr. Barber, in the bidding contest. Mr. Harlowe paid heavily for a cook book, while David Nesbit, for fifty cents, drew a splendid big fruit cake.

"It is so fortunate that that fruit cake fell into the hands of one of my friends," remarked Hippy, as David was about to walk off, his prize under his arm. "I adore fruit cake."

"That's no sign that you will ever get a chance at this one," replied David calmly.

"I shall, I know I shall," retorted Hippy, "You wouldn't betray my young confidence and dispel my fond hopes by eating it all yourself. You deserve an awful case of indigestion if you do."

"Children, children, stop squabbling," laughed Anne who, looking like a very demure little gypsy, had slipped up unnoticed. "Don't worry, Hippy, I'll see that you are remembered when the famous cake is cut."

"I feel relieved," said Hippy, giving her one of his Cheshire Cat grins. "I propose that you leave your treasure with this gypsy maid, David, for the time is flying and we have a great and glorious surprise to spring."

"See you later, Anne," said David, looking at his watch. Then taking Hippy by the arm the two young men hurried out of the hall, leaving Anne to wonder what the surprise might be.

Turning slowly she was making her way toward the gypsy camp when a voice called, "O Anne, wait a minute," and Marian Barber fluttered up accompanied by a tall, dark young man.

"Miss Pierson, allow me to present Mr. Hammond," she said.

The young man bowed rather too elaborately Anne thought, and a wave of dislike swept over her as she rather coldly acknowledged the introduction.

"Mr. Hammond has just come to Oakdale," Marian said eagerly. "He knows very few people as yet."

"Ah, yes," said Mr. Hammond, with a smile that was intended to be fascinating. "I am, indeed, a stranger. Miss Barber has kindly volunteered to introduce me to some of her charming friends, therefore I trust that in time they will be mine also."

Anne murmured some polite reply, and excusing herself walked away. "Horrid thing," she thought. "How cruel he looks when he smiles. I wonder where Marian met him. She seems to be delighted with him."

"Where have you been, Anne?" asked Grace, as Anne entered the tent where she and Miriam sat resting preparatory to beginning their dance, when enough people should gather outside to form a paying audience.

"Talking to Marian Barber and a young man who is trailing about with her."

"Did she introduce that man to you?" exclaimed Grace.

"Yes," replied Anne. "Did you meet him?"

"I did," was the answer. "Isn't he horrid?"

"That is precisely what I said," replied Anne. "There is something about his suave, silky manner that gives me the creeps."

493

"I hope Marian isn't seriously impressed with him," said Grace. "For there is something positively sinister about him."

Just then Hippy's voice was heard again above the crowd, and the three girls hurried to the opening in the tent

# CHAPTER VII

# A THIEF IN THE NIGHT

"Ladies and gentlemen," cried Hippy. "We have a noble animal for sale here. He is tame and gentle. A lady could ride him without fear. He sees equally well out of both eyes and is neither lame nor spavined. If you will just stand back a little we will let you see his paces."

The crowd drew back on either side of the lane between the rows of tents and booths and from somewhere in the back there was heard a great pawing and trampling, with cries of "Whoa, there! Whoa, there, Lightning!"

Then down the aisle there dashed the most absurd comic animal that had ever been seen in Oakdale. A dilapidated old horse, with crooked legs and sunken sides through which its ribs protruded. He had widely distended nostrils and his mouth drawn back over huge teeth. One ear lay flat, while the other stood up straight and wiggled, and his glazed eyes stared wildly. On his wobbly back sat David, dressed like a jockey and flourishing a whip.

"Gentlemen," went on Hippy, "you here behold an animal of splendid parts. He is pasture-fed and as gentle as a lamb, never kicks—"

The strange animal here kicked out one of his hind legs so wildly that David was obliged to hold on with both arms to keep from falling off.

"He has a happy, sunny nature, ladies. Is there any one present who would like to try his gait? Ten cents a ride."

The horse crossed his front legs and sat down on his haunches with an air of patient endurance. There were roars of laughter and no one enjoyed the fun more than Miss Thompson.

"I declare, Hippy, I should like to have a ride on the back of that animal!" she exclaimed, producing ten cents.

David leaped to the ground and gallantly assisted the principal to mount, while Hippy whispered something into the ear of the horse.

The animal trotted gently up to one end of the room and back, depositing Miss Thompson safely on her feet.

Miriam Nesbit then took a trial ride and no bucking bronco ever exhibited such traits of character as did that battered-looking quadruped. Miriam was obliged to jump down amid the cheers of the company. Many people rode that night, and rides went up to twenty-five and even fifty cents, until finally the poor, tired animal lay flat on the floor in an attitude of complete exhaustion. Then Hippy undid several hooks and eyes along the imaginary line which divided Lightning in half, and there came forth, very warm and fatigued, Tom Gray and Reddy Brooks.

On the whole the bazaar was proving an unqualified success. People entered into the spirit of the thing and spent their money without a murmur.

Eleanor's confetti proved a drawing card, and young people and old wandered about, bestowing handfuls of it upon their friends whenever a good opportunity presented itself.

Long before the fair was over Grace and Anne retired to one end of the gypsy encampment to begin counting the proceeds of their labors. The girls in charge of the various booths turned in their money almost as rapidly as they made it, and by the time the crowd had begun to thin the girls had arrived at a tolerably correct estimate of what the bazaar had netted them.

"Is it possible that I have counted correctly, Anne!" exclaimed Grace to her friend, who was helping to sort small silver into various piles.

"I don't know," said Anne, "it looks like a lot of money. How much does it all come to?"

"Roughly speaking, nearly five hundred dollars. Just think of that."

"Splendid!" cried Anne, clasping her hands joyfully. "But what shall we put it in?"

"I shall put it in this iron box of father's. You see, it has a combination lock and he loaned it to me to-night just for this purpose. As soon as the rest of the money is in I'll lock it and he will take charge of it. Will you go and find him?"

Anne departed and Grace began to deposit the money in the box, smiling to herself at the success of their undertaking.

The few remaining people who were now taking leave of each other had concentrated in one spot. There was a loud buzz of conversation and laughter, when suddenly, without a moment's warning, the electric lights went out. The gasoline torches had burned down by now and the place was in utter darkness.

Somewhere in the hall there was a cry, the sound of scuffling and then absolute silence.

Many of the men began to strike matches and peer into the darkness, and at last David groped his way over to a corner of the hall where he remembered he had seen the switch. As he felt for the electric button his hand encountered another hand, that grasped his with an iron grip, gave his wrist a vicious twist, pushed him violently away and was gone. David gave an involuntary cry of pain as he felt for the switch again. In another moment he had found it and the hall was again flooded with light. Instantly he looked about for the vicious person who had twisted his wrist, but he was alone in that part of the hall.

The excitements of that evening, however, were not yet at an end. People began running toward the last booth. There were cries and exclamations, and David, who had followed quickly after them, arrived there just in time to meet Mr. Harlowe carrying the limp figure of his daughter Grace in his arms. He deposited her on four chairs placed in a row, a bottle of smelling salts was put to her nose, while Hippy and Reddy ran for water.

Grace opened her eyes almost immediately and sat up.

"I'm not hurt," she said. "I was only stunned. Some one hit me on the head from behind, but my cap softened the blow. They were trying to get the box of money. Oh, is it gone?" she cried anxiously.

David and Tom examined the booth.

The money was gone.

## CHAPTER VIII

## MARIAN ASSERTS HER INDEPENDENCE

There was not the slightest clue to the thief who had stolen the iron box containing a little over five hundred dollars, for which the girls had worked so hard, but the loss was made good by Judge Putnam who, though on the bench at the state capital at the time the robbery occurred, had promptly sent Grace his check for the amount when Grace wrote him an account of it. For which generous act he became the idol of Oakdale High School.

"As for the thief," observed Mr. Harlowe, several mornings later at the breakfast table, after Grace had opened the letter and joyfully exhibited the check to her mother and father; "he'll have some trouble opening that box. It was the strongest box I have ever seen of the kind, made of iron reinforced with steel bands, with a combination lock that would baffle even your friend, Richards, Grace, who appeared to be a pretty sharp crook."

"How will the thief get at the money, then, father?" asked Grace.

"I can't imagine," answered Mr. Harlowe. "If he tries to blow up the box he runs the chance of blowing up all the money at the same time, and I don't believe there is an instrument made that would pry it open. He can't melt it and he can't knock a hole in it. Therefore, I don't just see what he can do, unless he finds some way to work the combination."

"It would be the irony of fate if the thief couldn't spend the money after all his trouble," observed Mrs. Harlowe.

"I hope he never, never can," cried Grace. "I hope he'll bruise all his knuckles and break all his finger nails trying to open the box, and still not make the slightest impression!"

"He certainly will if he tries to open the box with his finger nails and knuckles," replied her father, as he bestowed two kisses upon his wife and daughter, respectively, and departed to his business.

"Who is to be custodian of the fund, Grace? Are you to have charge of it?" asked Mrs. Harlowe.

"No, mother; Marian Barber was formally elected class treasurer last year. She likes to keep books and add up accounts and all those things.

498

So I shall just turn the check over to her to put in the bank until we give our next entertainment. Then, when we have about a thousand dollars, we'll give it all to Miss Thompson as our contribution toward rebuilding the gymnasium. I hear that the juniors are going to give a dance, but I don't think they will make any large amount like this, because they will have to pay for music and refreshments."

Grace could not help feeling proud of the success of the bazaar now that the judge's check had arrived, although at first she had demurred about accepting it. However, as the judge absolutely refused to take it back, it was therefore duly presented to Marian Barber, who, with a feeling of extreme importance at handling so much money in her own name, deposited it in the Upton Bank, and was the recipient, for the first time in her life, of a small, neat-looking check book. Later she showed it with great glee to the Phi Sigma Tau, who were drinking hot chocolate in the Harlowe's sitting room, the day after school began.

"I feel just like a millionaire," she exclaimed, "even though the money isn't mine. I'd just like to write one check to see how my name would look signed at the bottom here."

"It does seem like a lot of money," observed Anne thoughtfully, "but I'm afraid the check book won't be of much use to you, Marian, as you will probably draw it all out in a lump when the time comes to hand it over to Miss Thompson."

"Oh, I don't know," answered Marian, "we may have to give a few checks for expenses and things, the next entertainment we get up, and then I'll have an opportunity."

The girls laughed good-naturedly at Marian's evident eagerness to draw a check.

"We'll certainly have to incur some kind of expense for the express purpose of allowing Marian to draw a check," said Nora. "By the way, Grace, which booth made the most money, outside the auction, of course?"

"Eleanor Savelli's," replied Grace promptly. "They made most of it on confetti, too, although they sold quantities of flowers. They turned in seventy-five dollars."

"Eleanor certainly did work," observed Anne. "One feels as though one could forgive her all her sins after the success she made of her booth. It is a shame that so much ability and cleverness is choked and crowded out by willfulness and temper."

"Did you hear about the quarrel that she and Edna Wright had, after she attacked us?" asked Eva Allen.

"Yes," answered Grace. "I understand, too, that it has completely broken up their sorority. They carried their part of the bazaar through together and then Eleanor told Edna that she was practically done with her."

"You don't mean it! I hadn't heard that! Who told you so?" were the exclamations that followed this information.

"Daisy Culver told Ruth Deane, and Ruth told me," said Grace. "Ruth says that Edna feels dreadfully over it. She was really fond of Eleanor."

"Now I suppose that Miss Eleanor Vendetta de Savelli will be more impossible than ever," giggled Nora.

"Perhaps not," said Anne quietly. "I think it a very good thing that Edna and Eleanor have separated, for Eleanor Savelli is a far better girl at heart than Edna Wright. Eleanor is better off without her."

"I believe you are right, Anne," said Grace with conviction. "Although Eleanor's reformation is not for us. We've had experience."

"'Never too late to mend,'" quoted Jessica.

"True," retorted Nora, "but for my part I think the Phi Sigma Tau have done their share toward the mending process."

"Marian Barber!" exclaimed Grace. "Where in the world did you unearth that man you introduced us to, at the bazaar?"

"Yes, I should say so," echoed Nora. "I didn't like him one bit."

A flush overspread Marian Barber's plain face. She frowned, then said very stiffly:

"Really, girls, I can't see why anyone should dislike Mr. Hammond. I think he is a remarkably nice young man. Father and mother like him, too. He has called to see me twice since the bazaar, and I am going to the theatre with him to-morrow night. I like him very much better than any of these silly Oakdale schoolboys," she added a trifle maliciously.

The girls listened, thunderstruck. Was this good-natured, easy going Marian Barber who had spoken? To their knowledge Marian had never before received attentions from even "silly schoolboys." She was well liked among girls, but had always fought shy of young men.

"Forgive me, Marian," cried Nora impulsively. "I didn't dream that you were interested in Mr. Hammond."

"I am not half as much interested in him as he is interested in me," retorted Marian, bridling. "He prefers me to any Oakdale girl he has met."

The girls exchanged astonished glances at Marian's complacent statement.

"Where did you first meet him, Marian?" asked Anne gently.

"At the bazaar," replied Marian promptly.

"Who introduced him to you?" asked Grace curiously.

Marian hesitated a moment, then burst forth defiantly. "I suppose you girls will think it perfectly dreadful when I tell you that he introduced himself. He came up and asked me to tell him about some of the features of the bazaar. I did, then he went away, and after a while he came back and talked to me a long time. He is in the real estate business, and is going to have an office here in Oakdale. He was very much interested in the things I said to him, and when I told him about our Phi Sigma Tau he asked to be introduced to you girls. I never supposed you'd take such a dislike to him. I think he is perfectly splendid," she added with emphasis.

"Well, I don't agree with you," said hot-headed Nora. "And I don't think you should have noticed him, beyond being merely civil, without an introduction. Do you, Grace?"

"I don't know," said Grace slowly. "That is a question that no one save Marian can settle. I don't wish to seem hateful, Marian, but to tell you the truth, I wasn't favorably impressed with Mr. Hammond. Besides, he is ever so much older than you are. He must be at least twenty-five years old."

"He is twenty-nine," replied Marian coldly. "And I am glad that he isn't as young and foolish as most of the boys I have met."

"Does your mother know how you happened to meet him?" asked Jessica unthinkingly.

But this was a little too much. Marian rose to her feet, her voice choking with anger. "I don't blame Eleanor Savelli for calling you busy-bodies," she said. "And I shall be infinitely obliged to you if you will in future look to your own affairs and stop criticizing me."

With these words she rushed from the room, seized her wraps and was out on the street before any of the remaining girls had fully comprehended.

# CHAPTER IX

## THE JUDGE'S HOUSE PARTY

"There is nothing like congenial company when one travels," remarked Hippy Wingate, favoring his friends with a patronizing smile. "Now, when I came home from college I was obliged to consort with such grouches as David Nesbit and Reddy Brooks, who made me keep quiet when I wished to speak, and speak when I fain would have slept. But, observe the difference, all these fresh and charming damsels—"

"Charming we are, beyond a doubt," interrupted Nora O'Malley, "but fresh—never. The only fresh person aboard is named Wingate."

"If you two are going to disagree we'll bundle you both into the baggage car and let you fight it out," warned David. "Hippy ought to be exiled to that particular spot for having reviled Reddy and me."

"Keep quiet, Nora," said Hippy in a stage whisper. "We are in the hands of desperadoes."

It was a merry party who were speeding along their way to the state capital, for a wonderful visit was to be paid and the Phi Sigma Tau and their friends were to pay it. In short, Judge Putnam had invited them to spend Christmas at his beautiful home in the capital city, and for eight happy days they were to be his guests.

It was in reality Grace's party. The judge had written her, asking her to select as many guests as she chose. She had also received a prettily worded note from his sister, who had chaperoned them the previous summer in the Adirondacks, and who had taken charge of the judge's home in the capital for years.

Grace had at once invited the Phi Sigma Tau, and dispatched special delivery letters to Hippy, David and Reddy, not forgetting Tom Gray and Arnold Evans.

In order to make an even number of boys and girls, Grace had invited James Gardiner, an Oakdale boy, and last of all, very reluctantly, had sent a note to Mr. Henry Hammond.

This she had done solely to appease Marian Barber's wounded pride. For a week after the day that Marian had rushed angrily out of Grace's house, she had refused to go near her sorority. But one afternoon the six girls, headed by Grace, waylaid her as she was leaving the school and after much coaxing Marian allowed herself to be brought to a more reasonable frame of mind.

Then Grace, who honestly regretted having hurt Marian's feelings, had made an extra effort to treat Mr. Hammond cordially when they chanced to meet, and her friends had followed her example.

In spite of their feeling of dislike for him, they were forced to acknowledge that he seemed well-bred, was a young man of apparently good habits and that Oakdale people were rapidly taking him up. Grace privately thought Marian entirely too young to receive the attentions of a man so much older than herself, but Marian's father and mother permitted it, therefore Grace felt that she had no right to judge or object.

The longest journey seems brief when beguiled by gay companions, and the time slipped by like magic. It was with genuine surprise that the little party heard their station called. There was a great scurrying about for their various belongings, and well laden with suit cases and traveling bags the party hustled out of the train and were met on the platform by the judge's chauffeur, who conducted them to two waiting automobiles.

Off they whirled and in an incredibly short time the two machines drew up before the judge's stately home, where lights gleamed from every window. The guests alighted with much laughter and noise, and in a twinkling the massive front door opened and Judge Putnam appeared.

"Welcome, welcome!" he cried. "Now I am sure to have a Merry Christmas. I don't see how your fathers and mothers could spare you, and I owe them a debt of gratitude. Come in, come in. Here, Mary, are your children again."

The judge's sister came forward and greeted the young people warmly, kissing each girl in turn and shaking hands with the boys. Mr. Hammond and James Gardiner were duly presented to the judge and his sister, and then the boys were shown to their rooms by one of the servants, while Miss Putnam herself conducted the girls to theirs.

"We usually dine between seven and seven-thirty, my dears," said Miss Putnam, as they ascended. "I will send my maid, Annette, to you. Will you have separate rooms, or do you wish to do as you did last summer?"

"Oh, let two of us room together," said Grace eagerly. "But still, that isn't fair, for it will leave an odd one. You know we had Mabel with us last summer."

"Dear little Mabel," said Miss Putnam. "I am sure you must miss her greatly. Her finding of her mother was very wonderful. I received a letter from her last week. She says she is very happy, but that she misses her Oakdale friends, particularly Jessica."

"She is coming east for commencement," said Jessica with a wistful smile. "No one knows how much I miss her."

"Let us settle the question of rooms at once," interposed Grace, who knew that whenever the conversation turned to Mabel, Jessica invariably was attacked with the blues. "Who is willing to room alone?"

"I am," replied Miriam Nesbit, "only I stipulate that I be allowed to pay nocturnal visits to the rest of you whenever I get too bored with my own society."

"Very well, then," replied Grace. "How shall we arrange it?"

"You and Anne take one room, then," said Nora rather impatiently, "Jessica and I another and that leaves Marian and Eva together. Do hurry up about it, for I want to get the soot off my face, and the cinders out of my eyes."

The question of roommates being thus settled, the girls trooped into the rooms assigned them and began to dress for dinner. The matter of gowns had been discussed by the girls when the judge's invitation had first arrived. As they were to remain for a week, they would need trunks, but for the first dinner, in case the trunks did not arrive on time, it had been agreed that they each carry one simple gown in their suit cases.

Grace and Anne had both chosen white, Jessica a dainty flowered organdie, and Nora a pale pink dimity. Eva Allen also had selected white. Marian Barber alone refused to give her friends any satisfaction as to what she intended to wear. "Wait and see," she had answered. "I want my gown to be a complete surprise to all of you."

"How funny Marian acted about her gown," remarked Grace to Anne, as she fastened the last button on the latter's waist. The maid sent by Miss Putnam had offered her services, but the girls, wishing to be alone, had not required them.

"Yes," responded Anne. "I don't understand her at all of late. She has changed a great deal, and I believe it is due to the influence of that horrid Henry Hammond. I simply can't like that man."

"Nor I," said Grace. "It requires an effort on my part to be civil to him. I think, too, that the boys are not favorably impressed with him, although they are too polite to say so."

"I believe in first impressions," remarked Anne. "I think that nine times out of ten they are correct. I may be doing the man an injustice, but I can't help it. Every time that I talk with him I feel that he is playing a part, that underneath his polish he has a cruel, relentless nature."

"Are you girls ready!" called Nora's voice just outside their door.

"In a minute," answered Grace, and with a last glance at the mirror she and Anne stepped into the hall, where Nora, Jessica and Eva Allen stood waiting.

"Where's Marian?" asked Grace, noticing her absence.

"Don't ask me," said Eva, in a tone bordering on disgust. "She won't be out for some time."

"Shall we wait for her?" inquired Anne.

"No," replied Eva shortly. "Let us go, and don't ask me anything about her. When she does finally appear you'll understand."

"This sounds very mysterious," said Miriam Nesbit, who in a white dotted Swiss, with a sprig of holly in her black braids, looked particularly handsome. "Come on, girls, shall we go down?"

The six girls descended to the drawing room, looking the very incarnation of youth and charming girlhood, and the judge's eyes brightened at sight of them.

"A rosebud garden of girls," he cried gallantly, "but I seem to miss some one. Where is the seventh rosebud?"

"Marian will be here directly," said Grace, as they gathered about the big fireplace until dinner should be announced.

But ten minutes went by, and Marian still lingered.

"Dinner is served," announced the old butler.

The girls exchanged furtive glances, the judge looked rather uncomfortable, while Mr. Henry Hammond frowned openly.

Then there was another ten minutes' wait, that the girls tried to cover with conversation. Then—a rustle of silken skirts and a figure appeared in the archway that caused those assembled to stare in sheer amazement.

Was this fashionably attired person plain every-day Marian Barber? Her hair was drawn high upon her head, and topped with a huge cluster of false puffs, which made her look several years older than she had appeared in the afternoon, while her gown of blue satin was cut rather too low for a young girl, and had mere excuses in the way of sleeves. To cap the climax, however, it had a real train that persisted in getting in her way every time she attempted to move.

For a full minute no one spoke. Grace had an almost irrepressible desire to laugh aloud, as she caught the varied expressions on the faces of her friends. Mr. Hammond alone appeared unmoved. Grace fancied that she even detected a gleam of approval in his eyes as he glanced toward Marian.

"Shall we dine!" asked the judge, offering his arm to Grace, while Tom Gray escorted Miss Putnam, the other young men following with their friends.

The dinner passed off smoothly, although there was a curious constraint fell upon the young people that nothing could dispel.

Marian's gown had indeed proved a surprise to her young friends, and they could not shake off a certain sense of mortification at her lack of good taste.

"How could Marian Barber be so ridiculous, and why did her mother ever allow her to dress herself like that?" thought Grace as she glanced at Marian, who was simpering at some remark that Mr. Henry Hammond was making to her in a voice too low for the others to hear.

Then Grace suddenly remembered that Marian's mother had left Oakdale three weeks before on a three months' visit to a sister in a distant city.

"That deceitful old Henry Hammond is at the bottom of this," Grace decided. "He has probably put those ideas of dressing up into Marian's head. She needs some one to look after her. I'll ask mother if she can stay with me until her mother returns, that is if I can persuade her to come."

"Come out of your brown study, Grace," called Hippy. "I want you to settle an argument that has arisen between Miss O'Malley and myself. Never before have we had an argument. Timid, gentle creature that she is, she has always deferred to my superior intellect, but now—"

"Yes," retorted Nora scornfully, "now, he has been routed with slaughter, and so he has to call upon other people to rescue him from the fruits of his own folly."

"I am not asking aid," averred Hippy with dignity. "I plead for simple justice."

"Simple, indeed," interrupted David with a twinkle in his eye.

"I see very plainly," announced Hippy, "that I shall have to drop this O'Malley affair and defend myself against later unkind attacks. But first I shall eat my dessert, then I shall have greater strength to renew the fray."

"Then my services as a settler of arguments are not required," laughed Grace.

"Postponed, merely postponed," assured Hippy, and devoted himself assiduously to his dessert, refusing to be beguiled into further conversation.

Dinner over, the entire party repaired once more to the drawing room, where the young people performed for the judge's especial benefit the stunts for which they were already famous.

Much to Grace's annoyance, Henry Hammond attached himself to her, and try as she might she could not entirely rid herself of his attentions without absolute rudeness. Tom Gray looked a trifle surprised at this, and Marian Barber seemed openly displeased. Grace felt thoroughly out of patience, when toward the close of the evening, he approached her as she stood looking at a Japanese curio, and said:

"I wish to thank you, Miss Harlowe, for inviting me to become a member of this house party. I appreciate your invitation more than I can say."

"I hope you will enjoy yourself, Mr. Hammond," replied Grace rather coldly.

"There is little doubt of that," was the ready answer. "How well Marian is looking to-night. I am surprised at the difference a really grown-up gown makes in her."

Grace glanced at Marian, who in her eyes looked anything but well.

"Mr. Hammond," she said slowly, looking straight at him. "I do not in the least agree with you. Marian is not yet eighteen, and to-night she looks like anything but the school-girl that she did this afternoon. If her mother were at home I am sure that she would never allow Marian to have such a gown made, and I cannot fully understand what mischievous influence prompted her to make herself appear so utterly ridiculous to-night."

"Miss Harlowe," said the young man, his face darkening ominously, "your tone is decidedly offensive. Do I understand you to insinuate that I have in any way influenced Miss Barber as to her manner of dress?"

"I insinuate nothing," replied Grace, rather contemptuously. "If the coat fits you wear it."

"Miss Harlowe," answered the young man almost savagely, "I cannot understand why, after having included me in this house party, you deliberately insult me; but I advise you to be more careful in the future as to your remarks or I shall be tempted to forget the courtesy due a young woman, and repay you in your own coin."

"Mr. Hammond," replied Grace with cold scorn, "I acknowledge that my last remark to you was exceedingly rude, but nothing can palliate the offense of your reply. As a matter of interest, let me state that I am not in the least alarmed at your threat, for only a coward would ever attempt to bully a girl."

With these words Grace moved quickly away, leaving Mr. Henry Hammond to digest her answer as best he may.

# CHAPTER X

## CHRISTMAS WITH JUDGE

It was Christmas Eve, and the great soft flakes of snow that fell continuously gave every indication of a white Christmas. The north wind howled and blustered through the tree tops, making the judge and his young guests congratulate themselves on being safely sheltered from the storm.

The day had been clear and cold, and the entire party had driven on bob-sleds to the strip of woods just outside the town, where the boys had cut down a Christmas tree, and had brought it triumphantly home, while the girls had piled the sleds with evergreens and ground pine. On the return a stop had been made at the market, and great quantities of holly had been bought. Even the sprig of mistletoe for the chandelier in the hall had not been forgotten.

"We'll hurry up and get everything ready before the judge comes in," planned Grace. "We'll put this mistletoe right here, and Nora, you must see to it that you lead him over until he stands directly under it. Then we will all surround him. Miriam, will you tell Miss Putnam? We want her to be in it, too."

The young folks worked untiringly and a little before five the last trail of ground pine was in place, and the decorators stood back and reviewed their work with pride.

The great hall and drawing room had been transformed into a veritable corner of the forest, and the red holly berries peeping out from the green looked like little flame-colored heralds of Christmas. Here and there a poinsettia made a gorgeous blot of color, while on an old-fashioned mahogany what-not stood an immense bowl of deep-red roses, the joint contribution of the Phi Sigma Tau.

"It looks beautiful," sighed Jessica, "we really ought to feel proud of ourselves."

The entire party was grouped about the big drawing room.

"I am always proud of myself," asserted Hippy. "In the first place there is a great deal of me to be proud of; and in the second place I don't believe in hiding my light under a bushel."

"Now Jessica, you have started him," said David with a groan. "He'll talk about himself for an hour unless Reddy and I lead him out."

"I dare you to lead me out," defied Hippy.

"I never take a dare," replied David calmly, making a lunge for Hippy. "Come on, Reddy."

Reddy sprang forward and Hippy was hustled out, chanting as he went:

"Now children do not blame me, for I have somuch to say,That from myself I really cannot tear myselfaway,"

and remained outside for the space of two minutes, when he suddenly reappeared wearing Grace's coat and Miriam Nesbit's plumed hat and performed a wild dance down the middle of the room that made his friends shriek with laughter.

"Hippy, when will you be good?" inquired Miriam, as she rescued her hat, and smoothed its ruffled plumes.

"Never, I hope," replied Hippy promptly.

"That's the judge's ring," cried Grace as the sound of the bell echoed through the big room, and the guests flocked into the hall to welcome their host.

"This is what I call a warm reception," laughed Judge Putnam, as he stood surrounded by laughing faces.

"I claim the privilege of escorting Judge Putnam down the hall," cried Nora, and she conducted him directly to where the mistletoe hung.

"I must be an object of envy to you young men," chuckled the judge, as he walked unsuspectingly to his fate.

"The mistletoe! The mistletoe! You're standing under the mistletoe!" was the cry and the seven girls and Miss Putnam joined hands and circled around the judge. Then each girl in turn stepped up and imprinted a kiss on the good old judge's cheek.

The Girls Circled Around the Judge.

95

## The Girls Circled Around the Judge

---

"Well, I never!" exclaimed the old gentleman, but there were tears in his blue eyes and his voice trembled as he said to his sister, who was the last to salute him, "It takes me back over the years, Mary."

It was a merry party that ran upstairs to dress for dinner that night, and the spirit of Christmas seemed to have settled down upon the judge's borrowed household.

The only thing that had dimmed Grace Harlowe's pleasure in the least was the passage at arms that had occurred between herself and Henry Hammond. Grace's conscience smote her. She felt that she should not have spoken to him as she had, even though she disliked him. To be sure, his remark about Marian's gown had caused her inwardly to accuse him of influencing Marian to make herself ridiculous in the eyes of her friends, but she could not forgive herself for having unthinkingly spoken as she had done.

After due reflection Grace decided that she had acted unwisely, and made up her mind that she would try to make amends for her unkind retort. She decided, however, to see if she could not persuade Marian to go back to her usual style of dress.

Grace hurried through her dressing, and looking very sweet and wholesome in her dainty blue organdie, knocked at the door of the room occupied by Marian and Eva Allen.

"Come in," cried Eva's voice, and Grace entered, to find Eva completely dressed in a pretty white pongee, eyeing with great disfavor the tight-fitting princess gown of black silk that the maid was struggling to hook Marian into.

"Marian!" exclaimed Grace. "Whatever made you have a black evening gown? It makes you look years older than you are."

"That's exactly what I told her," said Eva Allen, "but she won't believe it." Marian looked sulky, then said rather sullenly: "I really can't see what difference it makes to you girls what I wear. I haven't interfered with you in the matter of your gowns, have I?"

"No," replied Grace truthfully, "but Marian, I think the judge likes to see us in the simple evening dresses we have been accustomed to wearing, and as we are his guests we ought to try and please him. Besides, you would look so much better in your white embroidered dress, or your pink silk, that you wore to commencement last year."

"I don't agree with, you at all," replied Marian so stiffly that the maid smiled openly, as she put the final touches to Marian's hair preparatory to adjusting the cluster of puffs that had completed her astonishing coiffure the night before. "Furthermore, I have been assured by persons of extreme good taste that my new gowns give me a distinct individuality I have never before possessed."

"That person of extreme good taste is named Hammond," thought Grace. "That remark about 'individuality' sounds just like him. I'll make one more appeal to her." Going over to where Marian stood viewing herself with satisfaction in the long mirror, Grace slipped her arm around her old friend.

"Listen, dear," she coaxed, "we mustn't quarrel on Christmas Eve. You know we are all Phi Sigma Taus and it seems so strange to see you looking so stately and grown up. Put on your white dress to-night, just to please me." But Marian drew away from her, frowning angrily. "Really, Grace," she exclaimed, "you are too provoking for any use, and I wish you would mind your own business and let me wear what I choose."

"Please pardon me, Marian," said Grace, turning toward the door. "I am sorry to have troubled you," and was gone like a flash.

"You ought to be ashamed of yourself, Marian Barber!" burst forth Eva. "The idea of telling Grace to mind her own business! You haven't been a bit like yourself lately, and I know that it's all on account of that Henry Hammond, the old snake."

"You will oblige me greatly, Eva, by referring more respectfully to my friend, Mr. Hammond," said Marian with offended dignity. Then she sailed out of the room, her train dragging half a yard behind her, while Eva turned to the mirror with a contemptuous sniff and powdered her little freckled nose almost savagely before following her irate roommate down stairs.

## CHAPTER XI

## SANTA CLAUS VISITS THE JUDGE

The moment that dinner was over the judge was hustled into the library by Nora and Miriam, and informed by them that they constituted a committee of two to amuse him until eleven o'clock. He was their prisoner and they dared him to try to escape.

Next to Grace, Nora, with her rosy cheeks and ready Irish wit was perhaps the judge's favorite, while he had a profound admiration for stately Miriam; so he was well satisfied with his captors, who triumphantly conducted him to the drawing room, where Miriam played and Nora sang Irish ballads with a delicious brogue that completely captivated the old gentleman.

At eleven o'clock there was a great jingling of bells and into the room dashed Santa Claus, looking as fat and jolly as a story-book Kris Kringle.

"Merry Christmas," he cried in a high squeaky voice. "It's a little early to wish you Merry Christmas, judge, but I've an engagement in China at midnight so I thought I'd drop in here a trifle early, leave a few toys for you and your little playmates and be gone. I always make it a point to remember good little boys. So hurry up, everybody, and follow me, for I haven't long to stay."

With these words Kris Kringle dashed through the hall followed by the judge who, entering fully into the spirit of the affair, seized Nora and Miriam by the hand and the three raced after their strange visitor at full speed, catching up with him at the door of the dining room which was closed. Here Santa Claus paused and gave three knocks on the oak door.

"Who is there?" demanded a voice, that sounded like David Nesbit's.

"Kris Kringle and three good children."

"Enter into the realm of Christmas," answered the voice, and the door was flung open.

The sight that greeted them was sufficiently brilliant to dazzle their eyes for a moment. In one corner of the dining room stood the great tree, radiant with gilt and silver ornaments. At the top was a huge silver star, while the branches were wound with glittering tinsel, and heavily laden with beribboned bundles of all shapes and sizes, while the space around the base of the tree was completely filled with presents.

At one side of the tree stood a graceful figure clad in a white robe that glittered and sparkled as though covered with diamonds. She wore a gilt crown on her head and carried a scepter, while over her shoulder trailed a long garland of holly fastened with scarlet ribbons. It was Grace Harlowe in a robe made of cotton wadding thickly sprinkled with diamond dust, gotten up to represent the spirit of Christmas.

On the other side of the tree lay old Father Time, apparently fast asleep, his sickle by his side. His long white cotton beard flowed realistically down to his waist, and in his folded hands was a placard bearing these words, "Gone to sleep for the next hundred years," while in the opposite corner his sister and the rest of the guests had grouped themselves, and as the old gentleman stepped over the threshold, a chorus of laughing voices rang out:

"Merry Christmas! Merry Christmas!"

Then Grace glided forward and escorted the judge to a sort of double throne that had been improvised from two easy chairs raised to a small platform constructed by the boys, and draped with the piano cover, and a couple of silken curtains, while Santa Claus performed the same office for Miss Putnam.

After they had been established with great pomp and ceremony, Santa Claus awoke Father Time by shaking him vigorously, apologizing to the company between each shake for doing so, and promising to put him to sleep the moment the festivities were over.

Then the fun of distributing the presents began, and for the next hour a great unwrapping and rattling of papers ensued, mingled with constant exclamations of surprise and delight from all present, as they opened and admired their gifts.

The judge was particularly pleased with the little personal gifts that the girls themselves had made for him, and exclaimed with the delight of a schoolboy as he opened each one. At last nothing remained save one rather imposing package.

"This must be something very remarkable," said the judge, as he untied the bow of scarlet ribbon and unwrapped the folds of tissue paper, disclosing a cut glass inkstand, with a heavy silver top, on which were engraved his initials in block letters.

There was a general murmur of admiration from all.

"Very fine, very fine," said the judge, picking up the card which read, "Merry Christmas, from Miss Barber."

"Miss Barber?" he repeated questioningly. Then it dawned upon him that this expensive gift was from one of his guests.

"Pardon me, my dear," he said turning to Marian, who looked half complacent, half embarrassed. "I am an old man and don't always remember names as well as I should. The beauty of your gift quite overcame me. Allow me to thank you and express my appreciation of it."

Marian smiled affectedly at the judge's words, in a manner so foreign to her former, blunt, good-natured self, that the girl chums watched her in silent amazement.

But the judge's inkstand was merely the fore-runner of surprises. A sudden cry from Grace attracted the attention of the others.

"Why, Marian Barber, what made you do it?"

Then other exclamations followed in quick succession as the Phi Sigma Taus rushed over to her in a body, each carrying a jeweler's box.

"You shouldn't have been so generous, Marian," said Grace. "I never dreamed of receiving this beautiful gold chain."

"Just look at my bracelet!" cried Jessica.

"And my lovely ring!" put in Nora.

"Not half so fine as my silver purse," commented Anne.

Miriam Nesbit was the recipient of a cut glass powder box with a silver top, while Eva Allen was in raptures over a gold chatelaine pin, that more than once she had vainly sighed for.

Even the boys had been so well remembered that they felt rather embarrassed when they compared their simple gifts to Marian with those she had given them. As for Mr. Henry Hammond, he had received a complete toilet set mounted in silver that was truly a magnificent affair, while Marian proudly exhibited a gold chain and locket set with small diamonds, which she had received from him.

When the last package had been opened, Santa Claus removed his huge white beard, slipped out of his scarlet bath robe bordered with cotton and stood forth as Hippy Wingate; while Father Time set his sickle carefully up in one corner, divested himself of his flowing beard and locks, took off David's gray dressing gown and appeared as Tom Gray.

It was long after midnight before the guests sought their rooms, their arms piled with gifts.

"Come into my room for an after-gathering," said Miriam to the girls, as they stood in a group at the head of the stairs.

"Wait until we deposit our spoils and get comfy," said Grace.

Fifteen minutes later the Phi Sigma Taus, with the exception of Marian Barber, wrapped in kimonos, were monopolizing the floor space around the big open fireplace in Miriam's room.

"Where's Marian?" asked Grace.

"Gone to bed," answered Eva laconically. "She said she didn't propose to stay up half the night to gossip."

"The very idea!" exclaimed Jessica. "We never do gossip, but I think she has furnished plenty of material so far for a gossiping match."

"And it looks as though we were in a fair way to start one, now," said Anne slyly.

"Anne, you rascal," said Jessica laughing. "I'll acknowledge my sins and change the subject."

"My presents were all beautiful!" said Miriam Nesbit, who, clad in a kimono of cream-colored silk bordered with red poppies, her long black braids hanging far below her waist, looked like a princess of the Orient.

"And mine," echoed Grace. "The chain Marian gave me is a dear."

She stopped abruptly. A sudden silence had fallen upon the group at her words. Grace instantly divined that in the minds of her friends there lurked a secret disapproval of Marian's extravagance in the matter of gifts.

# CHAPTER XII

## THE MISTLETOE BOUGH

After breakfast the next morning the judge proposed a sleigh ride, and soon the entire party were skimming over the ground in two big old-fashioned sleighs. Though the day was fairly cold, the guests were too warmly wrapped to pay any attention to the weather, and keenly enjoyed every moment of the ride.

After lunch a mysterious council took place in the library, and directly after a visit was made to the attic, Grace having received permission to rummage there. Later Reddy and Tom Gray were seen staggering down the stairs under the weight of a huge cedar chest, and later still the girls hurried down, their arms piled high with costumes of an earlier period.

Christmas dinner was to be a grand affair, and the judge had invited half a dozen friends of his own age to share "his borrowed children."

The girls had saved their prettiest gowns for the occasion, and the boys had put on evening dress. The judge viewed them with unmistakable pride as they stood grouped about the drawing room, awaiting the announcement of dinner. An almost imperceptible frown gathered between his brows, however, as his eyes rested upon Marian Barber, who was wearing a fearfully and wonderfully made gown of gold-colored silk, covered with spangles, that gave her a serpentine effect, and made her look ten years older than the other girls.

On going upstairs to dress, Marian had asked Eva Allen if she objected to dressing with Miriam Nesbit, and Eva had obligingly taken her belongings into Miriam's room after obtaining the latter's permission to do so. Marian had engaged the attention of Miss Putnam's maid for the greater part of an hour, and when she did appear the varied expressions upon the faces of her friends plainly showed that she had succeeded in creating a sensation.

"For goodness sake, what ails Marian!" growled Reddy Brooks in an undertone to David. "Can't the girls make her see that she looks like a fright beside them?"

"Anne told me that Grace and Eva have both talked to her," replied David in guarded tones. "Grace thinks Hammond has put this grown-up idea into her head."

"Humph!" growled Reddy in disgust. "She used to be a mighty pleasant, sensible girl, but lately she acts like a different person. I don't think much of that fellow Hammond. He's too good to be true."

"What have we here?" whispered Hippy to Nora under cover of general conversation. "I never before saw so many spingles and spangles collected in one spot."

"Sh-h-h!" pleaded Nora. "Don't make me laugh, Hippy. Marian is looking this way, and she'll be awfully cross if she thinks we are making sport of her."

"She reminds me of a song I once heard in a show which went something like this," and Hippy naughtily sang under his breath:

"My well-beloved circus queen, My human snake, my Angeline!"

There was a queer choking sound from Nora and she walked quickly down to the other end of the drawing room and earnestly fixed her gaze upon a portrait of one of the judge's ancestors, until she could gain control of her giggles.

The dinner was a memorable one to both the judge and his guests, and it was after nine o'clock before the last toast had been drunk in fruit punch. Then everyone repaired again to the drawing room.

Shortly after, Grace, Anne, Nora, Jessica, Eva and Miriam, accompanied by David, Tom, Hippy and Reddy disappeared, closing the massive doors between the drawing room and the wide hall. Half an hour later Arnold Evans announced that all those wishing to attend the pantomime, "The Mistletoe Bough," could obtain front seats in the hall.

There was a general rush for the hall where the spectators found rows of chairs arranged at one end.

Hardly had they seated themselves when the first notes of that quaint old ballad, "The Mistletoe Bough," sounded from the piano in the drawing room, Nora O'Malley appeared in the archway, and in her clear, sweet voice sang the first verse of the song.

As she finished, the strains of a wedding march were heard, and from the room at the opposite side of the hall came a wedding procession.

Anne, as the bride, was attired in an old-time, short-waisted gown of white satin with a long lace veil, yellow with age, while David in a square-cut costume with powdered wig, enacted the part of the bridegroom. Arnold Evans was the clergyman, Grace and Tom the parents of the bride, while Reddy, Jessica, Hippy and Eva were the wedding guests.

All were garbed in the fashion of "ye olden time," the boys in wigs and square cuts, the girls in short-waisted, low-necked gowns, with hair combed high and powdered.

Then the ceremony was performed in pantomime and the bride and groom received the congratulations of their friends. The groom bowed low over the bride's hand and led her to the center of the hall. The other couples formed in line behind them and a stately minuet was danced.

While the minuet was in progress the bride suddenly stopped in the midst of the figure and professing weariness of the dance, ran out of the room, after signifying to her husband and guests that she would hide, and after a brief interval they should seek for her.

Entering into her fun, the young husband and guests smilingly lingered a moment after her departure, and then ran eagerly off to find her. This closed the scene, and Nora again appeared and sang the next verse.

The cedar chest, brought from the attic by the boys, had been set on the broad landing at the turn of the open staircase, and in the next scene Anne appeared, alone, and discovering the chest climbed gleefully into it and drew the lid down.

Then followed the vain search for her and the deep despair of the young husband at the failure to find his bride, with the final departure of the wedding guests, their joy changed to sorrow over the bride's mysterious disappearance.

There was a brief wait until the next scene, during which another verse of the ballad was sung. Then the husband, grown old, appeared and in pantomime reviewed the story of the strange vanishing of his beautiful bride on her wedding night so many years before. In the next scene two servants appeared with orders to clean out and remove the old chest from the landing. Hippy and Jessica, as the two mischievous prying servants, enacted their part to perfection. Hippy carrying a broom and dust pan, did one of the eccentric dances, for which he was famous, while Jessica, armed with a huge duster, tried to drive him to work.

Finally both lay hold of the old chest, the rusted lock broke and the lid flew open. After one look both servants ran away in terror, and beckoned to the forsaken husband who had appeared in the meantime, seating himself on the oak settee in the lower hall. With eager gestures they motioned him to the landing where the old chest stood. The final tableau, depicted the stricken husband on his knees beside the chest with a portion of the wedding veil in his shaking hands, while the servants, ignorant of the story of the lost bride, looked on in wonder.

During the last tableau Nora softly sang the closing verse and the refrain. Even after the last note had died away the spectators sat perfectly still for a moment. Then the applause burst forth and David bowing in acknowledgment, turned and helped Anne out of the chest, where she had lain quietly after hiding.

The chest had been set with the side that opened toward the wall. While planning for the pantomime the boys had arranged the lid so that it did not close, yet the opening was not perceptible to those seated below. Thus there had been no danger of Anne meeting the fate of the ill-starred Ginevra, the heroine of the ballad.

"You clever children," cried the old judge. "How did you ever get up anything like that on such short notice? It was beautifully done. I have always been very fond of 'The Mistletoe Bough.' My sister used to sing it for me."

"Grace thought of it," said Anne. "We found all those costumes up in the garret in the old cedar chest. We knew the story by heart, and we knew the minuet. We danced it at an entertainment in Oakdale last winter. We had a very short rehearsal this afternoon in the garret and that's all."

"Anne arranged the scenes and coached David in his part of the pantomime," said Grace. "She did more than I."

The judge's guests, also, added their tribute of admiration to that of the judge.

"It was all so real. I could scarcely refrain from telling that poor young husband where his bride had hidden herself," laughed one old gentleman.

"Why don't you children have a little dance?" asked the judge. "This hall ought to make a good ball room, and you can take turns at the piano."

"Oh, may we, Judge?" cried Grace in delight. "I am simply dying to have a good waltz on this floor."

"I'll play for you for a while," volunteered Miriam, "then Eva and Jessica can take my place."

Five minutes later the young folks were gliding about the big hall to the strains of a Strauss' waltz, while the judge and his friends looked on, taking an almost melancholy pleasure in the gay scene of youthful enjoyment.

"Will you dance the next waltz with me, Miss Harlowe!" said Henry Hammond to Grace, as she sat resting after a two-step.

After a second's hesitation Grace replied in the affirmative. Despite her resolve to make peace with him, up to that moment Grace had been unable to bring herself to the point of speaking pleasantly to him.

The waltz began, and as they glided around the room she was obliged to acknowledge herself that Henry Hammond's dancing left nothing to be desired.

"Perhaps my impressions of him are unjust, after all," thought Grace. "I suppose I have no right to criticize him so severely, even though he was rude to me the other night. I was rude, too. Perhaps he will turn out—"

But Grace's reflections were cut short by her partner, who had stopped in the center of the hall.

"Miss Harlowe," he said with a disagreeable smile, "you are standing directly under the mistletoe. I suppose you know the penalty."

Grace looked at him with flashing eyes. "Mr. Hammond," she replied, flushing angrily, "you purposely halted under the mistletoe, and if for one minute you think that you can take advantage of a foolish tradition by so doing you are mistaken. When we girls coaxed Judge Putnam under the mistletoe the other night, it was merely with the view of offering a pretty courtesy to an elderly gentleman. None of our boys would think of being so silly, and I want you to distinctly understand that not one of our crowd is given to demonstrations of that sort."

"Miss Harlowe," replied Henry Hammond between his teeth, "you are an insolent, ill-bred young woman, and it is plain to be seen that you are determined to misconstrue my every action and incur my enmity. So be it, but let me warn you that my hatred is no light matter."

"Your friendship or your enmity are a matter of equal indifference to me, Mr. Hammond," answered Grace, and with a cool nod she crossed the room and joined Nora and Hippy, who were sitting on the stairs playing cats' cradle with the long silver chain of Nora's fan.

## CHAPTER XIII

## TOM AND GRACE SCENT TROUBLE

The time passed all too rapidly, and with many expressions of regret on both sides the judge and his youthful guests parted, two days before the New Year.

On account of the house party the Phi Sigma Tau had been obliged to postpone until New Year's Day entertaining as they had done the previous year the stray High School girls who were far from home. Therefore, the moment they arrived in Oakdale they found their hands full.

Mrs. Gray had been in California with her brother since September, and the girls greatly missed the sprightly old lady. It was the first Christmas since they had entered High School that she had not been with them, and they were looking forward with great eagerness to her return in February.

Julia Crosby, who was at Smith College, had accepted an invitation from her roommate to spend the holidays in Boston, much to Grace's disappointment, who had reckoned on Julia as one of the judge's house party.

New Year's Day the Phi Sigma Tau nobly lived up to their reputation as entertainers of those girls who they had originally pledged themselves to look out for, but New Year's Night the four girl chums had reserved for a special gathering which included the "eight originals" only. It was Miriam who had made this possible by inviting Eva Allen, James Gardiner, Arnold Evans, Marian Barber, and much against her will, Henry Hammond, to a dinner.

"Don't feel slighted at being left off my dinner list," she said to Grace, then added slyly, "Why don't the eight originals hold forth at Nora's?"

"You're a positive dear, Miriam," Grace replied. "We have been wanting to have an old-time frolic, but didn't wish to seem selfish and clannish."

"Opportunity is knocking at your gate, get busy," was Miriam's advice, which Grace was not slow to follow.

"At last there are signs of that spread that I was promised at the bazaar," proclaimed Hippy Wingate cheerfully, as attired in a long gingham apron belonging to Nora's elder sister, he energetically stirred fudge in a chafing dish and insisted every other minute that Nora should try it to see if it were done.

"You'll have to stir it a lot, yet," Nora informed him.

"But I'm so tired," protested Hippy. "I think Tom or Reddy might change jobs with me."

"Not so you could notice it," was the united reply from these two young men who sat with a basket of English walnuts between them and did great execution with nut crackers, while Anne and David separated the kernels from their shells.

The eight originals had repaired to the O'Malley kitchen immediately after their arrival, and were deep in the preparation of the spread, long deferred.

Grace stood by the gas range watching the chocolate she was making, while Nora and Jessica sat at a table making tiny sandwiches of white and brown bread with fancy fillings.

"This spread will taste much better because we've all had a hand in it," remarked David, as he handed Nora a dish of nut kernels, which she dropped into the mixture over which Hippy labored.

"I never fully realized my own cleverness until to-night," said Hippy modestly. "My powers as a fudge maker are simply marvelous."

"Humph!" jeered David, "you haven't done anything except stir it, and you tried to quit doing that."

"But no one paid any attention to my complaints, so I turned out successfully without aid," retorted Hippy, waving his spoon in triumph.

"Stop talking," ordered Nora, "and pour that fudge into this pan before it hardens."

"At your service," said Hippy, with a flourish of the chafing dish that almost resulted in sending its contents to the floor, and elicited Nora's stern disapproval.

"How fast the time has gone," remarked David to Anne. "Just to think that it's back to the college for us to-morrow."

"It will seem a long time until Easter," replied Anne rather sadly.

"And still longer to us," was David's answer.

"Oh, I don't know about that," put in Grace, who had heard the conversation. "I think it is always more lonely for those who are left behind. Oakdale will seem awfully dull and sleepy. We can't play basketball any more this year on account of the loss of the gym., and we seniors are going to give a concert instead of a play. So there are no exciting prospects ahead. There will be no class dances as we have no place to dance, unless we hire a hall, and we never have money enough for that."

"How about the five hundred dollars the judge sent?" asked Reddy.

"Oh, we have decided not to touch that. The money we take in at the concert will be added to it," said Nora. "That will be two entertainments for the seniors, and we think that is enough. We want the other classes to have a chance to make some money, too."

"If we only had the bazaar money that was stolen," said Anne regretfully.

"Strange that no trace of the thief was ever found," remarked David. "I know that my wrist was lame for a week from the twist that rascal gave it."

"I have always had a curious conviction that the man who took that money had been traveling around in the hall all evening," said Anne thoughtfully. "Whoever it was, he must have seen Grace deposit the money in the box, and he also knew the exact location of the switch."

"One would imagine the box too heavy to have been spirited away so easily," said Tom Gray. "The weight of all that silver must have been considerable."

"Yes, it did weigh heavily," replied Grace. "Still, we had a great many bills, too. In spite of the weight the thief did make a successful get away, and we owe Judge Putnam a heavy debt of gratitude for making good our loss."

"'Look not mournfully into the past,'" quoted Hippy, "but rather turn your attention to the important matter of refreshing the inner man."

"You fixed your attention on that matter years ago, Hippopotamus," said Reddy, "and since then you've never turned it in any other direction."

"Which proves me to be a person of excellent judgment and unqualified good taste," answered Hippy with a broad grin.

"More taste than judgment, I should say," remarked David.

"This conversation is becoming too personal," complained Hippy. "Excuse me, Nora, use that Irish wit of yours and lay these slanderers low."

"I am neither a life preserver nor a repairer of reputations," replied Nora cruelly. "Fight your own battles."

"All right, here goes," said Hippy. "Now Reddy Brooks and David Nesbit, I said, that what you said, and formerly have said to have said, was said, because you happened to have said something that I formerly was said to have said that never should have been said. What I really said—"

But what Hippy really did say was never revealed, for David and Reddy laid violent hands upon their garrulous friend and, escorting him to the kitchen door, shoved him outside and calmly locking the door, left him to meditate in the back yard, until Nora suddenly remembering that she had set the fudge on the steps to cool, opened the door in a hurry to find Hippy seated upon the lower step, a piece of fudge in either hand, looking the picture of content.

Hippy Sat With a Piece of Fudge in Either Hand.

125

## Hippy Sat With A Piece of Fudge in Either Hand

The party broke up at eleven o'clock, and the hard task of saying good-bye began. The boys were to leave early the next morning, so the girls would not see them again until Easter.

"Don't forget to write," called Nora after Hippy, as he hurried down the steps after the others, who had reached the gate.

"You'll hear from me as soon as we hit the knowledge shop," was the reassuring answer.

At the corner the little party separated, Hippy, Reddy and Jessica going in one direction, Anne and David in another, leaving Tom and Grace to pursue their homeward way alone. As they turned into Putnam Square, Grace gave a little exclamation, and seizing Tom by the arm, drew him behind a statue of Israel Putnam at the entrance of the square.

"Marian Barber is coming this way with that horrid Henry Hammond," she whispered. "I don't care to meet them. I have not spoken to him since the house party, and Marian will be so angry if I cut him deliberately when he is with her. I am sure they have not seen us. They were invited to Miriam's to-night. We'll stand here until they pass."

The two young people stood in the shadow quietly waiting, unseen by the approaching couple, who were completely absorbed in conversation.

"I tell you I can't do it," Grace heard Marian say impatiently. "It doesn't belong to me, and I have no right to touch it."

Hammond's reply was inaudible, but it was evident that Marian's remark had angered him, for he grasped her by the arm so savagely that she cried out: "Don't hold my arm so tightly, Henry, you are hurting me. I am not foolish to refuse to give it to you. Suppose you should lose it all—"

They had passed the statue by this time, and Grace and Tom heard no more of their conversation. There was a brief silence between them, then Grace spoke.

"Tom, what do you suppose that means?"

"I don't know, Grace," was the answer. "It didn't sound very promising."

"I should say not," said Grace decidedly. "I feel sure that Henry Hammond is a thoroughly unscrupulous person, and I shall not rest until

I find out what the conversation we overheard leads to."

"I believe you are right," said Tom, "and I'm only sorry I can't be here to help ferret the thing out."

"I'll write and keep you posted as to my progress," promised Grace, as she said good-bye to Tom at the Harlowe's door, a little later.

"Good-bye, Tom. Best wishes to Arnold. I'm sorry I didn't see him again."

"Good-night, Grace, and good-bye," said Tom, and with a hearty handshake they parted.

As Grace prepared for bed that night she turned Marian's words over and over in her mind, but could arrive at no logical conclusion, and finally dropped to sleep with the riddle still unsolved.

## CHAPTER XIV

## GRACE AND ANNE PLAN A STUDY CAMPAIGN

With the delights of the past holiday season still fresh in their memories, the pupils of Oakdale High School went back to their studies on the fourth of January, and in the course of a few days everything was again in smooth running order.

Semi-annual examinations were but three weeks away, and that meant a general brushing up in studies on the part of every pupil.

The senior class had, perhaps, less to do in the way of study than the three lower classes. A few of the seniors already had enough credits to insure graduation, although the majority expected the results of the January examinations to place them securely among the number to be graduated.

The members of the Phi Sigma Tau, with the exception of Anne, were among the latter, and had settled down to a three weeks' grind, from which no form of pleasure could beguile them.

As for Anne, she had carried five studies the entire time she had been in High School and had never failed in even one examination. She might have graduated a year earlier had she been so disposed.

Away down in her heart Anne cherished a faint hope that the way for a college career would yet be opened to her. She had made up her mind to try for a scholarship, and she prayed earnestly that before the close of her senior year she might hit upon some plan that would furnish the money for her support during her freshman year in college.

Grace was optimistic in regard to Anne's college career.

"You'll have some opportunity to earn money before the year is out, just see if you don't," she said to Anne one day at recess, when the latter had developed an unusual case of the blues. "If you just keep wishing hard enough for a thing you are pretty sure to get it. That is, if it's something that's good for you to have."

"I've been wishing for the same thing ever since I came to Oakdale, and I haven't got it yet," replied Anne rather mournfully. "I've been unusually short of money this year, too, because Mrs. Gray has been away, and the money I received from her work was a great help."

"Poor little Anne," said Grace sympathetically. "I wish you didn't have to worry over money. However, Mrs. Gray will be home in February, and you'll have her work until June."

"But even so, I can't have the use of it myself," was Anne's response. "I shall have to use it at home. We need every cent of it."

"Oh, dear," sighed Grace. "Why doesn't someone appear all of a sudden and offer you a fine position at about fifty dollars a week."

"Yes," said Anne, laughing in spite of her blues. "That is what really ought to happen, only the day for miracles is past."

"At any rate, I have always felt that you and I were going to college together, and I believe we shall," predicted Grace.

"I hope so, but I doubt it," replied Anne wistfully. "By the way, Grace, do you recite in any of Marian Barber's classes?"

"No," said Grace, "not this term. Why?"

"She is in my section in astronomy," answered Anne, "and lately she fails every day in recitation. You know it's a one-term study, and she will have to try an exam in it before long. I don't believe she'll pass, and she told Nora at the beginning of the year that if she failed in one study this year she wouldn't have enough credits to get through and graduate."

"Oh, she'll pull through, I think," said Grace. "She is really brilliant in mathematics, and always has kept up in other things."

"I know," persisted Anne, "but she has finished her mathematics' group, and her studies this year are things she doesn't care for, and consequently left them until the last. We wouldn't want a Phi Sigma Tau to fail, you know."

"I should say not," was Grace's emphatic response. "What shall we do about it?"

Anne pondered for a little. "We might take turns coaching her. We have all passed in astronomy. I don't know how she is in her other studies," she said. "Do you suppose she'd be angry if we proposed it to her?"

"I don't know," said Grace doubtfully. "She hasn't been to the last two Phi Sigma Tau meetings, and she is awfully cool to me. That's because I don't approve of Henry Hammond. To tell you the truth, I believe he absorbs her attention so completely that she doesn't have time for her studies."

"It's a pity her mother is away just at the time when Marian needs her most," Anne remarked.

"Yes," said Grace. "You know I asked her to come and stay with me, when we came back from the judge's, but she refused rather sharply, and practically told me that she was able to take care of herself."

Just then the gong sounded, and the girls had no further opportunity to discuss the subject until school closed for the day, then while waiting in the locker-room for Nora and Jessica, the talk was again renewed, and after swearing Anne to secrecy, Grace imparted to her the conversation between Marian and Henry Hammond that she and Tom had overheard on New Year's Night.

"I was so uneasy about it that I went all around town the next day to see what I could find out about him. I didn't get much satisfaction, however. He claims to be a real estate agent, and Mr. Furlow in the First National Bank says that he has interested a number of Oakdale citizens in land in the west. He is well liked, and it's surprising the way the business men have taken him up," concluded Grace.

"Perhaps what you heard him say to Marian was nothing of importance after all," said Anne.

But Grace shook her head obstinately. "No, Anne," she answered, "my intuitions never fail me. Henry Hammond is a rascal, and some day I shall prove it. As for Marian we'd better have a meeting of the Phi Sigma Tau to-morrow night and especially request her to be present. Then we'll all turn in and offer to help her get ready for the exams. Here come the girls now."

Nora, Jessica, Miriam and Eva Allen entered the senior locker-room together.

"Where's Marian?" asked Grace.

"You'd never guess if we told you," exclaimed Nora. "I never was more surprised in my life."

"Why? What's the matter?" asked Anne and Grace together.

"Who is the last person you'd expect to see her with?" asked Jessica.

"I don't know," said Grace. "Edna Wright?"

"Worse," was Nora's answer. "She's up in the study hall with Eleanor Savelli."

"Eleanor Savelli?" echoed Grace. "Why she is Marian's pet aversion."

"Past history," said Miriam Nesbit. "They appear to be thicker than thieves."

"I don't at all understand what ails her, but listen, girls, while I tell you my idea," and Grace rapidly narrated her plan of action.

"I foresee trouble, but I'll be on hand," said Miriam.

"We'll all be there!" was the chorus.

"Remember, Eva," were Grace's parting words, "I rely on you to coax Marian over to your house, then we'll surround her and make her accept our services."

"All right," responded Eva. "I'll do my best. Be careful what you say about Henry Hammond, or your mission may be in vain."

## CHAPTER XV

## THE PHI SIGMA TAUS MEET WITH A LOSS

After considerable coaxing, Eva finally wrung from Marian a promise to visit her that evening. She arrived about eight o'clock, and Eva tactfully producing a box of nut chocolates, a confection of which Marian was very fond, the two girls seated themselves in the Allen's cozy sitting room, with the box on a taboret between them.

Marian became more like her old self again, and the two girls were laughing merrily over the antics of Eva's Angora kitten when the doorbell rang, and Eva, looking rather conscious, went to the door.

At the sound of girlish voices, Marian rose, a look of intense annoyance on her face, which deepened as the Phi Sigma Tau trooped into the room, and laughingly surrounded her.

"How are you, Marian?" they cried. "You wouldn't come to us, so we planned a little surprise."

"So I see," replied Marian stiffly. "I am sorry, but I really must go, Eva. You should have told me that the girls were coming."

"Why, Marian Barber, what are you talking about?" asked Nora O'Malley in pretended surprise. "Why should you run away from the members of your own sorority?"

Marian did not answer, but half tried to free herself from the detaining hands of her friends. For a moment her expression softened, then she tossed her head and said, "Let me go, please."

"Marian," said Grace bluntly, "you have been acting very strangely toward us since we came back from the house party, and we don't understand it. You have stayed away from two sorority meetings and have deliberately avoided all of us, with the exception of Eva. We feel badly over it, because we have always liked you, and because you are a Phi Sigma Tau."

"Yes, Marian," interrupted Jessica, "have you forgotten the solemn initiation rites that were conducted at my house last year?"

"No," Marian admitted, smiling a little.

"Then listen, while Anne, who speaks more impressive English than the rest of us, tells you why we have thus entrapped you and used Eva for a bait. Speechify, Anne, and we will put in the applause at the proper intervals."

"Marian," began Anne, "Grace has already told you how kindly our feeling is for you, and the reason that we tried to see you to-night is because of something that I spoke of to Grace yesterday. I had noticed that you were having trouble in your astronomy recitations, and, of course, we all know that you must pass in all your subjects, both now and in June, in order to graduate; so I suggested that as the other girls have all passed in astronomy, we might take turns in coaching you. An hour or so of review every night from now until the exams, would put you in good condition."

"Yes, Marian," interrupted Nora. "Anne and Jessica did that for me last year in ancient history, and I never should have passed if they hadn't helped me."

Marian stood silently looking from one girl to the other, then she said with a mixture of hurt pride, anger and obstinacy in her voice:

"I don't need your help. In fact, I think the less we see of each other in future the better it will be for us all. The past three months have caused me to have an entirely different opinion than I used to have of you girls. You are all very nice as long as things go your way, but if one happens to make a friend or hold an opinion contrary to your views, then the Phi Sigma Taus feel bound to step in and interfere.

"Here is my sorority pin, and I sincerely hope you will elect another girl to my place. She is welcome to both the pin and your friendship. I am thankful that this is my last year in High School."

"You are a foolish girl, Marian Barber," cried Nora, "and you'll wake up some morning and find yourself awfully sorry for what you've just said. You are the last person I should have suspected of being so ridiculous. Why we've all played together since we were kiddies."

Marian tried to look dignified and unrelenting, but for an instant her lip quivered suspiciously.

Anne seeing that Marian showed signs of wavering, crossed over to her side, and slipping her arm around the obstinate girl, said gently:

"Better think it over before you do anything rash, dear. We are not trying in the least to interfere in your affairs. You know the primary object of the Phi Sigma Tau is to help one another. We thought that you would be glad to have us coach you in astronomy. You know how thankful Grace was for your help in trigonometry last year."

Marian hesitated as though at loss for an answer to this direct appeal to her common sense. The girls watched her anxiously, hoping that Anne's words had bridged the difficulty.

"Come on, Marian," said Nora O'Malley briskly. "Here's your sorority pin. Put it on and forget that you ever took it off. You are too sensible to nurse an imaginary grievance. Don't behave as Eleanor Savelli did. You know—"

But Nora was not allowed to finish the sentence, for Marian whirled upon her with flashing eyes, her temporary softness disappearing entirely.

"I don't wish to hear one word against Eleanor Savelli," she cried wrathfully. "She is my friend, and I shall stand up for her."

"Your friend?" was the united exclamation.

"Yes, my friend," reiterated Marian stormily, "and she is a true friend, too. Last year she was initiated into your sorority, and then deliberately slighted and left out of all your plans until in justice to herself she resigned.

"This year you are behaving in the same way with me. You began it by criticizing my friend, Henry Hammond, and invited him to the judge's house party for the express purpose of humiliating and insulting him. The boys of your crowd gave him the cold shoulder when he tried to be friendly and Grace was insufferably rude to him on two different occasions.

"Then you criticized my gowns and made fun of me behind my back, when in reality I was the only one of you who was properly dressed. You left Mr. Hammond and I both out of the pantomime, and made us last in everything.

"I tried to forgive and forget it all, and be just the same to you, but the first thing that Nora did when we reached Oakdale was to invite part of the crowd to her house and leave the rest of us out, and I am surprised that neither Miriam nor Eva resented the slight."

Here Grace and Miriam could not refrain from exchanging amused glances, but to Marian, who intercepted their glances, this was the last straw.

Dashing the sorority pin which Nora had previously shoved into her hand to the floor, with a sob of mingled anger and chagrin she exclaimed:

"How dare you ridicule me to my very face! I never want to speak to any of you again, and I shall not stay here to be laughed at."

With these words she fairly ran out of the room, and before anyone could expostulate with her, she had for the second time in three months rushed out of the house and away from her real friends.

"She is hopeless," sighed Grace, as they heard the outer door of the hall close noisily.

"Can you blame her?" said Anne earnestly. "She has been influenced all along by that Henry Hammond, and now she has fallen into Eleanor's hands. We know Eleanor's state of mind toward us, but why Henry Hammond should encourage Marian to break with her sorority is harder to understand. Yet he has undoubtedly used his influence against us for some purpose of his own. Marian's accusations are foolish and unjust. You all know that she was so engrossed with that miserable old trouble maker that she repeatedly refused to take part in the different things we planned."

"Of course, we know that," agreed Grace. "I don't even feel hurt at her outburst to-night. I wouldn't think of accepting her resignation from the Phi Sigma Tau, either. We won't try to make up with her, but we'll all keep a starboard eye upon her, and see that she doesn't come to grief."

"I had almost reduced her to reason," remarked Anne, with a rueful smile, "when Nora unfortunately mentioned Eleanor."

"Wasn't I an idiot, though?" asked Nora. "I forgot for the moment about having seen them together."

"I am going to turn detective," announced Grace.

"Are you going to detect or deduct?" asked Nora solemnly.

"Both," replied Grace confidently. "I am going to become a combination of Nick Carter and Sherlock Holmes, and my first efforts will be directed toward finding out who and what Mr. Henry Hammond really is."

## CHAPTER XVI

## THE UNEXPECTED HAPPENS

Grace lost no time in putting her resolution into practice, and left no stone unturned regarding the object of her distrust. But her efforts met with no better success than the first time she had instituted inquiry.

"Why are you so bitter against that young man, daughter?" asked her father rather curiously when she interviewed him as to the best means of finding out something of Henry Hammond's past. "He seems to be a good straight-forward young fellow."

"He's a villain, I know he is," asserted Grace, "but he's too sharp for me."

"Nonsense," laughed her father. "Having no basketball this winter you are bound to devote that surplus energy of yours to something. Are you making Hammond your victim?"

"You may tease me if you like," replied Grace with dignity, "but some day you'll acknowledge that I was right."

"All right, girlie," smiled her father. "Shall I say so, now?"

"You're a dear," laughed Grace, rubbing her soft cheek against his. "Only you will tease."

Since the evening that Marian Barber had repudiated her sorority, none of the members had spoken to her. She had studiously avoided going within speaking distance of them and had divided her time after school equally between Eleanor Savelli and Henry Hammond.

Eleanor had kept her word in reference to Edna Wright, and the two girls exchanged only the barest civilities whenever they chanced to meet. Eleanor had, however, gained considerable popularity with a number of the senior class, and wielded a tremendous influence over them. She had dropped her annoying tactics toward the teachers, and her conduct during the year had been irreproachable.

Anne Pierson's assertion that Eleanor would be better off away from

Edna had proved true, and unconsciously the spoiled, temperamental girl was receiving great benefit from her High School associations. She stood next to Anne Pierson in her classes, and her aptitude for study and brilliant recitations evoked the admiration of the entire class.

But despite these changes for the better, Eleanor still nursed her grudge against the Phi Sigma Tau, and held to her unrelenting resolve to be revenged upon them, individually or collectively, whenever the opportunity should arise.

In cautioning her friends the previous year against placing themselves in a position liable to put them at a disadvantage with Eleanor, Grace had unwittingly divined the former's intentions.

Now that Marian had strayed away from the Phi Sigma Tau and straight to their common enemy, Grace felt uneasy as to the result.

"I don't know what to think about Marian's sudden intimacy with Eleanor," she confided to Anne, one day at the beginning of the new term.

"So far nothing startling has happened," replied Anne. "Really, Eleanor happened along at a good time for Marian."

"Why did she?" asked Grace quickly.

"Because I understand that she coached Marian in astronomy and just simply made her cut out Henry Hammond for her books. It's due to Eleanor that she passed," answered Anne.

"I hadn't heard that," said Grace. "Isn't Eleanor a wonder in her studies? It's a pleasure to hear her recite."

"I do admire her ability," agreed Anne. "Perhaps she will see through Henry Hammond and persuade Marian to drop him."

"I don't know about that," said Grace dubiously. "I saw him with Eleanor in the run-about the other day. He was at the wheel, and they seemed to be having a very interesting session without Marian."

"He never did give me the impression of being a very constant swain," laughed Anne.

"I'm so glad that mid-year exams are over," sighed Grace. "I'm a sure enough graduate now, unless something serious happens."

"So am I," replied Anne. "If I could get clerical work to do this term I'd recite in the morning only and give my afternoons to earning a little money. It seems as though everything is against me. Did you know that Mrs. Gray has postponed coming home until March?"

"Yes," answered Grace. She understood Anne's growing despair as time went on, and the prospect of earning enough money to defray her college expenses grew less.

"I'm afraid I'll have to give it all up for next year at least, Grace," Anne's voice trembled a little. "But perhaps I can enter the year after. I can't give up the idea of being in the same college with you."

"Don't give up yet, dear," Grace pressed Anne's hand. "Maybe the unexpected will happen."

The girls separated at the corner and went their separate ways, Anne with the conviction that there was no use in wishing for the impossible and Grace deploring the fact that Anne was too proud to accept any help from her friends.

As Grace was about to curl herself up in a big chair before the fire that night with "Richard Carvel" in one hand and a box of peanut brittle in the other, she was startled by a loud ringing of the bell. Going to the door she beheld Anne who was fairly wriggling with excitement. Her cheeks were flushed and her dark eyes were like stars.

"Oh, Grace," she cried. "The unexpected has happened!"

"What are you talking about, Anne?" exclaimed Grace laughing. "Stop dancing up and down out there. Come in and explain yourself. That is if you can stand still long enough to do it."

"I have had the surprise of my life to-night, Grace," said Anne, as she entered the hall, while Grace unfastened her fur collar and pulled the pins from her hat. "I just couldn't wait until to-morrow to tell you about it. It's so wonderful I can't believe that it has happened to insignificant me."

"I know just as much now as I did at first, and perhaps a trifle less," said Grace.

Then taking Anne by the shoulders she marched her into the sitting room, shoved her into the easy-chair opposite her own and said, "Now, begin at the beginning, and don't leave out any details."

"Well," said Anne, drawing a long breath, "when I reached home after leaving you, I found a letter for me postmarked New York City. For an instant I thought it was from my father, but the hand writing was not his. I opened it, and who do you suppose it was from?"

"I don't know, and I'm a poor guesser, so tell me," responded Grace.

"It was from Mr. Everett Southard."

"No! Really?" cried Grace. "How nice of him to write to you."

"But I haven't told you the nicest part," continued Anne. "He wants me to go to New York to play a six-weeks' engagement in his company."

"Anne Pierson, you don't mean it," ejaculated Grace in intense astonishment.

"Grace Harlowe, I do mean it," retorted Anne. "Why it's the very opportunity that I've been yearning for, but never expected to get. Let me read you his letter."

Unfolding the letter that she had been holding in one hand, Anne read:

"MY DEAR MISS PIERSON:

"Remembering your exceptionally fine work as 'Rosalind' in the production of 'As You Like It,' given at your High School last year, I now write to offer you the same part in a six weeks' revival of the same play about to be presented in New York. Your acceptance will be a source of gratification to me, as it is very hard to engage actors who are particularly adapted to Shakespearian roles. The salary will be one hundred dollars per week with all traveling expenses paid.

"My sister extends a cordial invitation to you to make our home yours during your stay in New York, and will write you at once. I have already written Miss Tebbs regarding my offer. Hoping to receive an affirmative answer by return mail, with best wishes, I remain

"Yours sincerely,

"EVERETT SOUTHARD."

"Well, I should say the unexpected had happened," said Grace, as Anne finished reading. "One hundred dollars a week for six weeks! Why, Anne, think of it! You will have six hundred dollars for six weeks' work. I had no idea they paid such salaries."

"They pay more than that in companies like Mr. Southard's," replied Anne. "If I had acquired fame I could command twice that sum. I can't imagine why he ever chose me. Suppose I should fail entirely."

"Nonsense," retorted Grace. "You couldn't fail if you tried. The only thing that I am afraid of is that you'll be so carried away with the stage that you'll forget to come back to us again."

"Don't say that, Grace," said Anne quickly. "I never shall. I am wild to play this engagement, because it means that I am sure of at least two years in college, and I think if I can get tutoring to do, I can pull through the whole four. Aside from that, the stage is the last career in the world that I should choose. You know my views on that subject."

"I was only jesting, dear," Grace assured her, seeing the look of anxiety that crept into Anne's eyes. "I know you'll come back. We couldn't graduate without you. When shall you write to Mr. Southard?"

"I have already written," replied Anne gravely. "I knew that nothing could induce me to refuse, so I settled the matter at once."

"Confess, you bad child," said Grace, rising and putting one finger under Anne's chin. "Look me straight in the face and tell the truth. You thought I'd be shocked."

Anne colored, laughed a little and then said frankly, "Yes, I was afraid you wouldn't look at the matter in the same light. Now, I must go, because it is after nine and sister worries if I stay out late."

"Wait, I'll go to the corner with you," said Grace.

Slipping into her coat, and throwing a silk scarf over her head. Grace accompanied Anne into the street.

"Come as far as the next corner," begged Anne, and the two girls walked slowly on.

"Now I must go back," said Grace, as they neared the corner.

Just then Anne exclaimed very softly, "Look, Grace, isn't that Marian and her cavalier?"

"Where!" asked Grace, turning quickly.

"Across the street, coming in this direction. I do believe Marian is crying, too. They are crossing now, and will pass us. I don't think they've seen us yet."

Completely absorbed in their own affairs the approaching couple had not noticed either Grace or Anne.

"How could I have been so foolish!" the two girls heard Marian say tearfully.

"Don't be an idiot," her companion answered in rough tones. "You may win yet. I had inside information that it was safe to put the money on it. You act like a baby." Then he muttered something that was inaudible to the listeners.

"You are very unkind, Henry," wailed Marian.

But in the next instant Henry Hammond had seen the two girls. With a savage "cut it out, can't you! Don't let everyone know your business," his scowling expression changed to the polite smiling mask that he habitually wore.

But Grace, who in spite of her former disagreement with him, had for

Marian's sake favored him with a cool bow when he happened to cross her path even after Marian had stopped speaking, was up in arms at his display of rudeness to the girl who had cut herself off from her dearest friends to please him.

Marian averted her face as they passed opposite the chums, but her companion, who was preparing to bow, became suddenly disconcerted by the steady, scornful gaze of two pairs of eyes, that looked their full measure of contempt, and hastily turning his attention to Marian passed by without speaking.

"Contemptible coward!" raged Grace. "Did you hear what he said, Anne?"

"I should have cut his acquaintance on the spot."

"There is something queer about all this," mused Grace. "This is the second conversation of the sort that has taken place between those two that I have overheard. I wonder if he has persuaded Marian to put money into his real estate schemes, for I believe they are nothing but schemes."

"But Marian has no money of her own," protested Anne. "Don't you remember how delighted she was when she deposited the judge's check and received her first check book?"

"I wonder—"

Grace paused. A sudden suspicion entered her mind, that she instantly dismissed.

"You don't believe—" began Anne, but Grace stopped her.

"No, dear," she answered firmly. "We mustn't ever allow ourselves to entertain such a thought. Marian may have foolishly risked money of her own that we know nothing of, but as for anything else—Marian is still a member of our sorority and the honor of the Phi Sigma Tau is above reproach."

# CHAPTER XVII

## ANNE BECOMES FAMOUS

That Anne Pierson was to play a six weeks' engagement in New York under the management of the great Southard was a nine days' matter of wonder in Oakdale.

In spite of the fact that Anne tried to keep the news within her immediate circle of friends, it spread like wildfire.

"You'll just have to let me tell it, Anne," laughed Nora O'Malley. "I can't keep it to myself."

Rather to Anne's surprise, there was little disapproval expressed in regard to her coming engagement. Those who had seen her enact "Rosalind" in the High School production of "As You Like It," fully described in "GRACE HARLOWE'S JUNIOR YEAR AT HIGH SCHOOL," had been then convinced that her ability was little short of genius. But the interest of the thing deepened when the story crept about that this engagement meant a college career for her, and Anne became the idol of the hour.

"The whole town has gone mad over Anne," replied Jessica. "I expect to see a howling populace at the station when she leaves for New York to-morrow."

The three chums were seated upon the single bed in Anne's little room at the Pierson cottage, while Anne sat on the floor before an open trunk, busily engaged in packing.

"What shall we do without you!" lamented Grace. "Positively I have sorrowfully accompanied departing friends to the station so many times since school began that it's becoming second nature to me."

"Good-bye, forever; good-bye, forever," hummed Nora.

"Stop it instantly, Nora," commanded Grace. "Don't harrow my feelings until the time comes."

"Anne, you must write to us often," stipulated Jessica.

"Of course I shall," replied Anne. "Remember you are all coming down to see me, the very first Saturday that you can. I do hope the boys can make arrangements to be there at the same time."

"How lovely it was of Mrs. Gibson to suggest a theatre party and offer to chaperon us," said Nora.

"Everyone has been too sweet for anything," replied Anne, looking up from her task with a fond smile at the three eager faces of her friends.

"You didn't have the least bit of trouble about getting away from school, did you?" asked Jessica.

"No," replied Anne. "You see, I have enough counts to graduate now. I'm not depending on any of my June exams. I can easily make up the time when I come back."

"I imagine Marian Barber wishes that she hadn't been quite so hasty," said Nora. "She is going to miss an awfully nice trip."

"Perhaps we ought to send her an invitation," suggested Jessica.

"No, Jessica," said Grace gravely. "Marian must be the one to make advances. If she comes back to us, it must be of her own free will. We have done our part."

"Can we do anything to help you, Anne?" asked Grace.

"Yes," replied Anne, looking ruefully at the overflowing trunk. "You can all come over and sit upon this trunk. I never shall get the lid down any other way."

This having been successfully accomplished, the three girls took leave of Anne, who promised to be on hand for a final session that night at Grace's.

Before eight o'clock the next morning Anne departed for New York, laden with flowers, magazines and candy, bestowed upon her by the Phi Sigma Tau, who had risen before daybreak in order to be in time to see her off. She had purposely chosen an early train, as she wished to arrive in New York before the darkness of the winter evening closed in.

Mr. Southard and his sister were to meet her at the Jersey station, but careful little soul that she was, Anne decided that in case anything unforeseen arose to prevent their coming, she would have less difficulty in finding her way about in daylight.

"Take good care of yourself, Anne," commanded Nora, patting Anne on the shoulder.

"You do the same," replied Anne. "Don't forget that theatre party, either."

"We'll be there," Grace assured her, as she followed Anne up the aisle with her suit case. "By the way, Anne, here's my sweater. I thought you might need it during rehearsals. The stage is likely to be draughty."

"Grace Harlowe, you are too good to me," murmured Anne, as she reluctantly took the package that Grace thrust into her unwilling hands.

"All aboard," shouted the brakeman, and with a hasty kiss Grace hurried down the steps to join her friends, who stood on the station platform waving their farewells to the brown-eyed girl who was to separate from them for the first time since the beginning of their High School career.

The days slipped quickly away, and the girl chums heard frequently from Anne, who had arrived at her destination in safety, was met by the Southards and carried off to their comfortable home. She was enjoying every minute of her stay, she wrote them, and everyone was very kind to her. Miss Southard was a dear, and she was looking forward to the visit of the Phi Sigma Tau with almost as much enthusiasm as Anne herself.

The boys had been duly informed of Anne's good fortune, and the Saturday of the third week of Anne's engagement had been the date fixed upon for the theatre party. Tom Gray would bring Arnold Evans. Hippy, David and Reddy would join them in New York. Then the five boys would repair to the hotel where the girls were to stop, accompanied by Mrs. Gibson and James Gardiner, who was again invited to make the number even.

Intense excitement prevailed in school when it was learned that the Phi Sigma Tau were to go to New York to see Anne as "Rosalind," and the five girls were carried upon the top wave of popularity.

Marian and Eleanor alone remained aloof, evincing no outward interest in the news, although both thought rather enviously of the good time in New York that awaited the girls they had repudiated.

The eventful Saturday came at last, and the five girls, chaperoned by Mrs. Gibson, with James Gardiner for a bodyguard, boarded the same express that had carried Anne off and were whirled away to the metropolis.

As soon as they arrived in New York they were conveyed by taxicabs to their hotel and on entering the reception room were hailed with delight by the boys, who had arrived only half an hour before. While they were busily engaged in exchanging news, Anne hurried in from a rehearsal, was seized by Grace, then passed from one to the other until, freeing herself, she said, laughing:

"Do let me stand still for a second. I haven't had a really good look at any of you yet."

"What do you mean by becoming a Shakespearian star without consulting me first!" demanded David, with mock severity, although there was a rather wistful look in his eyes as they looked into Anne's. David preferred to keep Anne the little High School girl he had known for the past three years. Theatrical stars were somewhat out of his firmament.

"Don't worry," Anne assured him. "It's only for three more weeks. I'll be back in Oakdale in plenty of time to finish up my senior year with the girls."

"Anne, you haven't any idea of how much we have missed you," cried Nora. "We can't get used to being without you."

"I've missed you, too," responded Anne who stood with Grace's arm around her, smiling lovingly at her little circle of friends.

"Of course I have had a good many rehearsals—one every day, and sometimes two—so the time has fairly raced by; but when the play is over and I am on the way home at night, then I think of all of you, and it seems as though I must take the next train back to Oakdale."

"Do let me talk," interposed Hippy, who had hitherto been devoting his attention to Nora. "No one knows how I long to be back in Oakdale, fair village of my birth, home of the chafing dish and the cheerful chocolate cream. 'Tis there that the friends of my youth flourish, and the grass green banner of O'Malley waves. Take me back; oh, take me—"

"You will be taken away back and set down with a jar in about two seconds if you are seized with another of those spells," promised Tom Gray, turning a withering glance upon Hippy.

"What sort of jar," asked Hippy, with an interested grin. "A cookie jar or merely a glass candy jar? Be sure you make it a full one."

"It will be a full one," replied Tom with emphasis, "and will last you for a long time."

"I don't believe I'll take up with your proposition," said Hippy hastily. "There is something about the tone of your voice that makes my spinal column vibrate with nervous apprehension. I think I had better confine my conversation strictly to Nora. She is sympathetic and also skilled in argument."

With this, he took Nora by the arm and would have marched her out of the group had she not protested so vigorously that he turned from her in disgust and began questioning James Gardiner as to how he managed to survive the journey and what methods he had used to insure good behavior on the part of his charges, much to the embarrassment of that youth, who was anything but a "ladies' man."

"My dear young people," finally said Mrs. Gibson, laughingly, "this impromptu reception is liable to last all night unless it is checked by a stern hand. It is almost five o'clock, and we haven't even seen our rooms yet. Besides, Anne will have to leave before long for the theatre. Let us hurry with our dressing, order an early dinner and keep Anne here for it. Shall you be able to stay?" she asked, turning to Anne.

"I think so," replied Anne. "I do not have to be in the theatre until after seven. But I am not dressed for dinner," she added, looking doubtfully at her street costume. "You see, I came straight from rehearsal."

"Never mind, Anne," interposed Grace, "you are a star, and stars have the privilege of doing as they choose. At least that's what the Sunday papers say. Miriam and I are going to room together. Come up with us."

Mrs. Gibson had engaged rooms ahead for her party, and the girls soon found themselves in very luxurious quarters, with a trim maid on hand to attend to their wants.

The boys had engaged rooms on the floor above that occupied by Mrs. Gibson and the Phi Sigma Tau. James Gardiner heaved a sigh of relief as he deposited his suit case beside Tom's in the room to which they had been assigned.

"Girls are an awful responsibility," he remarked gloomily, with a care-worn expression that made Tom shout with laughter. "I like them all right enough, but not in bunches."

By making a special effort, the party was ready by six o'clock to descend to dinner, which was served to them in a private dining room, Mrs.

Gibson having thoughtfully made this arrangement, in order to give the young folks as much time together as possible.

They made a pretty picture as they sat at the round table, the delicate finery of the girls gaining in effect from the sombre evening coats of the boys. Mrs. Gibson, gowned in white silk with an overdress of black chiffon, sat at the head of the table and did the honors of the occasion.

"I feel frightfully out of place in this company of chivalry and beauty," Anne remarked, looking fondly about her at the friends whose presence told more plainly than words could have done the place she occupied in their hearts.

"Think how we shall fade into insignificance to-night when you hold forth with the great Southard," retorted Nora. "I shall consider myself honored by even a mere bow from you, after you have taken curtain calls before a New York audience."

"When I was with Edwin Booth," began Hippy reminiscently, "he often said to me, 'Hippy, my boy, my acting is nothing compared to yours. You are—'"

"A first cousin to Ananias and Sapphira," finished David derisively.

"Never heard of them," replied Hippy unabashed. "Not branches of our family tree. As I was saying—"

"Never mind what you were saying," said Nora in cutting tones. "Listen to me. It is seven o'clock. Anne must go, and in a taxicab, at that."

"Where shall we see you after the performance, dear?" asked Grace.

"Mr. Southard has obtained special permission for all of you to go behind the scenes after the play."

"How lovely!" cried the girls.

"My curiosity will at last be satisfied. I have always wanted to go behind the scenes of a New York theatre," remarked Mrs. Gibson.

"I have the dearest dressing room," said Anne, with enthusiasm. "Mr. and Miss Southard are going to carry you off to their house after the performance to-night. I almost forgot to tell you. So don't make any other plans."

"We are in the hands of our friends," said Hippy, with an exaggerated bow.

"You'll be in the hands of the law if you don't mend your ways," prophesied Reddy. "If we get you safely into the theatre without official assistance it will surprise me very much."

"Reddy, you amaze me," responded Hippy reproachfully. "I may make mistakes, but I am far from lawless. Neither do I flaunt the flame colored signal of anarchy every time I remove my hat."

There was a burst of good-natured laughter at Reddy's expense. His red hair was as common a subject of joke as was Hippy's behavior.

"That was a fair exchange of compliments," said Tom Gray. "Now forget it, both of you."

"Good-bye, every one, until eleven o'clock," cried Anne, who, knowing that she would be obliged to hurry away, had brought her wraps to the dining room with her.

David accompanied Anne to the entrance of the hotel, put her in a taxicab and walked into the hotel, hardly knowing whether he were glad or sorry that Anne had had greatness thrust upon her.

## CHAPTER XVIII

## THE THEATRE PARTY

It was a very merry party that took possession of the box that Mr. Southard had placed at their disposal and waited with ill-concealed impatience for the rise of the curtain.

Anne's friends had thought her the ideal "Rosalind" in the High School production of the piece, but her powers as an actress under the constant instruction of Everett Southard had increased tenfold. His own marvelous work was a source of inspiration to Anne, and from the instant that she set foot upon the stage until the final fall of the curtain she became and was "Rosalind."

Thrilling with pride as she eagerly watched Anne's triumph, Grace was in a maze of delight, and every round of applause that Anne received was as music to her ears. David, too, was more deeply moved than he liked to admit even to himself. In his own heart he had a distinct fear that in spite of her assertions to the contrary, Anne might after all yield to the call of her talent and seek a stage career. During the evening he became so unusually grave and silent that Grace, having an inkling of what was passing in his mind, leaned over and said:

"Don't worry, David, she won't. I am sure of it. Her mind is fixed upon college."

David drew a long breath of almost relief. "I believe it if you say so, Grace; it has worried me a lot, however. She is such a wonderful little actress."

"Nevertheless, take my word for it, she won't," was the assuring answer.

After the play was over, the visit behind the scenes being next on the programme, Mrs. Gibson and her charges were conducted through a long passage to the back of the house. The boys were taken to Mr. Southard's dressing room, and Mrs. Gibson and the five girls to Anne's.

There were many exclamations over the cozy dressing room which Anne occupied. As is the case in most of the recently built theatres, the star's dressing room had been comfortably furnished and was in direct comparison to the cheerless, barn-like rooms that make life on the road a terror to professional people.

"You see, I have had you right with me," smiled Anne, who was seated at a dressing table taking off her make-up with cold cream. She pointed to a photograph that the Phi Sigma Tau had had taken the previous summer.

"Only one face missing to-night," said Grace in low tones as she drew her chair close to Anne's.

"Have you found out anything else?" asked Anne in the same guarded tones.

"Nothing very important," replied Grace. "Marian and Henry Hammond have had some sort of quarrel. Nora saw them pass the other day without speaking."

"That's a step in the right direction", said Anne. "Once she has dropped him for good and all, she'll begin to see her own folly. Then she'll come back and be her old self again."

"I hope so," sighed Grace.

Then the conversation became general and the two girls had no further opportunity for discussion of the subject.

Just as Anne had completed her dressing, a knock sounded on the door, and Mr. Southard's deep voice called out:

"All aboard for the actors' retreat."

"Come in, Mr. Southard," said Anne, and the door opened to admit the eminent actor, who looked bigger and handsomer than ever in his long coat and soft black hat.

Then Anne presented him to Mrs. Gibson, and a general handshaking ensued.

For the third time that night they were handed into the "uncomplaining but over-worked taxicab," according to Nora's version, and set out for the Southard home.

The entire party promptly fell in love with Miss Southard, who was the counterpart of her brother, except that she was considerably older, and she apparently returned their liking from the moment of meeting.

"I know every one of you," she said. "Anne talks of no one else to me. Your fame has already preceded you."

The Southards proved to be hospitable entertainers, and exerted every effort in behalf of their young guests. The time slipped by on wings, and it was well after one o'clock before anyone thought of returning to the hotel.

"I am not a very reliable chaperon," laughed Mrs. Gibson, "to allow my charges to keep such late hours as this."

"It's only once in a life time," remarked Nora.

"How very cruel," said Mr. Southard solemnly. "I had hoped that you would all honor us again with your society."

"I didn't mean that," she cried, laughing a little. "I only meant that this was a red-letter night for us. We are basking in the light of greatness."

"Very pretty, indeed," was the actor's reply, and he gave Nora one of his rare, beautiful smiles that caused her to afterwards aver that he was truly the handsomest man in the whole world.

With many expressions of pleasure for the delightful hours they had passed, the revelers bade the Southards good night and good-bye.

"I am going to give a special party to the Phi Sigma Tau and these young men, when my season closes," announced the actor as they stood in the wide hall for a moment before leaving. "I trust that you may be able to again assume the role of chaperon," he added to Mrs. Gibson.

"I shall need no second invitation," replied Mrs. Gibson. "But may I not hope to see your sister and yourself at Hawks' Nest, in the near future?"

"You are indeed kind," responded Mr. Southard. "It would be a distinct pleasure and perhaps I may be able to arrange it. My season is to be a short one."

"Get your things and come with us, Anne," teased Grace. "We've loads of things to talk of, and you can breakfast with us, and go to the train, too. Please don't say no, because you won't see us again for three whole weeks."

"I give you my official permission to carry her off, this one time, Grace," laughed Mr. Southard.

"Better wear your long coat, dear. It is very cold," called Miss Southard as Anne ran upstairs after her wraps.

Then the final good-byes were said and the party were driven back to their hotel.

Mrs. Gibson invited Miriam to share her apartment, thus Grace and Anne were left to themselves, and indulged in one of their old heart-to-heart talks.

Breakfast the next morning was a late affair. After breakfast, the entire party went for a drive, and after a one-o'clock luncheon repaired to the station.

Mrs. Gibson, James Gardiner and the Phi Sigma Tau were to take the 2.30 train for Oakdale. The boys would leave at five o'clock. Tom and Arnold were to travel part of the journey with David, Hippy and Reddy. Then their ways diverged.

The girls kissed and embraced Anne tenderly, then there was a rush for the ferry. They stood on the deck waving to her until they could scarcely see the flutter of her handkerchief. After agreeing to meet the boys at the ferry, David escorted Anne back to the Southard's and spent a brief half hour with her.

"Promise me, Anne," said David earnestly, as he was leaving, "that you won't accept any engagement that you may receive an offer of."

"Of course not, you foolish David," replied Anne. "Notwithstanding the fact that you won't believe me, I solemnly promise to run from prospective managers, as I would from small-pox, and there's my hand upon it."

"I am satisfied," answered David, grasping her out-stretched hand. "I know you will keep your word."

## CHAPTER XIX

### GRACE MEETS WITH A REBUFF

During the journey to Oakdale, Anne and the Southards formed the chief topic of conversation. It was jointly agreed that Anne had been fortunate indeed in winning the friendship of the great actor and his charming sister.

"They treat her as though she were their own sister," remarked Eva Allen. "They will miss her sadly when she leaves them."

"Everyone misses Anne," said Miriam Nesbit. "She is so sweet and lovable that she simply draws one's affection to her. I am frightfully jealous of Grace."

"Yes, Grace is Anne's favorite," said Jessica. "Anne would give her life for Grace if it were necessary."

"And Mabel Allison feels the same way toward you, Jessica," interposed Grace.

"How I wish Mabel had been with us," sighed Jessica.

"I received a letter from Mrs. Allison, just before leaving Oakdale," said Mrs. Gibson. "She expects to come east in June. Mabel has set her heart upon being here for commencement week. I shall invite the Southards, too, and perhaps your people will lend you to me for the week following graduation."

"We should love to go," said Grace, and her friends echoed her answer.

Before their journey ended night closed in around them. They had dinner in the dining car, and after dinner the girls began to feel a trifle tired and sleepy.

James Gardiner had discovered a boy friend on the train and had been graciously granted permission by the Phi Sigma Tau to go over and cultivate his society.

"You have been an angel, James," said Nora, "and have proved yourself worthy of a little recreation. Don't forget to be on hand when the train stops, however. I never saw your equal as a luggage carrier."

One by one the five girls leaned against the comfortable backs of their seats and closed their eyes. Mrs. Gibson became absorbed in the pages of a new book.

Grace dozed for a brief space and then opening her eyes gazed idly about her. The seat on which she sat had been reversed in order that she and Nora might face Mrs. Gibson and Miriam. Their seats being near to the middle of the car, she could obtain a good view of a number of the other passengers. She noticed that the car was very full, every seat being occupied.

Her eye rested for a second upon a portly, well-dressed old gentleman in the last seat of the car, who was leaning back with closed eyes, then traveled on to the man who shared the seat.

"What a remarkable face that man has," she thought. "He looks like a combination of a snake and a fox. I never before saw such tricky eyes. He is rather good looking, but there is something about him that frightens one."

Grace found herself watching, with a kind of fascination, every move that the stranger made. Once her eyes met his and she shuddered slightly, there was a world of refined cruelty in their depths. She looked out of the window as the train rushed on through the darkness, then almost against her will turned her eyes again in the direction of the repellent stranger.

But what she saw this time caused her to stare in amazement. The stranger under cover of a newspaper was bent on extracting the handsome watch and chain that the elderly gentleman's open coat displayed. Although the paper hid the movement of his hands, Grace divined by the expression of the man's face what was taking place behind the paper screen.

Like a flash she was out of her seat and down the aisle. But quick as had been her movement, the thief was quicker. He straightened up, coolly turned to his paper, looking up at her with an air of bored inquiry as she paused before him.

Ignoring him completely, she touched the old man on the shoulder and said in a low tone, "Please pardon me, but if you value your watch you had better look to it. I just saw this man attempting to steal it."

The old gentleman bounded up like a rubber ball, saying excitedly, "What do you mean, young woman?"

"Just what I say," replied Grace.

The thief gave Grace a contemptuous look, then without stirring, said lazily, "The young lady is entirely mistaken. She must have been dreaming."

"I repeat my accusation," said Grace firmly. "I have been watching you for some time, and I saw you attempt it."

The old gentleman put his hand to his vest and drew out a particularly fine old-fashioned gold watch.

"My watch is safe enough," he growled testily, "and so is my chain. Anyone who steals from me will have to be pretty smart. I guess if this man had laid hands on my watch I'd have known it. Can't fool me."

"Certainly not," responded the tricky stranger. "If I were a thief you would be the last person I should attempt to practice upon."

"I should say so," grumbled the old gentleman. "Young woman, you have let your imagination run away with you. Be careful in the future or you may get yourself into serious trouble. This gentleman has taken your nonsense very good-naturedly."

As the two men were occupying the seat nearest the door, save for the old gentleman's first bounce, the little scene had been so quietly enacted that the other passengers were paying little attention to the trio.

"You had better go back to your friends," said the man whom Grace had accused, looking at her with cold hatred in his eyes. "That is, unless you wish to make yourself ridiculous."

Grace turned away without speaking. There were tears of mortification in her eyes. She had attempted to render a service and had been rudely rebuffed. She slipped into her place beside Nora, who was dozing, and had not missed her. Mrs. Gibson, too, had not marked her absence.

"Where were you, Grace?" said Miriam curiously. "I opened my eyes and you were gone. What's the matter? You look ready to cry."

"I am," replied Grace. "I could cry with sheer vexation." Then she briefly recounted what had occurred.

"What a crusty old man," sympathized Miriam. "It would serve him right if he did lose his old watch. Where are they sitting?"

"Down the aisle on the other side at the end," directed Grace.

Miriam turned around in her seat. "He looks capable of most anything," she remarked after a prolonged stare at the stranger, who was apparently absorbed in his paper. "Are you sure, however, that you were not mistaken, Grace? You can't always judge a man by his looks."

"You can this man," asserted Grace. "He is a polite villain of the deepest dye, and I know it."

It was after eleven o'clock when the train pulled into Oakdale. Mrs. Gibson's chauffeur awaited them with the big touring car, in which there was ample room for all of them.

"Keep a sharp lookout for that man," whispered Grace to Miriam. "I want to see if Oakdale is his destination."

The two girls lagged behind the others, eagerly scanning the platform.

"I think he must have gone on," said Miriam. "I don't see him. Don't worry any more about him, Grace."

Then she walked on ahead.

But Grace lingered. "That looks like him now," she thought. "He is just leaving the train. He seems to be waiting for someone."

She stood in the shadow of the station watching the man. Then she saw another man rapidly approaching. The newcomer walked straight up to the stranger and shook hands with him. Then the two men turned and she obtained a full-face view of them both.

Grace gave a little gasp of surprise, for the newcomer who had shaken the hand of the crook was Henry Hammond.

## CHAPTER XX

## MARIAN'S CONFESSION

Grace reached home that night with her head in a whirl. She could think of nothing save the fact that she had seen Henry Hammond warmly welcome a man whom she knew in her heart to be a professional crook. It formed the first link in the chain of evidence she hoped to forge against him. She had become so strongly imbued with the idea that Hammond was an impostor that the incident at the station only served to confirm her belief.

The Phi Sigma Tau were besieged with questions the next day, and at recess the five members held forth separately to groups of eager and admiring girls on the glories of the visit.

"Where is Marian Barber?" asked Grace of Ruth Deane, as they were leaving the senior locker-room at the close of the noon recess.

"She hasn't been in school to-day," replied Ruth. "I suppose what happened Friday was too much for her."

"What happened Friday?" repeated Grace. "Well, what did happen?"

"Oh, Eleanor Savelli and Marian had a quarrel in the locker-room. I was the only one who heard it, and I shouldn't have stayed but I know Eleanor of old, and I made up my mind that I had better stay and see that Marian had fair play. But I might as well have stayed away, for I wasn't of any use to either side. In fact, I doubt if either one realized I was there, they were so absorbed in their own troubles."

"It's a wonder that I wasn't around," remarked Grace. "I am really glad, however, that I wasn't. The Phi Sigma Tau were all in Miss Tebbs' classroom at recess last Friday. Miss Tebbs is a dear friend of the Southards, you know. She was invited to go with us, but had made a previous engagement that she could not break. We were talking things over with her. After school we all went straight home and I saw neither Eleanor nor Marian. Have you any idea what it was about?"

"I don't know," returned Ruth bluntly. "Marian and Eleanor came into the locker-room together. I heard Marian say something about telling Eleanor what she had in confidence. Then Eleanor just laughed scornfully and told Marian that she had told her secrets to the wrong person. Marian grew very angry, and called Eleanor treacherous and revengeful, and Eleanor said that Marian's opinion was a matter of indifference to her.

"Then she told Marian that she intended to call a class meeting for Thursday of this week and entertain them with the very interesting little story that Marian had told her the previous week.

"Marian wilted at that and cried like a baby, but Eleanor kept on laughing at her, and said that she would know better another time, and perhaps would think twice before she spoke once. She said that no one could trample upon her with impunity."

"Oh, pshaw," exclaimed Grace impatiently. "She always says that when she is angry. She said that last year."

"Well, Marian cried some more," continued Ruth, "and Eleanor made a number of other spiteful remarks and walked out with a perfectly hateful look of triumph on her face."

"And what about Marian?" asked Grace.

"She didn't go back to the study hall. She told Miss Thompson that she was ill and went home."

"Poor Marian," said Grace. "She certainly has been very foolish to leave her real friends and put her faith in people like Eleanor and that Henry Hammond. I have been afraid all along that she would be bitterly disillusioned. I think I'd better go to see her to-night."

"Why, I thought she wasn't on speaking terms with the Phi Sigma Tau!" exclaimed Ruth.

"Speaking terms or not, I'm going to find out what the trouble is and straighten it out if I can. Please don't tell that to any one, Ruth. I don't imagine it's anything serious. Eleanor always goes to extremes."

"Trust me, Grace, not to say a word," was the response.

"I wish Anne were here," mused Grace, as she took her seat and drew out her text-book on second year French. Then for the time being she dismissed Marian from her mind, and turned her attention to the lesson on hand.

By the time school closed that afternoon Grace had made up her mind to go to see Marian before going home. Leaving Nora and Jessica at the usual corner, she walked on for a block, then turned into the street where the Barbers lived.

Grace pulled the bell rather strenuously by way of expressing her feelings, and waited.

"Is Marian in?" she inquired of Alice, the old servant.

"Yes, Miss Grace," answered the woman, "She's in the sittin' room, walk right in there. It's a long time since I seen you here, Miss Grace."

"Yes, it is, Alice," replied Grace with a smile, then walked on into the room.

Over in one corner, huddled up on the wide leather couch, was Marian. Her eyes were swollen and red, and she looked ill and miserable.

"Marian," began Grace, "Ruth Deane told me you were ill, and so I came to see you."

"Go away," muttered Marian. "I don't wish to see you."

"I am not so sure of that," answered Grace. "I understand you have been having some trouble with Eleanor, and that she has threatened revenge."

"Who told you?" cried Marian, sitting up and looking angrily at Grace. "I can manage my own affairs, without any of your help."

"Very well," replied Grace quietly. "Then I had better go. I thought when I came that I might be able to help you. You look both ill and unhappy. I see I have been mistaken."

"You can't help me," replied Marian, her chin beginning to quiver. "Nobody can help me. I'm the most miserable girl—" her voice ended in a wail, and she rocked to and fro upon the couch, sobbing wildly.

"Listen to me, Marian," commanded Grace firmly. "You must stop crying and tell me every single thing about this trouble of yours. I have crossed swords with Eleanor before this, and I think I can bring her to reason."

"How can I tell you?" sobbed Marian. "Grace, I am a thief and may have to go to prison."

"A thief!" echoed Grace. "Nonsense, Marian. I don't believe you would steal a penny."

"But I am," persisted Marian tearfully. "I stole the class money, and it's all gone."

She began to sob again.

Grace let Marian finish her cry before interrogating her further. She wanted time to think. Her mind hastily reviewed the two conversations she had overheard between Marian and Henry Hammond. This, then, was the meaning of it all. The brief suspicion that had flashed into her mind and Anne's on the night that Marian and Henry Hammond had passed them, had been only too well founded. Marian had drawn the money from the bank and given it to him.

"Marian," asked Grace, "did you give the money the judge sent us to Henry Hammond?"

Marian nodded, too overcome as yet to speak.

"Can't you tell me about it?" continued Grace patiently.

Marian struggled for self-control, then began in a shaking voice.

"I have been a perfect idiot over that miserable Henry Hammond, and I deserve everything. I was not satisfied with being a school-girl, but thought it very smart to put up my hair and make a general goose of myself.

"It all began the night of the bazaar. I had no business to pay any attention to that man. He is really very clever, for before I realized what I had said I had told him all about our sorority and about being class treasurer, and a lot of things that were none of his business.

"After the bazaar I saw him often and told him about the judge's check.

"One day he asked me if I had any friends who had money that they would like to double. I had fifty dollars of my own that I had been saving for ever so long, and told him about it. He said that he manipulated stocks a little (whatever that is) in connection with his real estate business. He asked me to give him the money and let him prove to me how easily he could double it. I did, and he brought me back one hundred dollars.

"Of course, I was delighted. Then mother sent me fifty dollars for Christmas, and I bought all those presents. It took every cent I had, and I was awfully silly, for no one cared as much for them as if they'd been pretty little gifts that I made myself. That was my first folly.

"The next was those three gowns. They haven't been paid for yet. I haven't dared give father the bills, and I can never face mother. She would never have allowed me to order anything like them. Well, you know how badly I behaved at the house party, and how nice you all were to me, even when I was so hateful.

"On New Year's Night, when we were coming from Nesbits, Henry Hammond asked me for the class money. He said he had a chance to treble it, and that it was too good an opportunity to be lost.

"I refused point blank at first, and then he talked and talked in that smooth way of his until I began to think what a fine thing it would be to walk into the class and say, 'Girls, here are fifteen hundred dollars instead of five hundred.' I was feeling awfully cross at you girls just then, because he made me believe that you were slighting me and leaving me out of things. Besides, all of you had warned me against him, and I wanted to show you that I knew more than you did.

"I didn't promise to give it to him that night, but the more I thought of it the more I inclined toward his views, and the upshot of the matter was that I drew it out of the bank and let him have it."

Marian paused and looked piteously at Grace. Then she said brokenly:

"He lost it, Grace, every cent of it. The week after I gave it to him he told me that luck had been against him, and that it was all gone. When I asked him what he intended to do about it he promised that he would sell some real estate of his and turn the money over to me to give back to the class. He said it was his fault for persuading me to do it, and that I shouldn't suffer for it. But he never kept his word.

"Last week I asked him for the last time if he would refund the money, and he laughed at me and said that I had risked it and ought to accept my losses with good grace. I threatened to expose him, and he said if I did I should only succeed in making more trouble for myself than for him. He had only speculated with what I had given him. Where I obtained the money was none of his business, and as long as I had appropriated it I would have to abide by the consequences.

"Of course, I was desperate and didn't know what to do. I had no money of my own, and I didn't dare ask my father for it. I had to tell someone, so I told Eleanor."

"Eleanor!" exclaimed Grace aghast. "Oh, Marian, why did you tell her of all people."

"I thought she was my friend," declared Marian, "but I soon found out that she wasn't. As soon as I had told her, she changed entirely. She told me last Friday that she had been watching for a long time in the hope of revenging herself upon the Phi Sigma Tau for their insults, and that at last she had the means to do so.

"Her friendship for me was merely a pretense. She said that when I separated from my sorority she knew I was sure to do something foolish, so she decided to make advances to me and see what she could find out.

"She is going to call a class meeting for next Thursday after school, and she is going to expose me. She says that it is right that the class should know just what sort of material the Phi Sigma Tau is made up of, and that one of its members is a sneak and a thief."

"This is serious, and no mistake," replied Grace soberly. "Don't you remember, Marian, that back in our junior year, when Eleanor tried to get Anne's part in the play, I cautioned the girls to never put themselves in a position where Eleanor might injure them."

"Yes, I remember, now," Marian faltered, "but it is too late."

"I might try to checkmate her at her own game by threatening to tell the story of the missing costumes," reflected Grace aloud. "I'll try it at any rate. But even if we do succeed in silencing Eleanor, where are we to get the money to pay back the class fund? We can't arrest that miserable Henry Hammond without making the affair public, and this simply must remain a private matter. It is the hardest problem that I have ever been called upon to contend with.

"You must brace up, Marian, and go back to school to-morrow," directed Grace. "If you keep on this way it will serve to create suspicion. You have done a very foolish and really criminal act, but your own remorse has punished you severely enough. None of us are infallible. The thing to do now, is to find a way to make up this money."

Marian wiped her eyes, and, leaving the lounge, walked over to Grace, and, putting her arms about Grace's neck, said, with agonized earnestness:

"Grace, can you and the girls ever forgive me for being so hateful?"

"Why, of course, we can. There is nothing to forgive. We have never stopped thinking of you as a member of our sorority. We wouldn't ask anyone else to take your place."

An expression of intense relief shone in Marian's face.

"I am so glad," she said. "I can't help being happy, even with this cloud hanging over me."

"Cheer up, Marian," said Grace hopefully. "I have an idea that I shall straighten out this tangle yet. I must go now. Keep up your courage and whatever you do, don't tell anyone else what you have told me. There are too many in the secret now."

# CHAPTER XXI

## WHAT HAPPENED AT THE HAUNTED HOUSE

The moment that Grace left Marian, she set her active brain at work for some solution of the problem she had taken upon her own shoulders. She had no money, and the members of her sorority had none. Besides, Grace inwardly resolved not to tell the other girls were it possible to avoid doing so.

Mrs. Gray would be home before long, and Grace knew that the gentle old lady would gladly advance the money rather than see Marian disgraced. But Eleanor had planned to denounce Marian on Thursday, and it was now Monday.

There was but one course to pursue, and that was to go to Eleanor and beg her to renounce her scheme of vengeance. Grace felt very dubious as to the outcome of such an interview. Eleanor had in the past proved anything but tractable.

"I'll go to-night," decided Grace. "I'm not afraid of the dark. If mother objects, I'll take Bridget along for protection, although she's the greatest coward in the world."

Grace giggled a little as she thought of Bridget in the role of protector.

That night she hurried through her supper, and, barely tasting her dessert, said abruptly:

"Mother, may I go to Eleanor Savelli's this evening?"

"Away out to 'Heartsease,' Grace? Who is going with you?"

"No one," replied Grace truthfully. "Mother, please don't say no. I simply must see Eleanor at once."

"But I thought that you were not friendly with Eleanor," persisted Mrs. Harlowe.

"That is true," Grace answered, "but just now that is the very thing I want to be. It's this way, mother. Eleanor is going to try to make some trouble for Marian Barber in the class, and I must act at once if it is to be prevented."

"More school-girl difficulties," commented Mrs. Harlowe, with a smile. "But how does it happen that you always seem to be in the thick of the fight, Grace?"

"I don't know, mother," sighed Grace. "No one dislikes quarrels more than I do. May I go?"

"Yes," assented her mother, "but you must take Bridget with you. I'll see her at once and tell her to get ready."

It had been a raw, disagreeable day, and towards evening a cold rain had set in that was practically half snow. It was anything but an enviable night for a walk, and Bridget grumbled roundly under her breath as she wrapped herself in the voluminous folds of a water-proof cape and took down a huge, dark-green cotton umbrella from its accustomed nail behind the kitchen door.

"Miss Grace do be crazy to be goin' out this night. It's rheumatics I shall have to-morrow in all me bones," she growled.

She plodded along at Grace's side with such an injured expression that Grace felt like laughing outright at the picture of offended dignity that she presented.

Grace chatted gayly as they proceeded and Bridget answered her sallies with grunts and monosyllables. When they reached the turn of the road Grace said:

"Bridget, let's take the short cut. The walking is good and we'll save ten minutes' time by doing it."

"Phast that haunted house?" gasped Bridget. "Niver! May the saints presarve us from hants."

"Nonsense," laughed Grace. "There are no such things as ghosts, and you know it. If you're afraid you can go back and wait at your cousin's for me. She lives near here, doesn't she?"

"I will that," replied Bridget fervently, "but don't ye be too long gone, Miss Grace."

"I won't stay long," promised Grace, and hurried down the road, leaving Bridget to proceed with much grumbling to her cousin's house.

The house that Bridget had so flatly refused to pass was a two-story affair of brick that set well back from the highway. There were rumors afloat that a murder had once been committed there, and that the apparition of the victim, an old man, walked about at night moaning in true ghost fashion.

To be sure no one had as yet been found who had really seen the spectre old man, nevertheless the place kept its ghost reputation and was generally avoided.

Grace, who was nothing if not daring, never lost an opportunity to pass the old house, and jeered openly when any one talked seriously of the "ghost."

Now, she smiled to herself as she rapidly neared the house, at Bridget's evident fear of the supernatural.

"What a goose Bridget is," she murmured. "Just as though there were——" She stopped abruptly and stared in wonder at the old house. On the side away from the road was a small wing, and through one of the windows of this wing gleamed a tiny point of light.

"A light," she said aloud in surprise. "How strange. The ghost must be at home. Perhaps I was mistaken. No, there it is again. Ghost or no ghost, I'm going to see what it is."

Suiting the action to the words, Grace stole softly up the deserted walk and crouched under the window from whence the light had come. Clinging to the window ledge, she cautiously raised herself until her head was on a level with the glass. What she saw caused her to hold her breath with astonishment. Was she awake or did she dream? At one side of the room stood a small table, and on the table, in full view of her incredulous eyes, stood the strong box which had held the bazaar money that had been spirited away on Thanksgiving night. Bending over it, the light from his dark lantern shining full on the lock, was the man whom she had accused on the train.

Grace Held Her Breath in Astonishment.

195

## Grace Held Her Breath in Astonishment

572

Thrilled for the moment by her discovery, Grace forgot everything except what was going on inside the room. The man was making vain efforts to hit upon the combination. How long he had been there Grace had no idea. She could not take her eyes from the box which contained their hard-earned money.

Minutes went by, but still she watched in a fever of apprehension for fear he might accidentally discover the combination. Unsuccessful in his attempts, he finally straightened up with an exclamation of anger and disgust. Going over to a small cupboard built in the wall, he opened it, and, stooping, pressed his finger against some hidden spring. Then the wall opened and the light from the lantern disclosed an inside recess. Lifting the box, he carried it over and deposited it in the opening, and at his touch the panel slid back into place. Quickly locking the cupboard, he placed the key in his pocket, and, extinguishing the lantern, strode towards the door.

Once outside, he passed so close to Grace that by stretching out her hand she might easily have touched him, as she lay flat on the rain-soaked ground, scarcely daring to breathe.

The stranger paused to lock the door, and Grace heard him mutter: "Nice night to send a pal out in, and on a still hunt, too. Nothing short of soup'll open up that claim. If the rest of the jobs he's goin' to pull off are like this hand out, me to shake this rube joint."

The echo of his footsteps died away and Grace ventured to raise herself from her uncomfortable position. She peered into the blackness of the night, but could see nothing. Rising to her feet, she stealthily circled the house and set off at her best speed for "Heartsease."

"There'll be plenty of work for Eleanor and me to do this night," she thought. "If only she will help me now, and she must. She can't refuse. It's for the honor of the senior class."

Giving the old-fashioned knocker a vigorous pull, Grace waited impatiently for admittance.

"Is Miss Savelli at home?" asked Grace eagerly, the moment the maid opened the door.

"No, ma'am," answered the girl. "She and her aunt are in Oakdale to-night. We expect them any minute now."

Grace groaned inwardly.

"What shall I do?" she asked herself. "I must get that money away from there to-night. To-morrow may be too late, and besides I feel sure that that dreadful man won't return to-night. This is our opportunity and we mustn't neglect it."

The maid eyed her curiously. "You are Miss Harlowe, aren't you?" she asked.

"Yes," said Grace. "May I wait here for Miss Savelli?"

"Certainly, miss. Let me take your rain coat and cap. It's a terrible night, isn't it?"

Before Grace had time to answer the click of a latchkey was heard, and the maid said, "There they are."

Eleanor stepped part way into the hall before she became aware of Grace's presence. A look of surprise, followed by one of extreme dislike crossed her face. Drawing herself up, she was about to speak, when Grace exclaimed: "Don't say a word, Eleanor, until you hear what I have to say. I came here to-night to discuss a very personal matter with you, but something so strange has happened that I must defer what I had to say until another time and ask you if you will help me to-night."

"I don't understand," said Eleanor coldly. "Please explain yourself."

"Eleanor," Miss Nevin interposed, "Miss Harlowe is evidently very much agitated over something, therefore do not waste time over useless formality. I knew you, my dear, from the picture I saw of you at Mrs. Gray's," she added, turning to Grace, with a winning smile, that caused the young girl to love her immediately.

"Eleanor," said Grace quickly, "I have found the bazaar money that was stolen Thanksgiving night."

"Found it!" exclaimed Eleanor incredulously. "Where?"

"At the old haunted house," replied Grace.

Then she rapidly narrated the story of her walk, her curiosity as to the light, and the sight that it had revealed to her.

Eleanor and her aunt listened without interrupting.

"When I saw him put the money away and leave the house, I felt that he wouldn't try it again until daylight, so I came straight here," Grace continued. "If you will take your run-about down to the road where it runs near to the house, you and I can easily get the box and carry it to the machine. It will take two of us, because it's very heavy. I know I can find the secret of the panel, but we shall have to break open the door of the cupboard. I am not afraid, and, somehow, Eleanor, I felt that you would have plenty of the right brand of courage."

"I am not afraid," responded Eleanor, flushing at Grace's words, "but I know I should never have displayed the courage that you have. I should never have dared dashing up to a haunted house to investigate uncanny lights."

"My dear child," exclaimed Miss Nevin, "do you suppose that I would allow you two slips of girls to prowl around that old house alone, on a night like this?"

"Miss Nevin," Grace's voice rose in its earnestness, "we must get that money to-night, even if I have to go back there alone. It belongs to us, and we simply can't let it slip through our fingers."

"And so you shall get it," was the answer, "but with John, the coachman, for a bodyguard."

"May we go this minute?" chorused both girls.

"Yes," nodded Miss Nevin. "I'll send word to John to get out the run-about and take you at once."

Ten minutes later John, the coachman, and the two girls had squeezed into the run-about and were making as good time to the haunted house as the darkness would permit. The heavy outside door was found to be securely padlocked, and the windows were locked. With two blows of the small axe that he had brought with him, John shattered the glass of the very window through which Grace had peered, and, climbing in, helped the two girls in after him.

By the light of the two lanterns they had brought, the cupboard was easily located and opened and a diligent search was made for the hidden spring.

"Shall I smash in the paneling, miss?" asked the coachman.

"Perhaps you'd better," assented Grace. "I don't seem to be able to find the key to the riddle." She endeavored to step out of John's way, and as she did so, struck her foot smartly against the back wall of the cupboard near to the floor. There was a curious grating sound and the panel slid back, revealing the welcome sight of the strong box reposing in the recess.

Unwittingly Grace had touched the secret spring. Both girls cried out in triumph. Then, hurrying to the window, they climbed out, ready to receive the box. John set it on the window-sill, and, though very heavy, Grace and Eleanor combined forces and lowered it to the ground. Leaping over the sill, the coachman picked it up, and the three set off at full speed down the path.

The ride back to "Heartsease" was a memorable one to at least two of the occupants of the machine. But few remarks were exchanged. Each girl was busy with her own thoughts. The circumstances that had brought them together seemed too remarkable for mere words.

"'To the victors belong the spoils,'" called Grace as she hopped out of the run-about before John could assist her, with Eleanor at her heels, while the coachman followed more slowly, bearing the box.

The rain was still falling, but it was doubtful whether either girl was sensible to the fact that her hair was heavy with dampness and her clothing and shoes were wet.

"My dear, you had better allow Eleanor to provide you with dry clothing and remain with her to-night," suggested Miss Nevin as they entered the hall. Then ringing for the maid, she ordered hot chocolate.

"I wish you would stay with me, Grace," said Eleanor rather shyly. "I have a great deal to say to you."

"And I to you, Eleanor," Grace responded.

For a moment they stood facing one another. What they saw seemed to satisfy them. Their hands reached out simultaneously and met in a firm clasp.

"Will you kiss me, Grace?" was what Eleanor said.

"With all my heart," was the answer. And with that kiss all resentment and hard feeling died out forever.

"You are surely going to stay with me to-night," coaxed Eleanor. "We will send word to your mother."

But with Eleanor's remark the remembrance of her promise to her mother came back with a rush.

"Good gracious, Eleanor! I promised mother that I'd be home at nine o'clock. What time is it now?"

"It's half past ten," replied Eleanor, consulting her watch.

"Poor Bridget," mourned Grace. "She will be sure to think that the ghosts have spirited me away. I must go this minute, before search parties are sent out for me. But I'll see you to-morrow Eleanor, for I need your help."

Just then Miss Nevin, who had left the room, returned with a tray on which were tiny sandwiches and a pot of chocolate.

"You must have some refreshment, Grace," she said. "Eleanor, do the honors."

Grace was made to eat and drink, then, placing herself under John's protection, she returned to Oakdale in Eleanor's run-about, stopping on her way home at the house of Bridget's cousin, where she found the faithful though irate Bridget awaiting her in a state of anxiety bordering upon frenzy.

"Don't fuss, Bridget," consoled Grace. "The banshees didn't get me, and you're going to ride home in an automobile. That ought to make you feel better."

The prospect of the ride completely mollified Bridget, and by the time they reached home she fairly radiated good nature.

"Your ideas of time are somewhat peculiar, Grace," remarked her mother as Grace entered the living room, where her mother and father sat reading. "If Bridget had not been with you I should have been most uneasy."

But Grace was too full of her news to make other answer than cry out:

"Oh, mother, we found it! We did, truly!"

"What is the child talking about?" asked her father. And then Grace launched forth with an account of her night's doings.

"Well, I never!" was all Mr. Harlowe could find words for when his daughter had finished.

"What shall I do with you, Grace?" said her mother in despair. "You will be injured or killed yet, in some of your mad excursions."

"Trust to me to land right side up with care," answered Grace cheerfully.

"I'll call at the police station early to-morrow morning and have the chief send someone up to that old house," said Mr. Harlowe. "From what you heard the thief say, he must have a confederate. Perhaps the chief's men will get both of them."

"Perhaps so," replied Grace, but she had a shrewd idea as to who the confederate might be, and felt that if her suppositions were correct there was not much chance of his incriminating himself.

## CHAPTER XXII

## GRACE AND ELEANOR MAKE A FORMAL CALL

Before recess the next day the news that Grace Harlowe and Eleanor Savelli had been seen in earnest conversation together traveled like wild fire around the study hall. The members of the Phi Sigma Tau could scarcely believe their eyes, and when at recess they sought for enlightenment, Grace would give them no satisfaction save that she and Eleanor had really become friendly again.

"I love you all dearly, but I can't tell you about it yet, so please don't ask me. When I do tell you, you'll understand and be as glad as I am," she informed them affectionately, and with this they were obliged to content themselves.

At one o'clock that afternoon Grace was summoned from the study hall, and her friends' curiosity went up to the highest pitch and did not in the least abate when Eleanor Savelli was also excused and hurriedly followed Grace out.

"This must mean that they have caught him," said Eleanor, as she and Grace turned their steps in the direction of the police station.

Grace nodded silently. Her mind was busy with Marian's problem. She must get back the money that Henry Hammond had wheedled Marian into giving him. If the stranger had been apprehended and if Hammond were really his confederate, then the stranger might, under cross-examination, betray Hammond, who would at once be arrested.

Now that Eleanor had become her friend, Grace knew that she would never expose Marian in class meeting, but even with this menace removed, still nothing could disguise the fact that the judge's gift could not be honestly accounted for.

Grace believed that Henry Hammond had appropriated the money for his own use. She did not place any dependence in his story of having lost it through speculation. She therefore resolved that he should return it if she could devise any means of making him do so, without subjecting him to public exposure.

For Marian's sake, she would refrain from carrying the matter into court, and she reluctantly decided to say nothing about the meeting between

Hammond and the prisoner that she had witnessed at the station on the night of her return from New York.

Eleanor's surmise proved to be correct. At the door of the station house, Grace's father awaited them, and they were conducted into the court room, where the first thing that caught Grace's attention was the eyes of the prisoner, that glared ferociously at her.

"So you're the fresh kid that got me jugged, are you!" he snarled with a menacing gesture. "I'd like to get my hands on you for a couple of minutes."

"Silence!" roared Chief Burroughs.

Then the examination began. The strong box had been turned over to the police that morning by Miss Nevin, to be held as proof against the thief.

Grace identified the man as the one she had seen tampering with the lock the previous night, repeating what she had heard him say as he left the old house. She then told her story of the removal of the box, which was corroborated by Eleanor and John, the coachman.

"This is not the first time this man and I have met," declared Grace at the conclusion of her testimony. Then she related the incident of the train to the chief, while the prisoner glowered at her as though he would enjoy tearing her in pieces.

When examined, he gave his name as Jones, denied ever having seen Grace before, but under rigid cross-examination finally admitted the truth of her story, and that he had been in Oakdale on the previous Thanksgiving and had assisted in the theft of the strong box. He had left for New York the following morning, supposing that his confederate would have no trouble in unlocking the box.

"Why did you leave Oakdale?" questioned Chief Burroughs.

"Robbing kids was too small business for me," growled the man. "We heard this was a rich town, but when we got here I sized it up, and it didn't look good to me. So I beat it for New York the next day."

But no amount of grilling could induce him to reveal the identity of his partner.

"He's too good a pal to squeal on. Nothing doing in that line," was the unvarying answer.

When questioned as to his second visit to Oakdale, he said that his partner had been unable to open the strong box, and after looking about for some safe hiding place, had accidentally discovered the secret recess in the cupboard, while prowling about the haunted house.

This had seemed an ideal place of concealment, and he had secretly conveyed the box there until the prisoner, who was an expert cracksman, should be on hand to open it.

"And was that your sole object in coming to Oakdale?" was the chief's sharp query.

"Of course," replied the prisoner.

But the chief shook his head. "There is a good deal more back of this. You have not answered truthfully. Your real motive for coming here was robbery."

Grace and Eleanor were not detained throughout the entire examination. After giving their testimony, they were allowed to go. Once they were fairly outside the police station, Grace took Eleanor by the arm and said:

"Eleanor, I have a call to make, and I wish you to go with me. We haven't a moment to spare, for the First National Bank closes at three, and it's a quarter after two now."

"I am very glad to hear that useful and interesting fact about the First National Bank. Are you going to deposit money there!" asked Eleanor, laughing.

"No," answered Grace mysteriously. "I am going to draw money from there after I have called upon a certain person."

"But what have I to do with it!" questioned Eleanor.

"Come with me and see," Grace replied. "After we have succeeded in our undertaking, I'll answer any questions you may ask. I warn you, however, that the call I am about to make is not a friendly one. Are you willing to stand by me through what may be a rather disagreeable scene?"

"I certainly am," replied Eleanor emphatically. "You ought to know from past experiences that disagreeable scenes are my forte."

"I know that I'd rather have you with me on this expedition than anyone else I know," responded Grace. "You are not easily intimidated."

The two girls by this time had left Main Street and turned into Putnam Square.

"Grace," said Eleanor suddenly. "I believe I can guess the place you are headed for. You are going to Henry Hammond's office, aren't you?"

"Yes," said Grace, surprised at the accuracy of Eleanor's guess, "I am."

"And you are going there about the money that he stole from Marian. Am I right!"

"You are," answered Grace truthfully. "But how did you know?"

"Because," said Eleanor quietly, "I intended going there myself."

"Then you think that——" began Grace.

"I think that Henry Hammond is a thief and an impostor," finished Eleanor. "He tried to interest Aunt Margaret in some real estate, and called at 'Heartsease' on two different occasions. She is a very shrewd business woman and he couldn't fool her in the least. Both times he called he kept looking about him all the time, as though he were trying to see whether we had any valuables. He raved over the house, and hinted to be shown through it, but we weren't so foolish.

"When Chief Burroughs was questioning the prisoner to-day about his confederate, it suddenly flashed across me that it might be this man Hammond. He appeared here for the first time on the night of the bazaar and—"

"Eleanor," exclaimed Grace, "you've missed your vocation. You should have been a detective. I believe what you say to be the truth and have thought so for some time. We can hardly denounce Henry Hammond upon suspicion, but we can scare him and make him give back the class money. Perhaps we are defeating the ends of justice by not telling what we suspect, but if we have him arrested on suspicion, then the only way we can get back our money is to publicly charge him with extorting it from Marian. Think what a disgrace that would be for her in her graduating year, too," Grace added. "She would feel too ashamed to ever again face her best friends."

"I have thought of all that, too, and now that we are both of the same mind, let's on to victory," said Eleanor.

The two girls paused and shook hands as they entered the building in which Henry Hammond had his office, then mounted the stairs with the full determination of winning in their cause.

"Good afternoon, Mr. Hammond," called Eleanor, as she opened the door and walked serenely in, followed by Grace.

Henry Hammond started nervously up from his desk at the sound of her voice. The bland smile with which he greeted her changed to a frown as his eyes rested upon Grace, and he saluted her coldly.

"I am, indeed, honored, this afternoon," he said with sarcasm. "Miss Harlowe has never before visited my office."

"We had a few minutes to spare and thought we'd run in and tell you the news," replied Grace sweetly. "We have just come from the police station."

"Rather a peculiar place for two High School girls to visit, isn't it!" asked the man with a suspicion of a sneer.

"Yes, but we were the heroines in an adventure last night," replied Grace evenly. "We found the bazaar money that was stolen last Thanksgiving."

"What!" exploded Hammond. Then trying to conceal his agitation, he said with affected carelessness, "I believe I do remember something about that robbery."

"I was sure that you would," returned Grace, looking squarely at him. "That was the night of the day you came to Oakdale, was it not?"

"I really can't recollect the exact date," murmured Hammond.

"One of the thieves was caught to-day, at the old haunted house, where he had hidden the box," volunteered Eleanor.

A grayish pallor overspread Hammond's face. With a desperate effort at self-control, he said:

"Ah, there was more than one, then!"

"Oh, yes," declared Grace cheerfully. "There were two in it. The other will probably be apprehended soon. The prisoner hasn't revealed his identity, as yet. The funny thing is that I had seen the prisoner before. On the train that we took from New York, after seeing Anne Pierson in the play, I saw this same man try to steal a watch and chain from an old gentleman, who would not believe me when I warned him of his danger."

"When we finally reached Oakdale," continued Grace, "I watched to see if he got off the train, and he did. We saw a man meet him at the station, who—"

Henry Hammond sprang up and seizing his hat, said harshly, "I hope you young ladies will excuse me, what you have told me is so interesting that I believe I shall go over to the station house and get all the details. Will you remain until I return?" He fumbled in a drawer of his desk, and both girls saw him take out a bankbook.

"Thank you," said Grace politely. "We can't stay, but before we go we should like to have you write us a check for the five hundred dollars that Marian Barber foolishly loaned you. You see she had no right to do so. Besides, she is still a minor. If you do it at once we can cash it to-day. It is now fifteen minutes of three. I'll call the bank and tell them that I am coming. But first I must send a message to my father."

With these words, Grace walked to the telephone without giving Hammond time to answer. "Give me Main 268a, please," she said. With a bound he sprang to the door, but it closed in his face, and he heard the turn of the key in the lock, just as Grace calmly called, "Hello, is this Chief Burroughs? Is my father there?" Then she answered, "You say he is there? Well, this is his daughter, Grace. Please tell him that Miss Savelli and I are just about to leave Mr. Hammond's office, and wish him to meet us outside."

Hammond sprang toward Grace, but instantly realizing that it would be folly to molest her, drew back, scowling savagely.

Grace hung up the receiver and rang again. This time she called the bank, asking for the president. "Is this Mr. Furlow?" she said. "This is Grace Harlowe. I am at the office of Mr. Henry Hammond, who is about to write my father a check for five hundred dollars, which he wishes to cash before the bank closes. It is now ten minutes of three. He will be there inside of seven minutes. Thank you. Good-bye."

"Now," she commanded, turning to Hammond, the expression of whose face was a combination of baffled rage, disappointment and fear, "write the check."

With a muttered imprecation he went to his desk, jerked out a checkbook and wrote the desired check.

"To whom shall I make it payable?" he muttered.

"To Thomas G. Harlowe," replied Grace composedly.

Inserting her father's name, he fairly flung the check in her face, and strode to the door.

"Open this door," he commanded.

There was no response.

"You may open the door, Eleanor," called Grace. "Mr. Hammond is ready to go now."

The key turned in the lock. With a savage jerk, Henry Hammond flung open the door, and brushing Eleanor aside, bolted for the stairway.

Five seconds later the two girls reached the sidewalk and found Mr. Harlowe waiting for them.

"Father, dear," exclaimed Grace. "Here is a check for five hundred dollars, made payable to you by Mr. Henry Hammond. You have five minutes in which to cash it, before the bank closes. I'll tell you the story of it later. I haven't time now."

The First National Bank was just around the corner, and three minutes later Mr. Harlowe walked in, accompanied by Grace and Eleanor, and cashed the check without any trouble.

"Tom Harlowe must have made money on some deal with Hammond," thought the cashier, as he closed the window. "He is about the only one who has that I know of."

"And now, daughter, whose money is this, and what is it all about?" asked her father gravely, as they left the bank.

"I can have no better confidant than my father," declared Grace, and she thereupon told him the whole story.

Mr. Harlowe heard her story with mingled emotions of pride and disapproval.

"Never take such a risk again, Grace," he said sternly. "Suppose this man had carried a revolver. He might easily have turned the tables."

"I never stopped to think what he might do, father," said Grace ruefully. "The honor of the senior class was at stake, and I knew that I had to get that money somehow. Besides, I had notified Chief Burroughs as to my whereabouts, and sent word for you to wait for me, so he was really cornered, that's why Eleanor locked the door."

"Grace, you are incorrigible," sighed her father, "but if ever again you find yourself in a snarl over the rashness of your friends, then remember that I am the wisest person to consult. It may save you considerable worry, and will be at least a safer method."

Nevertheless, he could not refrain from smiling a little as he added, "What do you propose to do with this money?"

"Deposit it in Upton Bank, to-morrow," was Grace's prompt reply.

"And in whose name?" asked her father.

"In Marian Barber's father," said Grace steadily. "This time it will be safe, for she has learned her lesson."

## CHAPTER XXIII

## THE MESSAGE OF THE VIOLIN

The news of the finding of the lost money in the haunted house came out in the evening paper, and set the whole town of Oakdale agog with excitement.

The sensational robbery at the close of the Thanksgiving bazaar was too bold to have been forgotten, and the news of the recovery of the hard-earned money was a matter of delight to the public-spirited citizens of the little northern city.

The haunted house soon lost its ghost reputation, and was ransacked by small boys on the hunt for sliding panels and hidden treasure until the owner of the place, who had been absent from Oakdale, took a hand in things and threatened severe penalties for trespassing, which greatly cooled the ardor of the youthful treasure-seekers.

As for Grace Harlowe and Eleanor Savelli, they were the bright and shining lights of the town and the darlings of the senior class.

The two girls had become firm friends. After the excitement of the finding of the money had worn off, they had had a long talk and had cleared up all misunderstandings. Eleanor had confessed to Grace that long before they had been brought together she had secretly tired of the old grudge and had longed for peace.

"After Edna Wright and I quarreled, I began to see things in a different light," Eleanor had confided to Grace, "and the longing for the companionship of your kind of girls took hold of me so strongly it made me miserable at times.

"How I did envy you when you all went to the house party at Christmas, and I was wild to go to New York and see Anne, although I suppose I am the last person she would care to see.

"It wasn't just the good times, either, that I coveted, it was that sense of comradeship that existed among you girls that I didn't at all understand last year."

"But, Eleanor," Grace had said, "if you felt that way, why were you so determined to expose poor Marian Barber!"

"When Marian told me what she had done I felt the utmost contempt for her," Eleanor had replied. "My old idea of vengeance came to the front, and I thought of how completely I could humiliate you all through her. The day I quarreled with her in school I fully intended to expose her, but the more I thought about it, the less I liked the idea of it. I don't really believe that I could ever have stood up before those girls and betrayed her."

While Grace had listened to Eleanor, she had realized that the old whimsical, temperamental Eleanor was passing, and an entirely different girl was endeavoring to take her place. Grace exulted in her heart and dreamed great things for the Phi Sigma Tau when it should be restored to its original number of members.

Eleanor had announced herself ready and eager to take her old place in the sorority, while Marian Barber had, with tears in her eyes, humbly petitioned Grace for her old place in the Phi Sigma Tau.

"Silly girl," was Grace's answer. "You can't go back to what you never left, can you?"

No one save Grace, Eleanor and Mr. Harlowe knew of how near Marian had come to being discredited in the eyes of her class and friends, and they could be trusted with the secret.

Henry Hammond had left Oakdale the morning after he had been interviewed by Grace and Eleanor, and it was afterwards discovered that the land in which he had persuaded certain guileless citizens to invest money had proved worthless. The swindled ones joined forces and put the matter in the hands of a detective, but to no purpose, for no clue was found to his whereabouts.

The strong box was turned over to the girls and the money, which amounted to five hundred and ten dollars, was deposited in Upton Bank with the five hundred that had caused Marian Barber such anxiety and sorrow.

The thief whom Grace had assisted in capturing was found to be a noted crook, known to the police as "Larry the Locksmith," on account of his ability to pick locks. He was tried and sentenced to a number of years in the penitentiary, and departed from Oakdale stolidly refusing to furnish the police with the identity of his "pal."

Easter was drawing near, and Grace was radiantly happy. Anne, whose engagement had stretched into the eighth week, would be home the following day. Mrs. Gray was looked for hourly and the boys were coming from college on Monday.

"We certainly will have a reunion," Nora O'Malley exclaimed joyously, as she banged her books on the window sill of the senior locker-room to emphasize her remark.

"It seems good to have Grace with us once in a while," declared Jessica. "Her police court duties have kept her so busy that she has deserted her little playmates. Have you been asked to join the force yet, Grace!" she asked, trying to look innocent.

"That isn't fair, Jessica," retorted Grace, laughing. "I appeal to you girls," turning to the other members of the Phi Sigma Tau, who had one by one dropped into the locker-room. "Can you imagine me in the garb of an Oakdale policeman?"

"Not in our wildest nightmares," Miriam Nesbit gravely assured her.

"Anne will be home to-morrow," cried Eva Allen. "I'm so glad it's Saturday. We can celebrate. Will you come to my house?"

"We will," was the united answer.

"We'll all go to the train to meet Anne," planned Grace. "Then we'll give her about one hour to get acquainted with her family. After that we'll rush her off to Eva's, back to my house for supper (mother expects all of you), and then up to Mrs. Gray's."

"Poor Anne," said Marian Barber, "I can see her being carried home on a stretcher."

"We will meet at the station," directed Grace, as she left them. "Be there at 8.15. Don't one of you fail to be there."

As Anne Pierson stepped off the 8.15 train the next morning after an all-night ride, she was surrounded by seven laughing girls and marched in triumph to David Nesbit's big car, which Miriam used at her own pleasure during her brother's absence.

The eight girls managed to squeeze into it, and drove to the Pierson cottage with all speed. Here Anne was set down, told to make the most of her hour with her family and to be prepared upon their return to say good-bye to home for the rest of the day.

The programme outlined by Grace was carried out to the letter. The joy of Mrs. Gray at again seeing her adopted children was well worth witnessing.

"I don't know how I ever managed to stay away from you so long!" she exclaimed, as she looked fondly about her at the smiling, girlish faces. "How I wish you might all have been with me. I should have returned sooner, but dreaded the winter here. I do not thrive here—during these long, cold Oakdale winters. It is because I—"

Grace placed a soft hand upon Mrs. Gray's lips. "I can't allow you to finish that sentence," she laughed. "You are sixty-two years young, and you must always remember it."

The old lady laughed happily at Grace's remark, then under cover of general conversation said to her, "I am greatly surprised to see Eleanor here. How did it all come about? You never mentioned it in your letters."

"I know it," replied Grace, "I wanted to save it until you came home. I have been out to 'Heartsease' several times, too, and am quite in love with Miss Nevin. May Anne and I come to-morrow and have a good long gossip? You must hear all about Anne's triumphs in New York."

"Come and have dinner with me," replied Mrs. Gray.

"That will be fine," returned Grace. "We two are the only ones in the crowd who don't happen to have previous engagements, so the girls won't feel hurt at not being included."

"We are so glad that you came home in time for the concert," said Miriam Nesbit. "It is the last entertainment the senior class will have a chance to give. We hope to make a nice sum of money to add to the thousand we already have."

"I have not added my mite to your fund yet," said Mrs. Gray. "But now that I'm home I shall busy myself immediately with my High School girls. When and where is the concert to be held?"

"A week from next Monday, in Assembly Hall," replied Miriam. "We wish to give it before the boys go back to school. They have only ten days at home, you know."

"How anxious I am to see the boys," cried Mrs. Gray. "I found a letter from Tom waiting for me. He expects to arrive on Monday or Tuesday, and will bring Arnold with him."

"I received a letter from Tom, too," said Grace. "We have also heard from the boys. David is bringing home a friend of his, Donald Earle, who, he writes, is the most popular man in the freshman class."

The evening seemed all too short to Mrs. Gray and the Phi Sigma Tau.

"Why, we've only begun to talk," said Jessica, "and here it is after eleven o'clock."

"To be continued in our next," said Nora with a grin. "Introducing new features and startling revelations."

Sunday afternoon found Anne and Grace strolling up Chapel Hill toward Mrs. Gray's. Rather to their surprise they found Miss Nevin with Mrs. Gray in the library. The two women were in earnest conversation, and as Grace and Anne were ushered in, Grace's quick intuition told her that Miss Nevin was strongly agitated over something.

"How are my own children to-day," asked Mrs. Gray, coming forward and kissing both of them warmly. Anne was then presented to Miss Nevin, who took occasion to congratulate her upon her recent success. "Your fame has preceded you," she said with a sweet smile.

"You must tell us all about your stay in New York, Anne," said Mrs. Gray. "You are very young to have been chosen for so responsible an engagement, and I feel great pride in your success."

"Anne had two offers of engagements while in New York," interposed Grace. "One from Farman, the big manager, and one from Rupert Manton, the Shakespearian actor."

"But I am still in Oakdale," replied Anne smiling, "and have come to-day to beg for my secretary- ship again."

"You delightful child," cried Mrs. Gray. "I knew you would never desert me."

"Margaret," she said, turning to Miss Nevin, "would you care to tell my girls what you were telling me when they came in? I have already told them something of Eleanor's parentage. They know that Guido Savelli is her father. Perhaps they might be of assistance in helping you decide what is to be done. Grace is a famous suggester."

Miss Nevin flushed and looked hesitatingly at Anne and Grace, as though a trifle reluctant to speak.

"We shall consider anything you may choose to tell us strictly confidential, Miss Nevin," said Anne quietly.

"I am sure that you will," replied Miss Nevin. "What I have told Mrs. Gray is that I have received through my lawyers a letter from Eleanor's father. They enclosed his letter in one from them asking whether I were desirous of acquainting him with my whereabouts.

"He has written rather a sad letter. He seems to have awakened to a late remorse for having neglected my sister as he did. He asks for his child, and if he may see her. He has just finished a concert tour of America, and is at present in New York.

"Personally, I shall never forgive him, but have I the right to keep Eleanor from her father? He is both rich and famous, and she would adore him, for his music, if for nothing else. I have always said that when she became twenty-one years of age I should tell her of him, leaving to her the choice of claiming or ignoring him.

"But I never supposed for one instant that he would ever come forward and interest himself in her. A year ago I should not have considered her fit to choose, but she is greatly changed. The two years in which she has associated with girls of her own age have benefited her greatly. I feel as though I could not bear to give her up now. Moreover, this idea of claiming his child may be merely a whim on the part of her father. He is liable to forget her inside of six weeks."

Grace listened to Miss Nevin in breathless silence. It was all like a story-book romance.

Anne sat gazing off into space, thinking dreamily of the great virtuoso who had found after years of selfish pleasure and devotion to himself that blood was thicker than water. She fancied she could picture his pride when he beheld Eleanor and realized that she was his own child, and

Eleanor's rapture when she knew that her father was master of the violin she worshipped.

Suddenly an idea popped into Anne's head that was a positive inspiration.

"Why not ask him to come down for our concert?" she said, amazed at her own audacity in suggesting such a thing. "Eleanor need not know about him at all. She is to play at the concert, you know. If he hears her play he will realize more fully that she is really his own flesh and blood, and if he has any real fatherly feeling for her it will come to the surface. That will be the psychological moment in which to bring them together."

"Anne, you're a genius!" cried Grace. "You ought to be appointed Chief Arbiter of Destiny."

"Margaret," exclaimed Mrs. Gray, "I believe that Anne's idea is logical. Shall you try it!"

"I shall write to Guido at once," said Miss Nevin, rising. "Knowing his disposition as I do, it seems that I could find no better way of rousing his interest in Eleanor. Her love of the violin is a direct inheritance from him, and she may reach his heart through her music. At any rate, it is worth trying."

After Miss Nevin's departure Anne and Grace entertained Mrs. Gray with the promised gossip, and it was well toward ten o'clock before they turned their steps toward home.

The following week was a busy one. Every spare moment outside school the senior class zealously devoted to the concert. The High School Glee Club was to sing, and the mandolin and guitar club was to give two numbers. Nora O'Malley was to sing two songs from a late musical success, and Jessica and Miriam were to play a duet. James Gardiner, who was extremely proficient on the violincello, was down for a solo, while Eleanor was to play twice. The crowning feature of the concert, however, was to be contributed by Anne and Eleanor. Anne was to recite Tennyson's "Enoch Arden," and Eleanor was to accompany her on the piano with the music that she had arranged for it.

The two girls had worked incessantly upon it, rehearsing almost every day. Grace was the only one who had been permitted to hear a rehearsal of it, and she was enraptured with what she heard.

The boys had all arrived, and the Phi Sigma Tau divided their time equally between concert rehearsals and social gatherings. David's friend,

Donald Earle, was ably living up to his college reputation, and proved himself a source of unmitigated pleasure to the young people among whom he was thrown. It was soon discovered, however, that he was oftenest found in Eleanor's wake, and his eyes showed honest admiration for the beautiful girl every time he looked at her.

Hippy, who had established a reputation as a singer of humorous songs, was asked for his services.

"I have a number of new and choice ditties that I will render with pleasure, providing I am afterwards fed," he shrewdly declared, when interviewed on the subject.

"It will all depend upon how well you sing," stipulated Nora.

"Then I shan't warble at all," announced Hippy. "I am a man of few words, but when I say I must have food for my services as a soloist, I mean it. There must be no uncertainty. Do I feed or do I not?"

"You feed," laughed Nora.

The concert was to be held in Assembly Hall, and three days before every ticket issued had been sold. People who could not attend bought tickets and handed them back to be sold over again. The senior class, by reason of the popularity of the Phi Sigma Tau, was considered the class of classes.

"We'll have to put out a 'Standing Room Only' sign," declared Anne Pierson, as she viewed the packed house through a hole in the curtain.

The fateful night had arrived, and Anne, Eleanor and Grace stood in a group on the stage, while Anne industriously took note of the audience.

"Let me look for a minute, Anne," said Grace. "I don't believe there'll be standing room," she remarked, as she stepped aside to give Eleanor a chance to peer out.

"Come on, girls," called Nora O'Malley, as a burst of applause sounded from the other side of the curtain. "It's half past eight, and the curtain will go up in about two minutes."

The three girls scurried off the stage, the Glee Club filed on and arranged themselves, and the curtain rose.

Each number was applauded to the echo and in every instance the audience clamored for an encore.

594

As the time for Eleanor's first solo drew near, Anne and Grace felt their hearts beat a little faster. Nora was giving an encore to her first song. Eleanor was to follow her. As she stood in the wing her violin under her arm, Grace thought she had never appeared more beautiful.

Her gown was of some soft, white material and rather simply made. "I never like to wear fussy things when I play," she had confided to the girls.

Jessica stood directly behind her. She was to act as accompanist.

Nora O'Malley sang the concluding line of her song, favored the audience with a saucy little nod and made her exit.

"Come on, Eleanor," said Jessica. "It's our turn."

Well toward the back of the hall sat Miss Nevin, wearing a look of mingled anxiety and pain. Beside her sat a dark, distinguished man in the prime of life, who never took his eyes off the stage.

As one of the senior girls who had charge of the programme stepped forward and announced, "Solo, Miss Eleanor Savelli," he drew a deep breath, and such a look of longing crept into his eyes that Miss Nevin understood for the first time something of the loneliness of which he had written.

He covered his eyes with his hand as though reluctant to look. Then the full, soft notes of the violin were carried to his ears, and with a smothered cry of exultation he raised his eyes and saw for the first time his own child in her gown of white with the instrument he loved at her throat, while her slender hand drew the bow with the true skill of the artist.

Before Miss Nevin could stop him, he had risen in his seat, saying excitedly: "It is mia bella Edith. She has come again."

Then realizing what he had done, he sat down, and, burying his face in his hands, sobbed openly.

Persons around him, startled by his sudden cry, glared at him angrily for creating a commotion during Eleanor's exquisite number, then again turned their attention to the soloist.

"I must see her. I must see her," he muttered over and over again. "She is my child; mine."

"So you shall," whispered Miss Nevin soothingly, "but not until the concert is over. If we tell her now, Guido, it will upset her so that she can't appear again this evening, and she has two more numbers."

Unabashed by the emotion he had displayed, the virtuoso wiped his eyes, and sat waiting like one in a trance for his child to appear again.

Anne and Grace were alive with curiosity as to the outcome of Anne's suggestion. They had eagerly scanned the house before the concert began, but had failed to locate Miss Nevin and Eleanor's father.

"I'm going out in the audience and see if I can find them," Grace had whispered to Anne during Nora's song, as they stood in the wing on the opposite side from Jessica and Eleanor.

Anne had nodded silently, her attention focused upon Nora, whose singing always delighted her, and Grace, slipping quietly down to the door that led into the hall, made her way toward the back rows of seats just in time to witness Guido Savelli's emotion at first sight of his daughter.

Back to Anne she sped with her news, and the two friends held a quiet little jubilee of their own over the success of their plot.

There was a round of applause when "Enoch Arden" was announced. Eleanor took her place at the piano while Anne stepped forward and began the pathetic tale to the subdued strains of the music that Eleanor had fitted to it.

Anne's beautiful voice rose and fell with wonderful expression, while the music served to accentuate every word that she uttered. Her audience sat practically spell bound, and when she uttered poor Enoch's death cry, "A sail! A sail! I am saved!" there were many wet eyes throughout the assemblage. She paused for a second before delivering the three concluding lines, and Eleanor ended on the piano with a throbbing minor chord.

There was absolute silence as the performers made their exit. Then a perfect storm of enthusiasm burst forth. Anne and Eleanor returned to bow again and again, but the audience refused to be satisfied, until Anne, in her clear, musical voice, made a little speech of appreciation, which was received with acclamation.

The concert drew to a triumphant close. After Eleanor's second solo, she repaired to the dressing room, where she was immediately surrounded by a group of admiring girls and kept so busy answering questions as to how long she had studied the violin and where, that she did not see Grace Harlowe enter the right wing with Miss Nevin and a tall, dark-haired stranger who glanced quickly about as though in search of some one. "Where is she?" he said. "Find her at once. But, no, wait a moment. She shall hear me play! I will win the heart of my child through the music she loves, I may add one little solo to your programme?" he turned questioningly to Grace.

"Well, I should rather think so," gasped Grace. "It is an honor of which we never dreamed. This concert will be recorded in Oakdale history."

"It is well," said the virtuoso. "Bring me the violin of my child. I will speak to her through it."

Grace flew to the dressing room, where Eleanor's violin lay in its open case upon a table near the door. Hastily securing both violin and bow, she flitted out of the room—without having been noticed by the girls at the further end.

"Here it is," she breathed, as she handed it to Eleanor's father. "I will arrange for you to play after the Glee Club, who are just going on now."

"I thank you," replied the great man. "I pray you do not announce me. I shall need no one to accompany me."

"It shall be as you wish," promised Grace.

There was a moment's wait after the Glee Club had filed off the stage, then Guido Savelli appeared, violin in hand.

A faint ripple of surprise stirred the audience. Who was this distinguished stranger! They could not identify him as belonging among Oakdale musicians.

The virtuoso made a comprehensive survey of the house, then placing the violin almost caressingly to his throat, began to play.

His hearers listened in growing astonishment to the exquisite sounds that he drew from the instrument. There was a plaintive, insistent appeal in his music that was like the pleading of a human voice. It was a pathetic cry wrung from a hungry heart.

The dressing-room door stood partly open, and as the full, sweet notes of the violin were carried to her ears, Eleanor gave a cry of rapture.

"Who is playing?" she cried. "I must see at once." She ran out of the room and into the wing, where she could command a full view of the stage, and looked upon her father for the first time.

She stood, statue like, until the last note died away. Her eyes were full of tears, which she made no attempt to hide. Then she turned to Anne, who had slipped quietly up and now stood beside her:

"Anne," she said almost reverently, "he is a master. His music overwhelms me. I felt when he played as though—he were trying to give me some message, as though he were speaking to me alone. I suppose everyone in the audience felt the same. It is because he is a genius. Who is he, Anne, and where did he come from?"

"Eleanor," replied Anne, her voice trembling a little, "you must prepare yourself for the greatest surprise of your life. He was speaking to you when he played, and it was solely on your account that he played. He came here with your aunt to-night."

Eleanor paled a little.

"Anne, what does all this mean?" she said. "You and Grace have acted queerly all evening. What has this violinist to do with me!"

"That I cannot answer now," replied Anne, "but you will know within the next hour. Your aunt wishes you to get your wraps and meet her at once. She is outside in the carriage and he is with her."

"Are you and Grace coming with us?" questioned Eleanor.

"Not to-night," answered Anne, with a little smile. "You don't need either of us. Here's Grace," she added, as the latter hurried toward them.

"Eleanor," said Grace, "here is your cloak and your violin. Now, kiss both of us good night and trot along, for there's a big surprise waiting for you just around the corner, and it is the earnest wish of both Anne and I that it may prove a happy one."

## CHAPTER XXIV

## THE PARTING OF THE WAYS

With the passing of the Easter holidays unbroken quiet settled down over Oakdale High School.

The boys went back to college and the girls to High School to finish the little that remained to them of their senior year.

The proceeds of the concert had amounted to four hundred and seventy dollars, and with a contribution of five hundred dollars more from Mrs. Gray, the members of the senior class were the proud possessors of a fund of nineteen hundred and eighty dollars, which was to be presented to Miss Thompson on graduation night as their contribution toward the gymnasium.

The three lower classes had also raised considerable money, but collectively it had not reached the amount earned by the seniors.

The playing of the great Savelli at the concert was still a matter of comment in Oakdale. There were several persons in the audience who had previously heard him play, and had at once recognized him. More remarkable still was the fact of his being the father of Eleanor Savelli, and all sorts of rumors sprang up regarding his advent in Oakdale, and his affairs in general. As for Eleanor, it was some time before she could accustom herself to the idea of having a living father, and a famous one at that. She had gone down to the carriage on the night of the concert wondering what was in store for her, and had scarcely stepped inside before she had been clasped in the arms of the virtuoso, and addressed as his child. Shaking herself free from his clasp, she had demanded an explanation from her aunt, who had told her the truth, which to her at the time had seemed unbelievable.

Her first feeling toward her father had been entirely one of pride. Her aunt had been all in all to her since babyhood, therefore she experienced little of the feeling of affection toward him that he manifested for her. The fact that her father was a great artist was a source of infinite satisfaction to her, but gradually as she grew better acquainted with him she began to experience a degree of affection for him that in time became positive worship.

He was to remain at "Heartsease" until after her graduation, then, accompanied by Miss Nevin, Eleanor was to sail for Italy with him, there to remain until he should begin a European concert tour in the fall. Then she would go to Leipsig and enter the very conservatory where her mother and father had met. She had resumed the final "i" so long dropped from her name, and now proudly signed herself Savelli.

The Phi Sigma Tau, particularly Anne and Grace, became prime favorites with the great violinist and were frequently invited to "Heartsease" to hear him play, an honor which was accorded to no one else in Oakdale.

The days hurried by altogether too swiftly to suit Grace and her three closest friends, who looked forward to commencement week with mingled emotions of joy and regret. Graduation was the goal they had been striving for four years to reach, but graduation meant also the parting of the ways, and as the four chums looked back over their High School life it seemed to them that they could never again have quite the good times that they had enjoyed in one another's society.

"'We who are about to die salute you'" quoted Nora O'Malley, as the four girls strolled home from school on the Friday preceding commencement.

"What a cheerful remark," laughed Grace Harlowe.

"Well, that's the way I feel, at any rate," declared Nora. "I can't bear to think that next year we'll all be scattered to the four winds, or, rather, the two winds, because Jessica and I will be together, and so will you and Anne."

"Go to college with us, then," slyly tempted Grace.

"No," answered Nora decidedly. "I've set my heart on studying vocal music. I have always said that I should go to a conservatory, and since Eleanor's father has given me so much encouragement, I've made up my mind to become a concert singer if possible. I'll stay a year in the conservatory at least, and at the end of that time I'll know whether I am justified in going on studying."

"It's fortunate that I am going to study on the piano and that we can be at the same conservatory," said Jessica.

"And that Anne and I will be at the same college," added Grace, "if we ever make up our minds what college we wish to enter."

"There is still plenty of time for that," said Anne. "I am glad that scholarship doesn't stipulate as to what particular college—that is, if I win it."

"You won't know that until a week from to-night," said Jessica. "What a night that will be. This year there will be an extra feature, the presentation of the gym. money."

"I am so proud of our class," exclaimed Grace, "but I do wish we had an even two thousand dollars to give. We lack only twenty dollars. I wonder if the class would care to make it up."

"Why couldn't the Phi Sigma Tau make it up as a parting gift to Oakdale High School!" asked Nora. "That would be two dollars and a half apiece. I am willing to do with that much less fuss on my graduating gown, if the rest of you are."

"I am," said Grace.

"So am I," replied Jessica and Anne together.

"I am sure the other four girls will be of the same mind," said Grace. "I'll see them to-morrow."

The four other members of the Phi Sigma Tau were duly interviewed and by Monday of commencement week the twenty dollars had been added to the fund deposited in Upton Bank.

The prophecy made by Jessica on class day at the end of their sophomore year was about to be fulfilled to the letter, for the four chums had been appointed to the very honors to which she had jestingly assigned them two years before. Anne was chosen as class poet, and Jessica had composed both the words and music of the class song. Grace was to prophesy the futures of her various classmates, while Nora had been detailed to write the class grinds.

"To-day is the day of days," exclaimed Grace to her mother on Tuesday, as she smoothed out a tiny wrinkle in her class-day gown, which she lovingly inspected for the fifth time before putting it on. It was a pale blue marquisette embroidered in tiny daisies, and Grace declared it to be far prettier than her graduating gown of white organdie trimmed with fine lace.

"Nora has the dearest little pale green marquisette, mother," cried Grace with enthusiasm, "and Jessica's gown is pink silk, while Anne has a white silk muslin with violets scattered all over it. I've seen them all, but I must say that I think mine is the nicest and you're a perfect dear, mother, for having embroidered it for me," and, giving her mother a tempestuous hug, Grace gathered her class-day finery in her arms and rushed upstairs to dress for the afternoon that the senior class looked forward to more than to graduation night itself.

The Phi Sigma Tau met in the senior locker-room for the last time and proceeded to Assembly Hall in a body.

"How strange it seems to be going to Assembly Hall instead of the gym. for class day," remarked Miriam Nesbit to Grace.

"Yes, doesn't it?" returned Grace. "But when we come back here next year as post-graduates, we'll have the satisfaction of knowing that we helped a whole lot in getting the good old gym. ready for the next class, even if we couldn't hold forth in it."

The regular class day programme was carried out with tremendous enthusiasm. The girl chums were applauded to the echo for their capable handling of the honors assigned them. Nora in particular rose to heights of fame, her clever grinds provoking wholesale mirth.

"She must have made notes all year," whispered Anne to Jessica under cover of a laugh which was occasioned by the story of one absentminded senior who pushed her glasses up over her forehead, searched diligently for them through the halls and locker-room, and, convinced that she had lost them on the street, inserted an advertisement in one of the Oakdale newspapers before going home that night.

"She did," replied Jessica. "She has always said that she wanted the job of writing the grinds."

At the close of the exercises Grace delivered a spirited senior charge which was ably answered by the junior president. The class song composed by Jessica was sung, then graduates and audience joined in singing "Auld Lang Syne." Then the air was rent with class yells, while the graduates received the congratulations of their friends and then repaired to their banquet.

Wednesday brought Hippy, Reddy and David and also Donald Earle to Oakdale, while Tom Gray and Arnold Evans appeared on Thursday afternoon, to the relief of their young friends.

"Better late than never," called Tom Gray as he and Arnold hurried off the train to where David and his three friends stood eagerly scanning the train for them.

"We thought it would be never," retorted Hippy. "We were about to postpone commencement until sometime next week, and order the flags at half mast, but now things can proceed as usual."

"Hustle up, fellows," commanded David. "We're not the only ones who were anxious. The girls are all over at our house. There'll be a foregathering and a dinner there, and an after-gathering at your aunt's, Tom. So pile into my car and I'll take you up Chapel Hill on the double quick."

Inside of an hour the two young men were crossing the Nesbit's lawn and making for the broad veranda where a bevy of pretty girls stood ready to greet them.

"We are so glad you got here at last," cried Grace. "If you hadn't come on that train you wouldn't have seen us graduate. The next train from your part of the world doesn't get in until ten o'clock."

"We missed the early train and had to wait two hours," replied Tom, "but now that we are here, you'll find that you can't drive us away with a club."

"We shan't try to," said Nora. "Now, if you were Hippy—"

"Nothing could drive me from your presence," interrupted Hippy hastily, "so don't try it. Let's change the subject. That word club has an ugly sound. It makes me nervous."

"Never mind, Hippy," said Miriam. "Nora shall not tease you. I'll protect you."

"Nora, go away, I am protected!" exclaimed Hippy, and, getting behind Miriam, he peered forth at Nora with such a ludicrous expression that she laughed, and immediately declared a truce by allowing him to sit on the rustic seat beside her.

It was a memorable dinner. The girls in their dainty white graduating gowns, their eyes alight with the joy of youth, and the young men with their clean-cut, boyish faces made a picture that Mrs. Nesbit viewed with a feeling of pleasure that was akin to pain.

The start for Assembly Hall was made at a little after seven, as the girls were to join the senior class there, and proceed to the stage, where the class was to sit in a body. Nearly every member of the class carried flowers of some description that had been given to them by their families and friends.

Grace and her chums were supremely happy in that their little social world had turned out to do them honor. Mrs. Gray and Miss Nevin, accompanied by Eleanor's father, were seated near the front with Mrs. Gibson and the Southards, who had arrived at Hawk's Nest on the previous day. Grace's father and mother, Judge Putnam and his sister, Mrs. Nesbit, Nora's brothers and sister and Jessica's father were scattered about through the house.

When the graduates took their places upon the stage, there was tumultuous applause. To the citizens of Oakdale who had known the young women from babyhood, the present class seemed the finest Oakdale High School had yet turned out.

"Bless the dears," said Miss Thompson to Miss Tebbs, as the girls filed past them and on to the stage. "They are without exception the most brilliant lot of girls I have ever had charge of. But of them all there is no one of them quite equal to Grace. She is the ideal type of all that a High School girl should be, and when I say that I have paid her the highest compliment in my power."

The slight difficulty that had arisen between Grace and the principal during Grace's junior year had long since been adjusted by Eleanor, who had gone to Miss Thompson with a frank confession of her transgressions during her junior year. Miss Thompson had freely forgiven her and had fully appreciated the sense of honor that had prompted the deed.

As the class was large, fifteen girls from the entire number had been chosen to deliver essays and addresses. Among these were Anne, Eleanor, Grace, Miriam and Nora.

"I'm just as well satisfied that I was not chosen," Jessica whispered to Eva Allen, as Grace stepped forward to deliver the salutatory address.

"It's easy to see who is first in the hearts of Oakdale," returned Eva. "Grace won't be able to begin this evening if they don't stop it."

The moment that Grace had risen to deliver her address the commotion began, and it was not until Miss Thompson rose and smilingly held up her hand for silence that the noisy reception accorded Grace died away.

Anne, as valedictorian, was only a trifle less warmly received, and her eyes grew misty as she remembered how she had come to Oakdale poor and unknown, and entirely without friends, until Grace had so nobly championed her cause.

The bestowal of the freshman prize followed the graduates' addresses. Then came the announcement of the winners of the scholarships. There were two of these and every one of Anne's friends listened anxiously for her name. They were not disappointed, for Anne's name was the first called. She had won the Upton Scholarship of two hundred and fifty dollars a year, at whatever college she should decide to enter.

After the scholarships had been disposed of, a representative of each of the three lower classes in turn, beginning with the freshmen, presented the gymnasium money to Miss Thompson.

The freshmen had collected over three hundred dollars, the sophomores five hundred and the juniors six hundred and fifty dollars. Lastly, Grace rose from her place among her class and presented Miss Thompson with a check for the two thousand dollars, part of which had figured in the limelight of publicity. And there was one girl in the row of graduates whose heart beat uncomfortably faster for a moment as she thought of how differently it might have all ended for her had it not been for the fearless energy of Grace Harlowe.

It was over at last, the graduates received their diplomas and were admonished as to their future careers by the president of the Board of Education, whose speech concluded the exercises.

As they were leaving the stage, Jessica, whose eyes had been anxiously searching the audience from the beginning of the exercises, gave a little cry and hurrying down the steps, rushed straight into the arms of a brown-eyed girl in a traveling gown who stood waiting at the foot of the steps.

"Oh, you dear Mabel," cried Jessica joyously. "Where did you come from!"

"Mother and I didn't get in until almost nine o'clock, so we came here at once," replied Mabel Allison. "Mother is over there. Come and see her."

"I have been so disappointed," declared Jessica. "We hoped you would be here for class day, and when you didn't come to-day I gave up in despair."

"We intended to start last Friday, but mother was ill for a day or two, and that delayed us. You know it is quite a journey from Denver here."

Jessica and Mabel quickly made their way to Mrs. Allison, and a moment or two later were surrounded by the Phi Sigma Tau, and marched off in triumph to Mrs. Gray, who was in the midst of a group of her intimate friends.

After a great deal of handshaking and general greeting, the entire party of guests, young and old, set off for Mrs. Gray's beautiful home.

The young people had elected to walk and strolled along through the white moonlight, care free, the world before them.

The older members of the party who had ridden to the house were awaiting them on the veranda. Soon after they all repaired to the dining room, where a collation was served them at two long tables, at the close of which toasts were in order, and everyone was "drunk down" in the fruit punch provided for the occasion.

When the gamut of toasting had been finally run, Mr. Harlowe arose and said:

"I have been appointed as spokesman by a committee composed of the fathers, mothers, brothers and sisters of the eight young women who are the cause of all this celebration. The committee of which I speak may not in any sense compare with that august body known as the Phi Sigma Tau, but nevertheless it can boast of at least having held several secret sessions, the result of those sessions being this:

"A long time ago I promised my daughter Grace that my graduation gift to her should be a trip to Europe. Knowing what an addition to the trip the society of her young friends would be, I interviewed those responsible for the welfare of the Phi Sigma Tau, and it was decided that her sorority should accompany her.

"As certain members of the aforesaid committee also feel entitled to vacations, it is quite probable that the Phi Sigma Tau will sail with at least a round dozen of chaperons. In fact, I have seriously considered chartering a liner. Now I have done my duty and anyone who wishes may make remarks."

Then a perfect babble arose, and every one tried to express their opinion at once. As for the Phi Sigma Tau, they were in the seventh heaven of rapture.

Even Anne, who in spite of Mr. Harlowe's assurance, knew that for her the trip was practically impossible, rejoiced for her friends' sake.

"Come here, Anne," commanded Mrs. Gray from the head of the table.

"Anne is my own dear child," said the old lady. "In the past four years she has been not only my secretary, but a daughter as well. As her foster mother, I claim the privilege of sending her to Europe. It shall be my graduation gift to her."

"Three cheers for Mrs. Gray," proposed Hippy, rising, and they were given with a will.

"And are all of you boys going, too?" Grace asked delightedly of Tom Gray.

"Going? Well, I rather think so," he replied with emphasis.

"We are going all at once and with both feet foremost," declared Hippy. "First we shall all be sea sick. After that we shall prowl about Westminster Abbey and ruin our eyesight reading inscriptions on tombs. After that we shall be arrested in France for our Franco-American accent. We shall break our collar bones and bruise our shins doing strenuous Alpine stunts, and we shall turn a disapproving eye upon Russia and incidentally expose a few Nihilists. We shall fish in the Grand Canal at Venice and wear out our shoes prancing about Florence on a still hunt for old masters.

"Last, and by no means least, we shall sample everything to eat from English muffins to Hungarian goulash."

"I knew he'd end with something like that," sniffed Nora contemptuously.

"I am surprised that he ended at all," laughed David.

Those who have followed Grace Harlowe through her four years at High School, will hear from her again in college.

In "GRACE HARLOWE'S FIRST YEAR AT OVERTON COLLEGE" are set down the eventful happenings of her freshman year, and her many friends will find her to be the same generous, warm-hearted young woman who won their admiration and respect during her High School days.

## THE END.

# ABOUT THE AUTHOR

**Jessie Graham Flower** is apparently a pseudonym for American author Josephine Chase (died 1931) who was the author of the popular *Grace Harlowe* series of 27 books for girls, written between 1910 and 1929. The books fall into four separate series, including a high school series, college series, *Overseas* series, and *Overland Riders* series. Despite the popularity of these books, the huge impact Altemus Publishing had on the juvenile market in the years prior to WWI and their continuing availability on the used market, there is almost no information known about this most prolific of writers.

The author was also known by other pseudonyms including Pauline Lester (Marjorie Dean Series), Ames Thompson, Capt, Gordon Bates, and Dale Wilkinins Josephine Chase also penned the Khaki Boys series (1918-1920) under the pseudonym Captain Gordon Bates.

The Harlowe series follows the life of its heroine more or less chronologically from high school through college and beyond. Like Flower's other heroine, Grace is a role-model, already a "paragon when her story begins".

Chase blazed the trail of girls adventures that would be followed by the likes of Nancy Drew, Torchy Blaine, and Trixie Belden. They all used the same friends and fair play as a basic premise in their stories. While the plots and descriptions of Grace Harlowe's adventures seem very tame by today's standards, it harkens back to a time when small town values and small town heroes won in the end.

Made in the USA
Las Vegas, NV
23 December 2023

83477375R00341